CARDBOARD

DOUG TENNAPEL

AN IMPRINT OF

■ SCHOLASTIC

New York Toronto London Auckland Sydney Mexico City New Delhi Hong Kong

This book is dedicated to The Chestertonians.

Library of Congress Control Number: 2011934533

ISBN 978-0-545-41872-0 (hardcover)
ISBN 978-0-545-41873-7 (paperback)
12 11 10   14 15 16
Printed in China   38

First edition, August 2012
Book design by Phil Falco

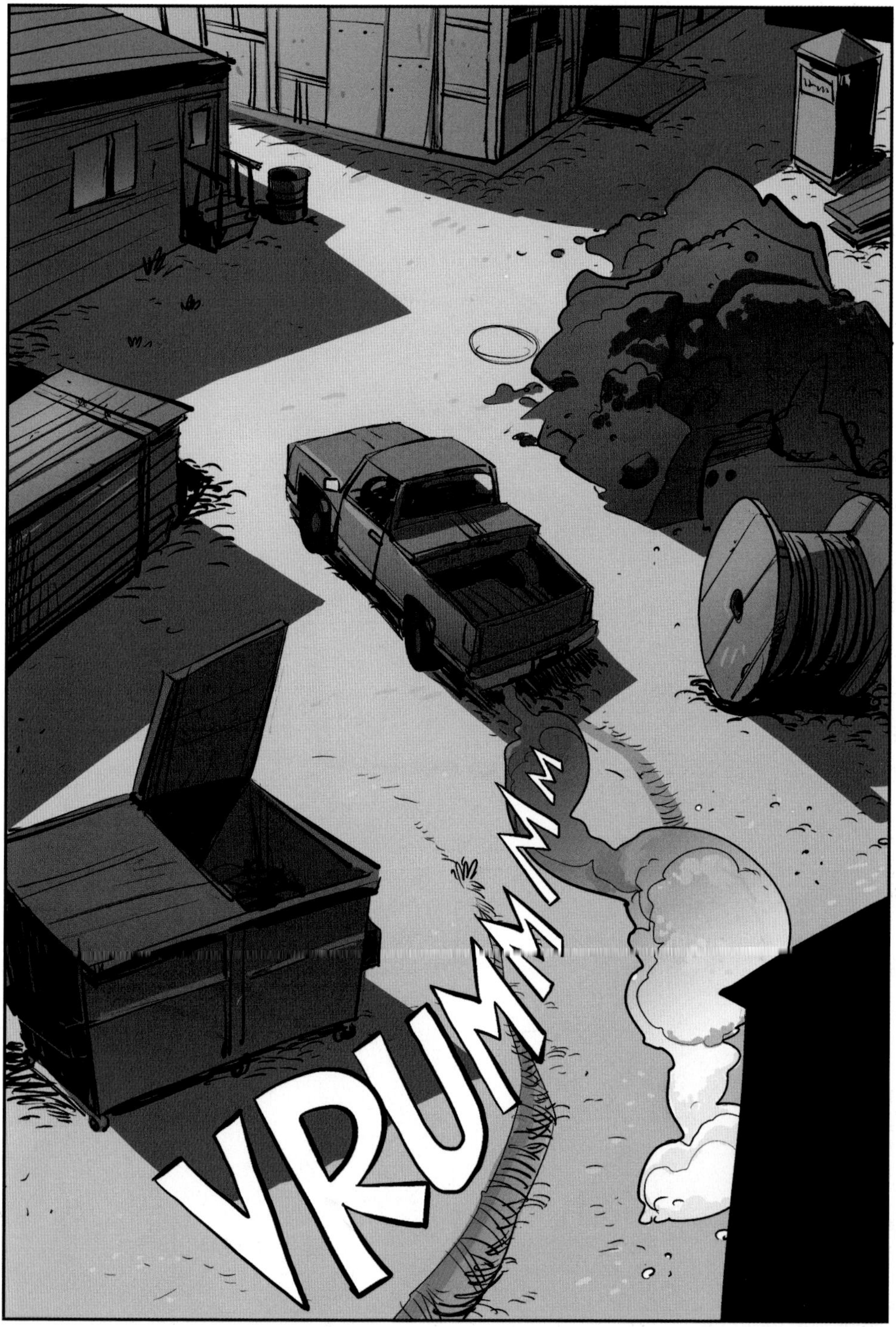
VRUMMMMM

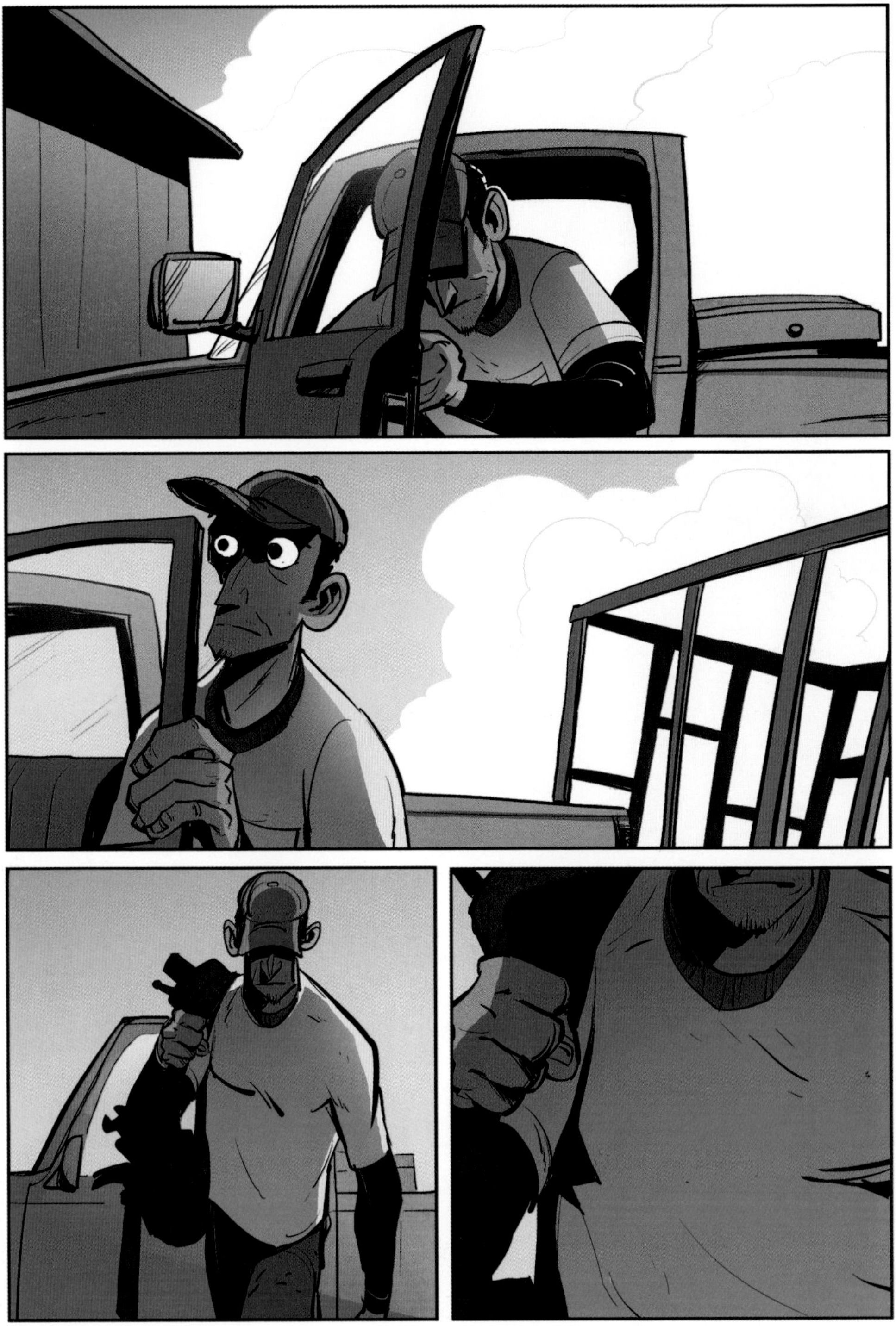

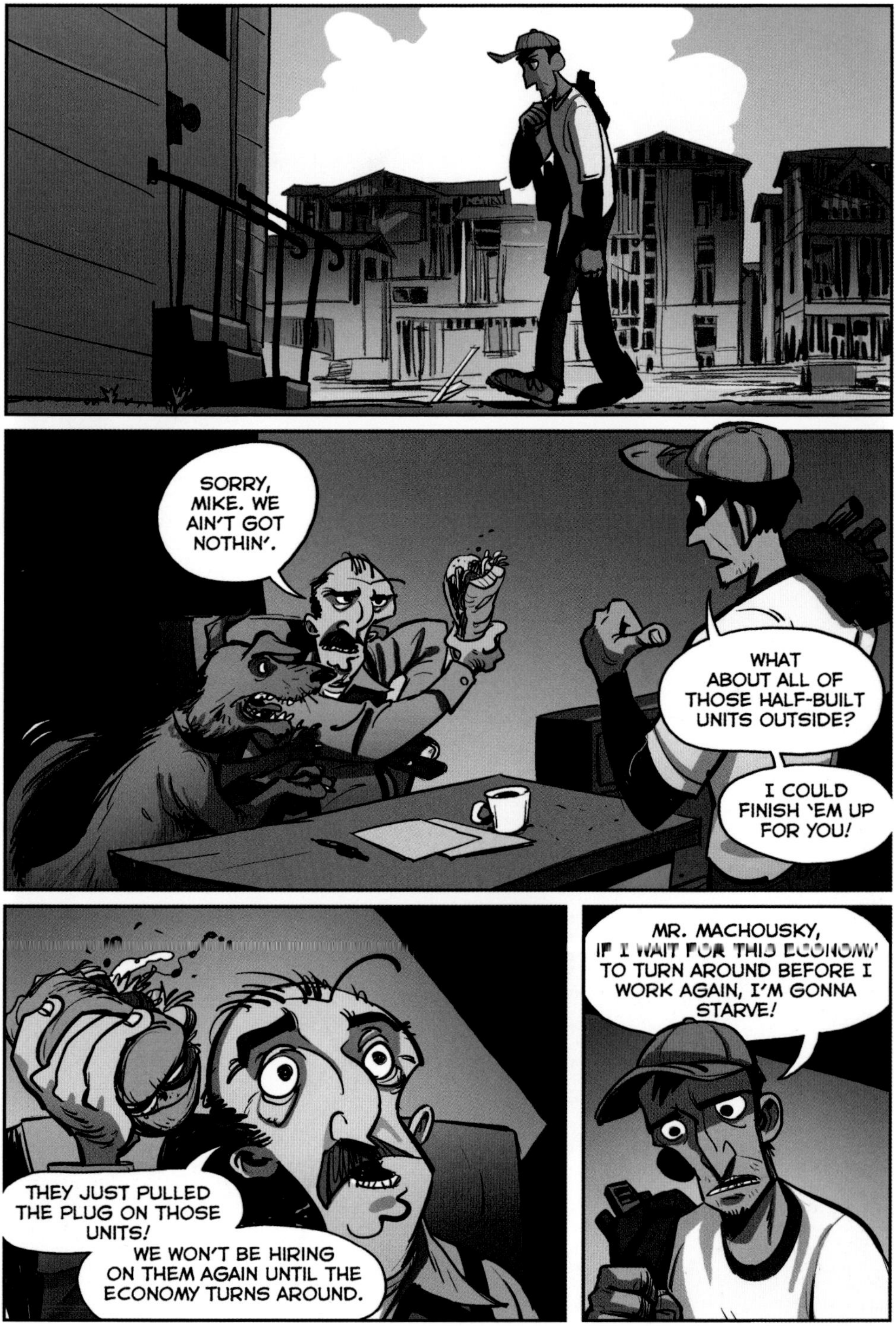
SORRY, MIKE. WE AIN'T GOT NOTHIN'.
WHAT ABOUT ALL OF THOSE HALF-BUILT UNITS OUTSIDE?
I COULD FINISH 'EM UP FOR YOU!
THEY JUST PULLED THE PLUG ON THOSE UNITS!
WE WON'T BE HIRING ON THEM AGAIN UNTIL THE ECONOMY TURNS AROUND.
MR. MACHOUSKY, IF I WAIT FOR THIS ECONOMY TO TURN AROUND BEFORE I WORK AGAIN, I'M GONNA STARVE!

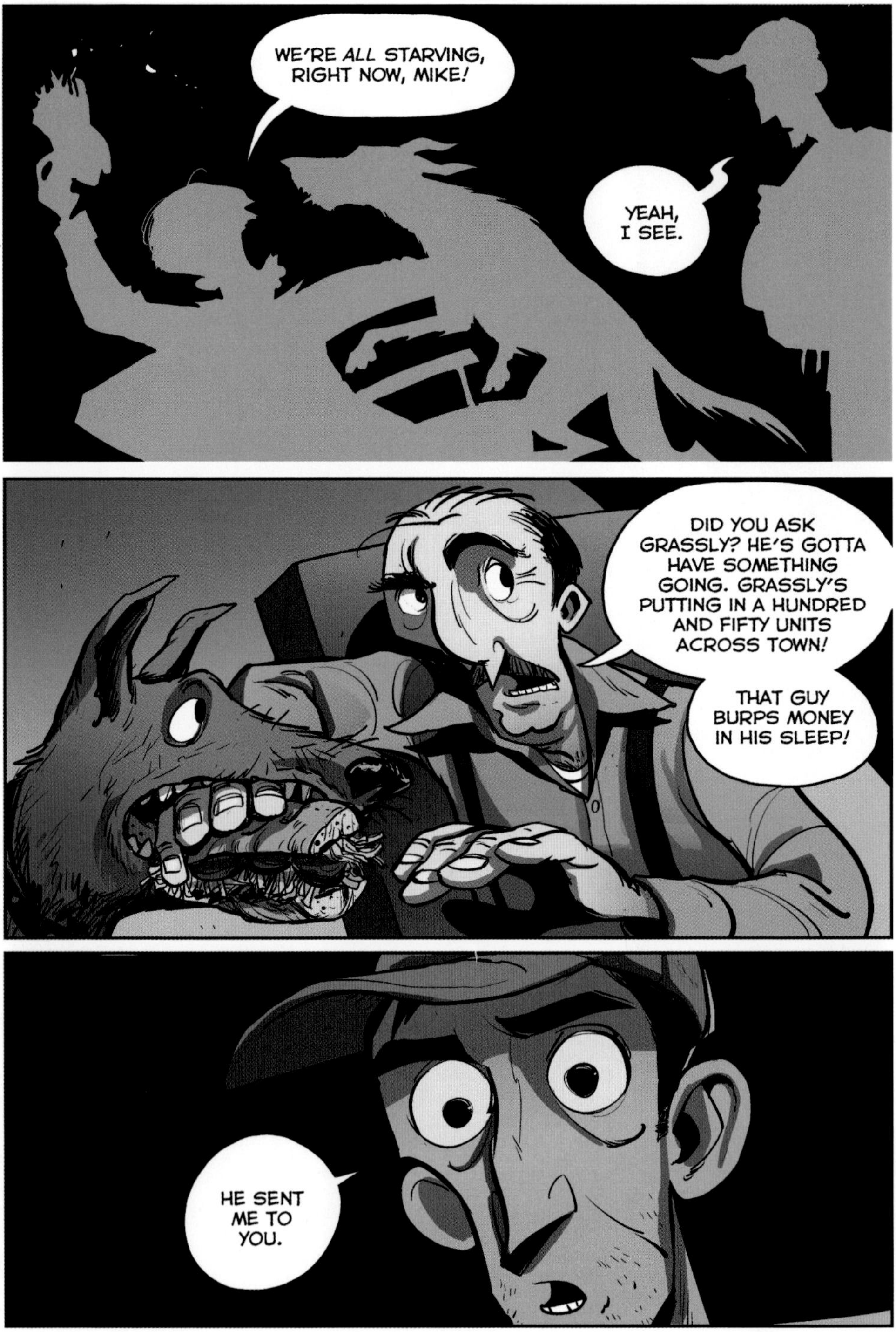
WE'RE *ALL* STARVING, RIGHT NOW, MIKE!
YEAH, I SEE.
DID YOU ASK GRASSLY? HE'S GOTTA HAVE SOMETHING GOING. GRASSLY'S PUTTING IN A HUNDRED AND FIFTY UNITS ACROSS TOWN!
THAT GUY BURPS MONEY IN HIS SLEEP!
HE SENT ME TO YOU.

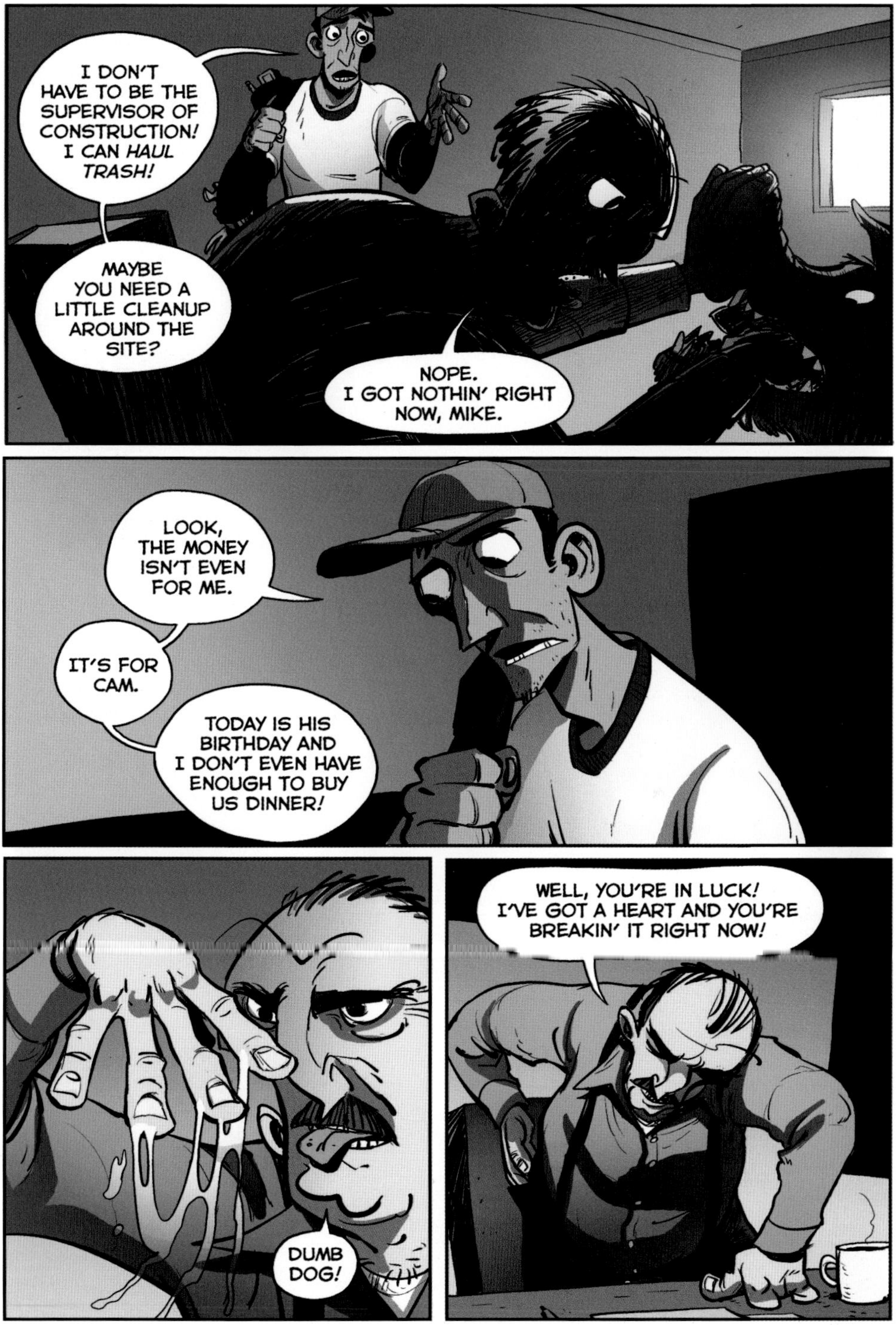
I DON'T HAVE TO BE THE SUPERVISOR OF CONSTRUCTION! I CAN *HAUL TRASH!*
MAYBE YOU NEED A LITTLE CLEANUP AROUND THE SITE?
NOPE. I GOT NOTHIN' RIGHT NOW, MIKE.
LOOK, THE MONEY ISN'T EVEN FOR ME.
IT'S FOR CAM.
TODAY IS HIS BIRTHDAY AND I DON'T EVEN HAVE ENOUGH TO BUY US DINNER!
DUMB DOG!
WELL, YOU'RE IN LUCK! I'VE GOT A HEART AND YOU'RE BREAKIN' IT RIGHT NOW!

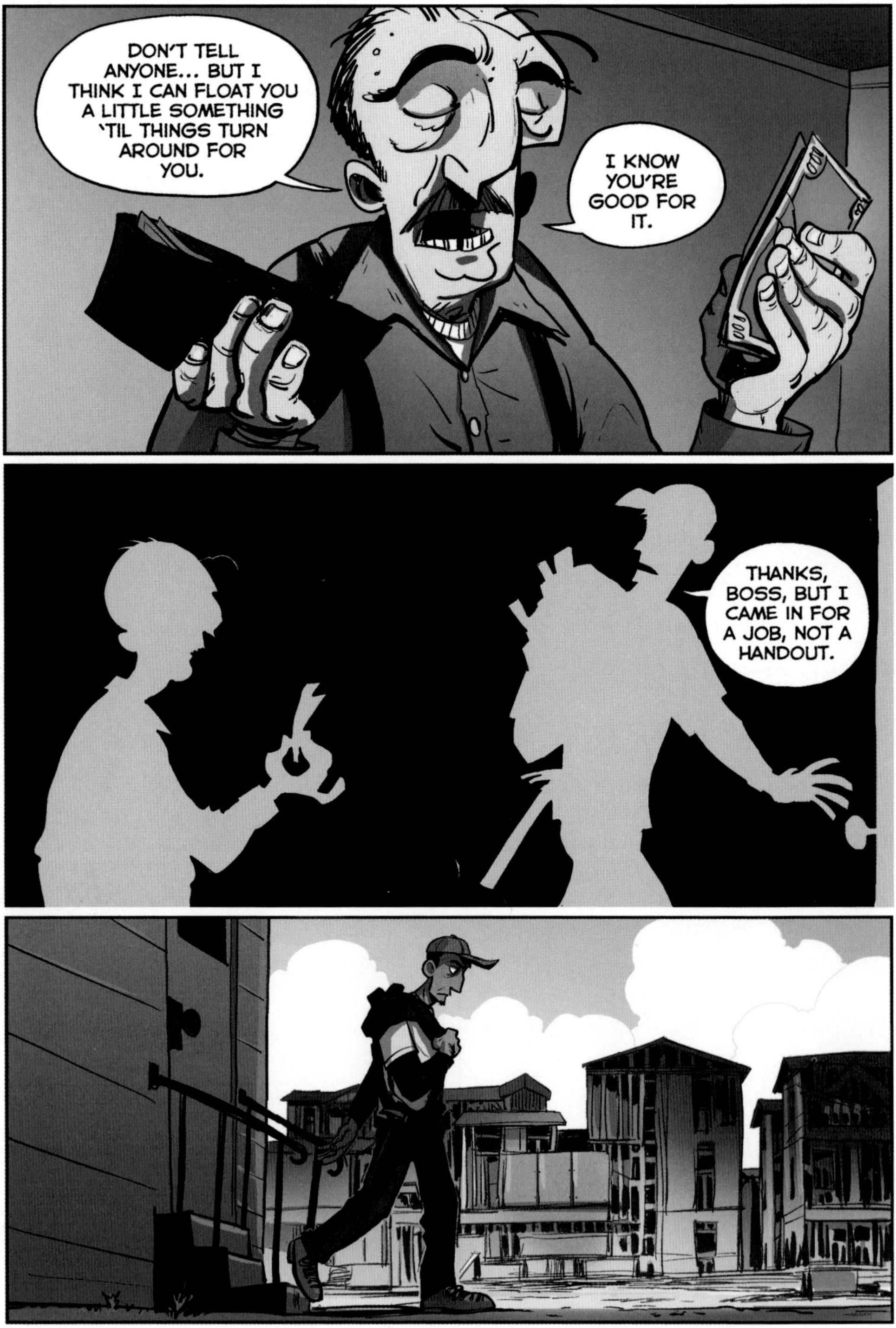
DON'T TELL ANYONE... BUT I THINK I CAN FLOAT YOU A LITTLE SOMETHING 'TIL THINGS TURN AROUND FOR YOU.
I KNOW YOU'RE GOOD FOR IT.
THANKS, BOSS, BUT I CAME IN FOR A JOB, NOT A HANDOUT.

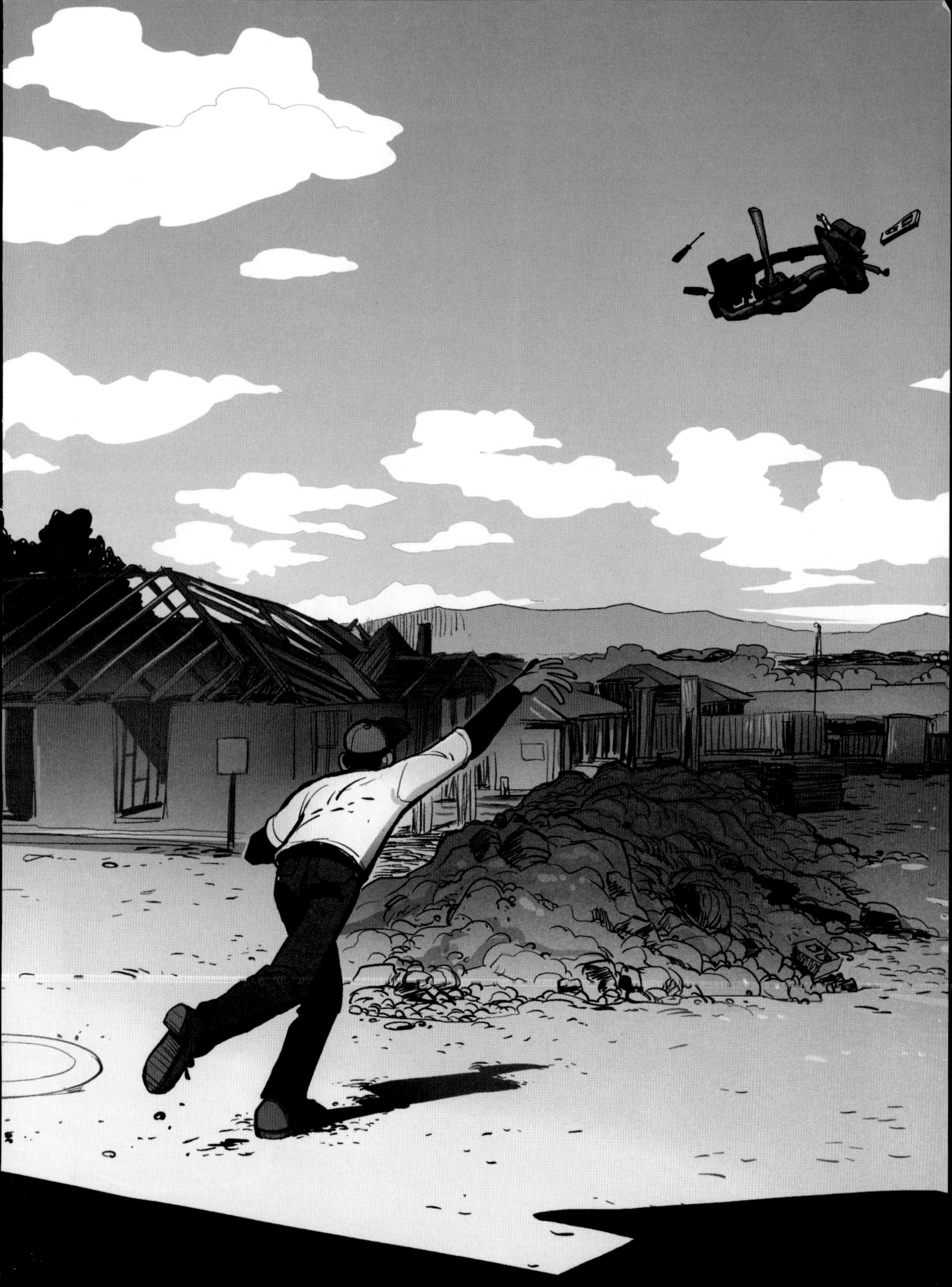

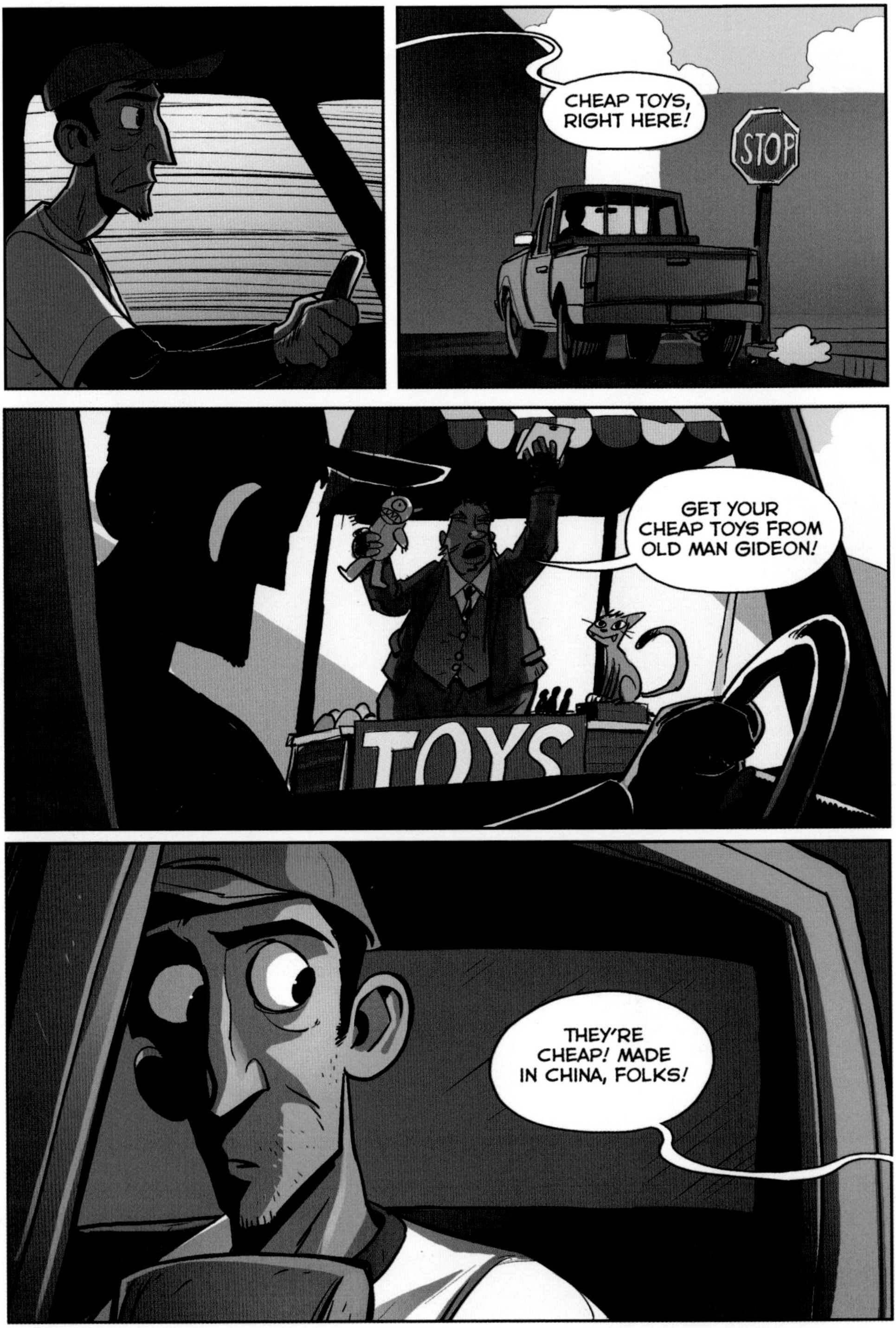
CHEAP TOYS, RIGHT HERE!
STOP
GET YOUR CHEAP TOYS FROM OLD MAN GIDEON!
TOYS
THEY'RE CHEAP! MADE IN CHINA, FOLKS!

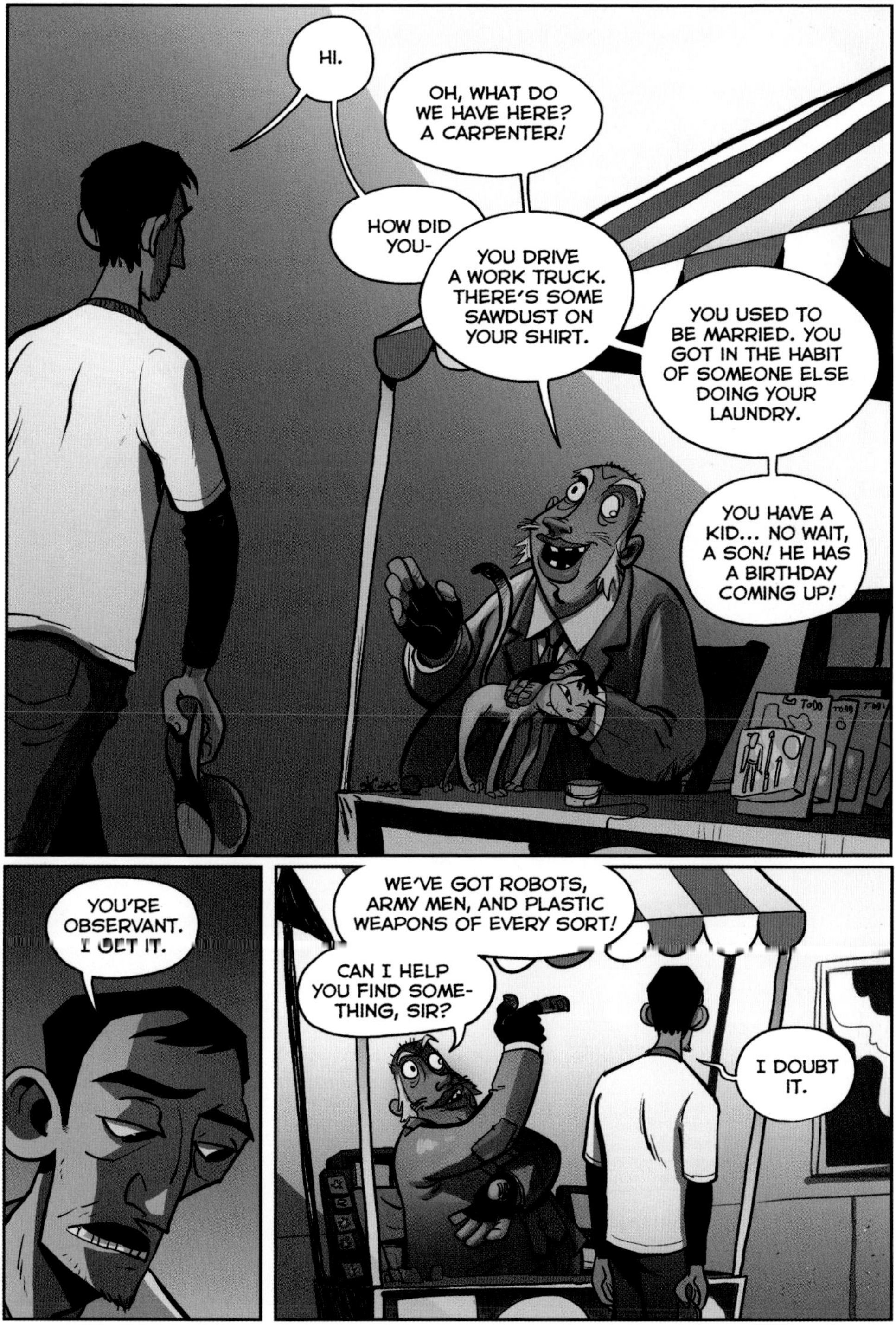
HI.
OH, WHAT DO WE HAVE HERE? A CARPENTER!
HOW DID YOU-
YOU DRIVE A WORK TRUCK. THERE'S SOME SAWDUST ON YOUR SHIRT.
YOU USED TO BE MARRIED. YOU GOT IN THE HABIT OF SOMEONE ELSE DOING YOUR LAUNDRY.
YOU HAVE A KID... NO WAIT, A SON! HE HAS A BIRTHDAY COMING UP!
YOU'RE OBSERVANT. I GET IT.
WE'VE GOT ROBOTS, ARMY MEN, AND PLASTIC WEAPONS OF EVERY SORT!
CAN I HELP YOU FIND SOME-THING, SIR?
I DOUBT IT.

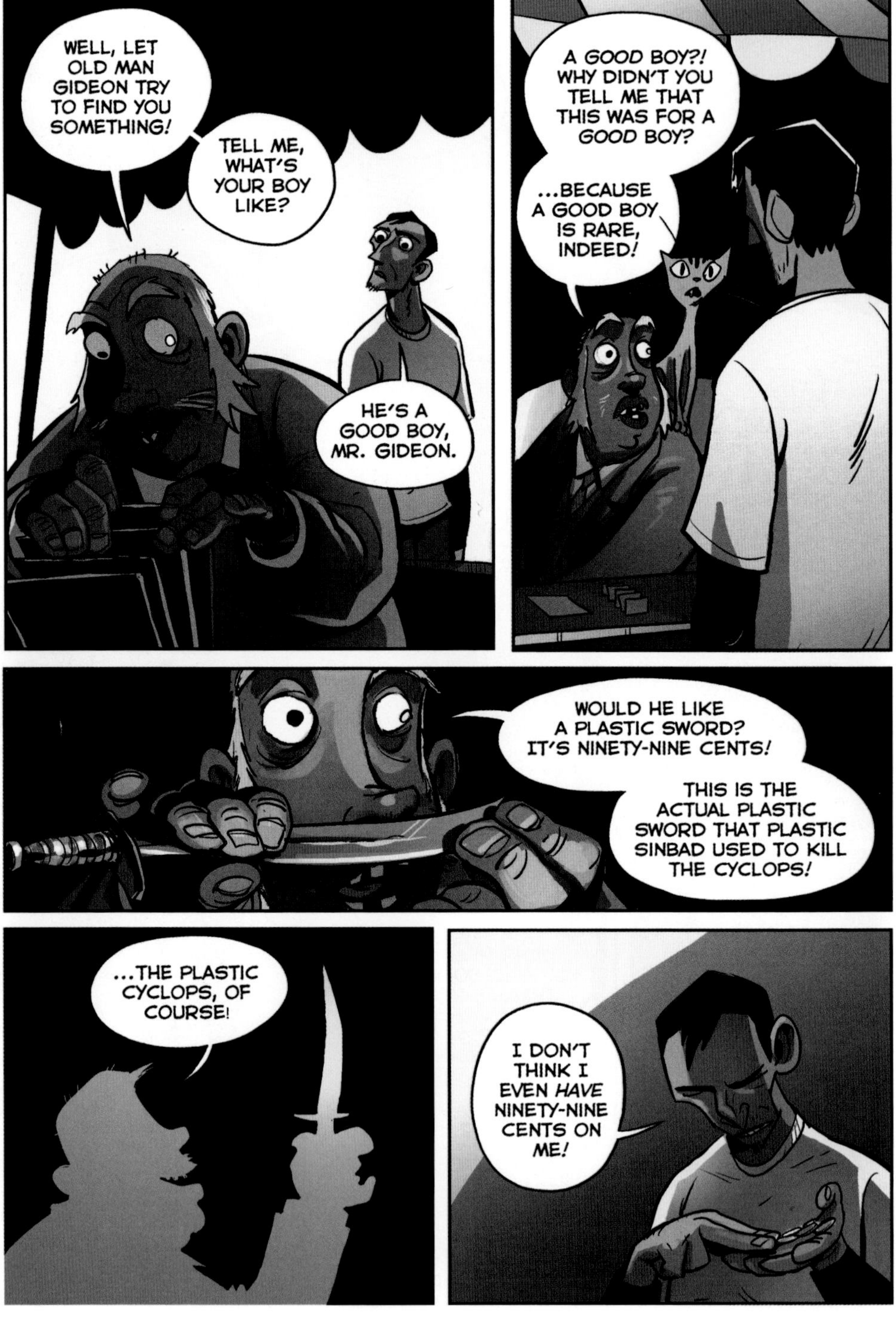
WELL, LET OLD MAN GIDEON TRY TO FIND YOU SOMETHING!
TELL ME, WHAT'S YOUR BOY LIKE?
HE'S A GOOD BOY, MR. GIDEON.
A *GOOD* BOY?! WHY DIDN'T YOU TELL ME THAT THIS WAS FOR A *GOOD* BOY?
...BECAUSE A GOOD BOY IS RARE, INDEED!
WOULD HE LIKE A PLASTIC SWORD? IT'S NINETY-NINE CENTS!
THIS IS THE ACTUAL PLASTIC SWORD THAT PLASTIC SINBAD USED TO KILL THE *CYCLOPS!*
...THE PLASTIC CYCLOPS, OF COURSE!
I DON'T THINK I EVEN *HAVE* NINETY-NINE CENTS ON ME!

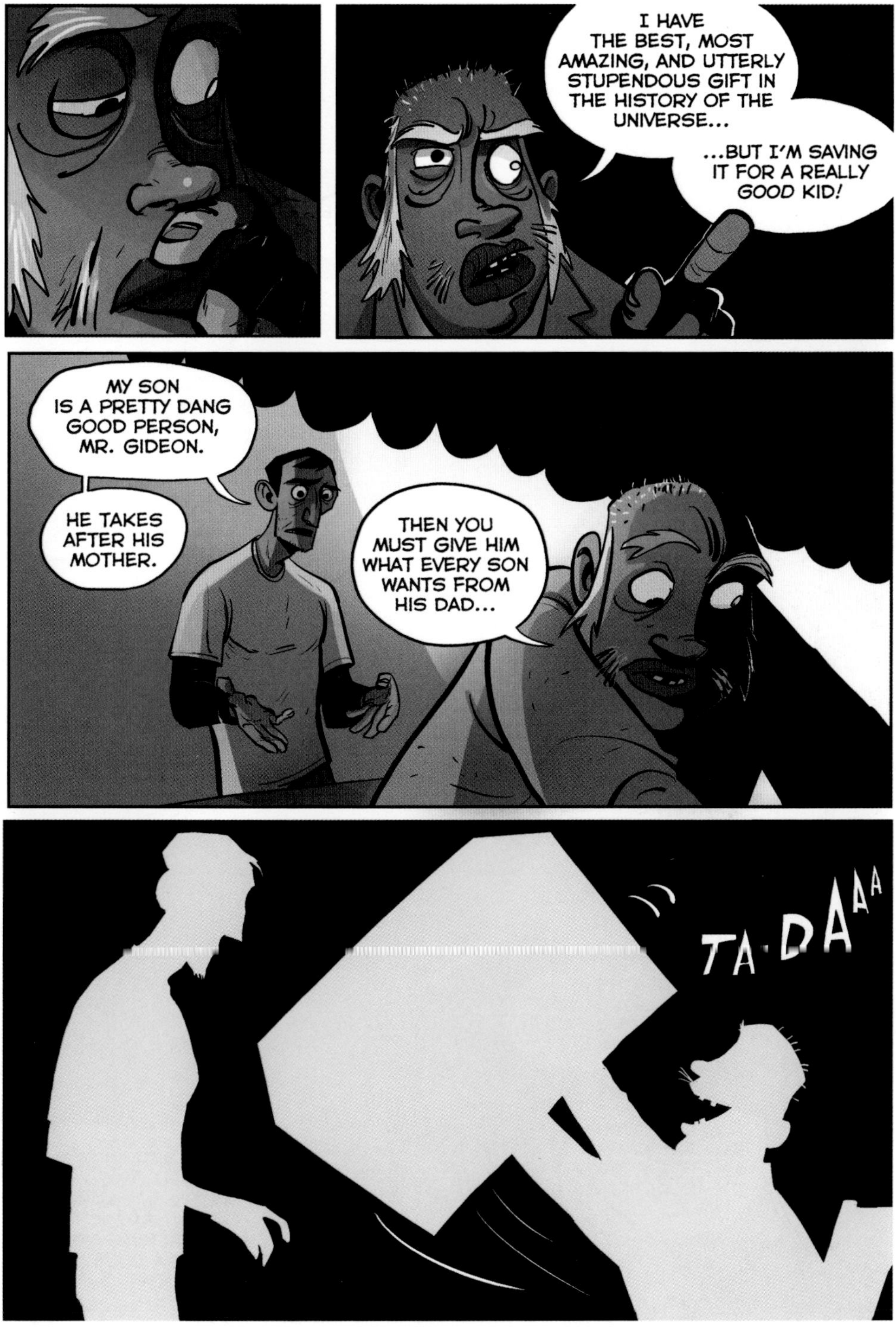
I HAVE THE BEST, MOST AMAZING, AND UTTERLY STUPENDOUS GIFT IN THE HISTORY OF THE UNIVERSE...
...BUT I'M SAVING IT FOR A REALLY *GOOD* KID!
MY SON IS A PRETTY DANG GOOD PERSON, MR. GIDEON.
HE TAKES AFTER HIS MOTHER.
THEN YOU MUST GIVE HIM WHAT EVERY SON WANTS FROM HIS DAD...
TA-DAAAA

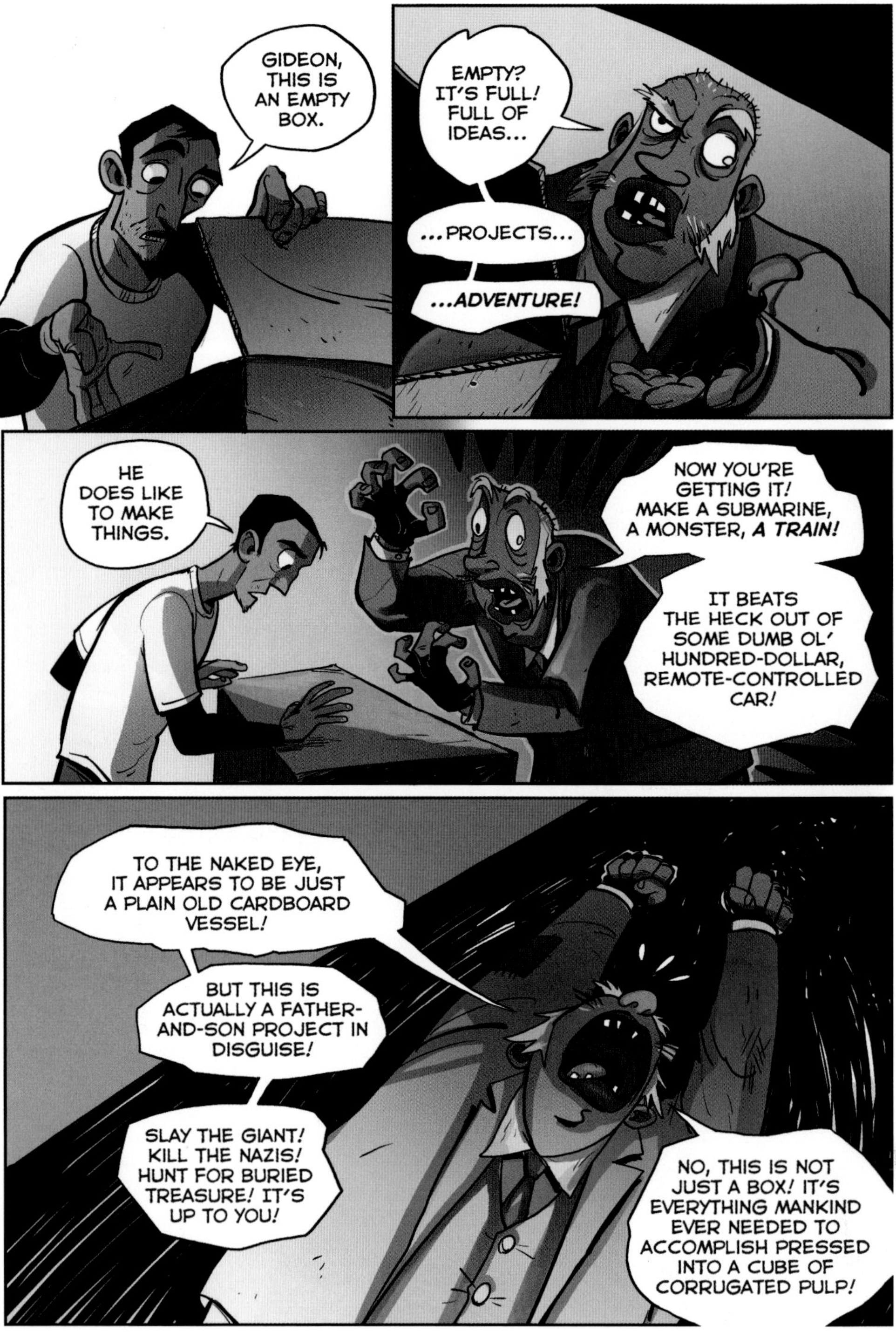
GIDEON, THIS IS AN EMPTY BOX.
EMPTY? IT'S FULL! FULL OF IDEAS...
...PROJECTS...
...ADVENTURE!
HE DOES LIKE TO MAKE THINGS.
NOW YOU'RE GETTING IT! MAKE A SUBMARINE, A MONSTER, A TRAIN!
IT BEATS THE HECK OUT OF SOME DUMB OL' HUNDRED-DOLLAR, REMOTE-CONTROLLED CAR!
TO THE NAKED EYE, IT APPEARS TO BE JUST A PLAIN OLD CARDBOARD VESSEL!
BUT THIS IS ACTUALLY A FATHER-AND-SON PROJECT IN DISGUISE!
SLAY THE GIANT! KILL THE NAZIS! HUNT FOR BURIED TREASURE! IT'S UP TO YOU!
NO, THIS IS NOT JUST A BOX! IT'S EVERYTHING MANKIND EVER NEEDED TO ACCOMPLISH PRESSED INTO A CUBE OF CORRUGATED PULP!

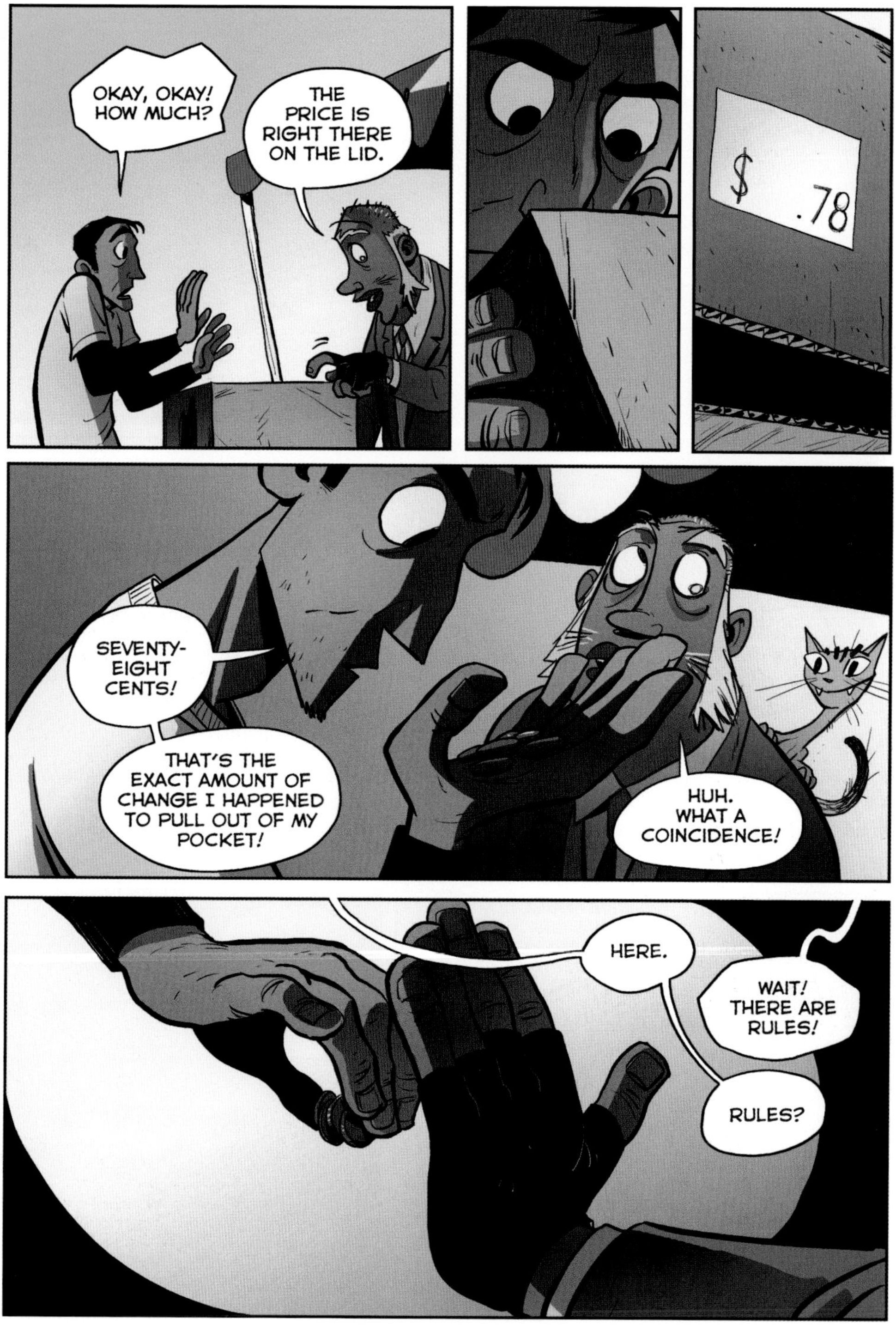
OKAY, OKAY! HOW MUCH?
THE PRICE IS RIGHT THERE ON THE LID.
$ .78
SEVENTY-EIGHT CENTS!
THAT'S THE EXACT AMOUNT OF CHANGE I HAPPENED TO PULL OUT OF MY POCKET!
HUH. WHAT A COINCIDENCE!
HERE.
WAIT! THERE ARE RULES!
RULES?

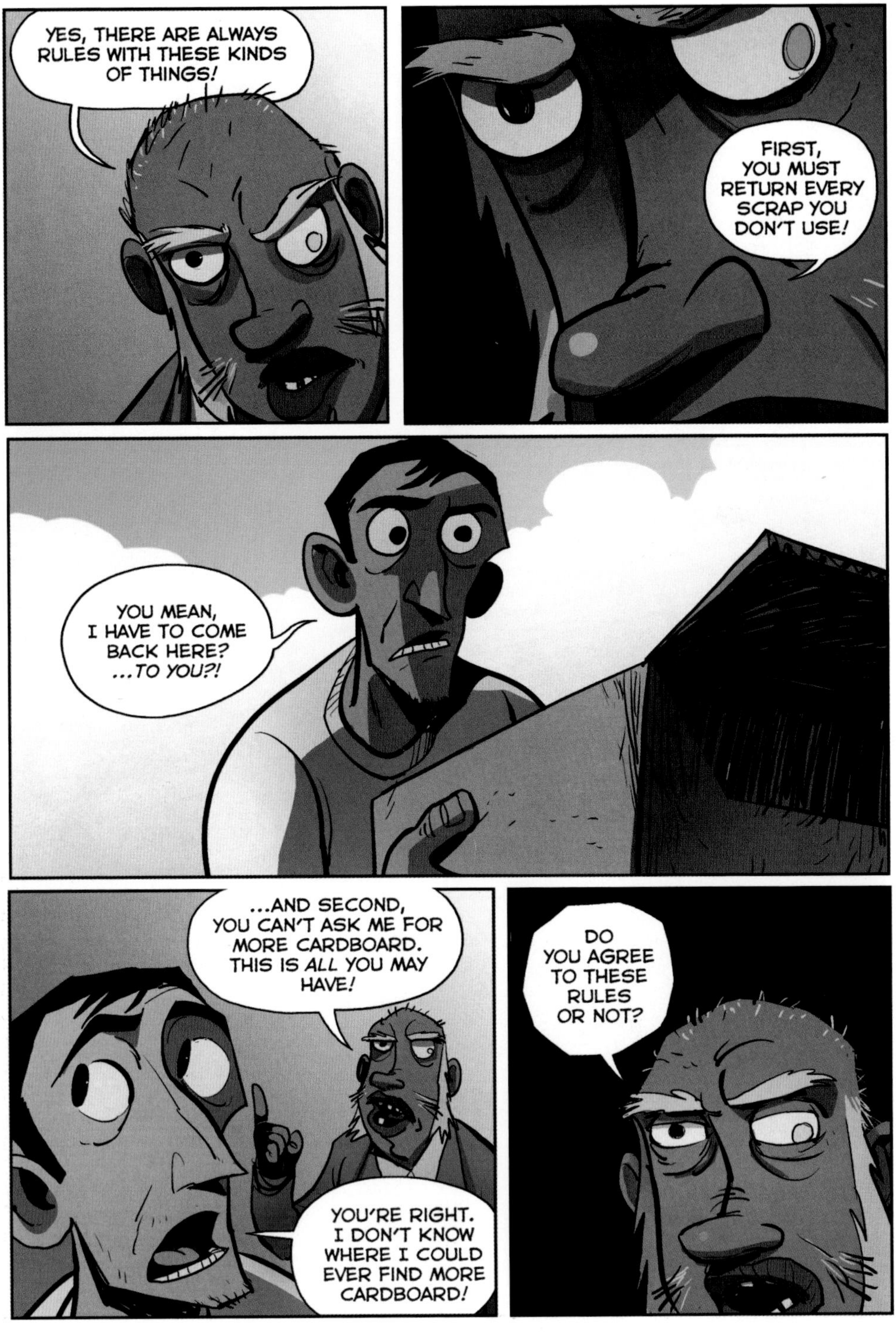
YES, THERE ARE ALWAYS RULES WITH THESE KINDS OF THINGS!
FIRST, YOU MUST RETURN EVERY SCRAP YOU DON'T USE!
YOU MEAN, I HAVE TO COME BACK HERE? ...TO YOU?!
...AND SECOND, YOU CAN'T ASK ME FOR MORE CARDBOARD. THIS IS *ALL* YOU MAY HAVE!
YOU'RE RIGHT. I DON'T KNOW WHERE I COULD EVER FIND MORE CARDBOARD!
DO YOU AGREE TO THESE RULES OR NOT?

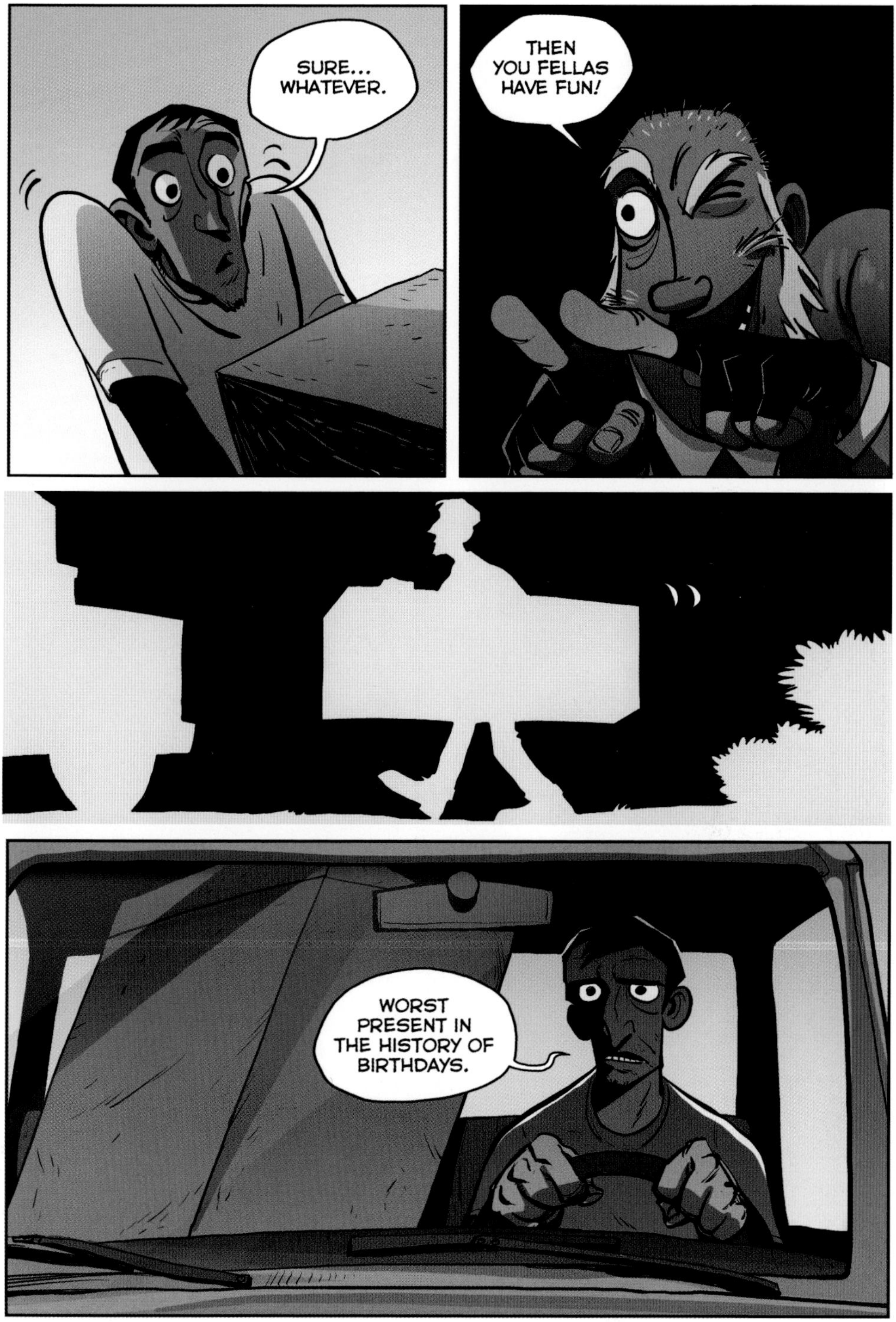
SURE... WHATEVER.
THEN YOU FELLAS HAVE FUN!
WORST PRESENT IN THE HISTORY OF BIRTHDAYS.

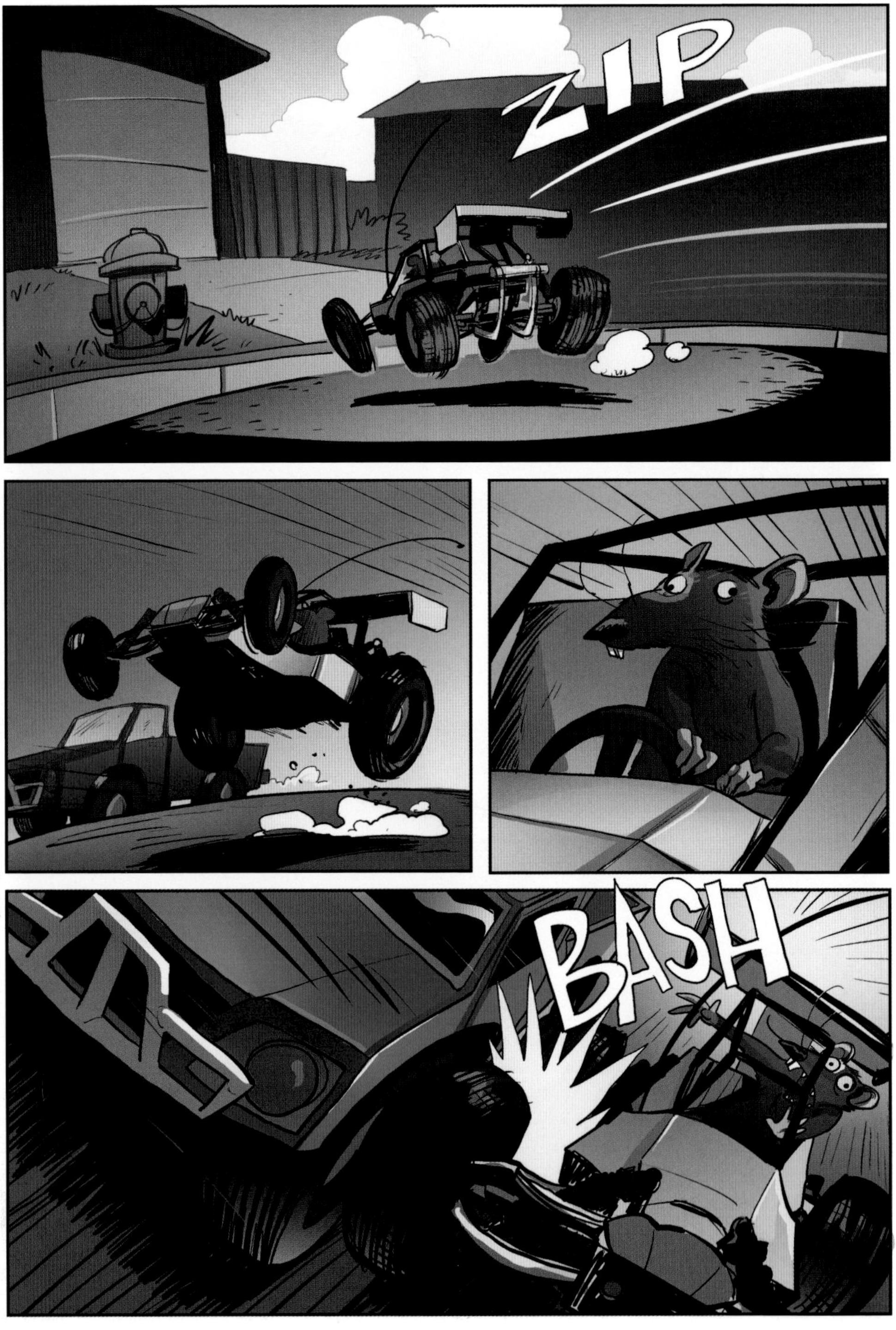
ZIP
BASH

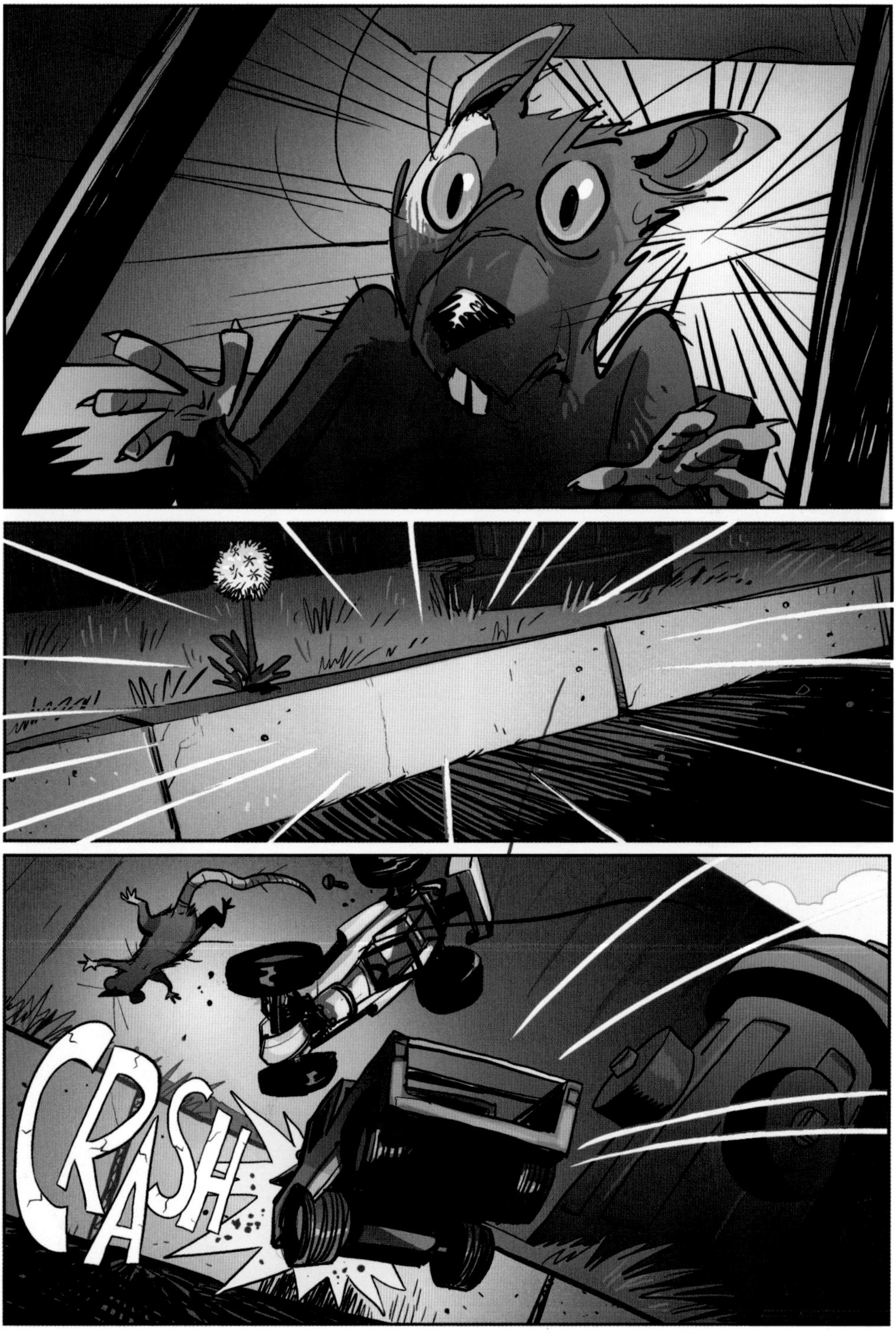
CRASH

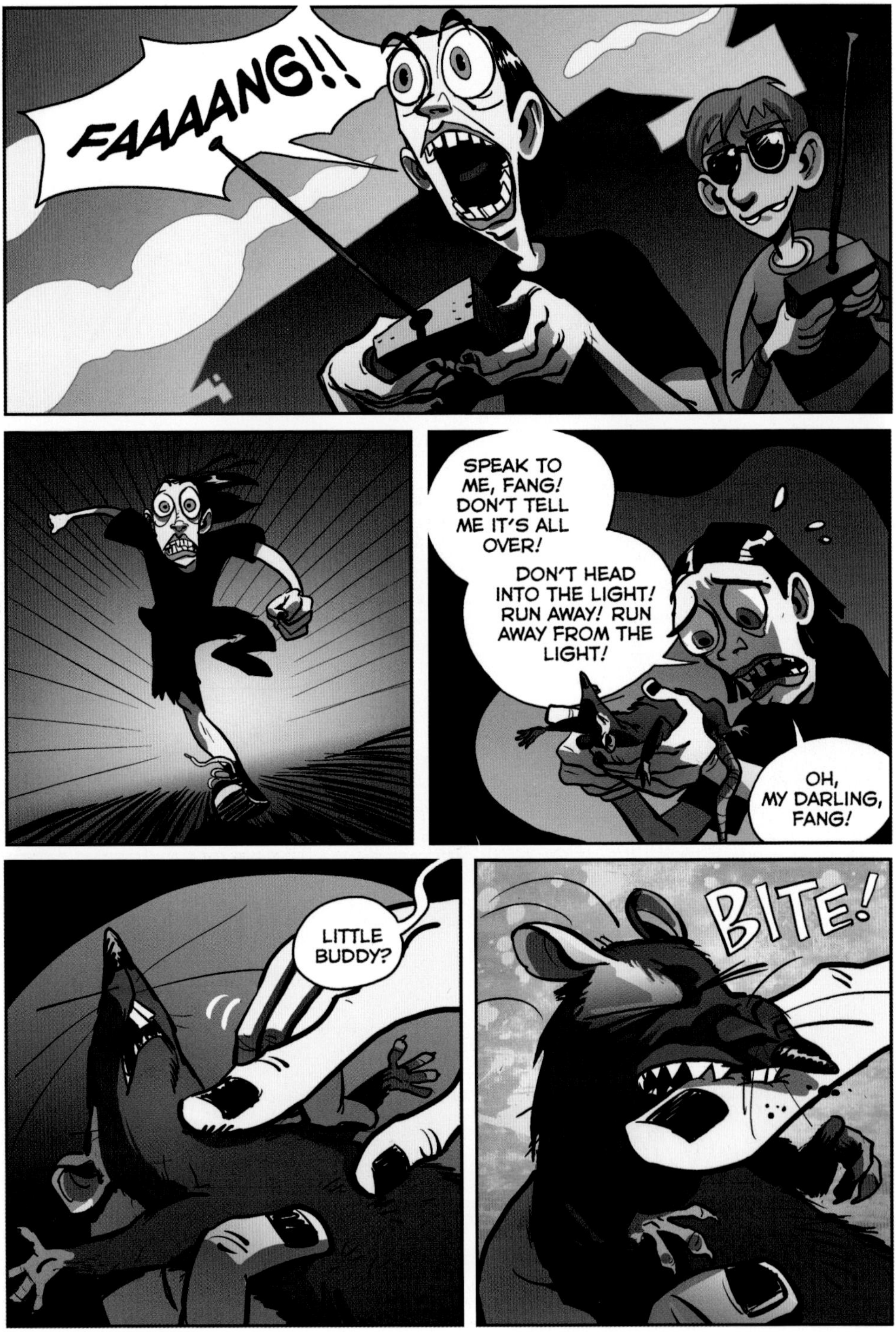
FAAAANG!!
SPEAK TO ME, FANG! DON'T TELL ME IT'S ALL OVER!
DON'T HEAD INTO THE LIGHT! RUN AWAY! RUN AWAY FROM THE LIGHT!
OH, MY DARLING, FANG!
LITTLE BUDDY?
BITE!

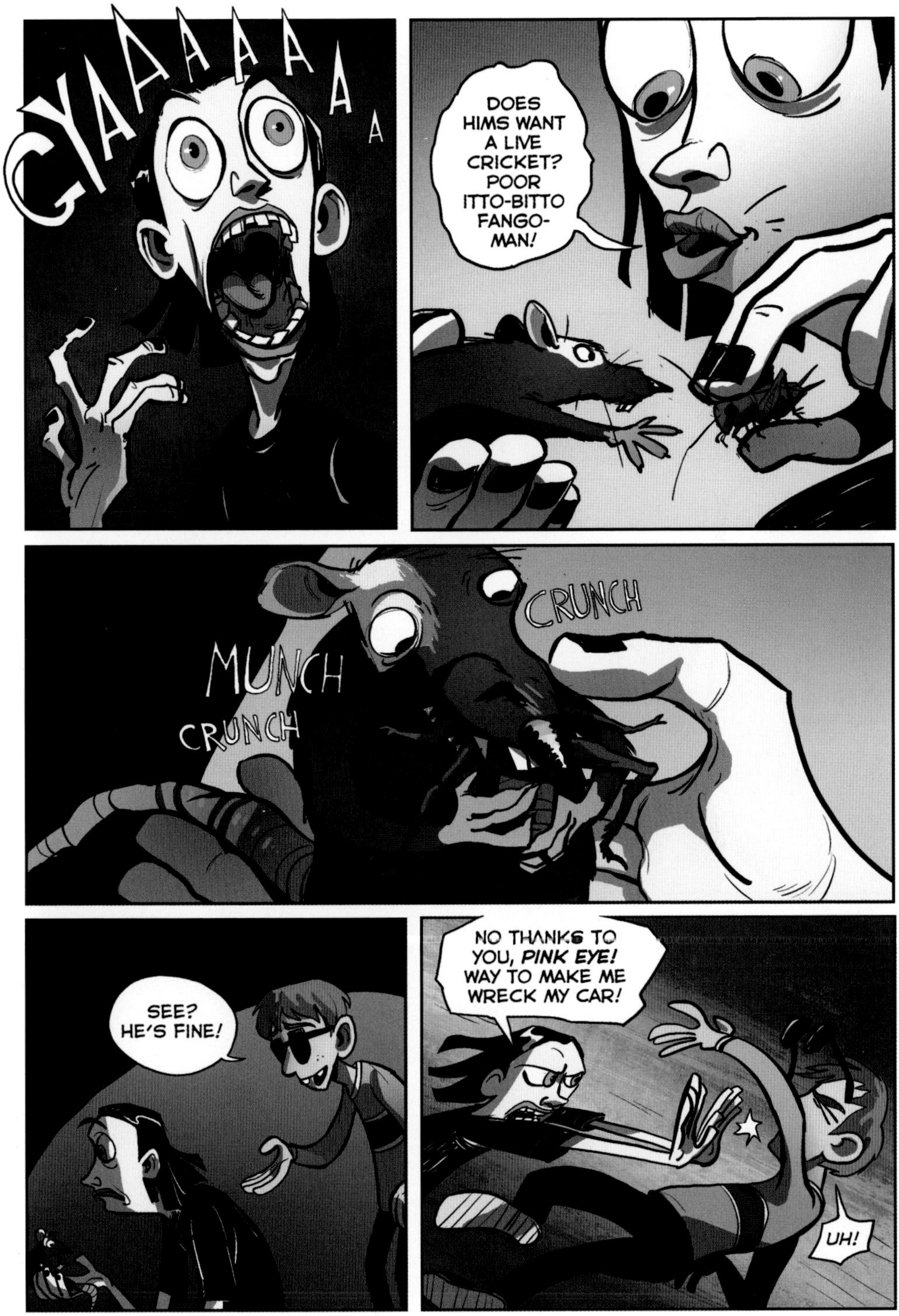
GYAAAAAAAA
DOES HIMS WANT A LIVE CRICKET? POOR ITTO-BITTO FANGO-MAN!
CRUNCH
MUNCH
CRUNCH
SEE? HE'S FINE!
NO THANKS TO YOU, *PINK EYE!* WAY TO MAKE ME WRECK MY CAR!
UH!

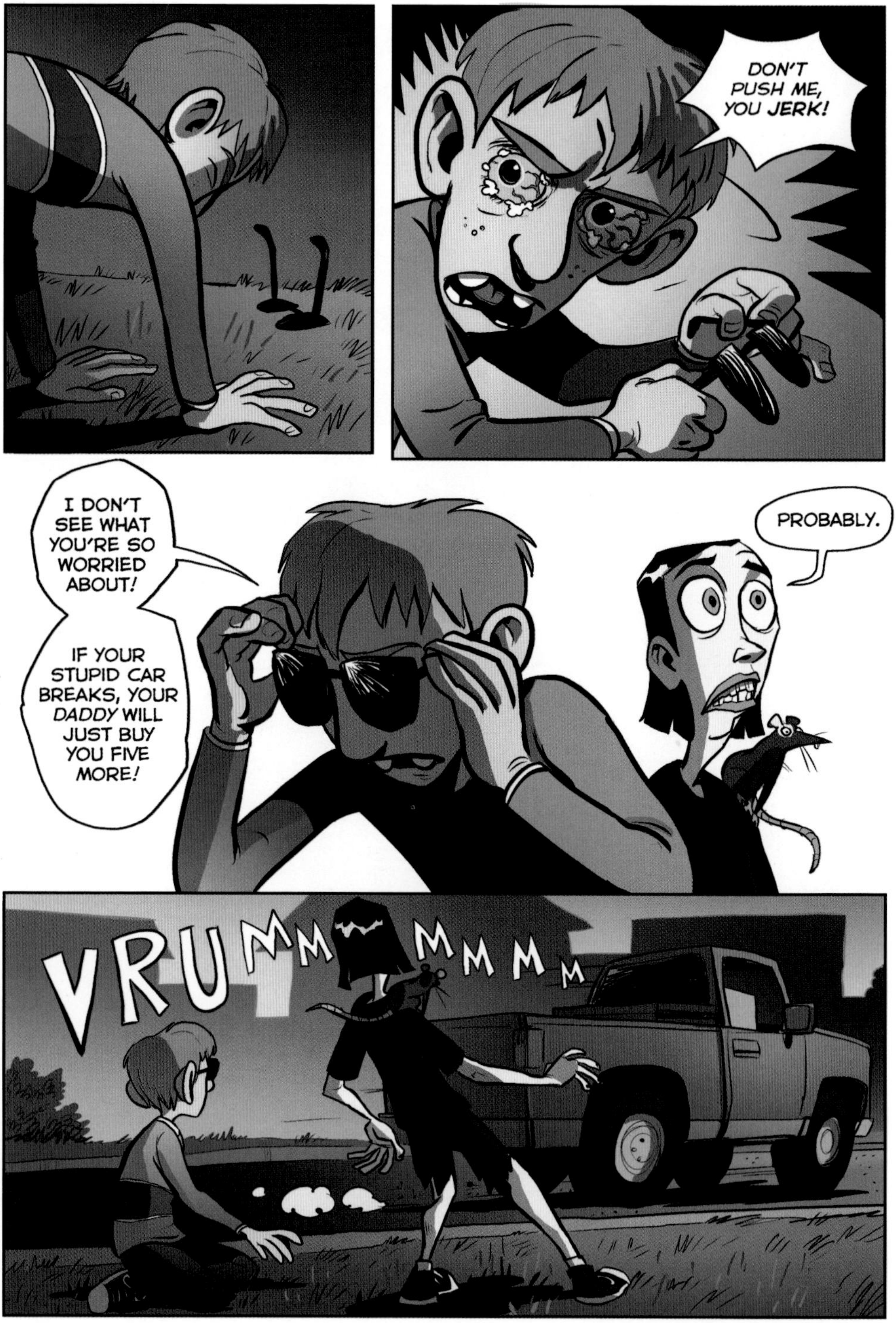
DON'T PUSH ME, YOU JERK!
I DON'T SEE WHAT YOU'RE SO WORRIED ABOUT!
IF YOUR STUPID CAR BREAKS, YOUR DADDY WILL JUST BUY YOU FIVE MORE!
PROBABLY.
VRUMMMMMMM

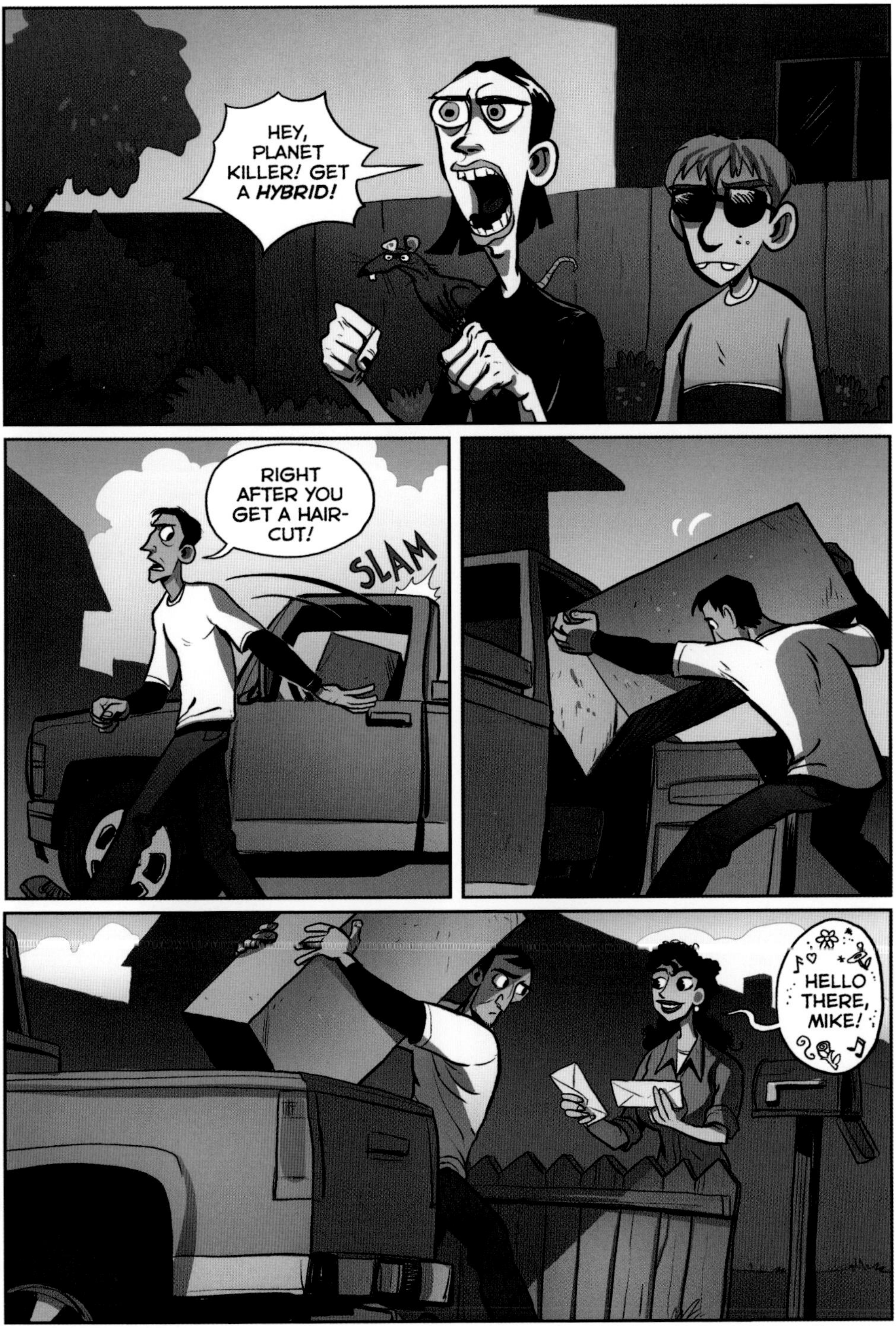
HEY, PLANET KILLER! GET A HYBRID!
RIGHT AFTER YOU GET A HAIR-CUT!
SLAM
HELLO THERE, MIKE!

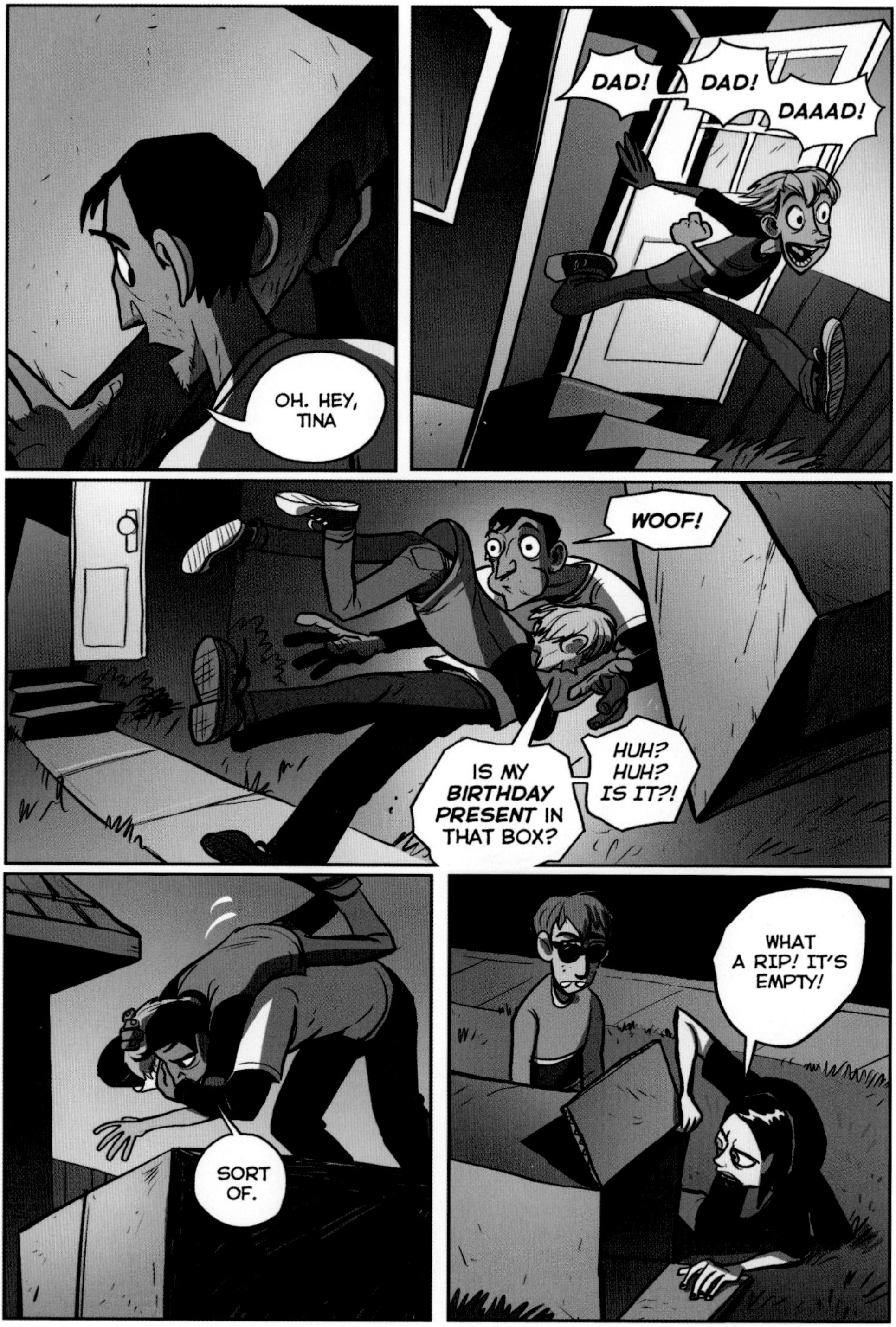
OH. HEY, TINA
DAD! DAD! DAAAD!
WOOF!
IS MY *BIRTHDAY PRESENT* IN THAT BOX?
HUH? HUH? IS IT?!
SORT OF.
WHAT A RIP! IT'S EMPTY!

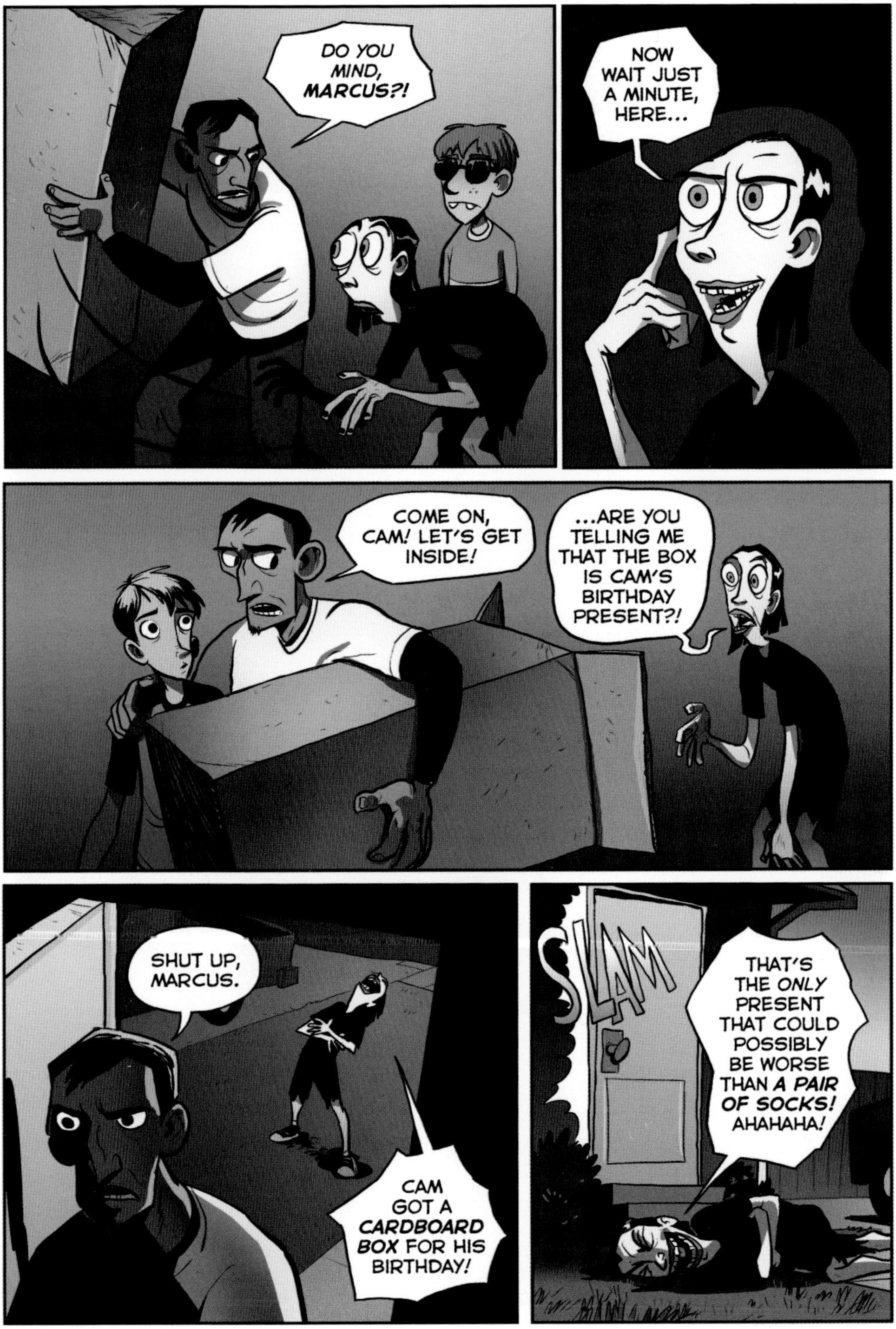
DO YOU MIND, MARCUS?!
NOW WAIT JUST A MINUTE, HERE...
COME ON, CAM! LET'S GET INSIDE!
...ARE YOU TELLING ME THAT THE BOX IS CAM'S BIRTHDAY PRESENT?!
SHUT UP, MARCUS.
CAM GOT A CARDBOARD BOX FOR HIS BIRTHDAY!
SLAM
THAT'S THE ONLY PRESENT THAT COULD POSSIBLY BE WORSE THAN A PAIR OF SOCKS! AHAHAHA!

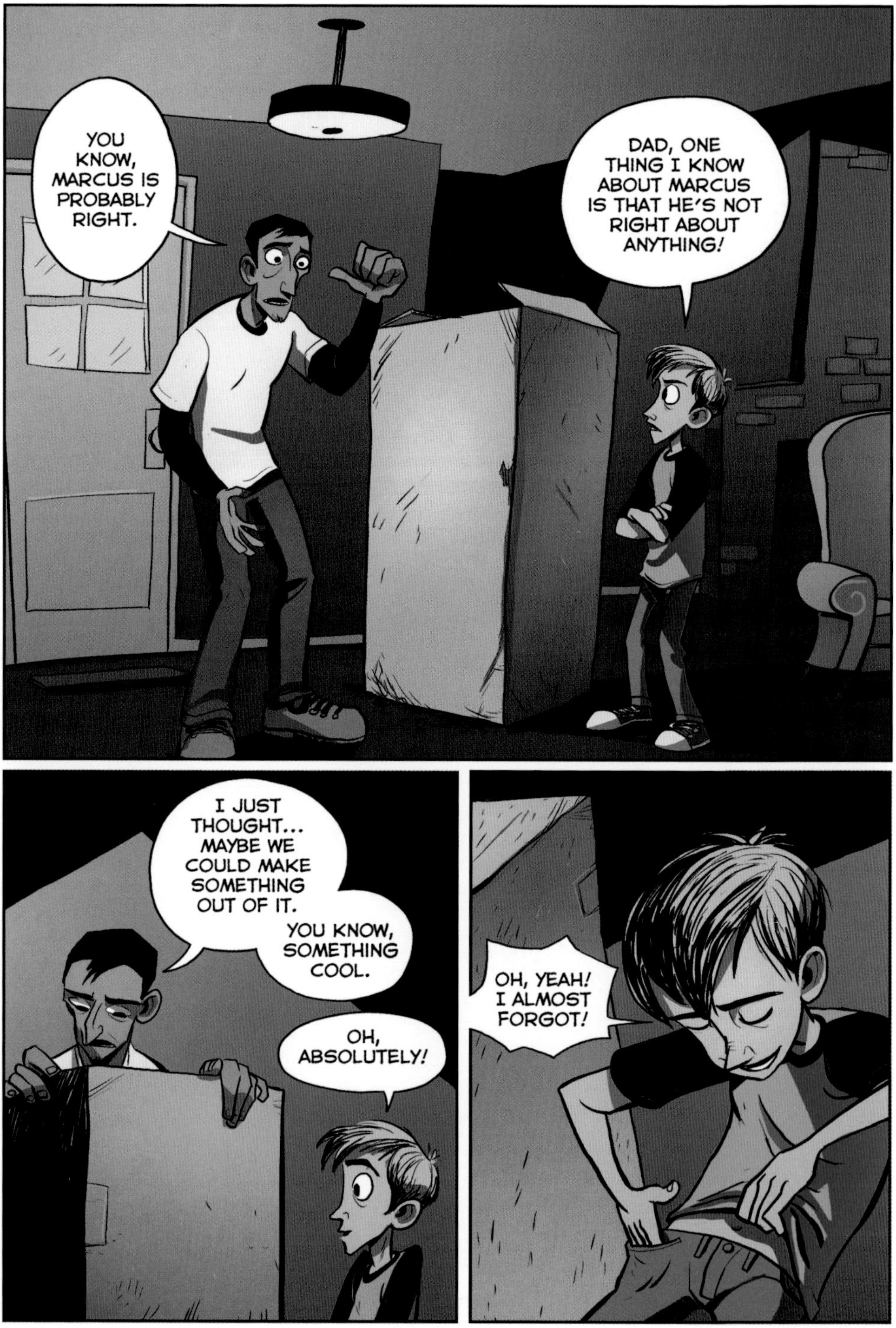
YOU KNOW, MARCUS IS PROBABLY RIGHT.
DAD, ONE THING I KNOW ABOUT MARCUS IS THAT HE'S NOT RIGHT ABOUT ANYTHING!
I JUST THOUGHT... MAYBE WE COULD MAKE SOMETHING OUT OF IT.
YOU KNOW, SOMETHING COOL.
OH, ABSOLUTELY!
OH, YEAH! I ALMOST FORGOT!

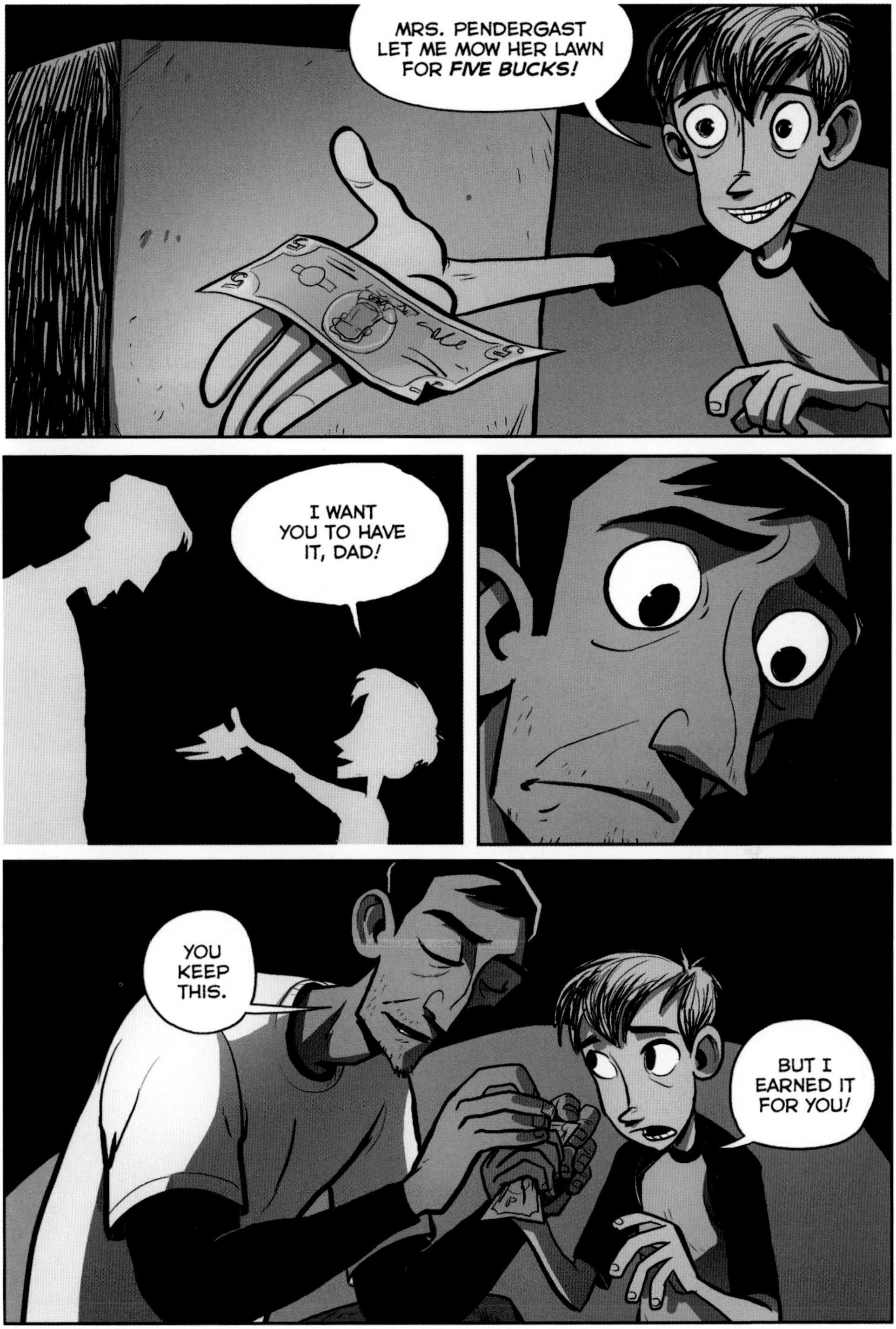
MRS. PENDERGAST LET ME MOW HER LAWN FOR *FIVE BUCKS!*
I WANT YOU TO HAVE IT, DAD!
YOU KEEP THIS.
BUT I EARNED IT FOR YOU!

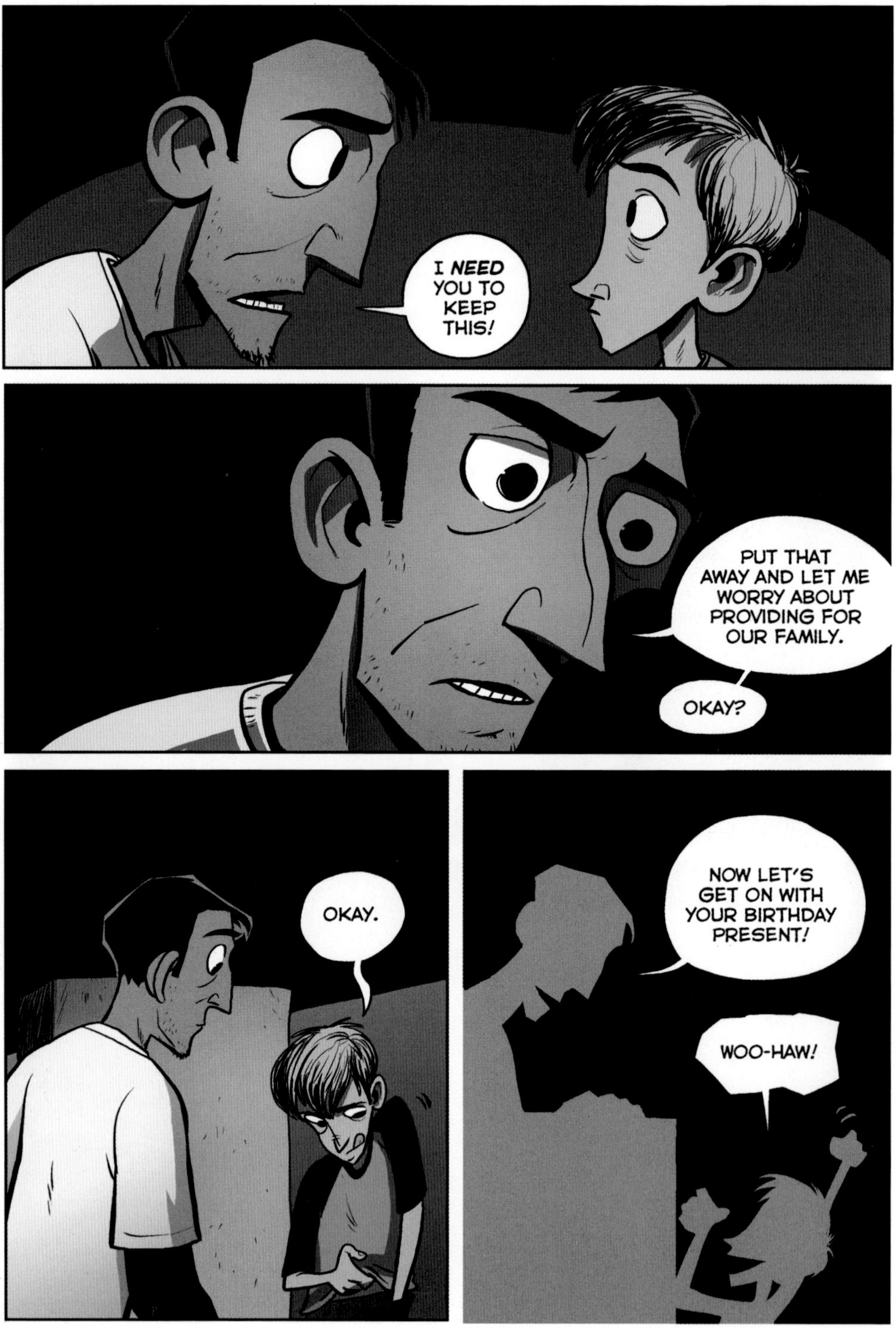
I NEED YOU TO KEEP THIS!
PUT THAT AWAY AND LET ME WORRY ABOUT PROVIDING FOR OUR FAMILY.
OKAY?
OKAY.
NOW LET'S GET ON WITH YOUR BIRTHDAY PRESENT!
WOO-HAW!

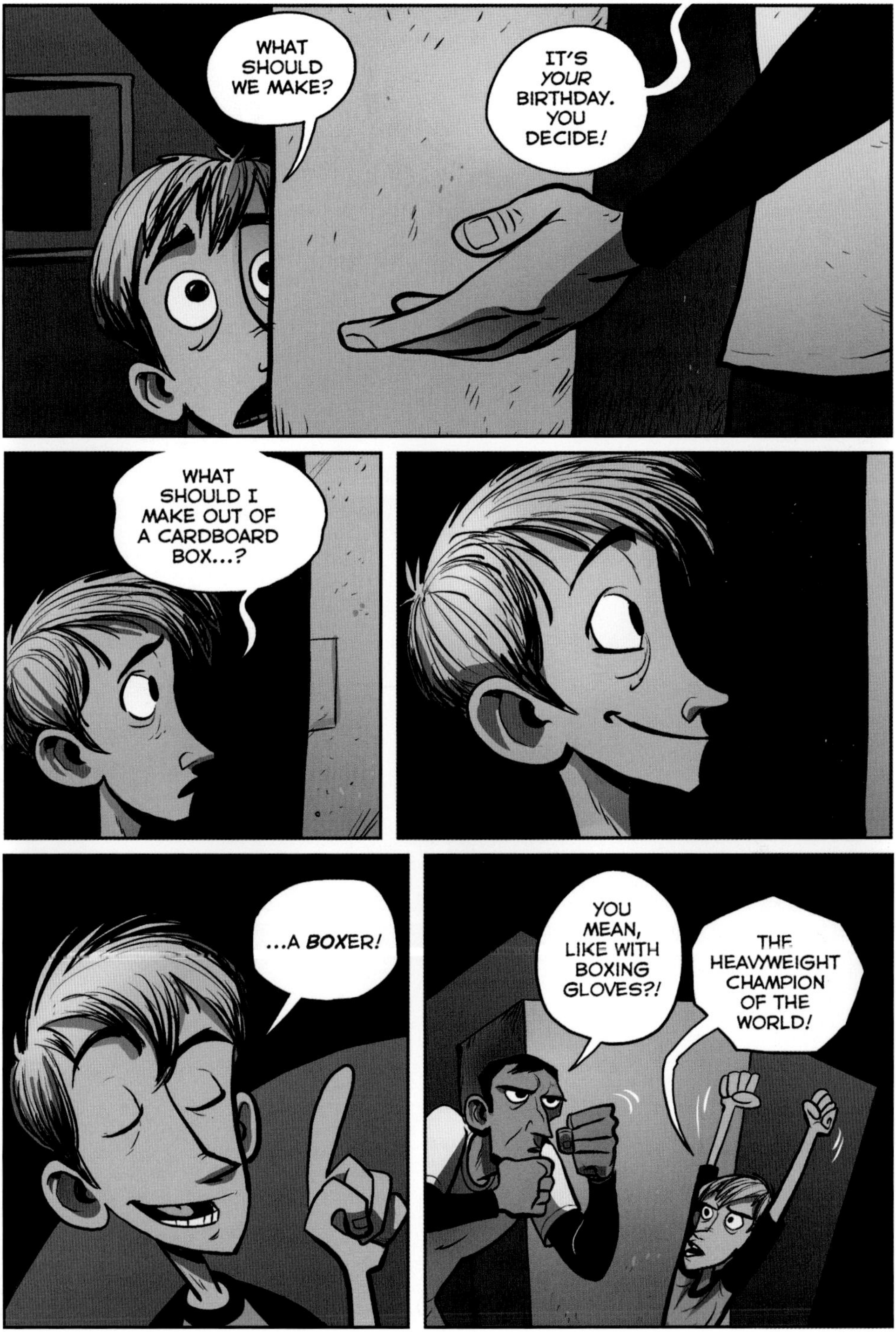
WHAT SHOULD WE MAKE?
IT'S *YOUR* BIRTHDAY. YOU DECIDE!
WHAT SHOULD I MAKE OUT OF A CARDBOARD BOX...?
...A *BOXER!*
YOU MEAN, LIKE WITH BOXING GLOVES?!
THE HEAVYWEIGHT CHAMPION OF THE WORLD!

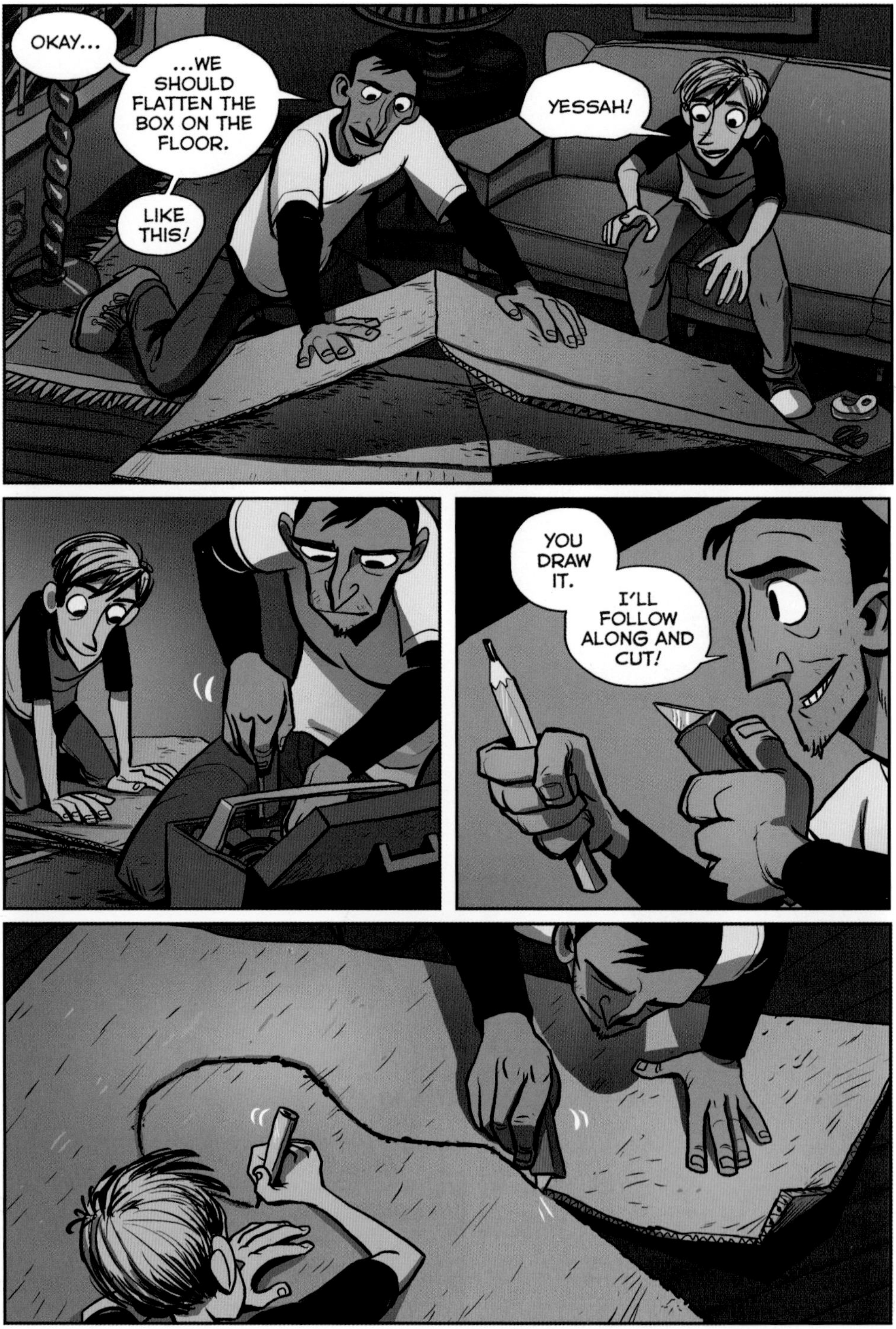
OKAY...
...WE SHOULD FLATTEN THE BOX ON THE FLOOR.
LIKE THIS!
YESSAH!
YOU DRAW IT.
I'LL FOLLOW ALONG AND CUT!

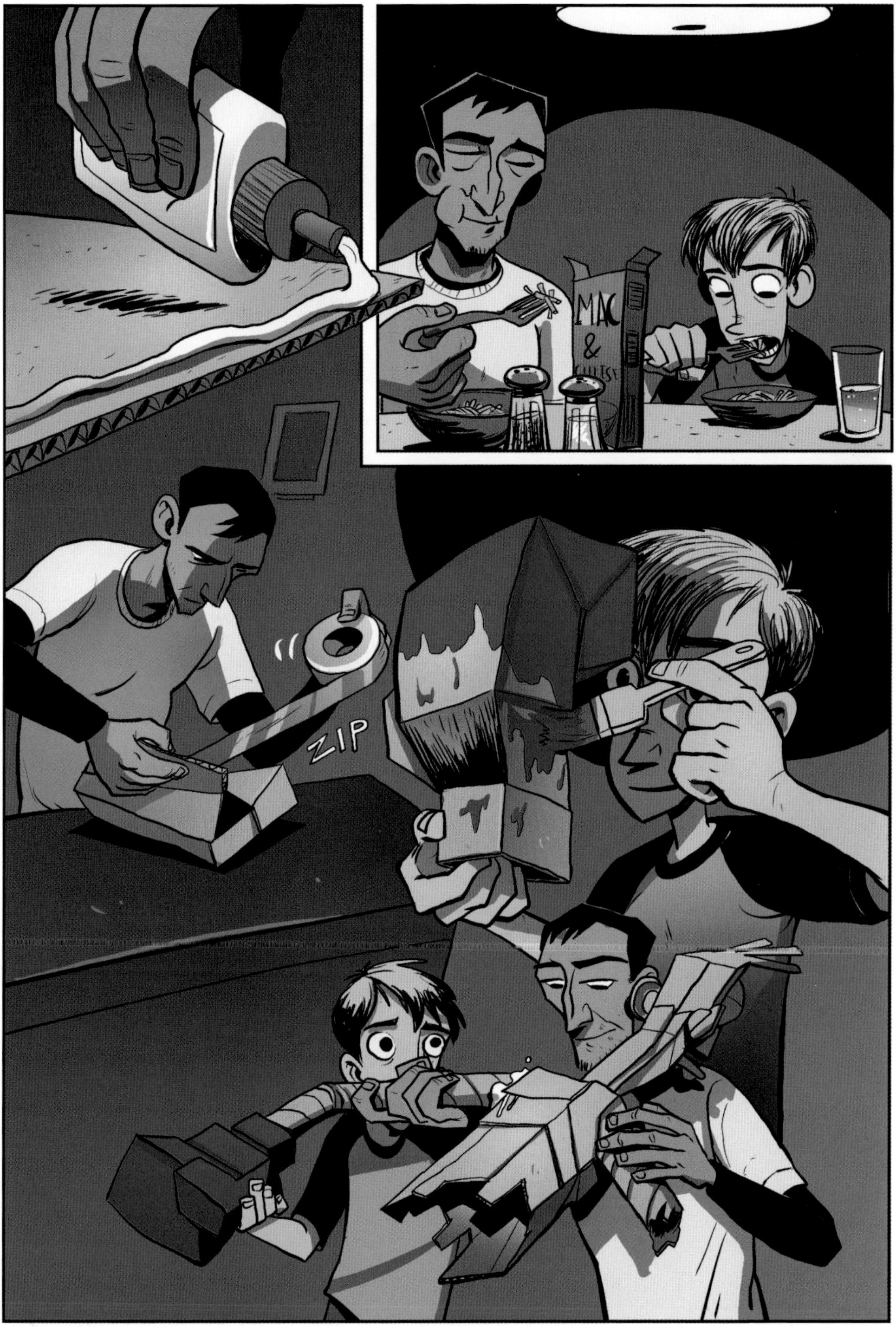
MAC & CHEESE
ZIP

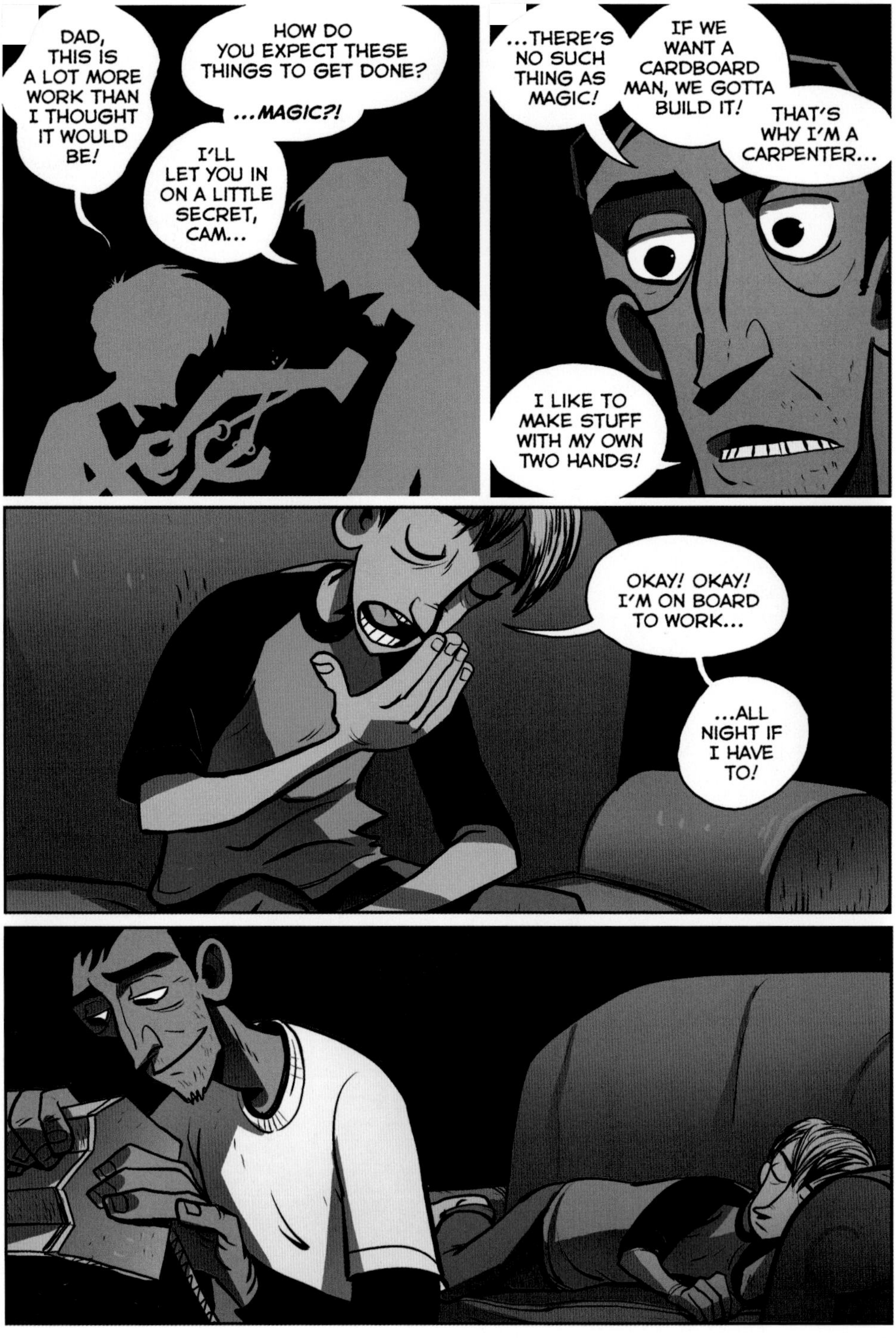
DAD, THIS IS A LOT MORE WORK THAN I THOUGHT IT WOULD BE!
HOW DO YOU EXPECT THESE THINGS TO GET DONE?
...MAGIC?!
I'LL LET YOU IN ON A LITTLE SECRET, CAM...
...THERE'S NO SUCH THING AS MAGIC!
IF WE WANT A CARDBOARD MAN, WE GOTTA BUILD IT!
THAT'S WHY I'M A CARPENTER...
I LIKE TO MAKE STUFF WITH MY OWN TWO HANDS!
OKAY! OKAY! I'M ON BOARD TO WORK...
...ALL NIGHT IF I HAVE TO!

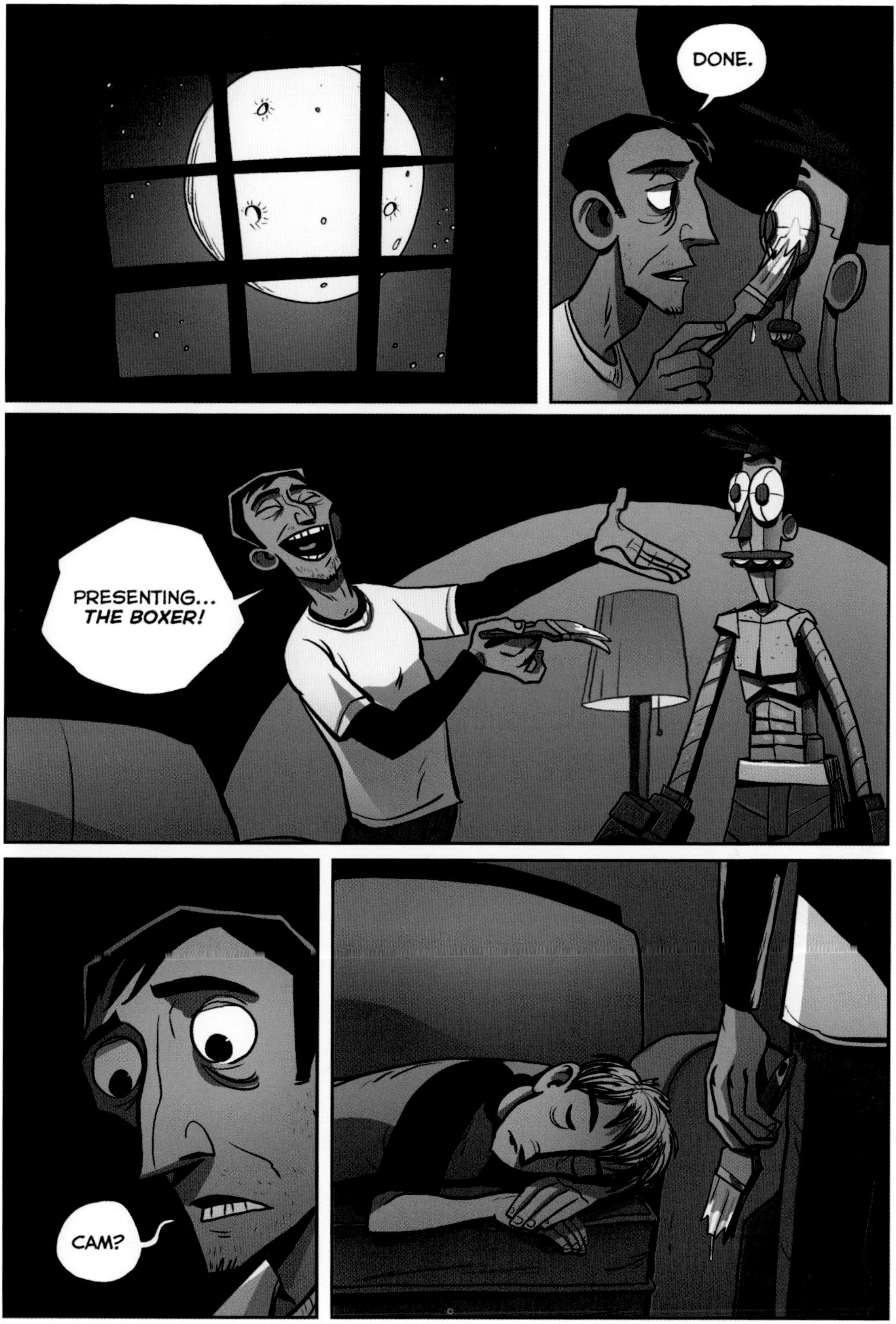
DONE.
PRESENTING... *THE BOXER!*
CAM?

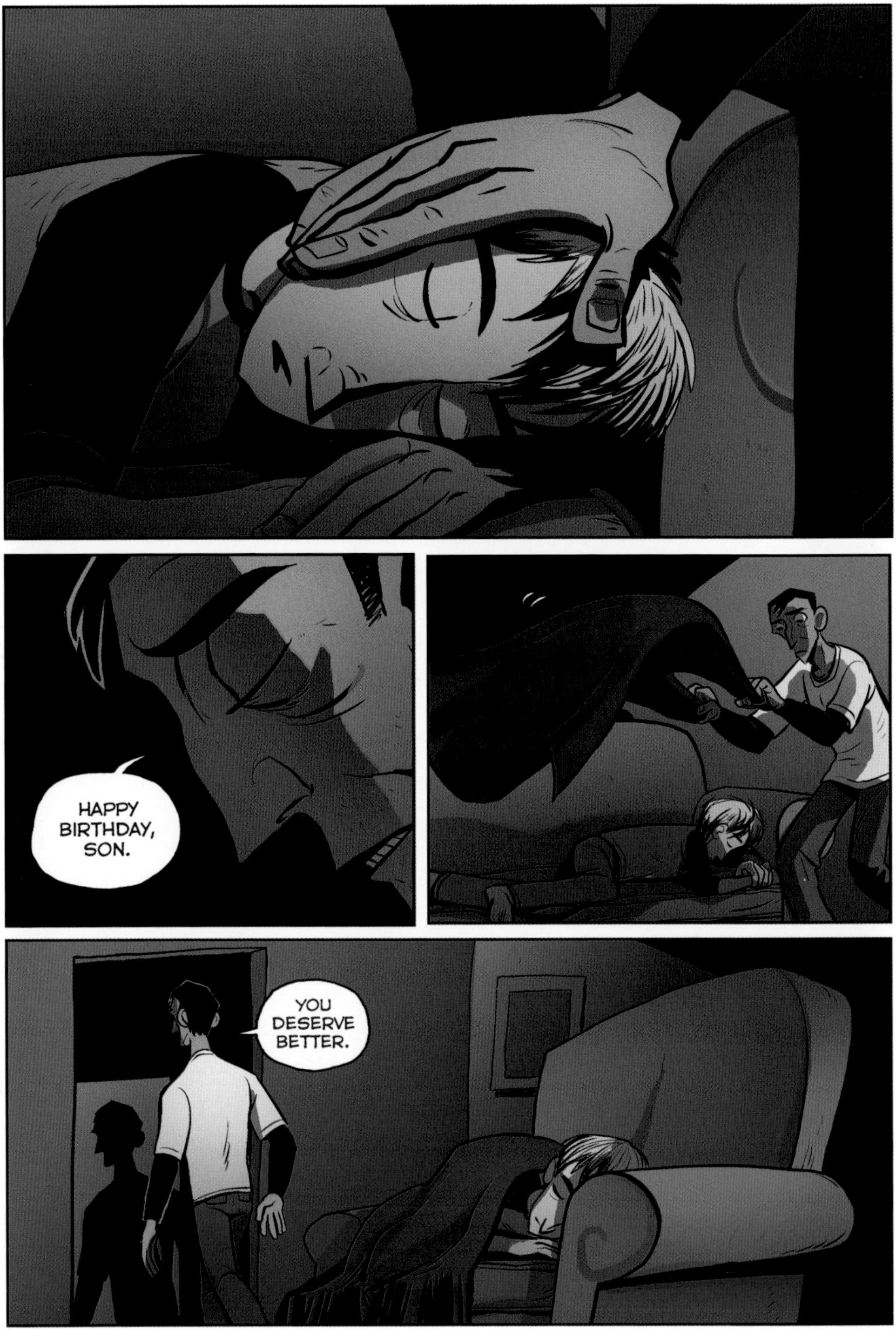
HAPPY BIRTHDAY, SON.
YOU DESERVE BETTER.

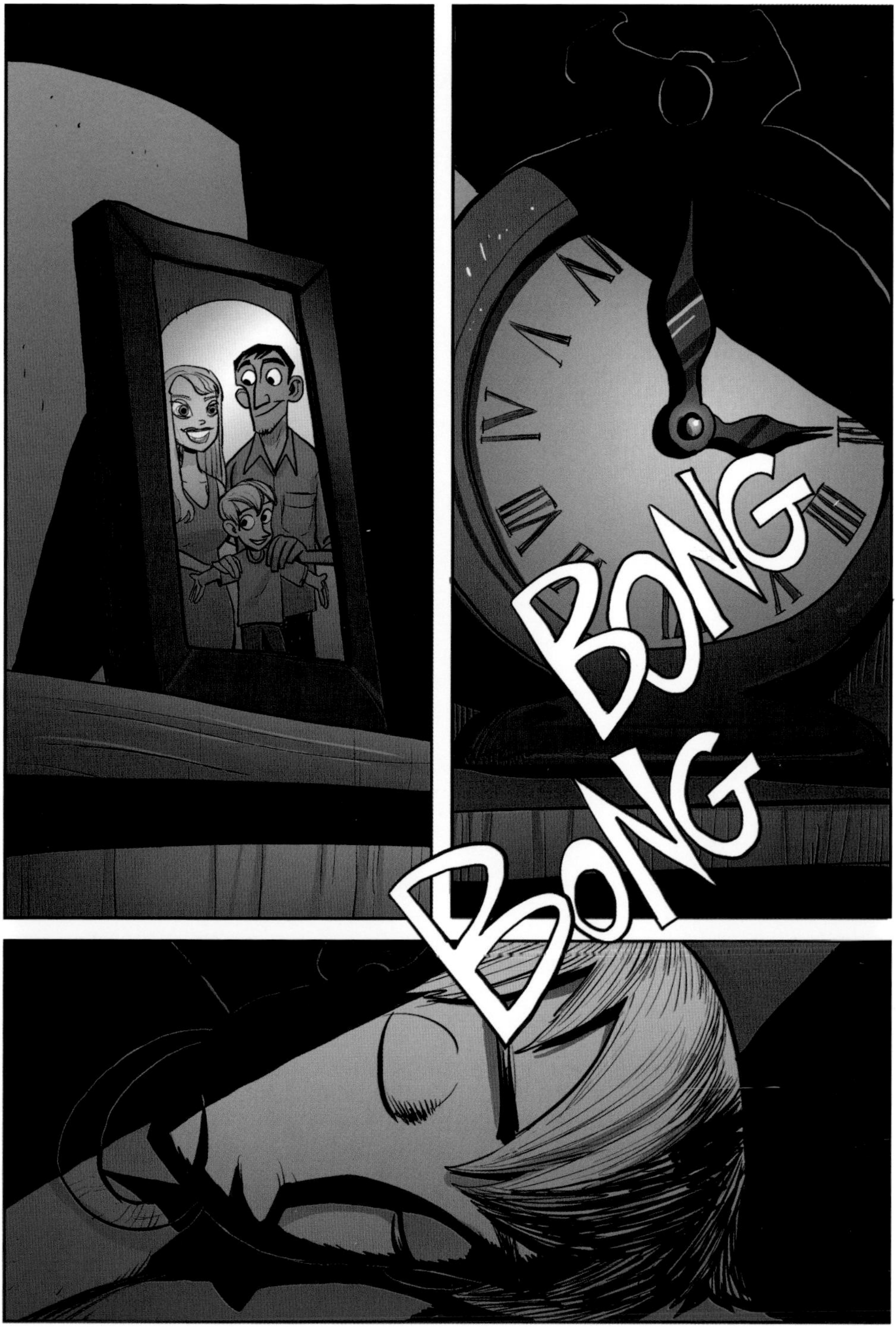
BONG
BONG

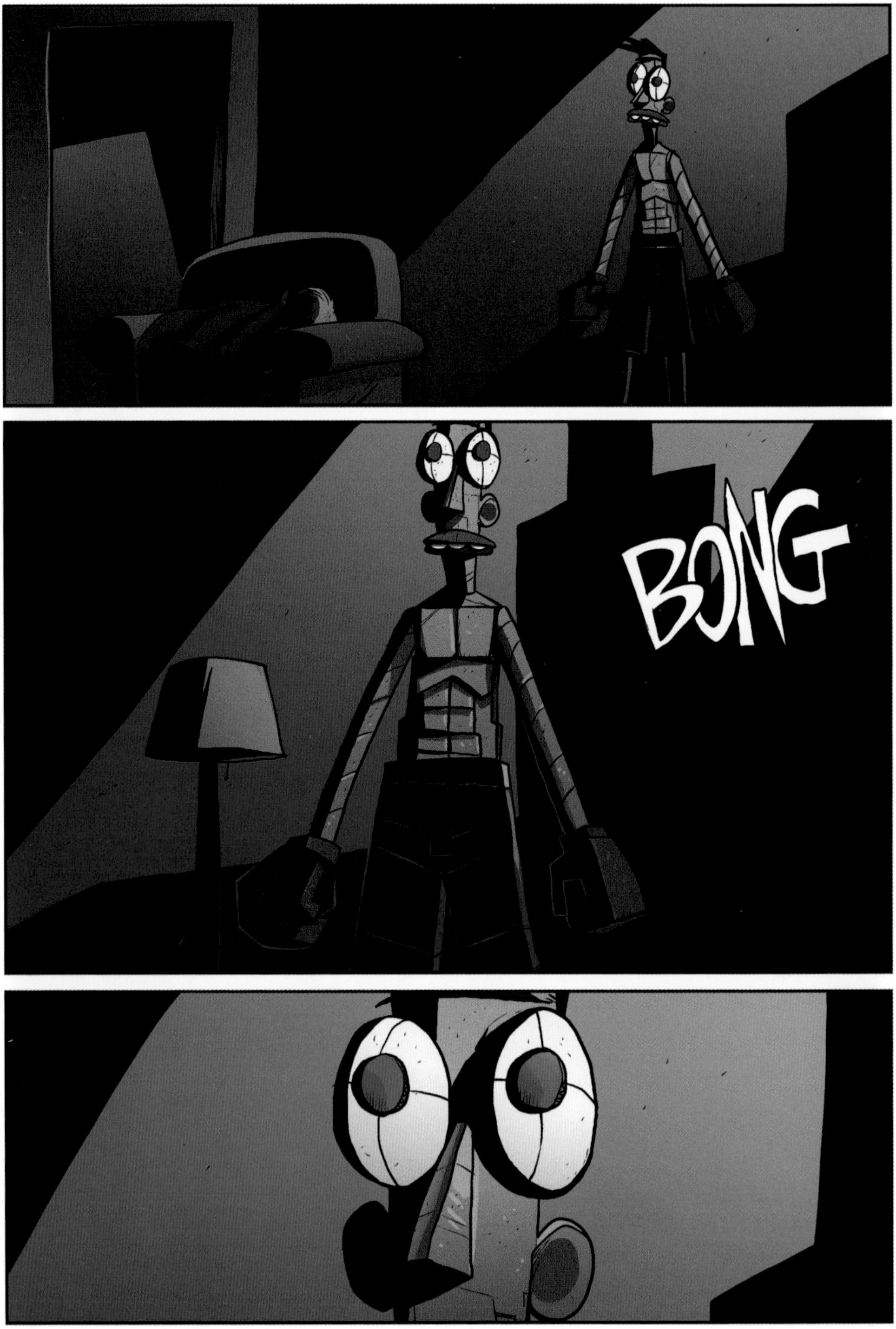
BONG

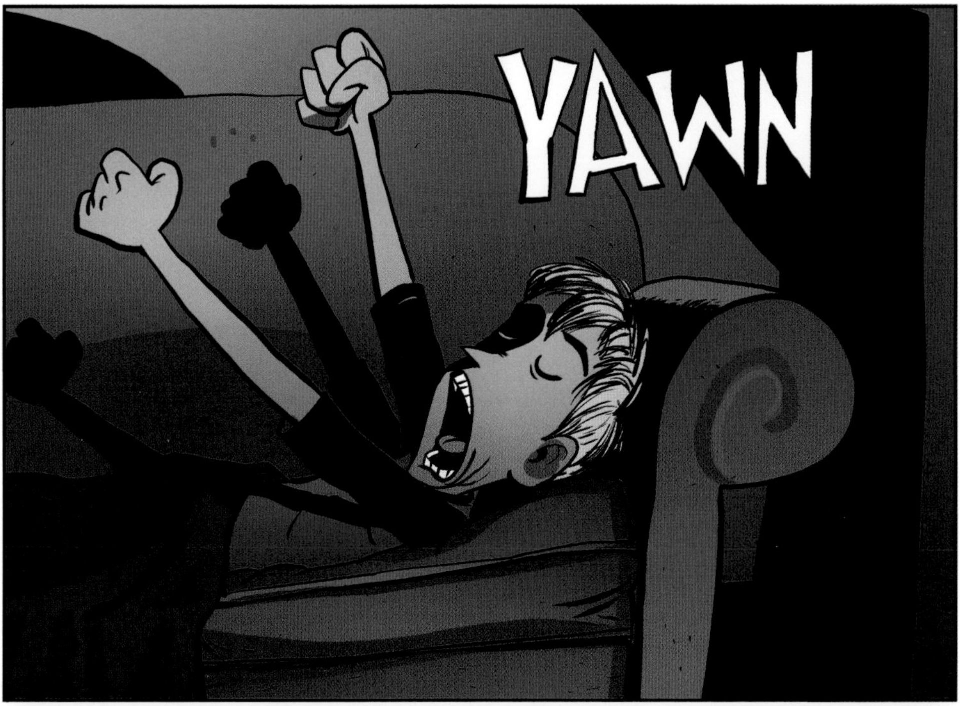
YAWN

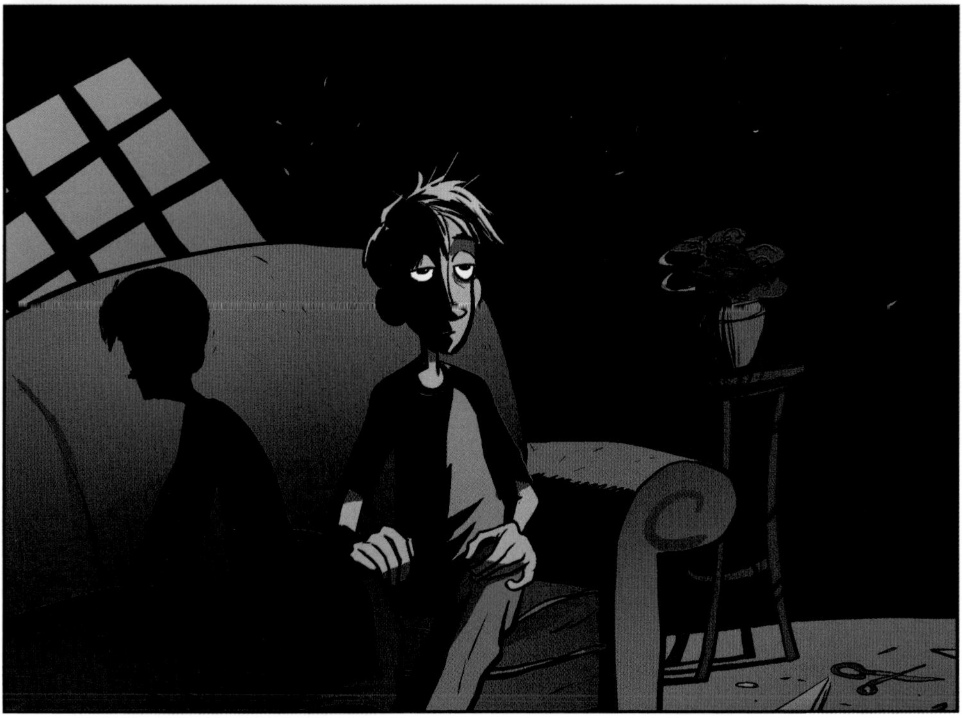

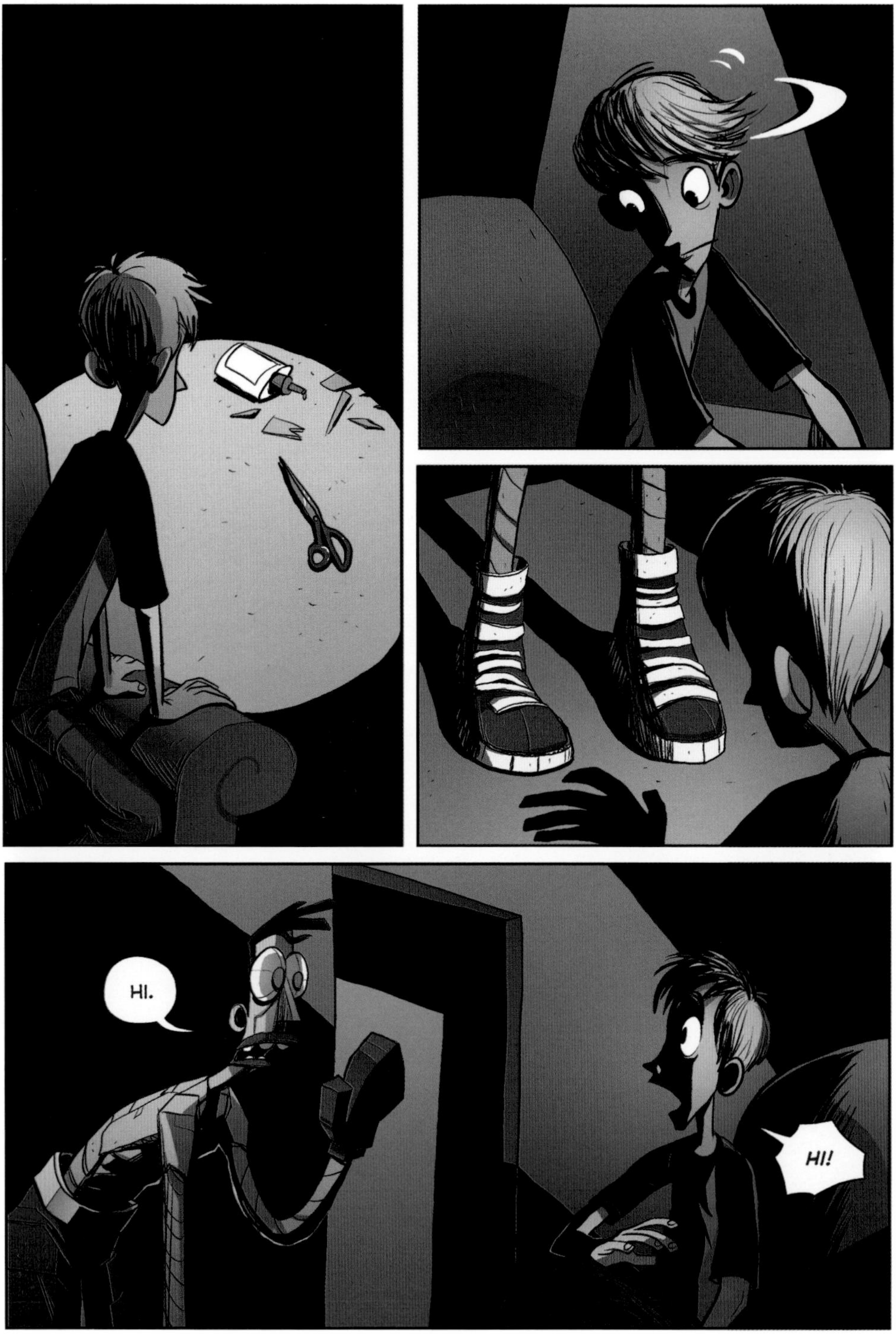
HI.
HI!

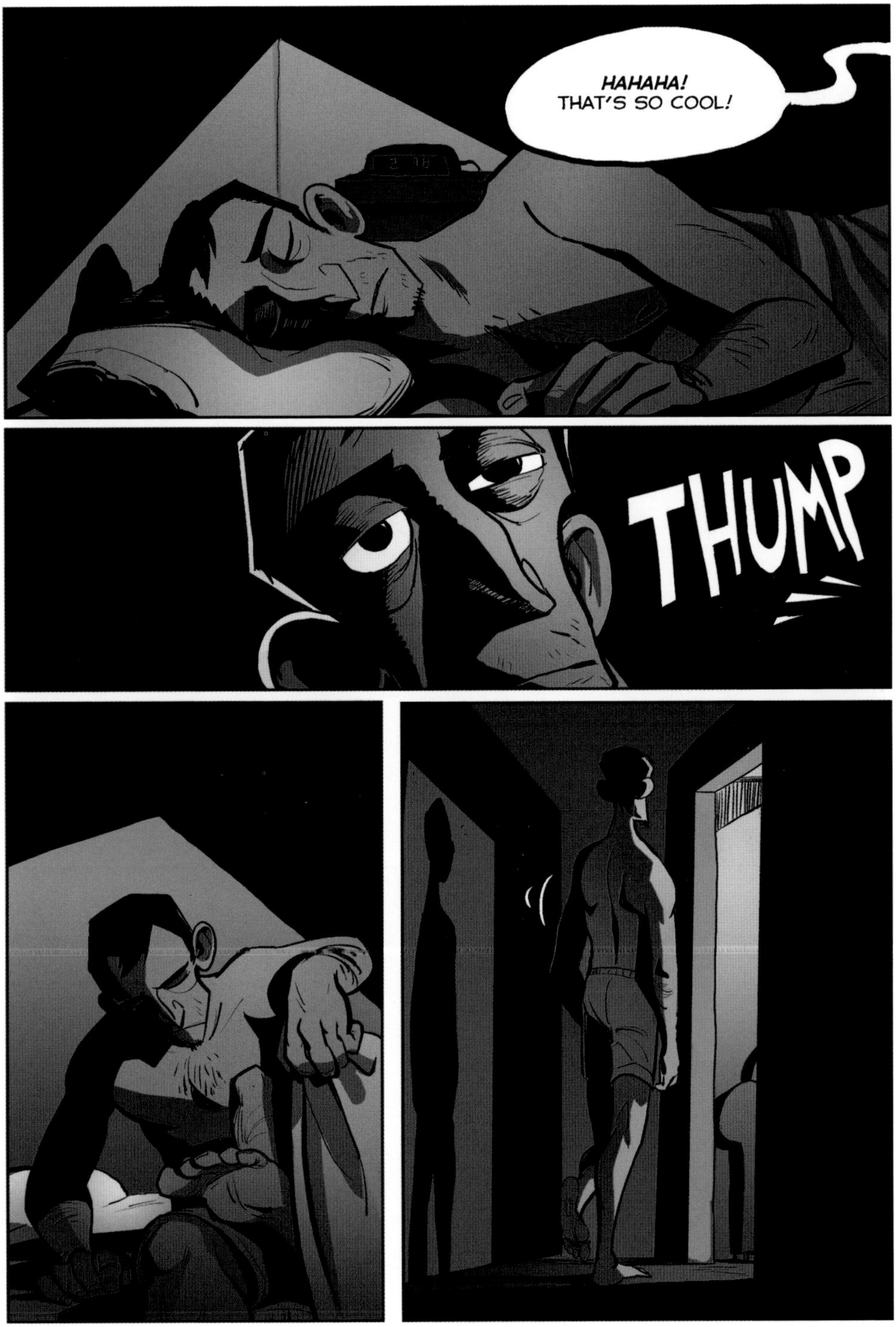
HAHAHA!
THAT'S SO COOL!
THUMP

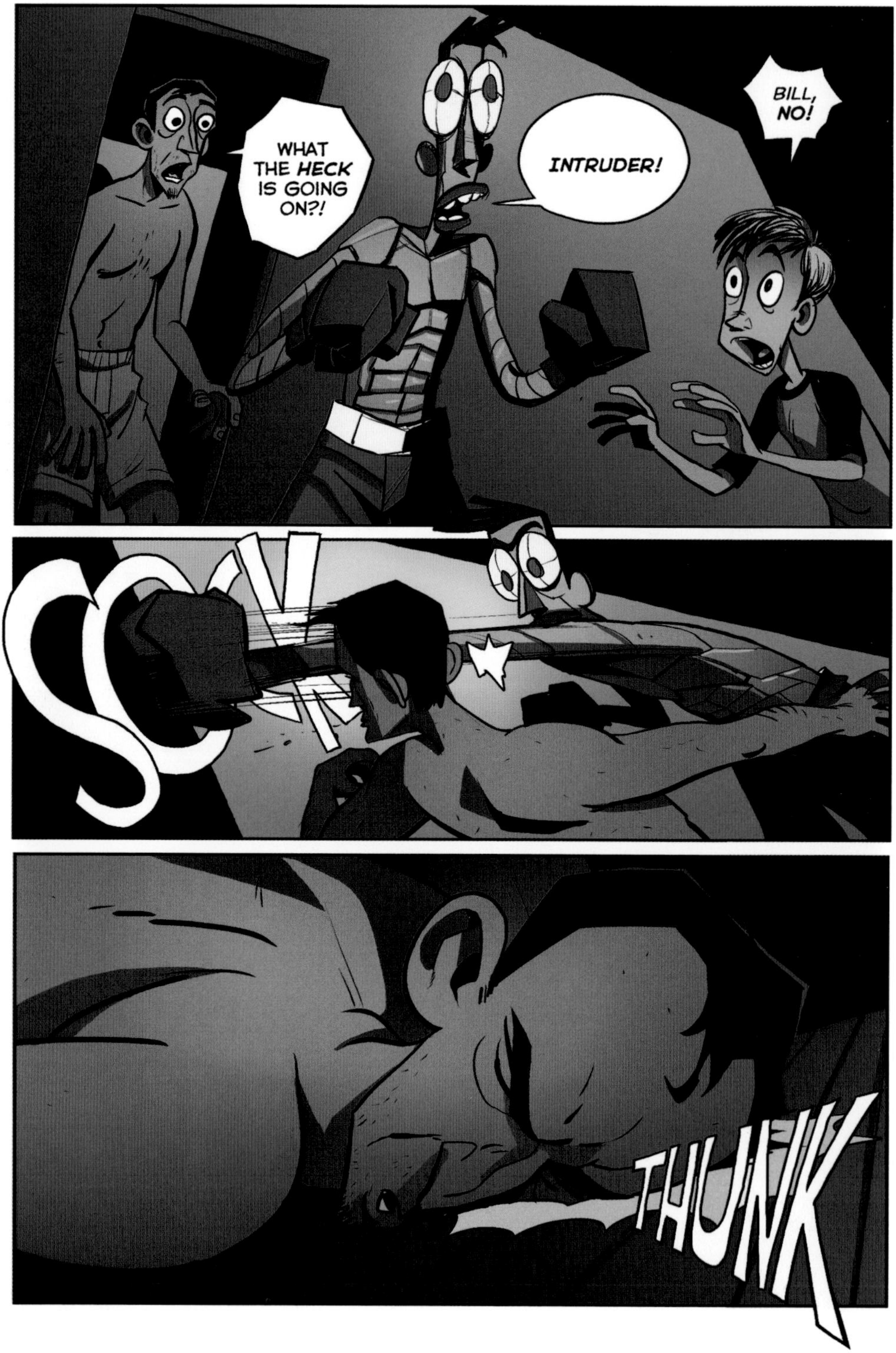
WHAT THE HECK IS GOING ON?!
INTRUDER!
BILL, NO!
THUNK

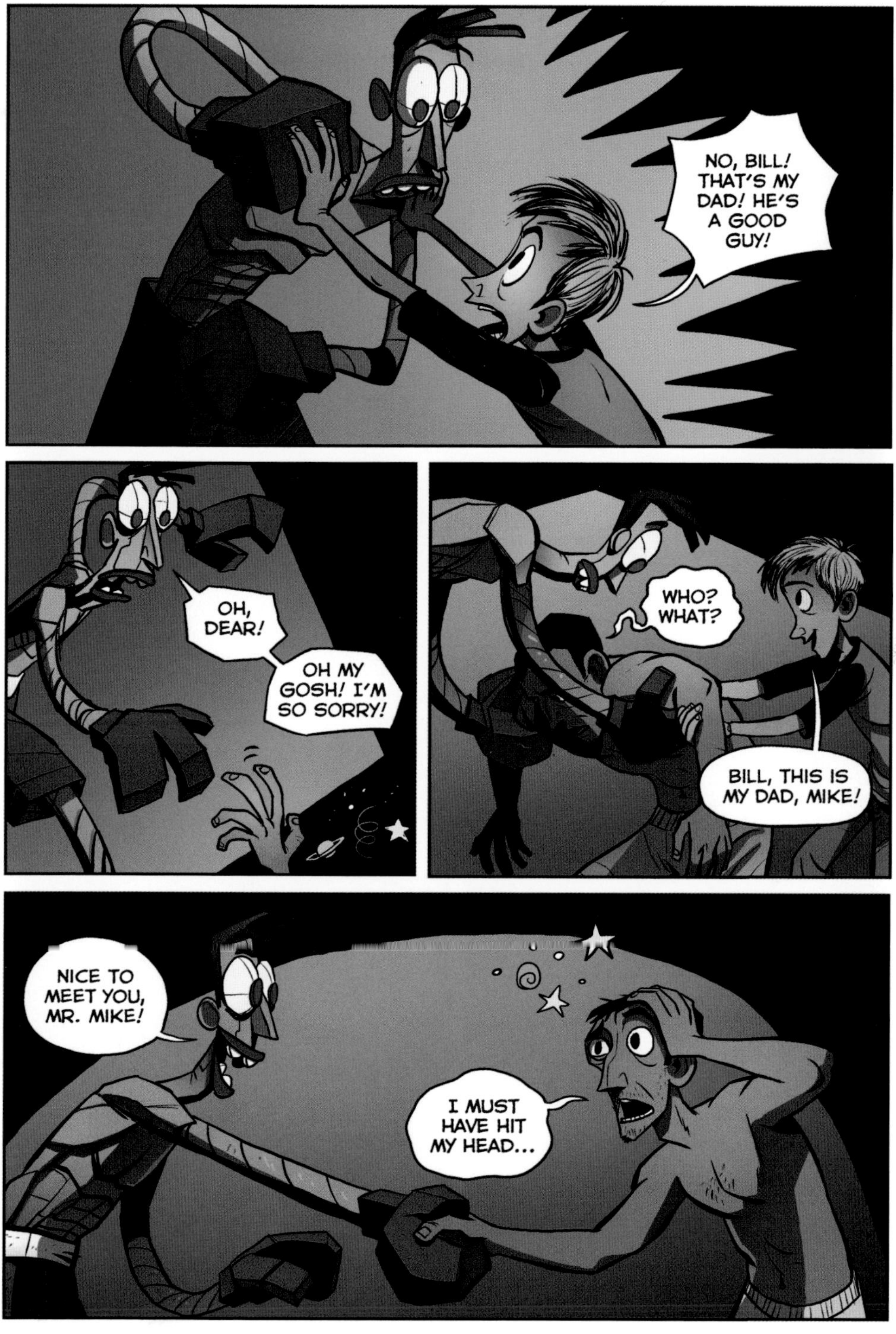
NO, BILL! THAT'S MY DAD! HE'S A GOOD GUY!
OH, DEAR!
OH MY GOSH! I'M SO SORRY!
WHO? WHAT?
BILL, THIS IS MY DAD, MIKE!
NICE TO MEET YOU, MR. MIKE!
I MUST HAVE HIT MY HEAD...

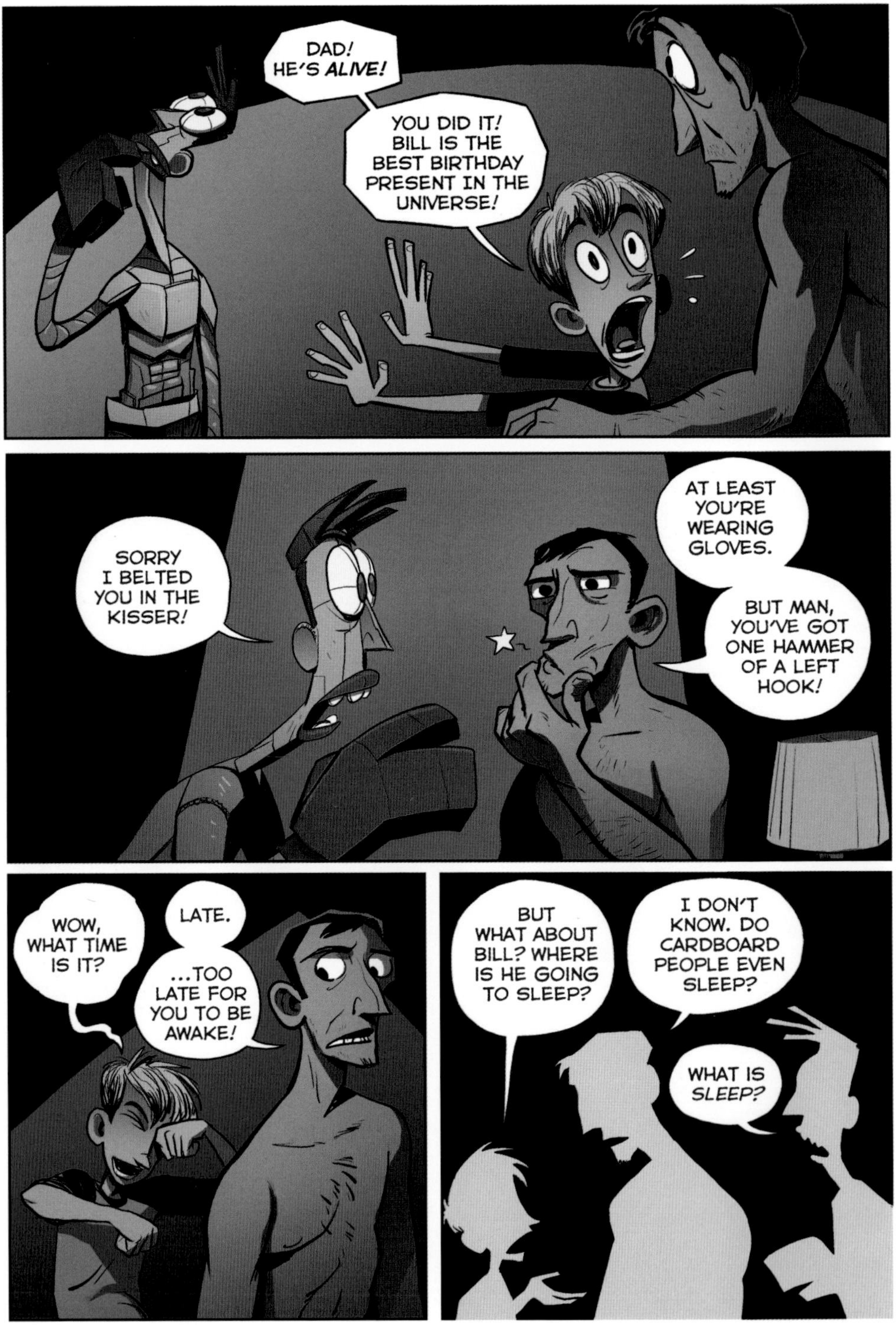
DAD! HE'S *ALIVE!*
YOU DID IT! BILL IS THE BEST BIRTHDAY PRESENT IN THE UNIVERSE!
SORRY I BELTED YOU IN THE KISSER!
AT LEAST YOU'RE WEARING GLOVES.
BUT MAN, YOU'VE GOT ONE HAMMER OF A LEFT HOOK!
WOW, WHAT TIME IS IT?
LATE.
...TOO LATE FOR YOU TO BE AWAKE!
BUT WHAT ABOUT BILL? WHERE IS HE GOING TO SLEEP?
I DON'T KNOW. DO CARDBOARD PEOPLE EVEN SLEEP?
WHAT IS *SLEEP?*

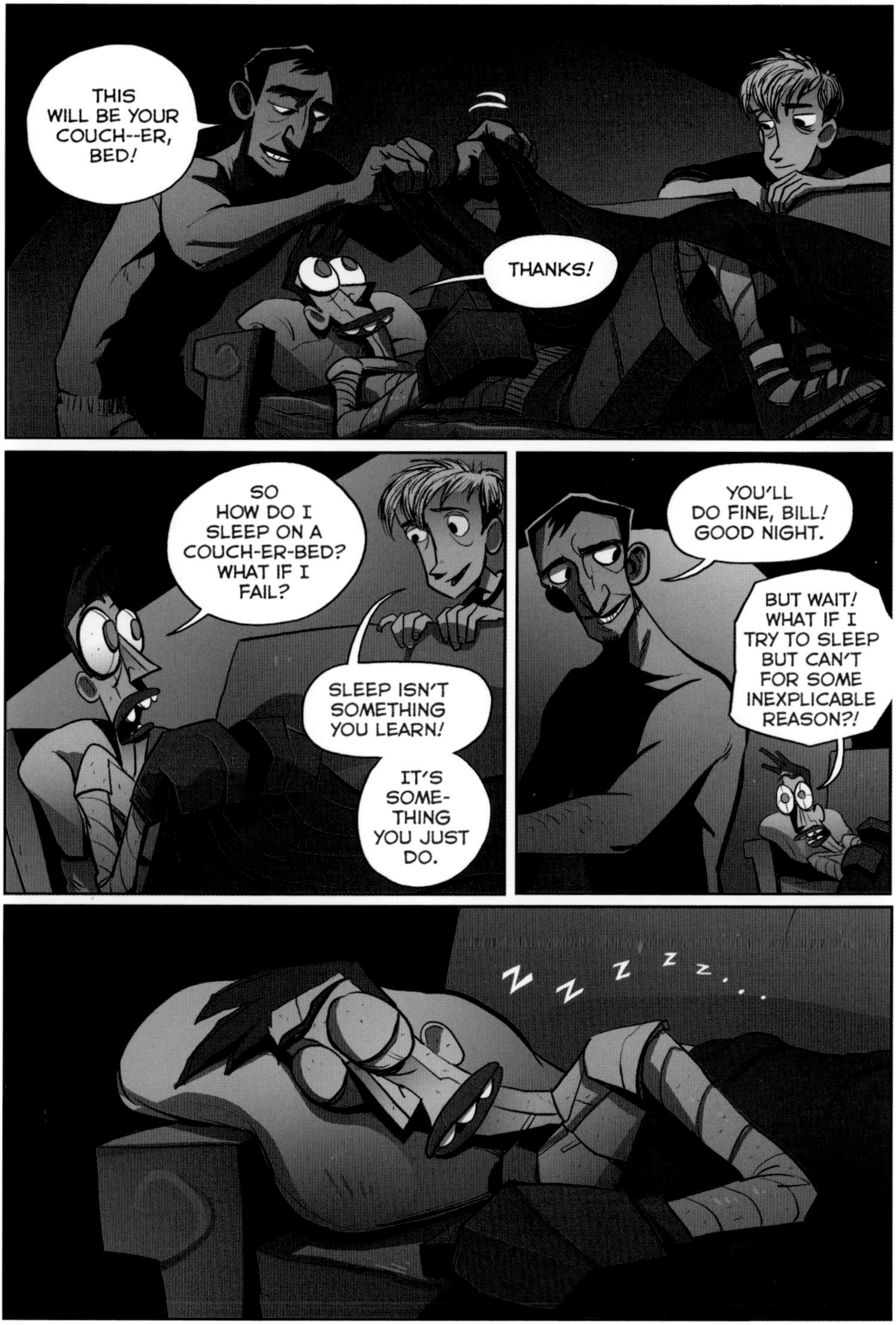
THIS WILL BE YOUR COUCH--ER, BED!
THANKS!
SO HOW DO I SLEEP ON A COUCH-ER-BED? WHAT IF I FAIL?
SLEEP ISN'T SOMETHING YOU LEARN!
IT'S SOME-THING YOU JUST DO.
YOU'LL DO FINE, BILL! GOOD NIGHT.
BUT WAIT! WHAT IF I TRY TO SLEEP BUT CAN'T FOR SOME INEXPLICABLE REASON?!
Z Z Z Z Z . . .

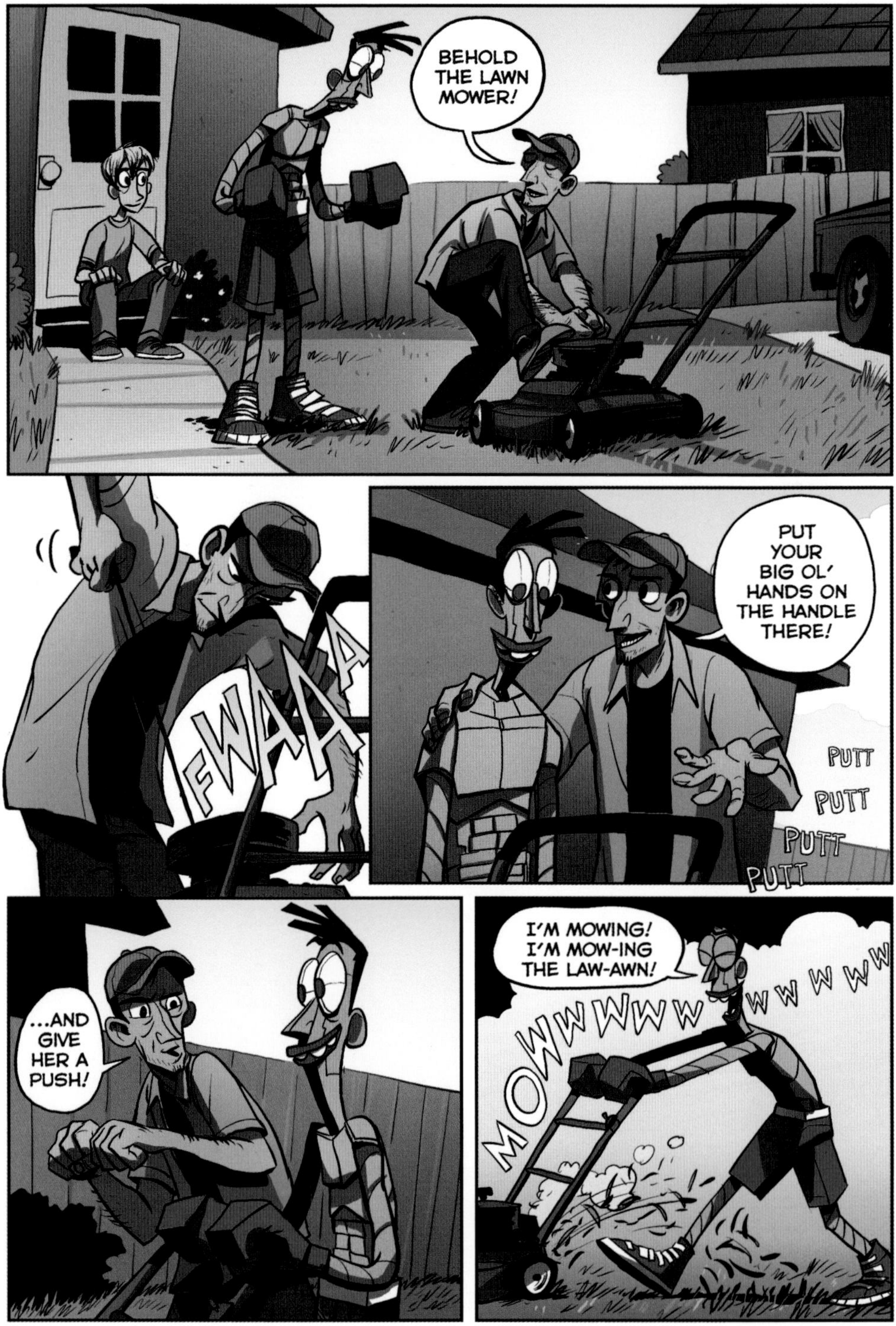
BEHOLD THE LAWN MOWER!
FWAAA
PUT YOUR BIG OL' HANDS ON THE HANDLE THERE!
PUTT PUTT PUTT PUTT
...AND GIVE HER A PUSH!
I'M MOWING! I'M MOW-ING THE LAW-AWN!
MOWWWWWWW W W W W W W

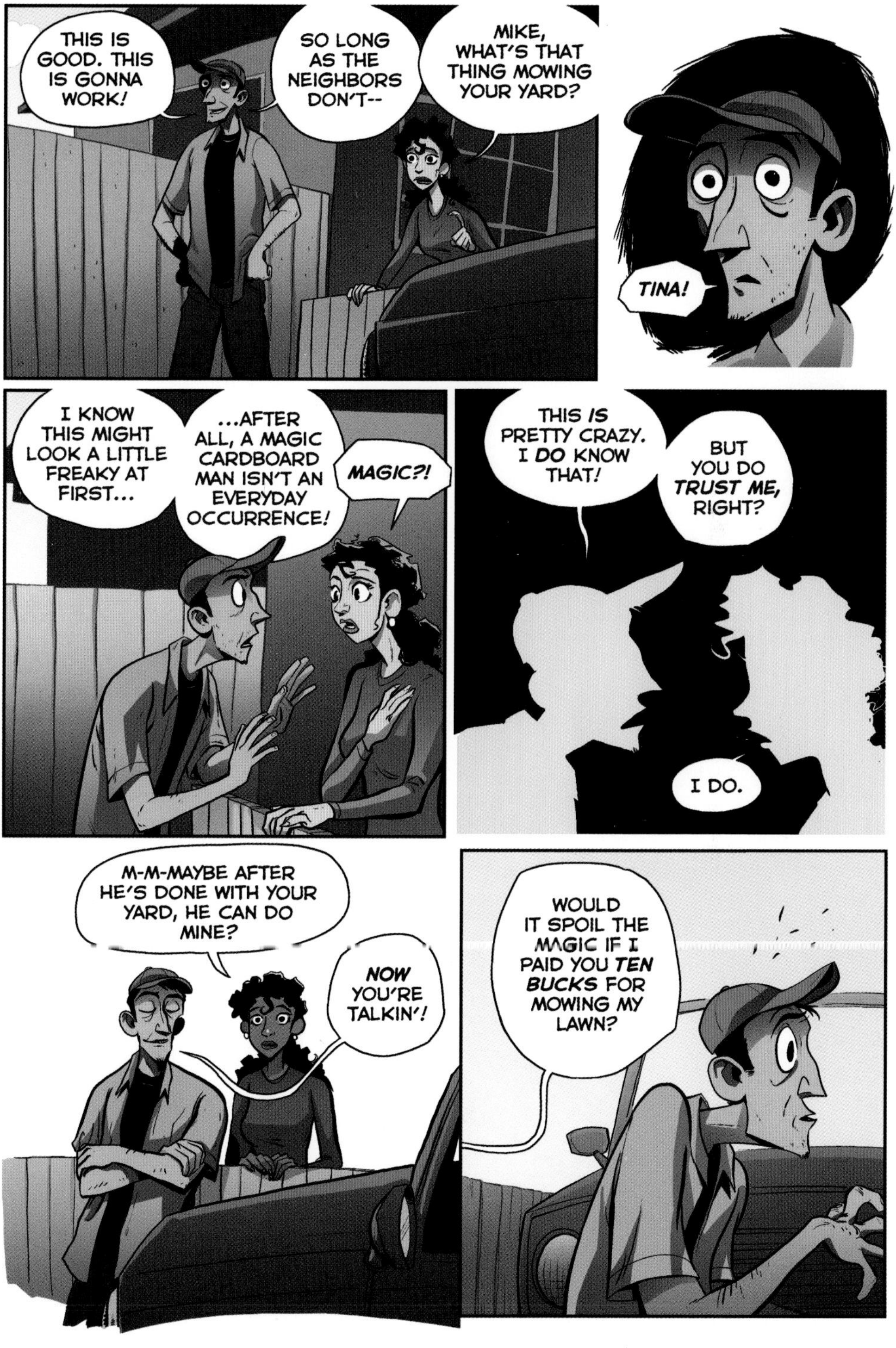
THIS IS GOOD. THIS IS GONNA WORK!
SO LONG AS THE NEIGHBORS DON'T--
MIKE, WHAT'S THAT THING MOWING YOUR YARD?
TINA!
I KNOW THIS MIGHT LOOK A LITTLE FREAKY AT FIRST...
...AFTER ALL, A MAGIC CARDBOARD MAN ISN'T AN EVERYDAY OCCURRENCE!
MAGIC?!
THIS IS PRETTY CRAZY. I DO KNOW THAT!
BUT YOU DO TRUST ME, RIGHT?
I DO.
M-M-MAYBE AFTER HE'S DONE WITH YOUR YARD, HE CAN DO MINE?
NOW YOU'RE TALKIN'!
WOULD IT SPOIL THE MAGIC IF I PAID YOU TEN BUCKS FOR MOWING MY LAWN?

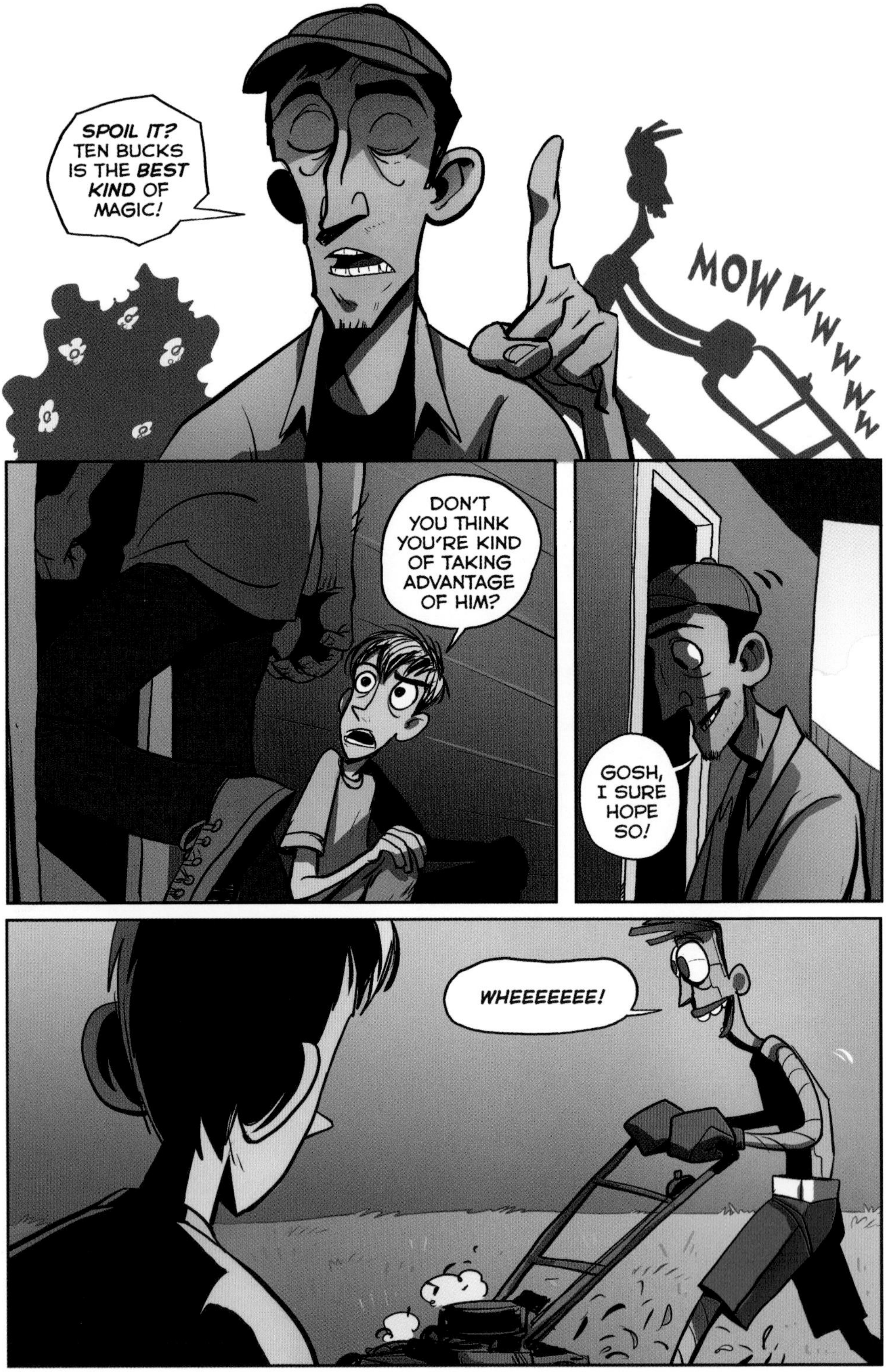
SPOIL IT? TEN BUCKS IS THE BEST KIND OF MAGIC!
MOWWWWWWW
DON'T YOU THINK YOU'RE KIND OF TAKING ADVANTAGE OF HIM?
GOSH, I SURE HOPE SO!
WHEEEEEEE!

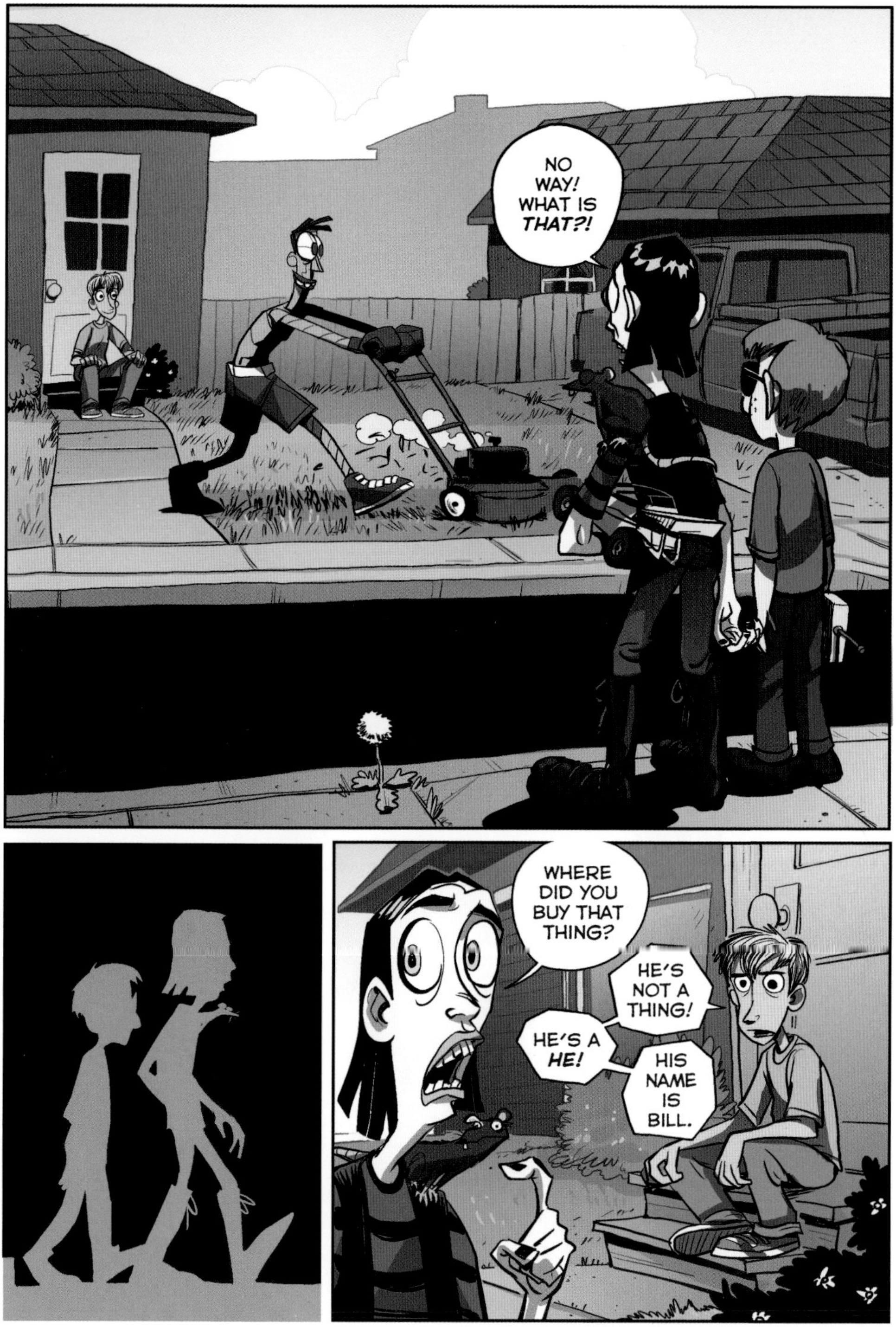
NO WAY! WHAT IS *THAT?!*
WHERE DID YOU BUY THAT THING?
HE'S NOT A THING!
HE'S A *HE!*
HIS NAME IS BILL.

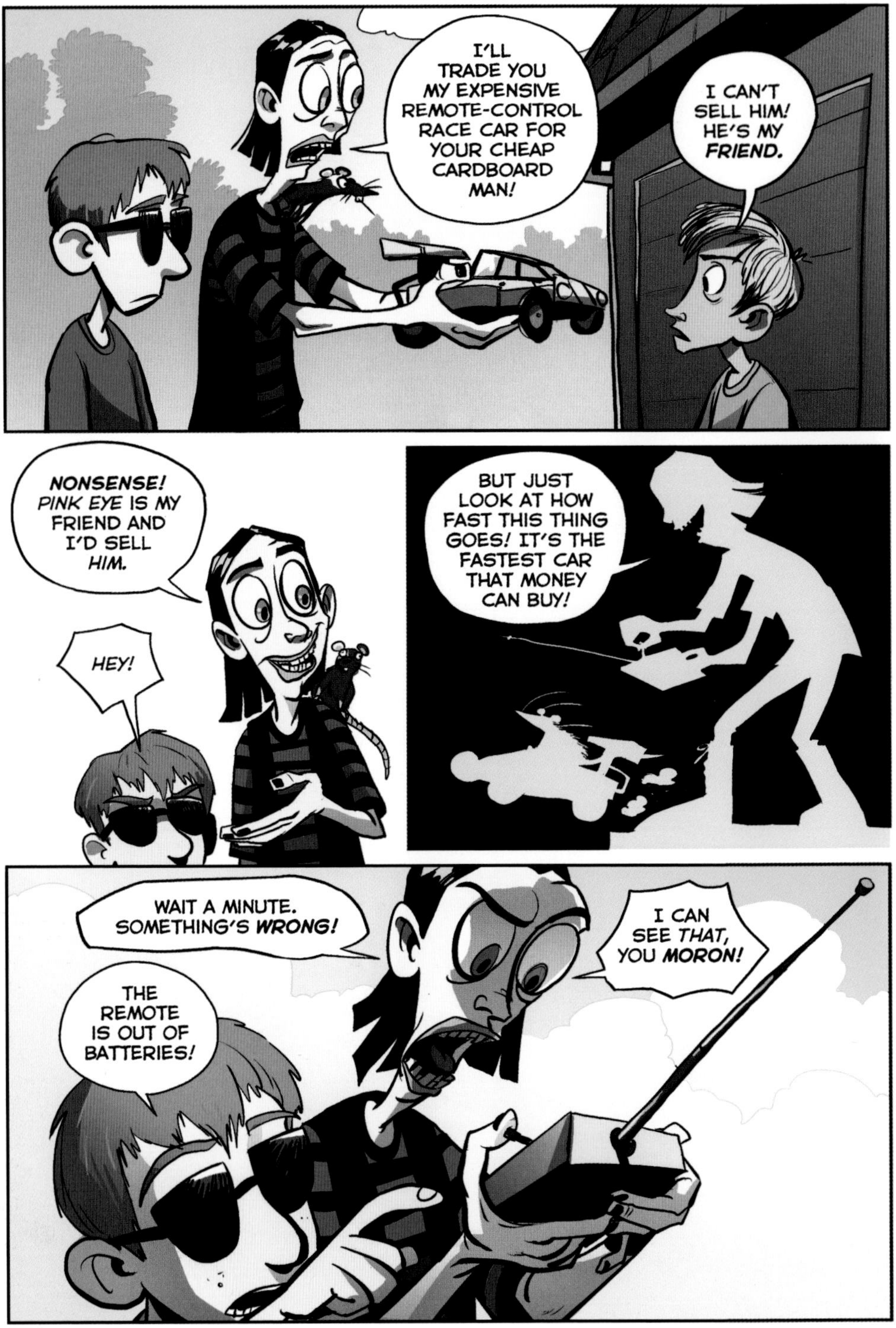
I'LL TRADE YOU MY EXPENSIVE REMOTE-CONTROL RACE CAR FOR YOUR CHEAP CARDBOARD MAN!
I CAN'T SELL HIM! HE'S MY ***FRIEND.***
NONSENSE! *PINK EYE* IS MY FRIEND AND I'D SELL *HIM.*
HEY!
BUT JUST LOOK AT HOW FAST THIS THING GOES! IT'S THE FASTEST CAR THAT MONEY CAN BUY!
WAIT A MINUTE. SOMETHING'S ***WRONG!***
THE REMOTE IS OUT OF BATTERIES!
I CAN SEE *THAT,* YOU ***MORON!***

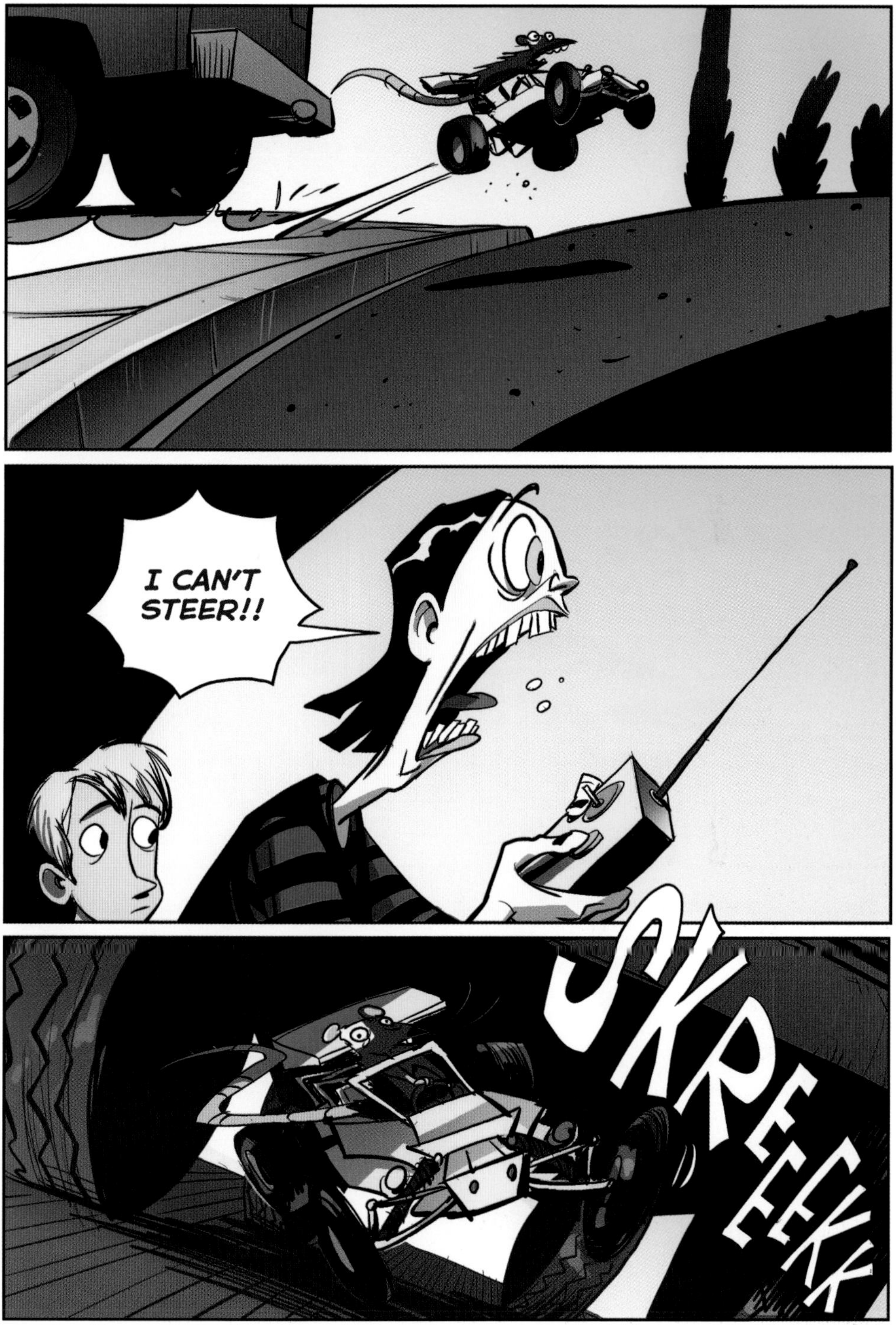
I CAN'T STEER!!
SKREEEKK

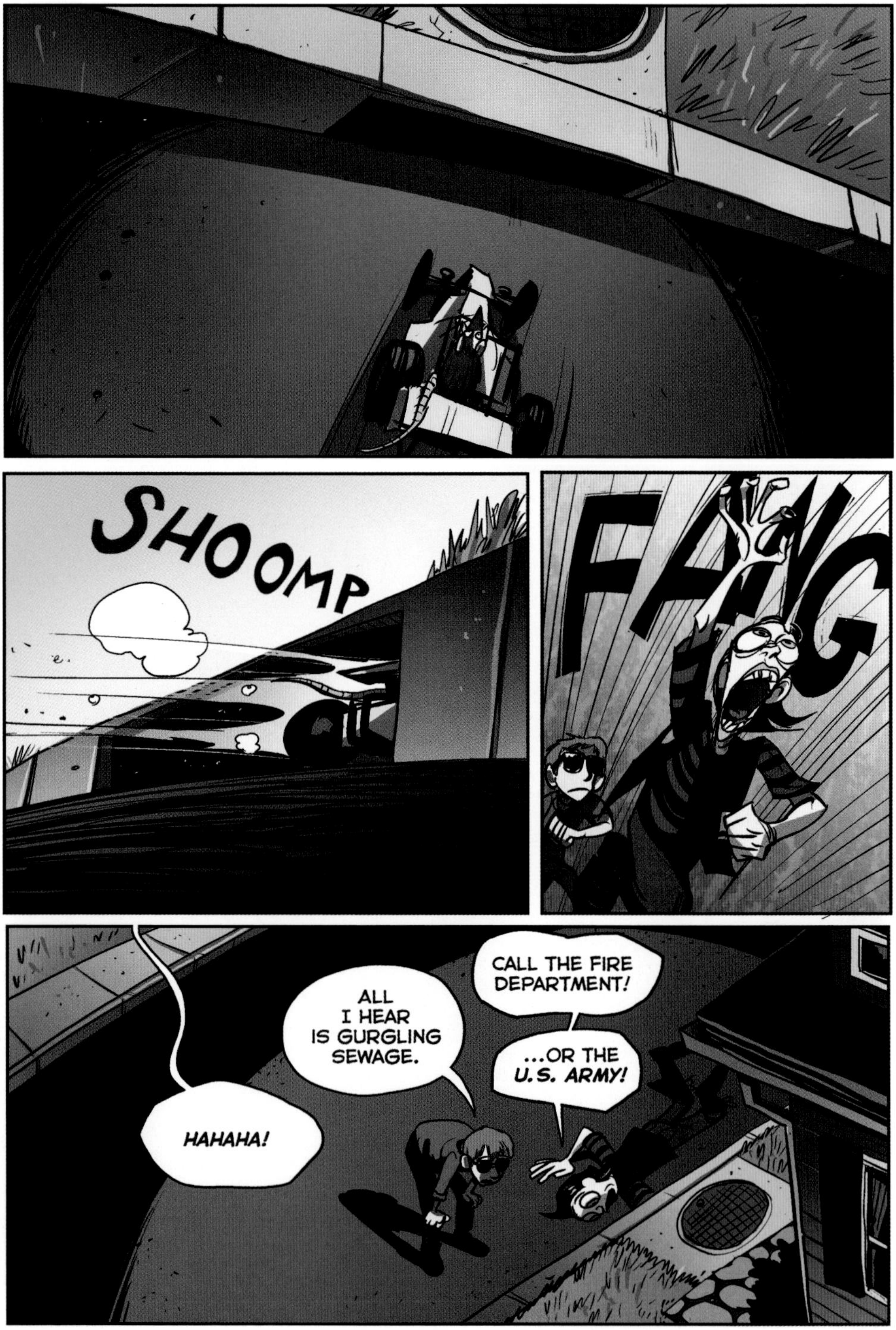
SHOOMP
FANG
ALL I HEAR IS GURGLING SEWAGE.
CALL THE FIRE DEPARTMENT!
...OR THE U.S. ARMY!
HAHAHA!

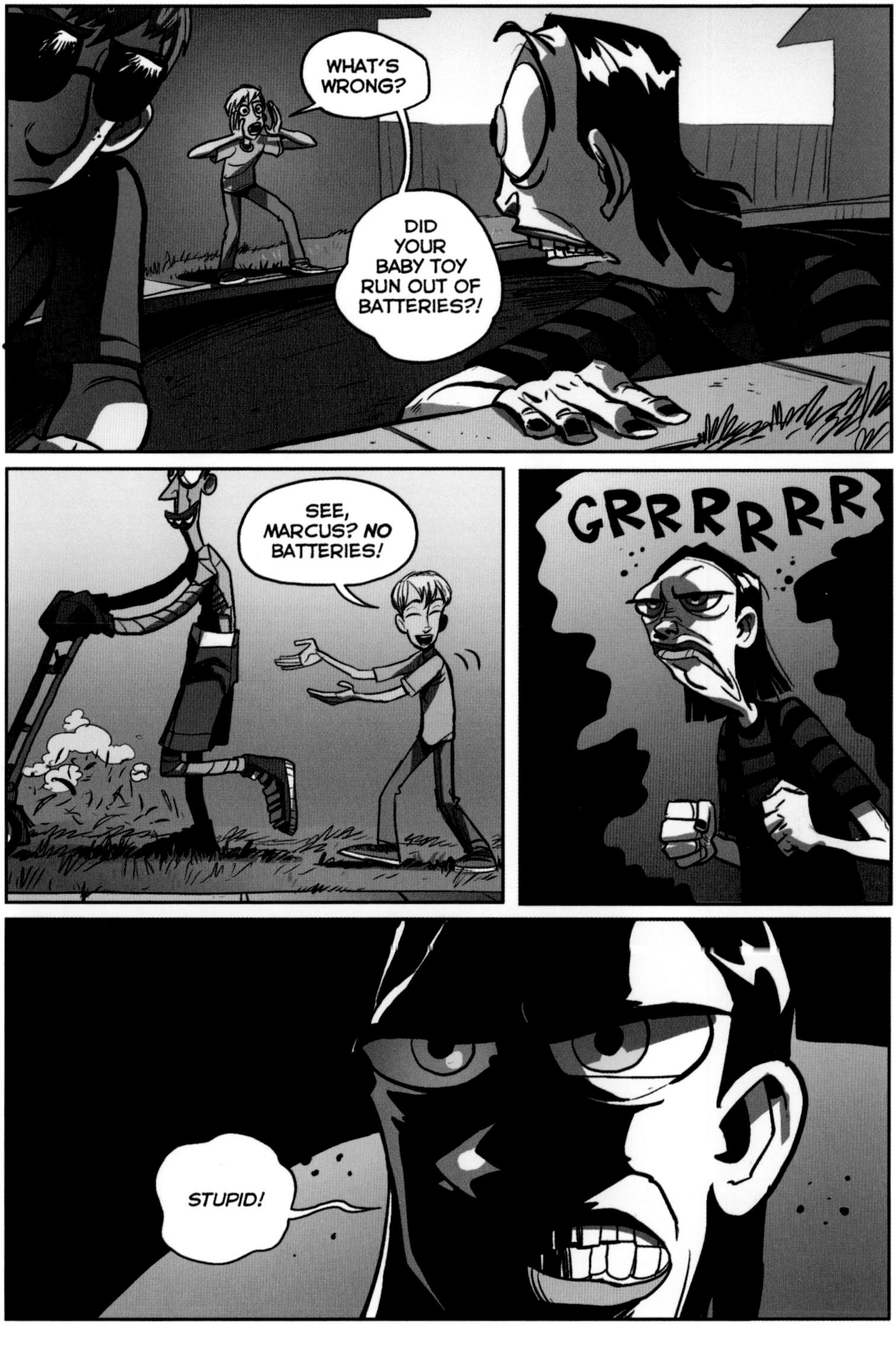
WHAT'S WRONG?
DID YOUR BABY TOY RUN OUT OF BATTERIES?!
SEE, MARCUS? NO BATTERIES!
GRRRRRR
STUPID!

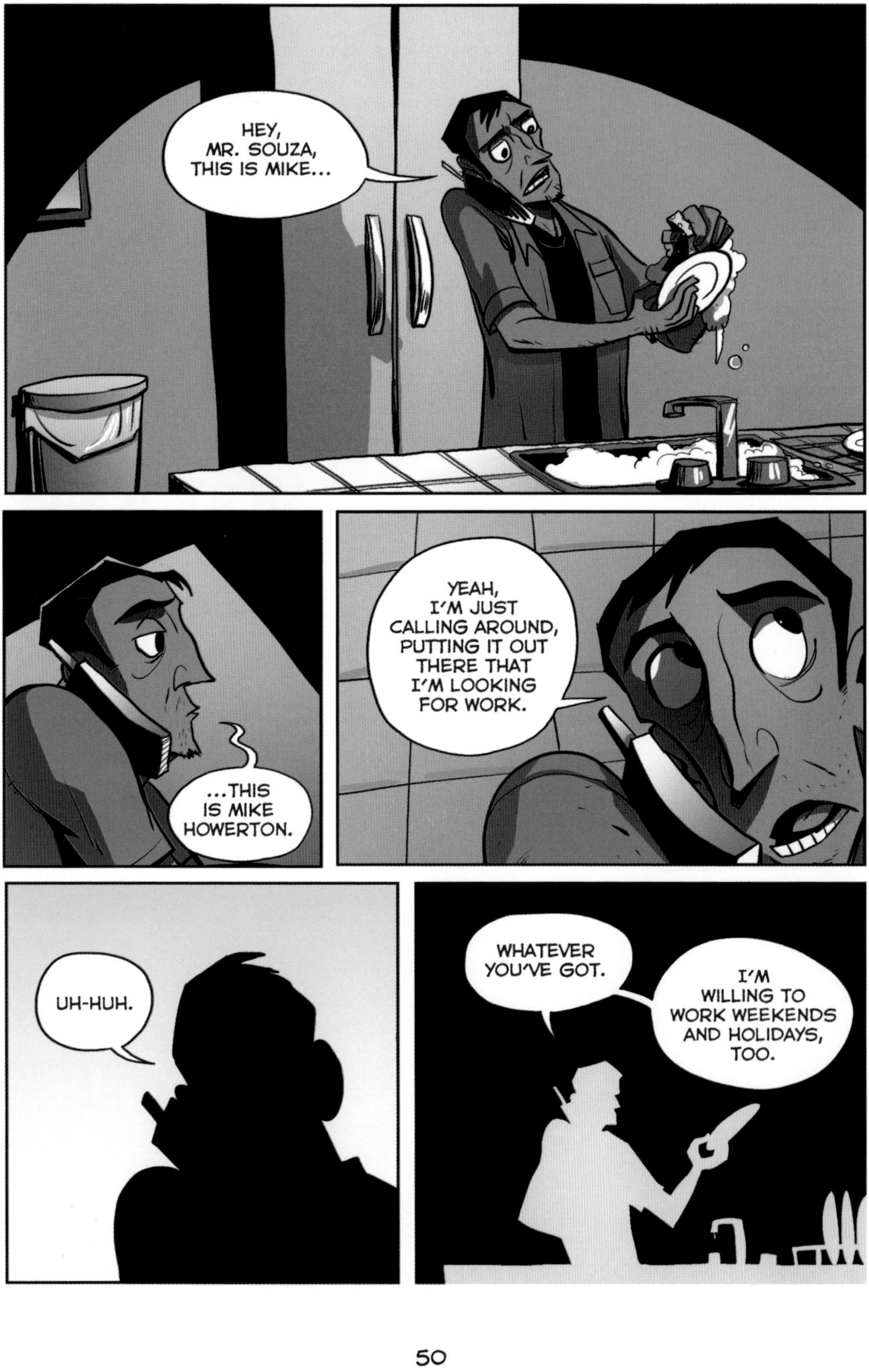
HEY, MR. SOUZA, THIS IS MIKE...
...THIS IS MIKE HOWERTON.
YEAH, I'M JUST CALLING AROUND, PUTTING IT OUT THERE THAT I'M LOOKING FOR WORK.
UH-HUH.
WHATEVER YOU'VE GOT.
I'M WILLING TO WORK WEEKENDS AND HOLIDAYS, TOO.

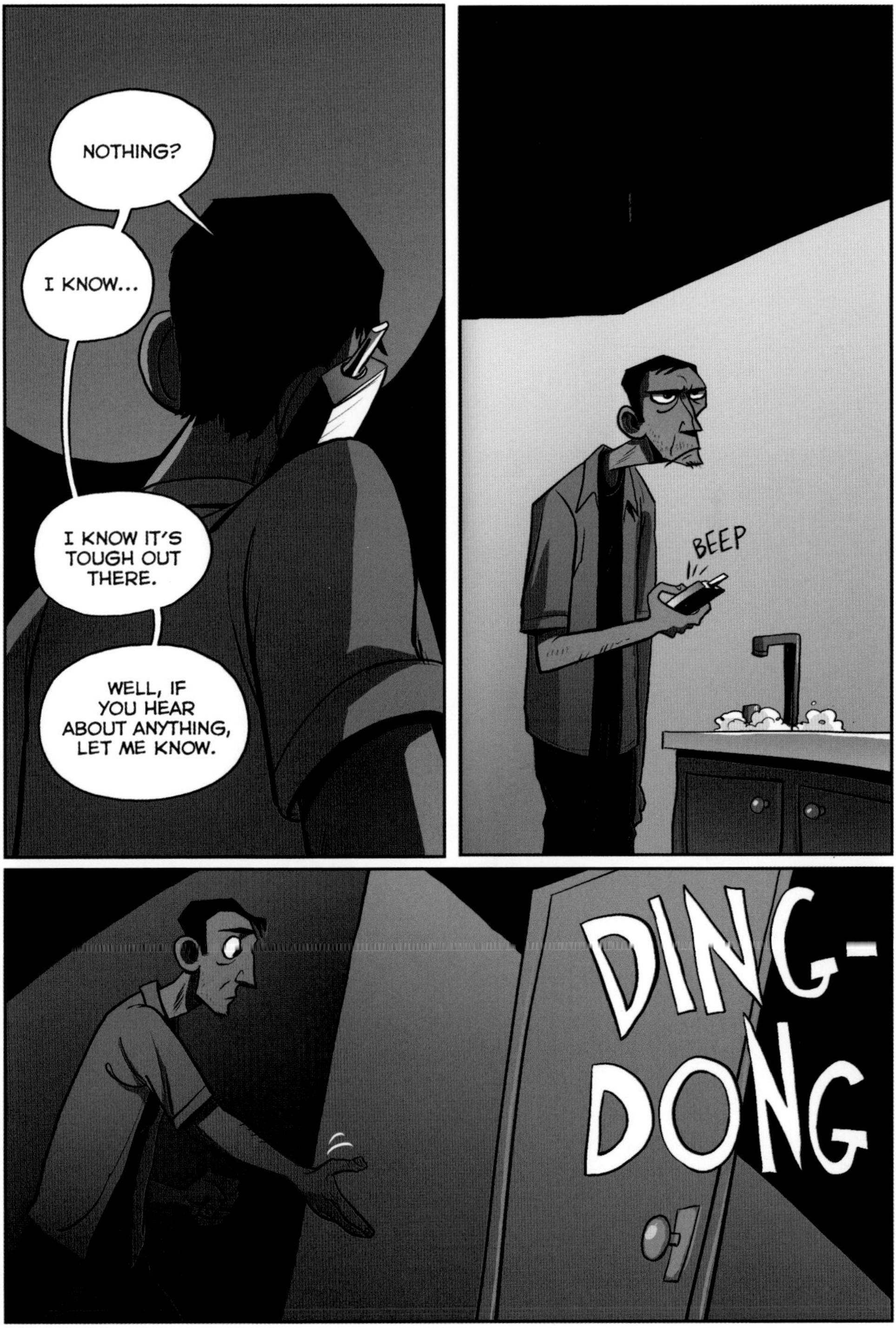
NOTHING?
I KNOW...
I KNOW IT'S TOUGH OUT THERE.
WELL, IF YOU HEAR ABOUT ANYTHING, LET ME KNOW.
BEEP
DING-DONG

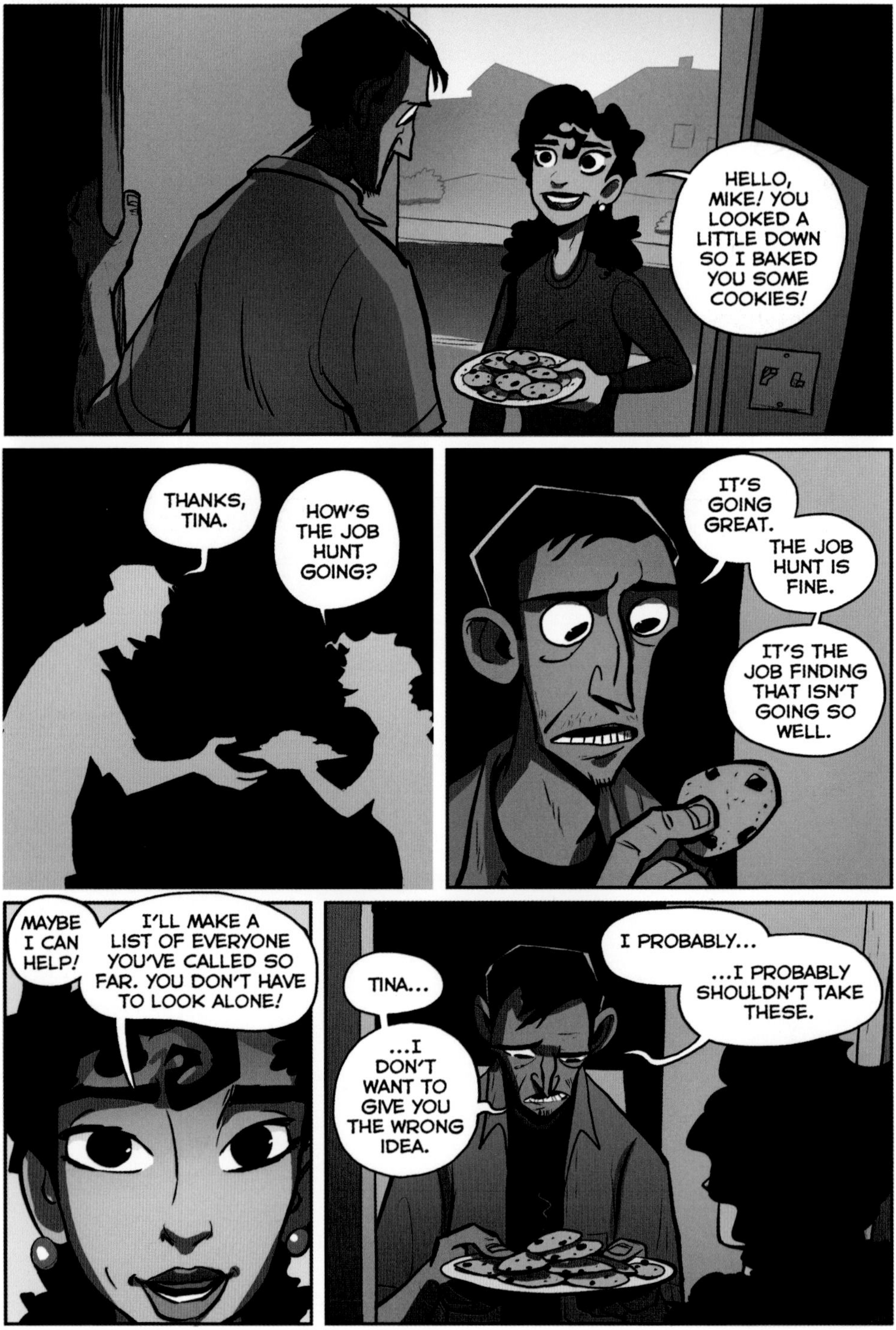
HELLO, MIKE! YOU LOOKED A LITTLE DOWN SO I BAKED YOU SOME COOKIES!
THANKS, TINA.
HOW'S THE JOB HUNT GOING?
IT'S GOING GREAT.
THE JOB HUNT IS FINE.
IT'S THE JOB FINDING THAT ISN'T GOING SO WELL.
MAYBE I CAN HELP!
I'LL MAKE A LIST OF EVERYONE YOU'VE CALLED SO FAR. YOU DON'T HAVE TO LOOK ALONE!
TINA...
...I DON'T WANT TO GIVE YOU THE WRONG IDEA.
I PROBABLY...
...I PROBABLY SHOULDN'T TAKE THESE.

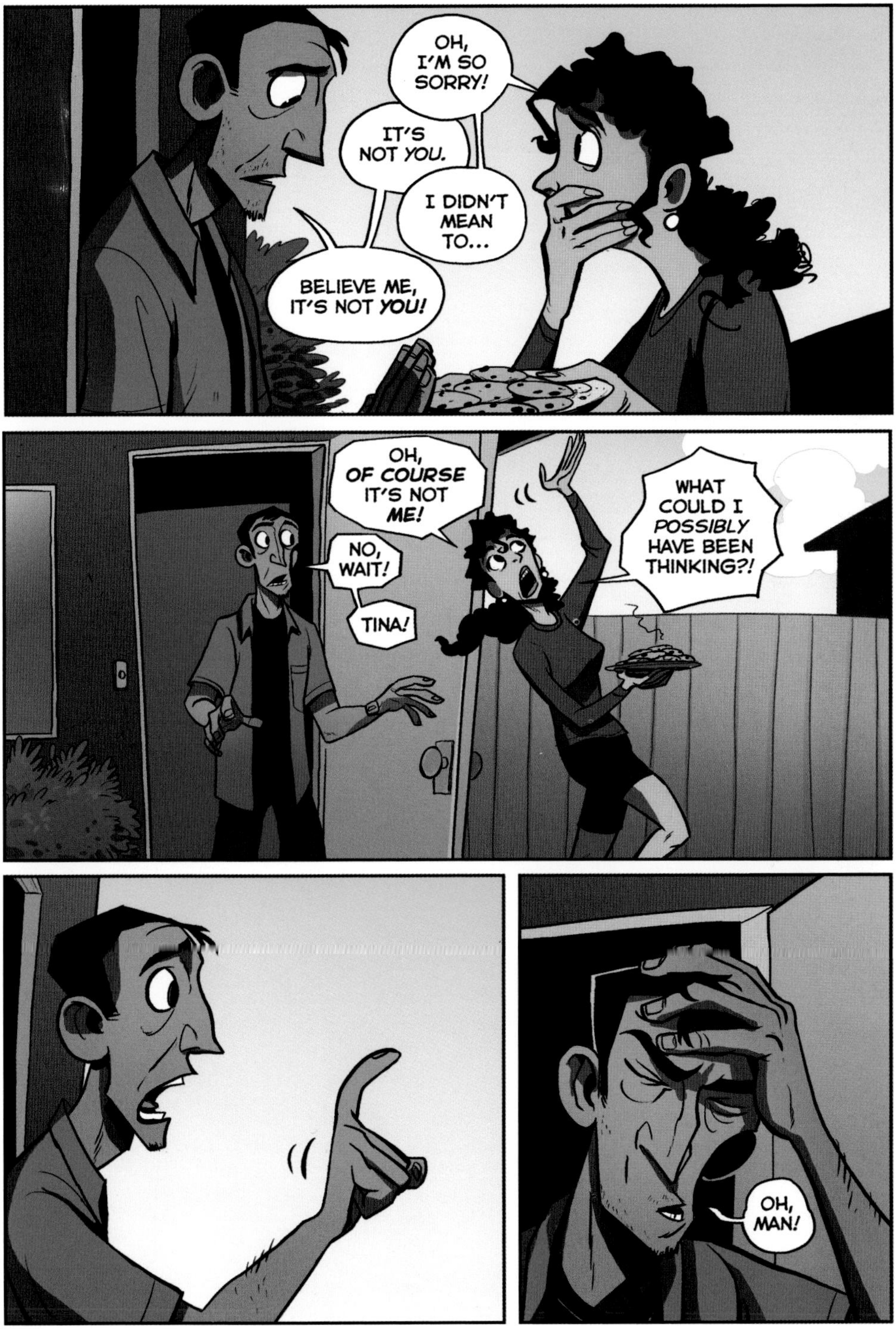
OH, I'M SO SORRY!
IT'S NOT *YOU.*
I DIDN'T MEAN TO...
BELIEVE ME, IT'S NOT ***YOU!***
OH, ***OF COURSE*** IT'S NOT ***ME!***
NO, WAIT!
TINA!
WHAT COULD I *POSSIBLY* HAVE BEEN THINKING?!
OH, MAN!

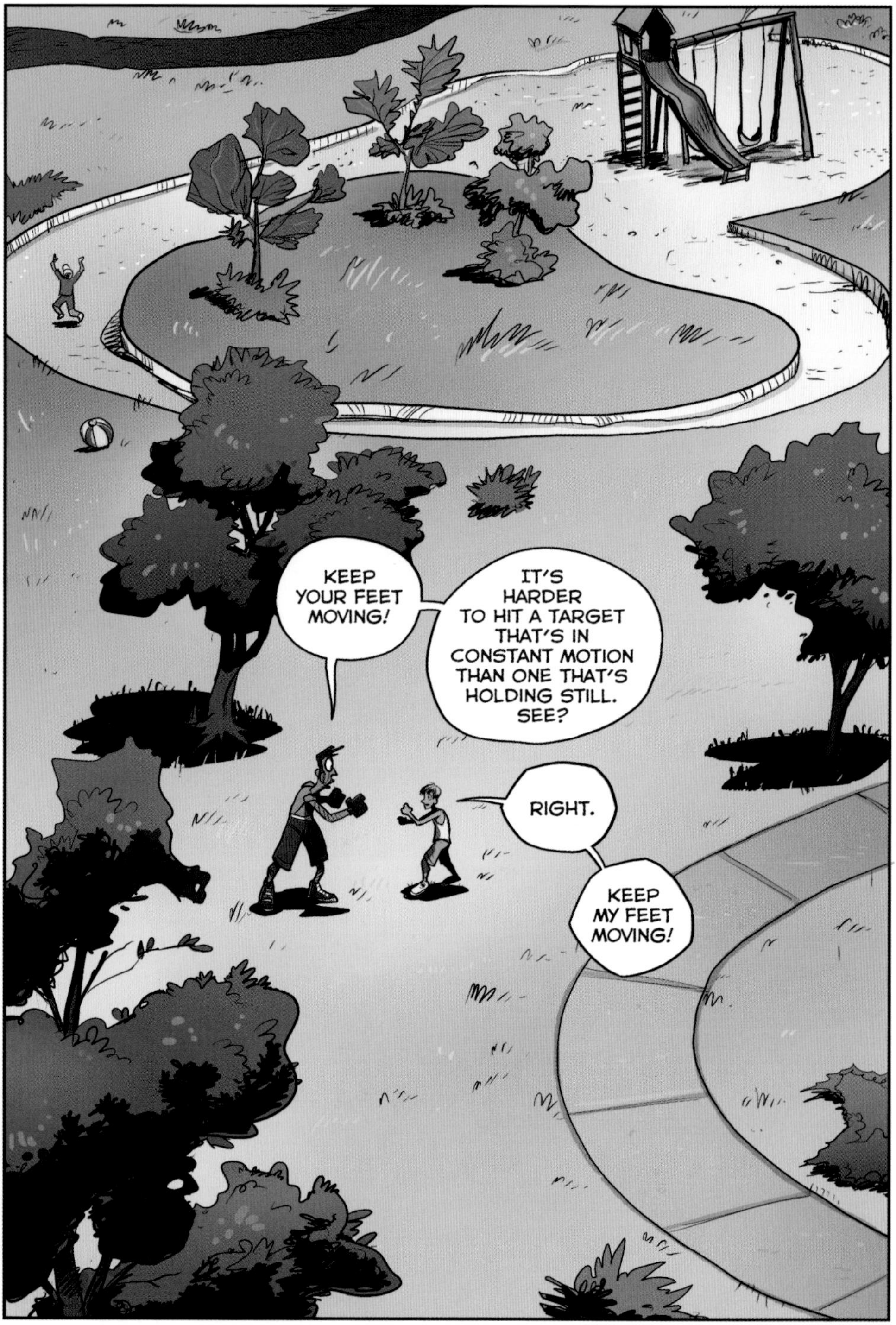
KEEP YOUR FEET MOVING!
IT'S HARDER TO HIT A TARGET THAT'S IN CONSTANT MOTION THAN ONE THAT'S HOLDING STILL. SEE?
RIGHT.
KEEP MY FEET MOVING!

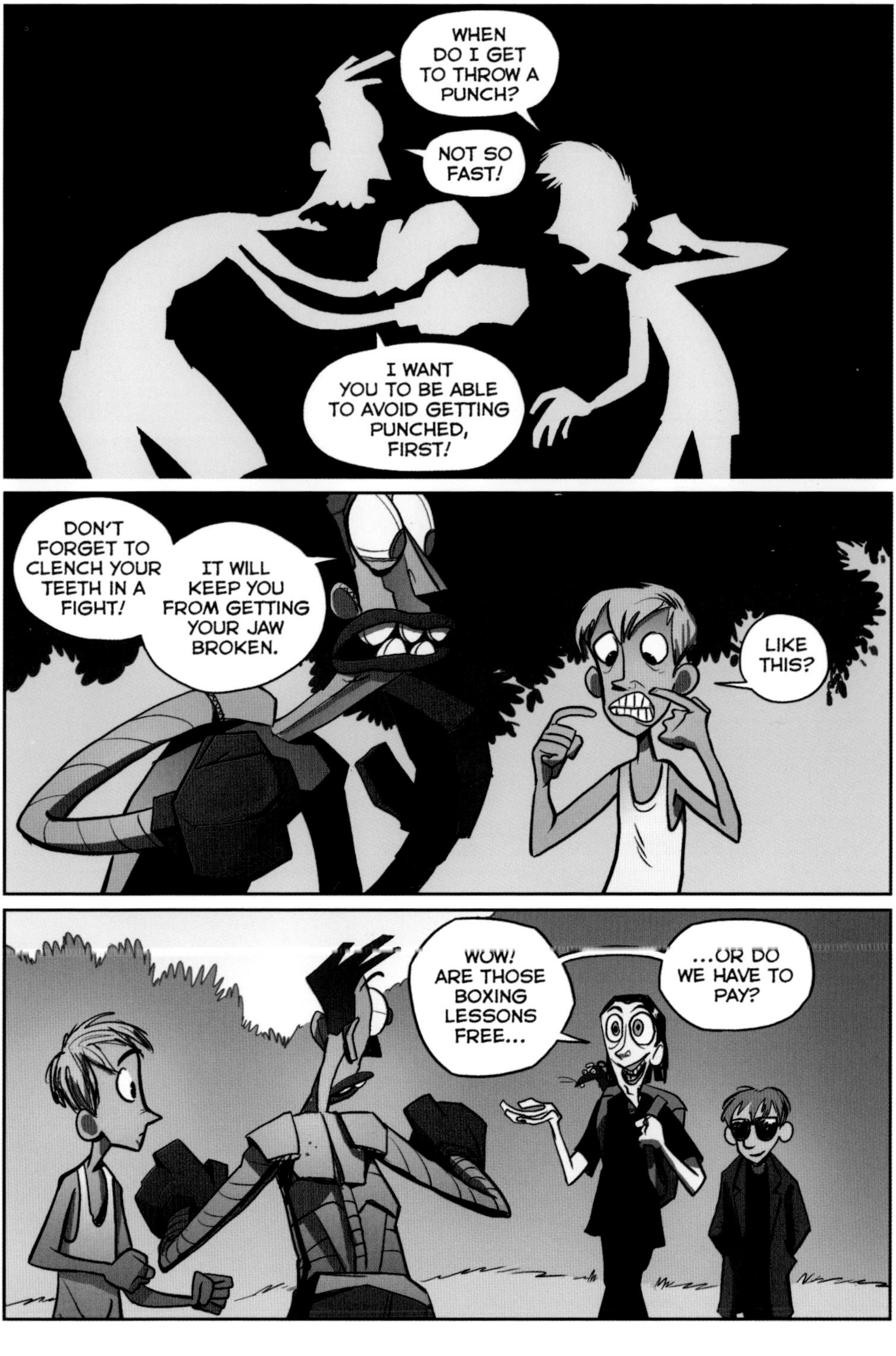
WHEN DO I GET TO THROW A PUNCH?
NOT SO FAST!
I WANT YOU TO BE ABLE TO AVOID GETTING PUNCHED, FIRST!
DON'T FORGET TO CLENCH YOUR TEETH IN A FIGHT!
IT WILL KEEP YOU FROM GETTING YOUR JAW BROKEN.
LIKE THIS?
WOW! ARE THOSE BOXING LESSONS FREE...
...OR DO WE HAVE TO PAY?

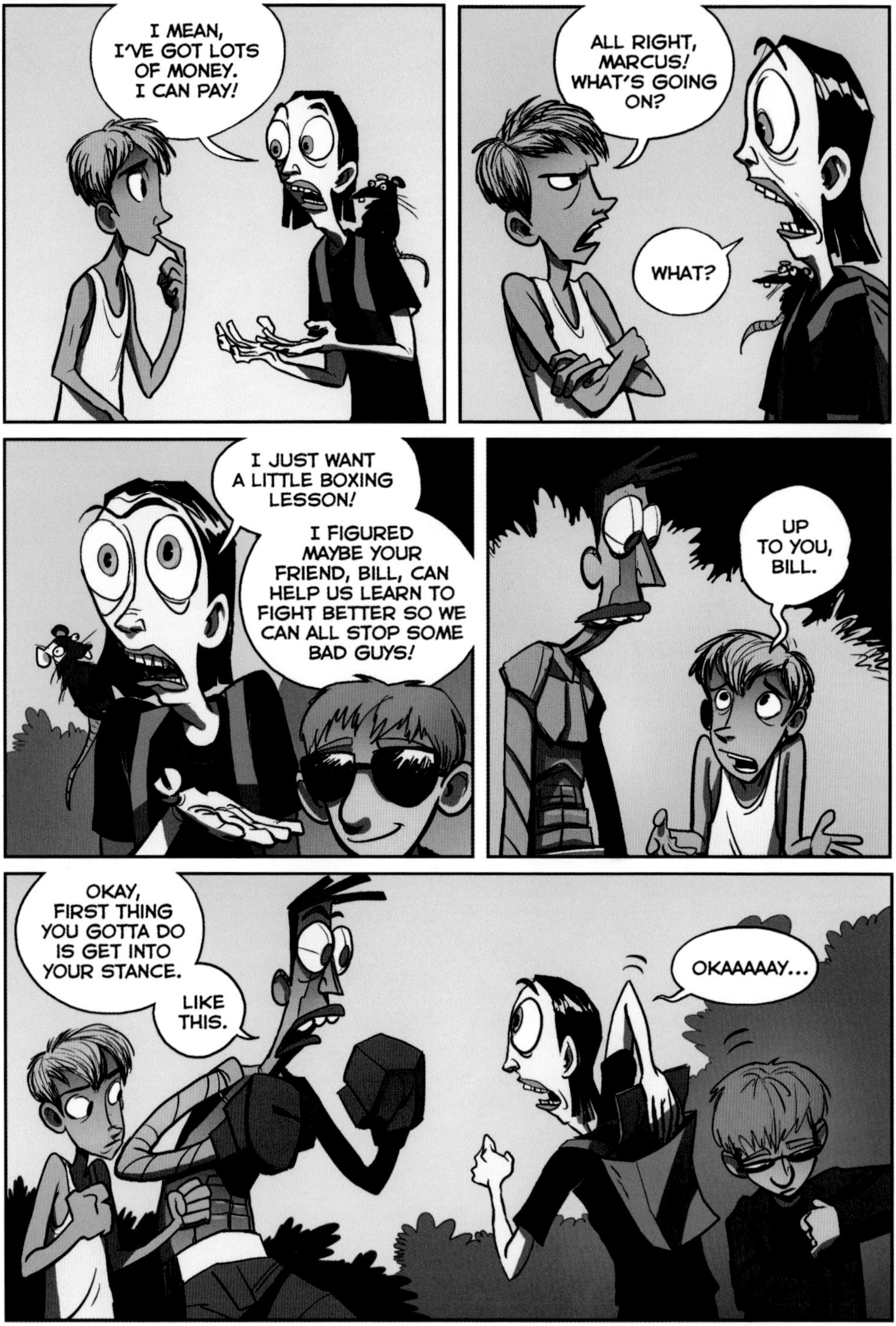
I MEAN, I'VE GOT LOTS OF MONEY. I CAN PAY!
ALL RIGHT, MARCUS! WHAT'S GOING ON?
WHAT?
I JUST WANT A LITTLE BOXING LESSON!
I FIGURED MAYBE YOUR FRIEND, BILL, CAN HELP US LEARN TO FIGHT BETTER SO WE CAN ALL STOP SOME BAD GUYS!
UP TO YOU, BILL.
OKAY, FIRST THING YOU GOTTA DO IS GET INTO YOUR STANCE.
LIKE THIS.
OKAAAAAY...

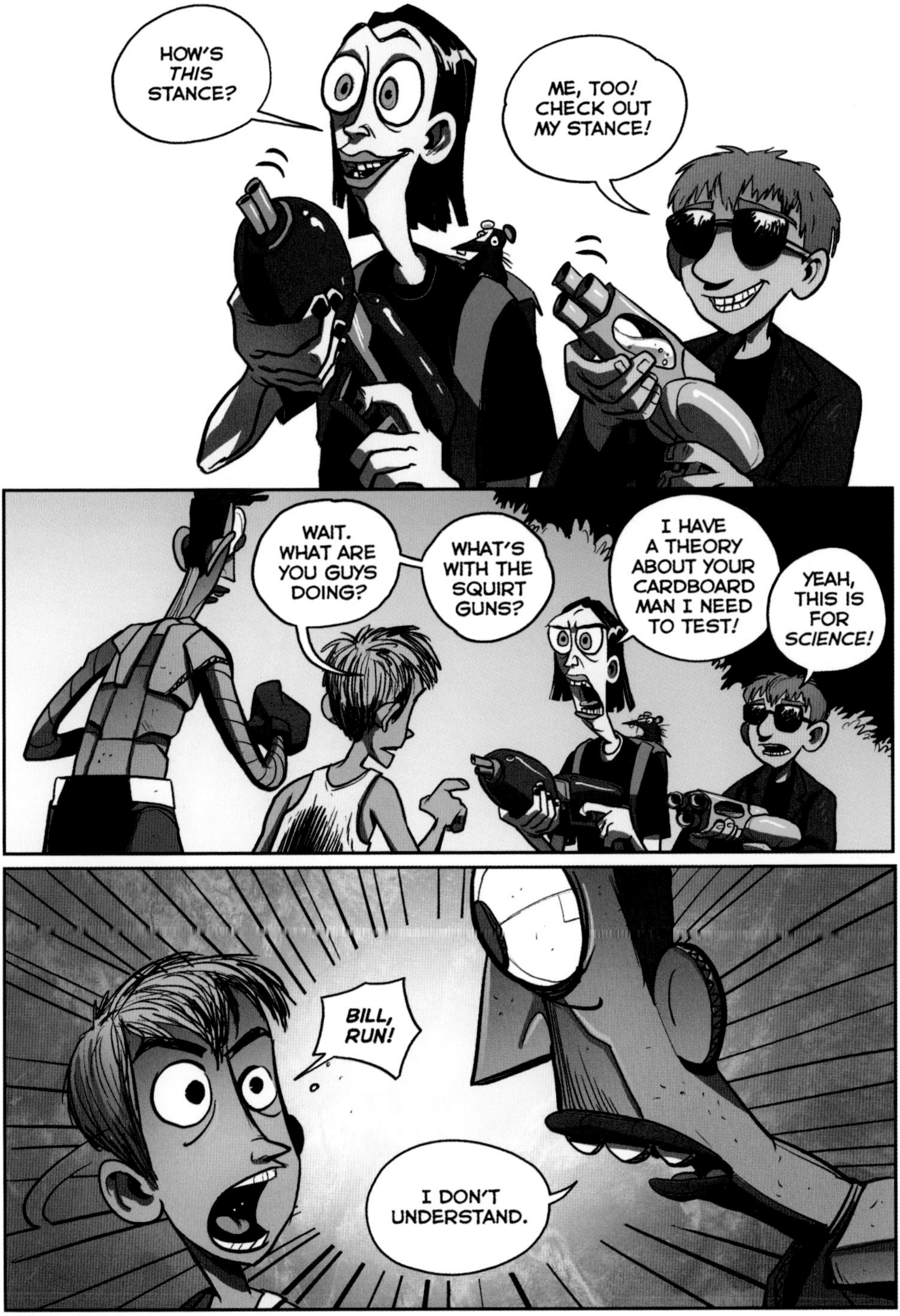
HOW'S *THIS* STANCE?
ME, TOO! CHECK OUT MY STANCE!
WAIT. WHAT ARE YOU GUYS DOING?
WHAT'S WITH THE SQUIRT GUNS?
I HAVE A THEORY ABOUT YOUR CARDBOARD MAN I NEED TO TEST!
YEAH, THIS IS FOR *SCIENCE!*
BILL, RUN!
I DON'T UNDERSTAND.

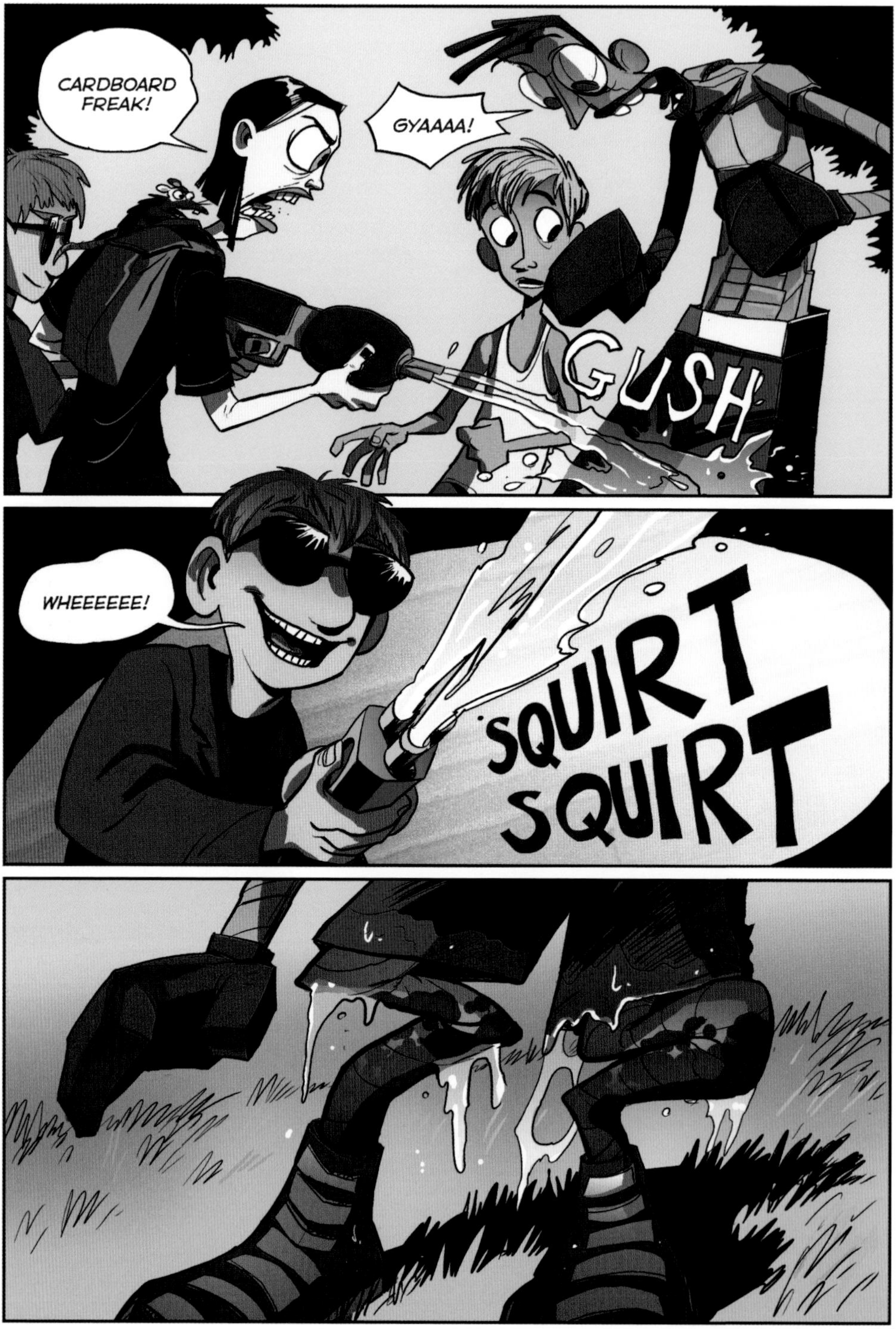
CARDBOARD FREAK!
GYAAAA!
GUSH
WHEEEEEE!
SQUIRT SQUIRT

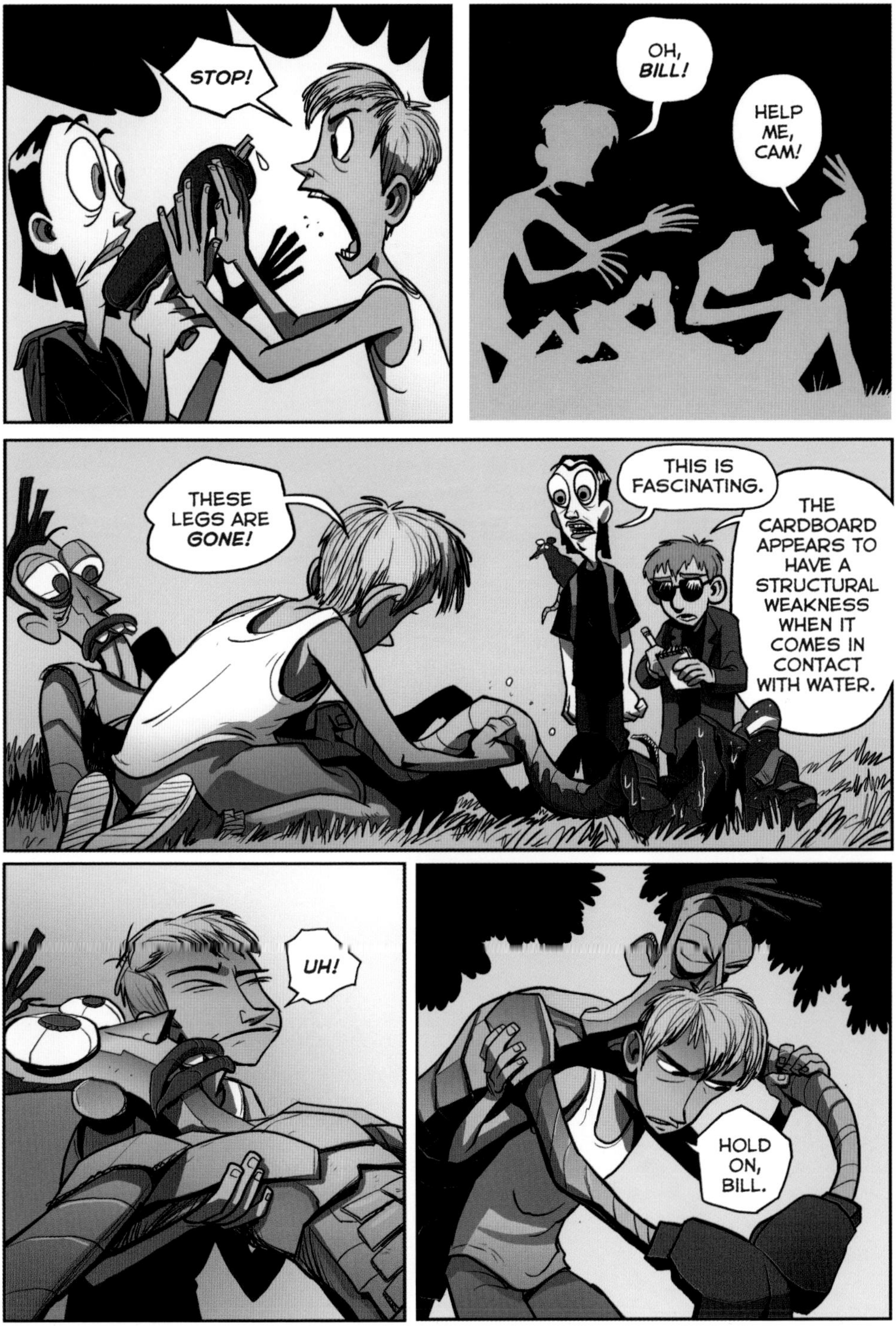
STOP!
OH, BILL!
HELP ME, CAM!
THESE LEGS ARE GONE!
THIS IS FASCINATING.
THE CARDBOARD APPEARS TO HAVE A STRUCTURAL WEAKNESS WHEN IT COMES IN CONTACT WITH WATER.
UH!
HOLD ON, BILL.

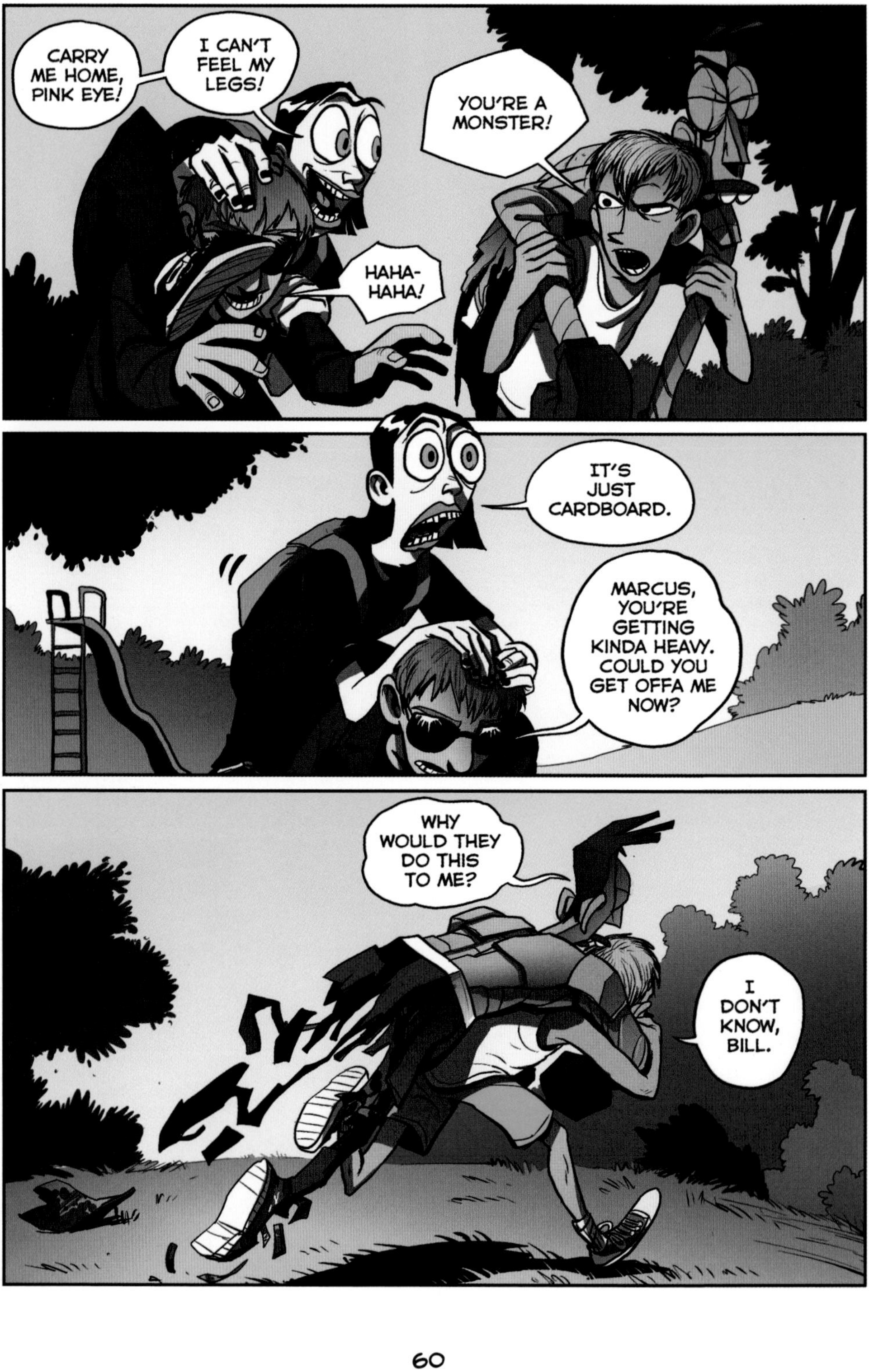
CARRY ME HOME, PINK EYE!
I CAN'T FEEL MY LEGS!
YOU'RE A MONSTER!
HAHA-HAHA!
IT'S JUST CARDBOARD.
MARCUS, YOU'RE GETTING KINDA HEAVY. COULD YOU GET OFFA ME NOW?
WHY WOULD THEY DO THIS TO ME?
I DON'T KNOW, BILL.

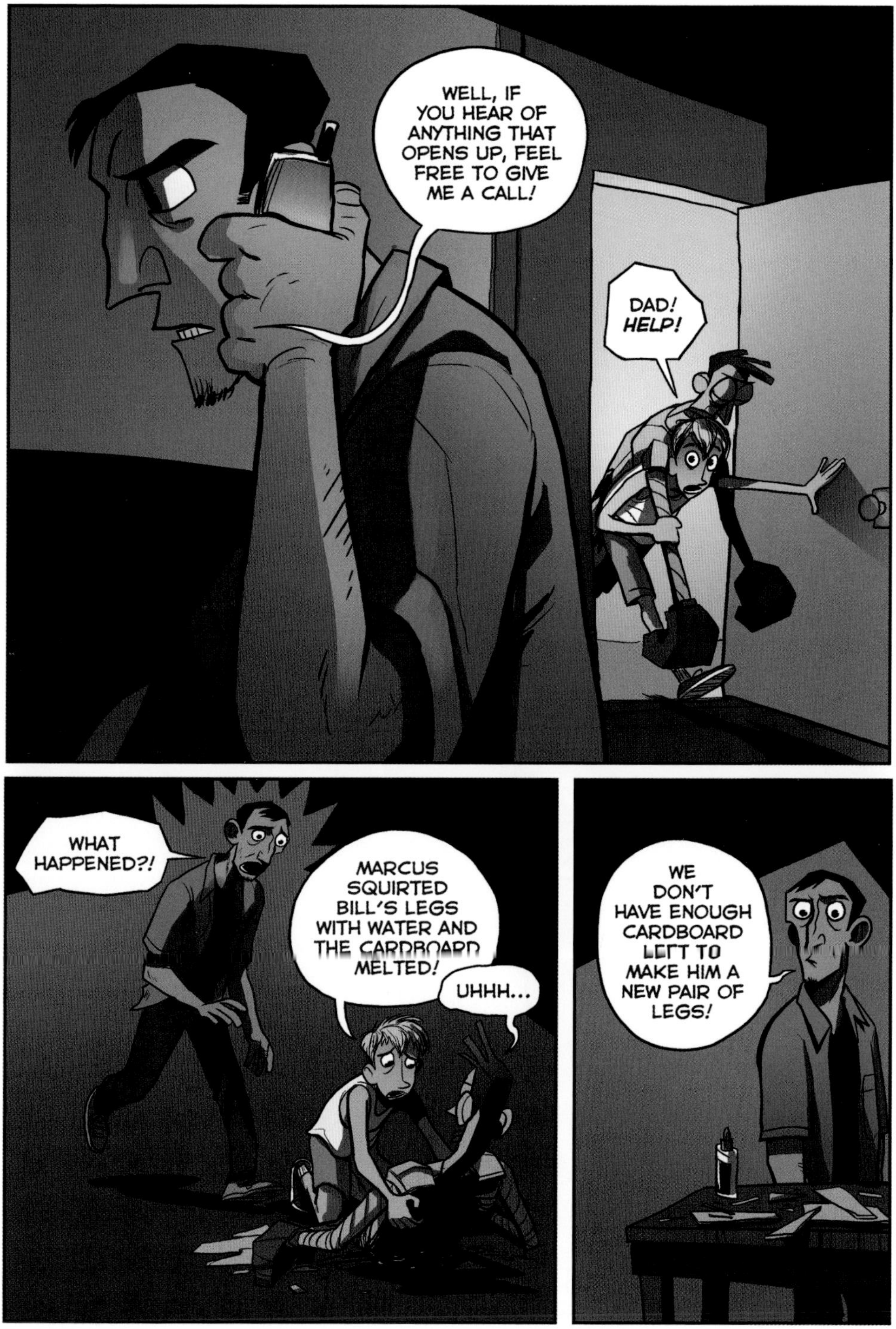
WELL, IF YOU HEAR OF ANYTHING THAT OPENS UP, FEEL FREE TO GIVE ME A CALL!
DAD! HELP!
WHAT HAPPENED?!
MARCUS SQUIRTED BILL'S LEGS WITH WATER AND THE CARDBOARD MELTED!
UHHH...
WE DON'T HAVE ENOUGH CARDBOARD LEFT TO MAKE HIM A NEW PAIR OF LEGS!

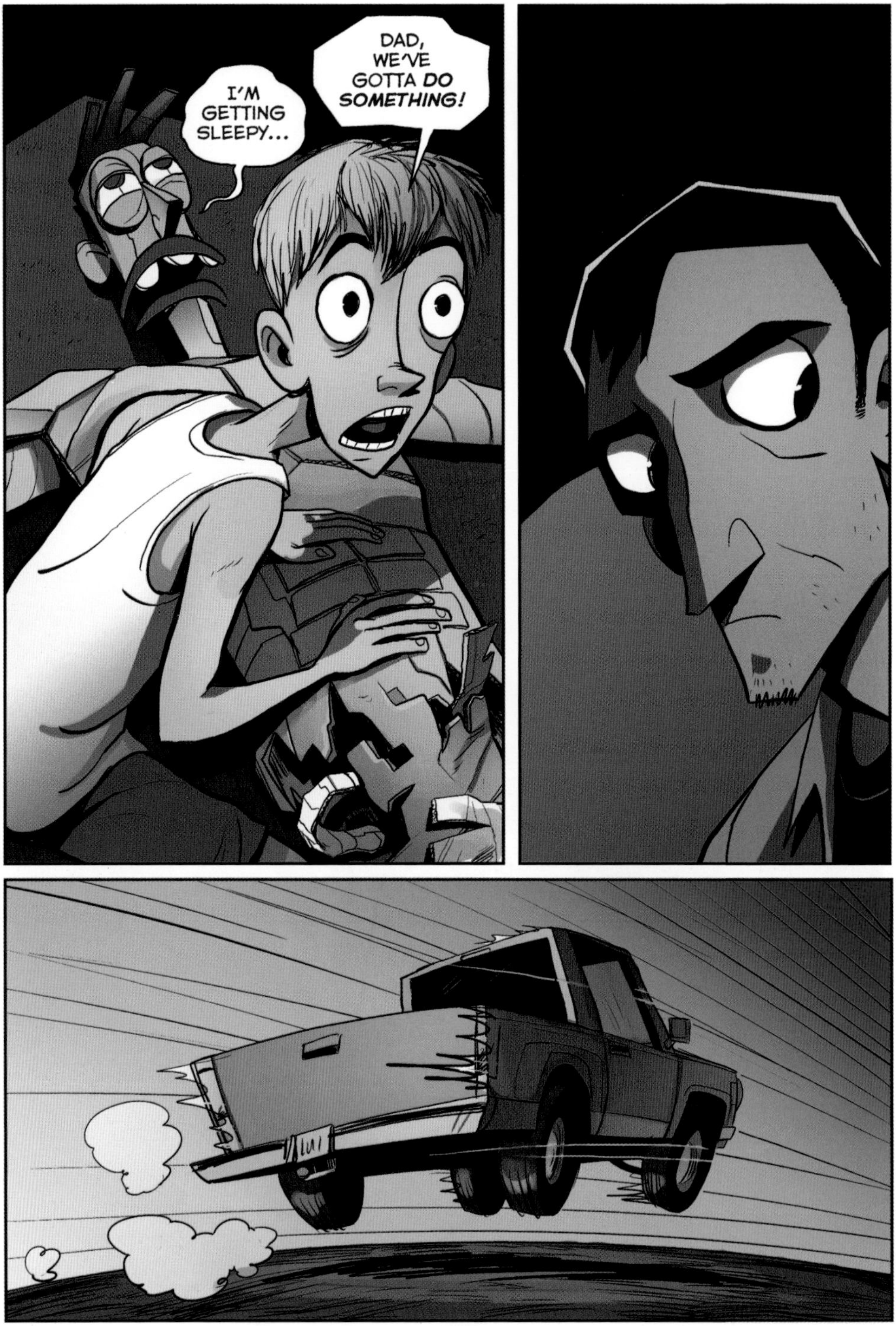
I'M GETTING SLEEPY...
DAD, WE'VE GOTTA DO SOMETHING!

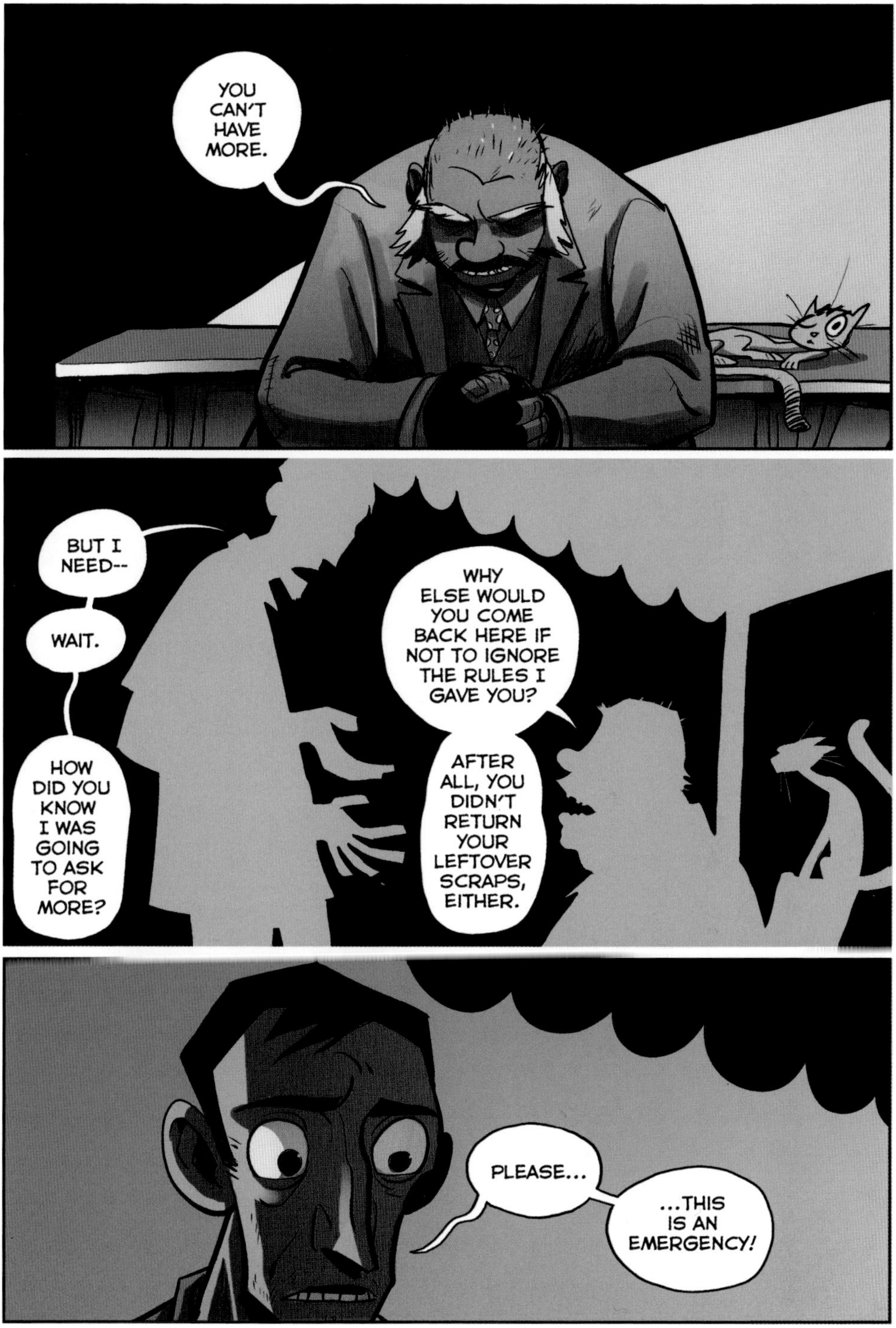
YOU CAN'T HAVE MORE.
BUT I NEED--
WAIT.
HOW DID YOU KNOW I WAS GOING TO ASK FOR MORE?
WHY ELSE WOULD YOU COME BACK HERE IF NOT TO IGNORE THE RULES I GAVE YOU?
AFTER ALL, YOU DIDN'T RETURN YOUR LEFTOVER SCRAPS, EITHER.
PLEASE...
...THIS IS AN EMERGENCY!

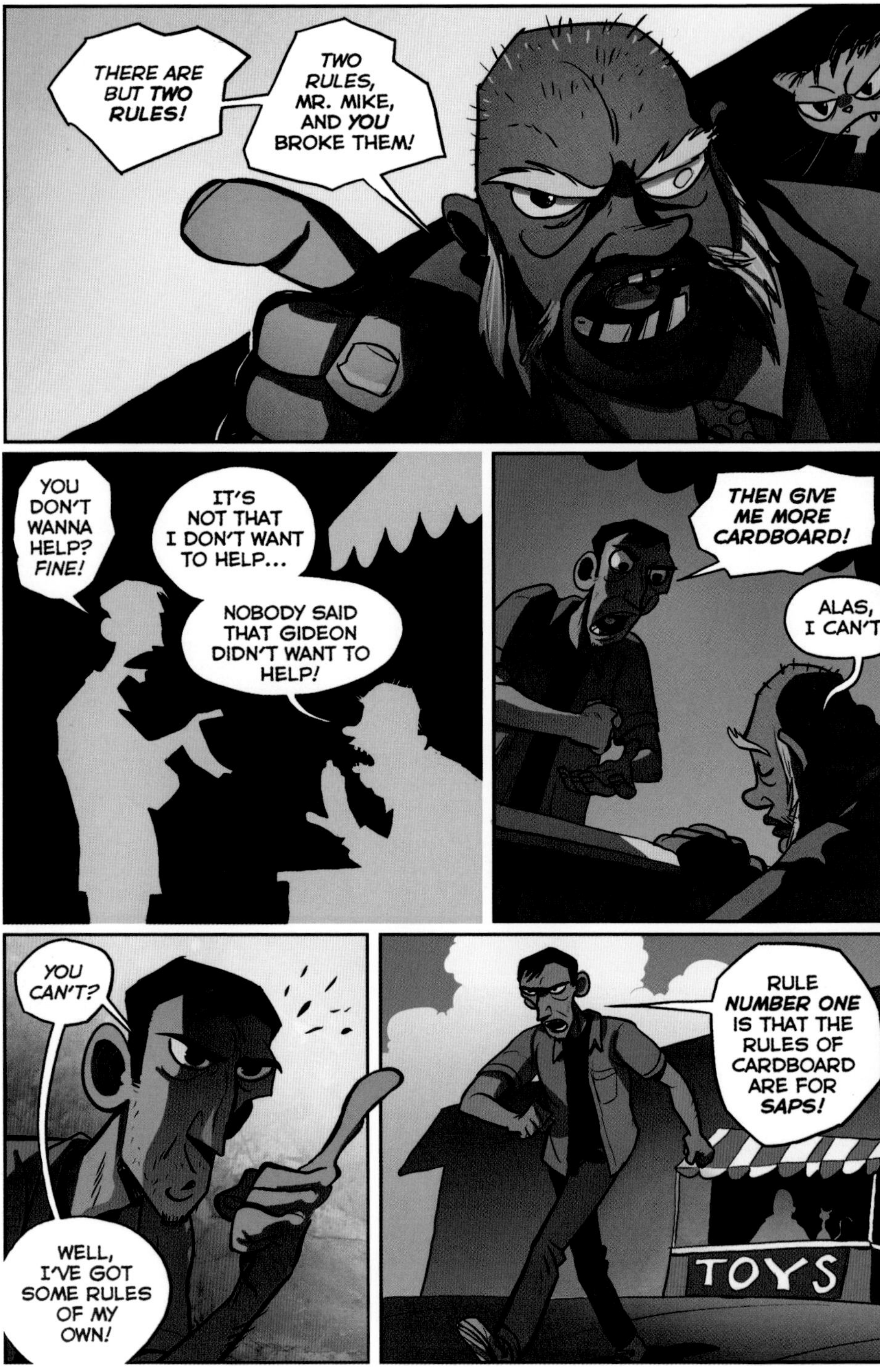
THERE ARE BUT TWO RULES!
TWO RULES, MR. MIKE, AND YOU BROKE THEM!
YOU DON'T WANNA HELP? FINE!
IT'S NOT THAT I DON'T WANT TO HELP...
NOBODY SAID THAT GIDEON DIDN'T WANT TO HELP!
THEN GIVE ME MORE CARDBOARD!
ALAS, I CAN'T.
YOU CAN'T?
WELL, I'VE GOT SOME RULES OF MY OWN!
RULE NUMBER ONE IS THAT THE RULES OF CARDBOARD ARE FOR SAPS!
TOYS

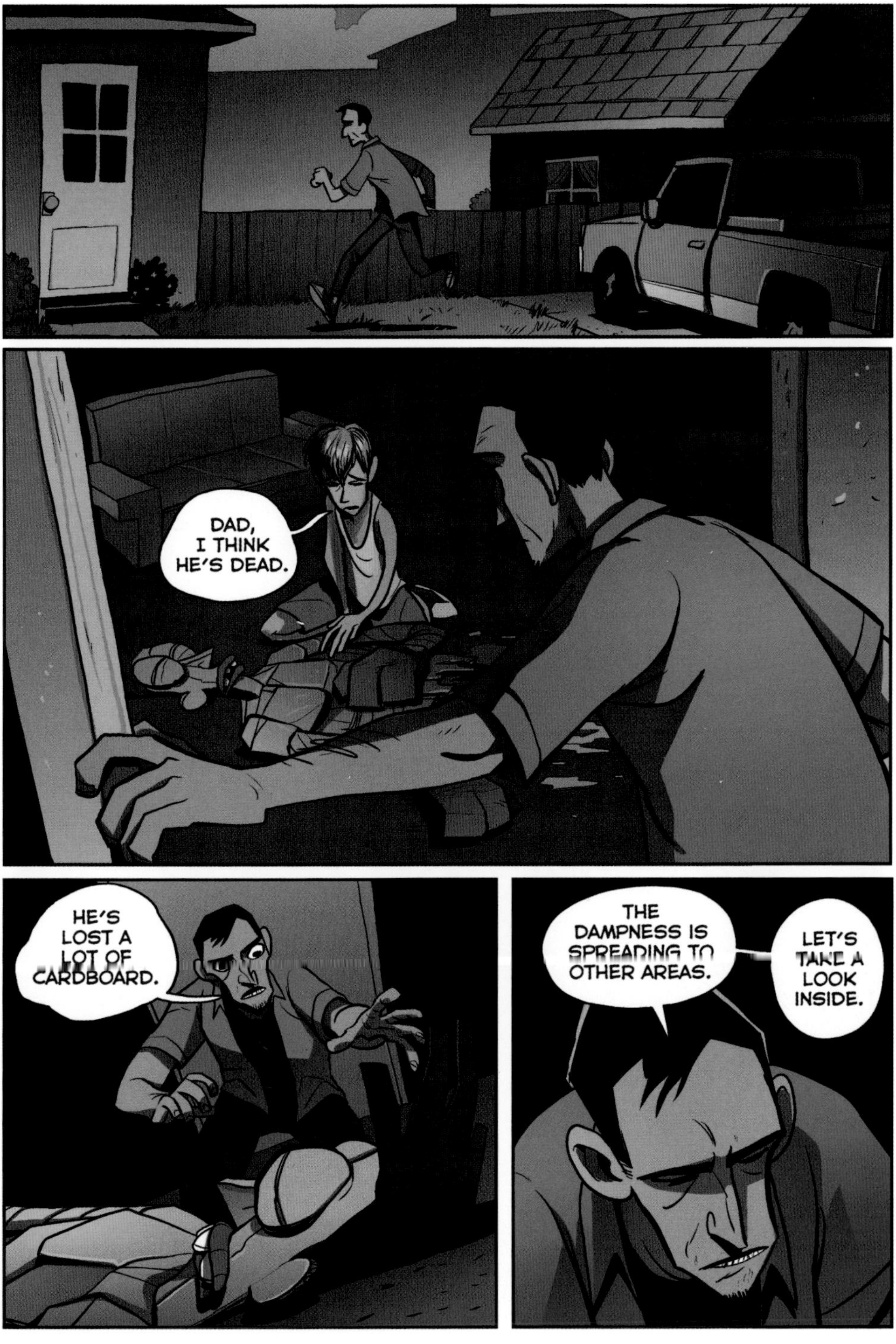
DAD, I THINK HE'S DEAD.
HE'S LOST A LOT OF CARDBOARD.
THE DAMPNESS IS SPREADING TO OTHER AREAS.
LET'S TAKE A LOOK INSIDE.

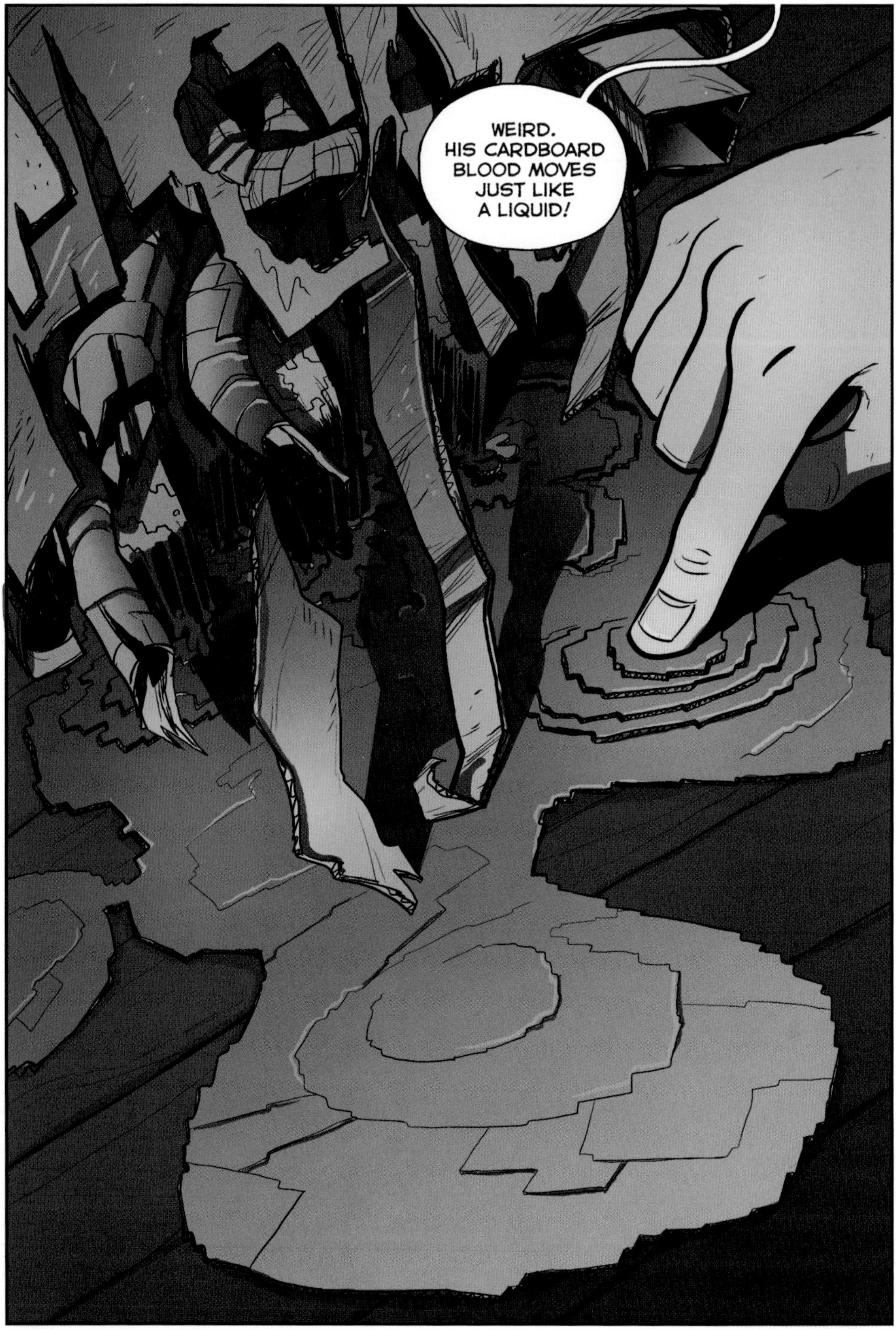
WEIRD. HIS CARDBOARD BLOOD MOVES JUST LIKE A LIQUID!

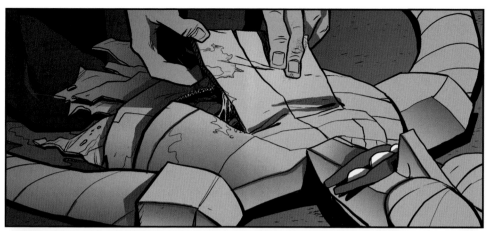

BA-BUMP
BA-THUMP
BA-BUMP

HIS HEART'S STILL PUMPING.

HE'S NOT DEAD YET!

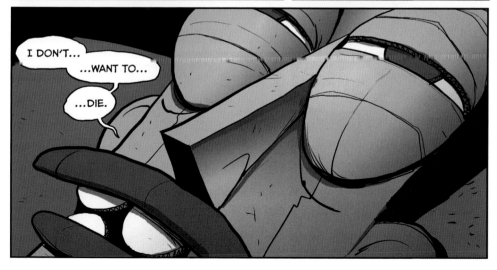

I DON'T...

...WANT TO...

...DIE.

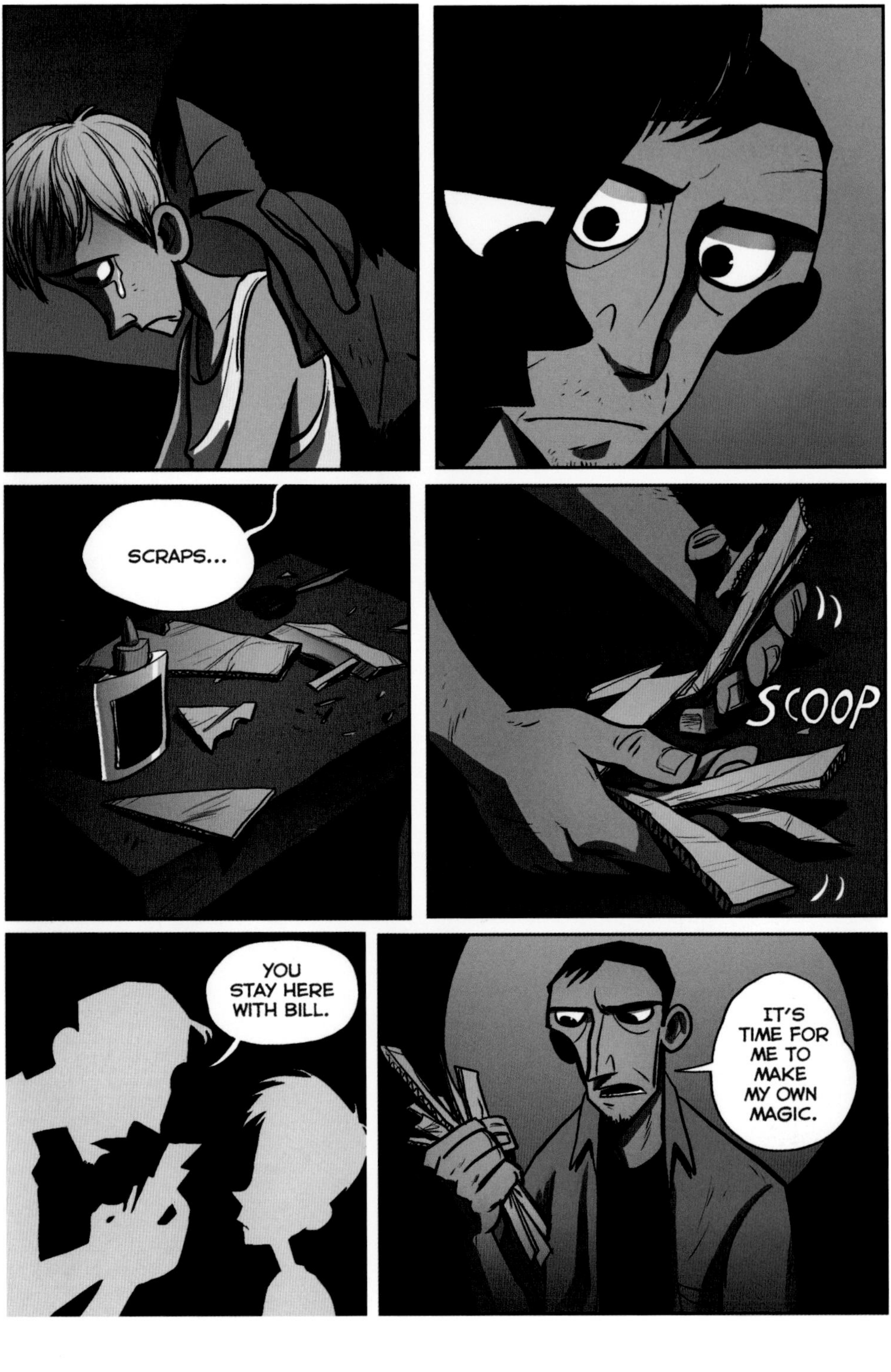
SCRAPS...
SCOOP
YOU STAY HERE WITH BILL.
IT'S TIME FOR ME TO MAKE MY OWN MAGIC.

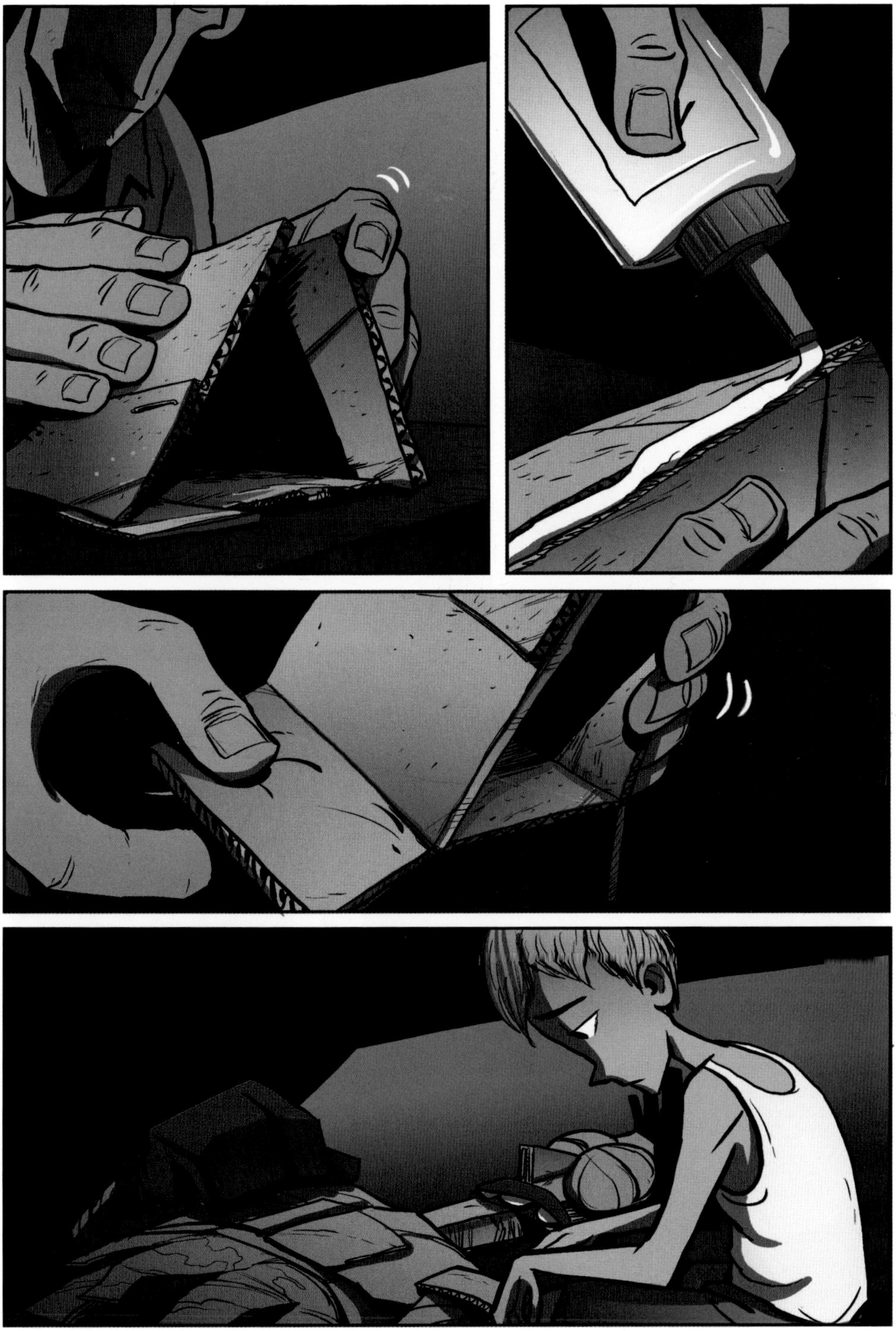

FLESH.

YOU ARE A FLESH...

...PERSON.

YOU'RE AWAKE!

HOW DO YOU FEEL?!

CAM... ...YOU ARE A GOOD PERSON...

...NOT A CARDBOARD THING LIKE ME.

WELL, DOGS AREN'T MADE OF CARDBOARD...

...THEY'RE MADE OF FLESH AND THEY'RE NOT AS HUMAN AS YOU ARE!

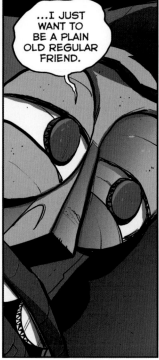

...I JUST WANT TO BE A PLAIN OLD REGULAR FRIEND.

YOU MAY BE MADE OF CARDBOARD, BUT I THINK OF YOU AS A REAL PERSON!

I DON'T WANT TO BE A CARDBOARD FRIEND.

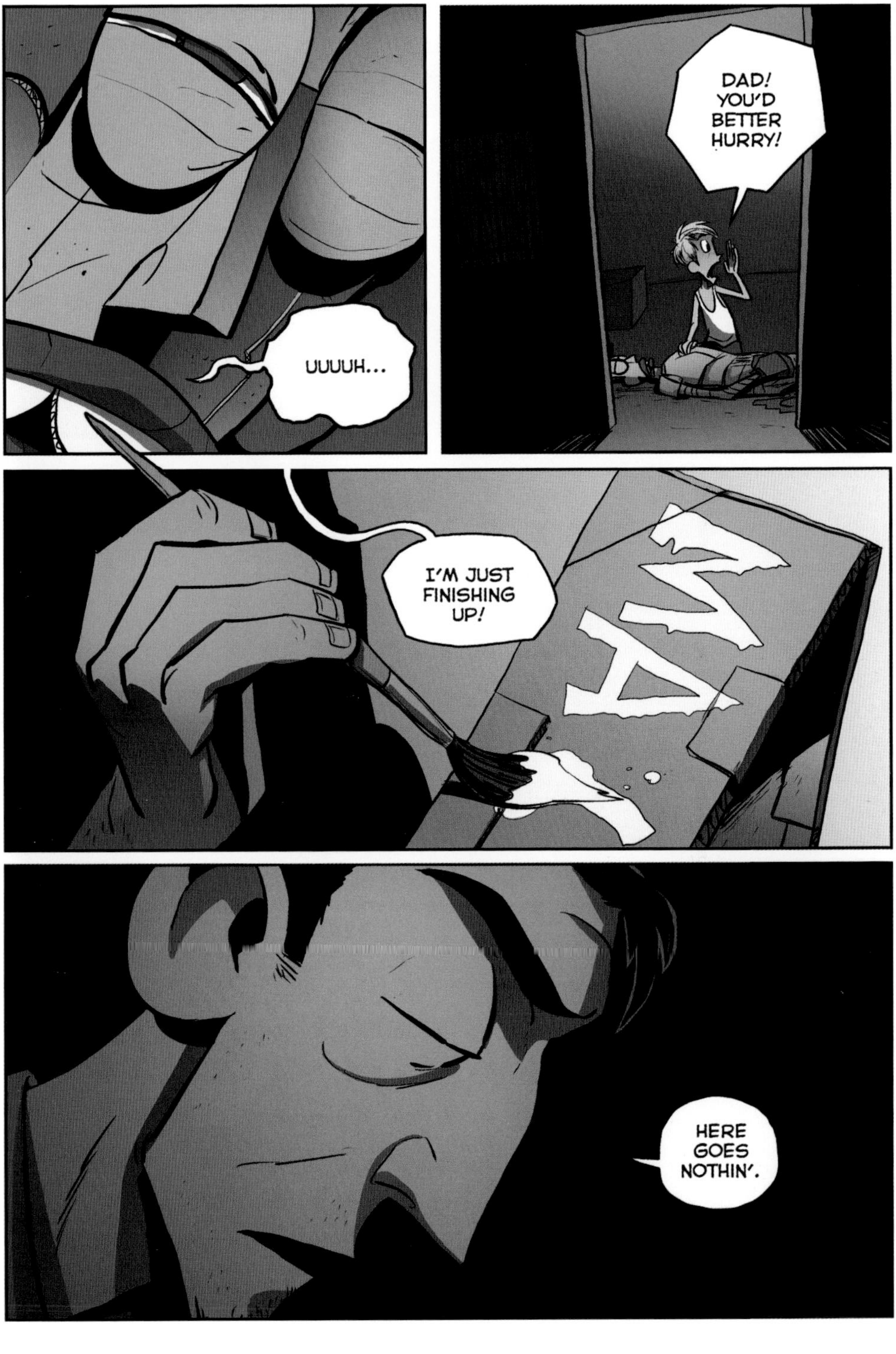
UUUUH...
DAD! YOU'D BETTER HURRY!
I'M JUST FINISHING UP!
HERE GOES NOTHIN'.

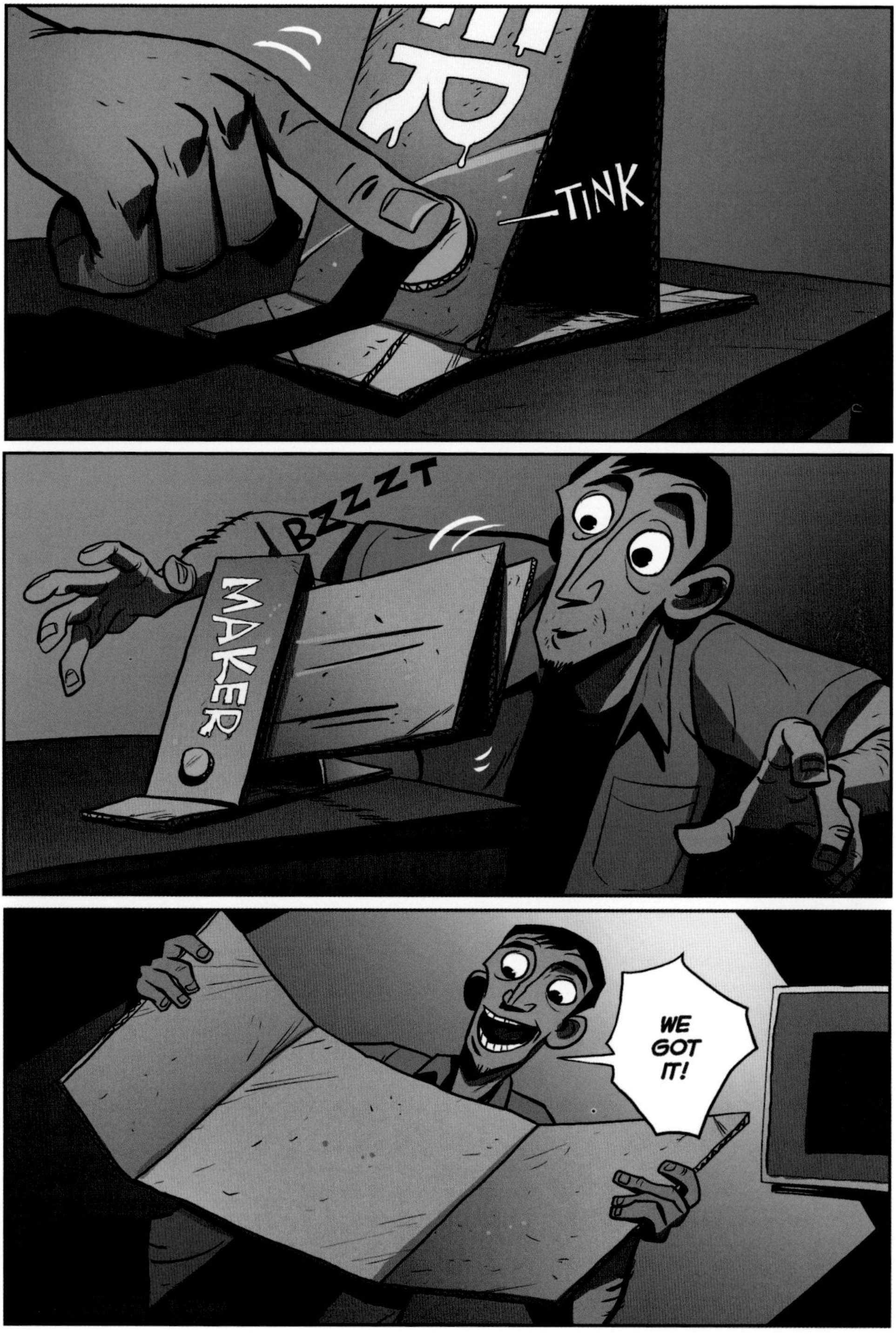
TINK
BZZZT
MAKER
WE GOT IT!

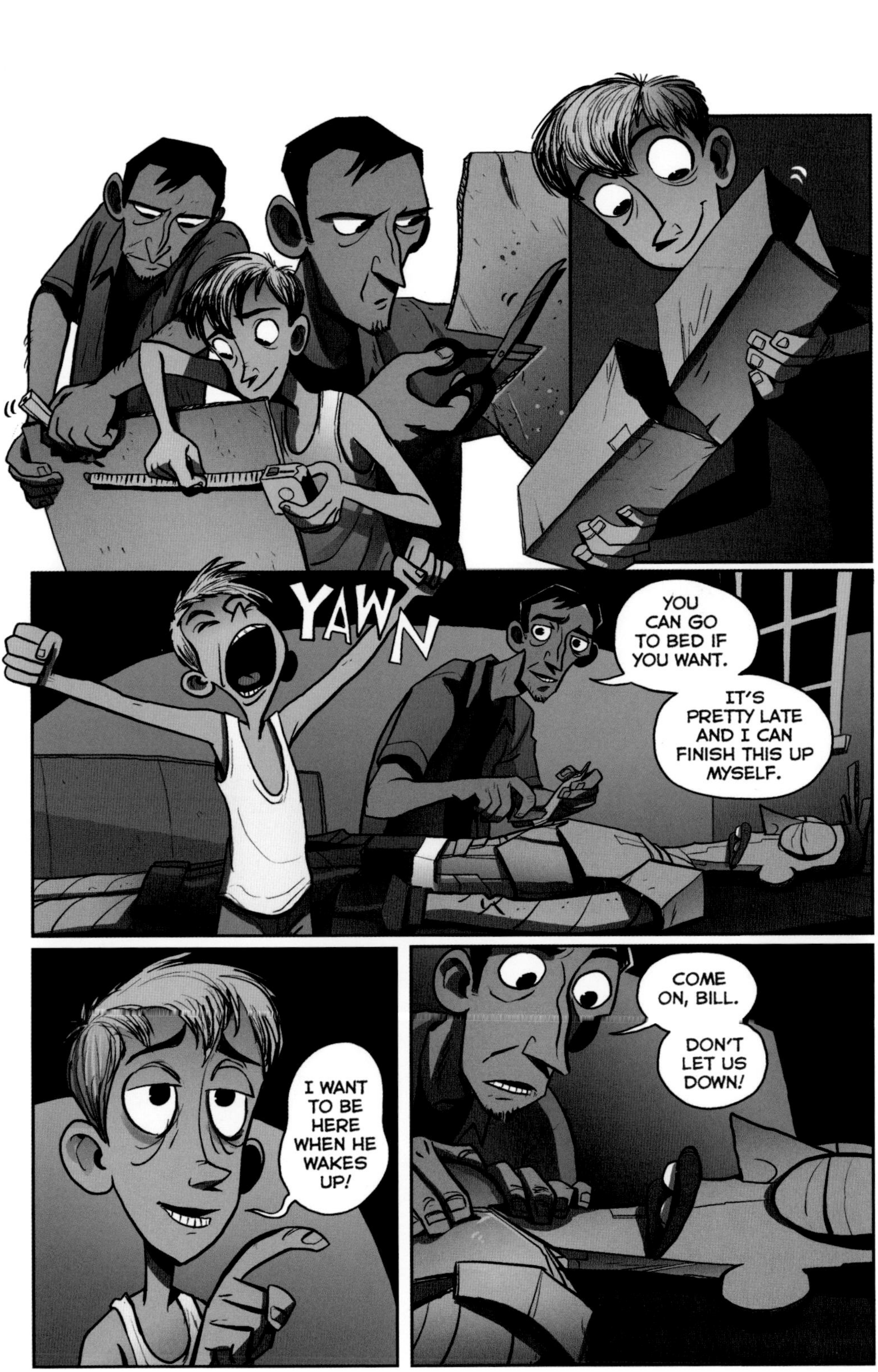
YAWN
YOU CAN GO TO BED IF YOU WANT.
IT'S PRETTY LATE AND I CAN FINISH THIS UP MYSELF.
I WANT TO BE HERE WHEN HE WAKES UP!
COME ON, BILL.
DON'T LET US DOWN!

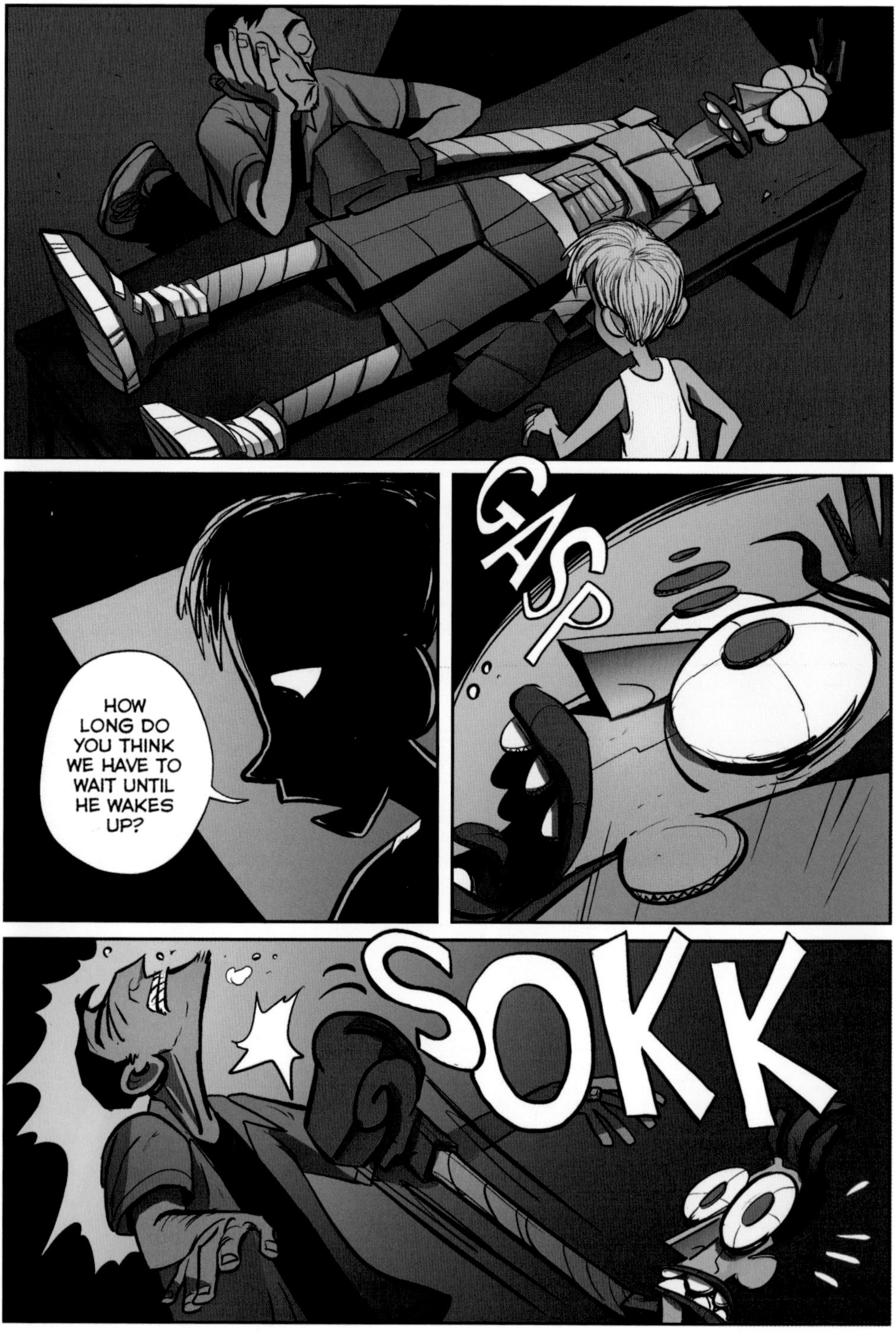
HOW LONG DO YOU THINK WE HAVE TO WAIT UNTIL HE WAKES UP?
GASP
SOKK

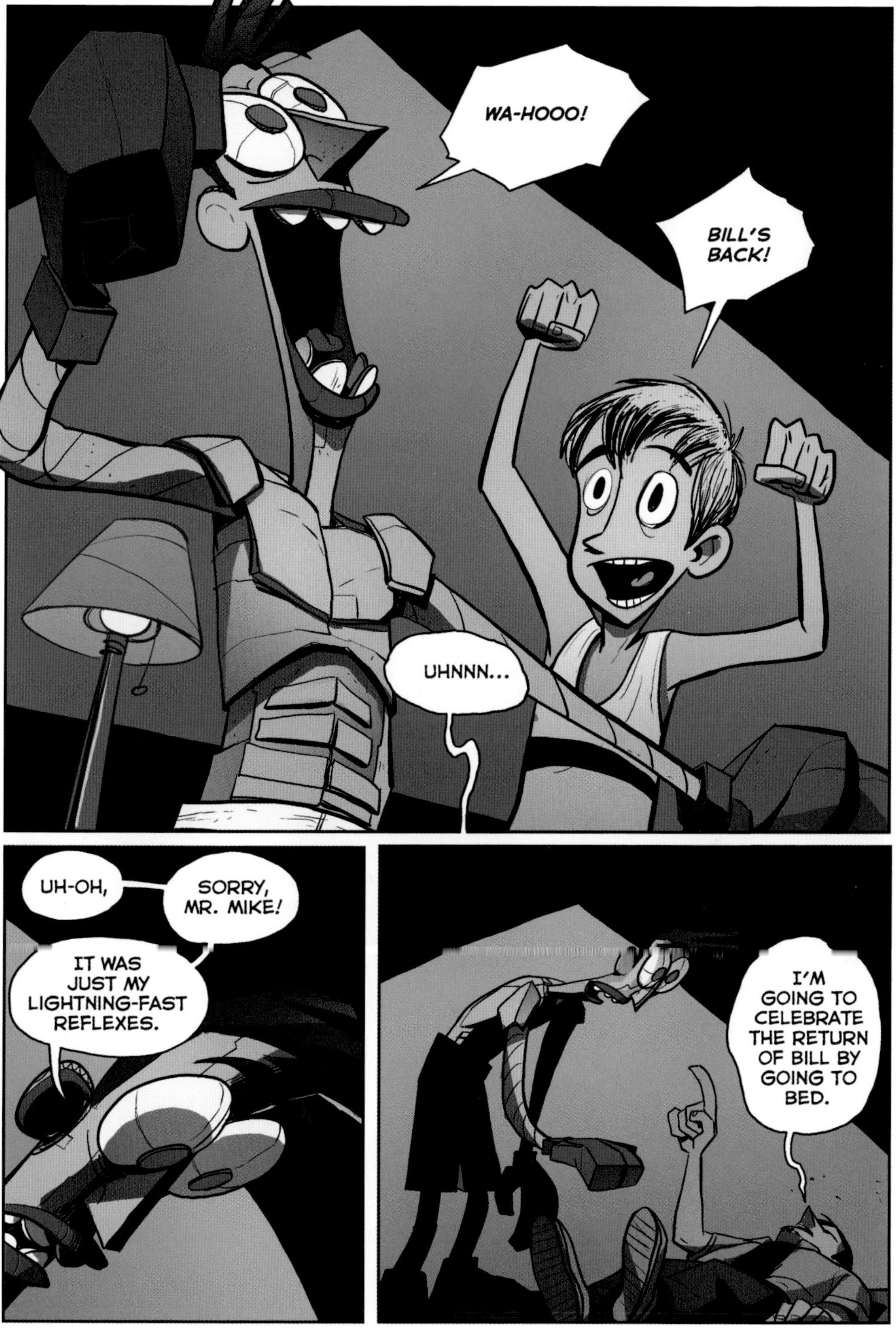
WA-HOOO!
BILL'S BACK!
UHNNN...
UH-OH,
SORRY, MR. MIKE!
IT WAS JUST MY LIGHTNING-FAST REFLEXES.
I'M GOING TO CELEBRATE THE RETURN OF BILL BY GOING TO BED.

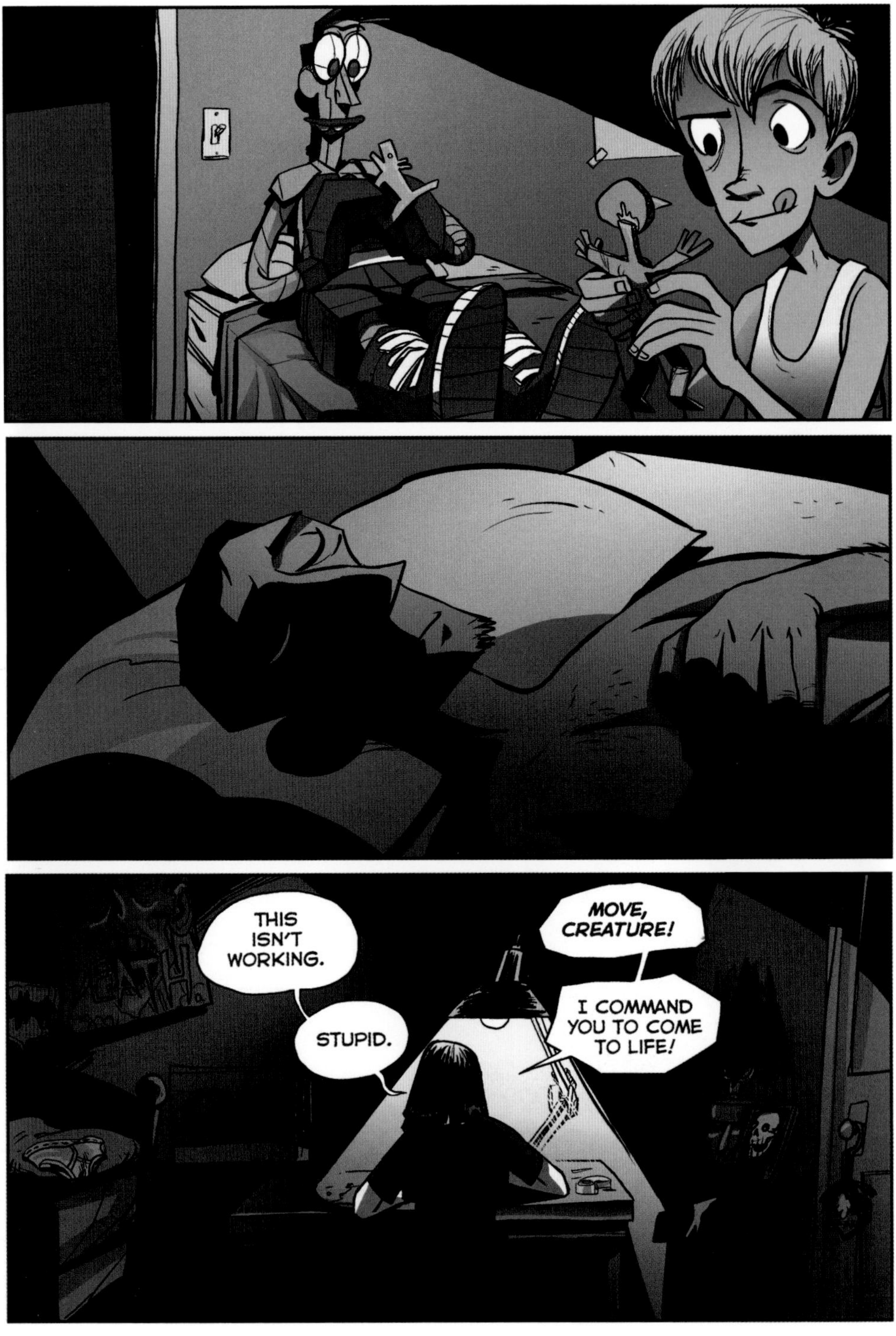
THIS ISN'T WORKING.
STUPID.
MOVE, CREATURE!
I COMMAND YOU TO COME TO LIFE!

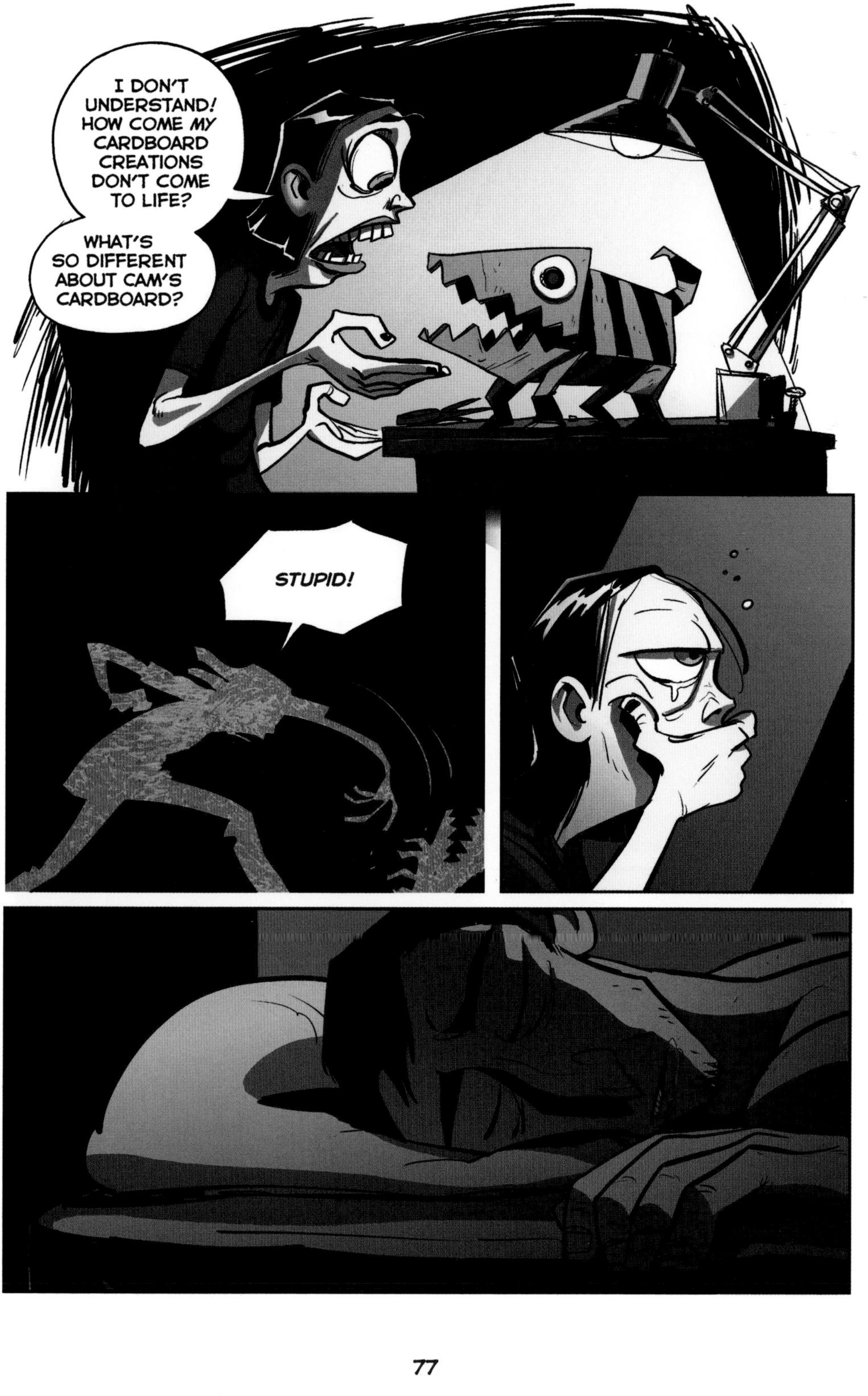
I DON'T UNDERSTAND! HOW COME *MY* CARDBOARD CREATIONS DON'T COME TO LIFE?
WHAT'S SO DIFFERENT ABOUT CAM'S CARDBOARD?
STUPID!

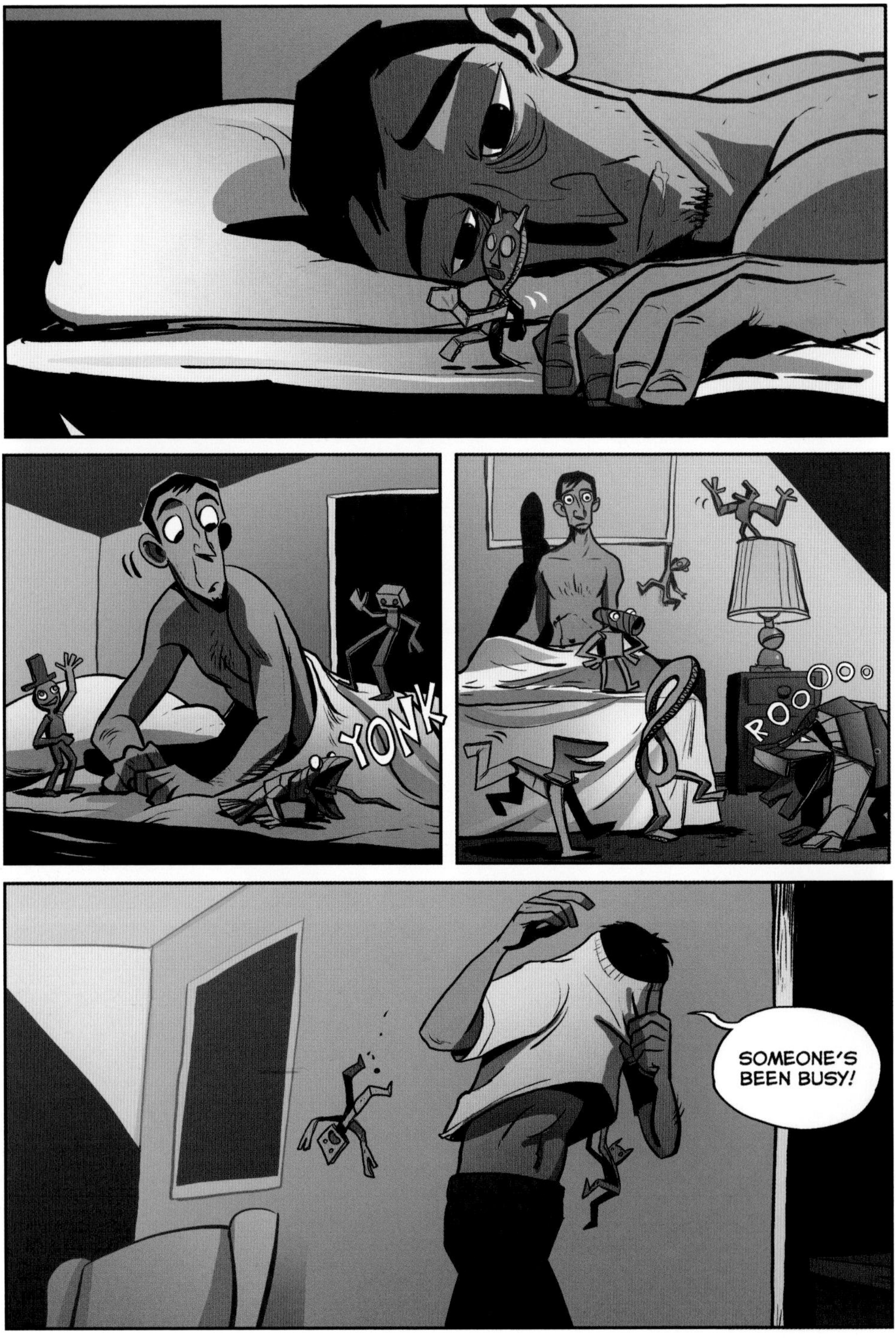
YONK
ROOOOO
SOMEONE'S BEEN BUSY!

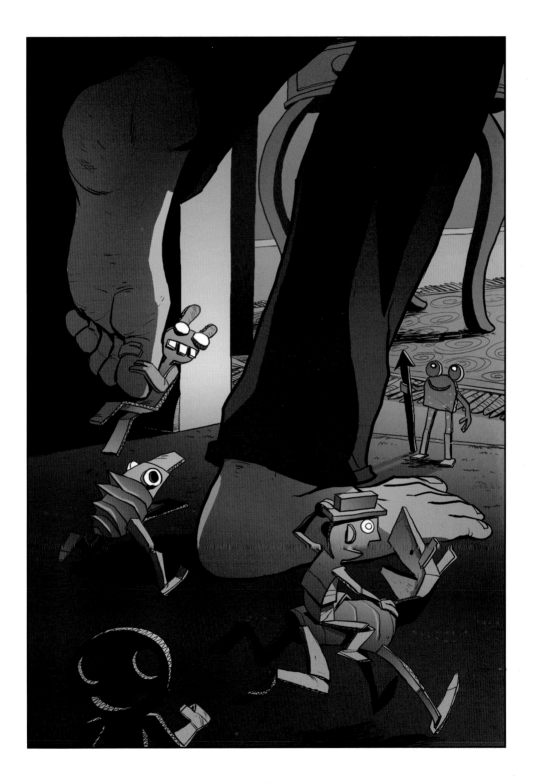

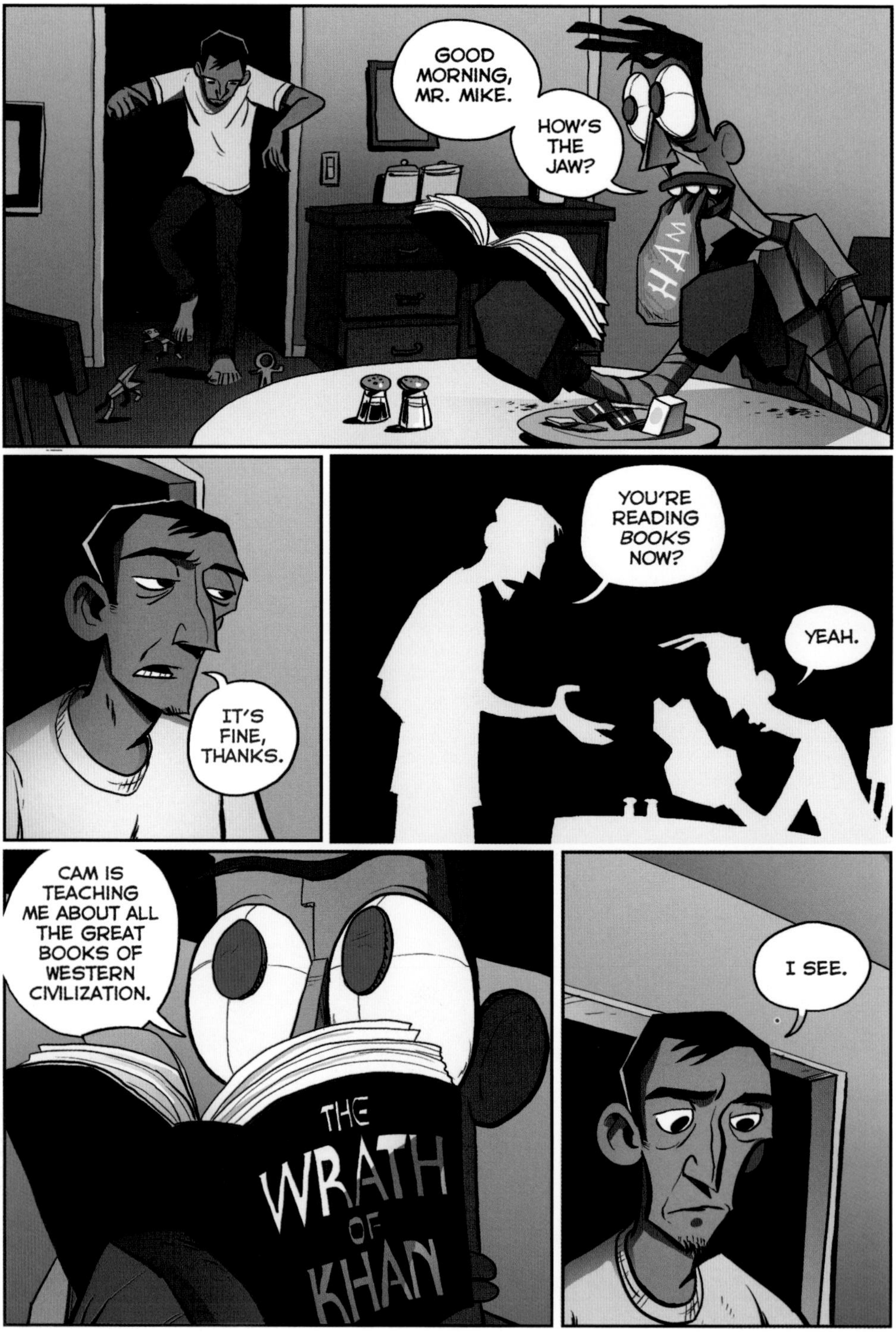
GOOD MORNING, MR. MIKE.
HOW'S THE JAW?
HAM
IT'S FINE, THANKS.
YOU'RE READING *BOOKS* NOW?
YEAH.
CAM IS TEACHING ME ABOUT ALL THE GREAT BOOKS OF WESTERN CIVILIZATION.
THE WRATH OF KHAN
I SEE.

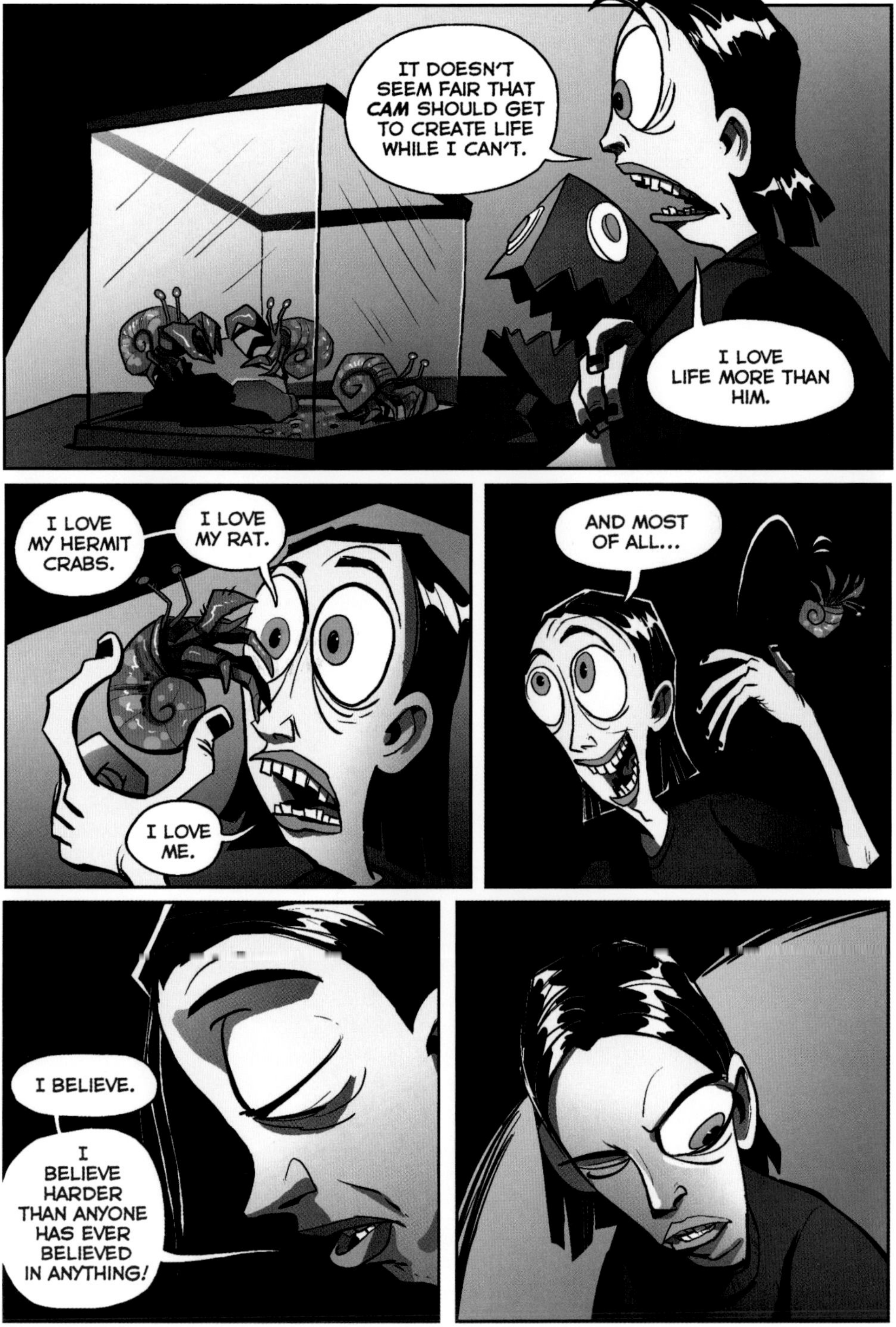
IT DOESN'T SEEM FAIR THAT CAM SHOULD GET TO CREATE LIFE WHILE I CAN'T.
I LOVE LIFE MORE THAN HIM.
I LOVE MY HERMIT CRABS.
I LOVE MY RAT.
I LOVE ME.
AND MOST OF ALL...
I BELIEVE.
I BELIEVE HARDER THAN ANYONE HAS EVER BELIEVED IN ANYTHING!

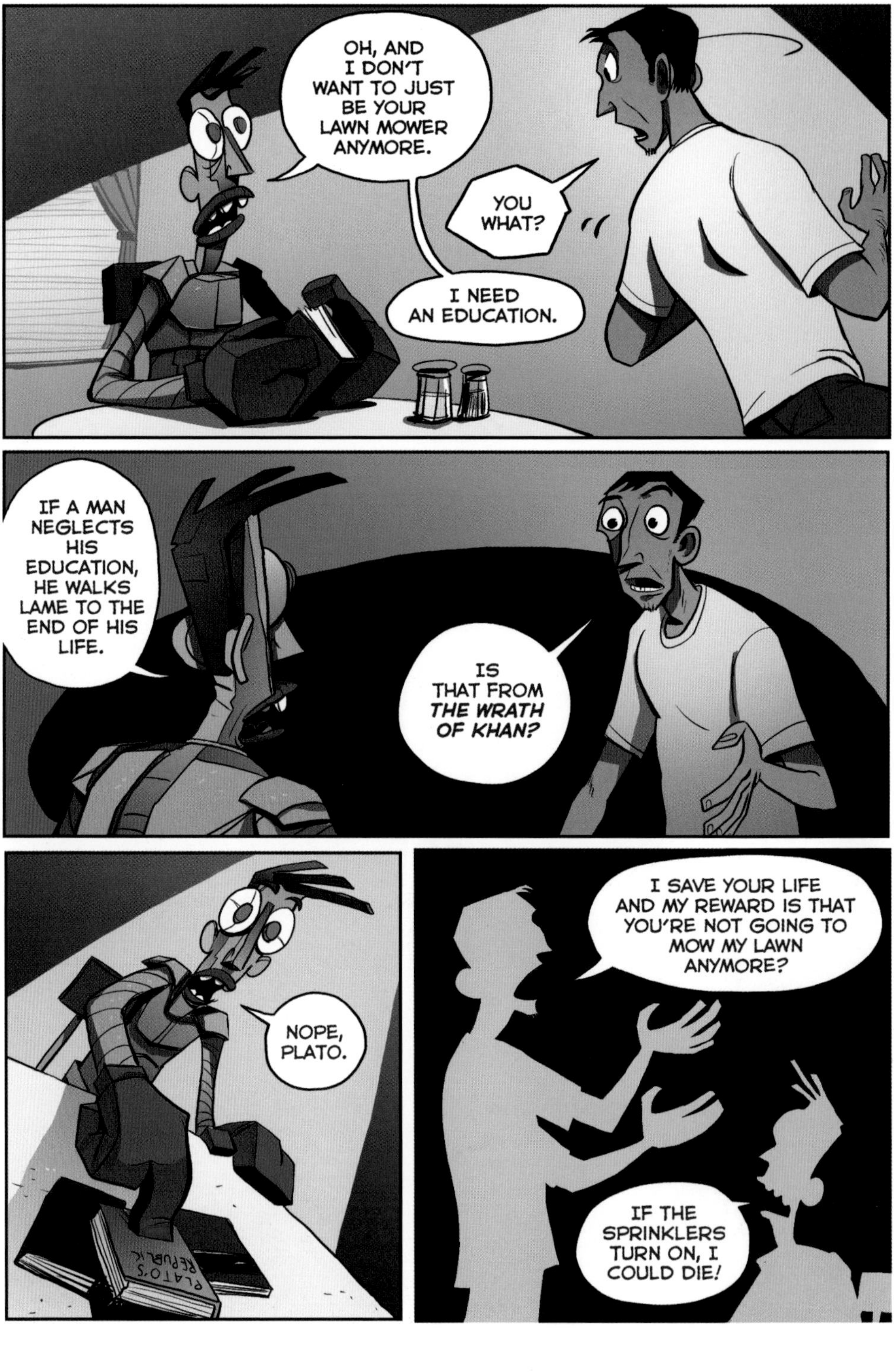
OH, AND I DON'T WANT TO JUST BE YOUR LAWN MOWER ANYMORE.
YOU WHAT?
I NEED AN EDUCATION.
IF A MAN NEGLECTS HIS EDUCATION, HE WALKS LAME TO THE END OF HIS LIFE.
IS THAT FROM *THE WRATH OF KHAN?*
NOPE, PLATO.
PLATO'S REPUBLIC
I SAVE YOUR LIFE AND MY REWARD IS THAT YOU'RE NOT GOING TO MOW MY LAWN ANYMORE?
IF THE SPRINKLERS TURN ON, I COULD DIE!

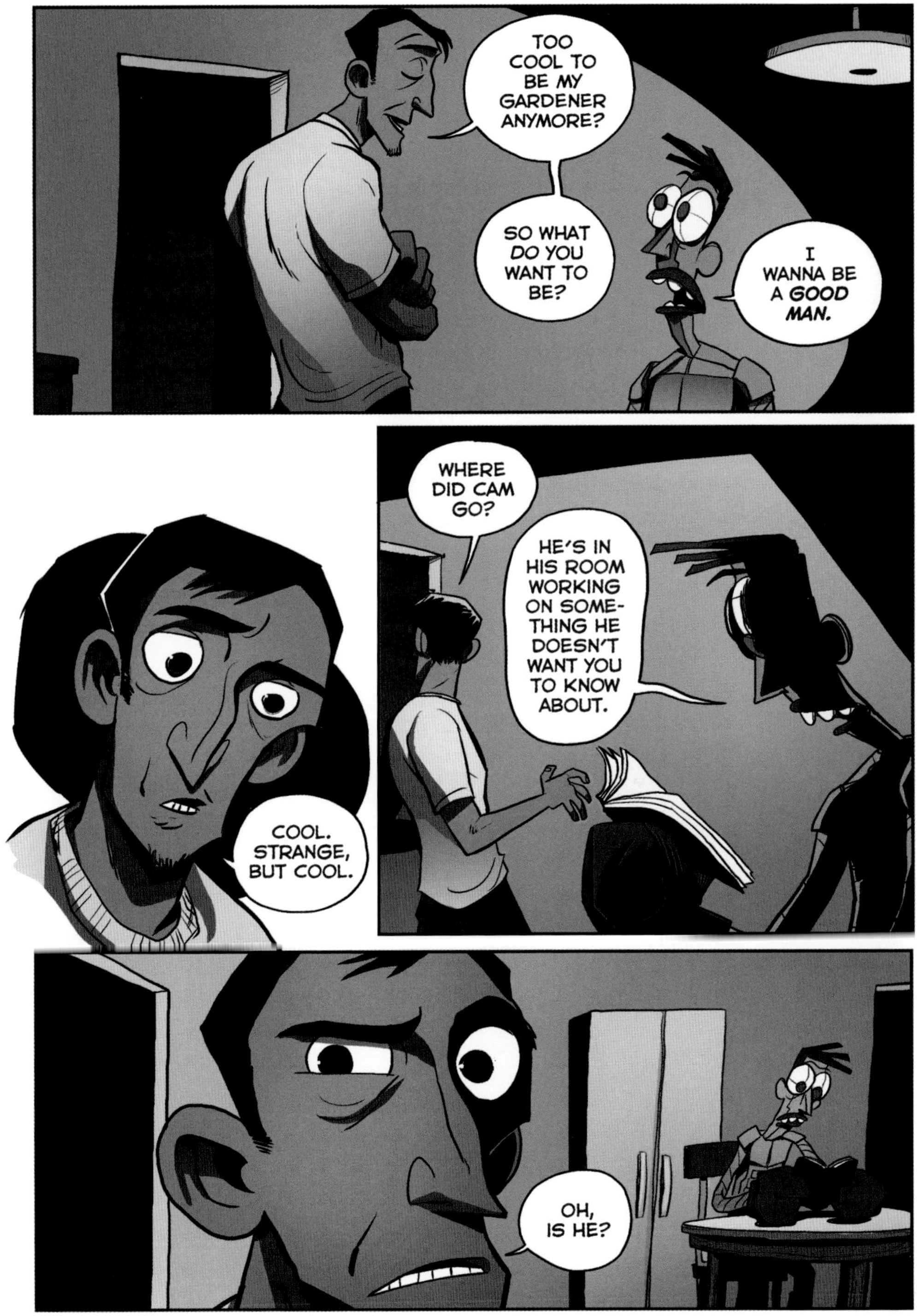
TOO COOL TO BE MY GARDENER ANYMORE?
SO WHAT *DO* YOU WANT TO BE?
I WANNA BE A ***GOOD MAN.***
WHERE DID CAM GO?
HE'S IN HIS ROOM WORKING ON SOME-THING HE DOESN'T WANT YOU TO KNOW ABOUT.
COOL. STRANGE, BUT COOL.
OH, IS HE?

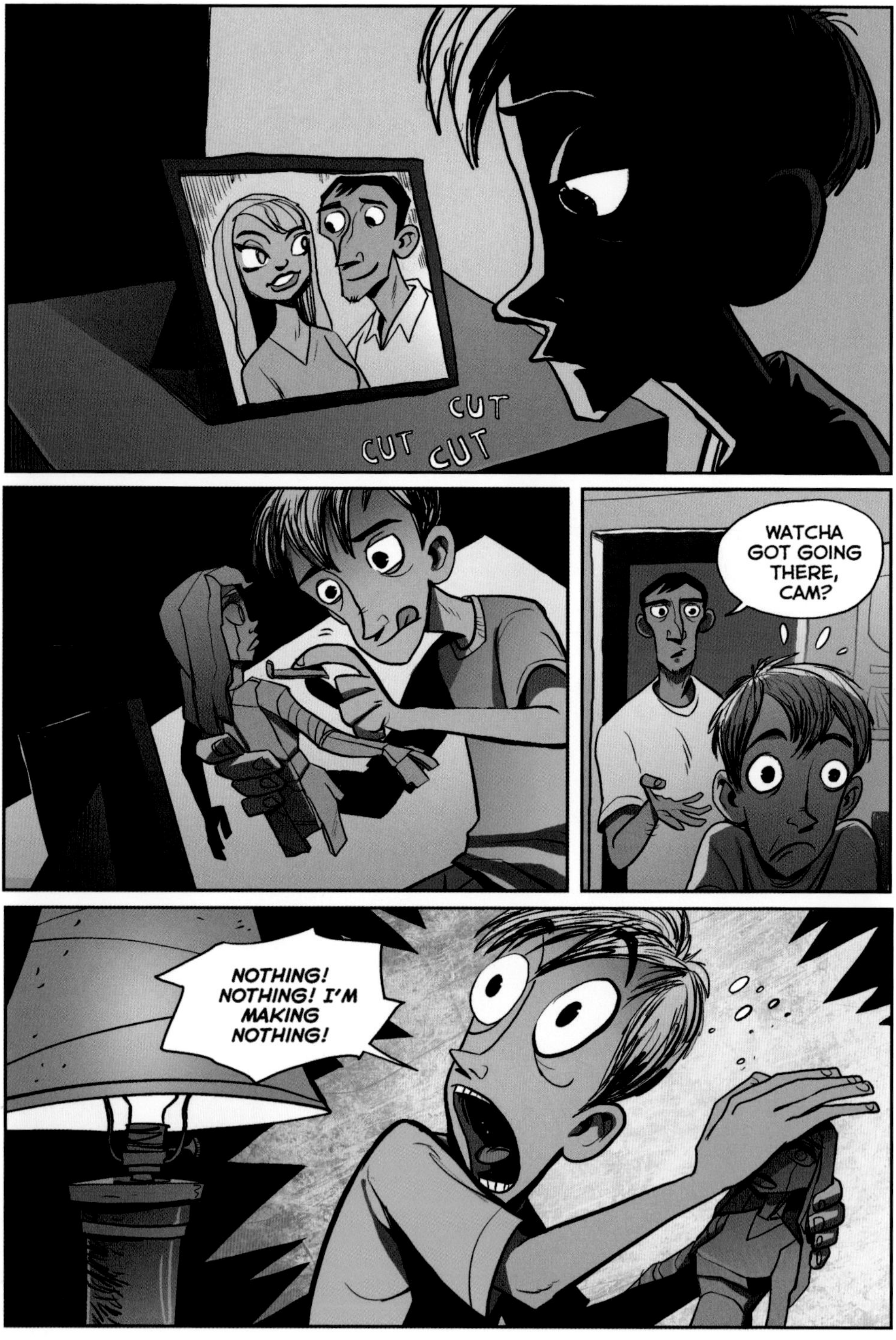
CUT
CUT
CUT
WATCHA GOT GOING THERE, CAM?
NOTHING! NOTHING! I'M MAKING NOTHING!

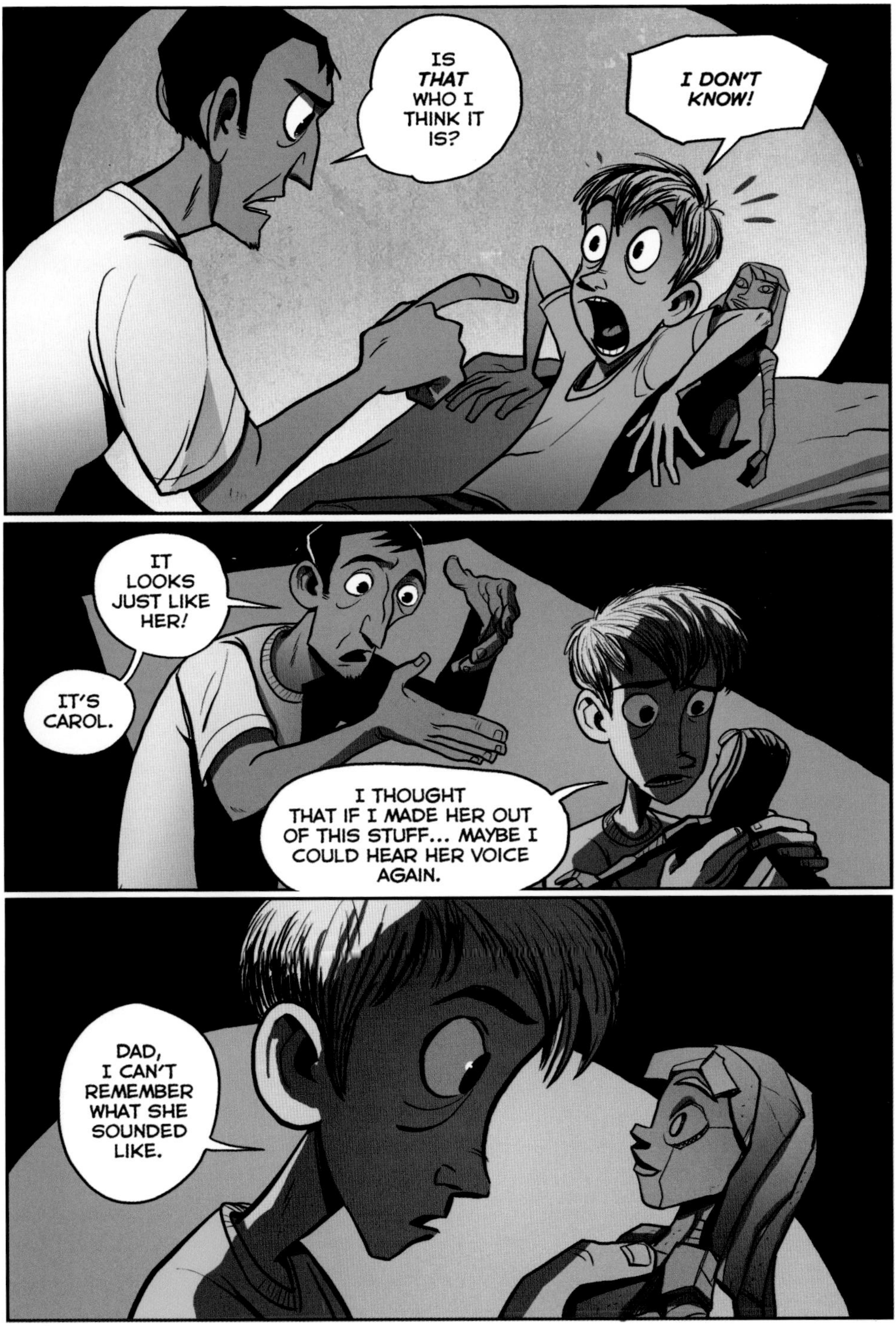
IS *THAT* WHO I THINK IT IS?
I DON'T KNOW!
IT LOOKS JUST LIKE HER!
IT'S CAROL.
I THOUGHT THAT IF I MADE HER OUT OF THIS STUFF... MAYBE I COULD HEAR HER VOICE AGAIN.
DAD, I CAN'T REMEMBER WHAT SHE SOUNDED LIKE.

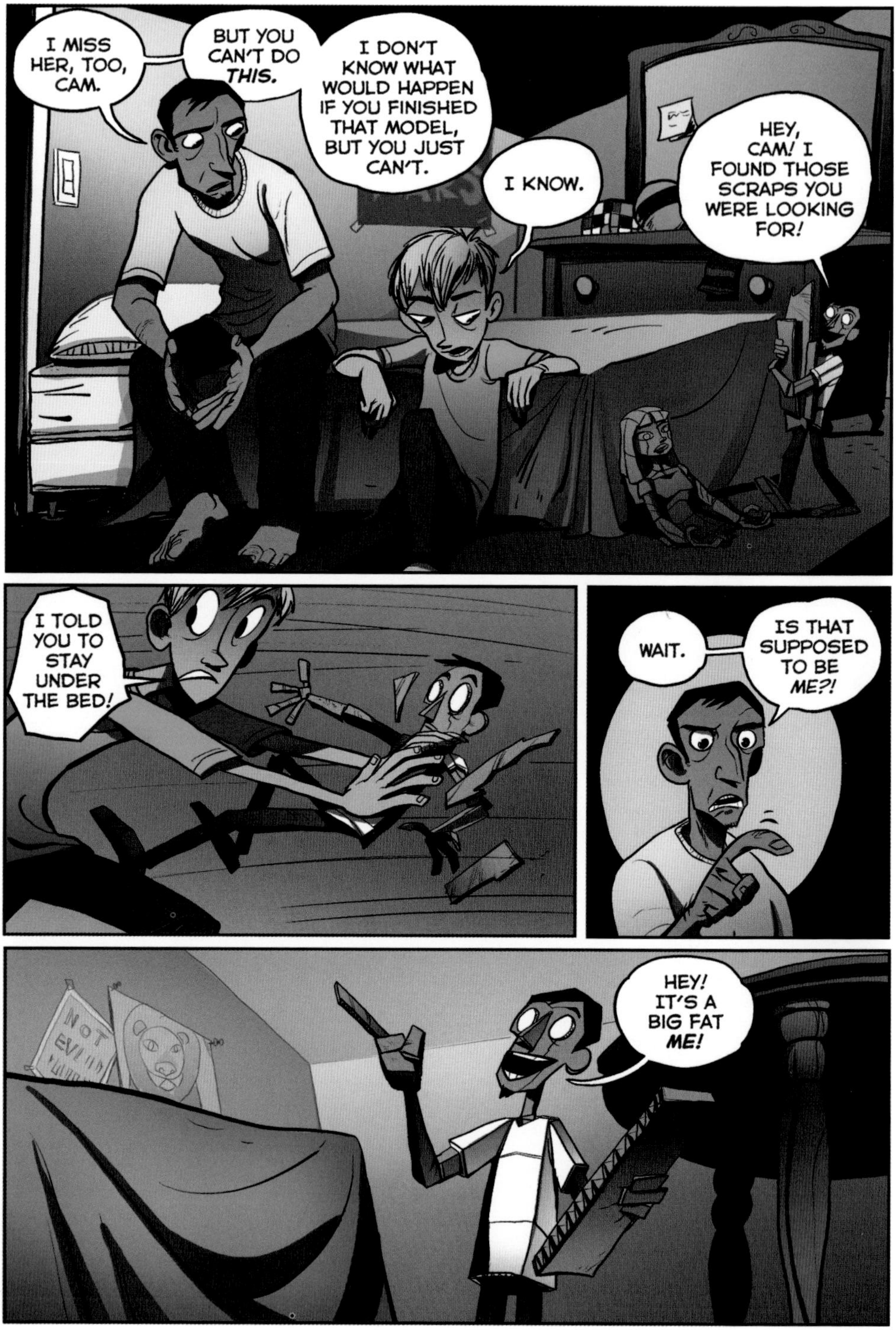
I MISS HER, TOO, CAM.
BUT YOU CAN'T DO *THIS.*
I DON'T KNOW WHAT WOULD HAPPEN IF YOU FINISHED THAT MODEL, BUT YOU JUST CAN'T.
I KNOW.
HEY, CAM! I FOUND THOSE SCRAPS YOU WERE LOOKING FOR!
I TOLD YOU TO STAY UNDER THE BED!
WAIT.
IS THAT SUPPOSED TO BE *ME?!*
HEY! IT'S A BIG FAT *ME!*

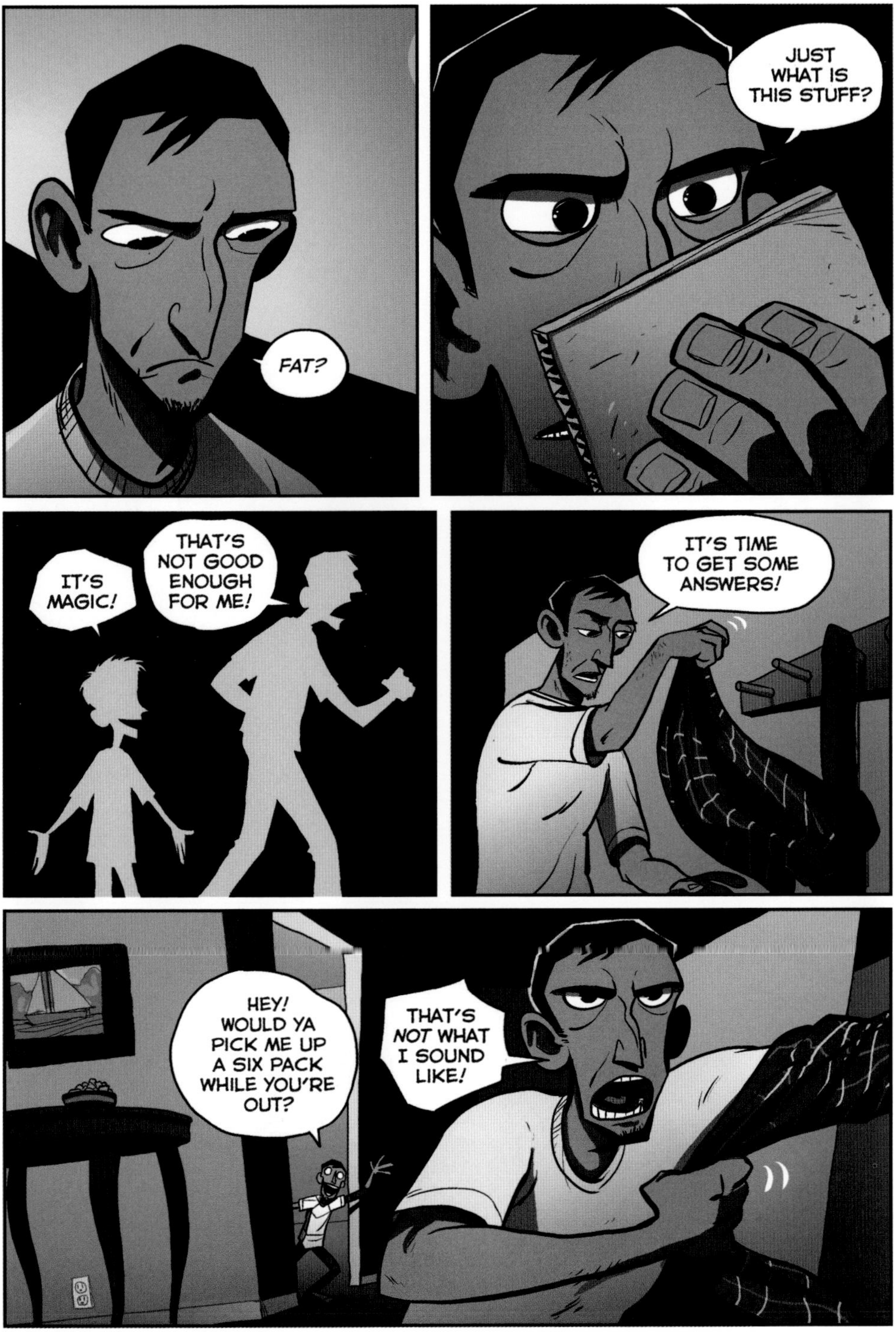
FAT?
JUST WHAT IS THIS STUFF?
IT'S MAGIC!
THAT'S NOT GOOD ENOUGH FOR ME!
IT'S TIME TO GET SOME ANSWERS!
HEY! WOULD YA PICK ME UP A SIX PACK WHILE YOU'RE OUT?
THAT'S *NOT* WHAT I SOUND LIKE!

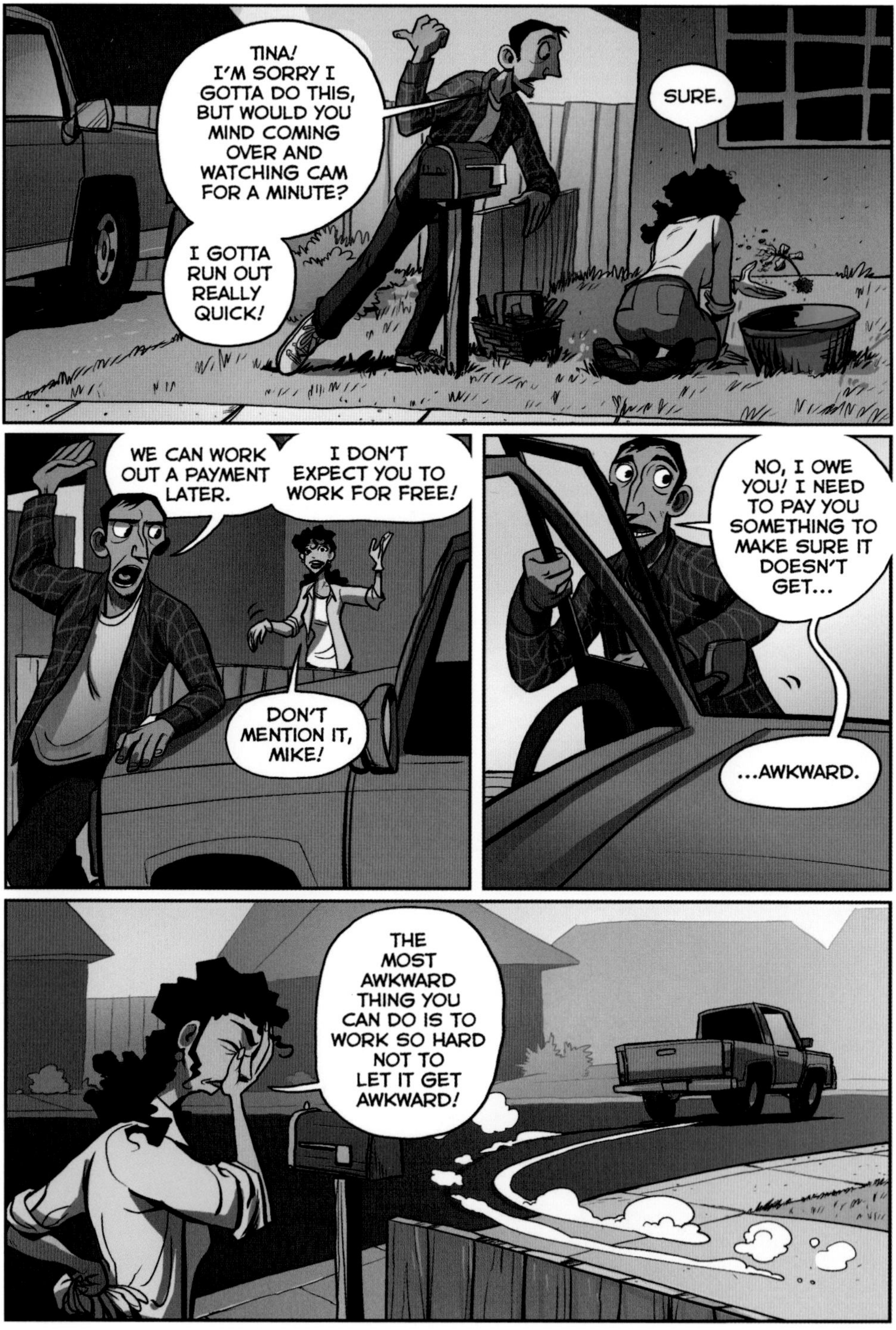
TINA! I'M SORRY I GOTTA DO THIS, BUT WOULD YOU MIND COMING OVER AND WATCHING CAM FOR A MINUTE?
I GOTTA RUN OUT REALLY QUICK!
SURE.
WE CAN WORK OUT A PAYMENT LATER.
I DON'T EXPECT YOU TO WORK FOR FREE!
DON'T MENTION IT, MIKE!
NO, I OWE YOU! I NEED TO PAY YOU SOMETHING TO MAKE SURE IT DOESN'T GET...
...AWKWARD.
THE MOST AWKWARD THING YOU CAN DO IS TO WORK SO HARD NOT TO LET IT GET AWKWARD!

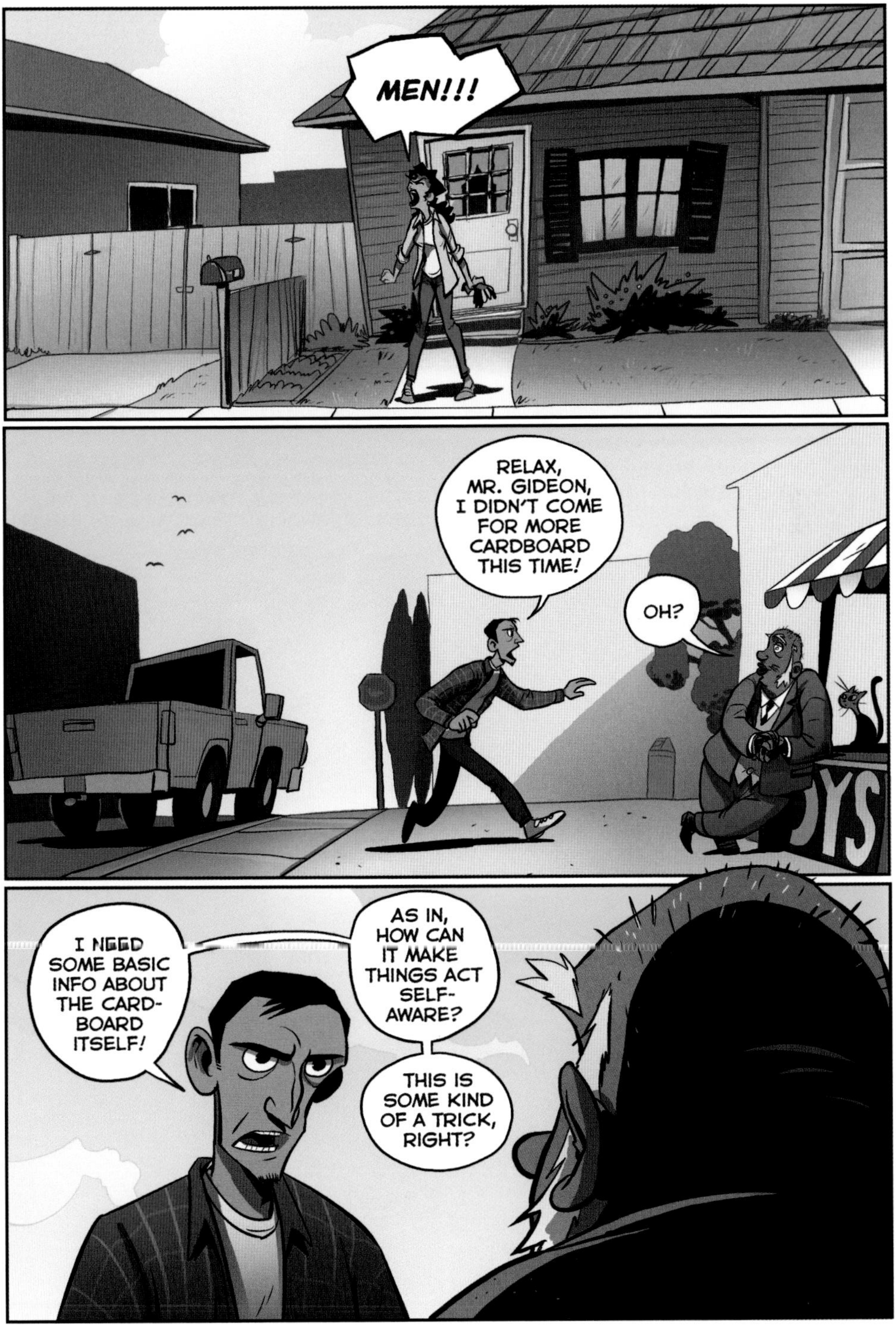
MEN!!!
RELAX, MR. GIDEON, I DIDN'T COME FOR MORE CARDBOARD THIS TIME!
OH?
I NEED SOME BASIC INFO ABOUT THE CARD-BOARD ITSELF!
AS IN, HOW CAN IT MAKE THINGS ACT SELF-AWARE?
THIS IS SOME KIND OF A TRICK, RIGHT?

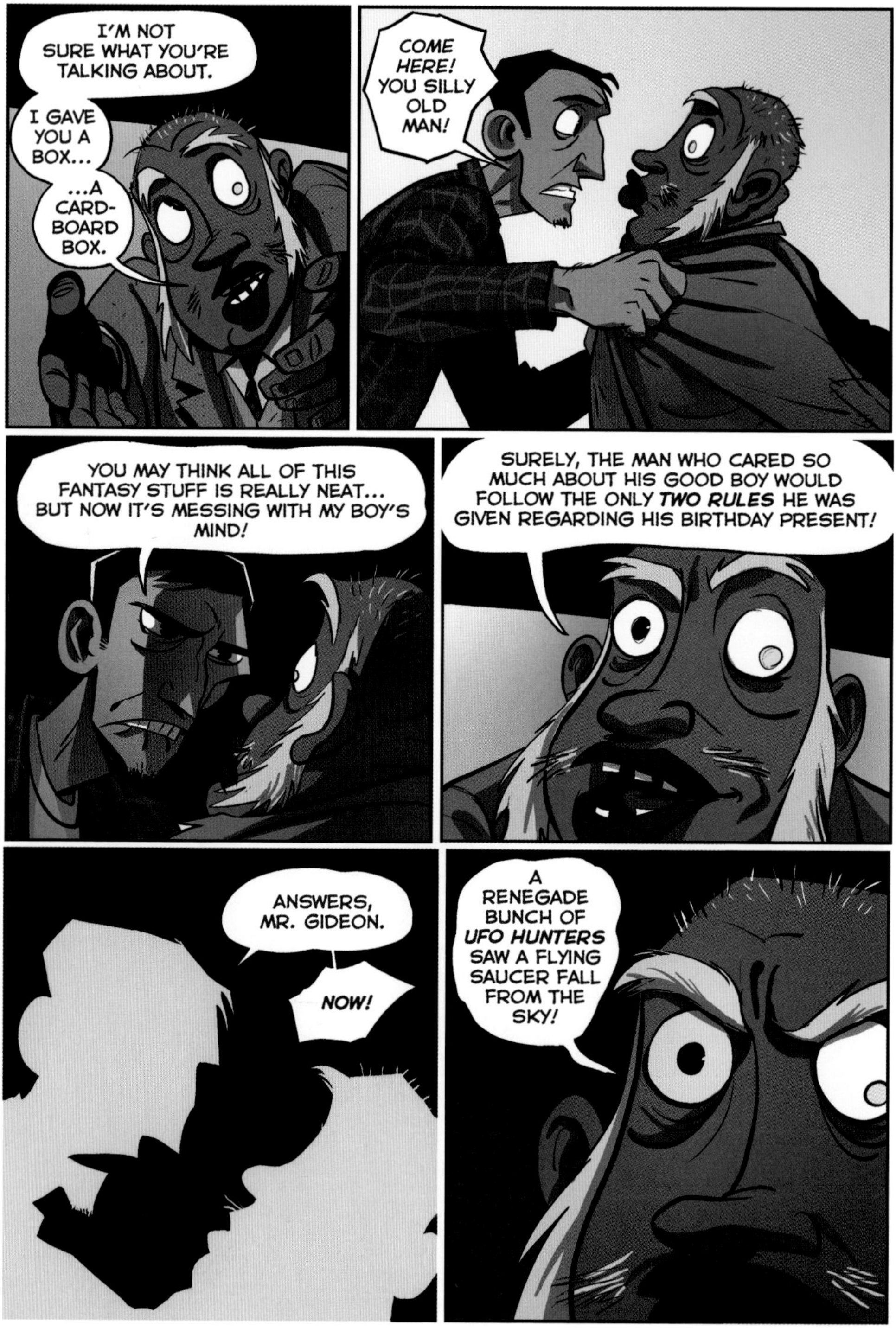
I'M NOT SURE WHAT YOU'RE TALKING ABOUT.
I GAVE YOU A BOX...
...A CARD-BOARD BOX.
COME HERE! YOU SILLY OLD MAN!
YOU MAY THINK ALL OF THIS FANTASY STUFF IS REALLY NEAT... BUT NOW IT'S MESSING WITH MY BOY'S MIND!
SURELY, THE MAN WHO CARED SO MUCH ABOUT HIS GOOD BOY WOULD FOLLOW THE ONLY TWO RULES HE WAS GIVEN REGARDING HIS BIRTHDAY PRESENT!
ANSWERS, MR. GIDEON.
NOW!
A RENEGADE BUNCH OF UFO HUNTERS SAW A FLYING SAUCER FALL FROM THE SKY!

A CRASHED ALIEN SHIP! GO ON!

THE HUNTERS FOUND THE CRASH SITE BEFORE ANYONE ELSE EVEN KNEW ABOUT IT!

THEY SALVAGED PARTS OF THE ALIEN CRAFT...

...THEN PACKED THEM INTO CARDBOARD BOXES TO BE MAILED TO A TESTING FACILITY IN NEW MEXICO!

BUT WHEN THE PACKAGES ARRIVED AT THEIR DESTINATION...

...THE BOXES WERE EMPTY!

MAYBE THE CONTENTS WERE STOLEN!

THAT'S WHAT EVERYONE THOUGHT AT FIRST!

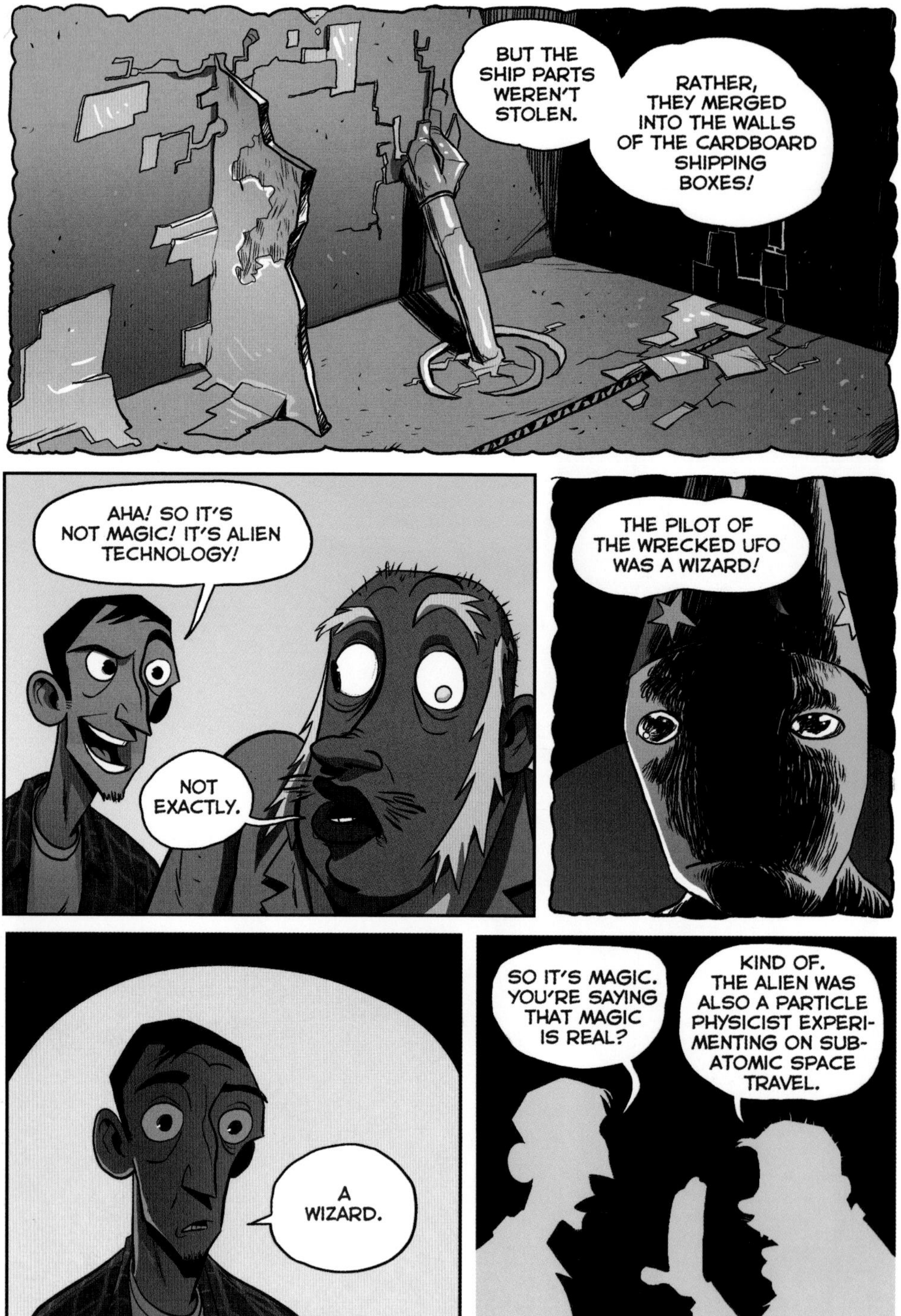
BUT THE SHIP PARTS WEREN'T STOLEN.
RATHER, THEY MERGED INTO THE WALLS OF THE CARDBOARD SHIPPING BOXES!
AHA! SO IT'S NOT MAGIC! IT'S ALIEN TECHNOLOGY!
NOT EXACTLY.
THE PILOT OF THE WRECKED UFO WAS A WIZARD!
A WIZARD.
SO IT'S MAGIC. YOU'RE SAYING THAT MAGIC IS REAL?
KIND OF. THE ALIEN WAS ALSO A PARTICLE PHYSICIST EXPERI- MENTING ON SUB- ATOMIC SPACE TRAVEL.

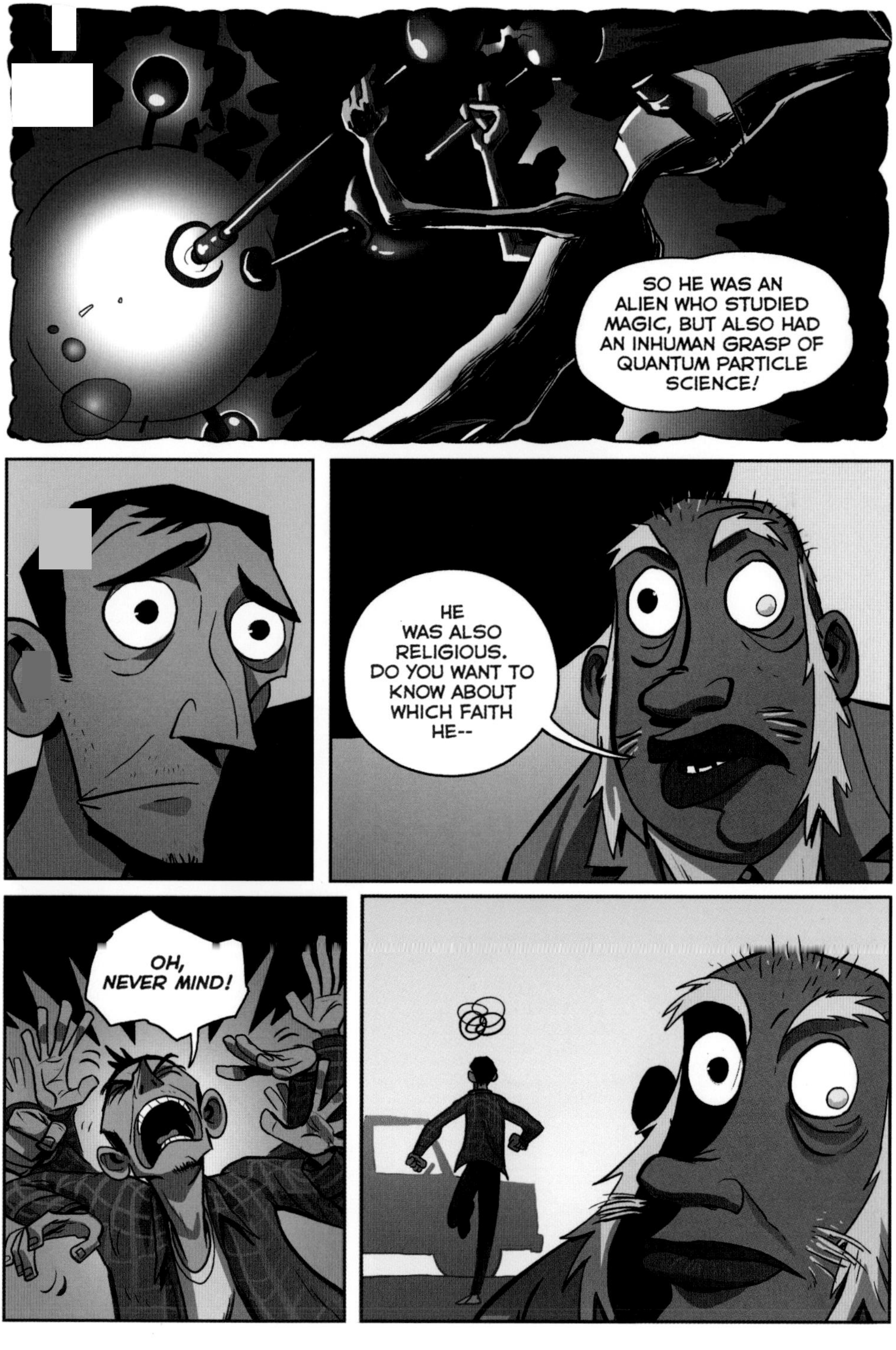
SO HE WAS AN ALIEN WHO STUDIED MAGIC, BUT ALSO HAD AN INHUMAN GRASP OF QUANTUM PARTICLE SCIENCE!
HE WAS ALSO RELIGIOUS. DO YOU WANT TO KNOW ABOUT WHICH FAITH HE--
OH, NEVER MIND!

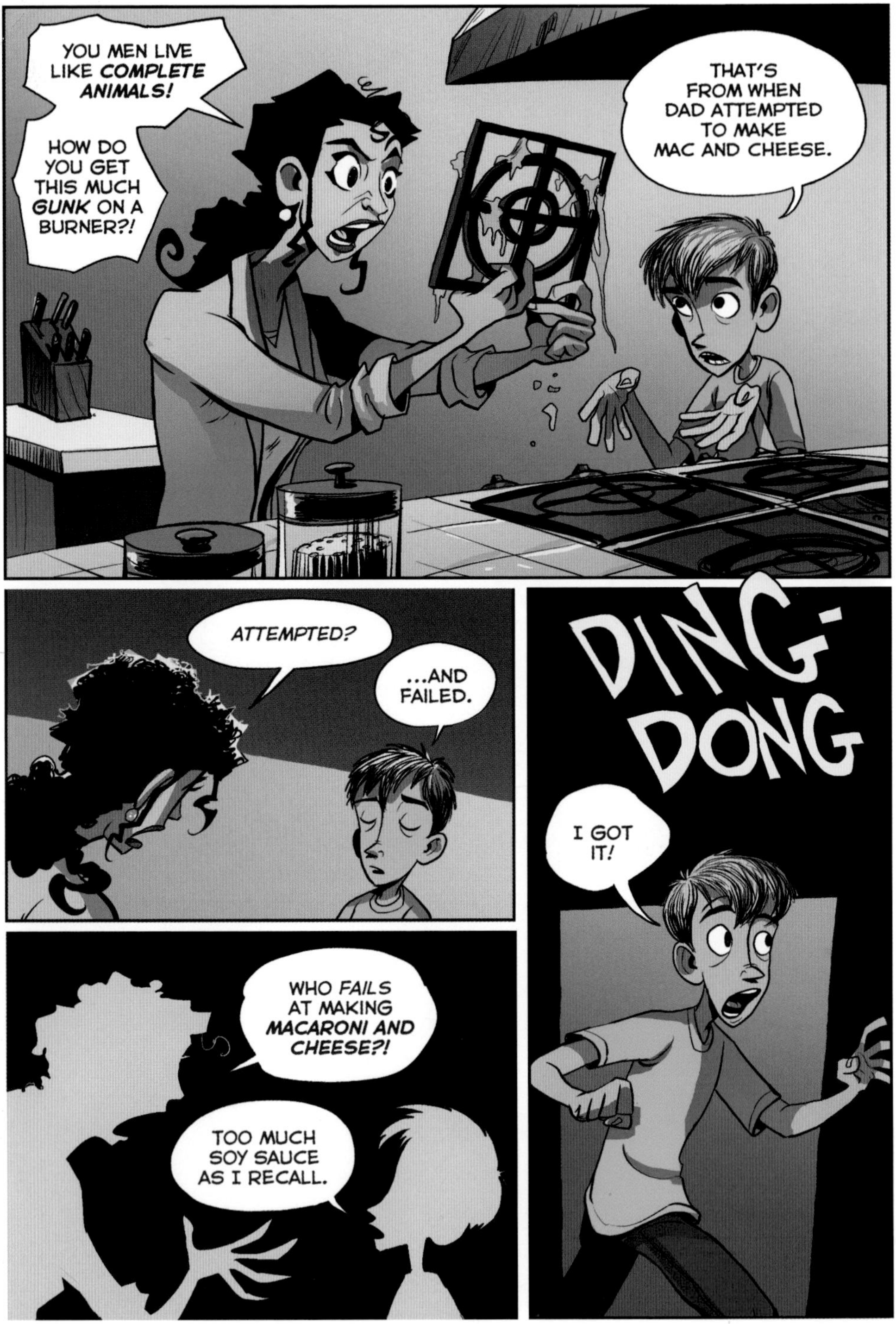
YOU MEN LIVE LIKE **COMPLETE ANIMALS!**
HOW DO YOU GET THIS MUCH **GUNK** ON A BURNER?!
THAT'S FROM WHEN DAD ATTEMPTED TO MAKE MAC AND CHEESE.
ATTEMPTED?
...AND FAILED.
WHO *FAILS* AT MAKING ***MACARONI AND CHEESE?!***
TOO MUCH SOY SAUCE AS I RECALL.
DING-DONG
I GOT IT!

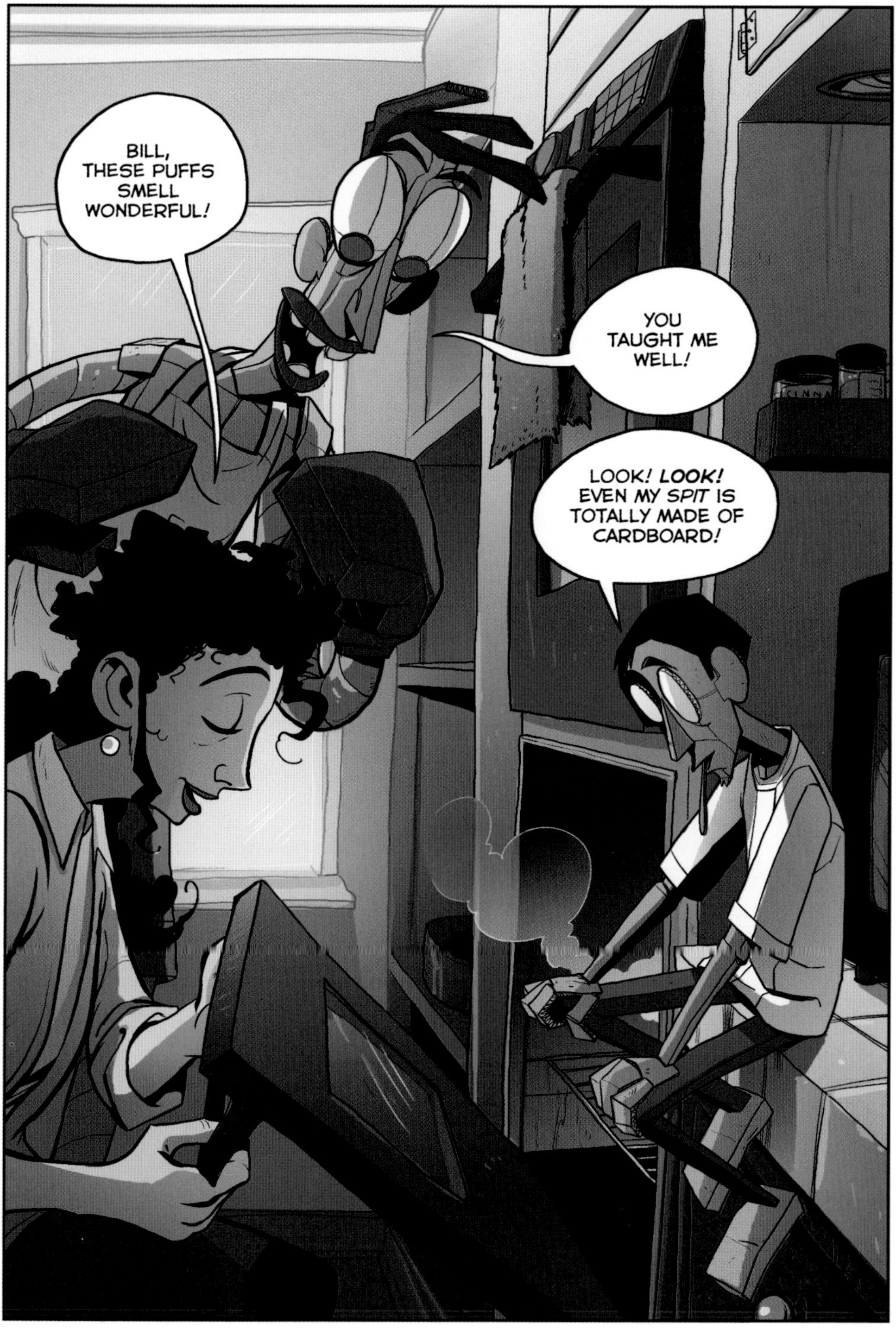
BILL, THESE PUFFS SMELL WONDERFUL!
YOU TAUGHT ME WELL!
LOOK! LOOK! EVEN MY SPIT IS TOTALLY MADE OF CARDBOARD!

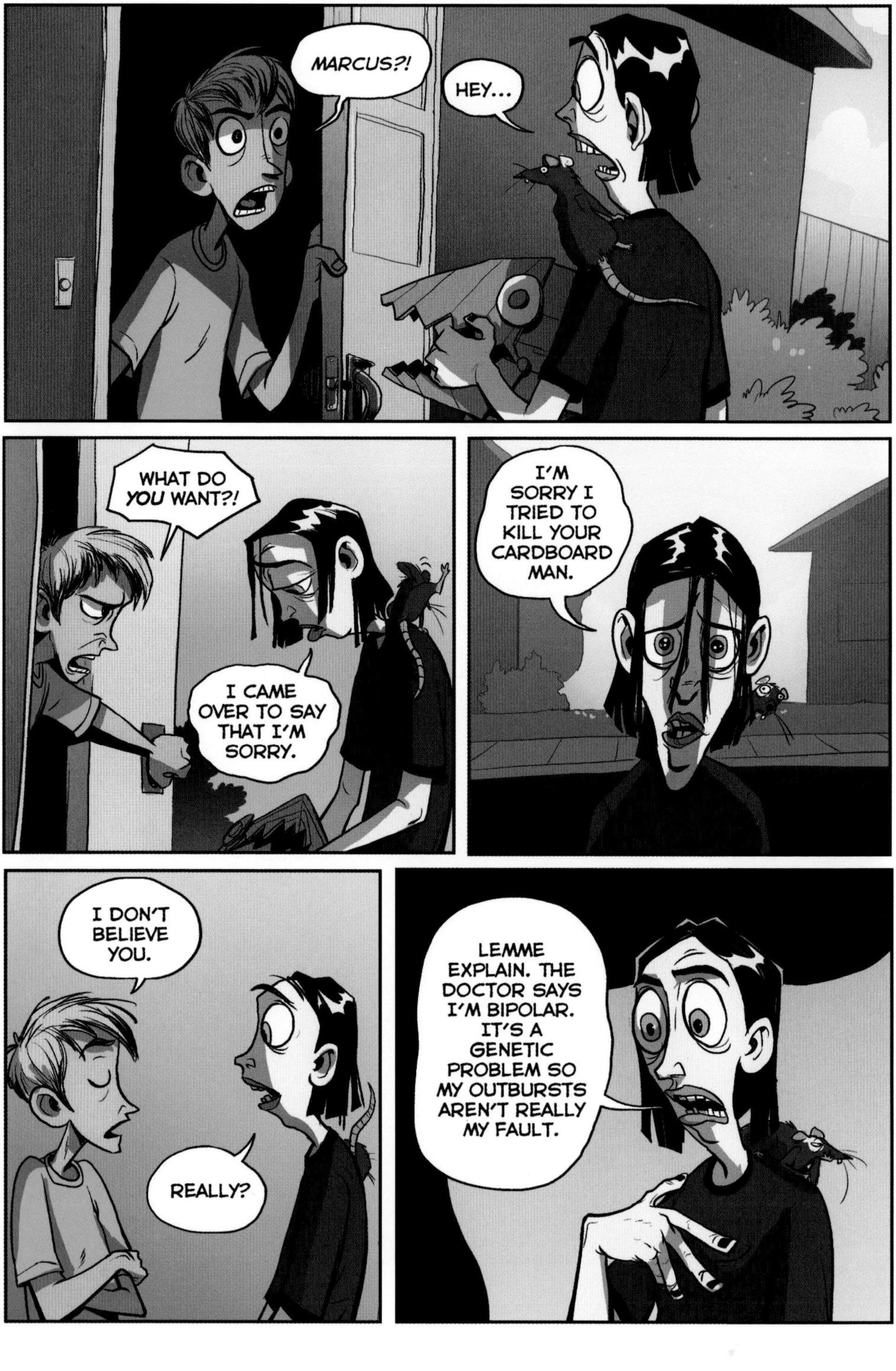
MARCUS?!
HEY...
WHAT DO YOU WANT?!
I CAME OVER TO SAY THAT I'M SORRY.
I'M SORRY I TRIED TO KILL YOUR CARDBOARD MAN.
I DON'T BELIEVE YOU.
REALLY?
LEMME EXPLAIN. THE DOCTOR SAYS I'M BIPOLAR. IT'S A GENETIC PROBLEM SO MY OUTBURSTS AREN'T REALLY MY FAULT.

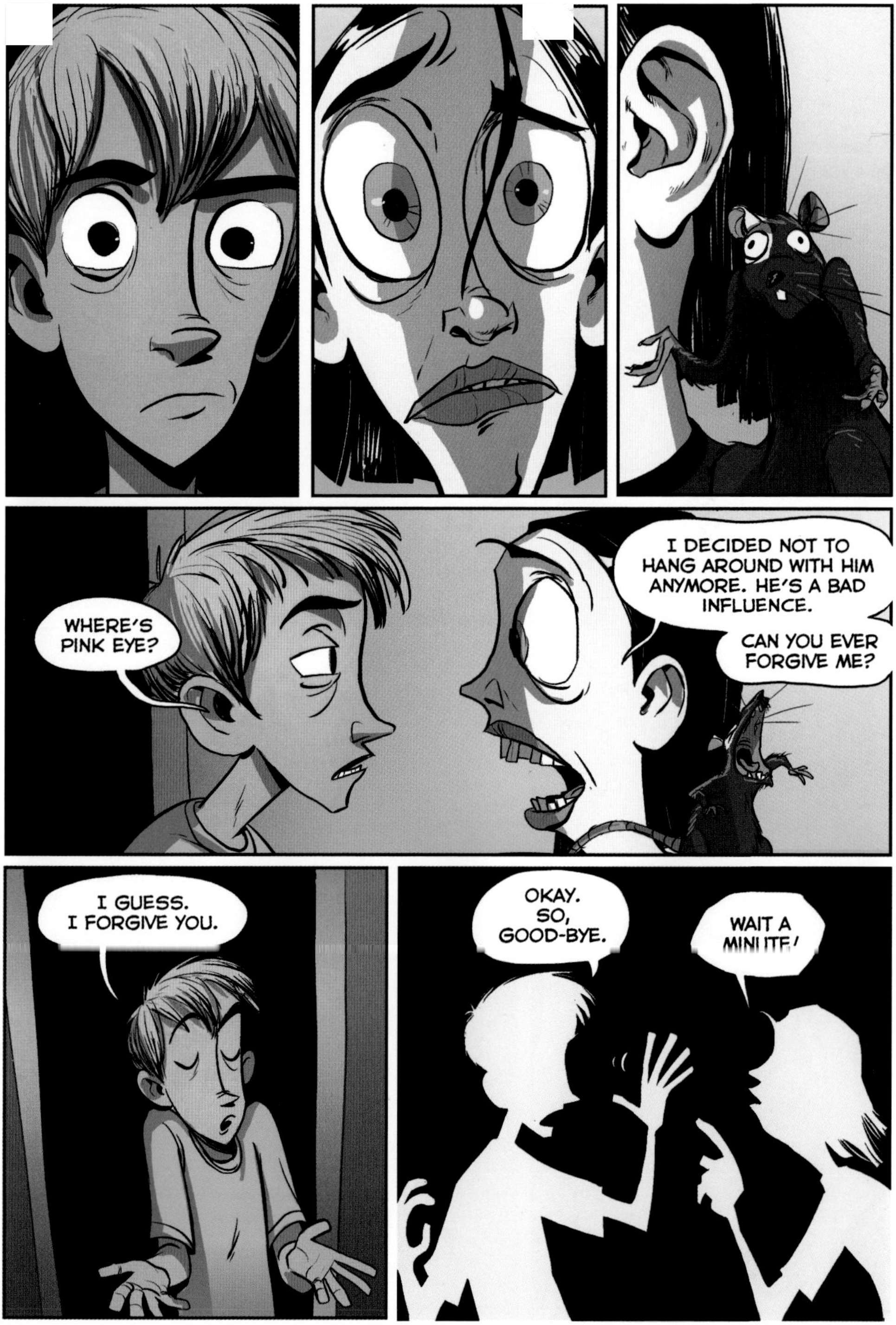
WHERE'S PINK EYE?
I DECIDED NOT TO HANG AROUND WITH HIM ANYMORE. HE'S A BAD INFLUENCE.
CAN YOU EVER FORGIVE ME?
I GUESS. I FORGIVE YOU.
OKAY. SO, GOOD-BYE.
WAIT A MINUTE!

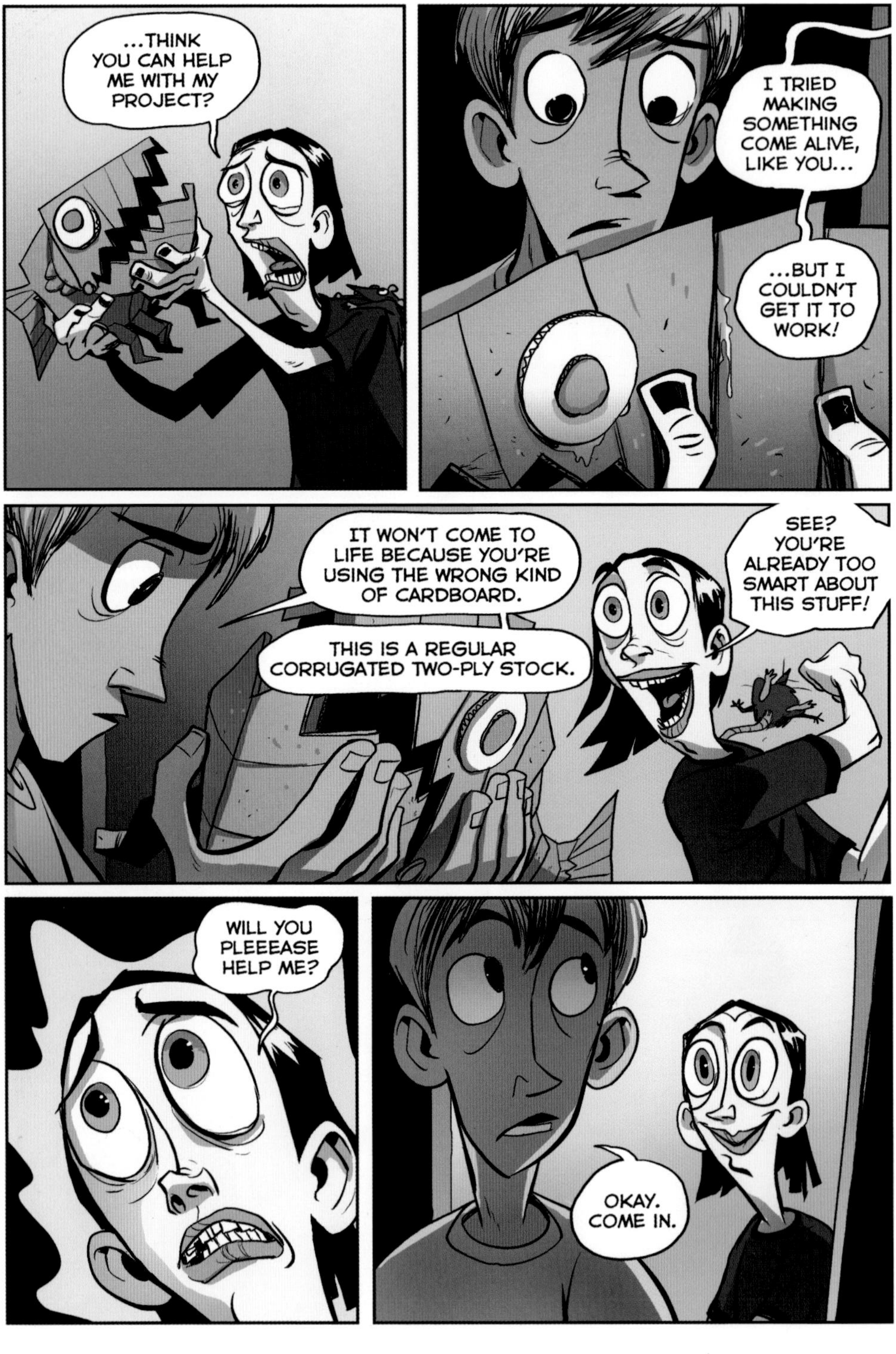
...THINK YOU CAN HELP ME WITH MY PROJECT?
I TRIED MAKING SOMETHING COME ALIVE, LIKE YOU...
...BUT I COULDN'T GET IT TO WORK!
IT WON'T COME TO LIFE BECAUSE YOU'RE USING THE WRONG KIND OF CARDBOARD.
THIS IS A REGULAR CORRUGATED TWO-PLY STOCK.
SEE? YOU'RE ALREADY TOO SMART ABOUT THIS STUFF!
WILL YOU PLEEEASE HELP ME?
OKAY. COME IN.

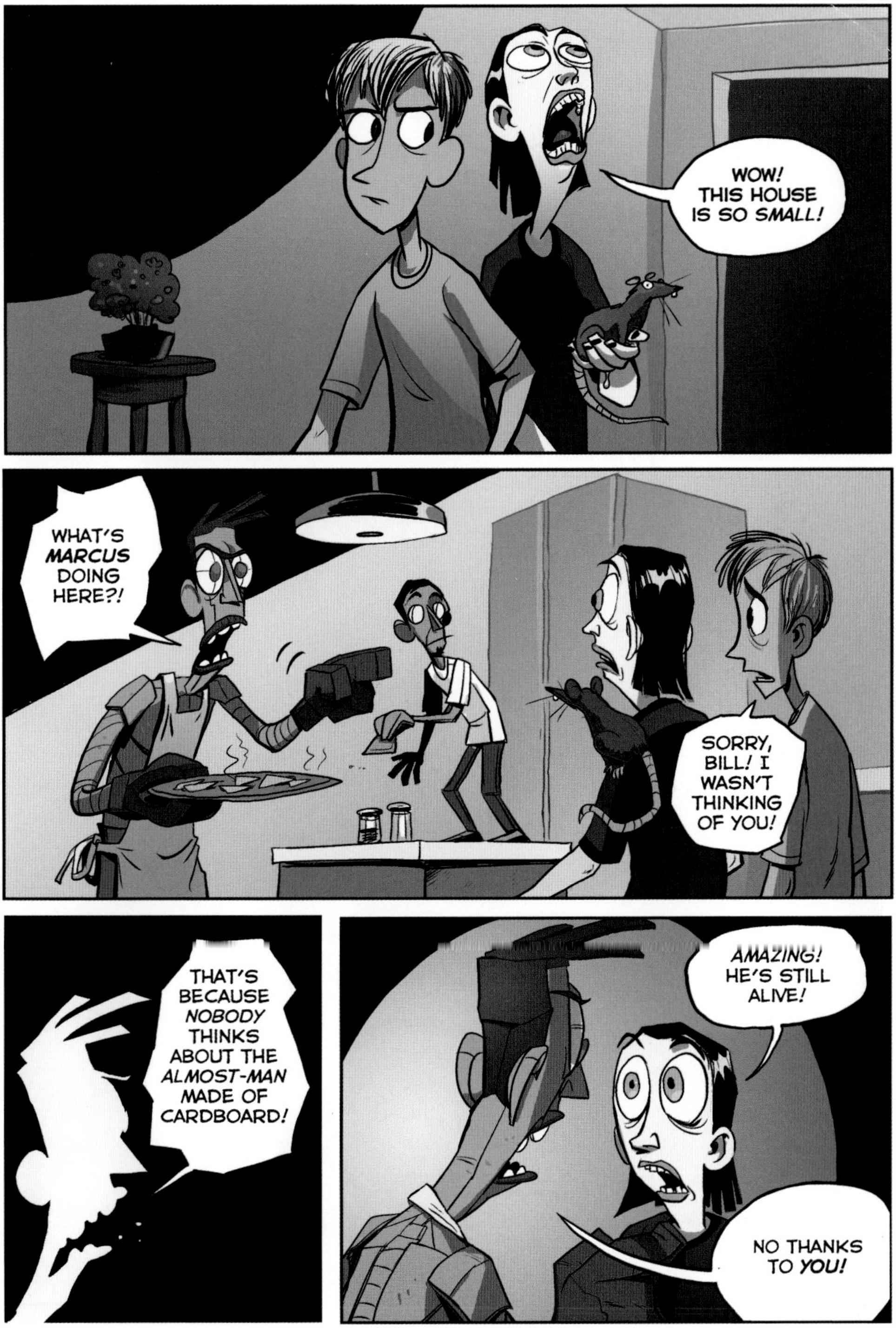
WOW! THIS HOUSE IS SO SMALL!
WHAT'S MARCUS DOING HERE?!
SORRY, BILL! I WASN'T THINKING OF YOU!
THAT'S BECAUSE NOBODY THINKS ABOUT THE ALMOST-MAN MADE OF CARDBOARD!
AMAZING! HE'S STILL ALIVE!
NO THANKS TO YOU!

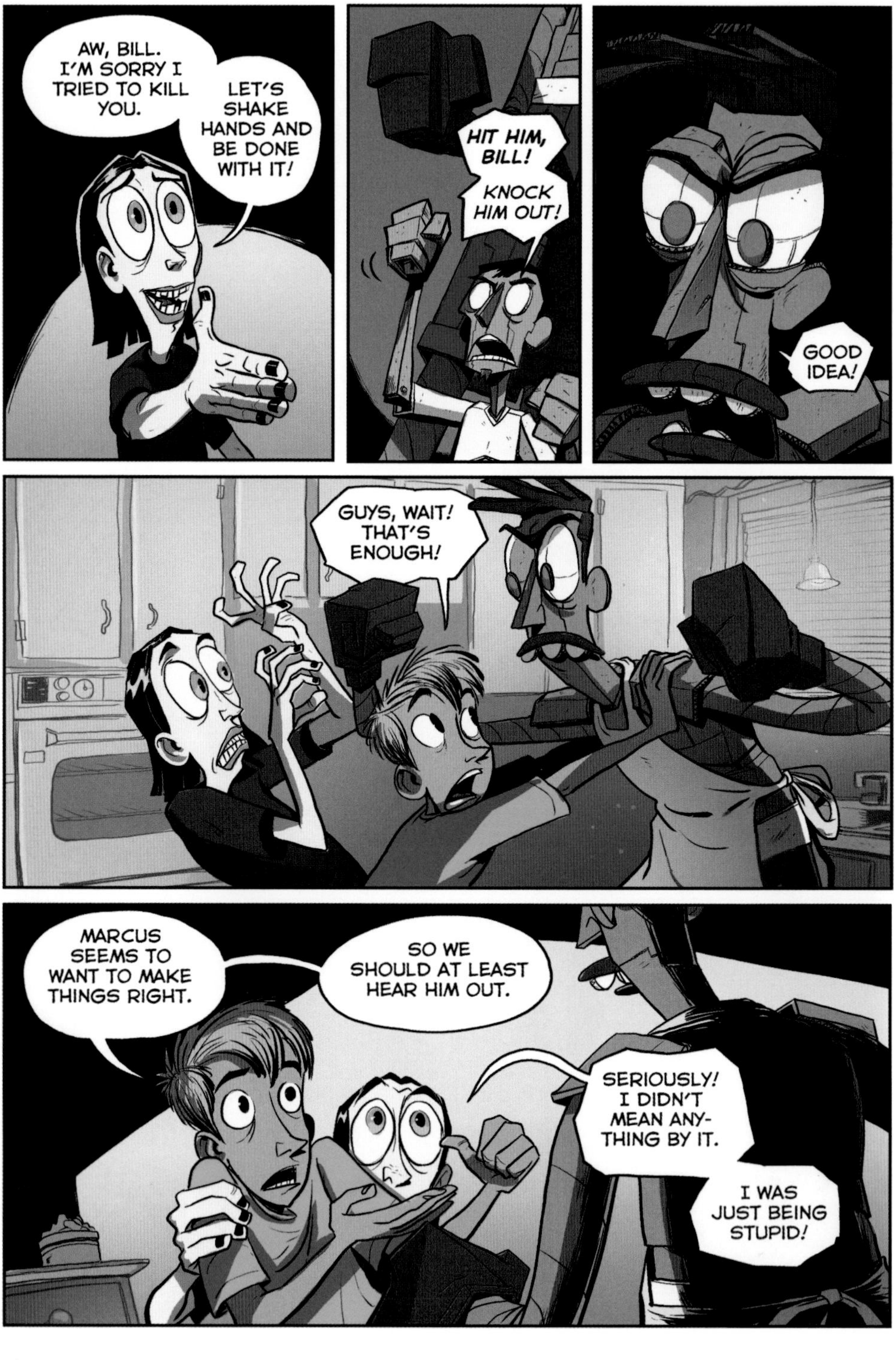
AW, BILL. I'M SORRY I TRIED TO KILL YOU.
LET'S SHAKE HANDS AND BE DONE WITH IT!
HIT HIM, BILL!
KNOCK HIM OUT!
GOOD IDEA!
GUYS, WAIT! THAT'S ENOUGH!
MARCUS SEEMS TO WANT TO MAKE THINGS RIGHT.
SO WE SHOULD AT LEAST HEAR HIM OUT.
SERIOUSLY! I DIDN'T MEAN ANY-THING BY IT.
I WAS JUST BEING STUPID!

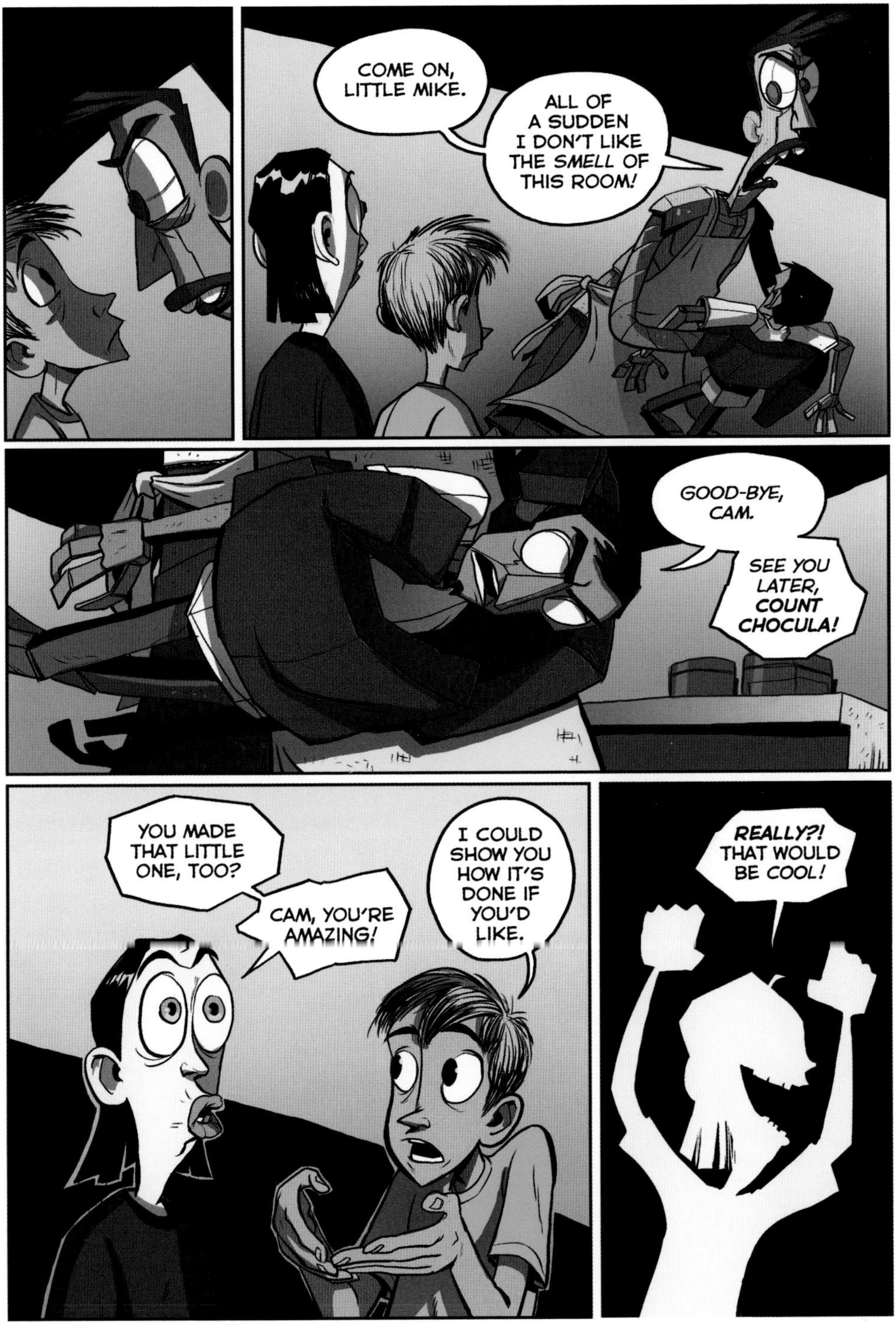
COME ON, LITTLE MIKE.
ALL OF A SUDDEN I DON'T LIKE THE *SMELL* OF THIS ROOM!
GOOD-BYE, CAM.
SEE YOU LATER, **COUNT CHOCULA!**
YOU MADE THAT LITTLE ONE, TOO?
CAM, YOU'RE AMAZING!
I COULD SHOW YOU HOW IT'S DONE IF YOU'D LIKE.
REALLY?! THAT WOULD BE *COOL!*

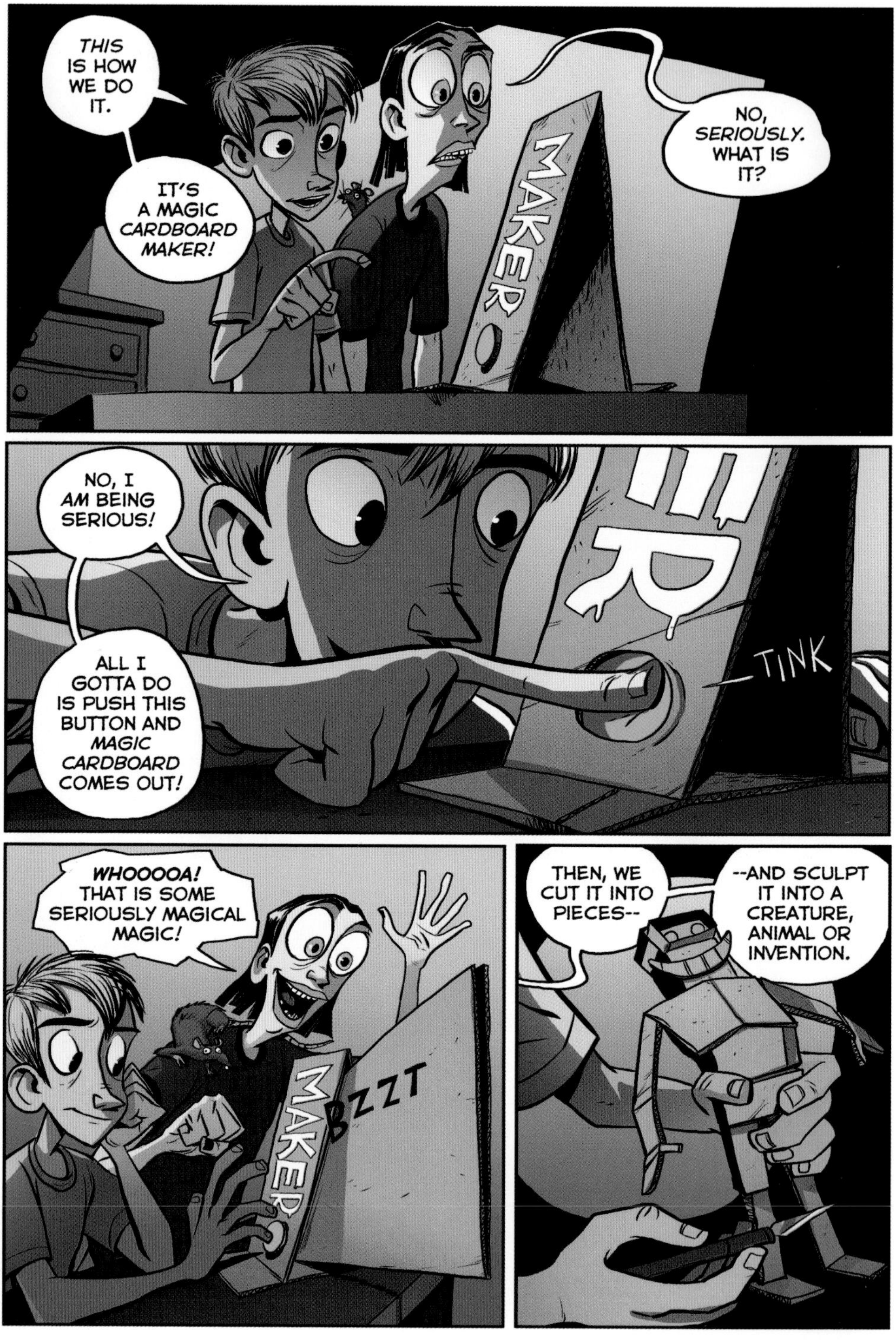
THIS IS HOW WE DO IT.
IT'S A MAGIC CARDBOARD MAKER!
NO, SERIOUSLY. WHAT IS IT?
MAKER
NO, I AM BEING SERIOUS!
ALL I GOTTA DO IS PUSH THIS BUTTON AND MAGIC CARDBOARD COMES OUT!
TINK
WHOOOOA! THAT IS SOME SERIOUSLY MAGICAL MAGIC!
MAKER
BZZT
THEN, WE CUT IT INTO PIECES--
--AND SCULPT IT INTO A CREATURE, ANIMAL OR INVENTION.

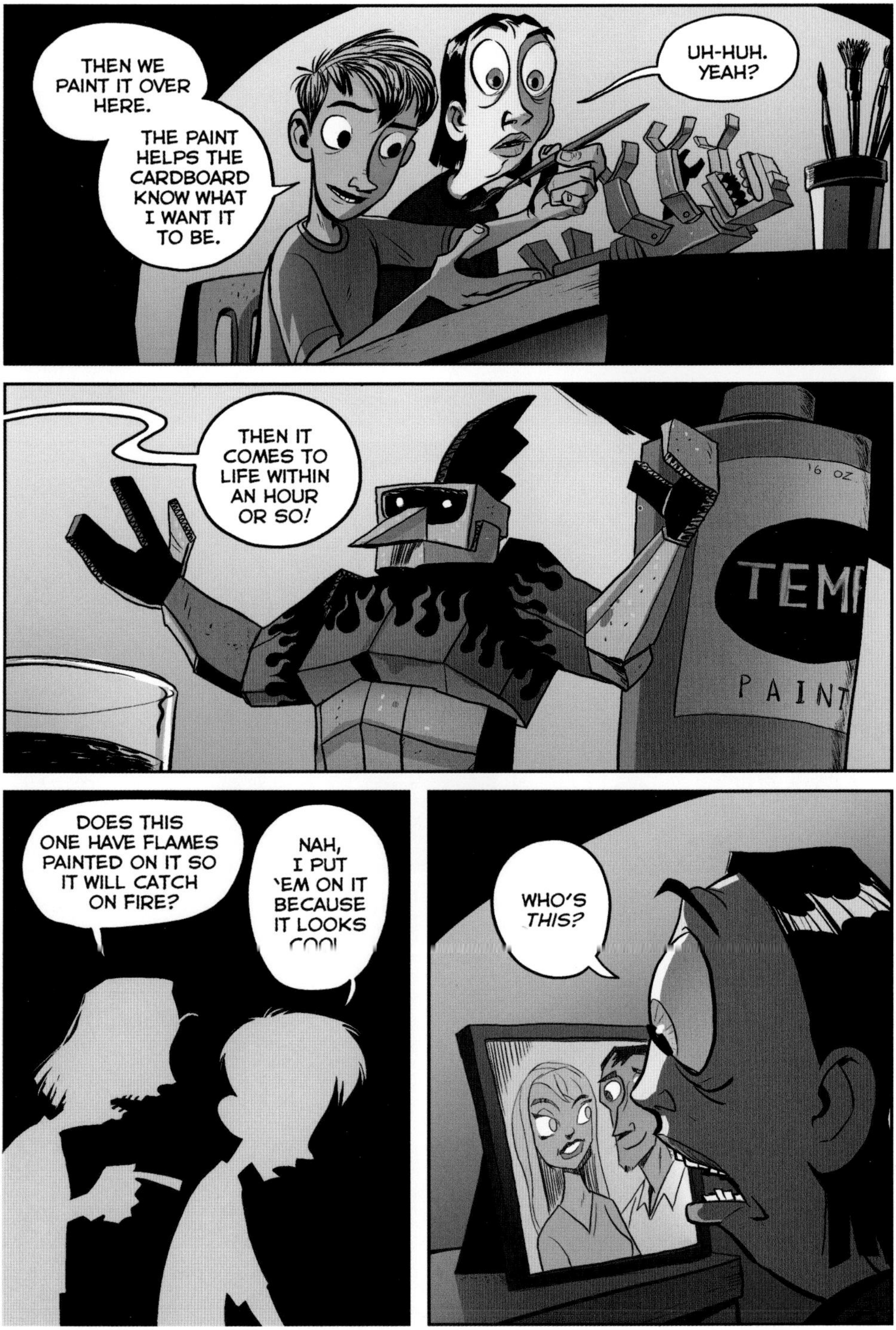
THEN WE PAINT IT OVER HERE.
THE PAINT HELPS THE CARDBOARD KNOW WHAT I WANT IT TO BE.
UH-HUH. YEAH?
THEN IT COMES TO LIFE WITHIN AN HOUR OR SO!
16 OZ
TEMP
PAINT
DOES THIS ONE HAVE FLAMES PAINTED ON IT SO IT WILL CATCH ON FIRE?
NAH, I PUT 'EM ON IT BECAUSE IT LOOKS COOL
WHO'S THIS?

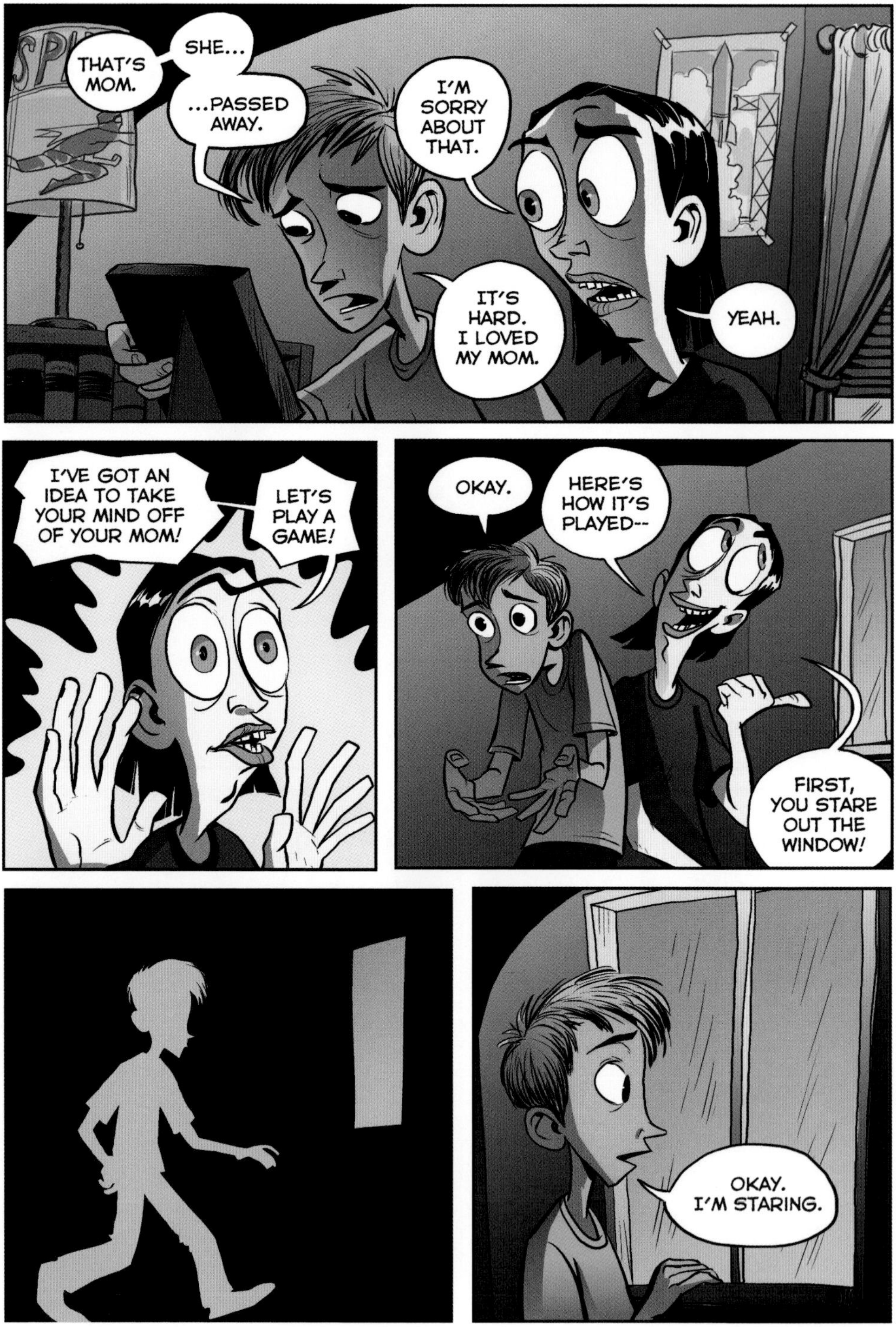
THAT'S MOM.
SHE...
...PASSED AWAY.
I'M SORRY ABOUT THAT.
IT'S HARD. I LOVED MY MOM.
YEAH.
I'VE GOT AN IDEA TO TAKE YOUR MIND OFF OF YOUR MOM!
LET'S PLAY A GAME!
OKAY.
HERE'S HOW IT'S PLAYED--
FIRST, YOU STARE OUT THE WINDOW!
OKAY. I'M STARING.

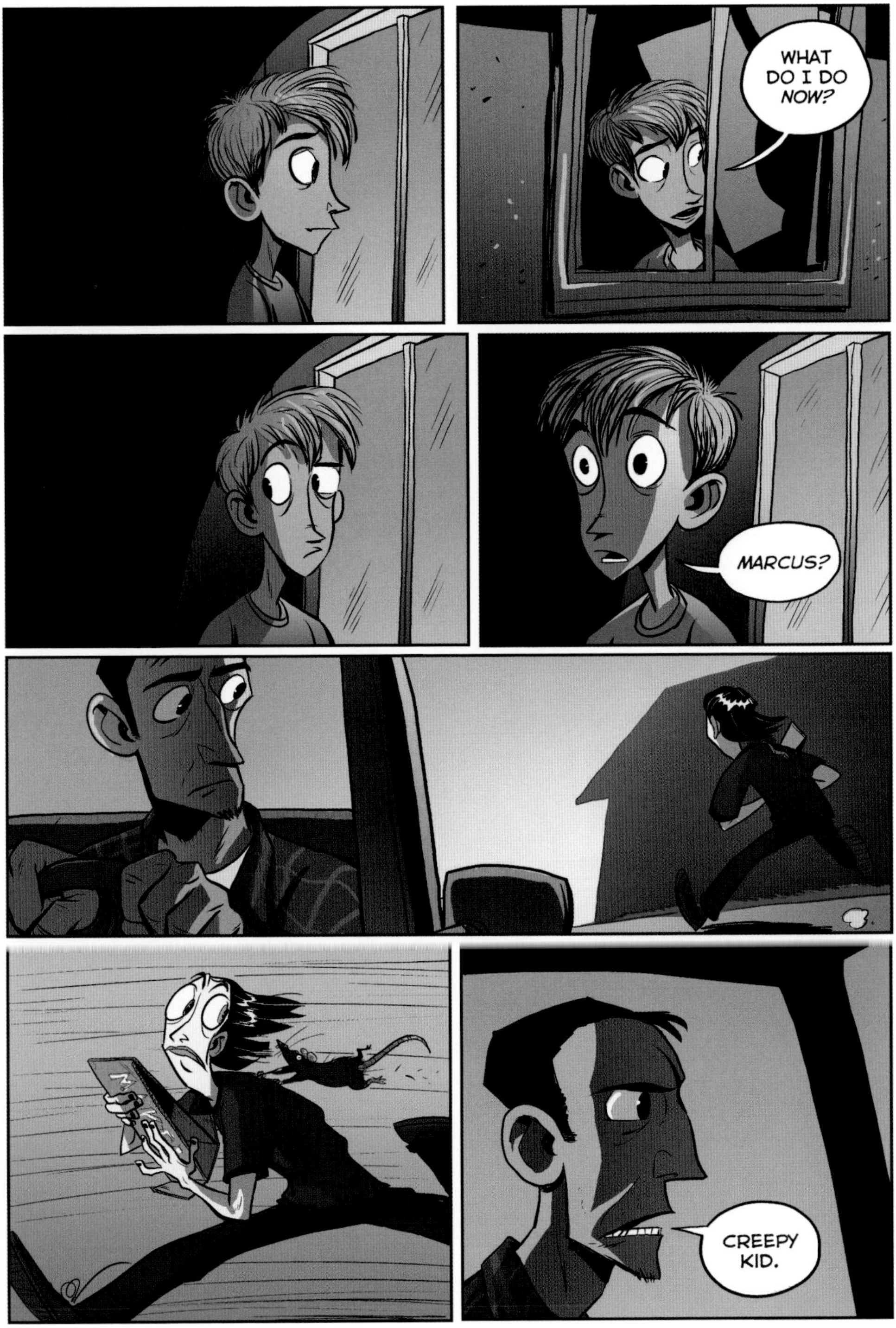
WHAT DO I DO NOW?
MARCUS?
CREEPY KID.

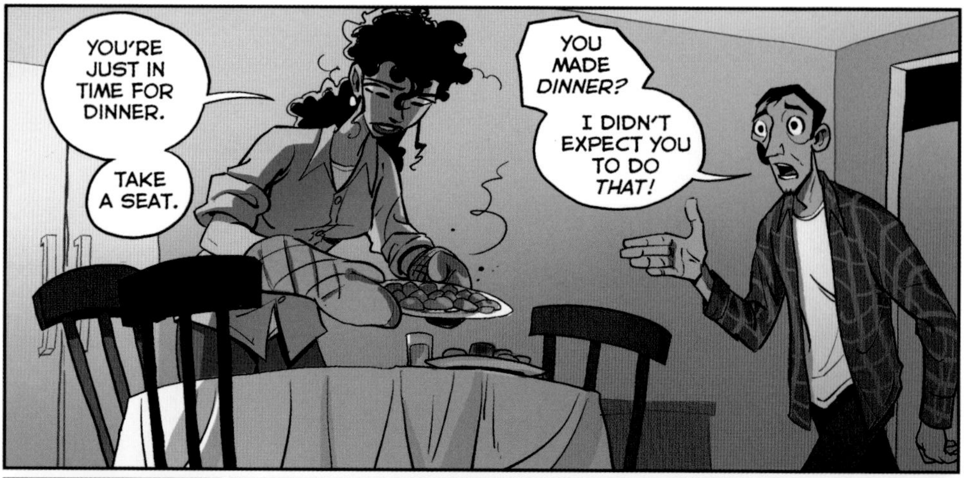
YOU'RE JUST IN TIME FOR DINNER.
TAKE A SEAT.
YOU MADE *DINNER?*
I DIDN'T EXPECT YOU TO DO *THAT!*
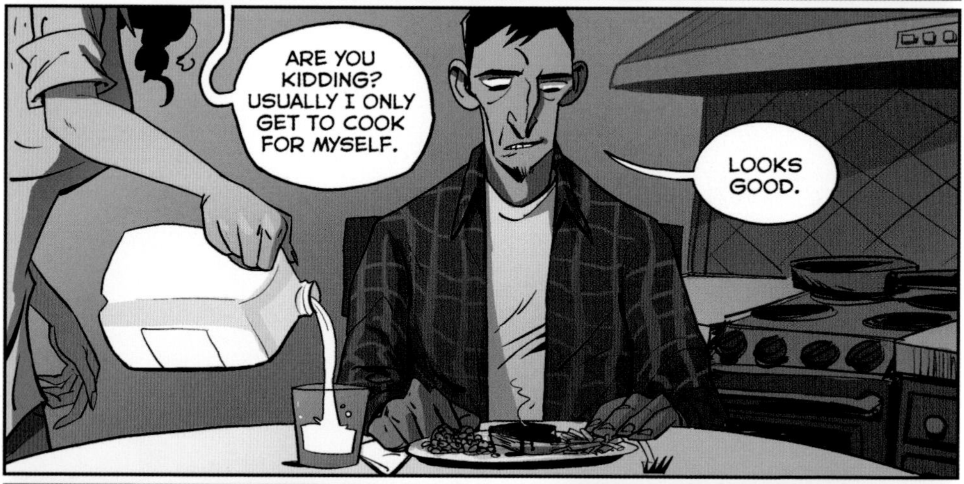
ARE YOU KIDDING? USUALLY I ONLY GET TO COOK FOR MYSELF.
LOOKS GOOD.
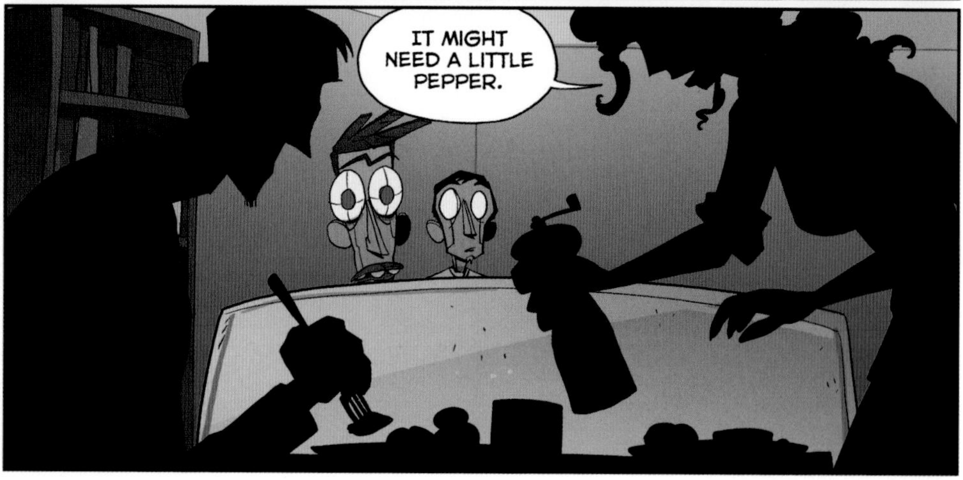
IT MIGHT NEED A LITTLE PEPPER.

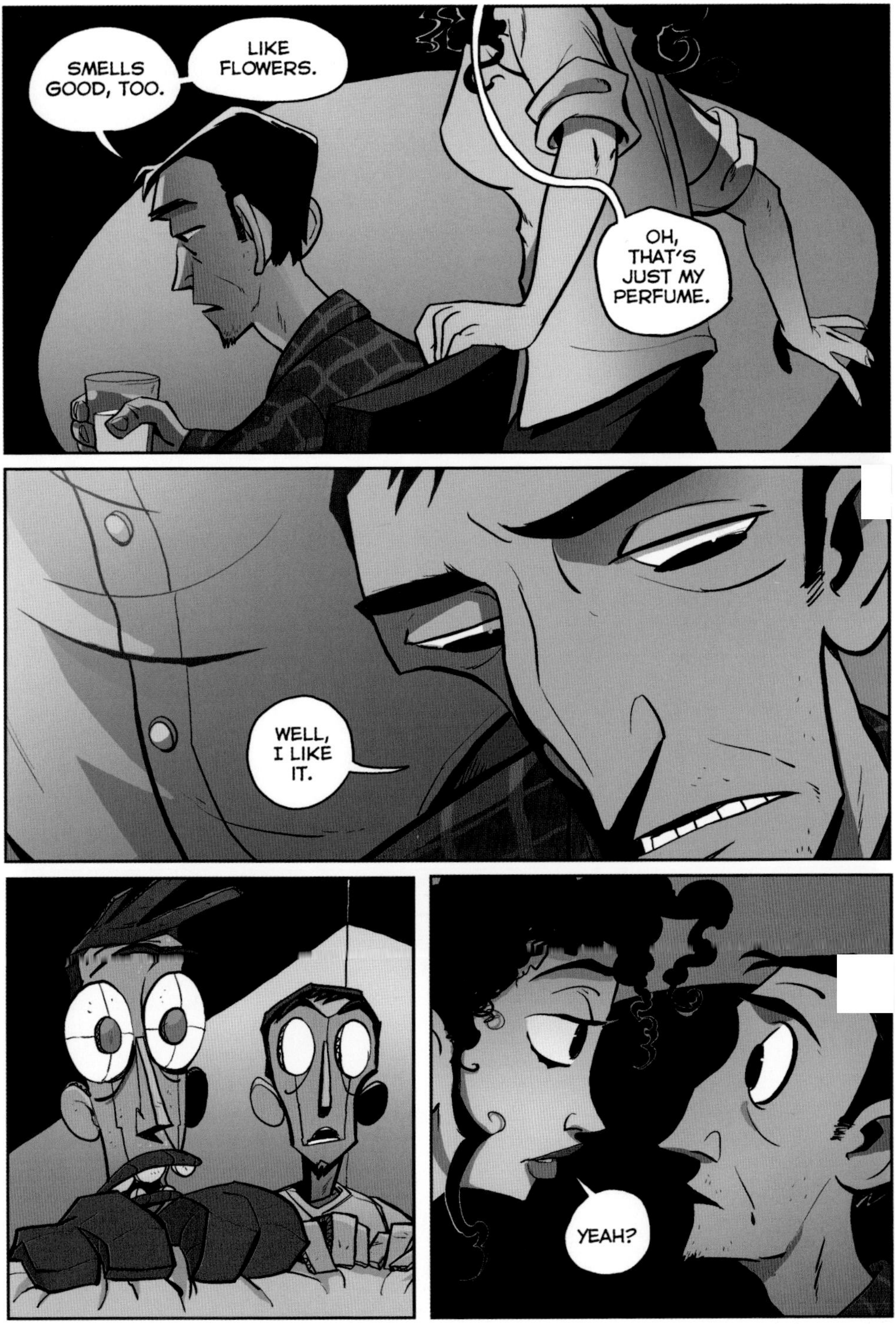
SMELLS GOOD, TOO.
LIKE FLOWERS.
OH, THAT'S JUST MY PERFUME.
WELL, I LIKE IT.
YEAH?

WAIT.

I'M SORRY.

WHAT?!

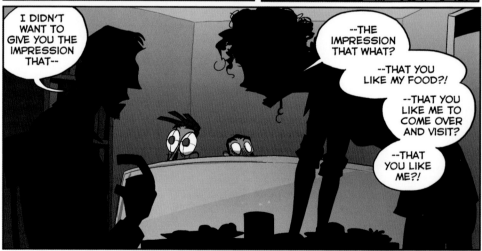

I DIDN'T WANT TO GIVE YOU THE IMPRESSION THAT--

--THE IMPRESSION THAT WHAT?

--THAT YOU LIKE MY FOOD?!

--THAT YOU LIKE ME TO COME OVER AND VISIT?

--THAT YOU LIKE ME?!

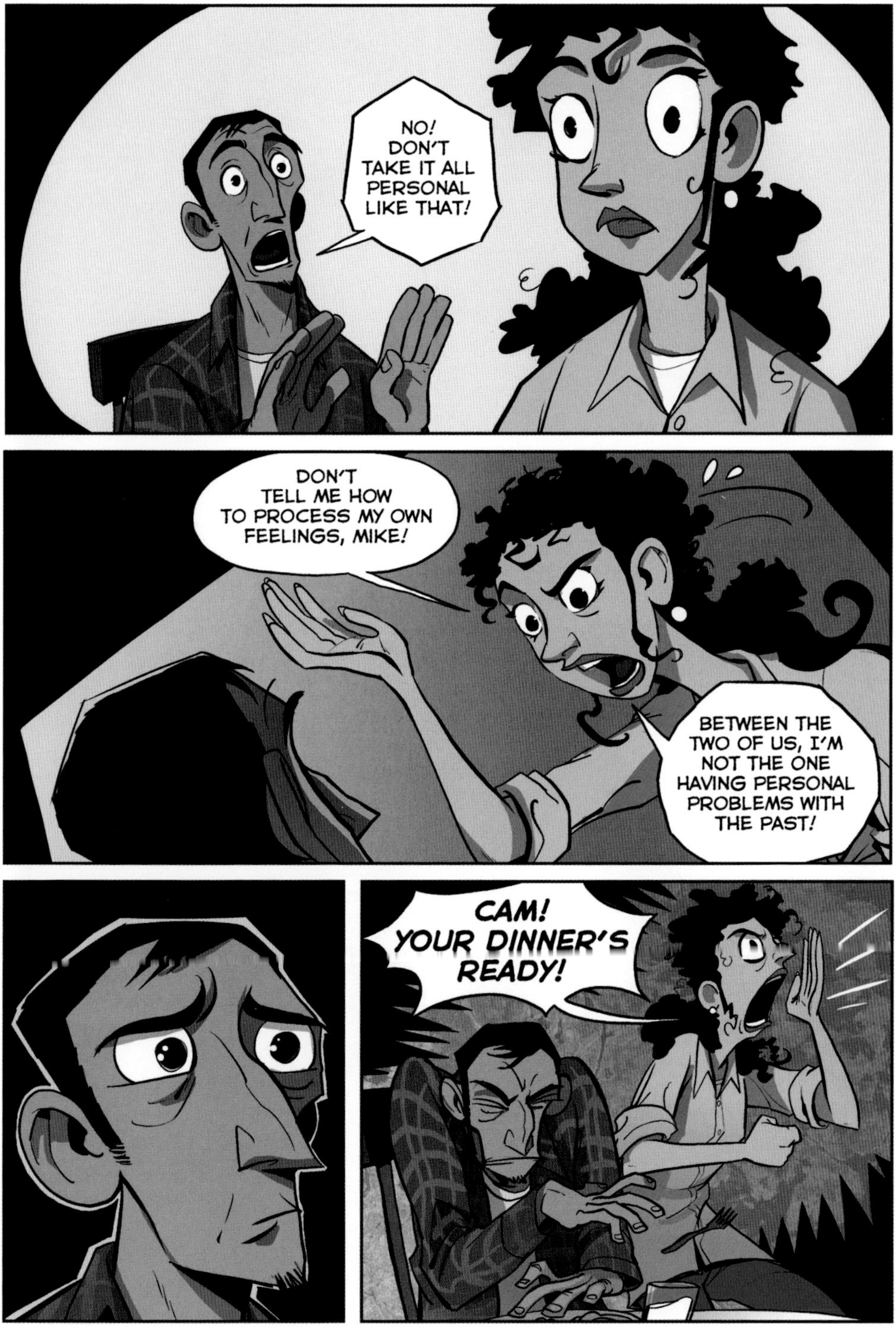
NO! DON'T TAKE IT ALL PERSONAL LIKE THAT!
DON'T TELL ME HOW TO PROCESS MY OWN FEELINGS, MIKE!
BETWEEN THE TWO OF US, I'M NOT THE ONE HAVING PERSONAL PROBLEMS WITH THE PAST!
CAM! YOUR DINNER'S READY!

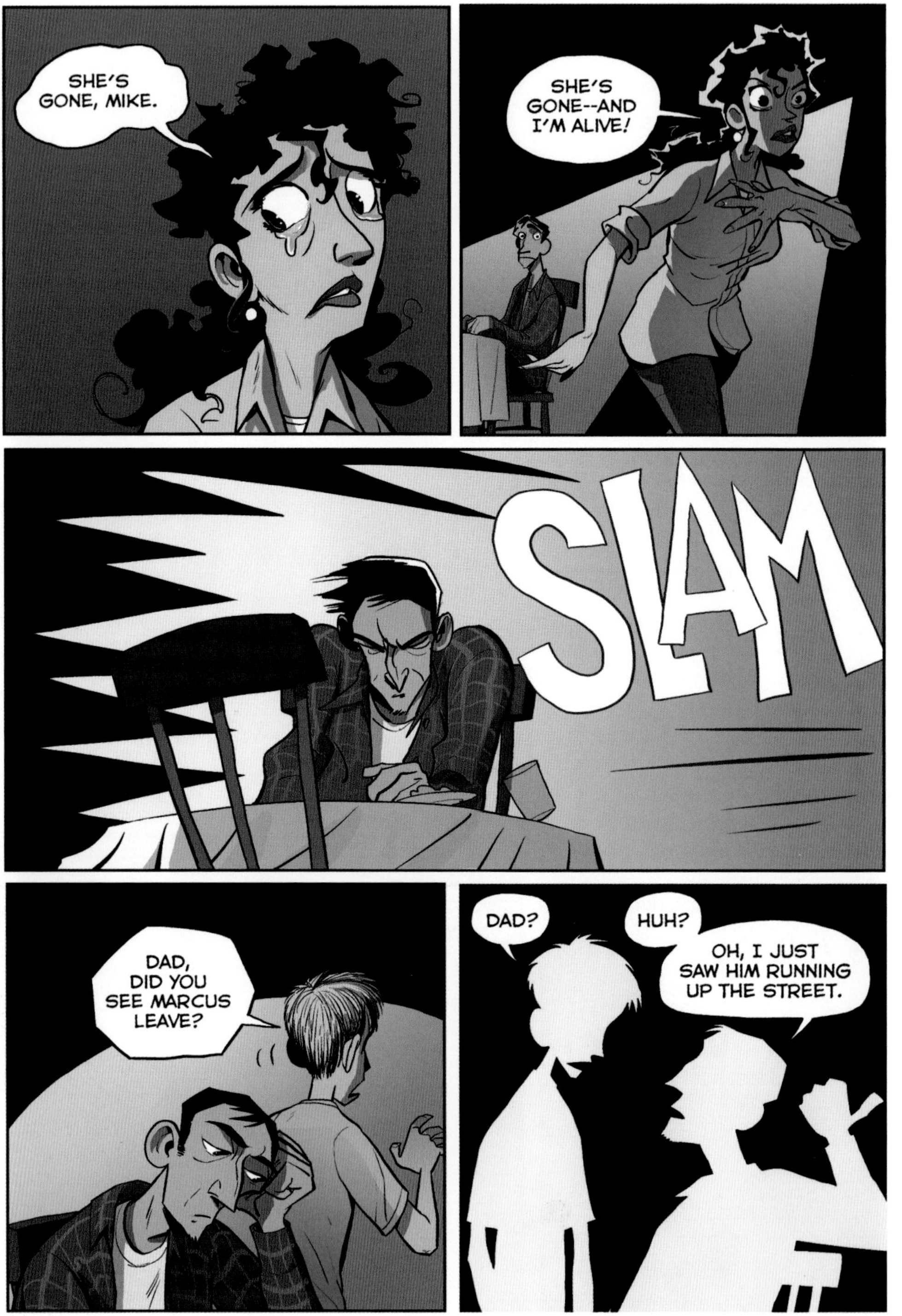
SHE'S GONE, MIKE.
SHE'S GONE--AND I'M ALIVE!
SLAM
DAD, DID YOU SEE MARCUS LEAVE?
DAD?
HUH?
OH, I JUST SAW HIM RUNNING UP THE STREET.

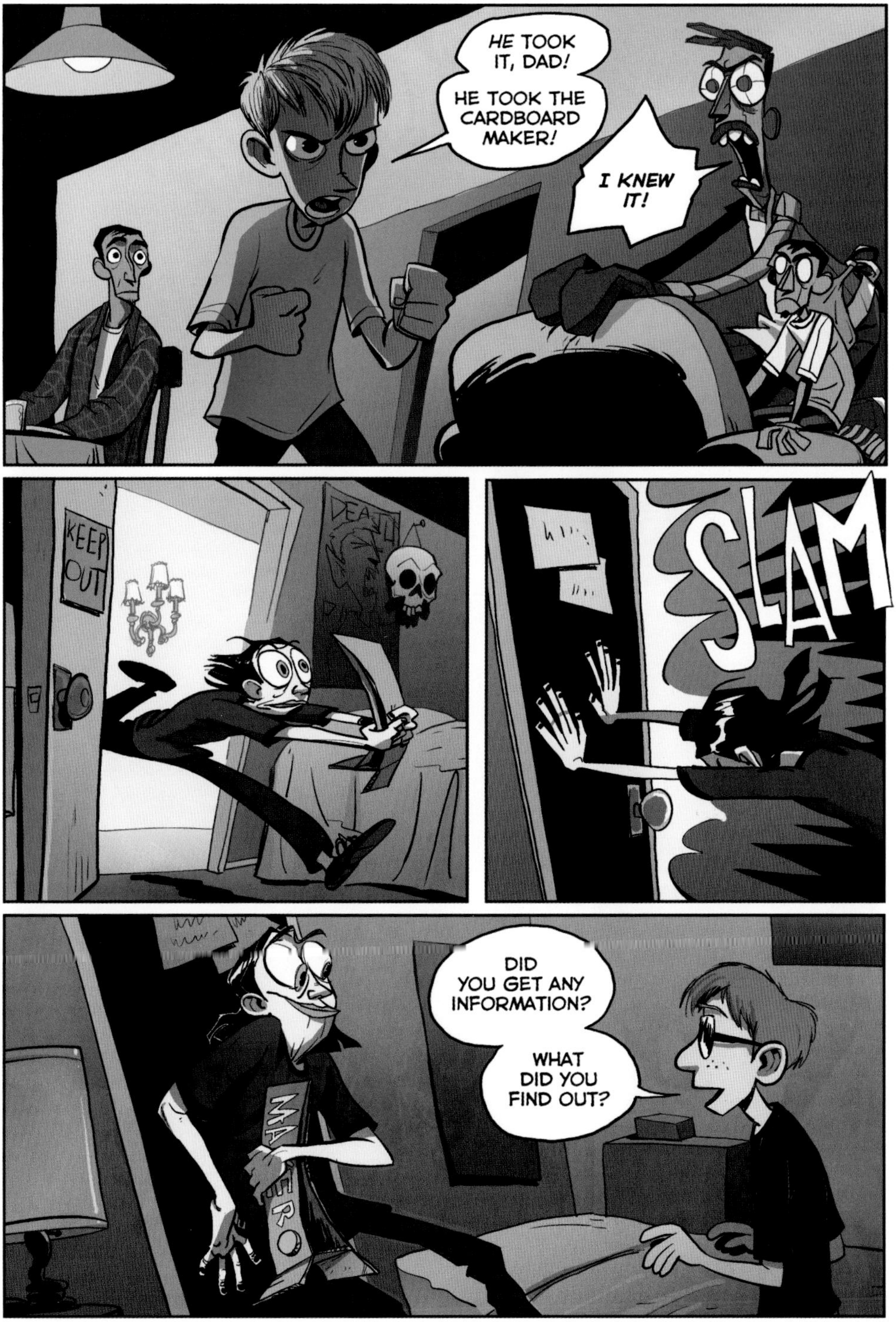
HE TOOK IT, DAD!
HE TOOK THE CARDBOARD MAKER!
I KNEW IT!
KEEP OUT
SLAM
DID YOU GET ANY INFORMATION?
WHAT DID YOU FIND OUT?

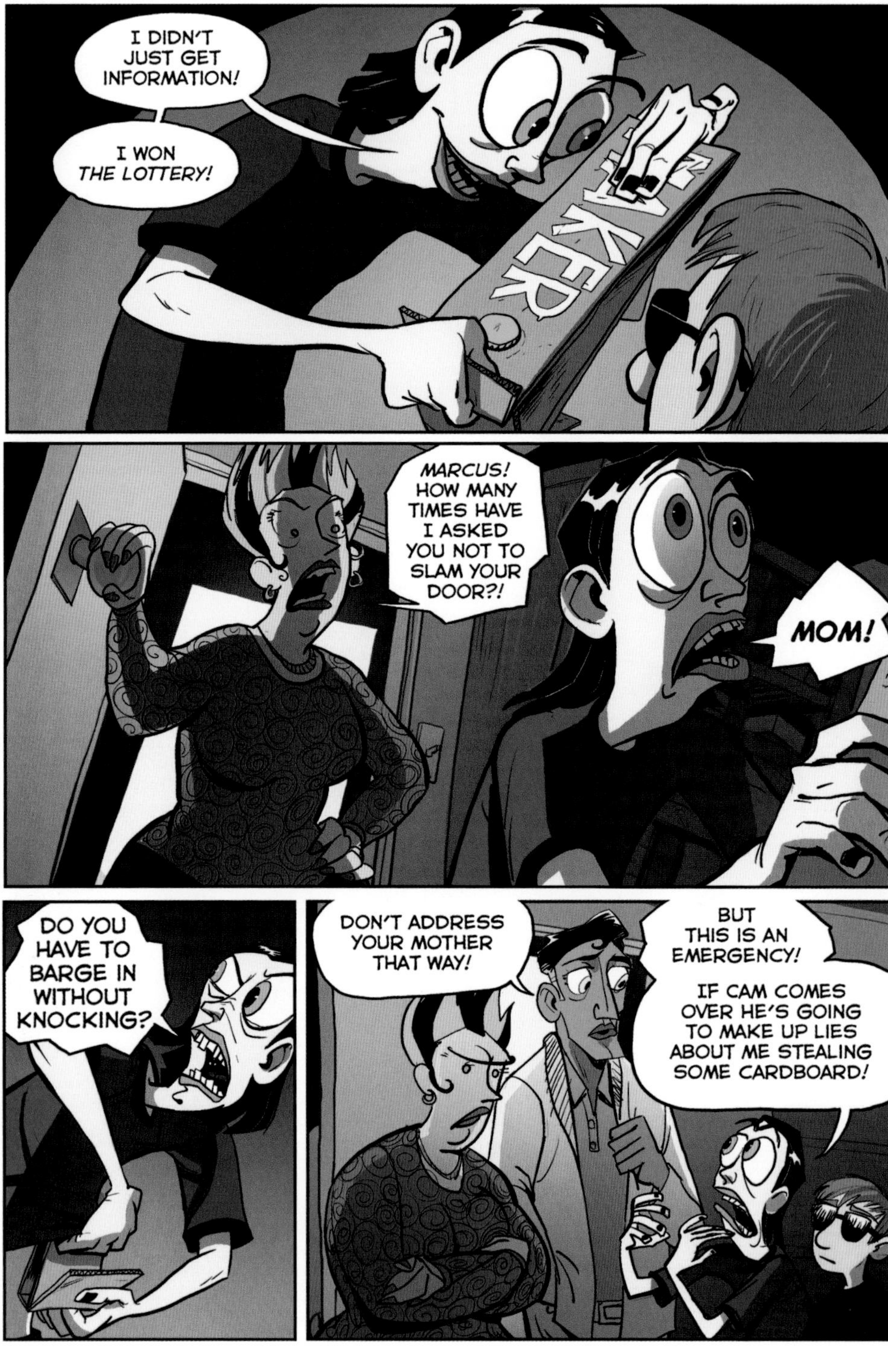
I DIDN'T JUST GET INFORMATION!
I WON THE LOTTERY!
MARCUS! HOW MANY TIMES HAVE I ASKED YOU NOT TO SLAM YOUR DOOR?!
MOM!
DO YOU HAVE TO BARGE IN WITHOUT KNOCKING?
DON'T ADDRESS YOUR MOTHER THAT WAY!
BUT THIS IS AN EMERGENCY!
IF CAM COMES OVER HE'S GOING TO MAKE UP LIES ABOUT ME STEALING SOME CARDBOARD!

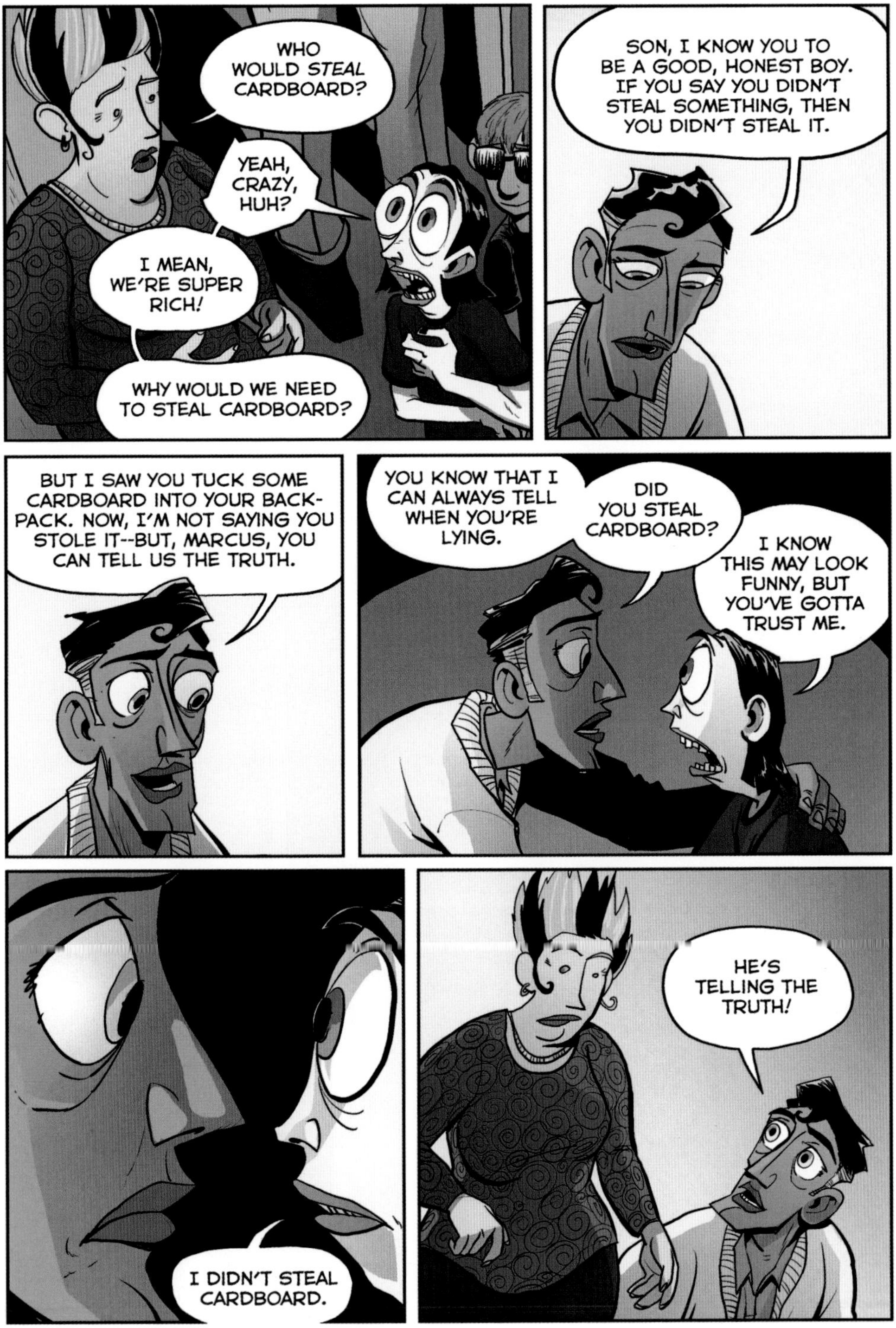
WHO WOULD STEAL CARDBOARD?
YEAH, CRAZY, HUH?
I MEAN, WE'RE SUPER RICH!
WHY WOULD WE NEED TO STEAL CARDBOARD?
SON, I KNOW YOU TO BE A GOOD, HONEST BOY. IF YOU SAY YOU DIDN'T STEAL SOMETHING, THEN YOU DIDN'T STEAL IT.
BUT I SAW YOU TUCK SOME CARDBOARD INTO YOUR BACK-PACK. NOW, I'M NOT SAYING YOU STOLE IT--BUT, MARCUS, YOU CAN TELL US THE TRUTH.
YOU KNOW THAT I CAN ALWAYS TELL WHEN YOU'RE LYING.
DID YOU STEAL CARDBOARD?
I KNOW THIS MAY LOOK FUNNY, BUT YOU'VE GOTTA TRUST ME.
I DIDN'T STEAL CARDBOARD.
HE'S TELLING THE TRUTH!

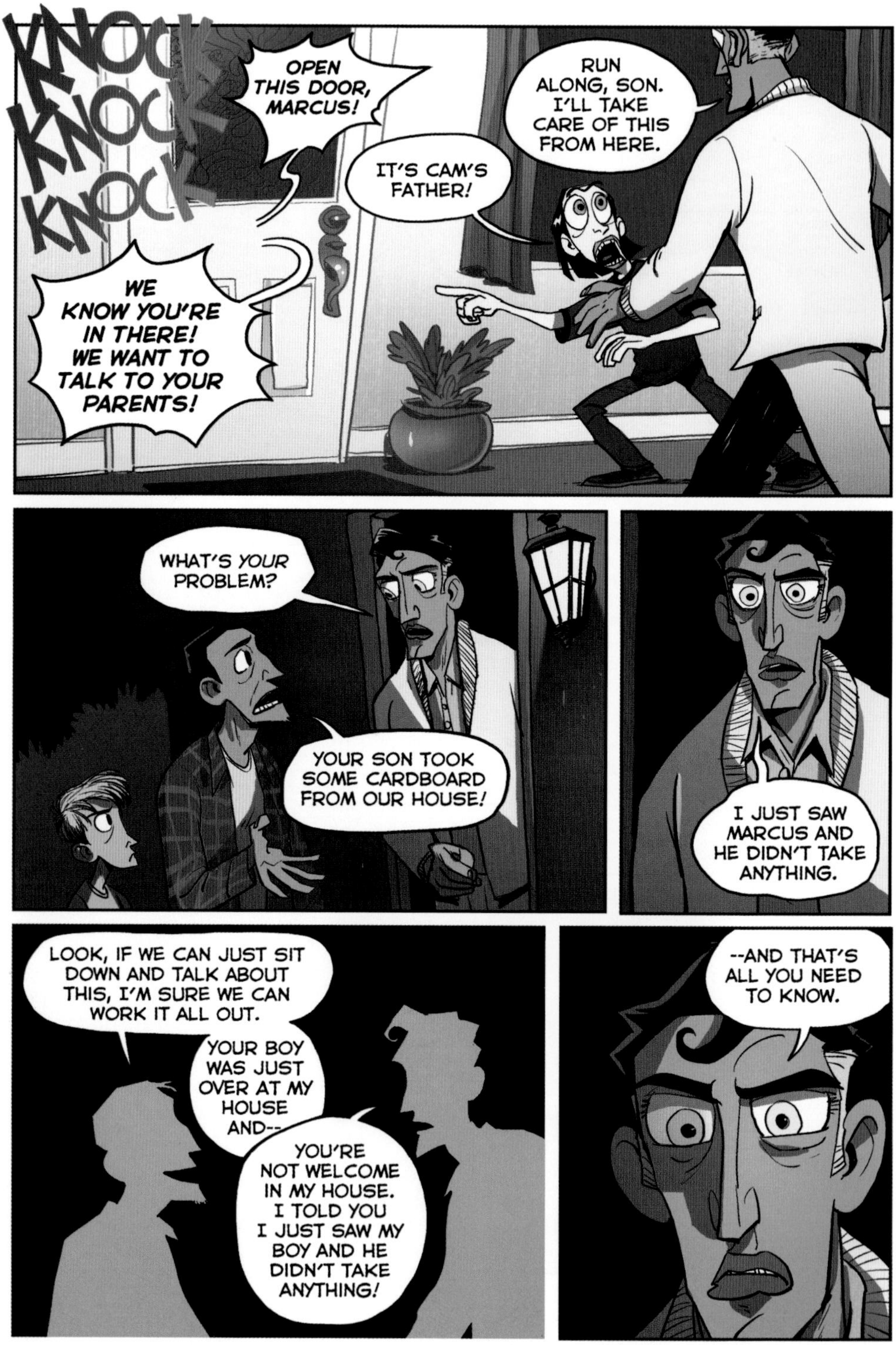
KNOCK KNOCK KNOCK
OPEN THIS DOOR, MARCUS!
WE KNOW YOU'RE IN THERE! WE WANT TO TALK TO YOUR PARENTS!
IT'S CAM'S FATHER!
RUN ALONG, SON. I'LL TAKE CARE OF THIS FROM HERE.
WHAT'S *YOUR* PROBLEM?
YOUR SON TOOK SOME CARDBOARD FROM OUR HOUSE!
I JUST SAW MARCUS AND HE DIDN'T TAKE ANYTHING.
LOOK, IF WE CAN JUST SIT DOWN AND TALK ABOUT THIS, I'M SURE WE CAN WORK IT ALL OUT.
YOUR BOY WAS JUST OVER AT MY HOUSE AND--
YOU'RE NOT WELCOME IN MY HOUSE. I TOLD YOU I JUST SAW MY BOY AND HE DIDN'T TAKE ANYTHING!
--AND THAT'S ALL YOU NEED TO KNOW.

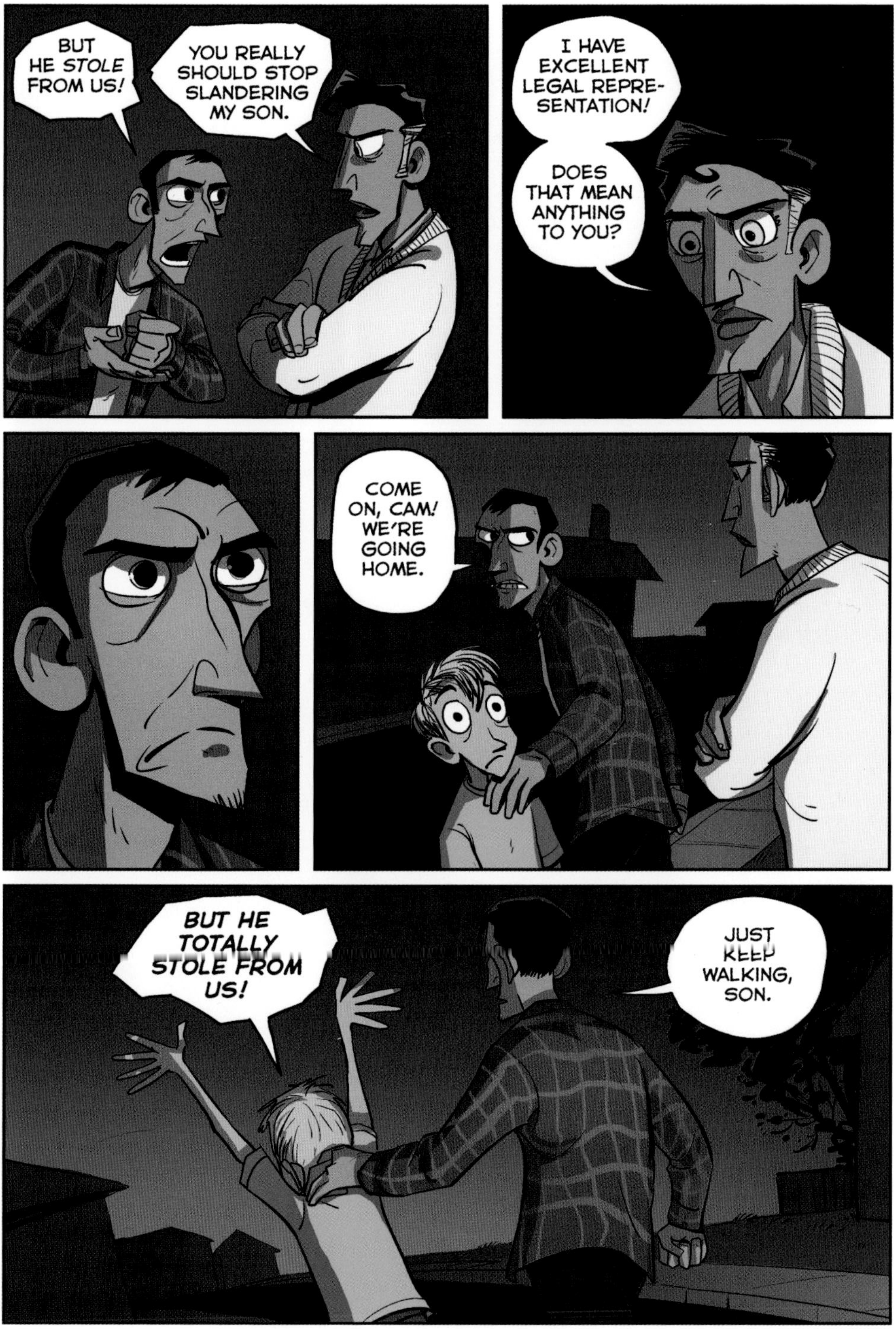
BUT HE *STOLE* FROM US!
YOU REALLY SHOULD STOP SLANDERING MY SON.
I HAVE EXCELLENT LEGAL REPRESENTATION!
DOES THAT MEAN ANYTHING TO YOU?
COME ON, CAM! WE'RE GOING HOME.
BUT HE TOTALLY STOLE FROM US!
JUST KEEP WALKING, SON.

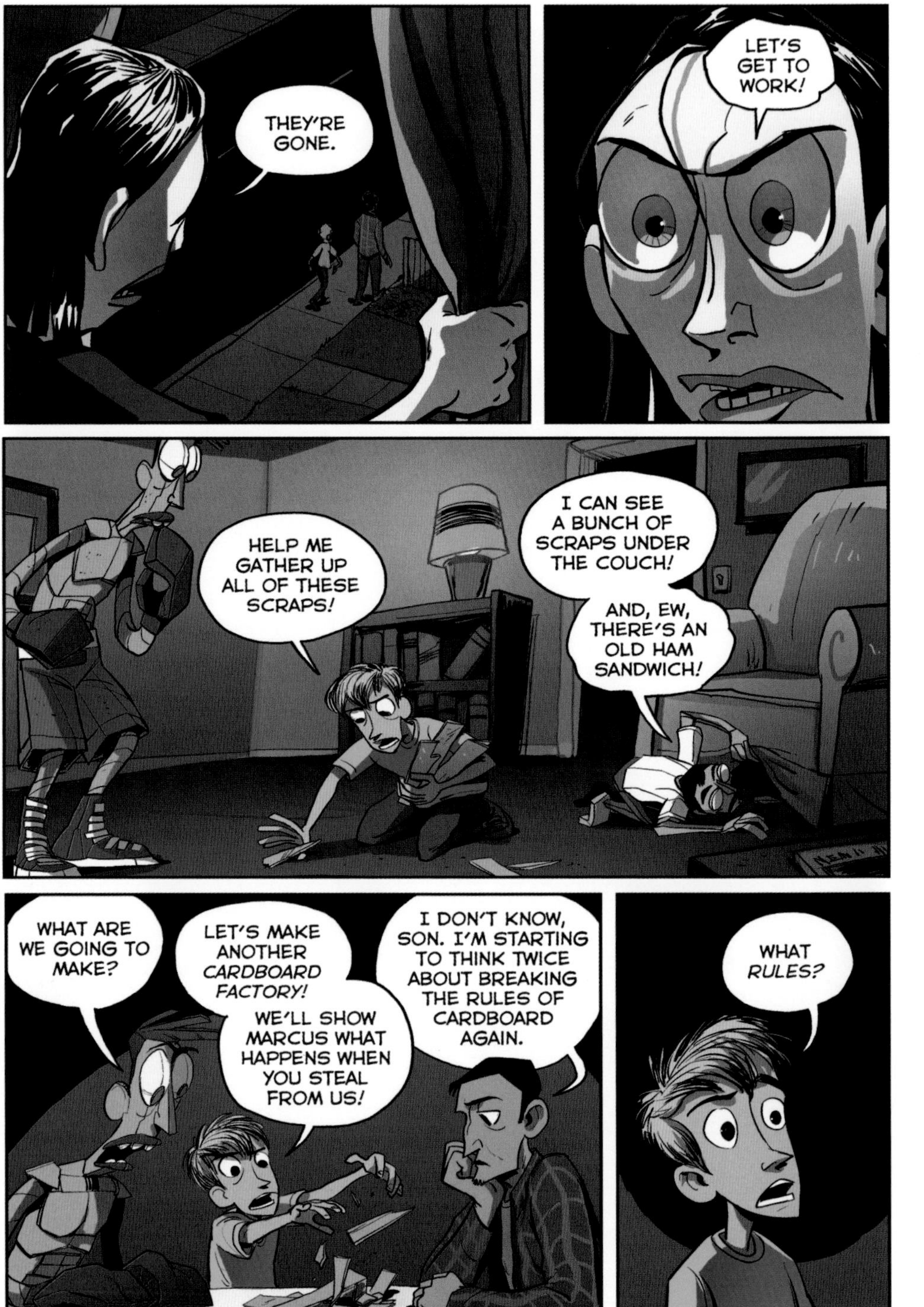
THEY'RE GONE.
LET'S GET TO WORK!
HELP ME GATHER UP ALL OF THESE SCRAPS!
I CAN SEE A BUNCH OF SCRAPS UNDER THE COUCH!
AND, EW, THERE'S AN OLD HAM SANDWICH!
WHAT ARE WE GOING TO MAKE?
LET'S MAKE ANOTHER *CARDBOARD FACTORY!*
WE'LL SHOW MARCUS WHAT HAPPENS WHEN YOU STEAL FROM US!
I DON'T KNOW, SON. I'M STARTING TO THINK TWICE ABOUT BREAKING THE RULES OF CARDBOARD AGAIN.
WHAT *RULES?*

THERE WAS THIS OLD MAN WHO SOLD ME THAT FIRST CARDBOARD BOX AND HE GAVE ME THESE RULES I HAD TO FOLLOW.

--LIKE THAT WE'RE SUPPOSED TO BRING ALL OF THESE SCRAPS BACK TO HIM.

THIS ISN'T FAIR! WHY SHOULD MARCUS GET TO HAVE A CARDBOARD MAKER BUT I DON'T?!

HE'S RICH, DAD! HE'S GOT EVERY-THING!

HE DOES HAVE A HUGE EGO.

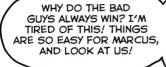

WHY DO THE BAD GUYS ALWAYS WIN? I'M TIRED OF THIS! THINGS ARE SO EASY FOR MARCUS, AND LOOK AT US!

WE CAN'T EVEN AFFORD TO HAVE MEAT WITH OUR MAC AND CHEESE!

I'M TIRED OF ALWAYS BEING POOR, DAD!

HE'S RIGHT, MIKE. IT'S NOT FAIR THAT A BAD KID WOULD GET MORE THAN A GOOD KID!

WELL, I'LL JUST PUT A CALL IN TO THE LIFE-ISN'T-FAIR POLICE!

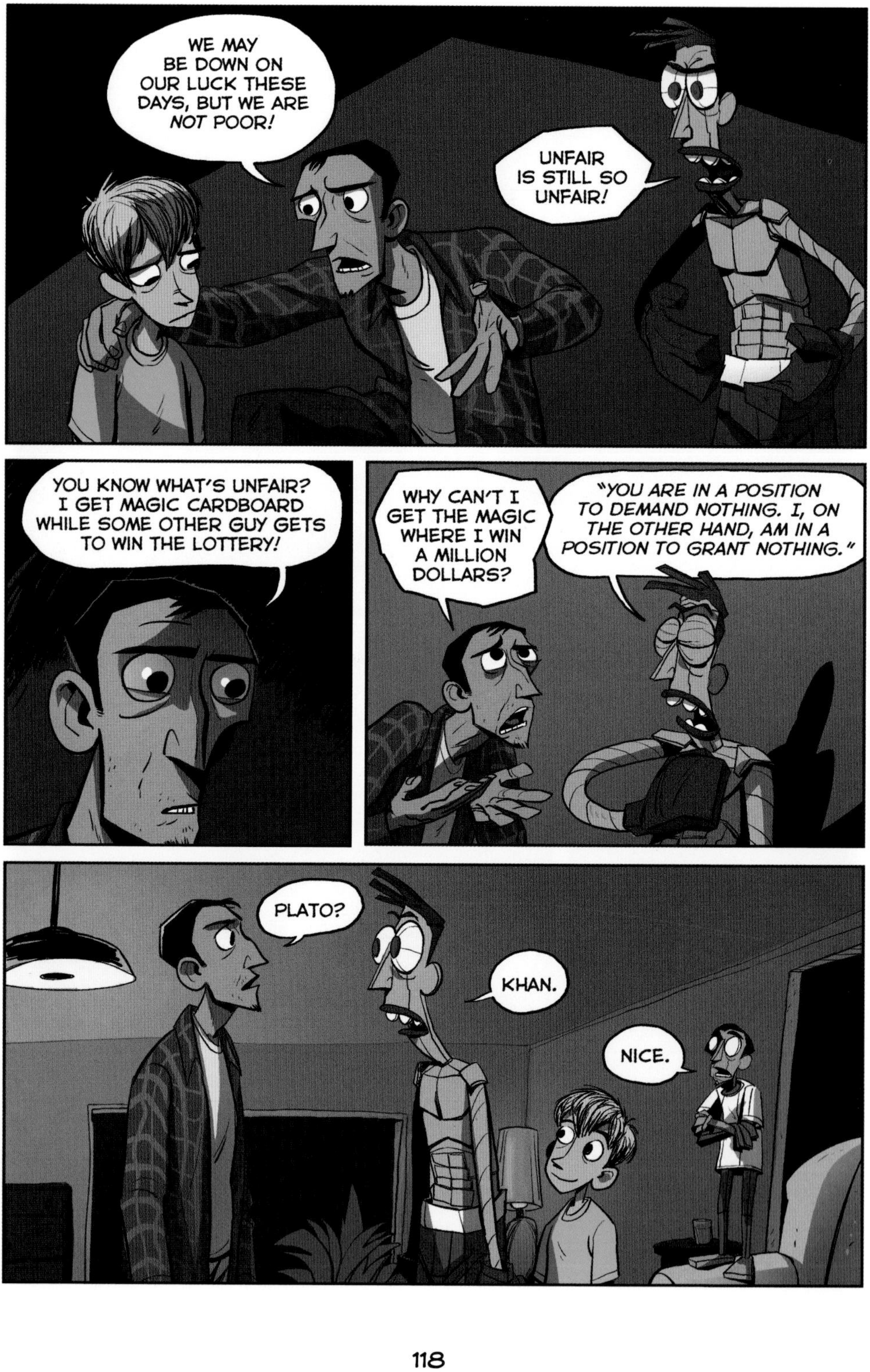
WE MAY BE DOWN ON OUR LUCK THESE DAYS, BUT WE ARE *NOT* POOR!
UNFAIR IS STILL SO UNFAIR!
YOU KNOW WHAT'S UNFAIR? I GET MAGIC CARDBOARD WHILE SOME OTHER GUY GETS TO WIN THE LOTTERY!
WHY CAN'T I GET THE MAGIC WHERE I WIN A MILLION DOLLARS?
"YOU ARE IN A POSITION TO DEMAND NOTHING. I, ON THE OTHER HAND, AM IN A POSITION TO GRANT NOTHING."
PLATO?
KHAN.
NICE.

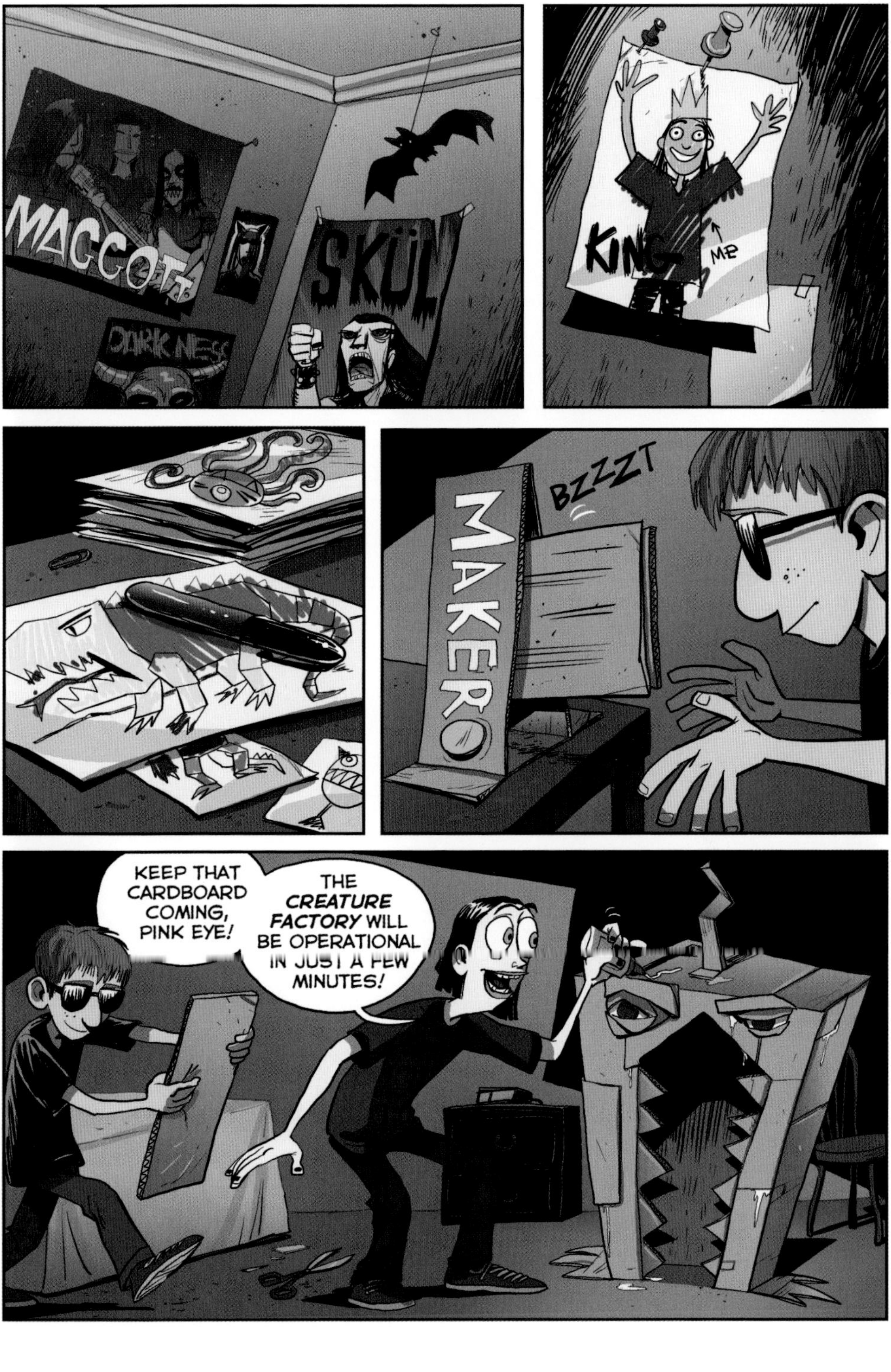
MAGGOTT
DARKNESS
SKÜL
KING
ME
MAKER
BZZZT
KEEP THAT CARDBOARD COMING, PINK EYE!
THE CREATURE FACTORY WILL BE OPERATIONAL IN JUST A FEW MINUTES!

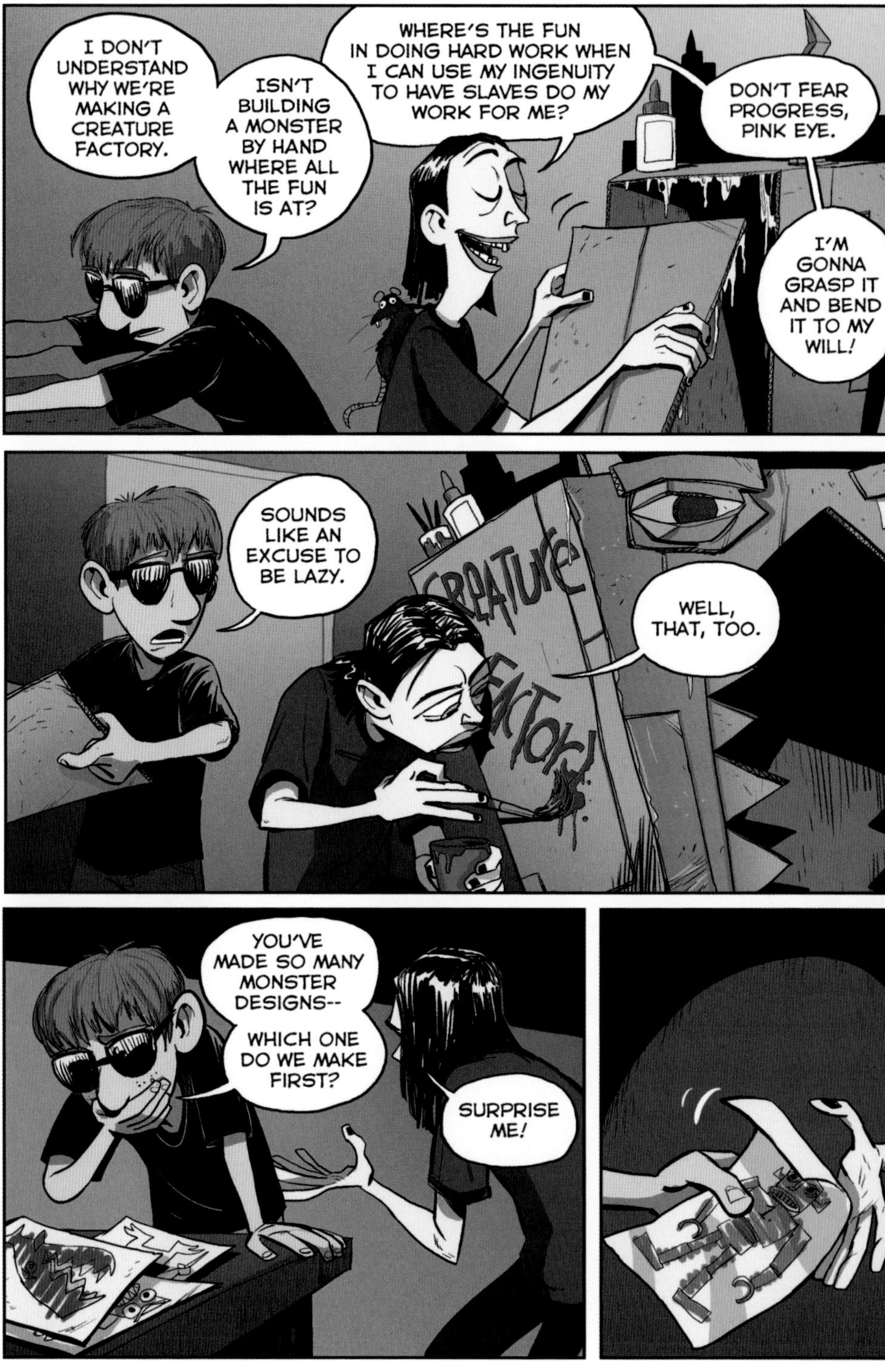
I DON'T UNDERSTAND WHY WE'RE MAKING A CREATURE FACTORY.
ISN'T BUILDING A MONSTER BY HAND WHERE ALL THE FUN IS AT?
WHERE'S THE FUN IN DOING HARD WORK WHEN I CAN USE MY INGENUITY TO HAVE SLAVES DO MY WORK FOR ME?
DON'T FEAR PROGRESS, PINK EYE.
I'M GONNA GRASP IT AND BEND IT TO MY WILL!
SOUNDS LIKE AN EXCUSE TO BE LAZY.
CREATURE FACTORY
WELL, THAT, TOO.
YOU'VE MADE SO MANY MONSTER DESIGNS--
WHICH ONE DO WE MAKE FIRST?
SURPRISE ME!

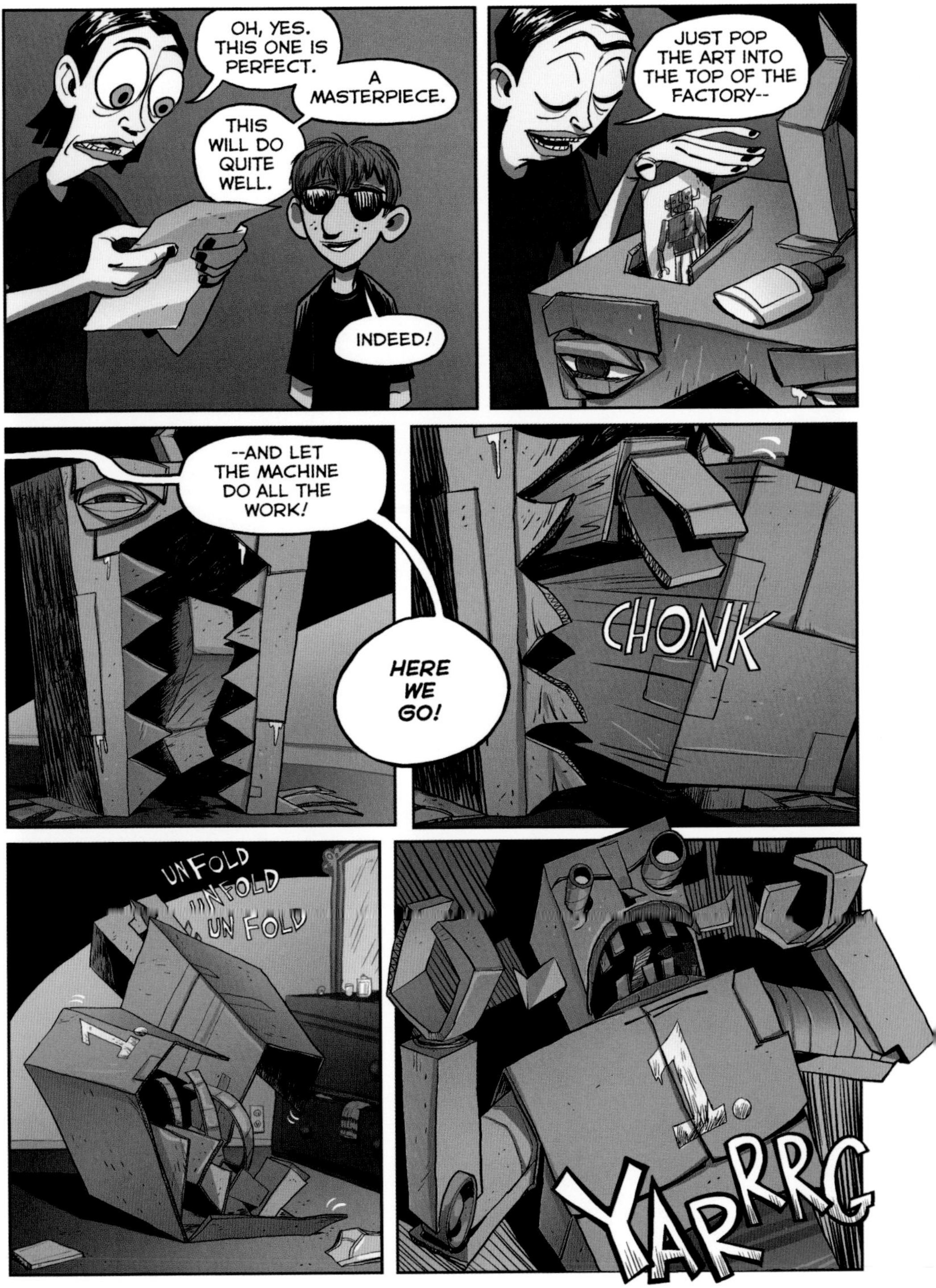
OH, YES. THIS ONE IS PERFECT.
A MASTERPIECE.
THIS WILL DO QUITE WELL.
INDEED!
JUST POP THE ART INTO THE TOP OF THE FACTORY--
--AND LET THE MACHINE DO ALL THE WORK!
HERE WE GO!
CHONK
UNFOLD
UNFOLD
UN FOLD
YARRRG

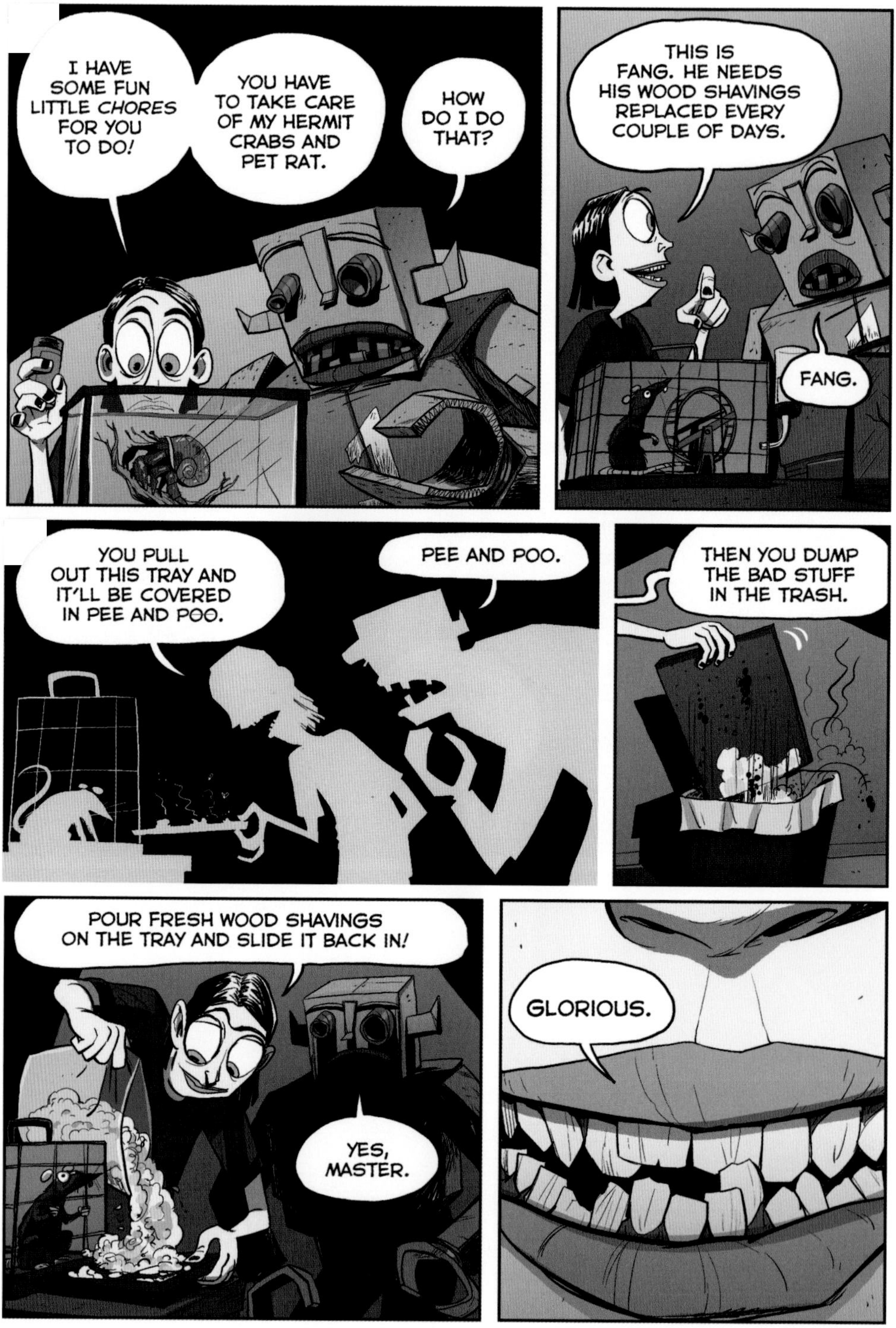
I HAVE SOME FUN LITTLE *CHORES* FOR YOU TO DO!
YOU HAVE TO TAKE CARE OF MY HERMIT CRABS AND PET RAT.
HOW DO I DO THAT?
THIS IS FANG. HE NEEDS HIS WOOD SHAVINGS REPLACED EVERY COUPLE OF DAYS.
FANG.
YOU PULL OUT THIS TRAY AND IT'LL BE COVERED IN PEE AND POO.
PEE AND POO.
THEN YOU DUMP THE BAD STUFF IN THE TRASH.
POUR FRESH WOOD SHAVINGS ON THE TRAY AND SLIDE IT BACK IN!
YES, MASTER.
GLORIOUS.

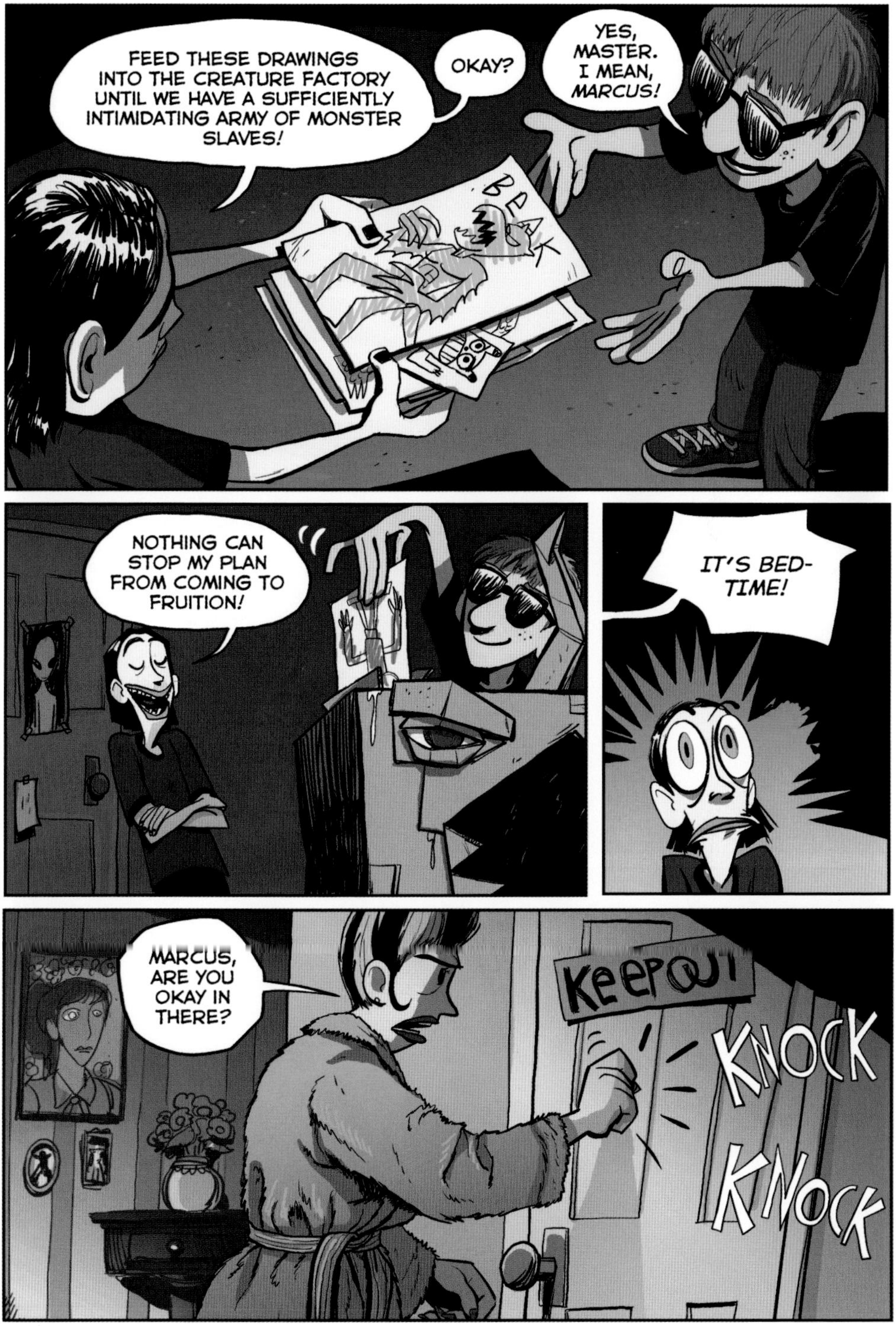
FEED THESE DRAWINGS INTO THE CREATURE FACTORY UNTIL WE HAVE A SUFFICIENTLY INTIMIDATING ARMY OF MONSTER SLAVES!
OKAY?
YES, MASTER. I MEAN, MARCUS!
BEAK
NOTHING CAN STOP MY PLAN FROM COMING TO FRUITION!
IT'S BED-TIME!
MARCUS, ARE YOU OKAY IN THERE?
KEEP OUT
KNOCK
KNOCK

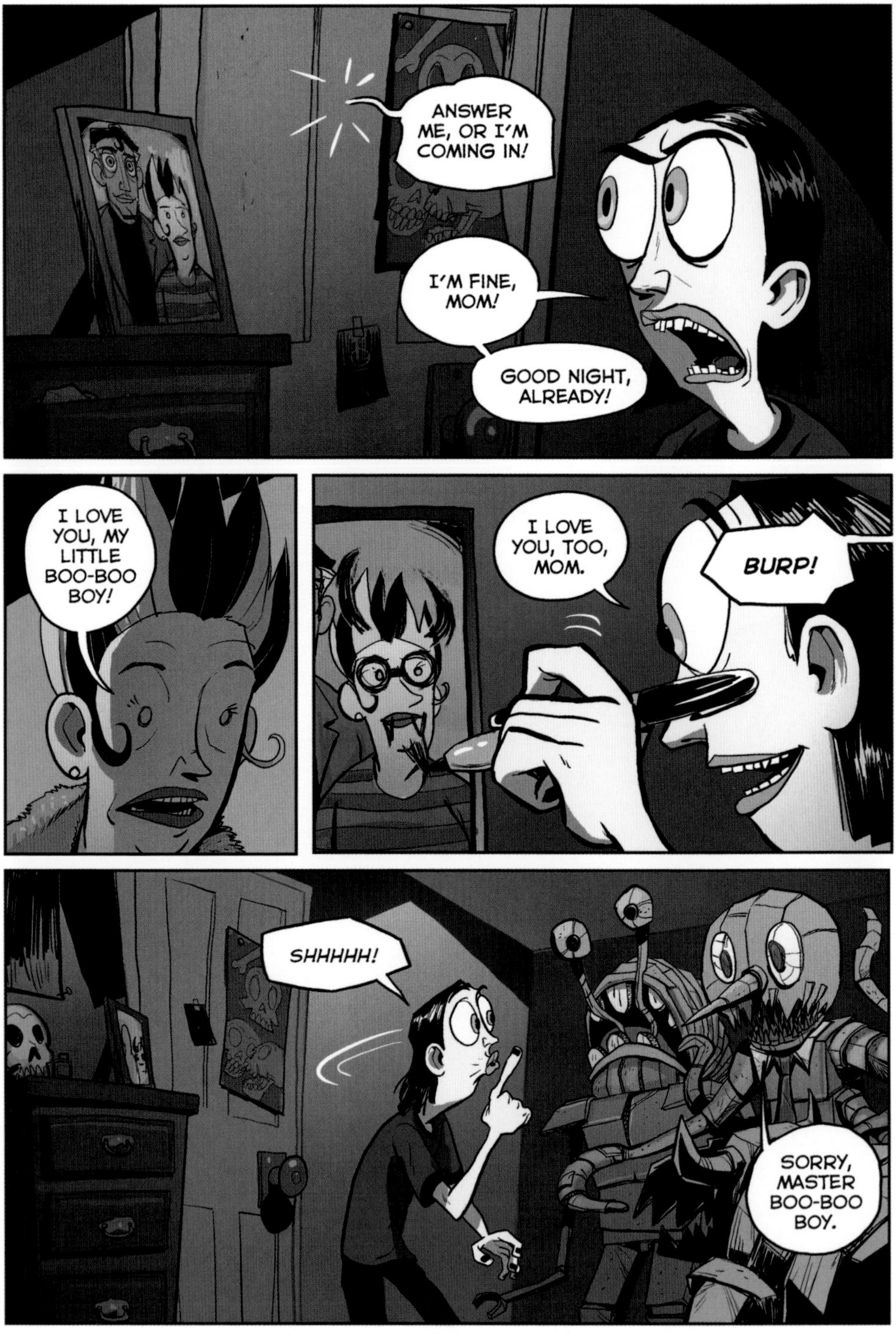
ANSWER ME, OR I'M COMING IN!
I'M FINE, MOM!
GOOD NIGHT, ALREADY!
I LOVE YOU, MY LITTLE BOO-BOO BOY!
I LOVE YOU, TOO, MOM.
BURP!
SHHHHH!
SORRY, MASTER BOO-BOO BOY.

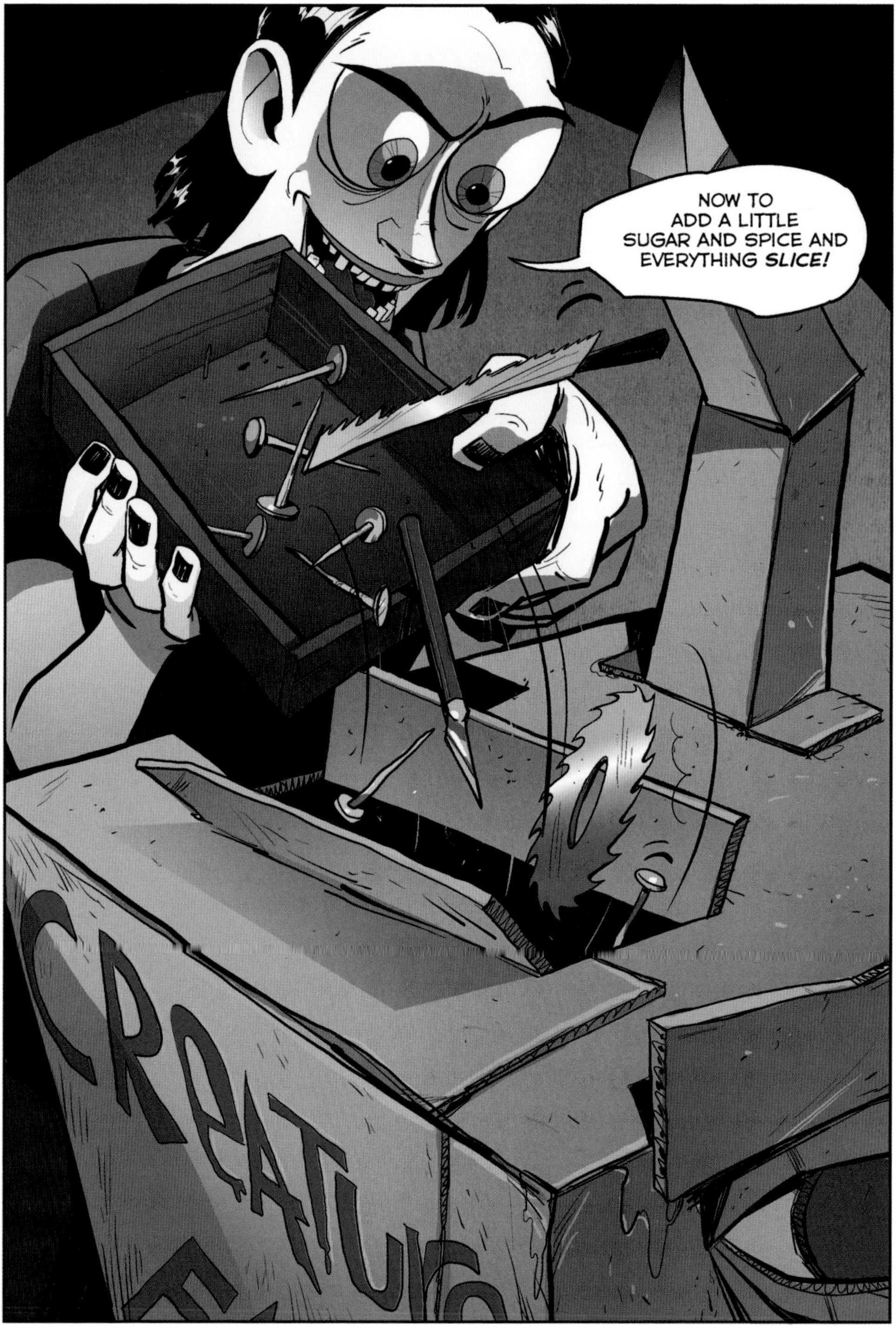
NOW TO ADD A LITTLE SUGAR AND SPICE AND EVERYTHING *SLICE!*
CREATURE F

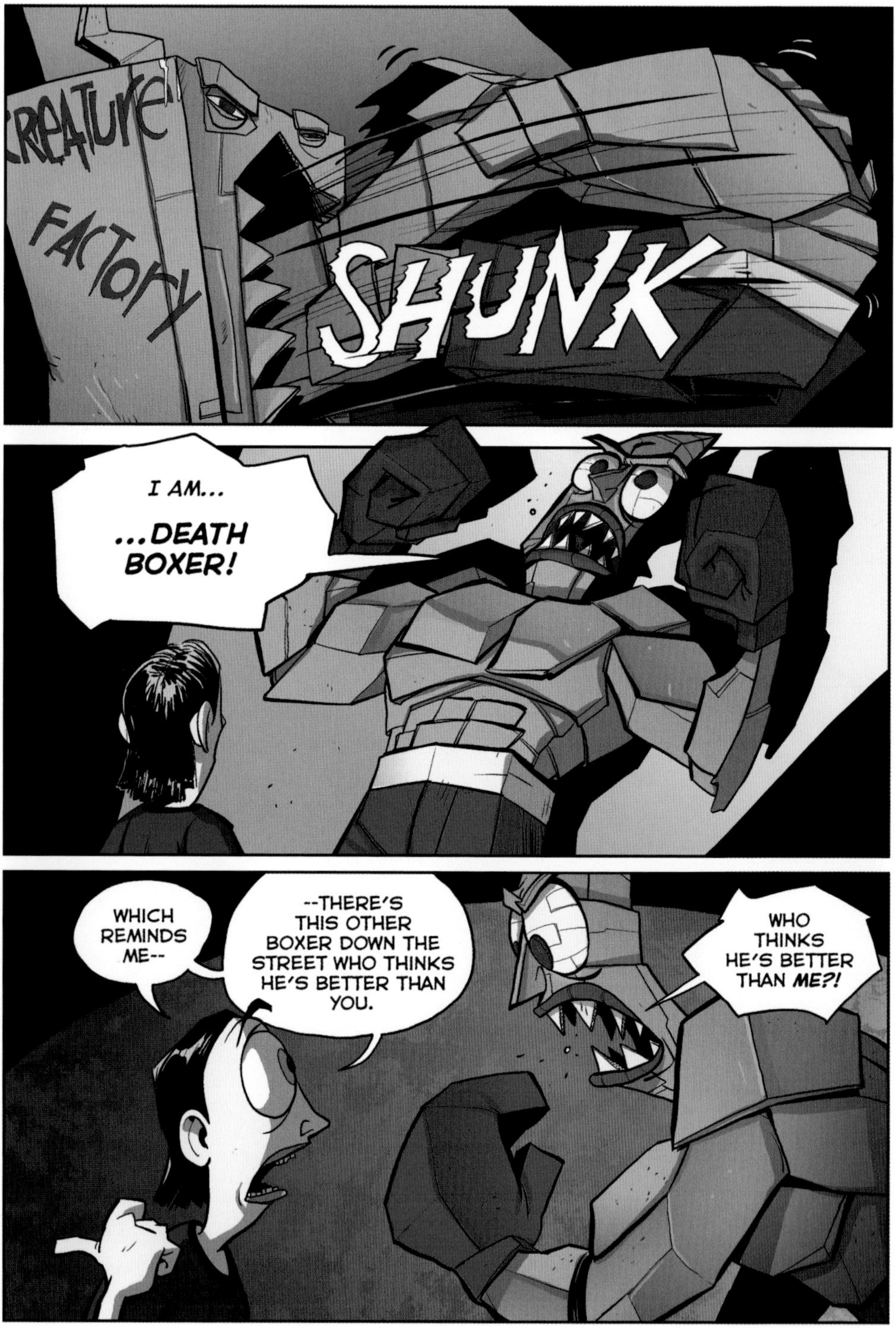
CREATURE FACTORY
SHUNK
I AM...
...DEATH BOXER!
WHICH REMINDS ME--
--THERE'S THIS OTHER BOXER DOWN THE STREET WHO THINKS HE'S BETTER THAN YOU.
WHO THINKS HE'S BETTER THAN *ME?!*

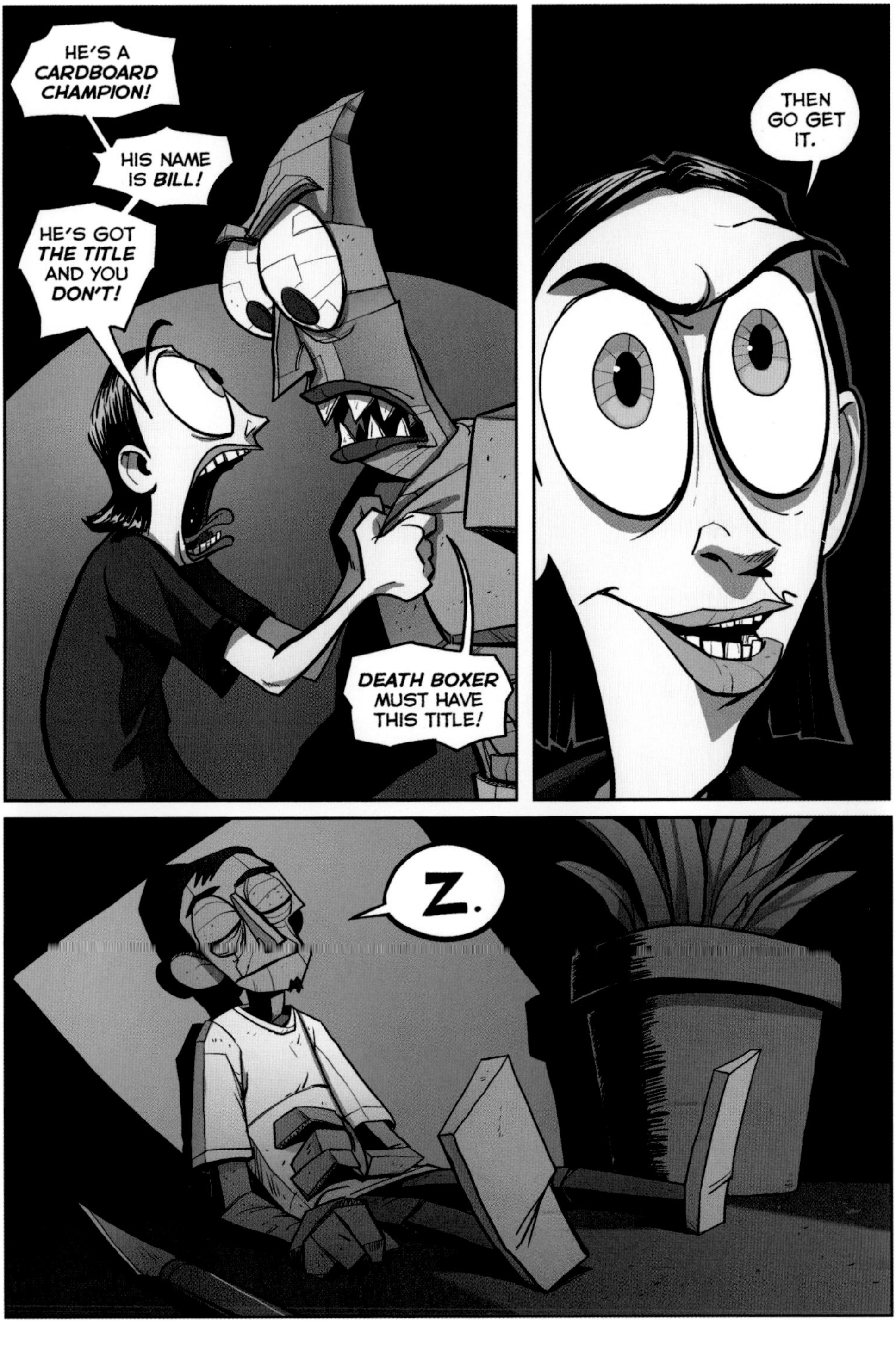
HE'S A CARDBOARD CHAMPION!
HIS NAME IS BILL!
HE'S GOT THE TITLE AND YOU DON'T!
DEATH BOXER MUST HAVE THIS TITLE!
THEN GO GET IT.
Z.

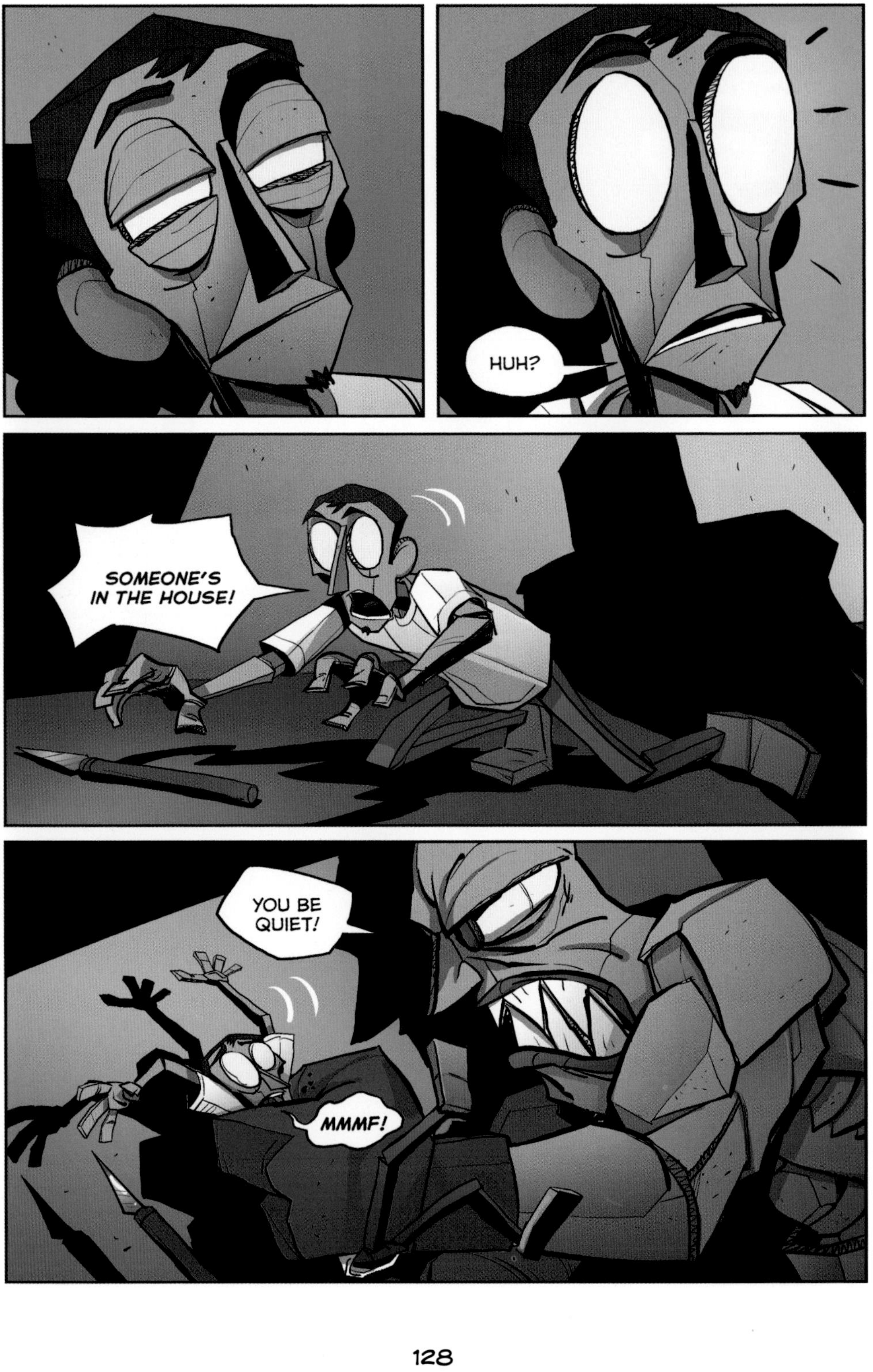
HUH?
SOMEONE'S IN THE HOUSE!
YOU BE QUIET!
MMMF!

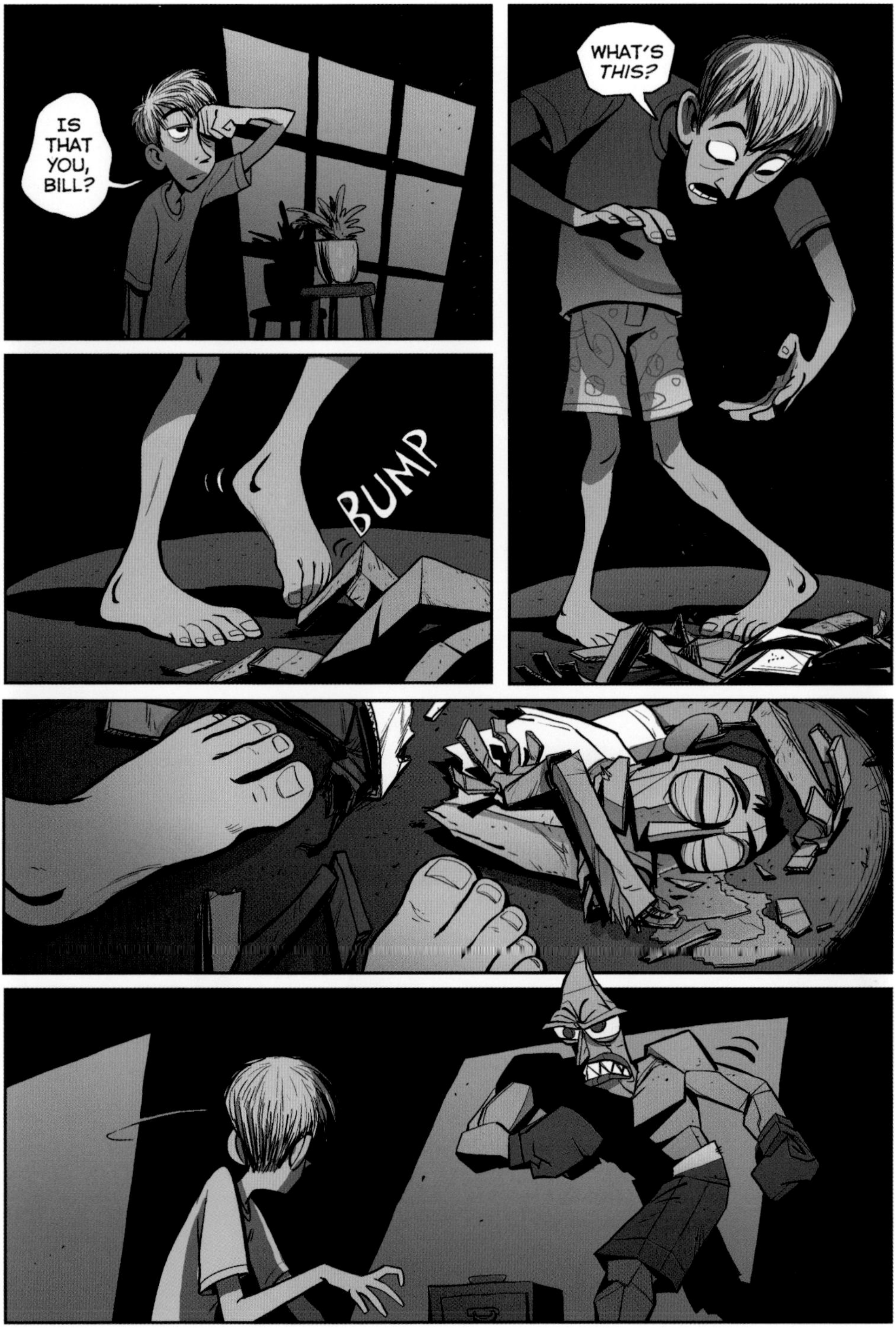
IS THAT YOU, BILL?
WHAT'S THIS?
BUMP

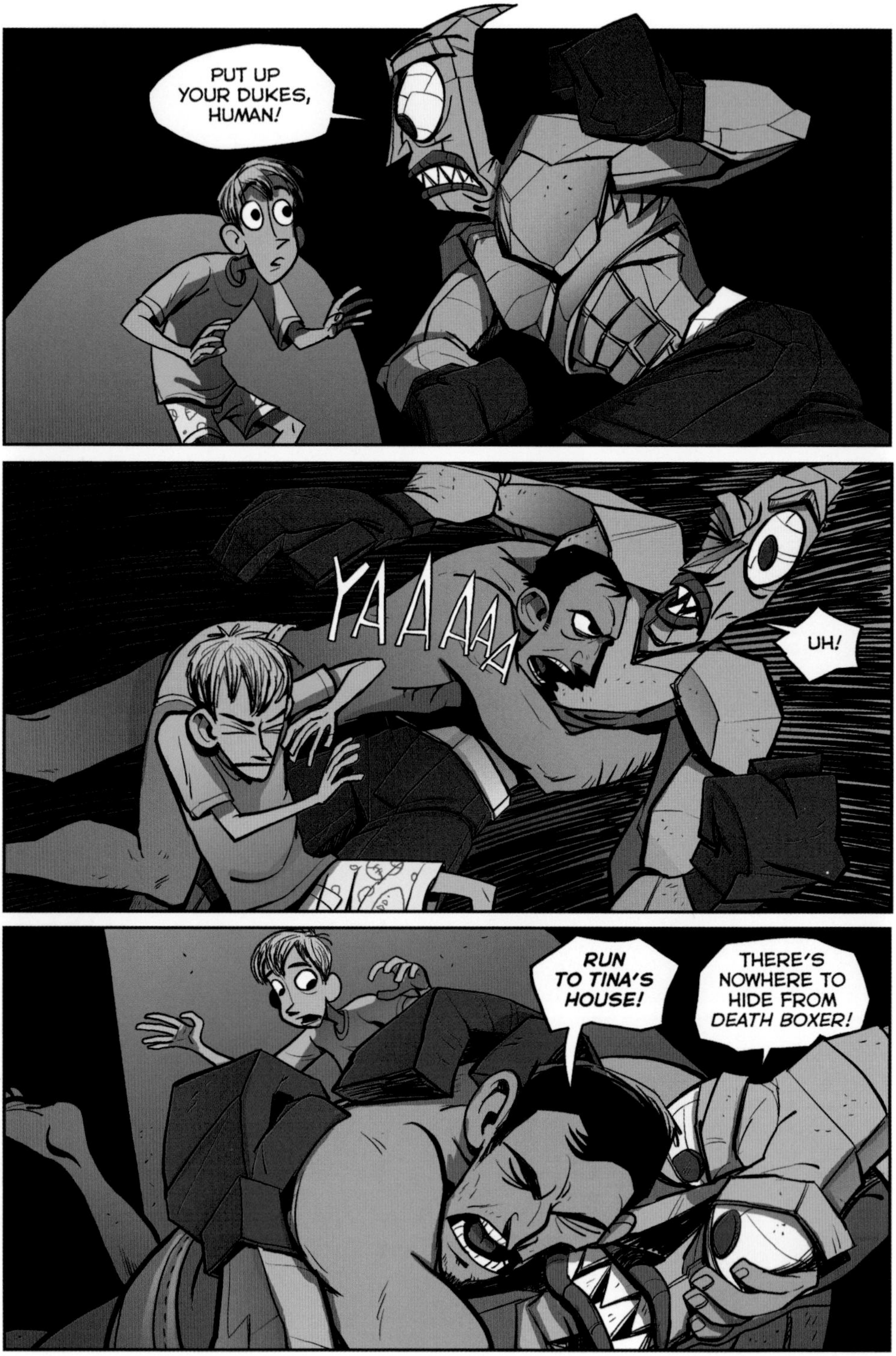
PUT UP YOUR DUKES, HUMAN!
YAAAAA
UH!
RUN TO TINA'S HOUSE!
THERE'S NOWHERE TO HIDE FROM *DEATH BOXER!*

YOUR BOXING...IS WEAK! LET ME GIVE YOU A FEW POINTERS!

OAF!

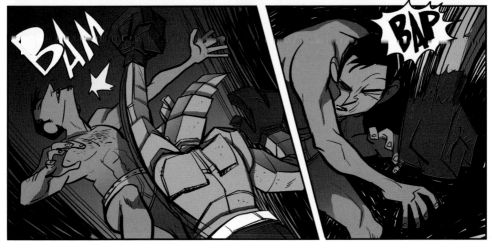

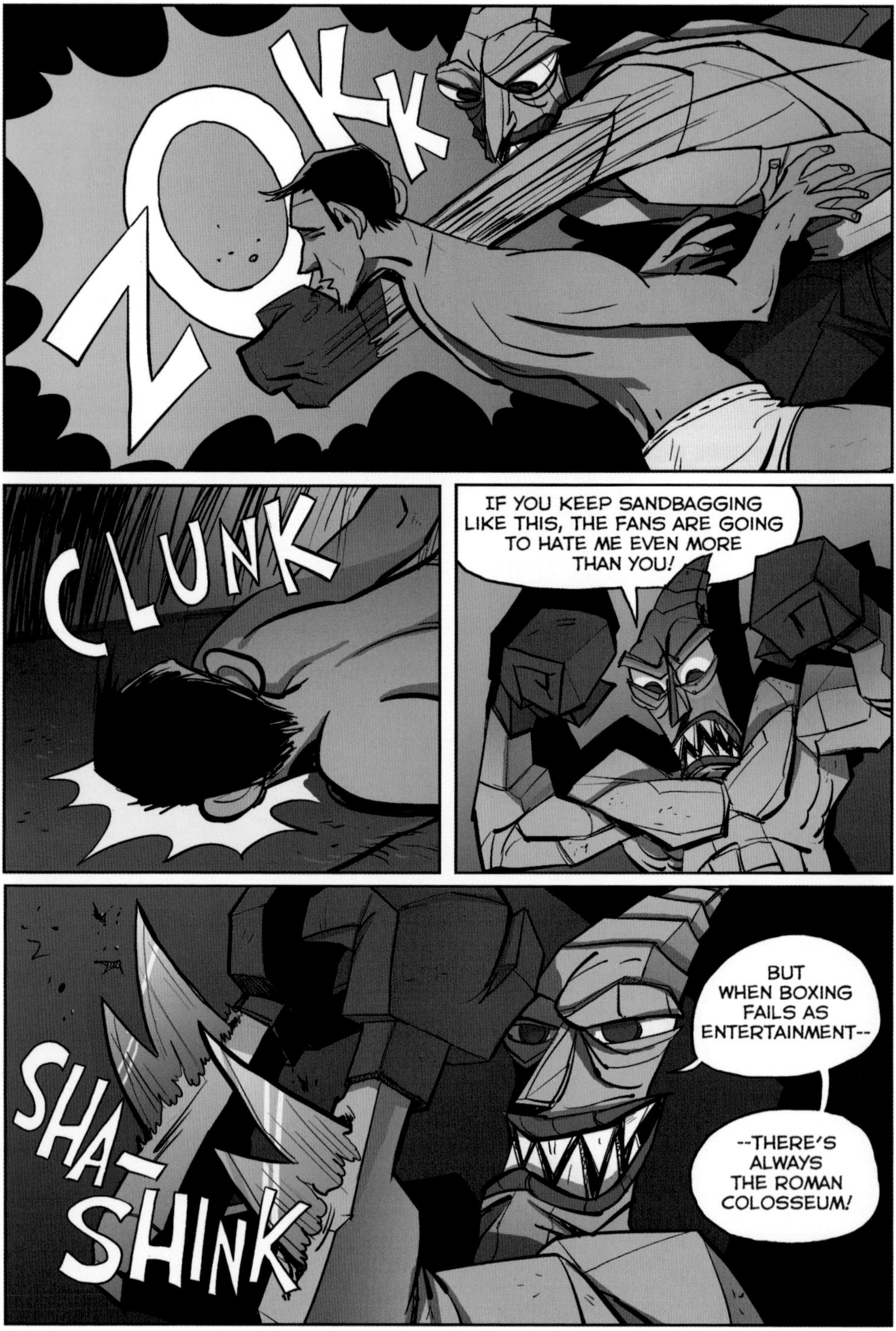
ZOKK
CLUNK
IF YOU KEEP SANDBAGGING LIKE THIS, THE FANS ARE GOING TO HATE ME EVEN MORE THAN YOU!
SHA-SHINK
BUT WHEN BOXING FAILS AS ENTERTAINMENT--
--THERE'S ALWAYS THE ROMAN COLOSSEUM!

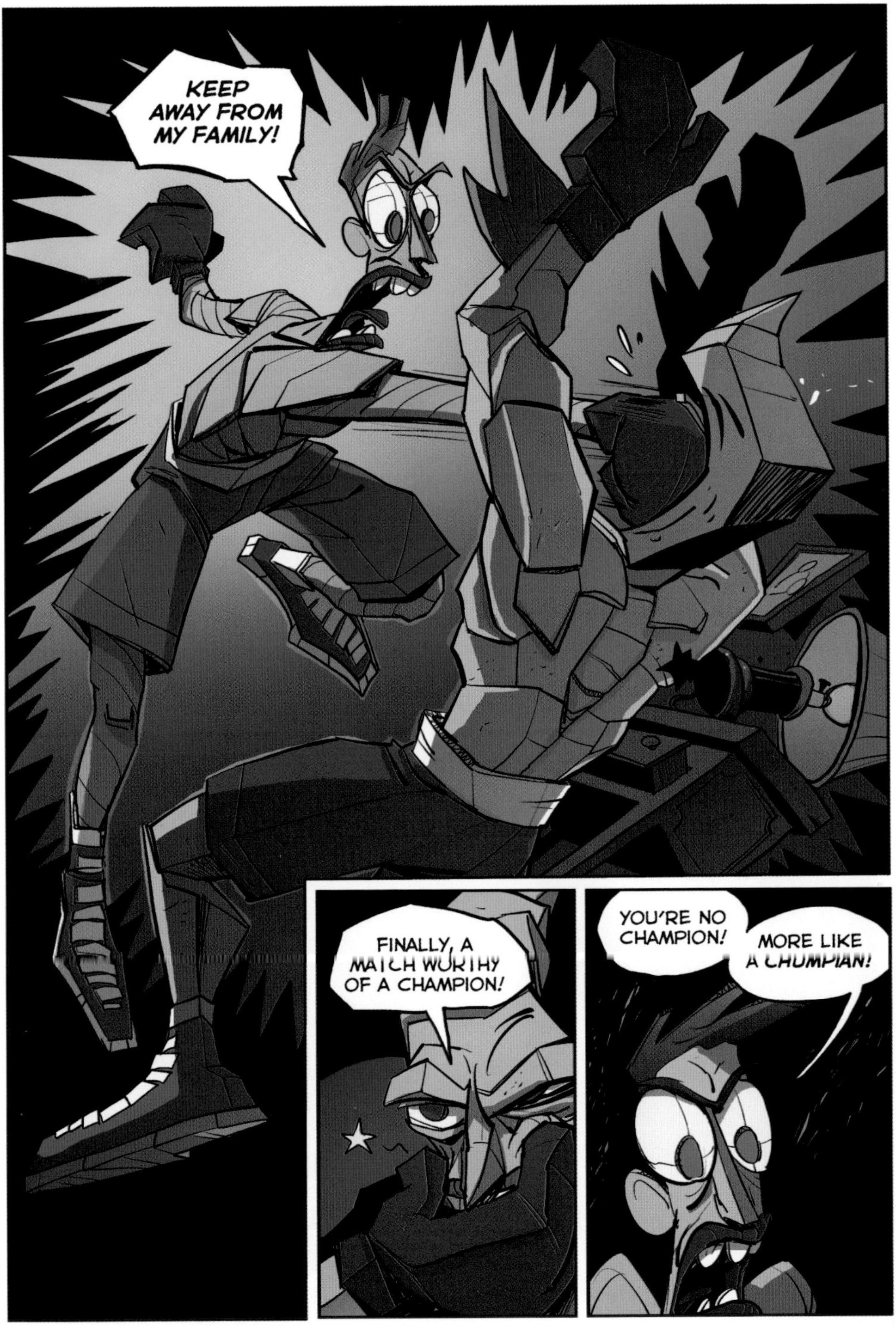
KEEP AWAY FROM MY FAMILY!
FINALLY, A MATCH WORTHY OF A CHAMPION!
YOU'RE NO CHAMPION!
MORE LIKE A CHUMPIAN!

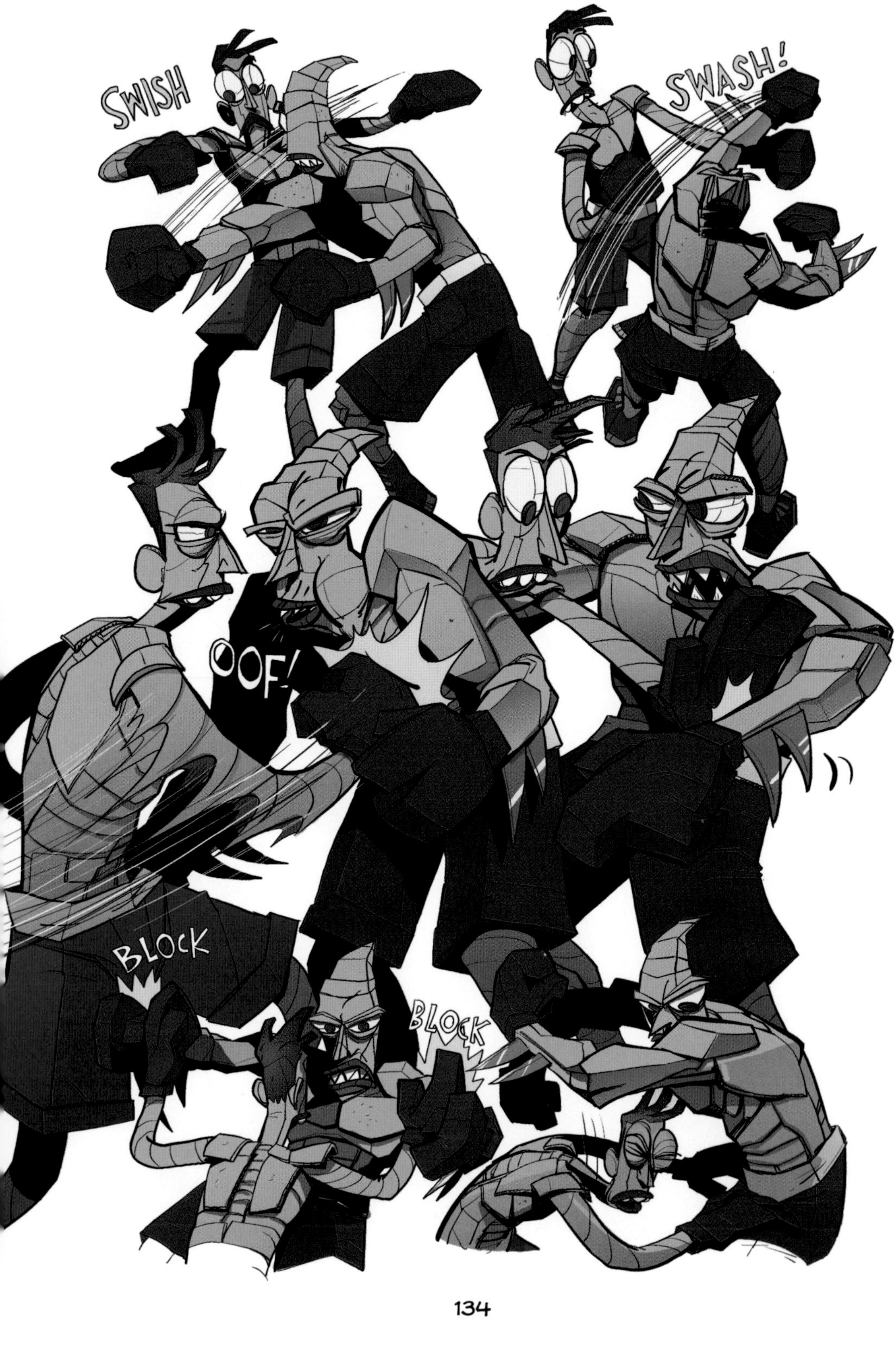
SWISH
SWASH!
OOF!
BLOCK
BLOCK

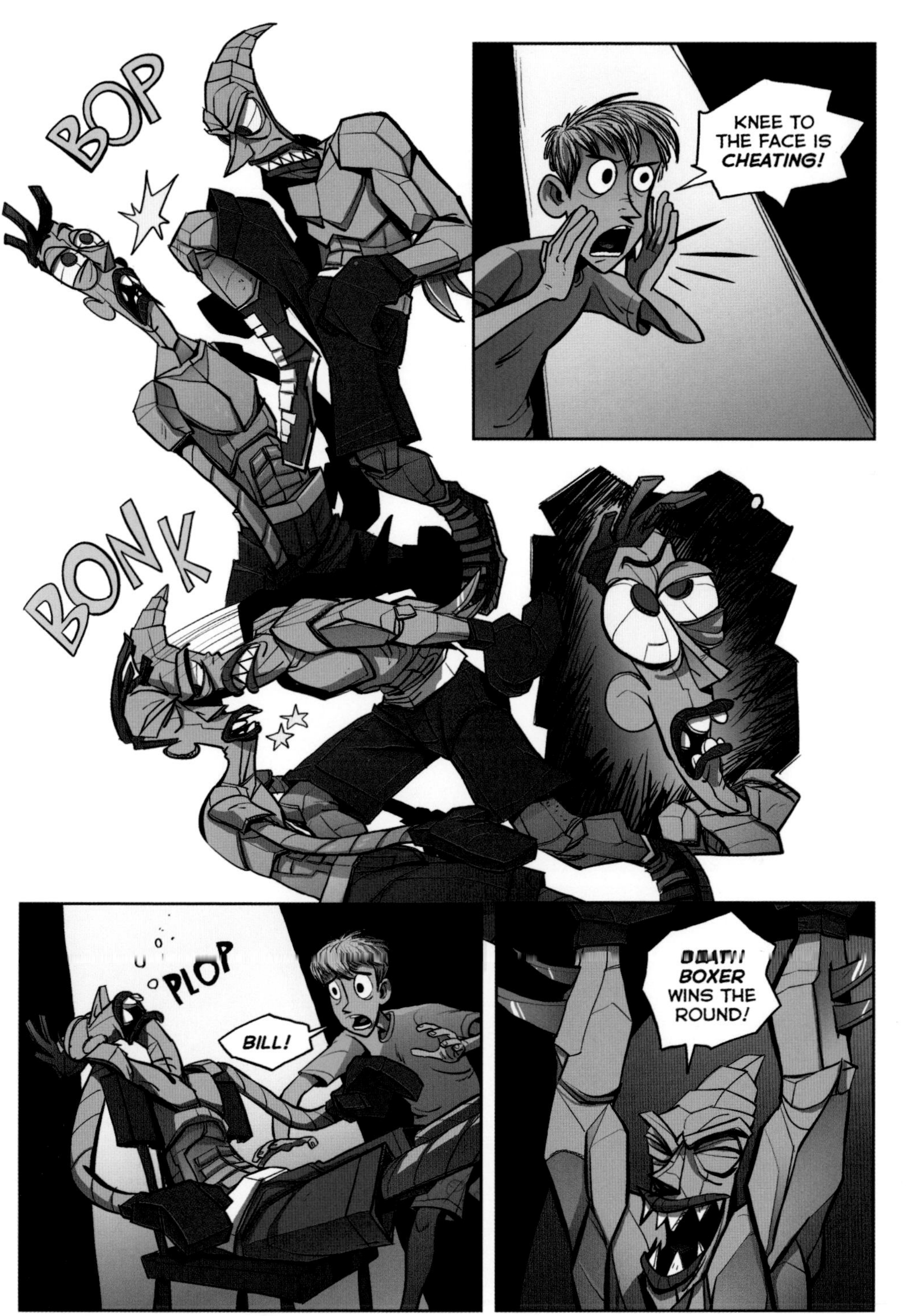
BOP
KNEE TO THE FACE IS CHEATING!
BONK
PLOP
BILL!
BOXER WINS THE ROUND!

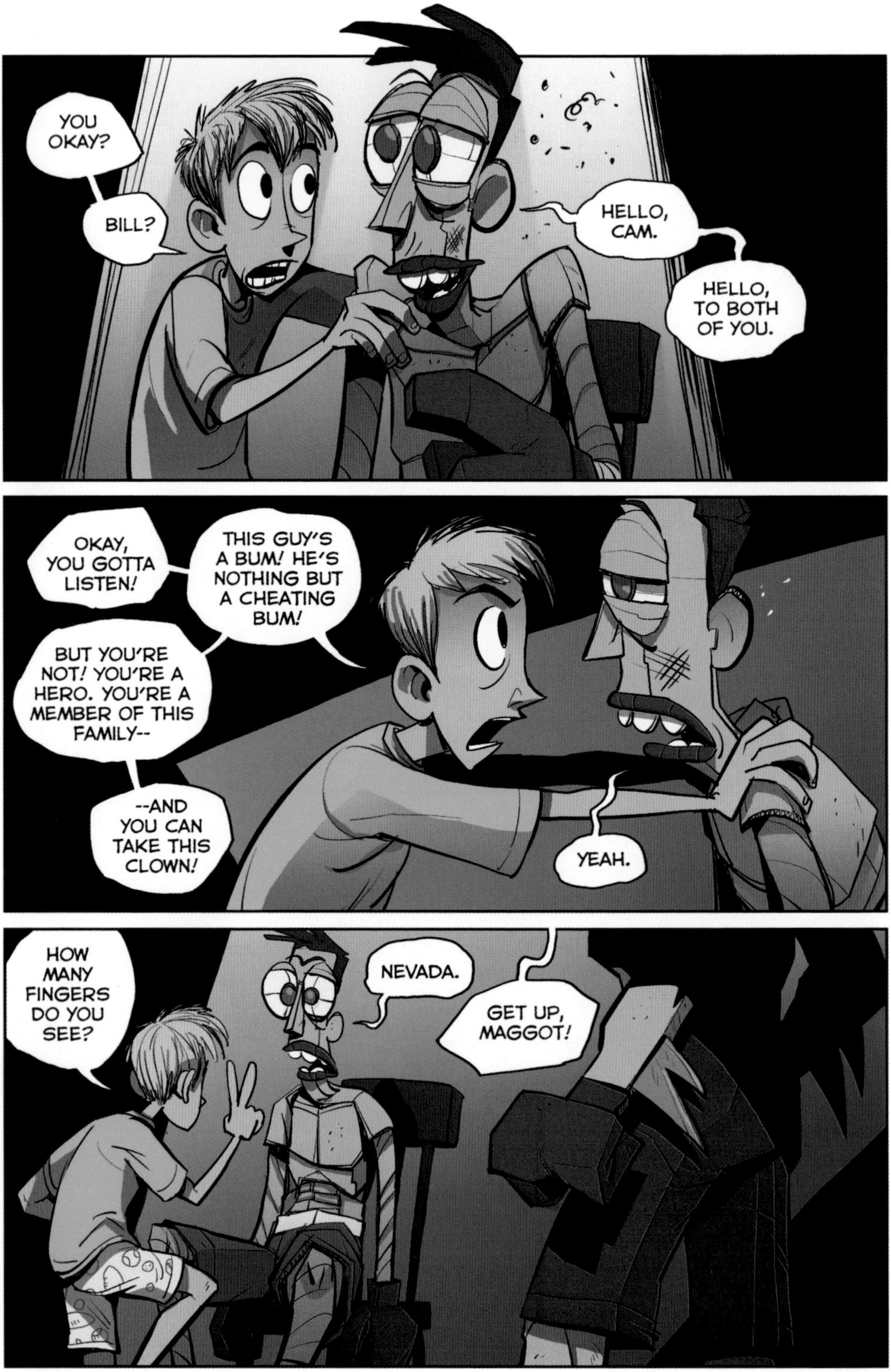
YOU OKAY?
BILL?
HELLO, CAM.
HELLO, TO BOTH OF YOU.
OKAY, YOU GOTTA LISTEN!
THIS GUY'S A BUM! HE'S NOTHING BUT A CHEATING BUM!
BUT YOU'RE NOT! YOU'RE A HERO. YOU'RE A MEMBER OF THIS FAMILY--
--AND YOU CAN TAKE THIS CLOWN!
YEAH.
HOW MANY FINGERS DO YOU SEE?
NEVADA.
GET UP, MAGGOT!

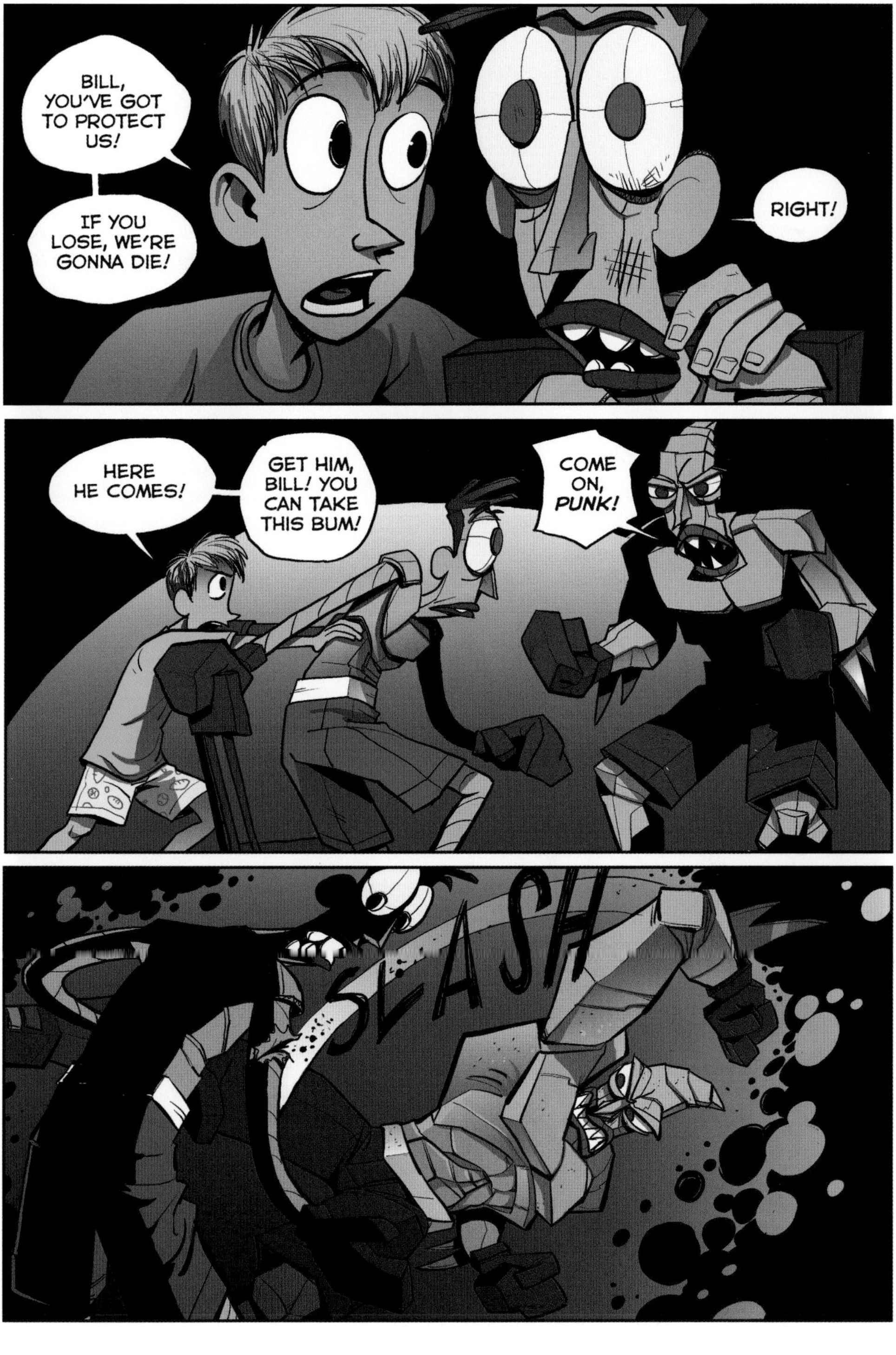
BILL, YOU'VE GOT TO PROTECT US!
IF YOU LOSE, WE'RE GONNA DIE!
RIGHT!
HERE HE COMES!
GET HIM, BILL! YOU CAN TAKE THIS BUM!
COME ON, PUNK!
SLASH

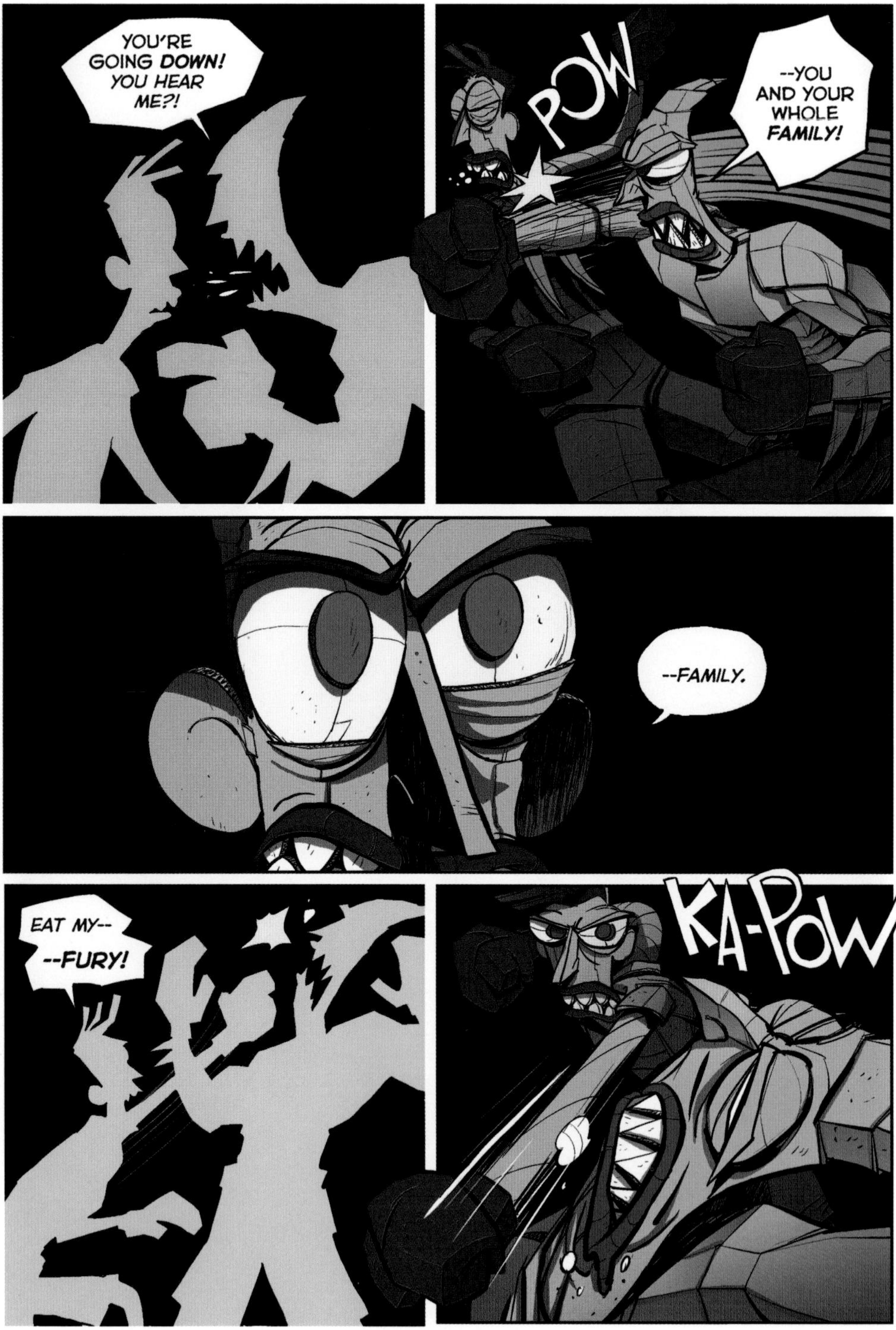
YOU'RE GOING DOWN! YOU HEAR ME?!
POW
--YOU AND YOUR WHOLE FAMILY!
--FAMILY.
EAT MY--
--FURY!
KA-POW

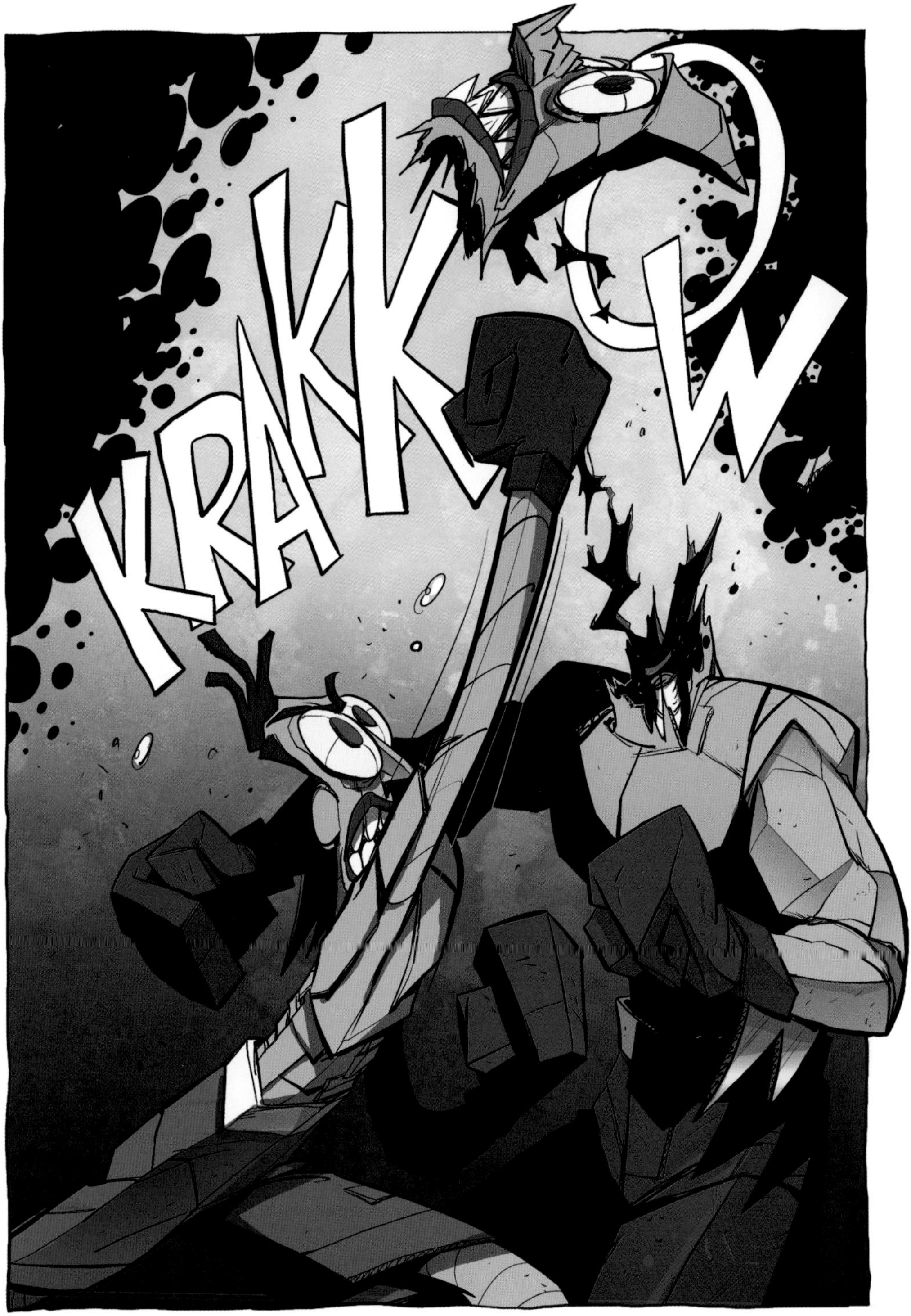
KRAKKOW

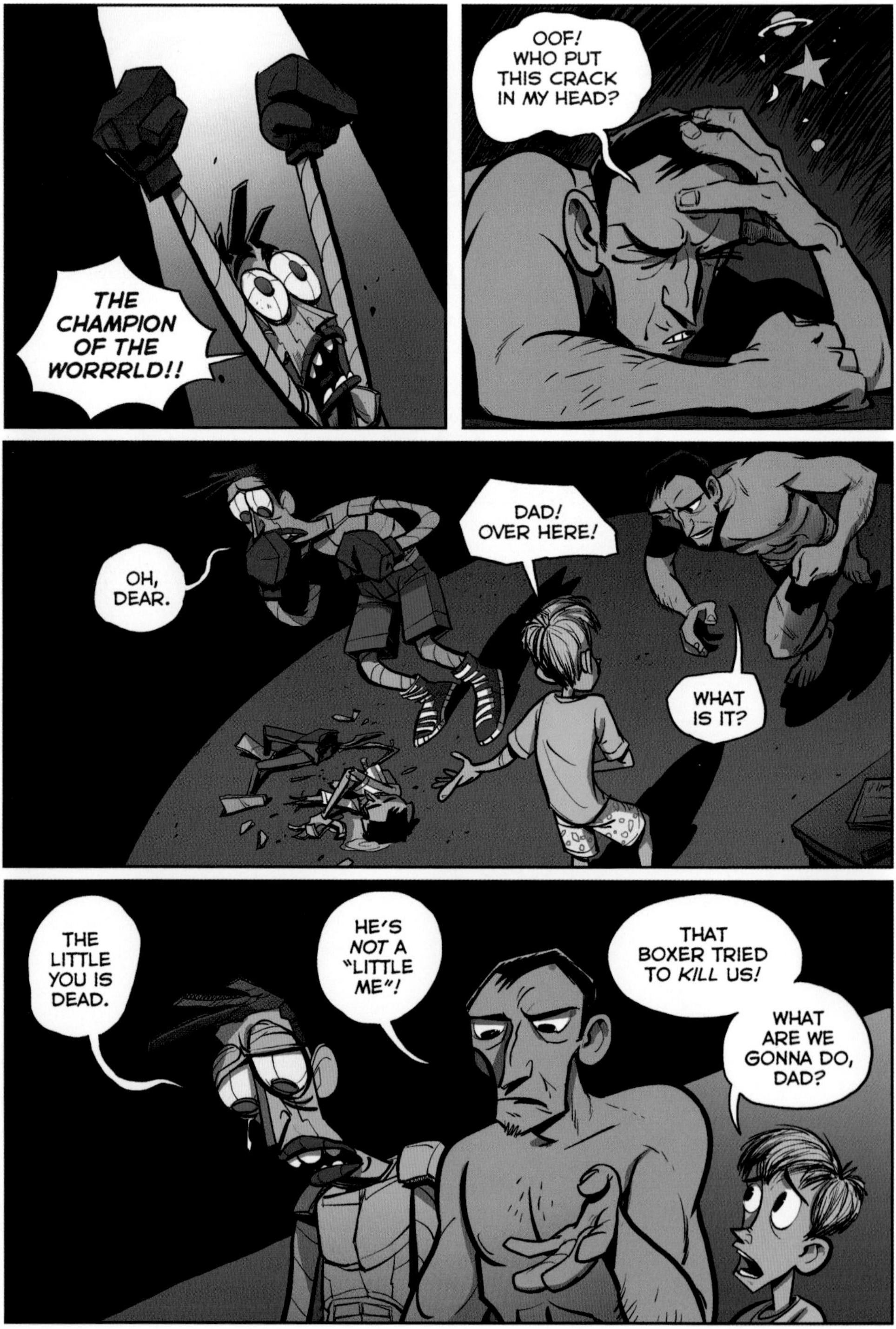
THE CHAMPION OF THE WORRRLD!!
OOF! WHO PUT THIS CRACK IN MY HEAD?
OH, DEAR.
DAD! OVER HERE!
WHAT IS IT?
THE LITTLE YOU IS DEAD.
HE'S *NOT* A "LITTLE ME"!
THAT BOXER TRIED TO *KILL* US!
WHAT ARE WE GONNA DO, DAD?

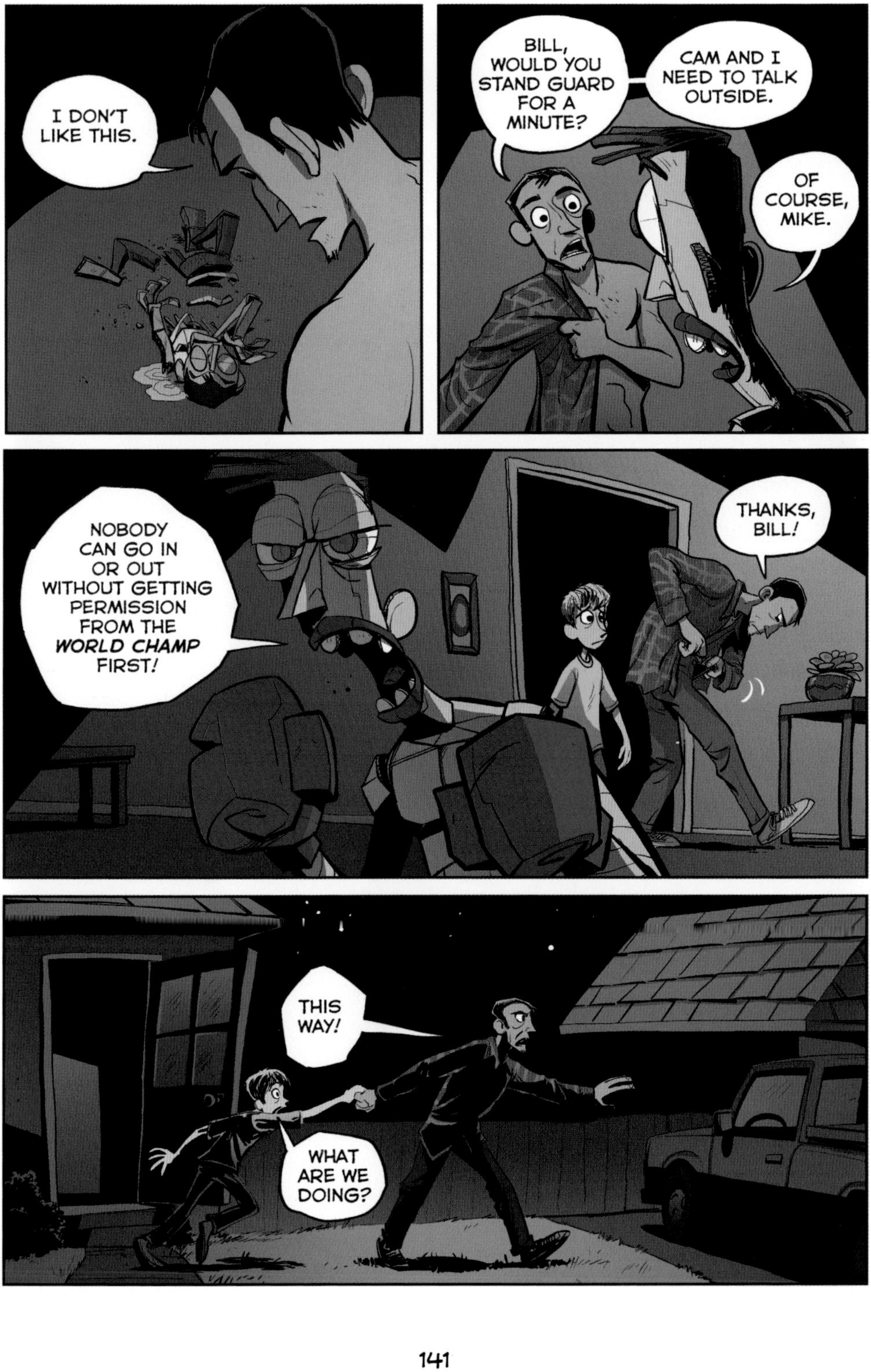
I DON'T LIKE THIS.
BILL, WOULD YOU STAND GUARD FOR A MINUTE?
CAM AND I NEED TO TALK OUTSIDE.
OF COURSE, MIKE.
NOBODY CAN GO IN OR OUT WITHOUT GETTING PERMISSION FROM THE *WORLD CHAMP* FIRST!
THANKS, BILL!
THIS WAY!
WHAT ARE WE DOING?

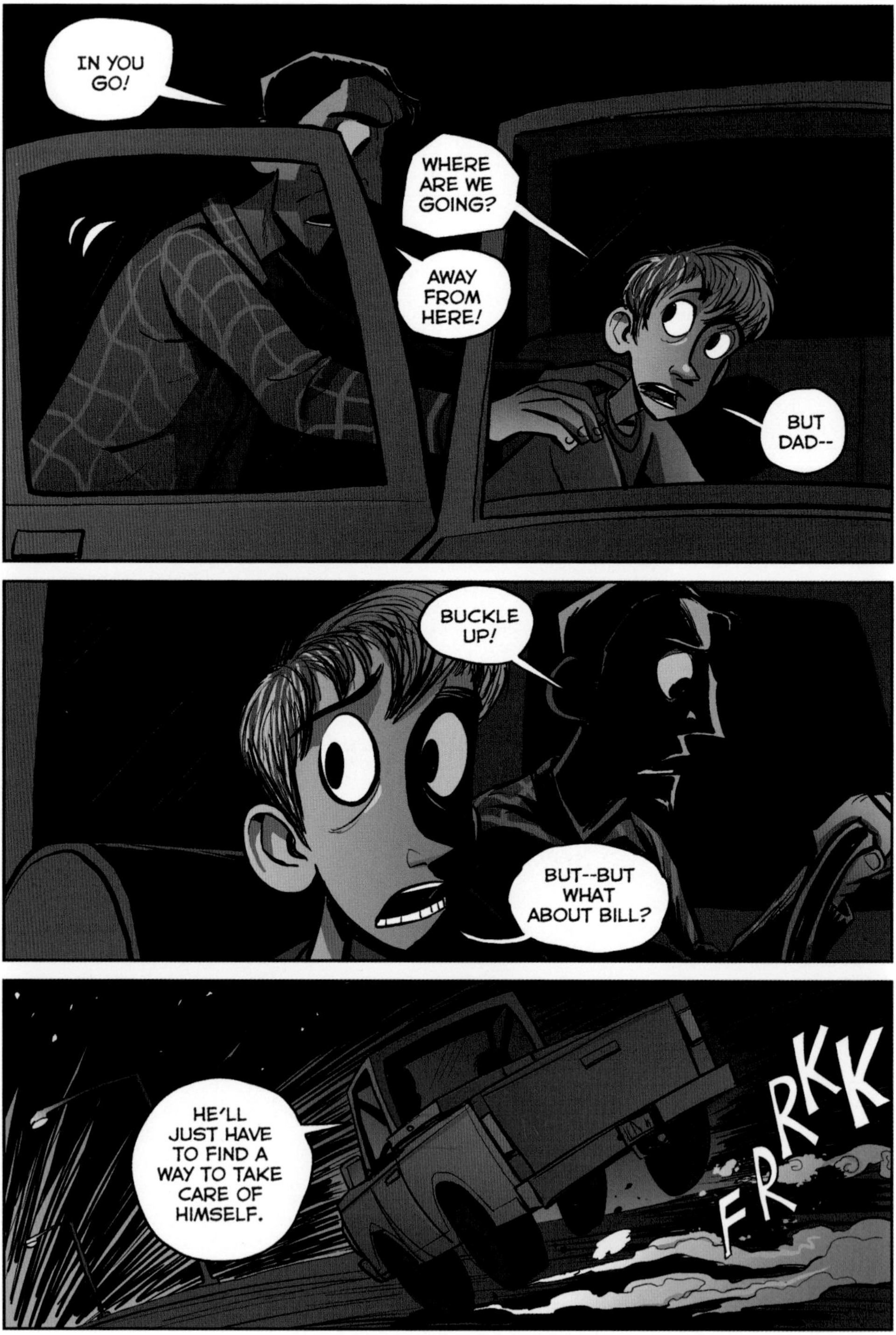
IN YOU GO!
WHERE ARE WE GOING?
AWAY FROM HERE!
BUT DAD--
BUCKLE UP!
BUT--BUT WHAT ABOUT BILL?
HE'LL JUST HAVE TO FIND A WAY TO TAKE CARE OF HIMSELF.
FRRKK

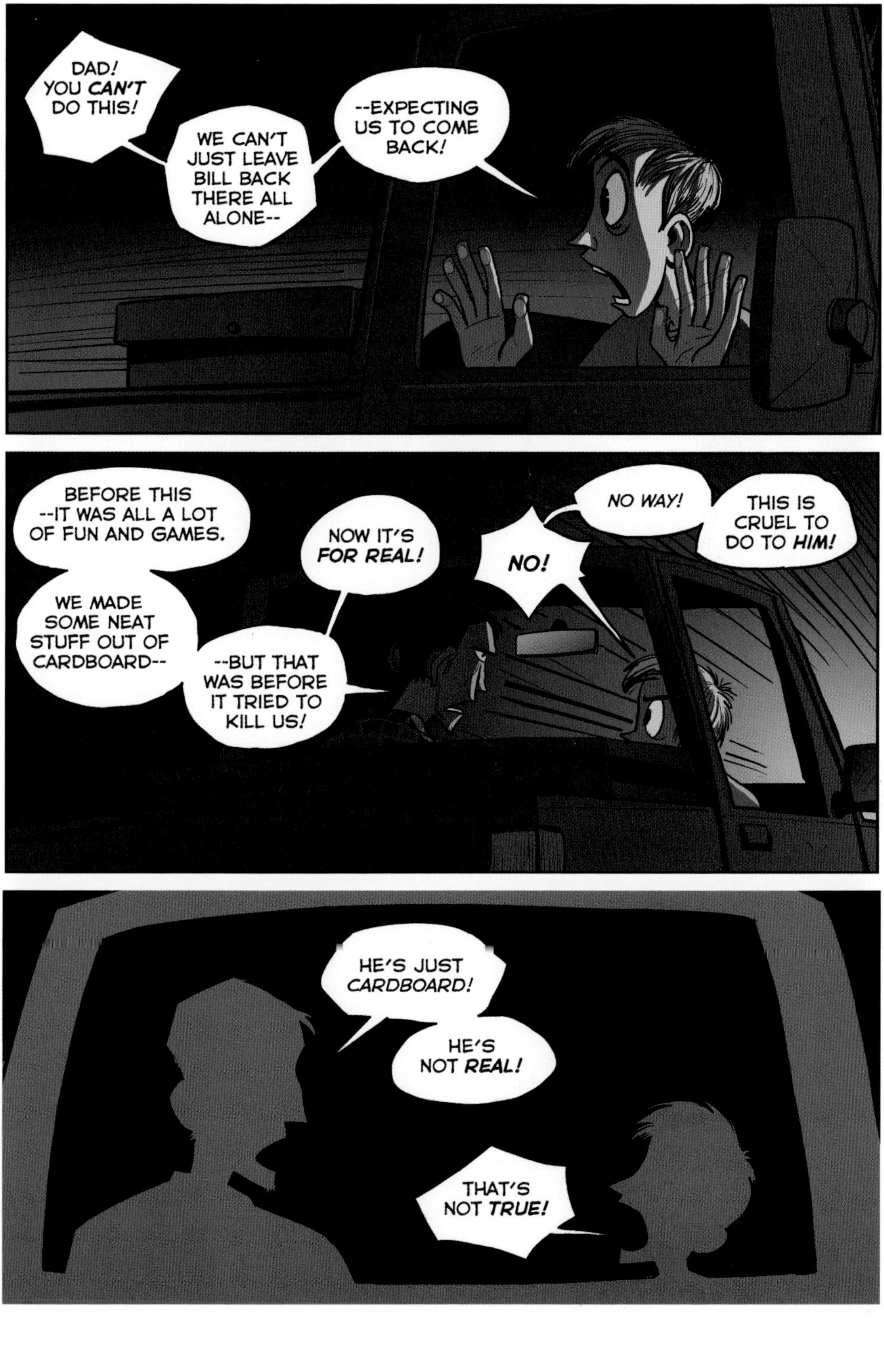
DAD! YOU CAN'T DO THIS!
WE CAN'T JUST LEAVE BILL BACK THERE ALL ALONE--
--EXPECTING US TO COME BACK!
BEFORE THIS --IT WAS ALL A LOT OF FUN AND GAMES.
WE MADE SOME NEAT STUFF OUT OF CARDBOARD--
NOW IT'S FOR REAL!
--BUT THAT WAS BEFORE IT TRIED TO KILL US!
NO!
NO WAY!
THIS IS CRUEL TO DO TO HIM!
HE'S JUST CARDBOARD!
HE'S NOT REAL!
THAT'S NOT TRUE!

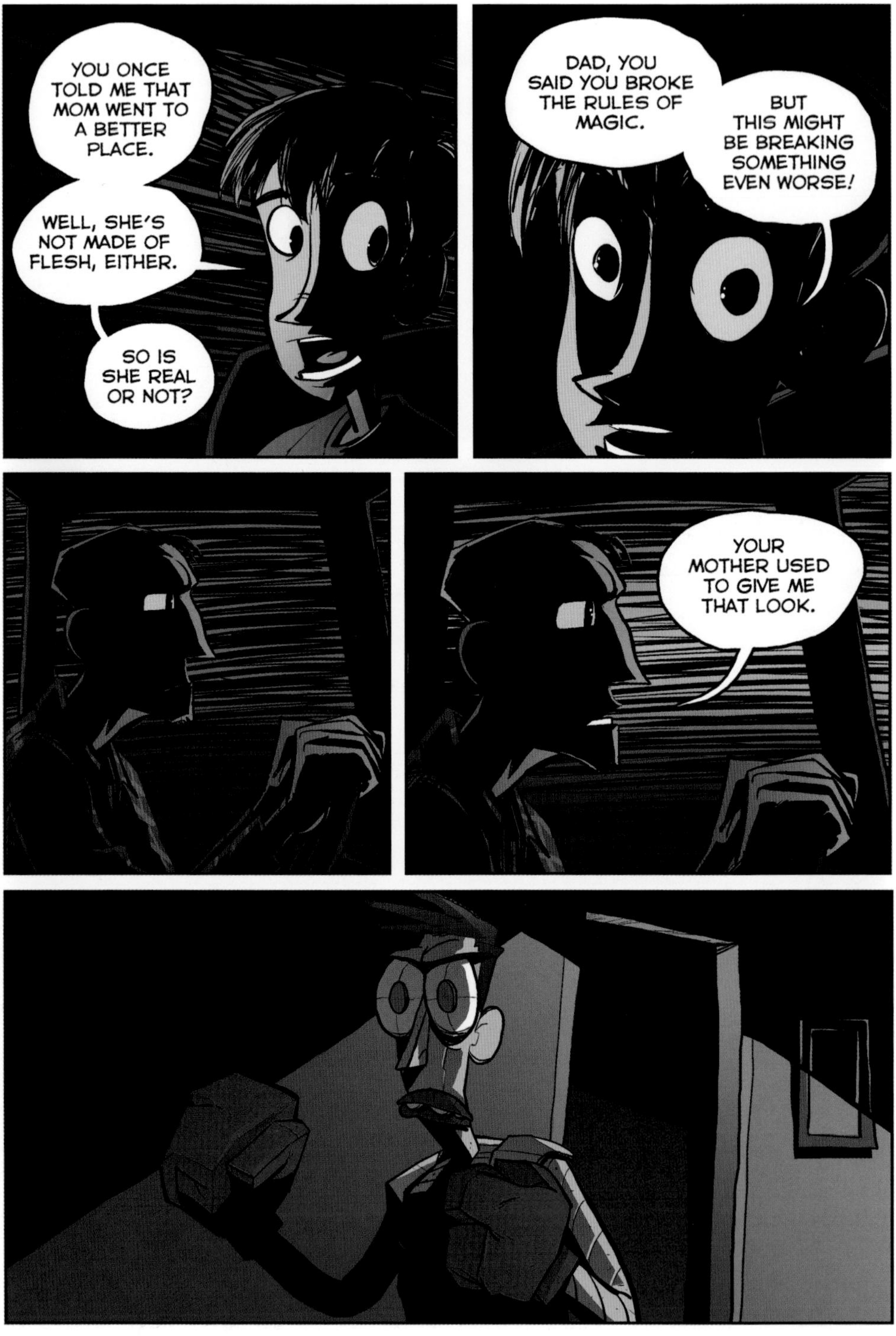
YOU ONCE TOLD ME THAT MOM WENT TO A BETTER PLACE.
WELL, SHE'S NOT MADE OF FLESH, EITHER.
SO IS SHE REAL OR NOT?
DAD, YOU SAID YOU BROKE THE RULES OF MAGIC.
BUT THIS MIGHT BE BREAKING SOMETHING EVEN WORSE!
YOUR MOTHER USED TO GIVE ME THAT LOOK.

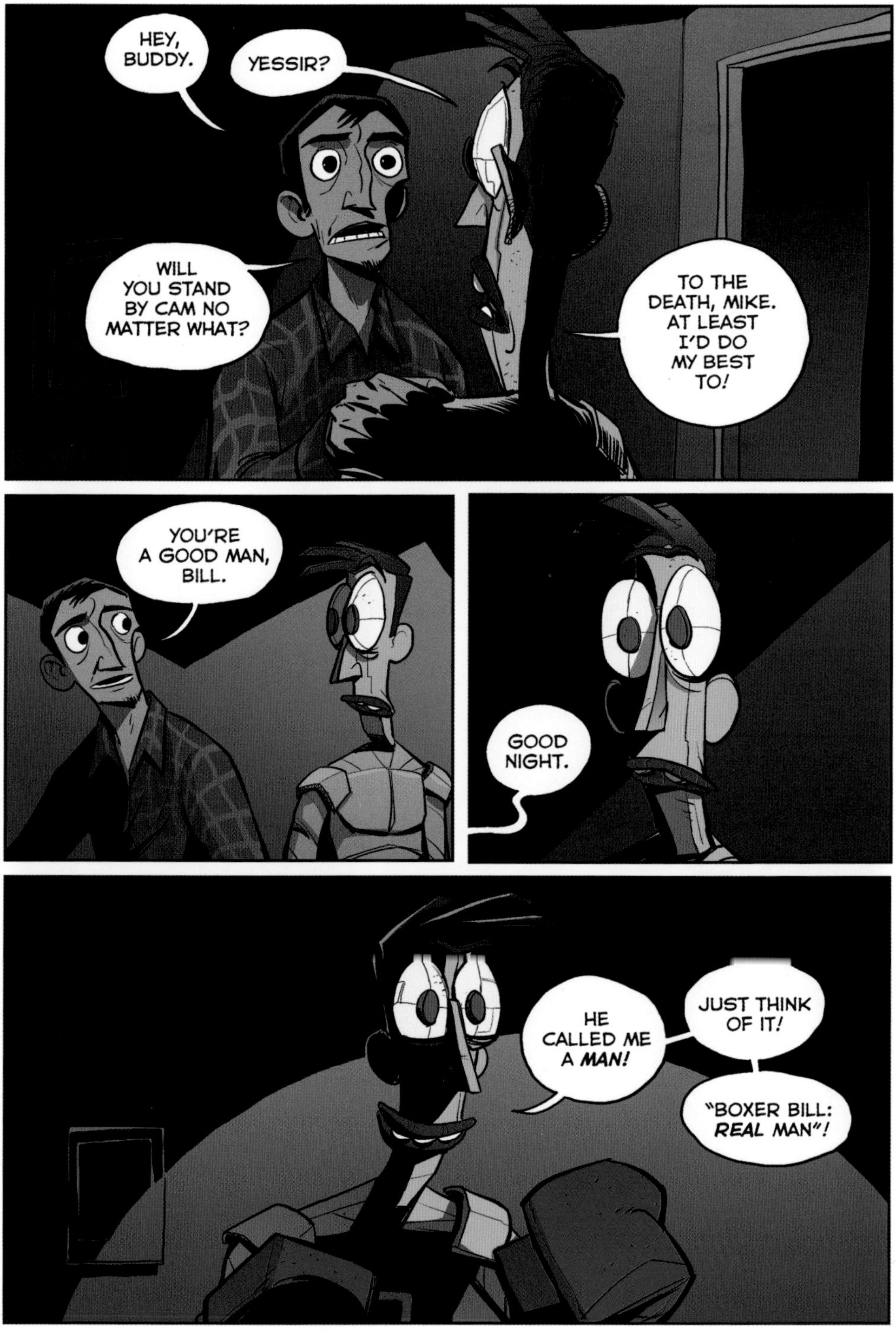
HEY, BUDDY.
YESSIR?
WILL YOU STAND BY CAM NO MATTER WHAT?
TO THE DEATH, MIKE. AT LEAST I'D DO MY BEST TO!
YOU'RE A GOOD MAN, BILL.
GOOD NIGHT.
HE CALLED ME A *MAN!*
JUST THINK OF IT!
"BOXER BILL: *REAL* MAN"!

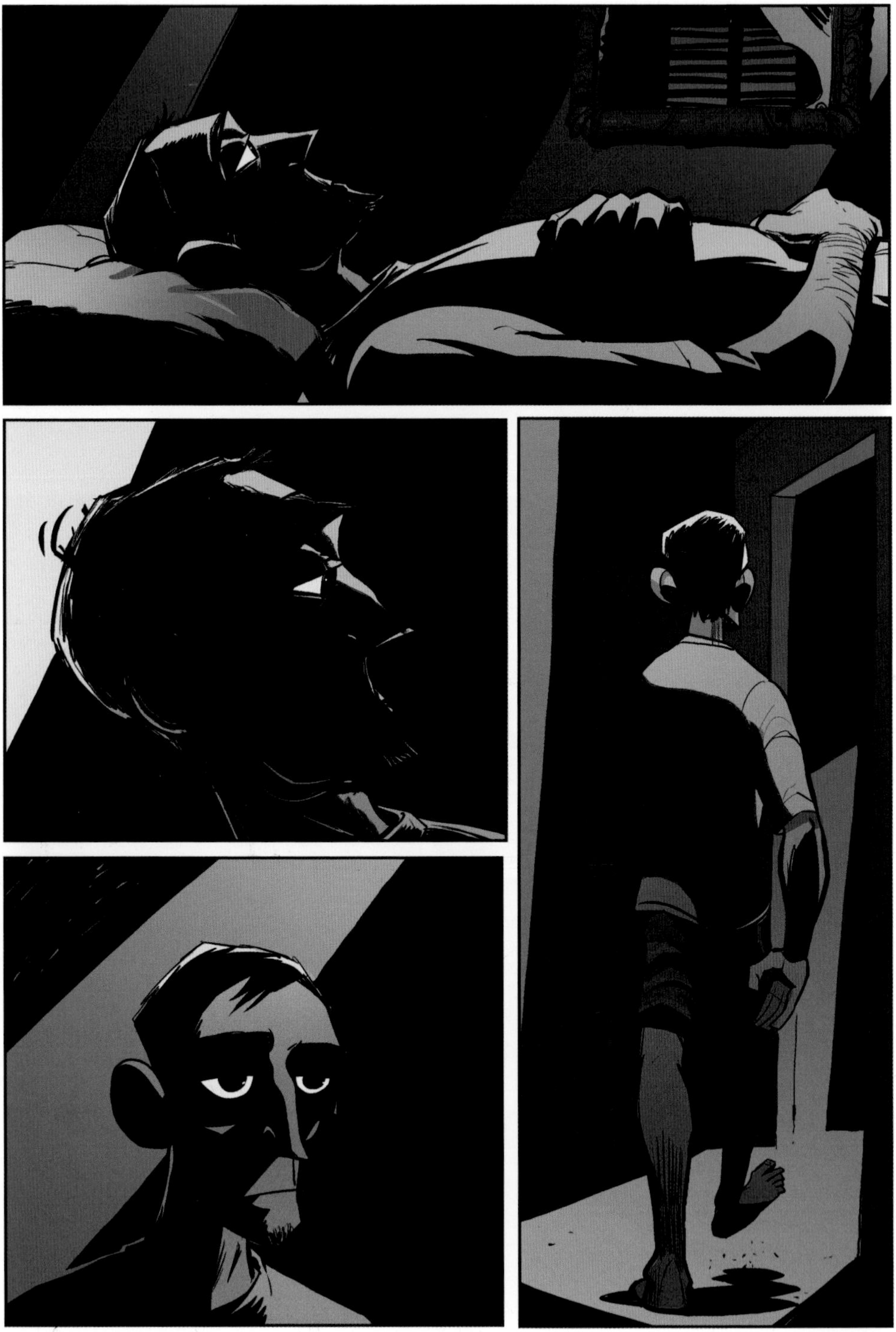

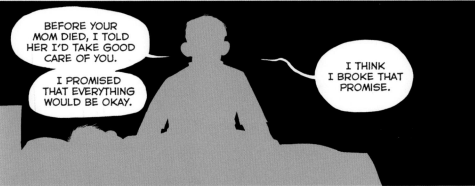

BEFORE YOUR MOM DIED, I TOLD HER I'D TAKE GOOD CARE OF YOU.

I PROMISED THAT EVERYTHING WOULD BE OKAY.

I THINK I BROKE THAT PROMISE.

YOU'RE ASLEEP SO I CAN TELL YOU MY SECRET-- I DONT KNOW ANYTHING ABOUT HOW TO BE A FATHER.

I ALWAYS THOUGHT I WAS JUST BORN TO SWING A HAMMER. IT'S THE ONLY THING I'M REALLY GOOD AT.

BUT WHAT AM I SUPPOSED TO DO WHEN NOBODY IN THE STATE NEEDS THE ONLY THING I'M GOOD AT?

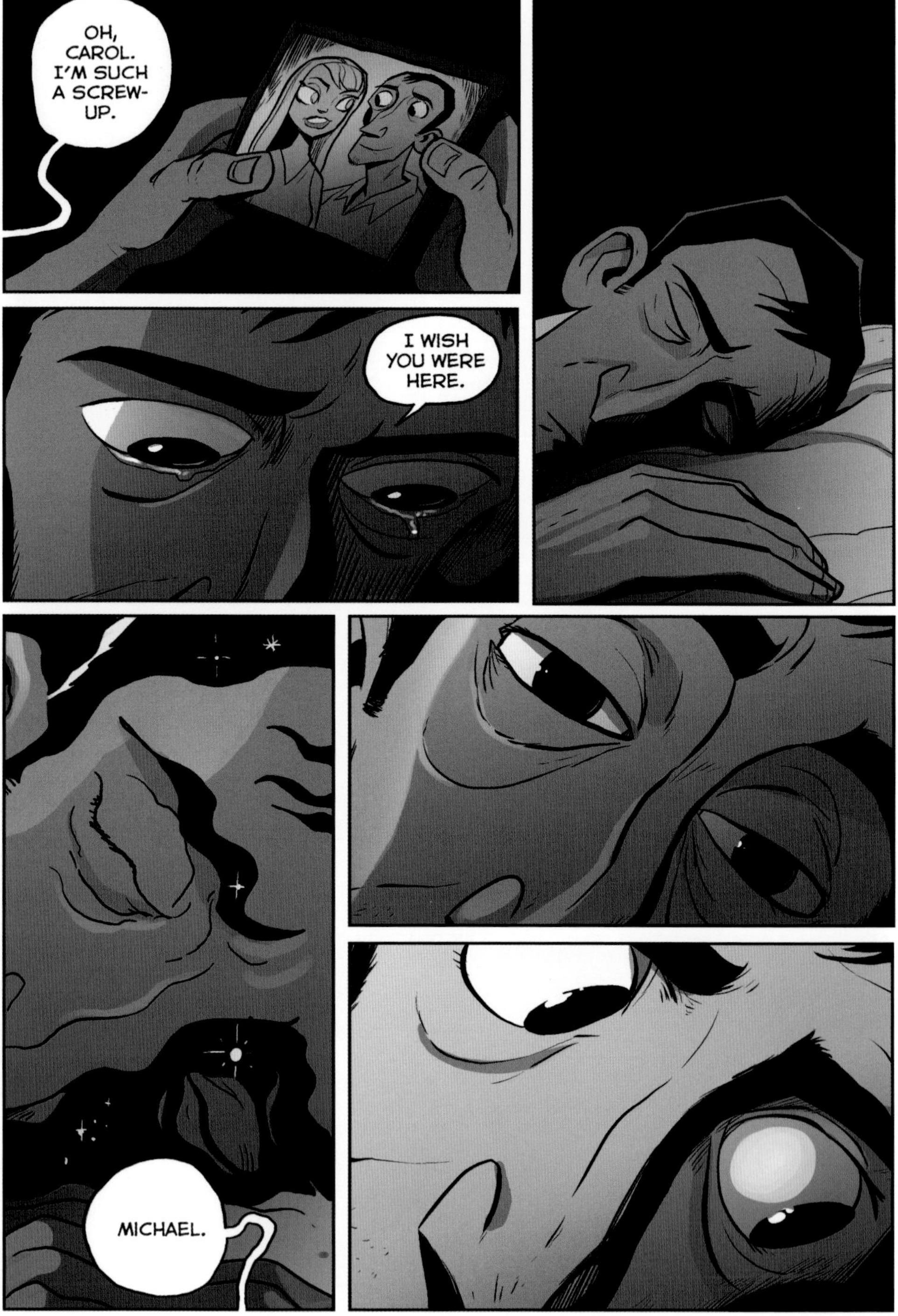
OH, CAROL. I'M SUCH A SCREW-UP.
I WISH YOU WERE HERE.
MICHAEL.

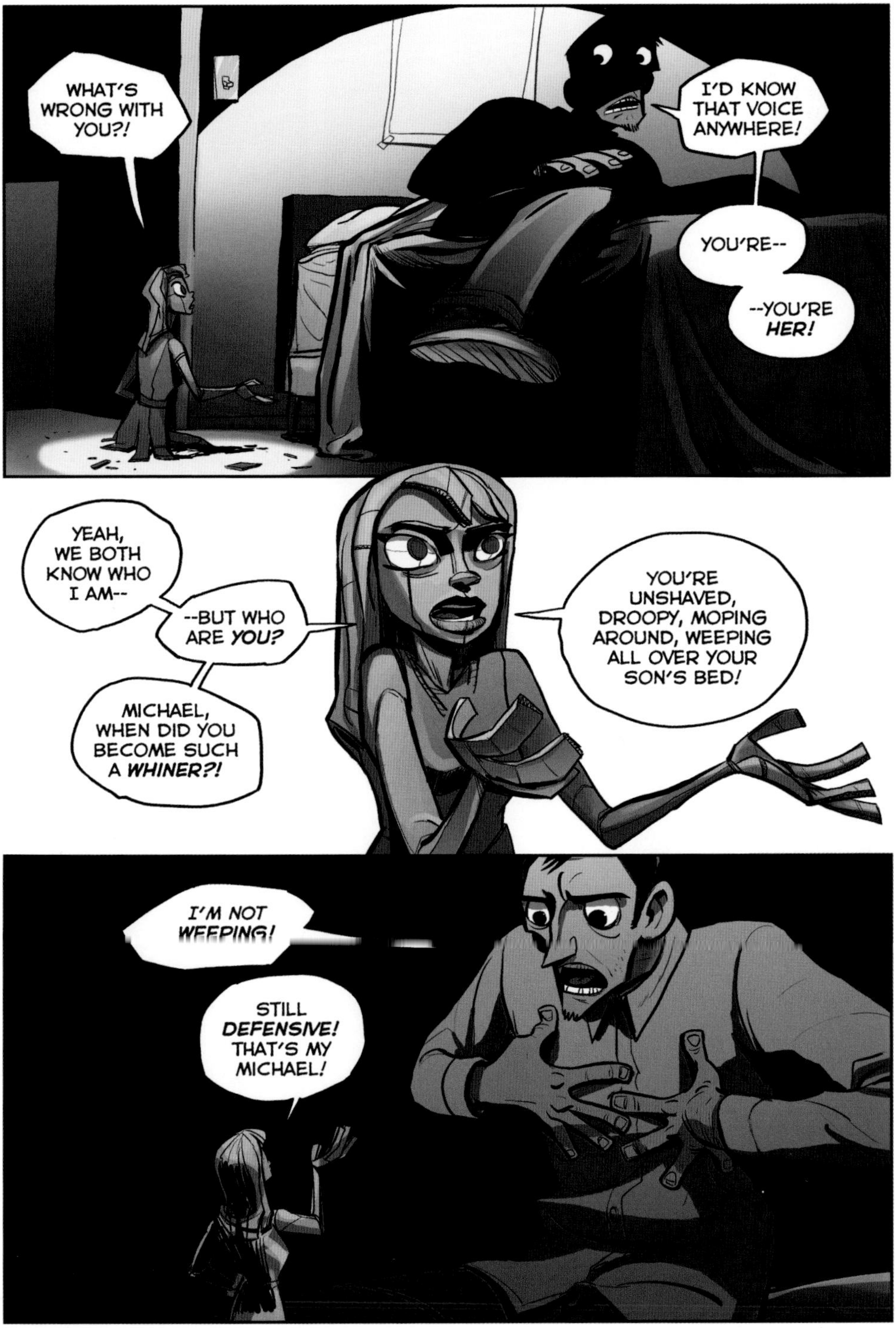
WHAT'S WRONG WITH YOU?!
I'D KNOW THAT VOICE ANYWHERE!
YOU'RE--
--YOU'RE HER!
YEAH, WE BOTH KNOW WHO I AM--
--BUT WHO ARE YOU?
MICHAEL, WHEN DID YOU BECOME SUCH A WHINER?!
YOU'RE UNSHAVED, DROOPY, MOPING AROUND, WEEPING ALL OVER YOUR SON'S BED!
I'M NOT WEEPING!
STILL DEFENSIVE! THAT'S MY MICHAEL!

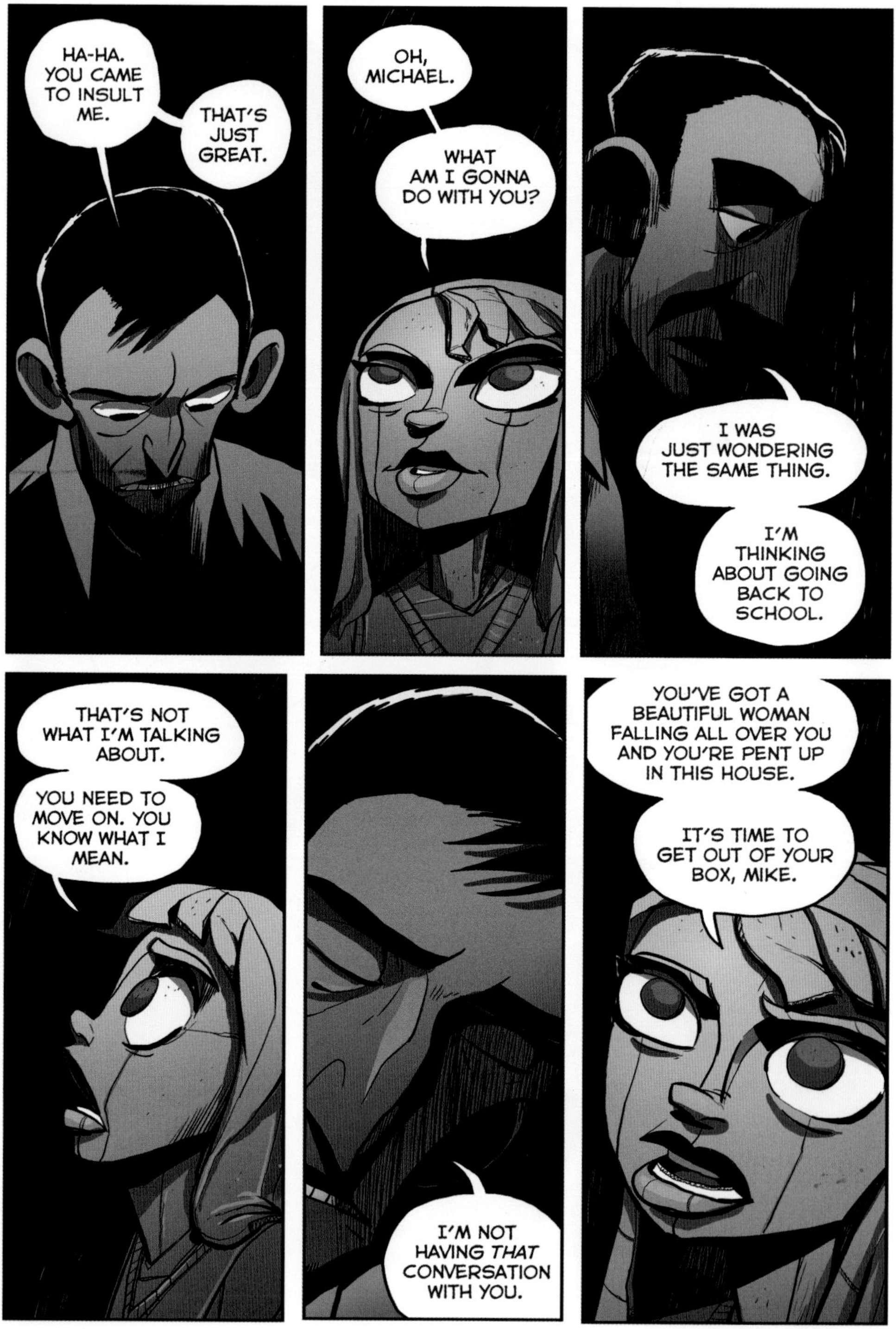
HA-HA. YOU CAME TO INSULT ME.
THAT'S JUST GREAT.
OH, MICHAEL.
WHAT AM I GONNA DO WITH YOU?
I WAS JUST WONDERING THE SAME THING.
I'M THINKING ABOUT GOING BACK TO SCHOOL.
THAT'S NOT WHAT I'M TALKING ABOUT.
YOU NEED TO MOVE ON. YOU KNOW WHAT I MEAN.
I'M NOT HAVING *THAT* CONVERSATION WITH YOU.
YOU'VE GOT A BEAUTIFUL WOMAN FALLING ALL OVER YOU AND YOU'RE PENT UP IN THIS HOUSE.
IT'S TIME TO GET OUT OF YOUR BOX, MIKE.

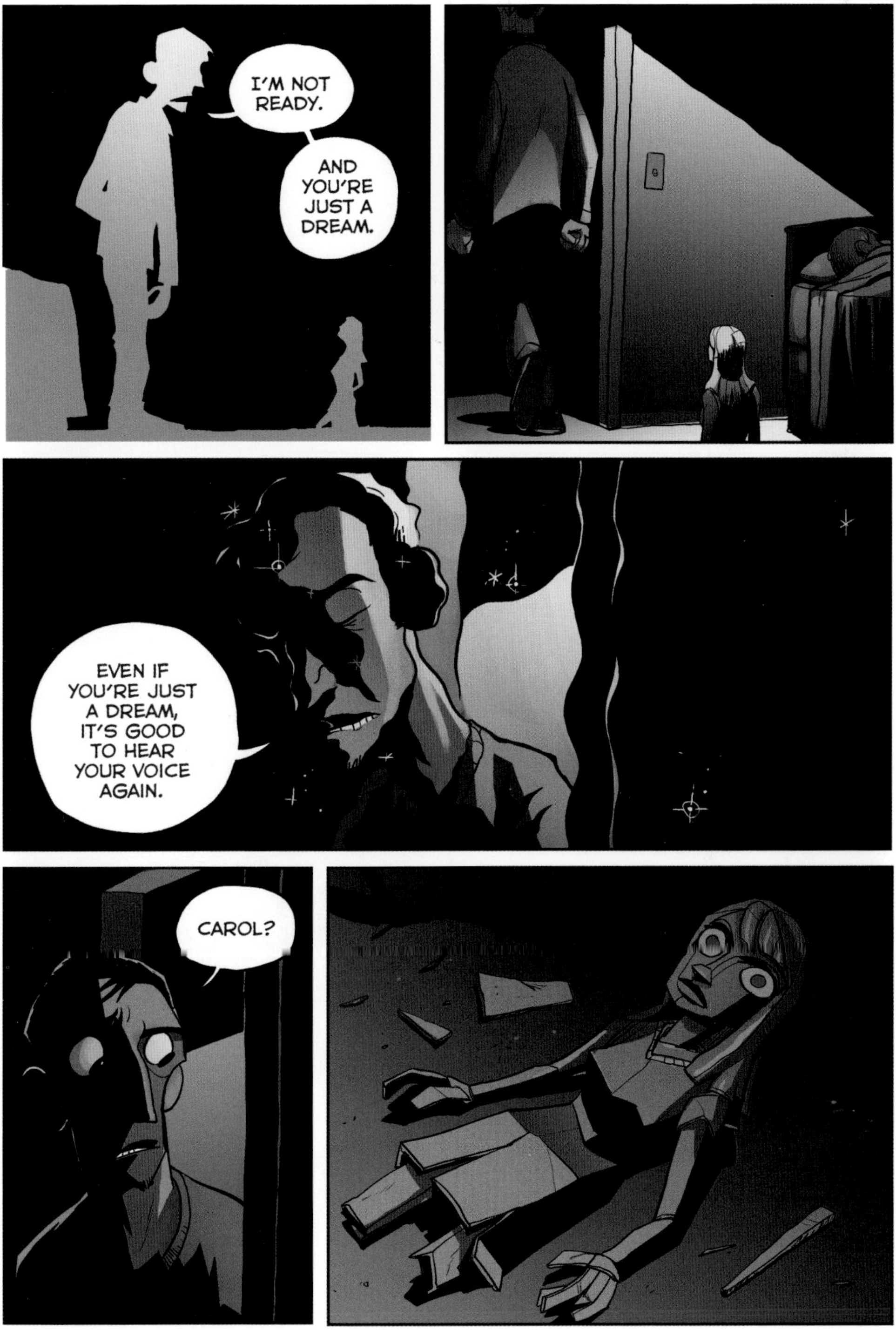
I'M NOT READY.
AND YOU'RE JUST A DREAM.
EVEN IF YOU'RE JUST A DREAM, IT'S GOOD TO HEAR YOUR VOICE AGAIN.
CAROL?

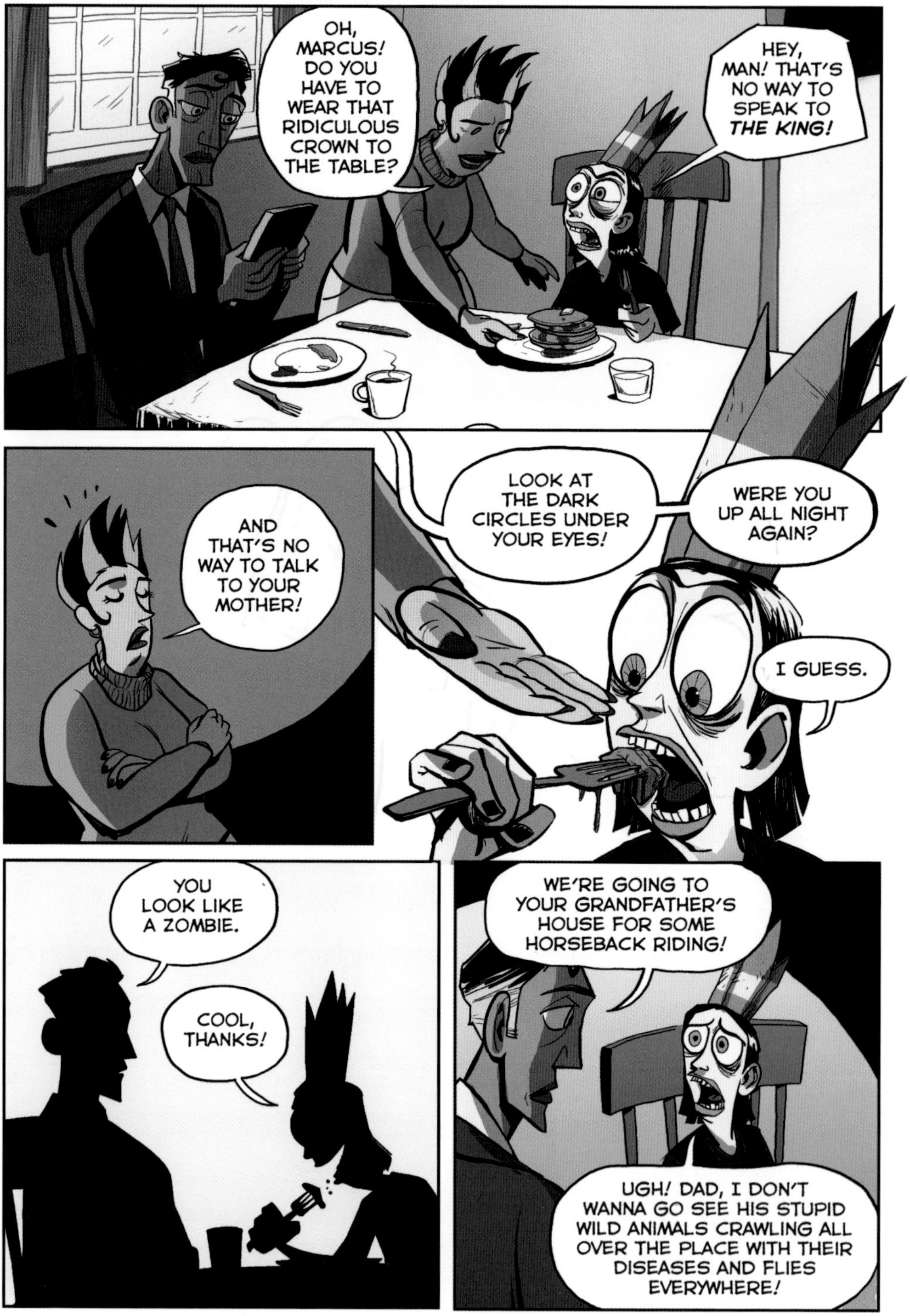
OH, MARCUS! DO YOU HAVE TO WEAR THAT RIDICULOUS CROWN TO THE TABLE?
HEY, MAN! THAT'S NO WAY TO SPEAK TO THE KING!
AND THAT'S NO WAY TO TALK TO YOUR MOTHER!
LOOK AT THE DARK CIRCLES UNDER YOUR EYES!
WERE YOU UP ALL NIGHT AGAIN?
I GUESS.
YOU LOOK LIKE A ZOMBIE.
COOL, THANKS!
WE'RE GOING TO YOUR GRANDFATHER'S HOUSE FOR SOME HORSEBACK RIDING!
UGH! DAD, I DON'T WANNA GO SEE HIS STUPID WILD ANIMALS CRAWLING ALL OVER THE PLACE WITH THEIR DISEASES AND FLIES EVERYWHERE!

BESIDES, NOW THAT HIS DIABETES IS RAGING, GRAMPA DOESN'T HAVE ANY ICE CREAM IN THE FRIDGE!

WHAT A *TERRIBLE* THING TO SAY!

SEE? THAT'S WHY I SHOULDN'T HAVE TO GO! BECAUSE I'M GOING TO EMBARRASS YOU WITH SOMETHING I'M GOING TO SAY!

HE'S GOT A POINT.

WHY CAN'T I JUST STAY HOME?

DAD, I'M ALMOST A MAN, AND IT'S ABOUT TIME YOU EXPANDED SOME OF MY RESPONSIBILITIES TO REFLECT THAT FACT.

I THINK YOU'RE RIGHT!

I AM?

I WAS ABOUT YOUR AGE WHEN MY PARENTS TRUSTED ME TO MAKE MORE OF MY OWN DECISIONS.

BUT YOU HAVE TO PROMISE THAT WHILE WE'RE GONE, YOU'LL EAT ONLY HEALTHY, ORGANIC FOODS AND KEEP THE MTV DOWN TO LESS THAN FOUR HOURS A NIGHT.

MMMMM, OKAY.

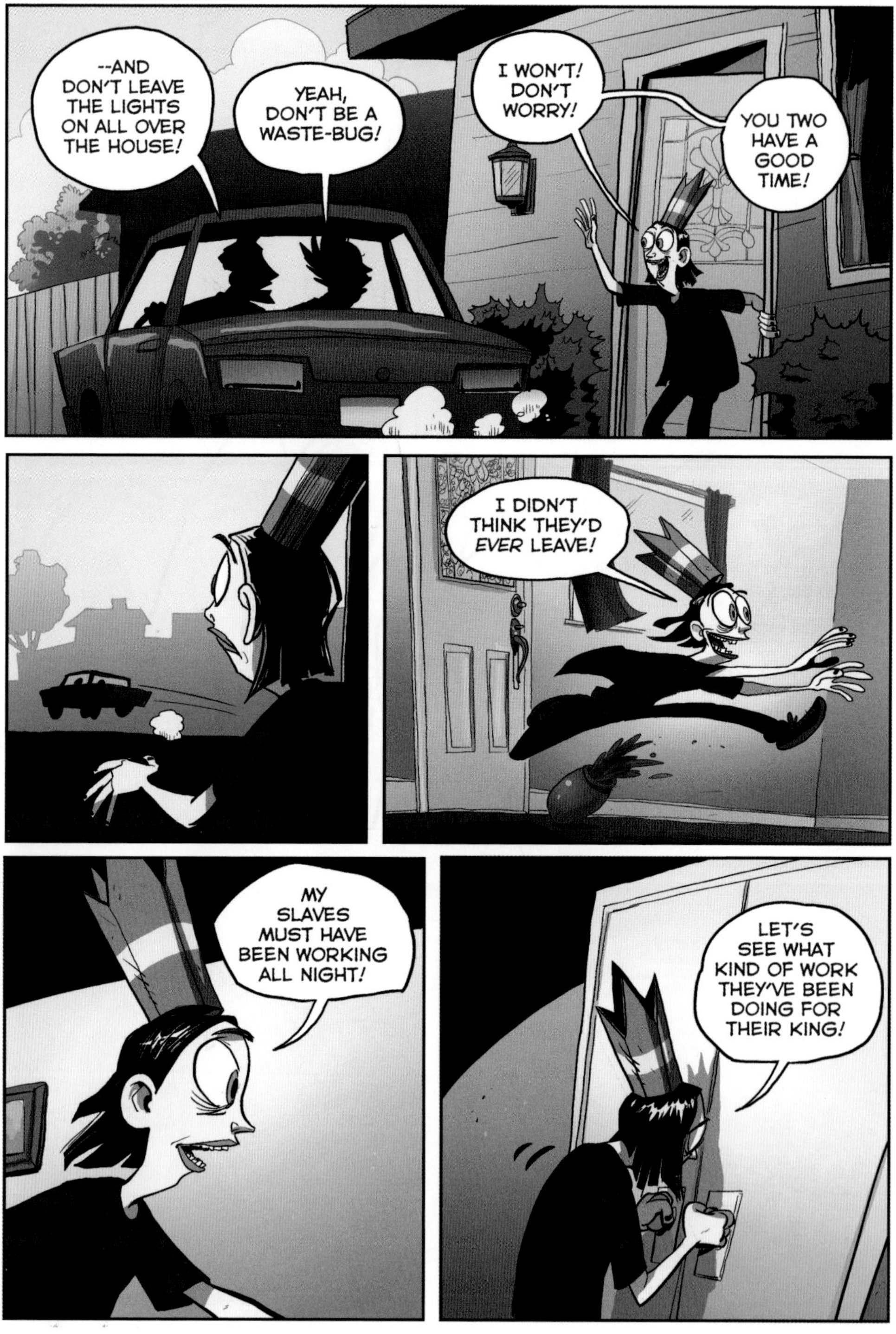
--AND DON'T LEAVE THE LIGHTS ON ALL OVER THE HOUSE!
YEAH, DON'T BE A WASTE-BUG!
I WON'T! DON'T WORRY!
YOU TWO HAVE A GOOD TIME!
I DIDN'T THINK THEY'D *EVER* LEAVE!
MY SLAVES MUST HAVE BEEN WORKING ALL NIGHT!
LET'S SEE WHAT KIND OF WORK THEY'VE BEEN DOING FOR THEIR KING!

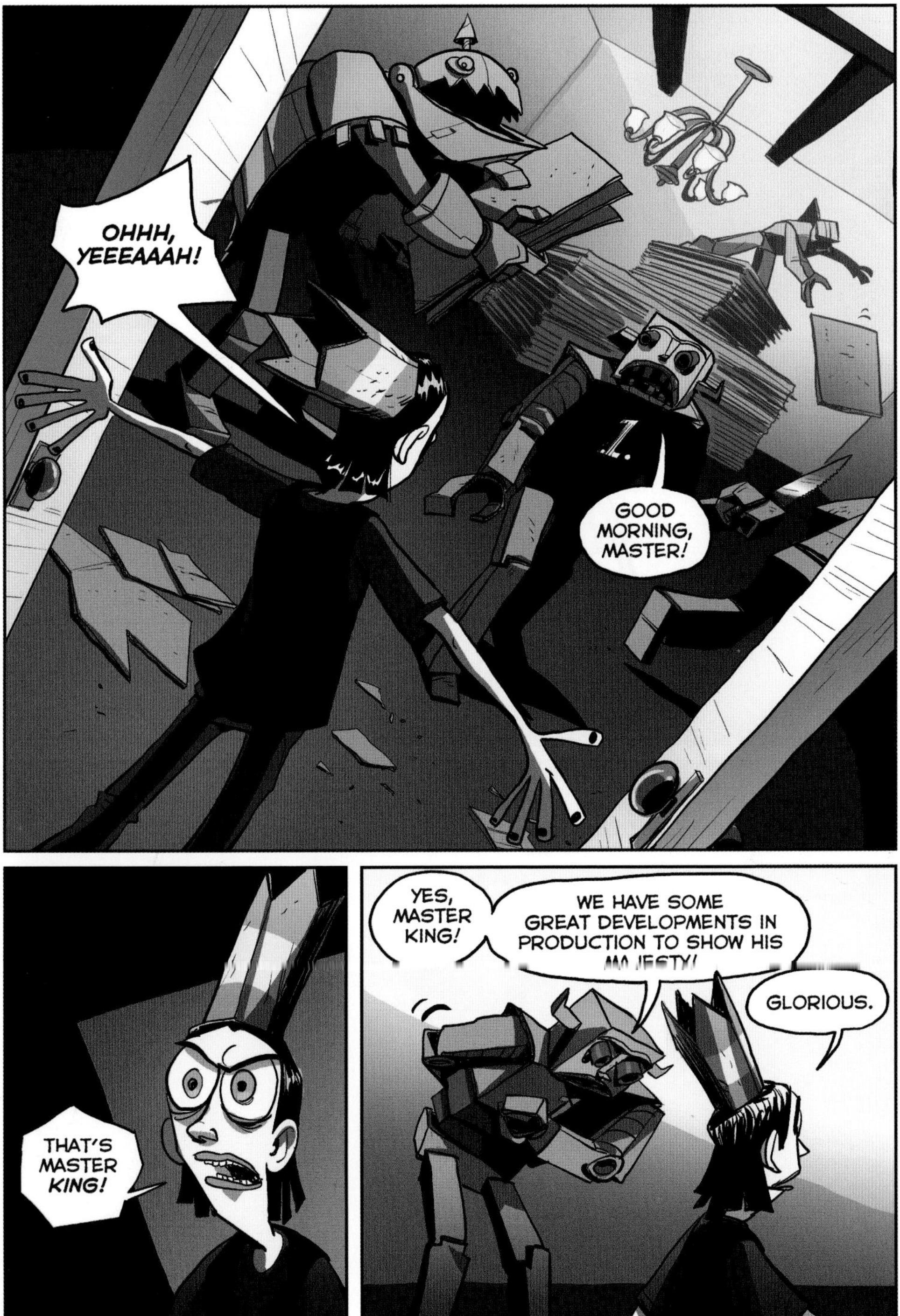
OHHH, YEEEAAAH!
GOOD MORNING, MASTER!
THAT'S MASTER KING!
YES, MASTER KING!
WE HAVE SOME GREAT DEVELOPMENTS IN PRODUCTION TO SHOW HIS
GLORIOUS.

WE'VE NOW STREAMLINED CARDBOARD PRODUCTION AND DISTRIBUTION TO A SCIENCE! IT'S PRODUCED, CATALOGUED, THEN STORED ON THE BACK PATIO.

WELL DONE, HERMES. I JUST DECIDED YOUR NEW NAME IS HERMES.

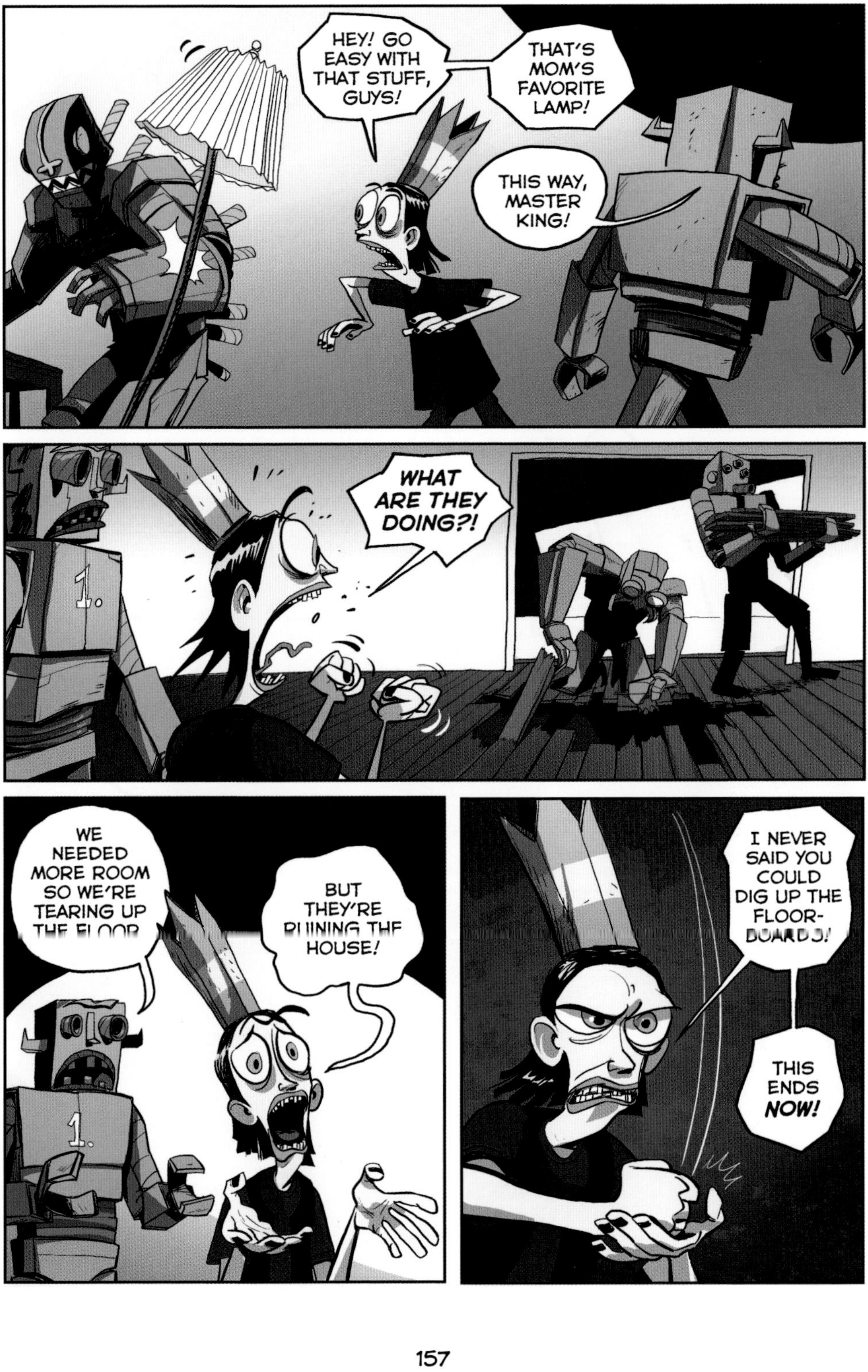

HEY! GO EASY WITH THAT STUFF, GUYS!
THAT'S MOM'S FAVORITE LAMP!
THIS WAY, MASTER KING!
WHAT ARE THEY DOING?!
WE NEEDED MORE ROOM SO WE'RE TEARING UP THE FLOOR
BUT THEY'RE RUINING THE HOUSE!
I NEVER SAID YOU COULD DIG UP THE FLOOR-BOARDS!
THIS ENDS NOW!

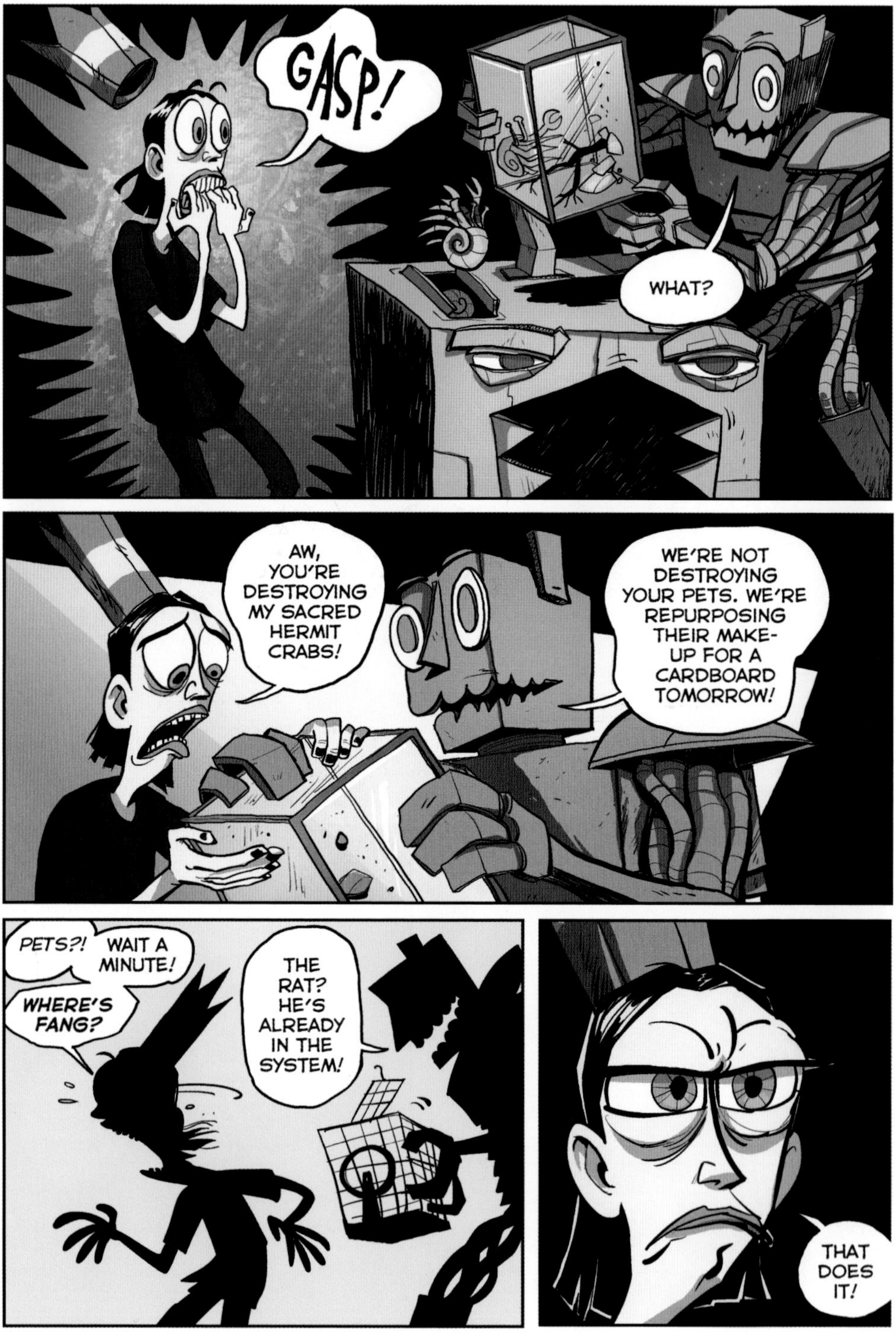
GASP!
WHAT?
AW, YOU'RE DESTROYING MY SACRED HERMIT CRABS!
WE'RE NOT DESTROYING YOUR PETS. WE'RE REPURPOSING THEIR MAKE-UP FOR A CARDBOARD TOMORROW!
PETS?!
WAIT A MINUTE!
WHERE'S FANG?
THE RAT? HE'S ALREADY IN THE SYSTEM!
THAT DOES IT!

STOP WORKING! I COMMAND ALL OF YOU TO STOP DIGGING UP MY HOUSE!

LOOK, YOU HAVE YOUR JOB AND I HAVE MINE. MY JOB IS TO DIG UP THESE FLOORS, AND YOURS--

--IS TO WEAR A FUNNY LITTLE CROWN.

I DON'T LIKE YOUR TONE, SLAVE!

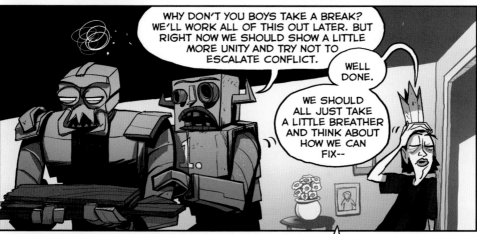

WHY DON'T YOU BOYS TAKE A BREAK? WE'LL WORK ALL OF THIS OUT LATER. BUT RIGHT NOW WE SHOULD SHOW A LITTLE MORE UNITY AND TRY NOT TO ESCALATE CONFLICT.

WELL DONE.

WE SHOULD ALL JUST TAKE A LITTLE BREATHER AND THINK ABOUT HOW WE CAN FIX--

CHOOM

EEK!

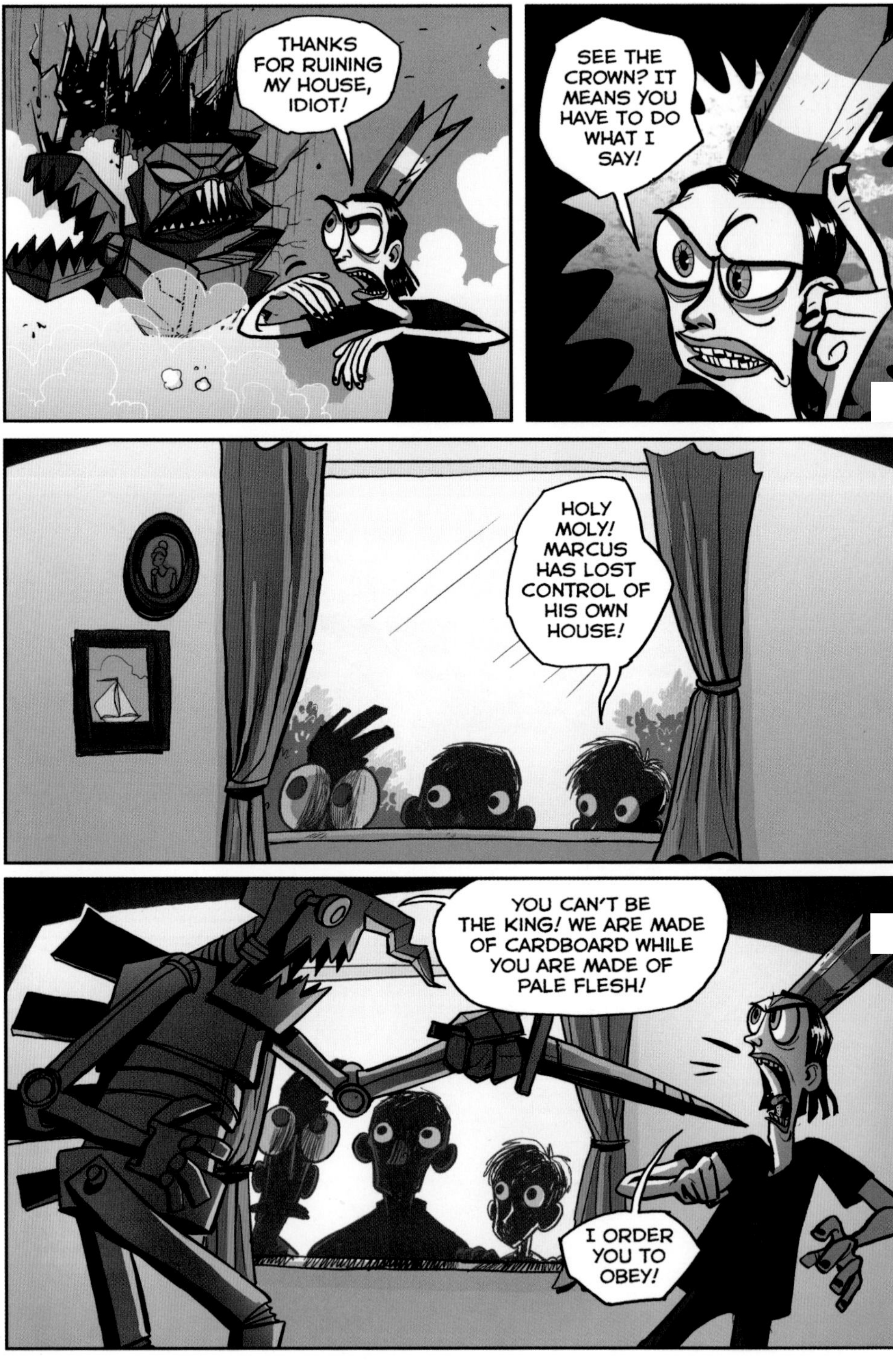
THANKS FOR RUINING MY HOUSE, IDIOT!
SEE THE CROWN? IT MEANS YOU HAVE TO DO WHAT I SAY!
HOLY MOLY! MARCUS HAS LOST CONTROL OF HIS OWN HOUSE!
YOU CAN'T BE THE KING! WE ARE MADE OF CARDBOARD WHILE YOU ARE MADE OF PALE FLESH!
I ORDER YOU TO OBEY!

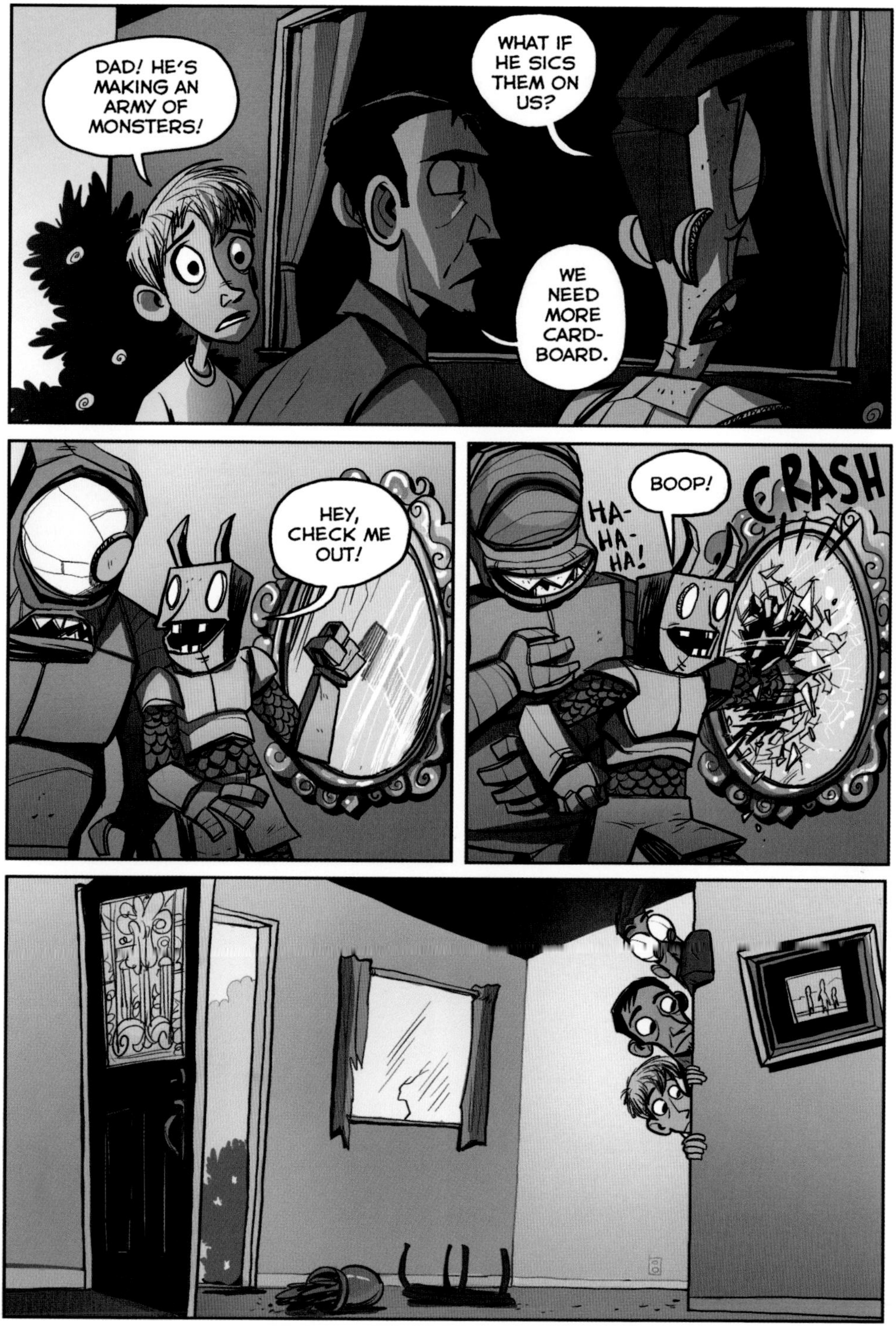
DAD! HE'S MAKING AN ARMY OF MONSTERS!
WHAT IF HE SICS THEM ON US?
WE NEED MORE CARD-BOARD.
HEY, CHECK ME OUT!
HA-HA-HA!
BOOP!
CRASH

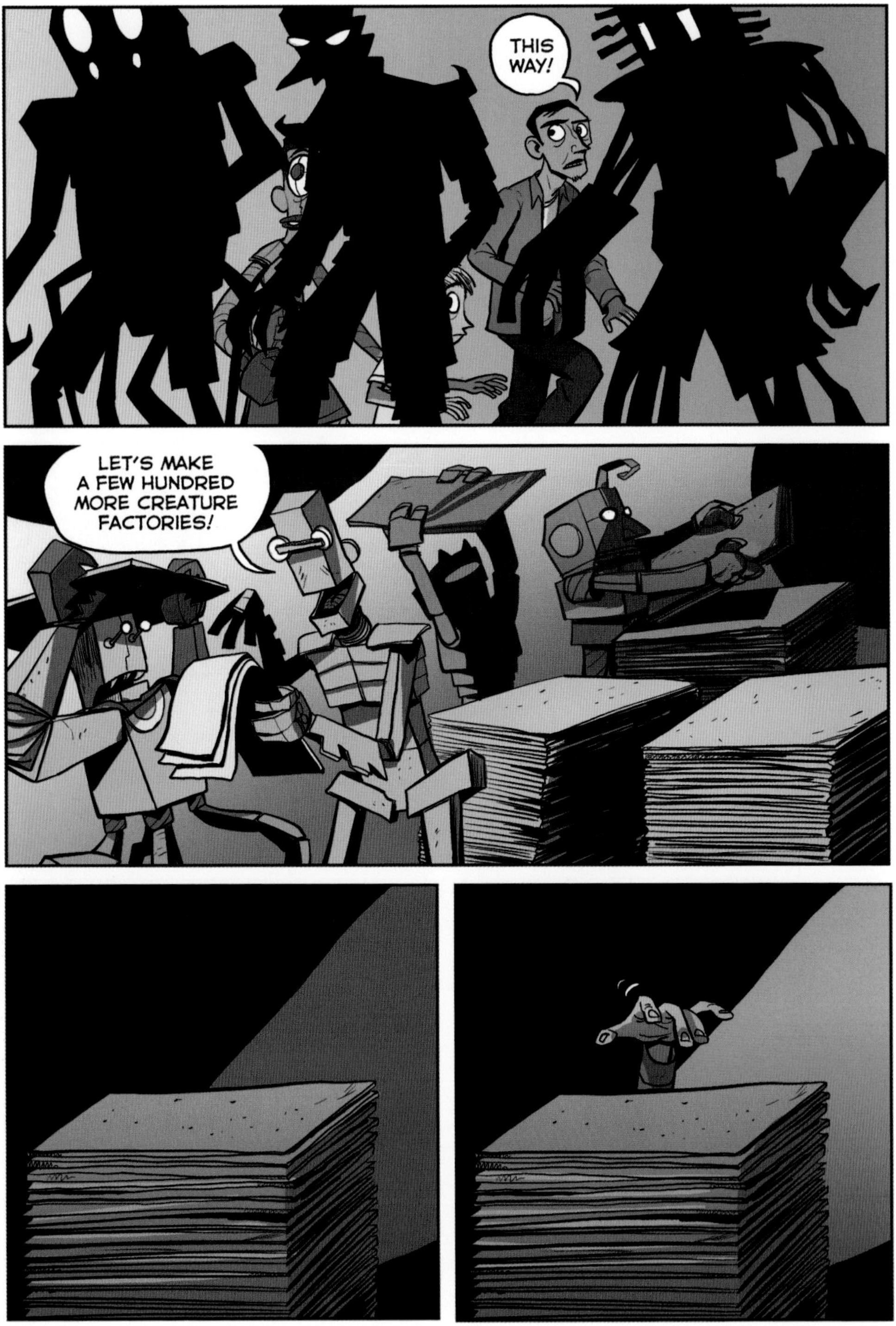
THIS WAY!
LET'S MAKE A FEW HUNDRED MORE CREATURE FACTORIES!

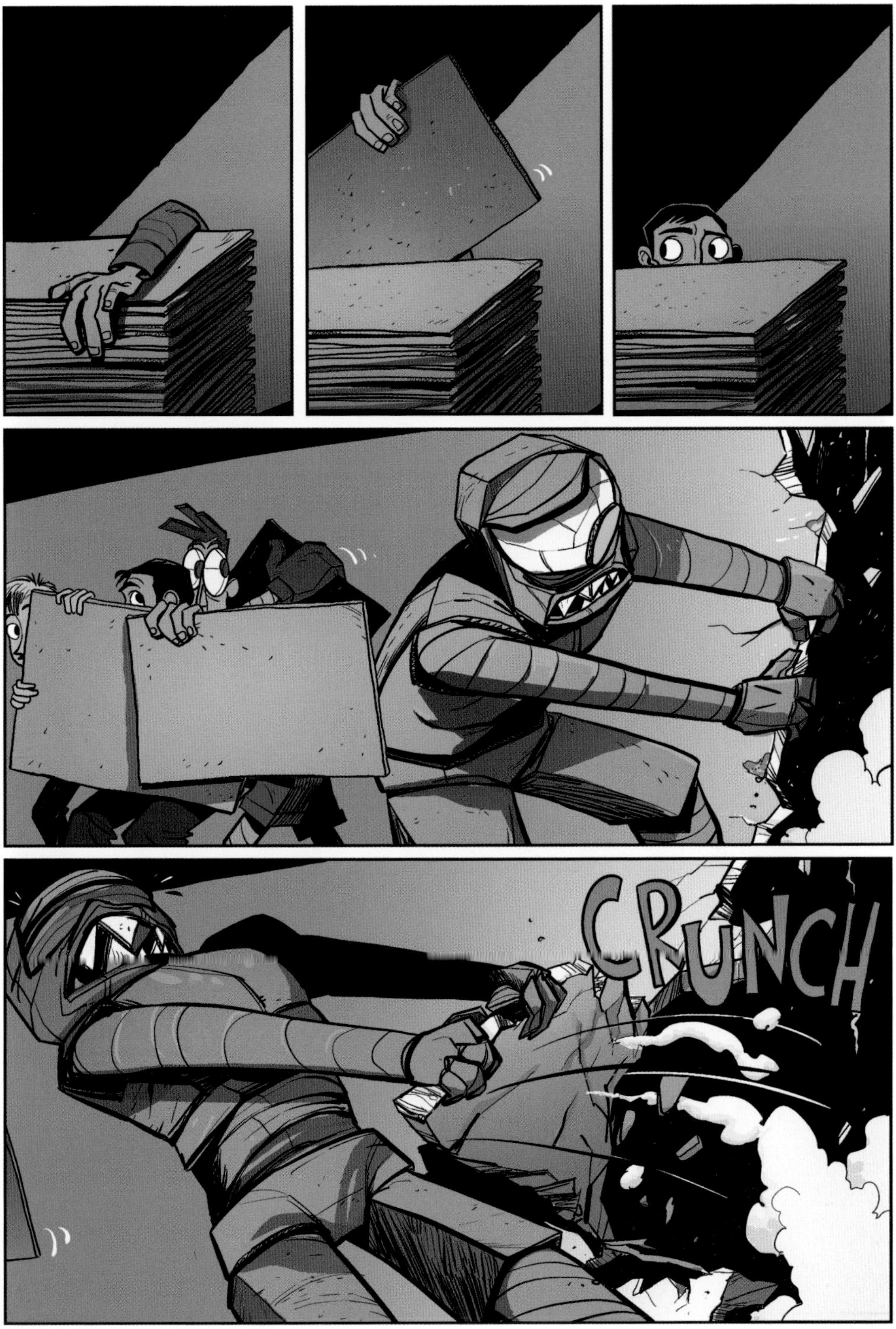
CRUNCH

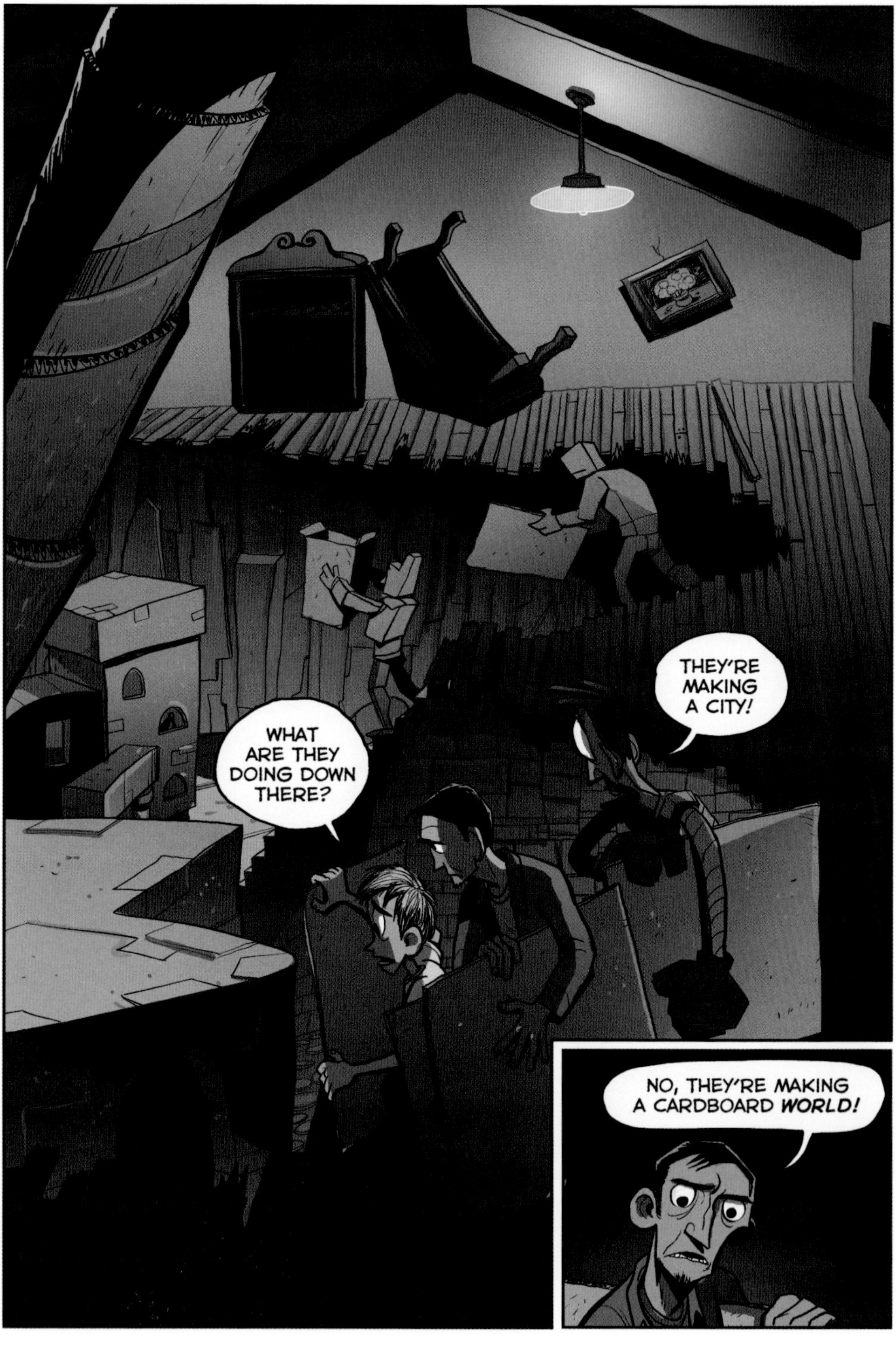

WHAT ARE THEY DOING DOWN THERE?
THEY'RE MAKING A CITY!
NO, THEY'RE MAKING A CARDBOARD ***WORLD!***

WHAT HAVE WE DONE?
MARCUS, AREN'T YOUR PARENTS GOING TO BE UPSET WHEN THEY--
PINK EYE!
YOU'VE GOTTA HELP ME!
ARE YOU CRAZY? YOUR HOUSE IS OVER-RUN BY EVIL CARDBOARD. I'M OUTTA HERE!
NO, DON'T GO! YOU'VE ALWAYS BEEN THERE FOR ME!

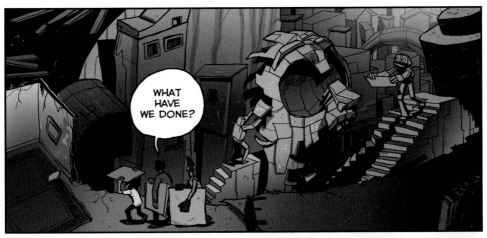

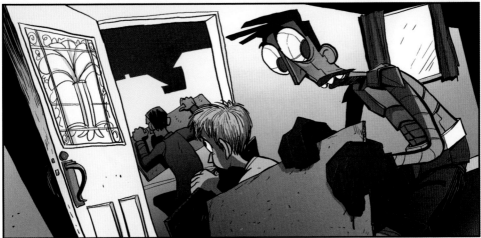

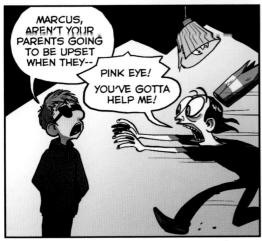

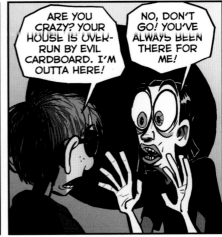

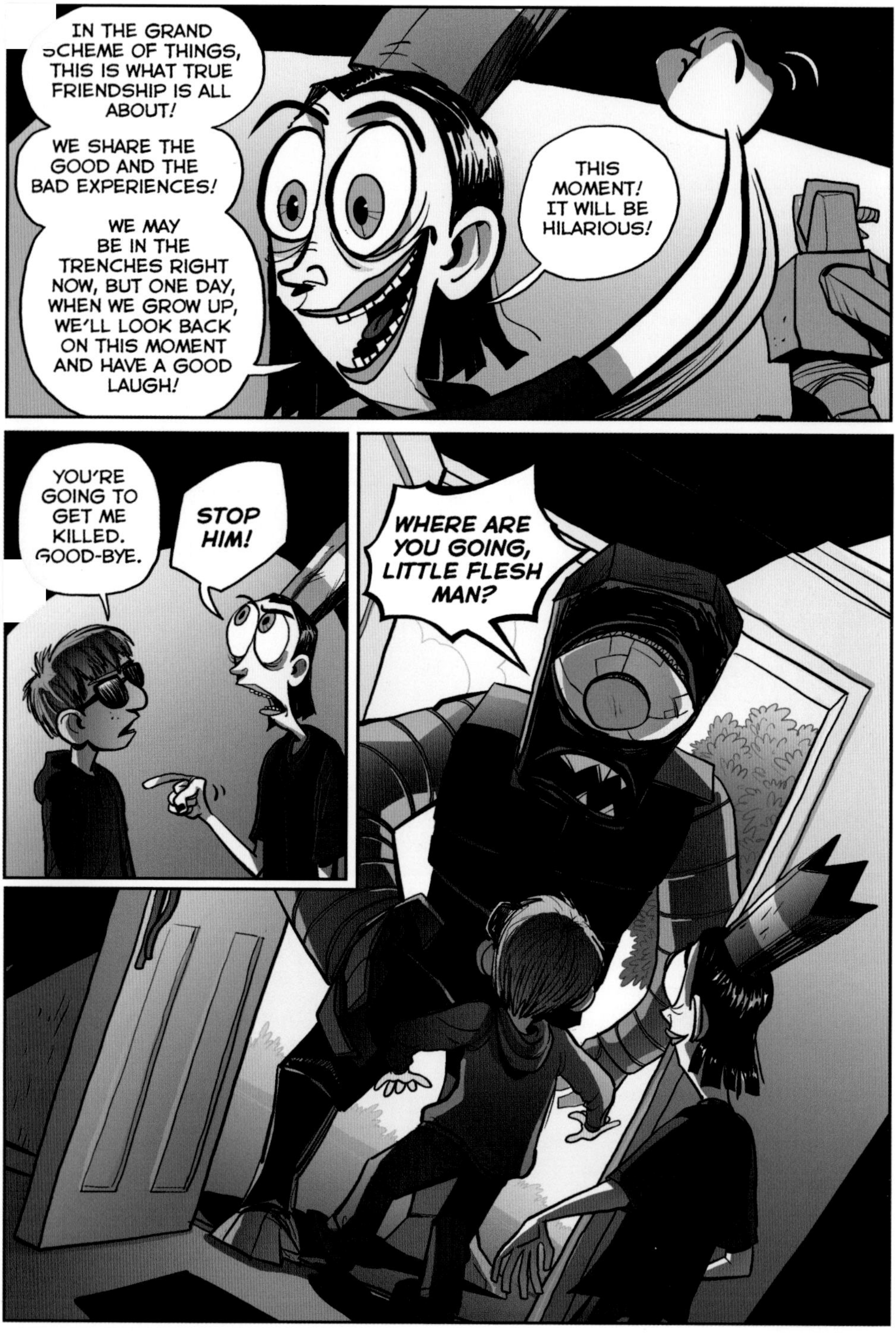
IN THE GRAND SCHEME OF THINGS, THIS IS WHAT TRUE FRIENDSHIP IS ALL ABOUT!
WE SHARE THE GOOD AND THE BAD EXPERIENCES!
WE MAY BE IN THE TRENCHES RIGHT NOW, BUT ONE DAY, WHEN WE GROW UP, WE'LL LOOK BACK ON THIS MOMENT AND HAVE A GOOD LAUGH!
THIS MOMENT! IT WILL BE HILARIOUS!
YOU'RE GOING TO GET ME KILLED. GOOD-BYE.
STOP HIM!
WHERE ARE YOU GOING, LITTLE FLESH MAN?

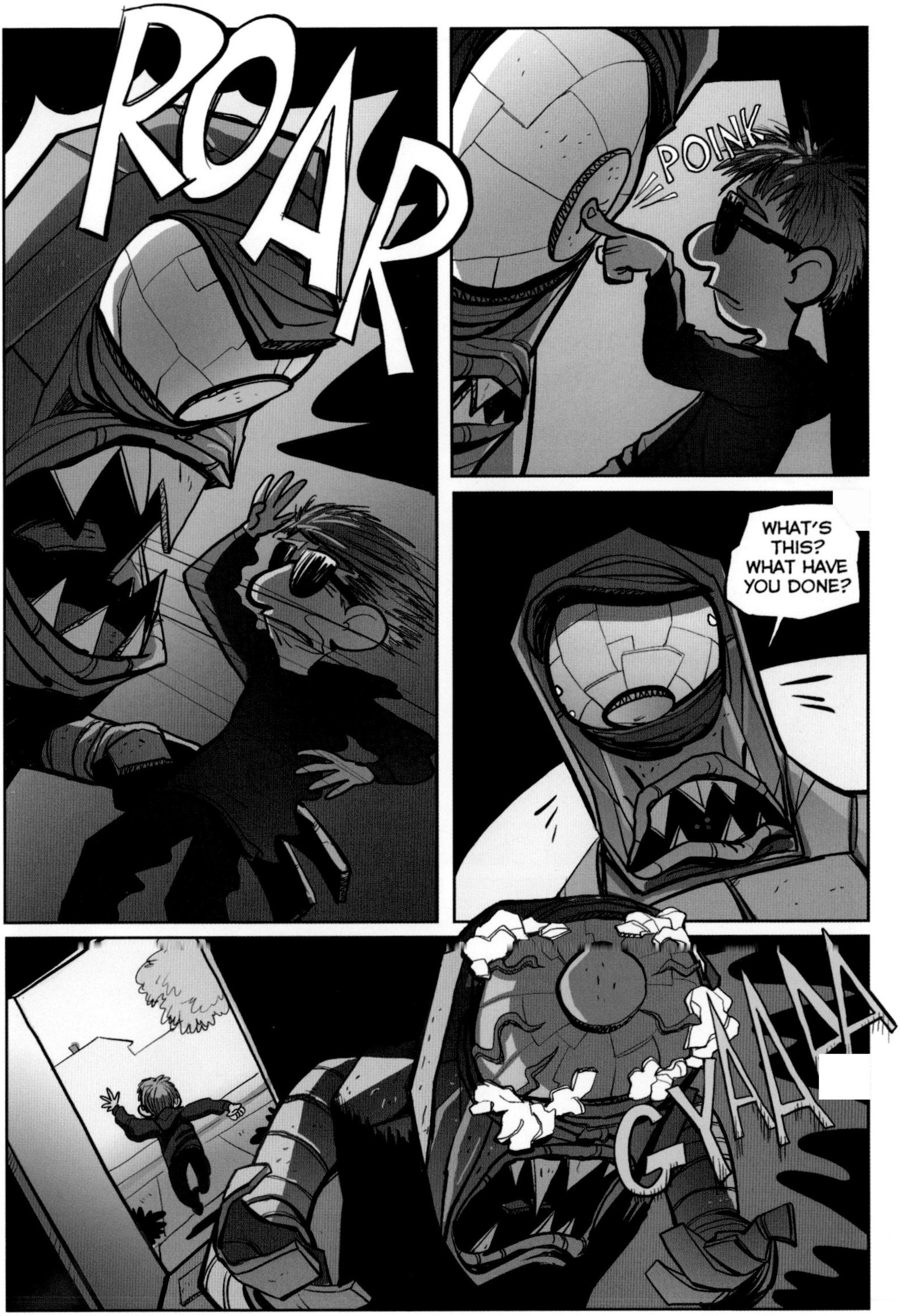
ROAR
POINK
WHAT'S THIS? WHAT HAVE YOU DONE?
GYAAAA

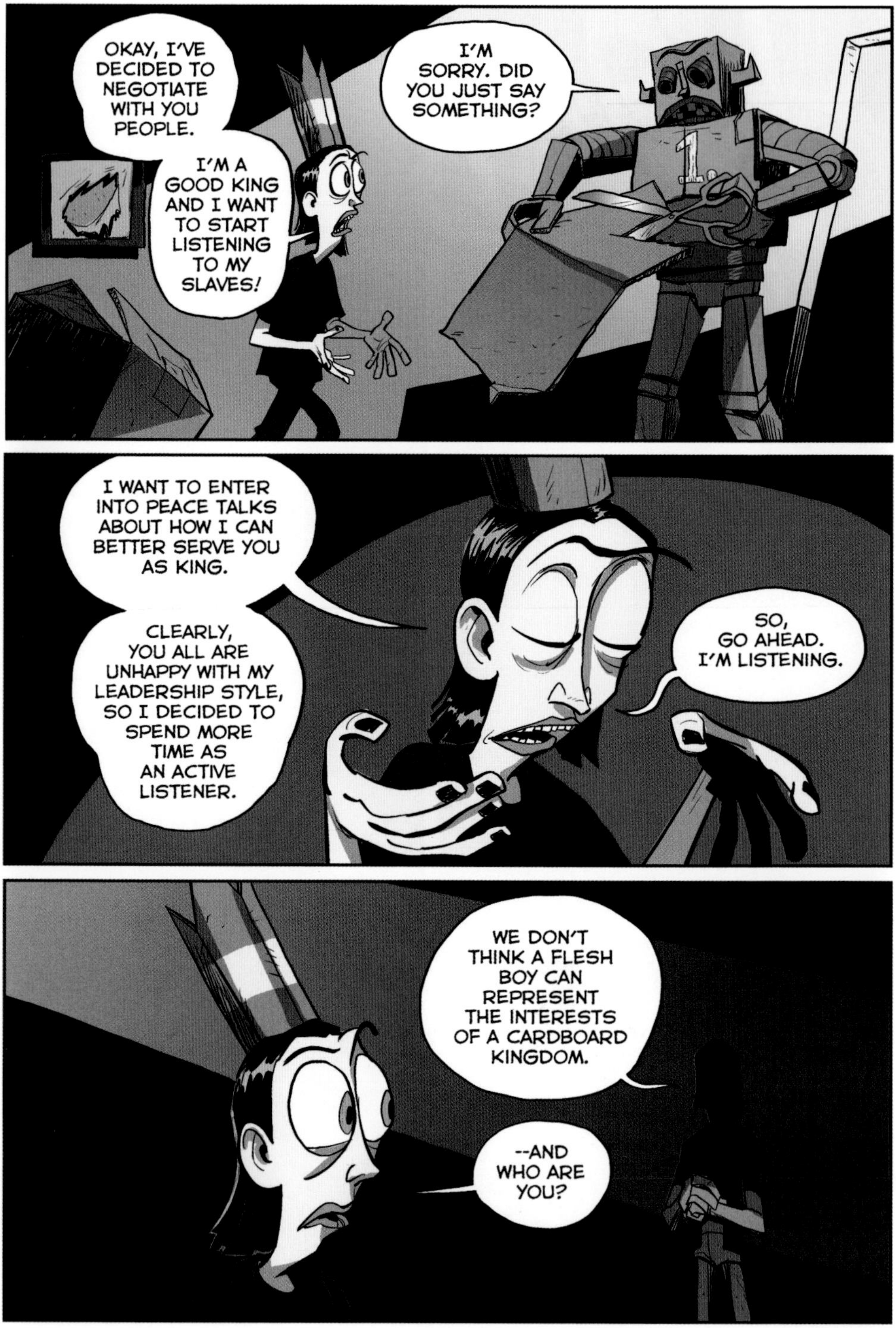
OKAY, I'VE DECIDED TO NEGOTIATE WITH YOU PEOPLE.
I'M A GOOD KING AND I WANT TO START LISTENING TO MY SLAVES!
I'M SORRY. DID YOU JUST SAY SOMETHING?
I WANT TO ENTER INTO PEACE TALKS ABOUT HOW I CAN BETTER SERVE YOU AS KING.
CLEARLY, YOU ALL ARE UNHAPPY WITH MY LEADERSHIP STYLE, SO I DECIDED TO SPEND MORE TIME AS AN ACTIVE LISTENER.
SO, GO AHEAD. I'M LISTENING.
WE DON'T THINK A FLESH BOY CAN REPRESENT THE INTERESTS OF A CARDBOARD KINGDOM.
--AND WHO ARE YOU?

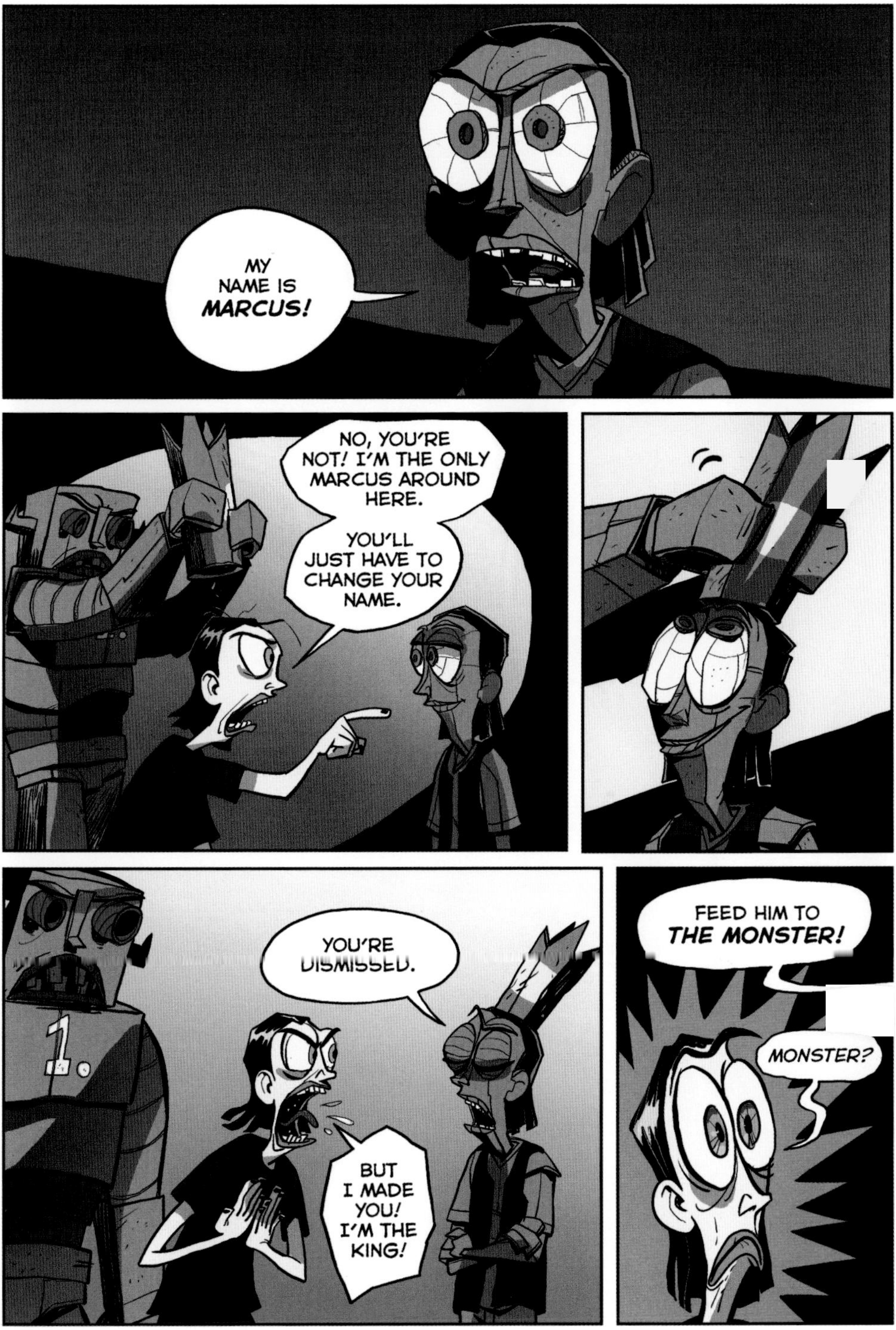
MY NAME IS MARCUS!
NO, YOU'RE NOT! I'M THE ONLY MARCUS AROUND HERE.
YOU'LL JUST HAVE TO CHANGE YOUR NAME.
YOU'RE DISMISSED.
BUT I MADE YOU! I'M THE KING!
FEED HIM TO THE MONSTER!
MONSTER?

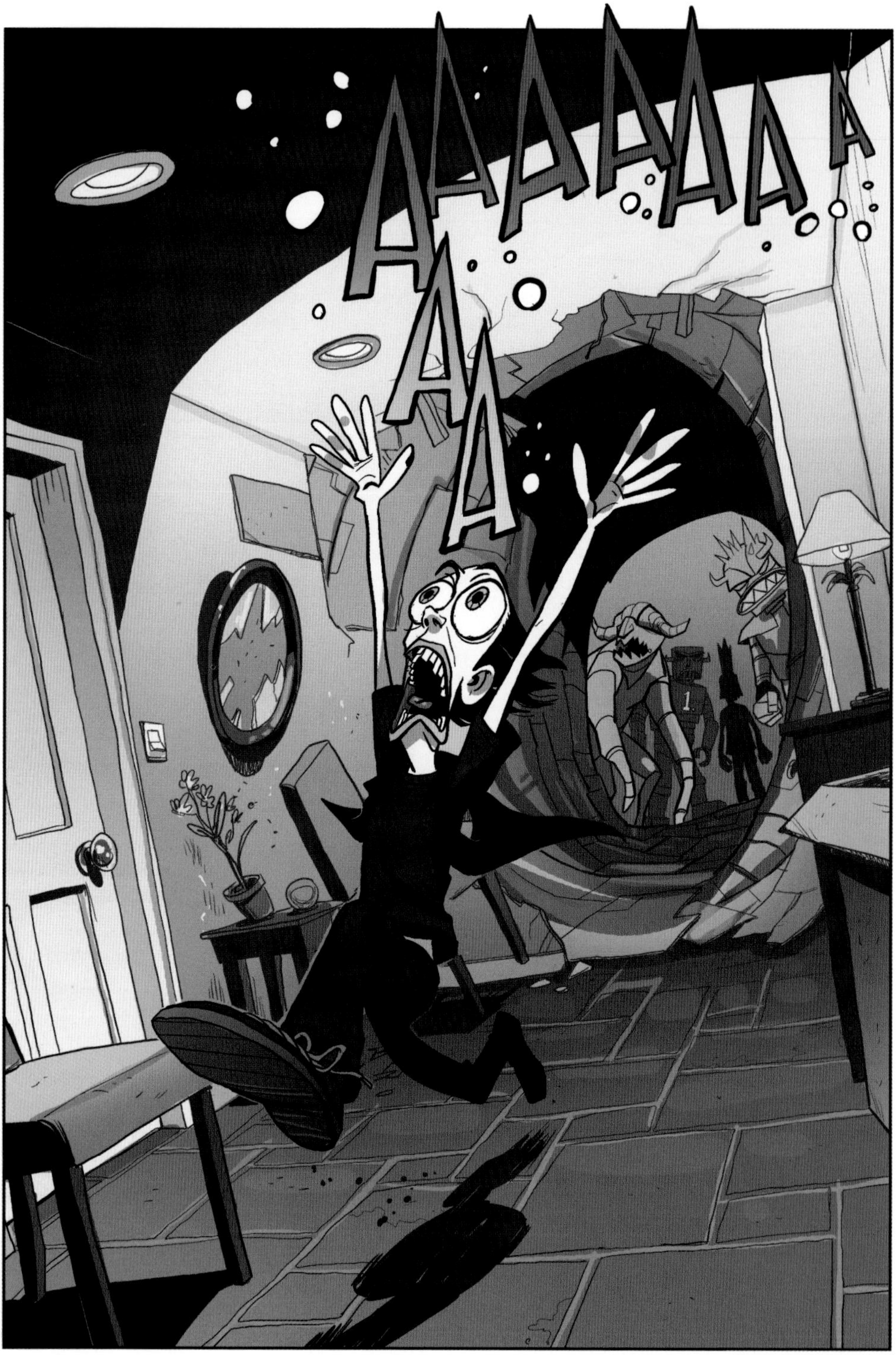
AAAAAAAAAA

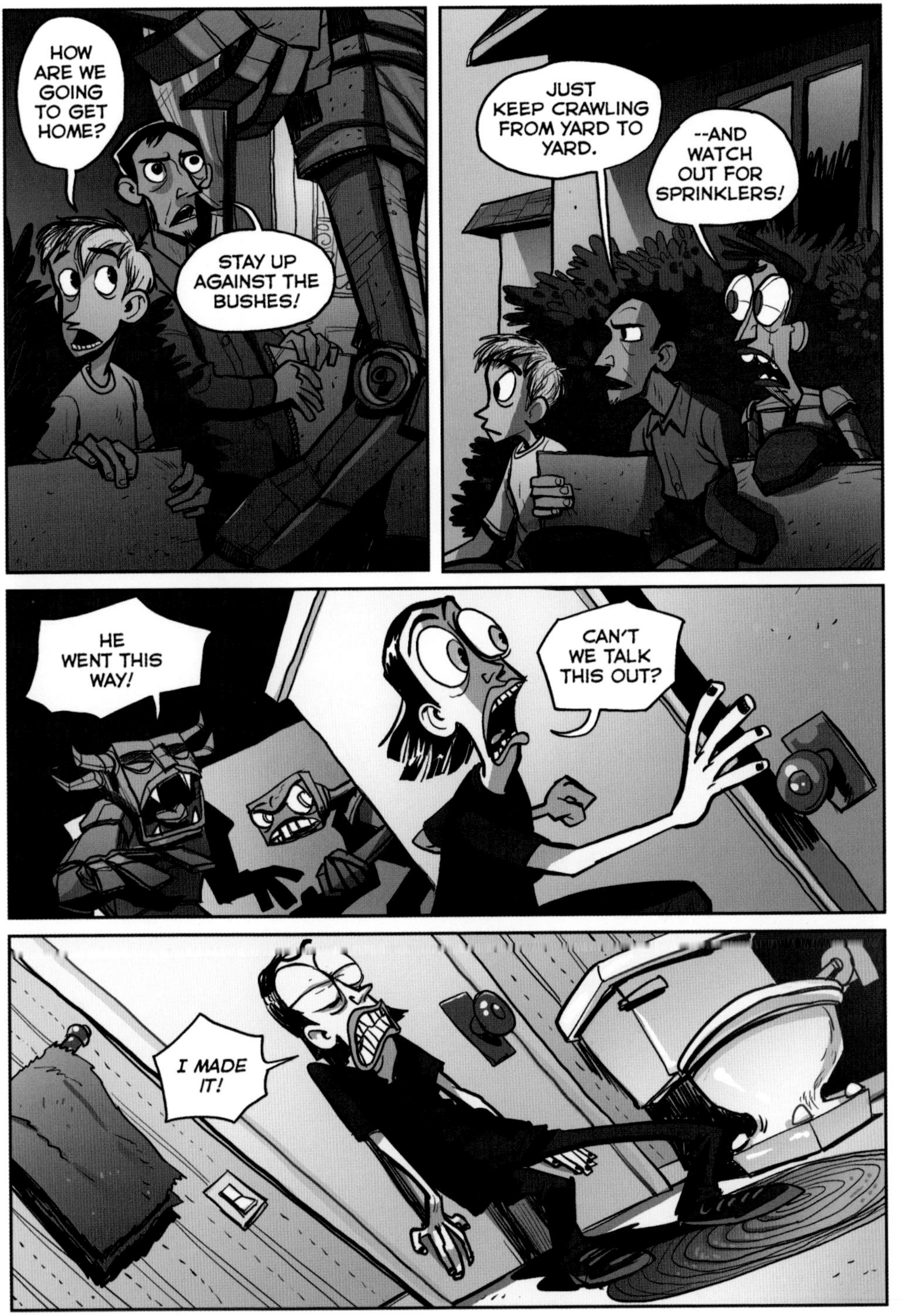
HOW ARE WE GOING TO GET HOME?
STAY UP AGAINST THE BUSHES!
JUST KEEP CRAWLING FROM YARD TO YARD.
--AND WATCH OUT FOR SPRINKLERS!
HE WENT THIS WAY!
CAN'T WE TALK THIS OUT?
I MADE IT!

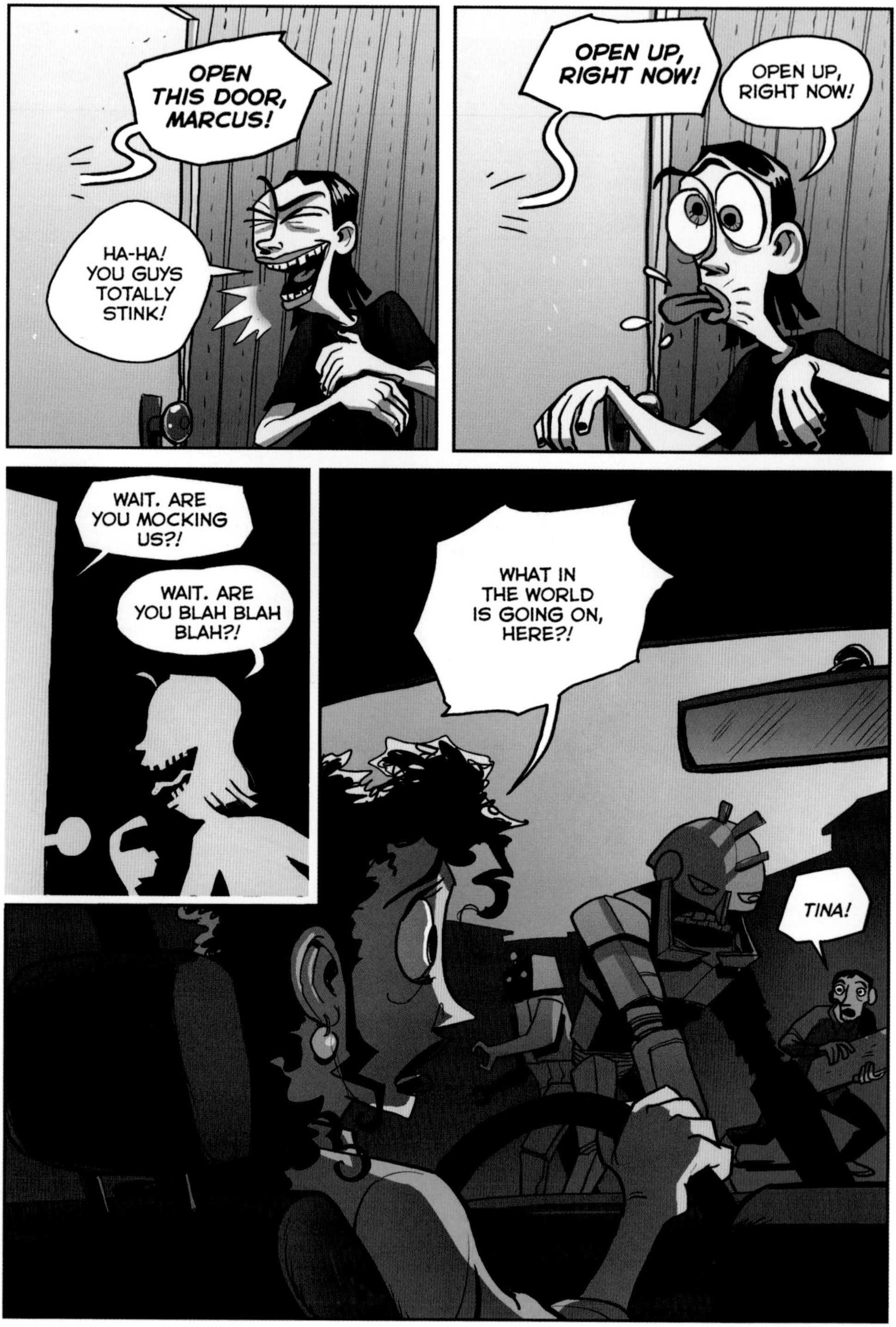
OPEN THIS DOOR, MARCUS!
HA-HA! YOU GUYS TOTALLY STINK!
OPEN UP, RIGHT NOW!
OPEN UP, RIGHT NOW!
WAIT. ARE YOU MOCKING US?!
WAIT. ARE YOU BLAH BLAH BLAH?!
WHAT IN THE WORLD IS GOING ON, HERE?!
TINA!

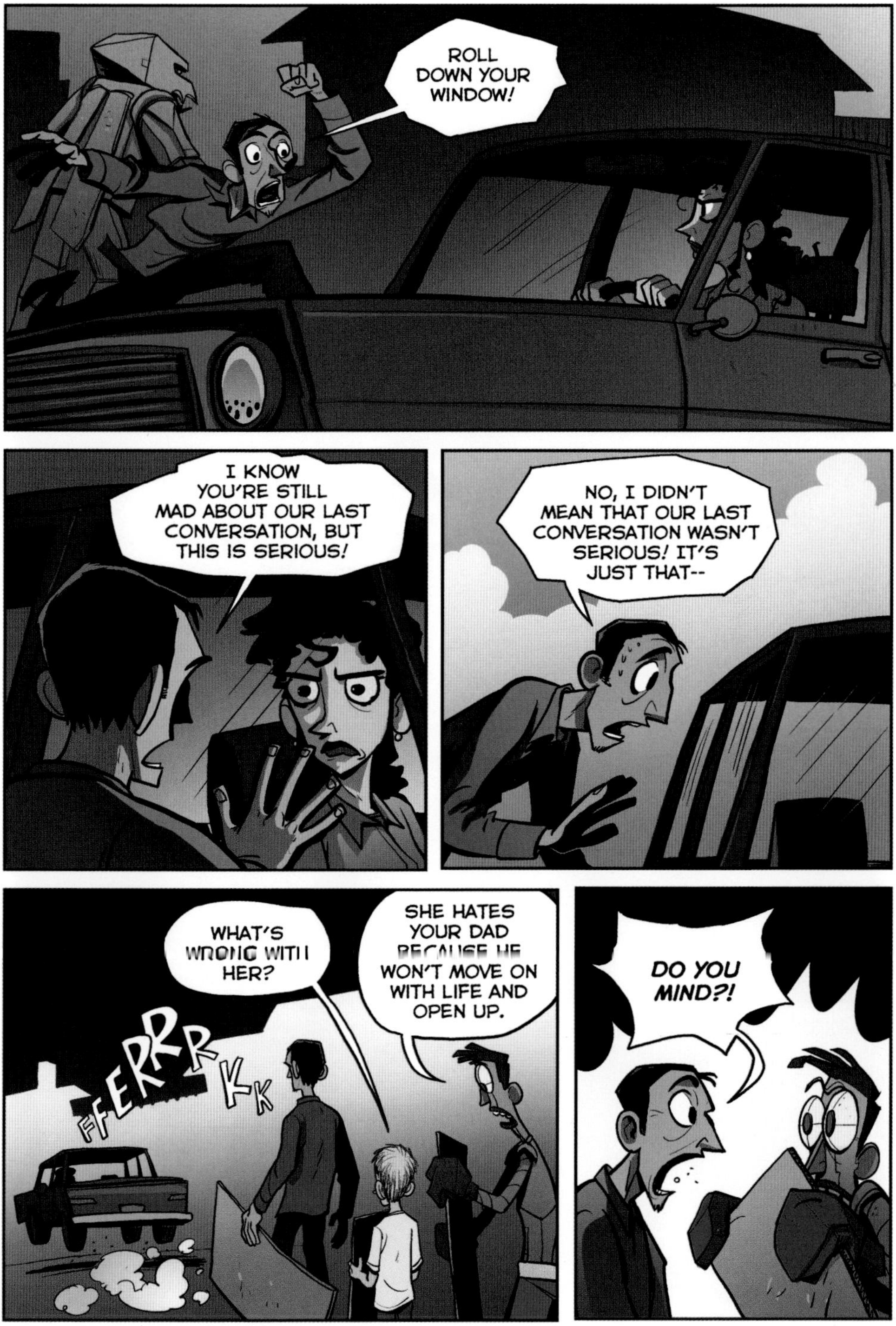
ROLL DOWN YOUR WINDOW!
I KNOW YOU'RE STILL MAD ABOUT OUR LAST CONVERSATION, BUT THIS IS SERIOUS!
NO, I DIDN'T MEAN THAT OUR LAST CONVERSATION WASN'T SERIOUS! IT'S JUST THAT--
WHAT'S WRONG WITH HER?
SHE HATES YOUR DAD BECAUSE HE WON'T MOVE ON WITH LIFE AND OPEN UP.
FFERRRKK
DO YOU MIND?!

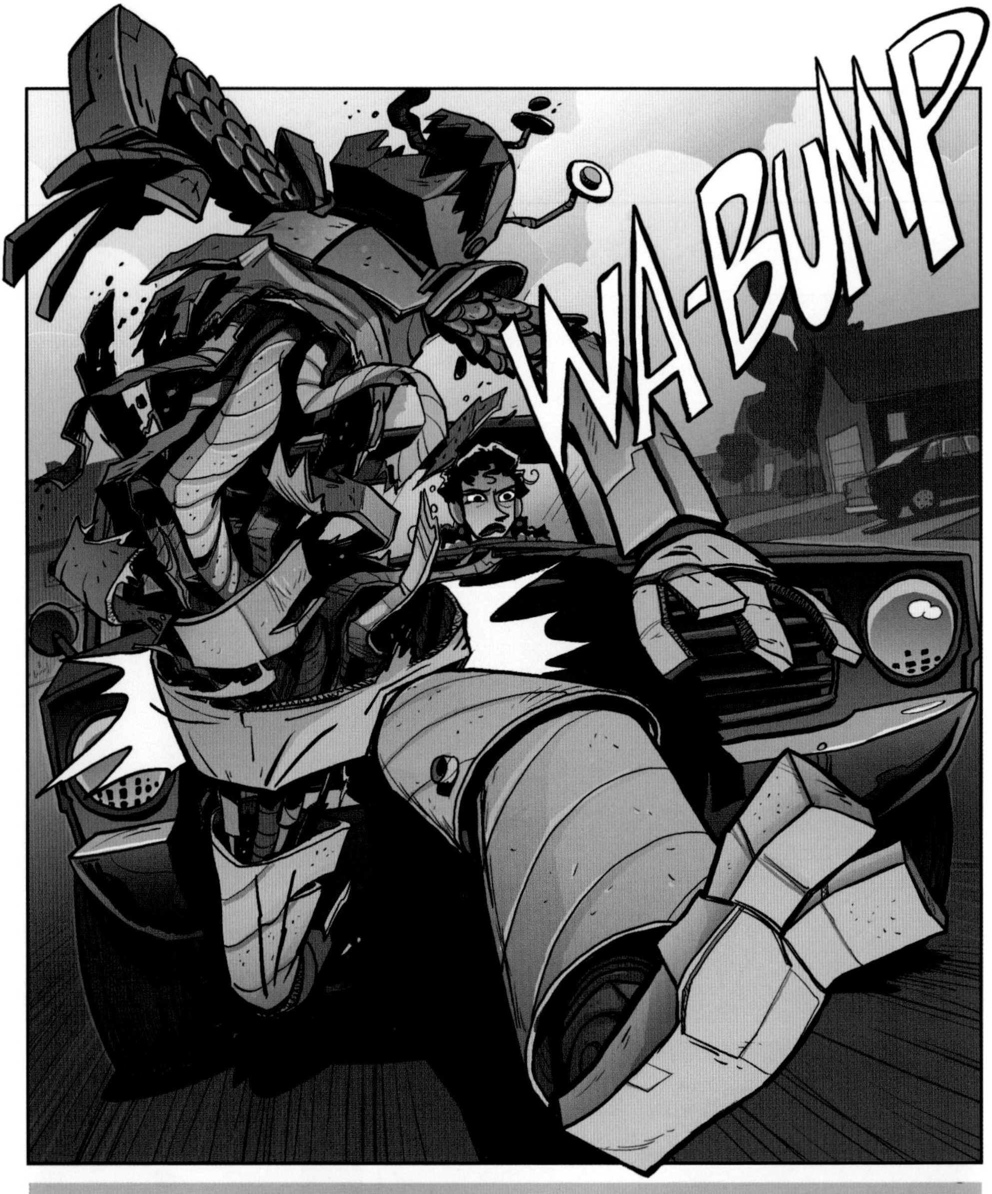
WA-BUMP

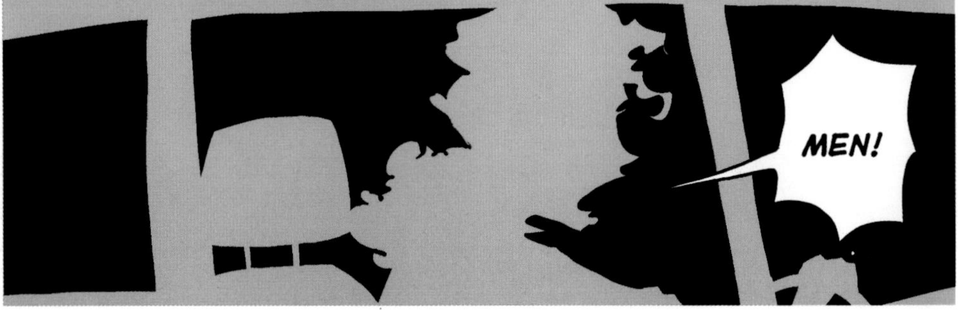
MEN!

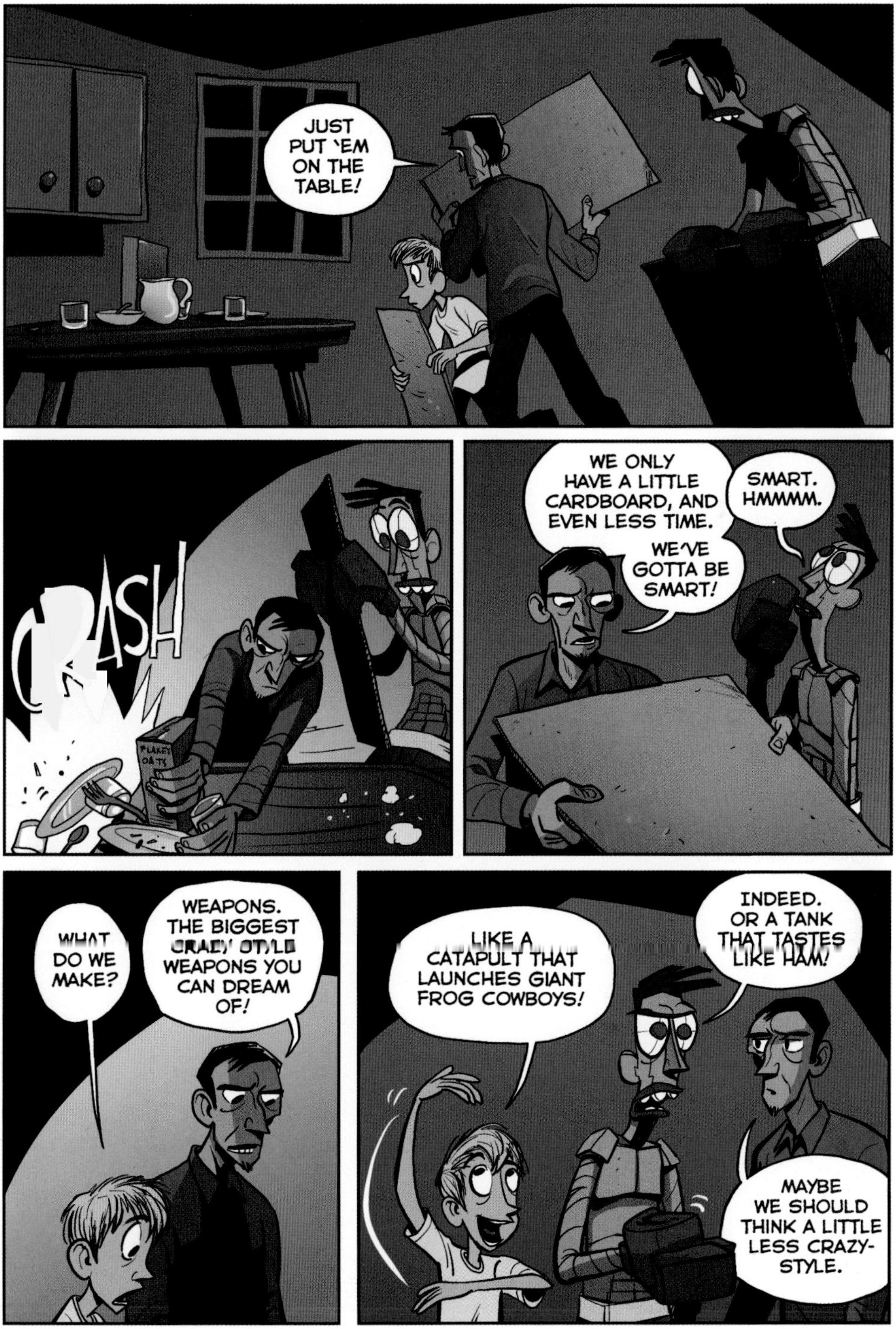
JUST PUT 'EM ON THE TABLE!
WE ONLY HAVE A LITTLE CARDBOARD, AND EVEN LESS TIME.
WE'VE GOTTA BE SMART!
SMART. HMMMM.
WHAT DO WE MAKE?
WEAPONS. THE BIGGEST CRAZY STYLE WEAPONS YOU CAN DREAM OF!
LIKE A CATAPULT THAT LAUNCHES GIANT FROG COWBOYS!
INDEED. OR A TANK THAT TASTES LIKE HAM!
MAYBE WE SHOULD THINK A LITTLE LESS CRAZY-STYLE.

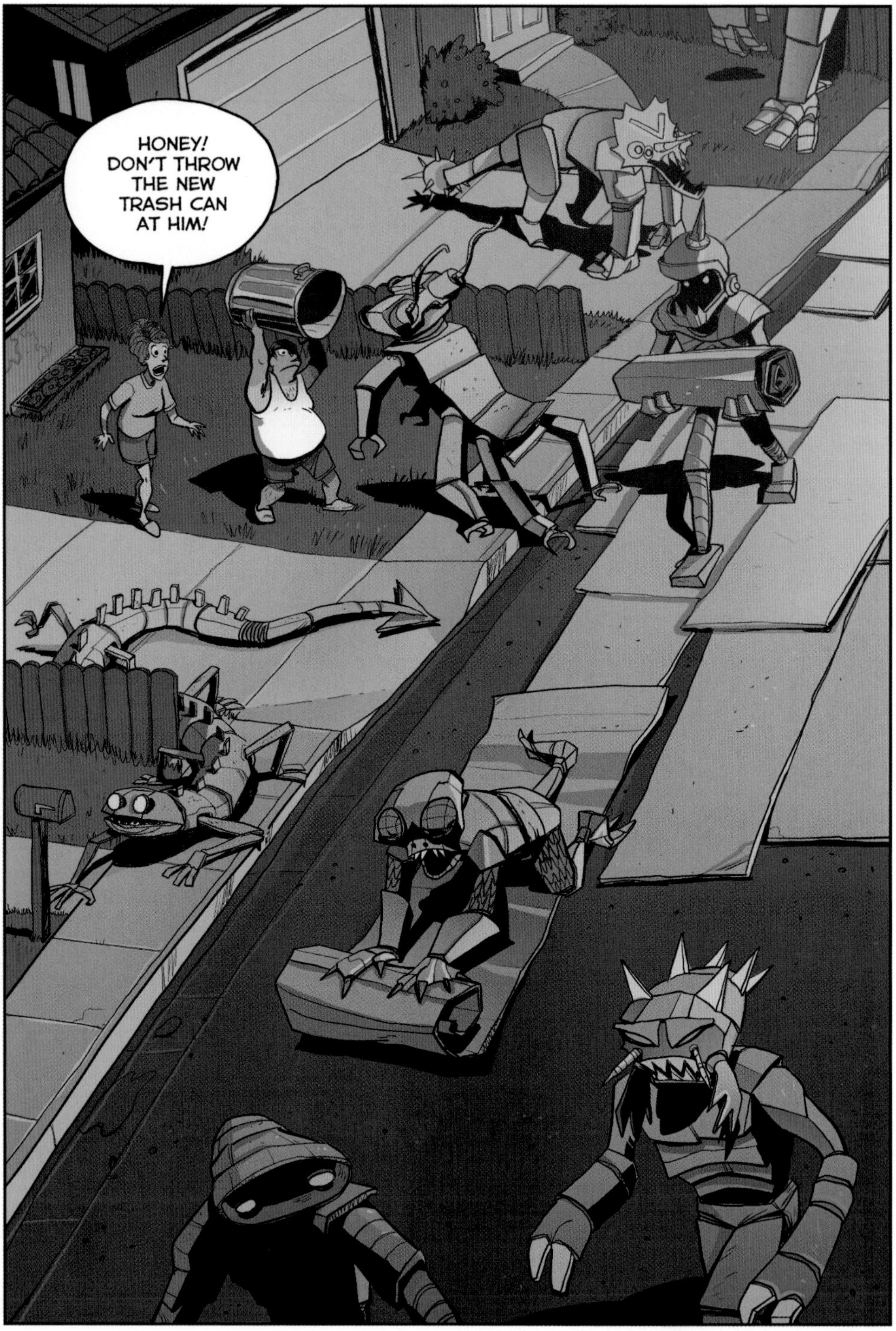
HONEY! DON'T THROW THE NEW TRASH CAN AT HIM!

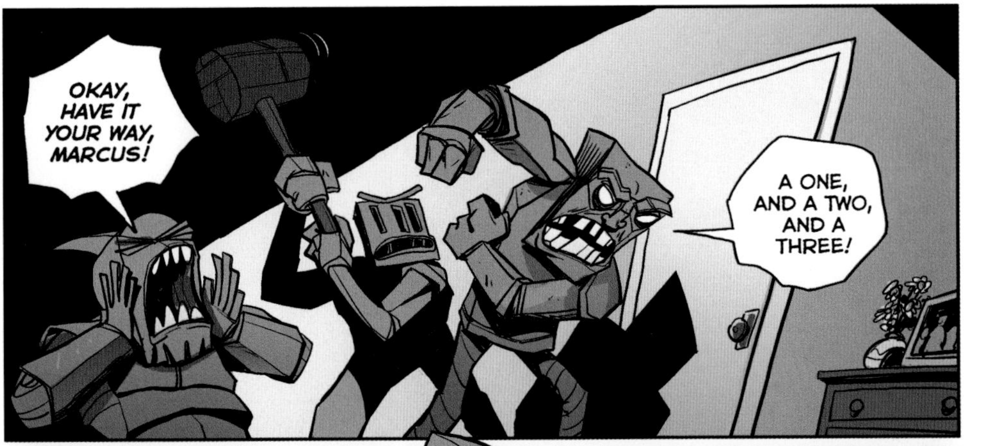
OKAY, HAVE IT YOUR WAY, MARCUS!
A ONE, AND A TWO, AND A THREE!

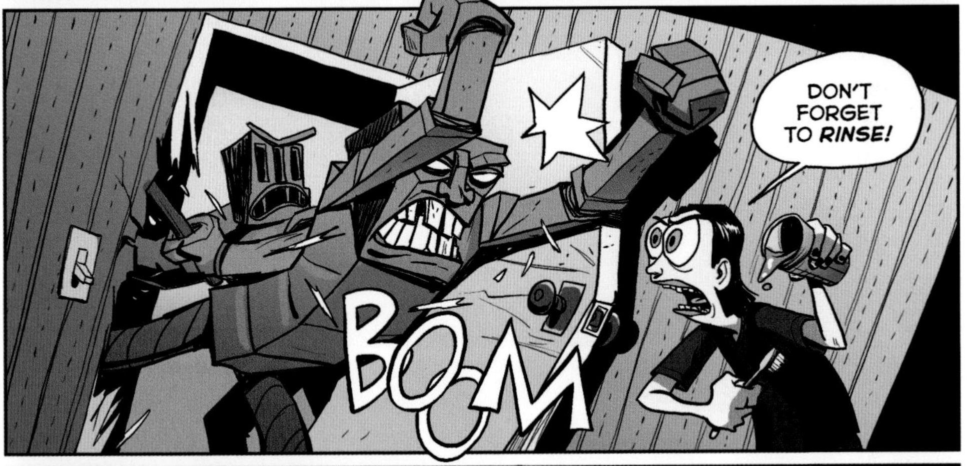
DON'T FORGET TO *RINSE!*
BOOOM

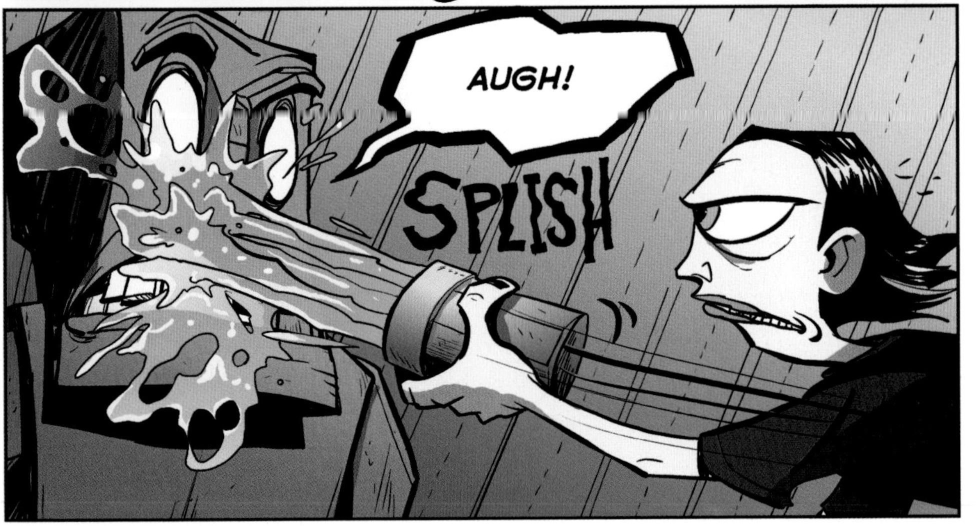
AUGH!
SPLISH

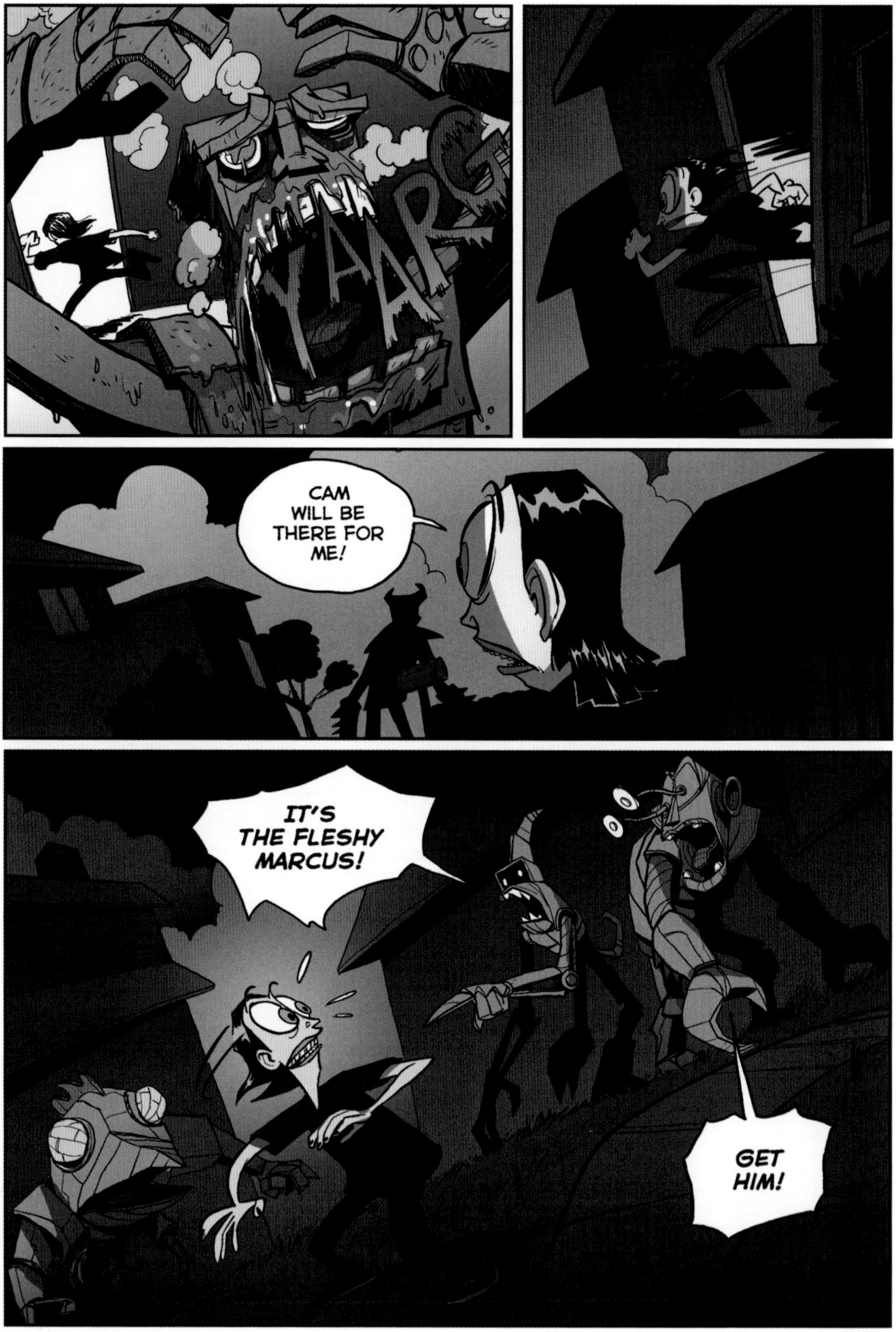
YAARG
CAM WILL BE THERE FOR ME!
IT'S THE FLESHY MARCUS!
GET HIM!

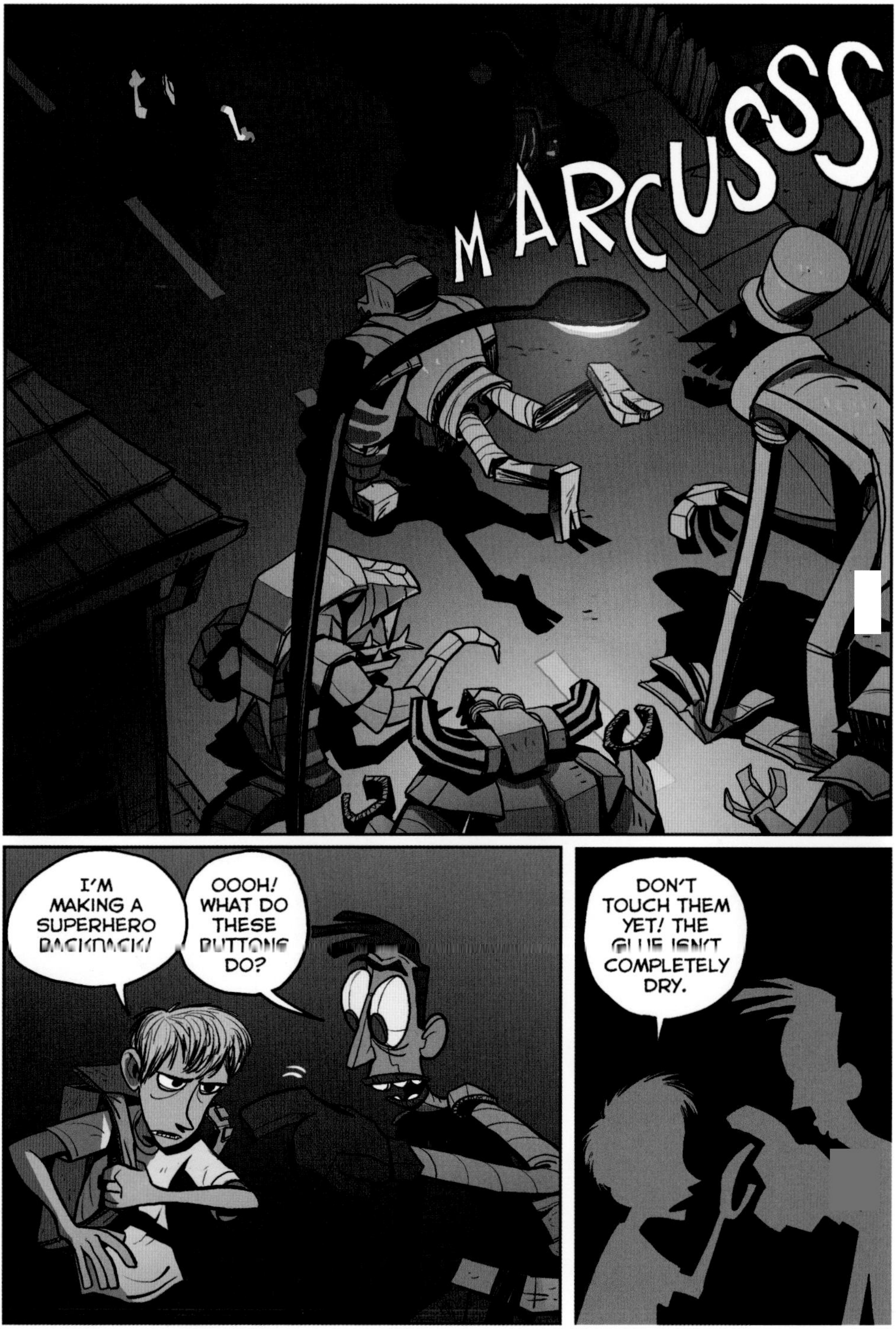
MARCUSSS
I'M MAKING A SUPERHERO BACKPACK!
OOOH! WHAT DO THESE BUTTONS DO?
DON'T TOUCH THEM YET! THE GLUE ISN'T COMPLETELY DRY.

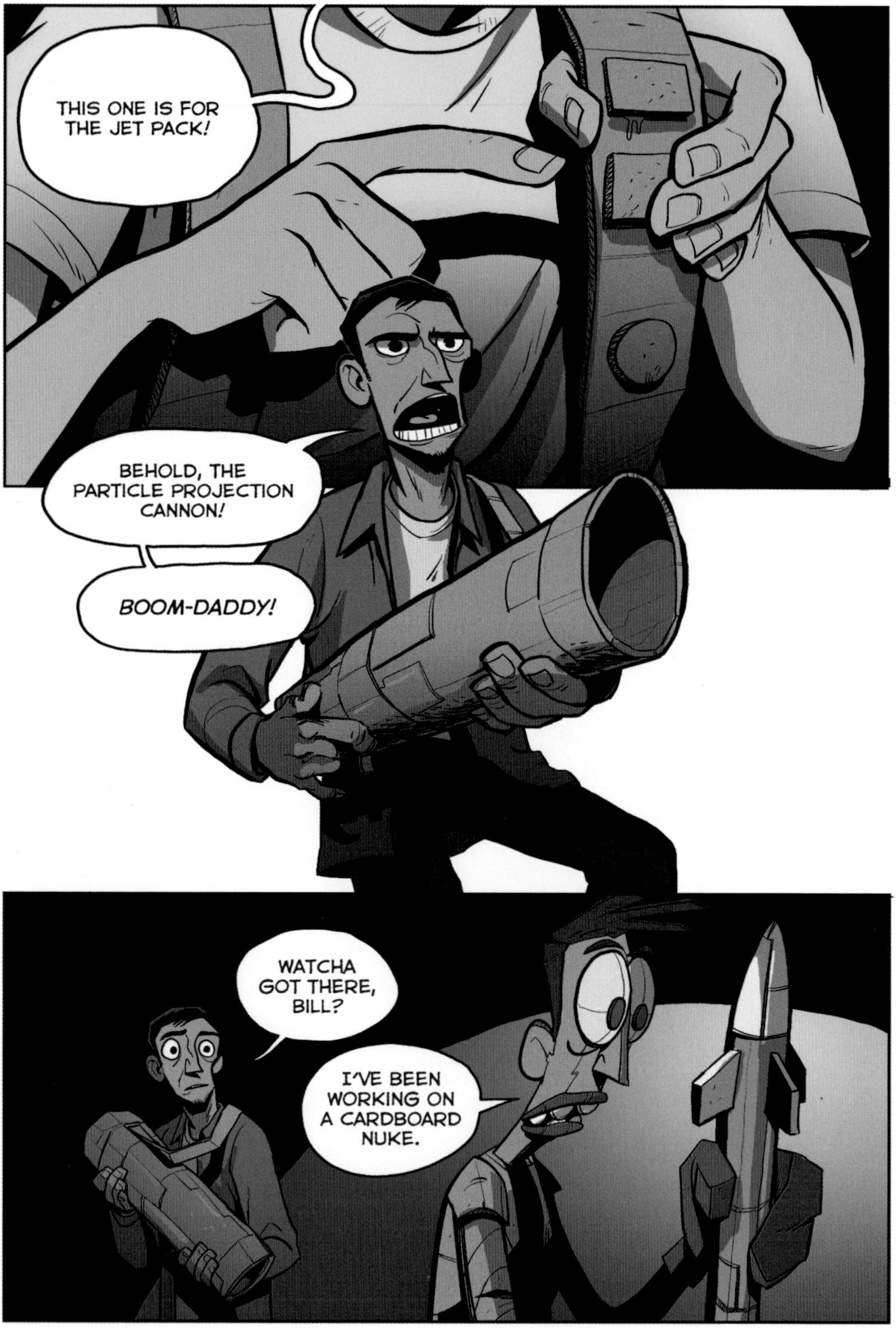
THIS ONE IS FOR THE JET PACK!
BEHOLD, THE PARTICLE PROJECTION CANNON!
BOOM-DADDY!
WATCHA GOT THERE, BILL?
I'VE BEEN WORKING ON A CARDBOARD NUKE.

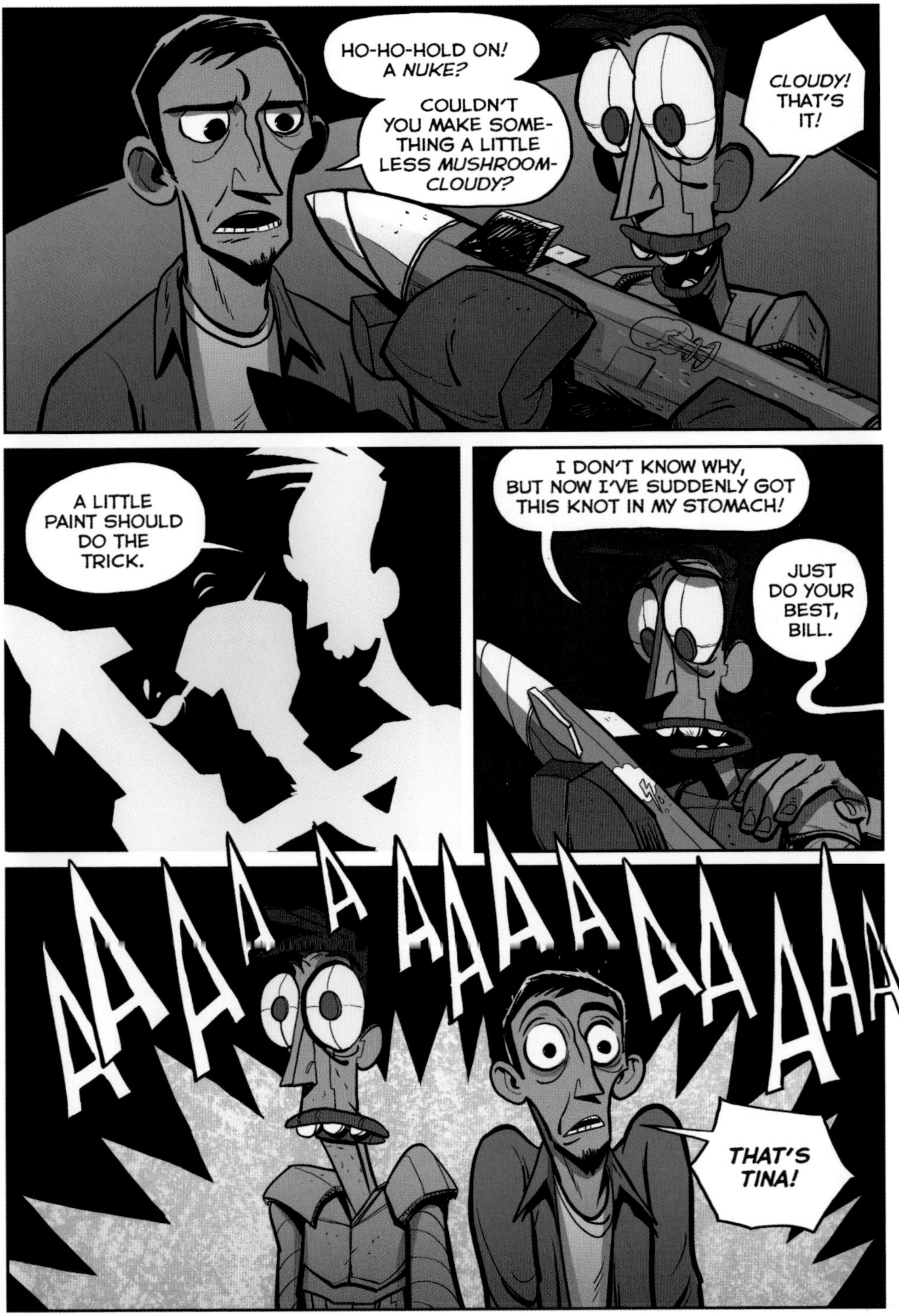
HO-HO-HOLD ON! A NUKE?
COULDN'T YOU MAKE SOME-THING A LITTLE LESS MUSHROOM-CLOUDY?
CLOUDY! THAT'S IT!
A LITTLE PAINT SHOULD DO THE TRICK.
I DON'T KNOW WHY, BUT NOW I'VE SUDDENLY GOT THIS KNOT IN MY STOMACH!
JUST DO YOUR BEST, BILL.
AAAAAAAAAAAAAAA
THAT'S TINA!

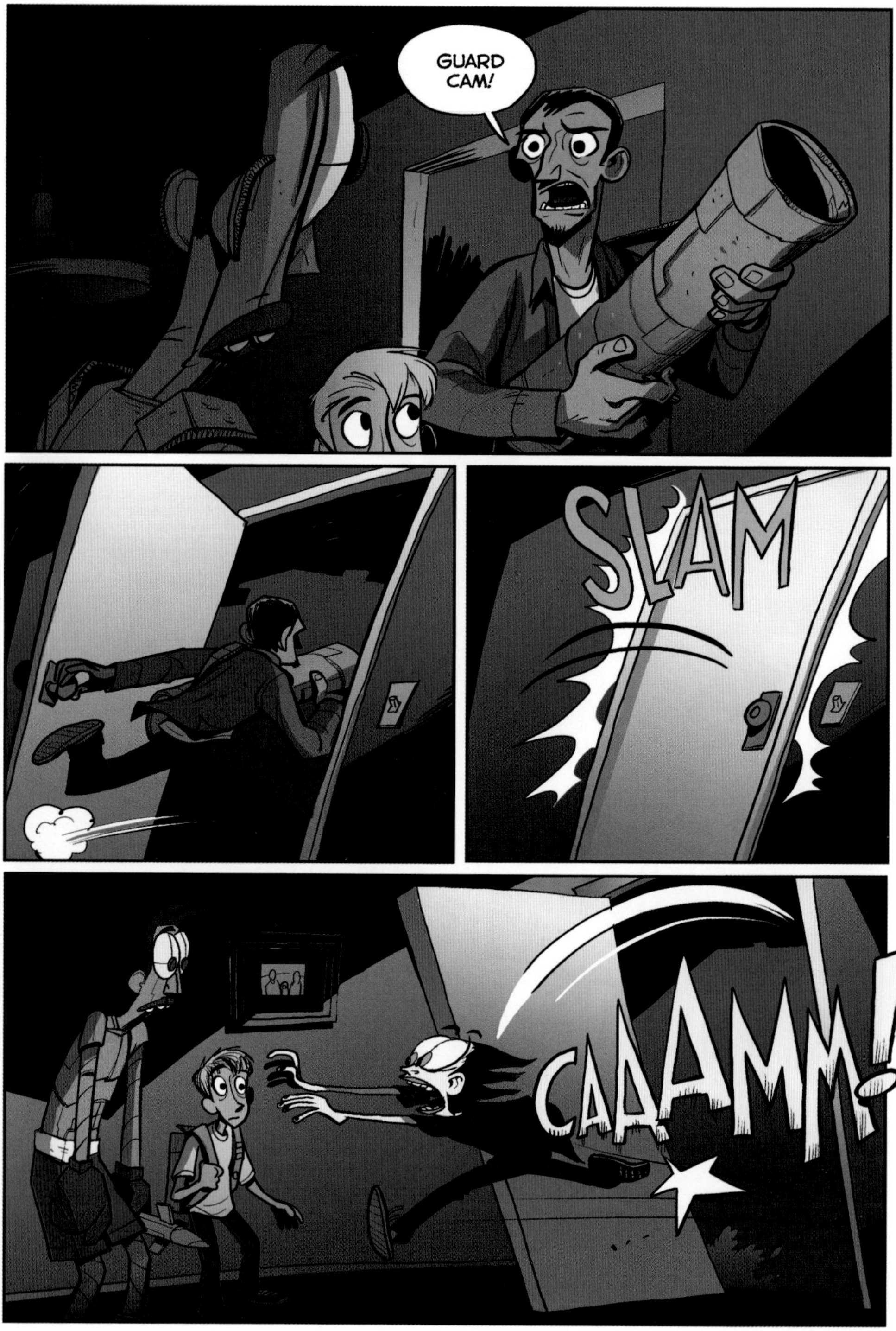
GUARD CAM!
SLAM
CAAAMM!

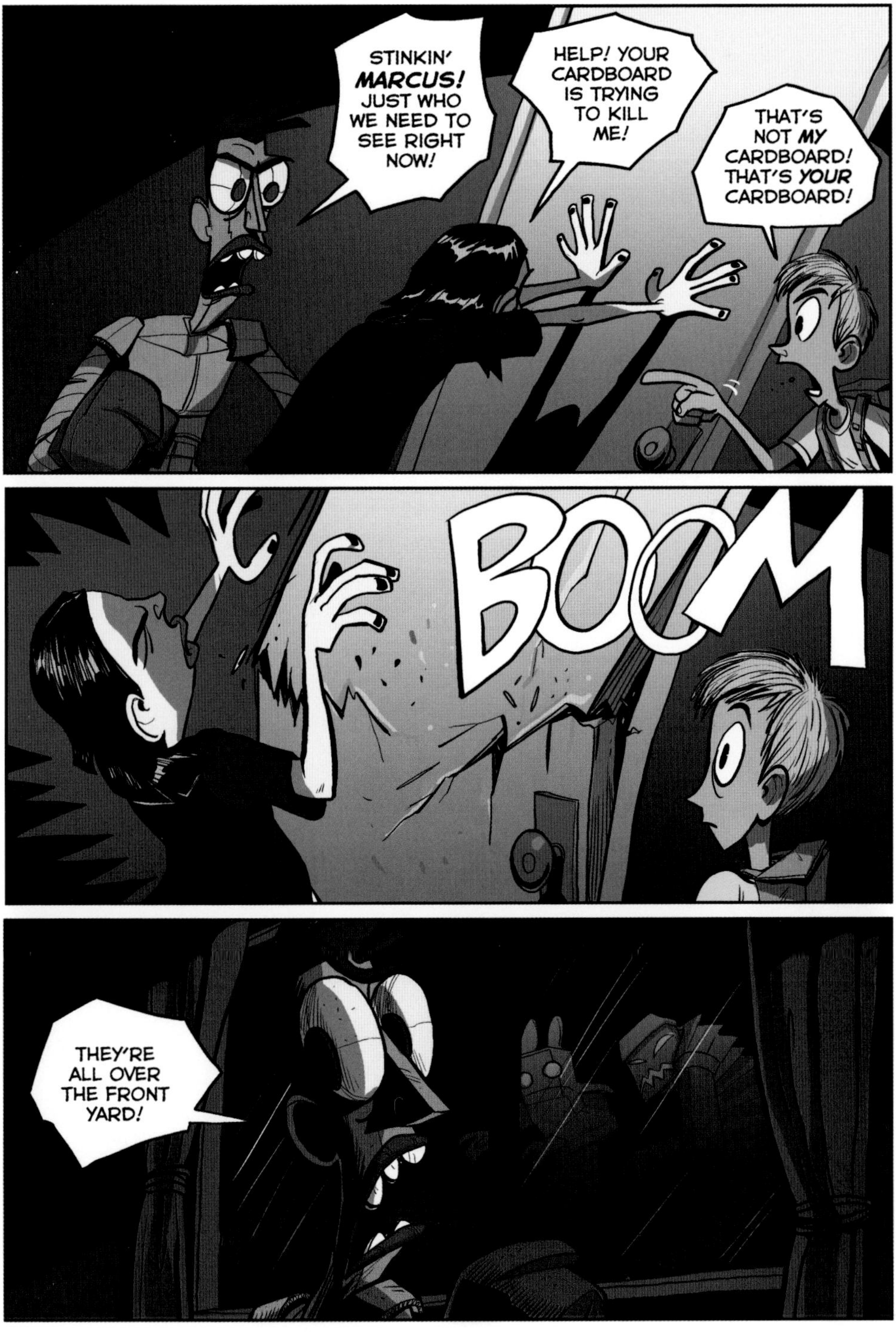
STINKIN' **MARCUS!** JUST WHO WE NEED TO SEE RIGHT NOW!
HELP! YOUR CARDBOARD IS TRYING TO KILL ME!
THAT'S NOT ***MY*** CARDBOARD! THAT'S ***YOUR*** CARDBOARD!
BOOM
THEY'RE ALL OVER THE FRONT YARD!

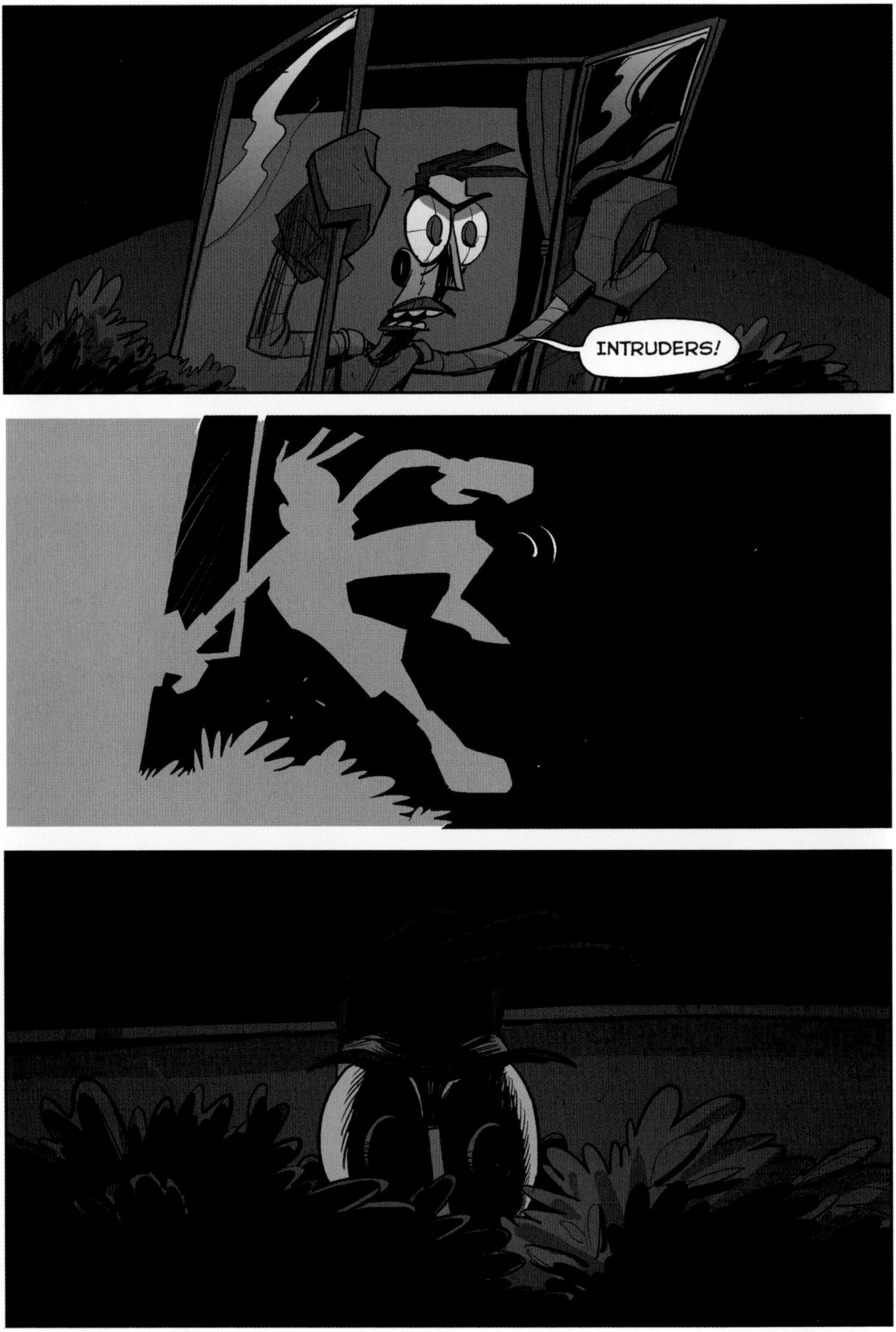
INTRUDERS!

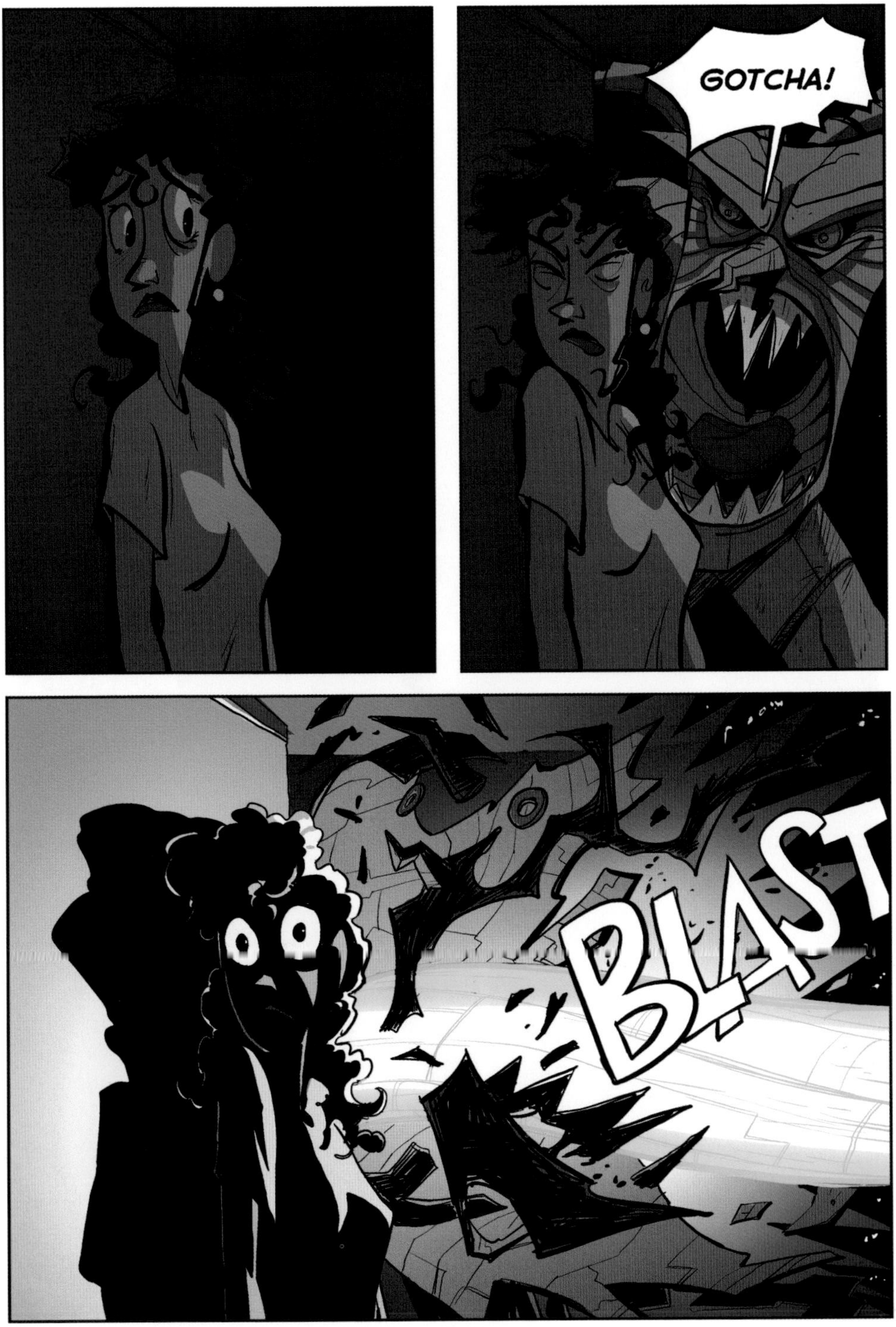
GOTCHA!
BLAST

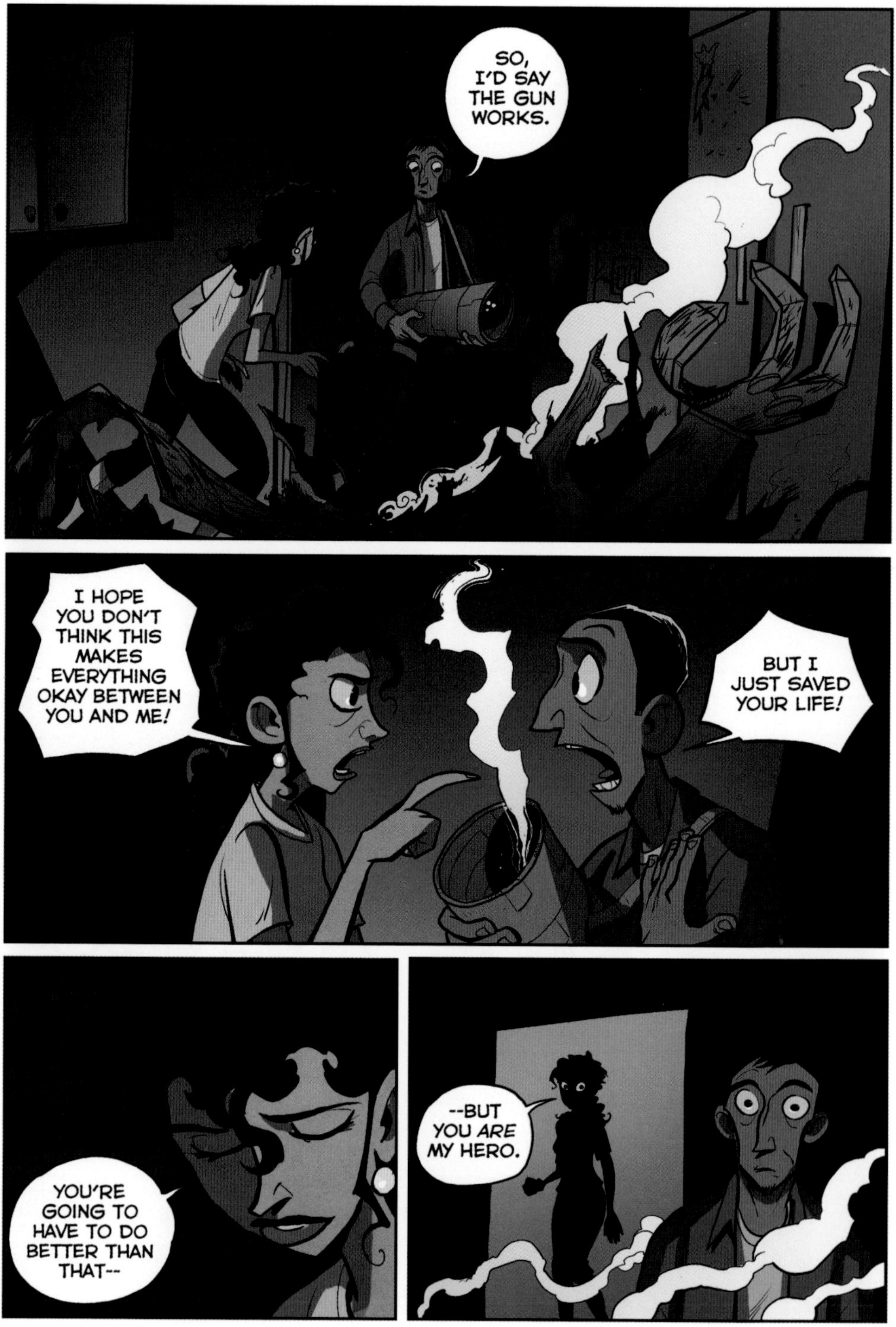
SO, I'D SAY THE GUN WORKS.
I HOPE YOU DON'T THINK THIS MAKES EVERYTHING OKAY BETWEEN YOU AND ME!
BUT I JUST SAVED YOUR LIFE!
YOU'RE GOING TO HAVE TO DO BETTER THAN THAT--
--BUT YOU *ARE* MY HERO.

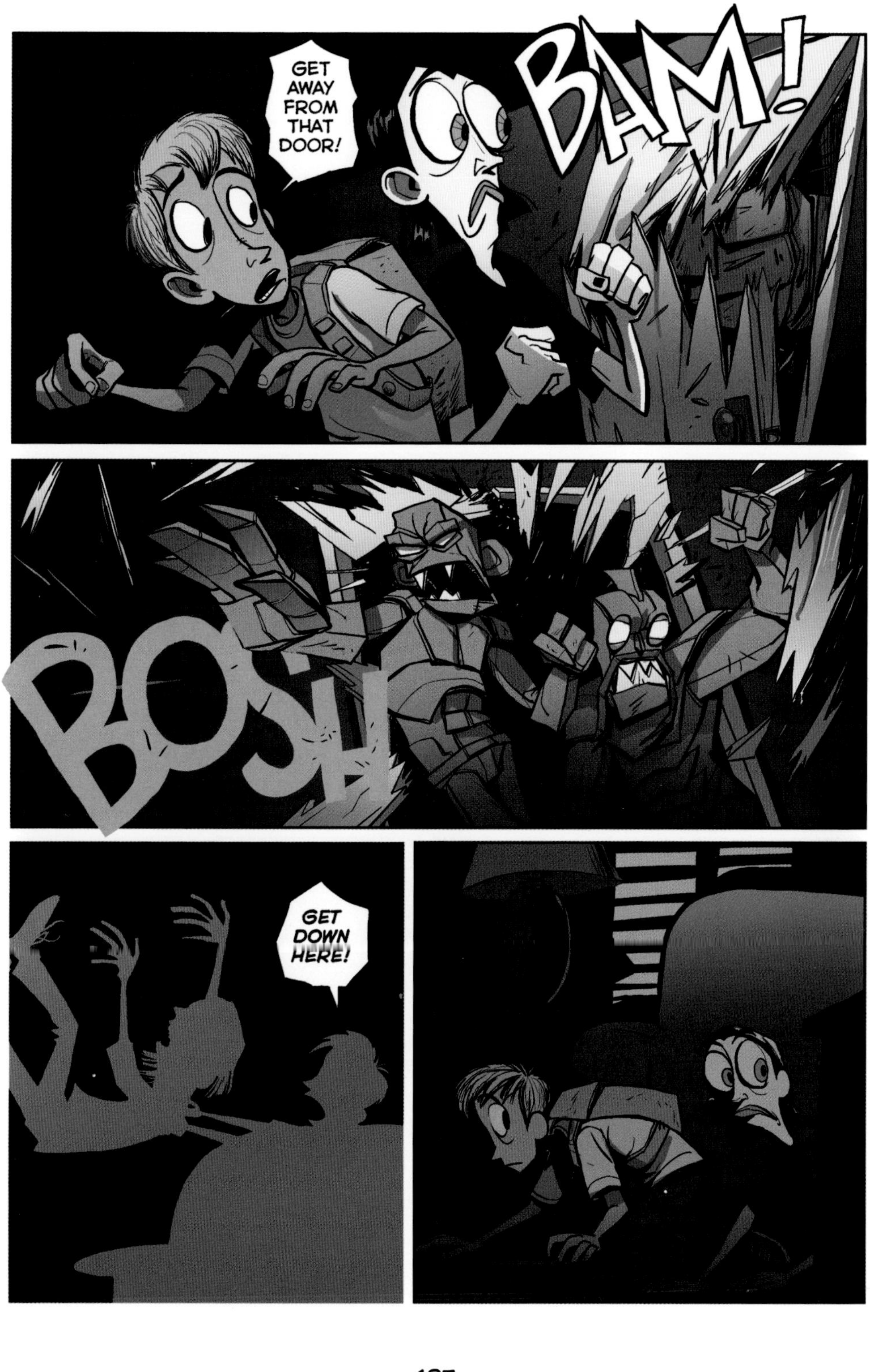
GET AWAY FROM THAT DOOR!
BAM!
BOSH
GET DOWN HERE!

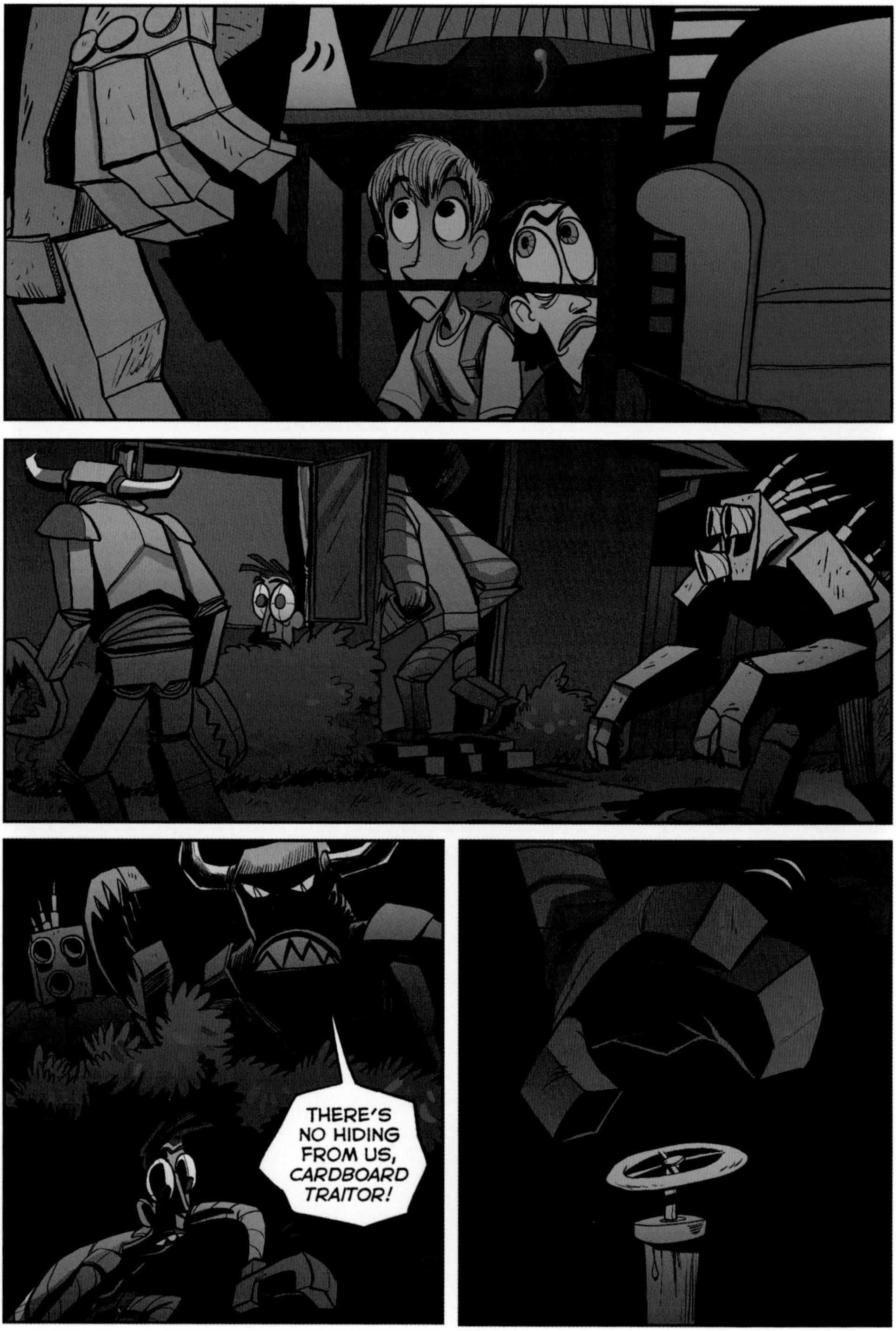
THERE'S NO HIDING FROM US, CARDBOARD TRAITOR!

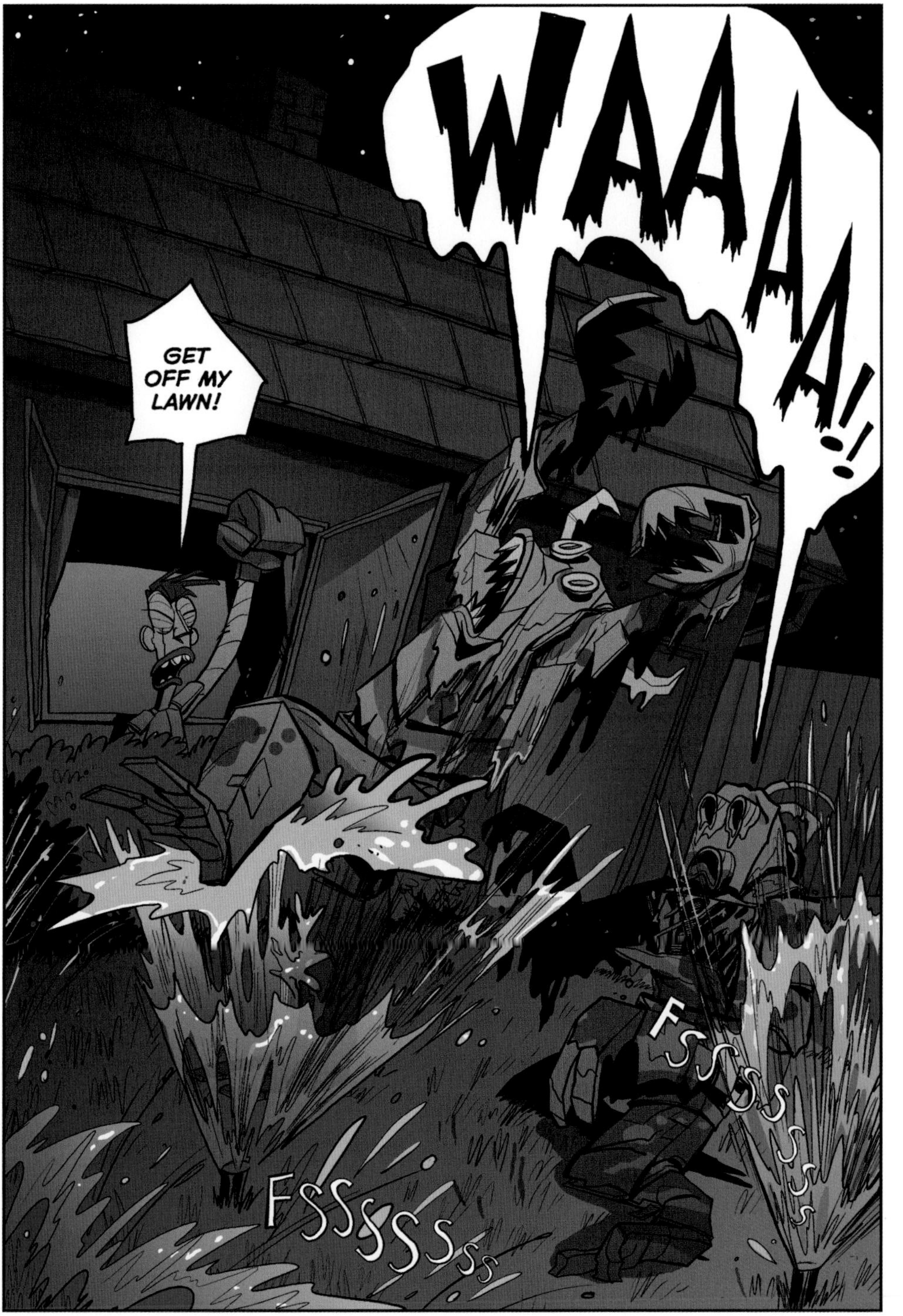
WAAAAA!!
GET OFF MY LAWN!
FSSSSSSSS
FSSSSSSSS

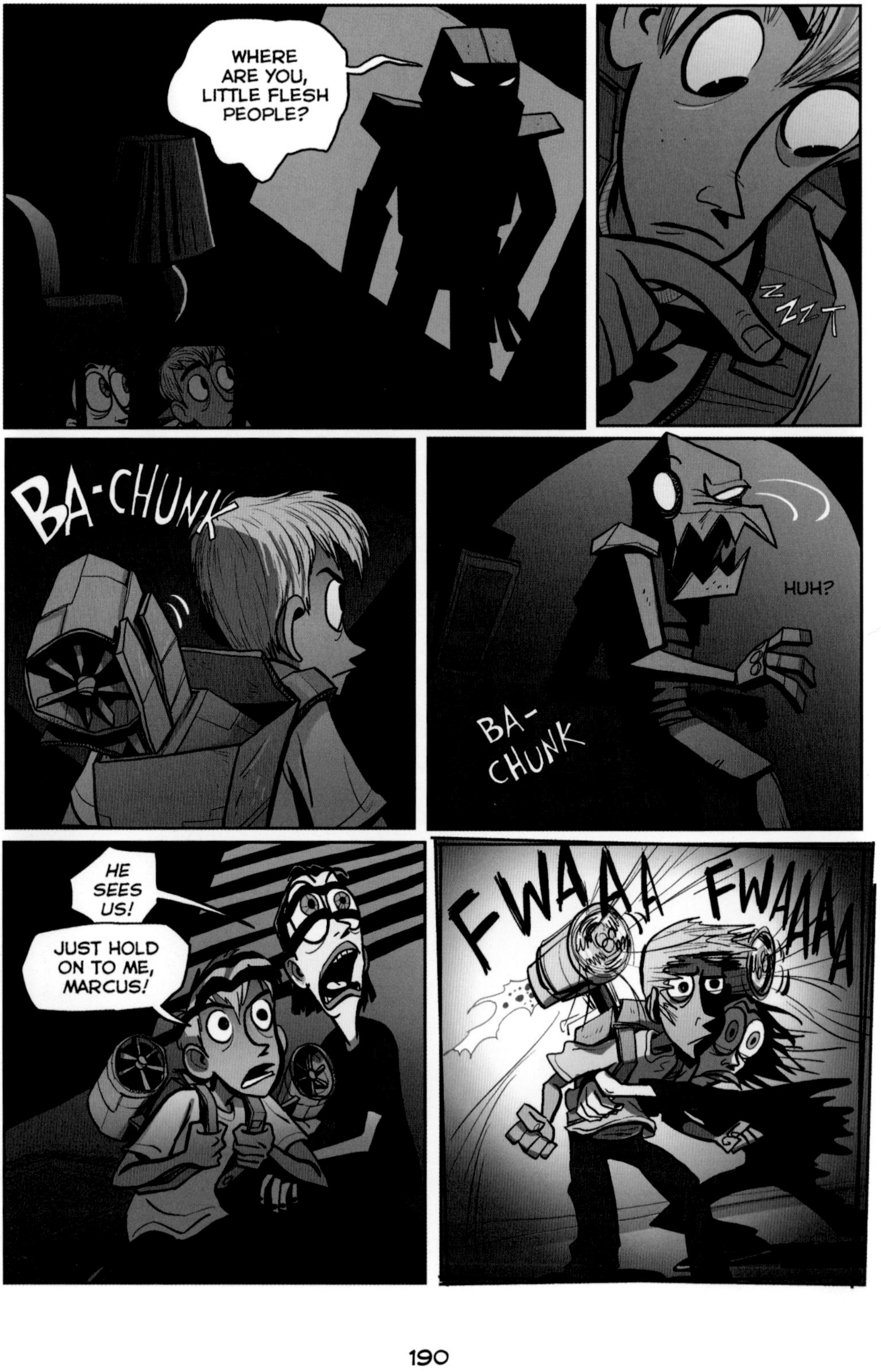

WHERE ARE YOU, LITTLE FLESH PEOPLE?
ZZZT
BA-CHUNK
HUH?
BA-CHUNK
HE SEES US!
JUST HOLD ON TO ME, MARCUS!
FWAAA FWAAAA

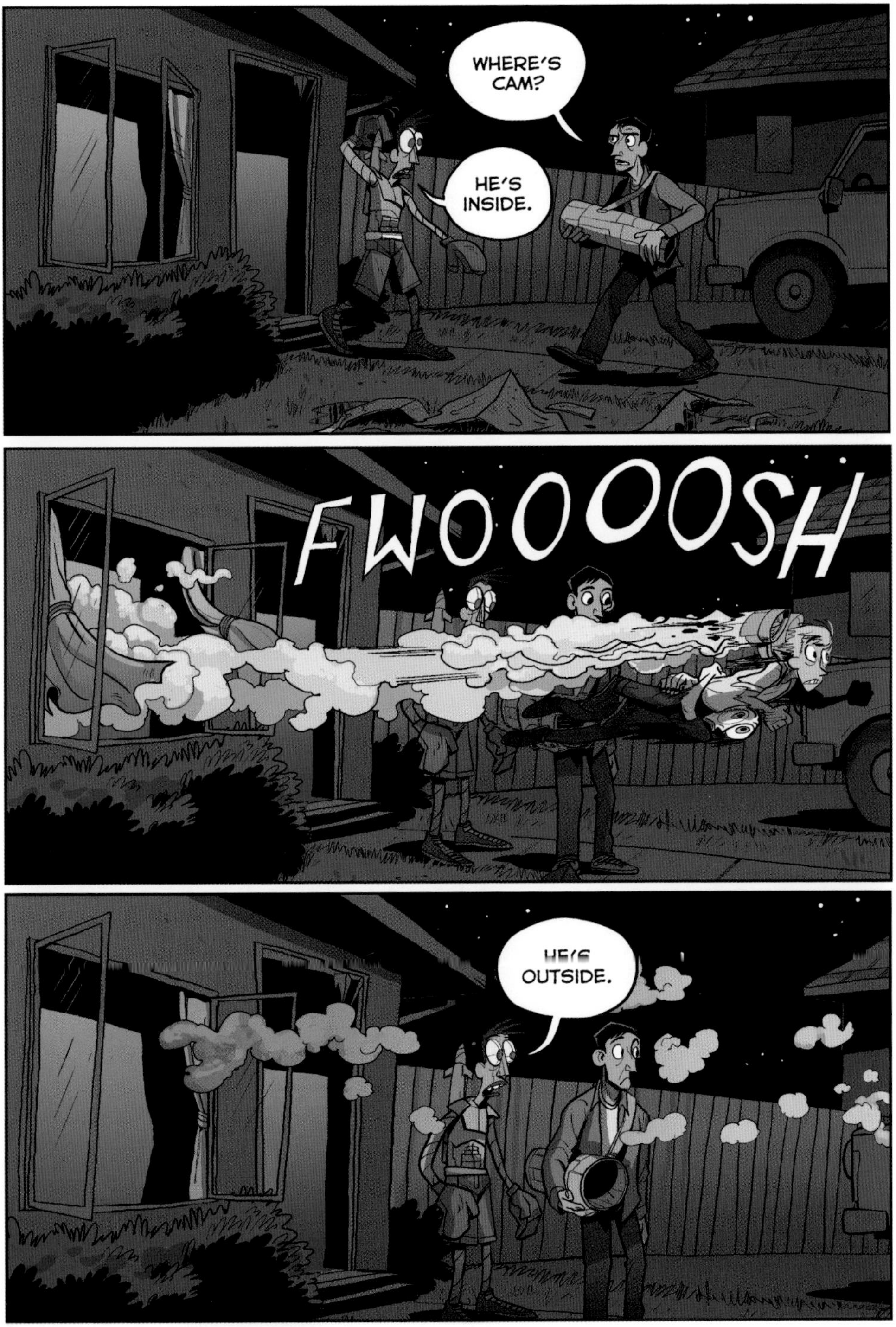
WHERE'S CAM?
HE'S INSIDE.
FWOOOOSH
HE'S OUTSIDE.

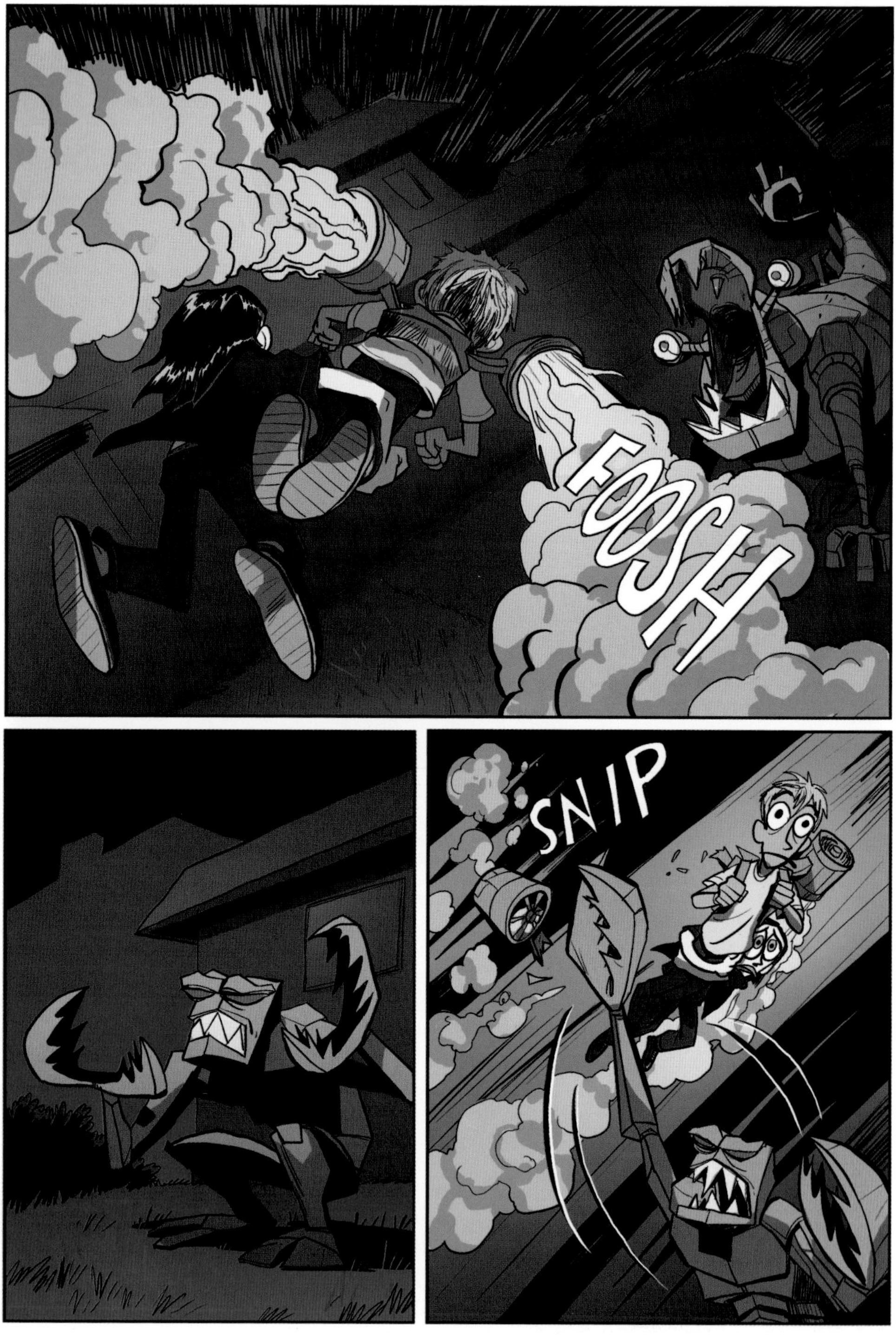
FOOSH
SNIP

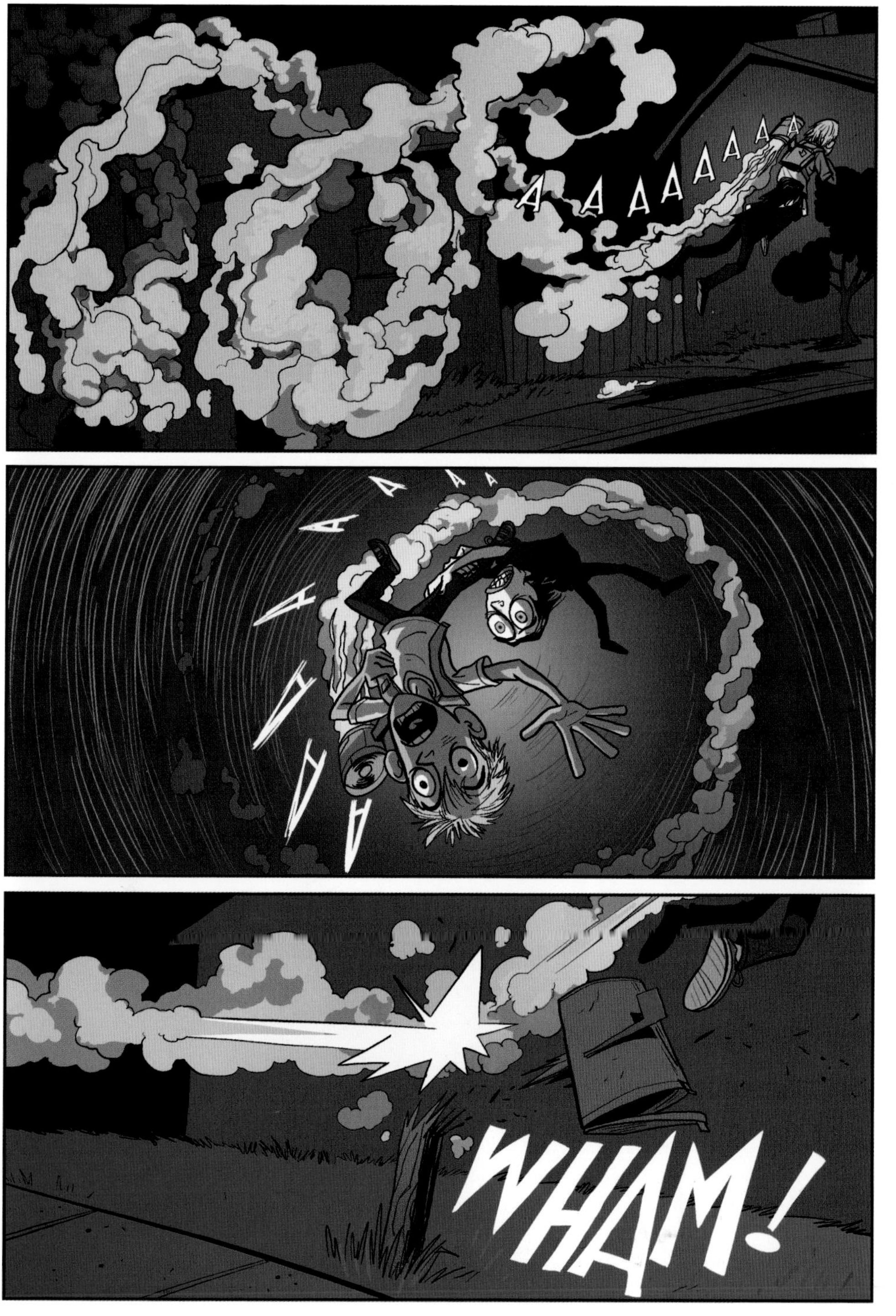
AAAAAAAA
AAAAAAAAAAA
WHAM!

OH, MY NECK IS THRASHED!

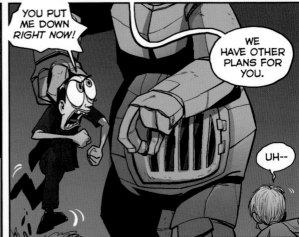

YOU PUT ME DOWN *RIGHT NOW!*

WE HAVE OTHER PLANS FOR YOU.

UH--

LET HIM GO!

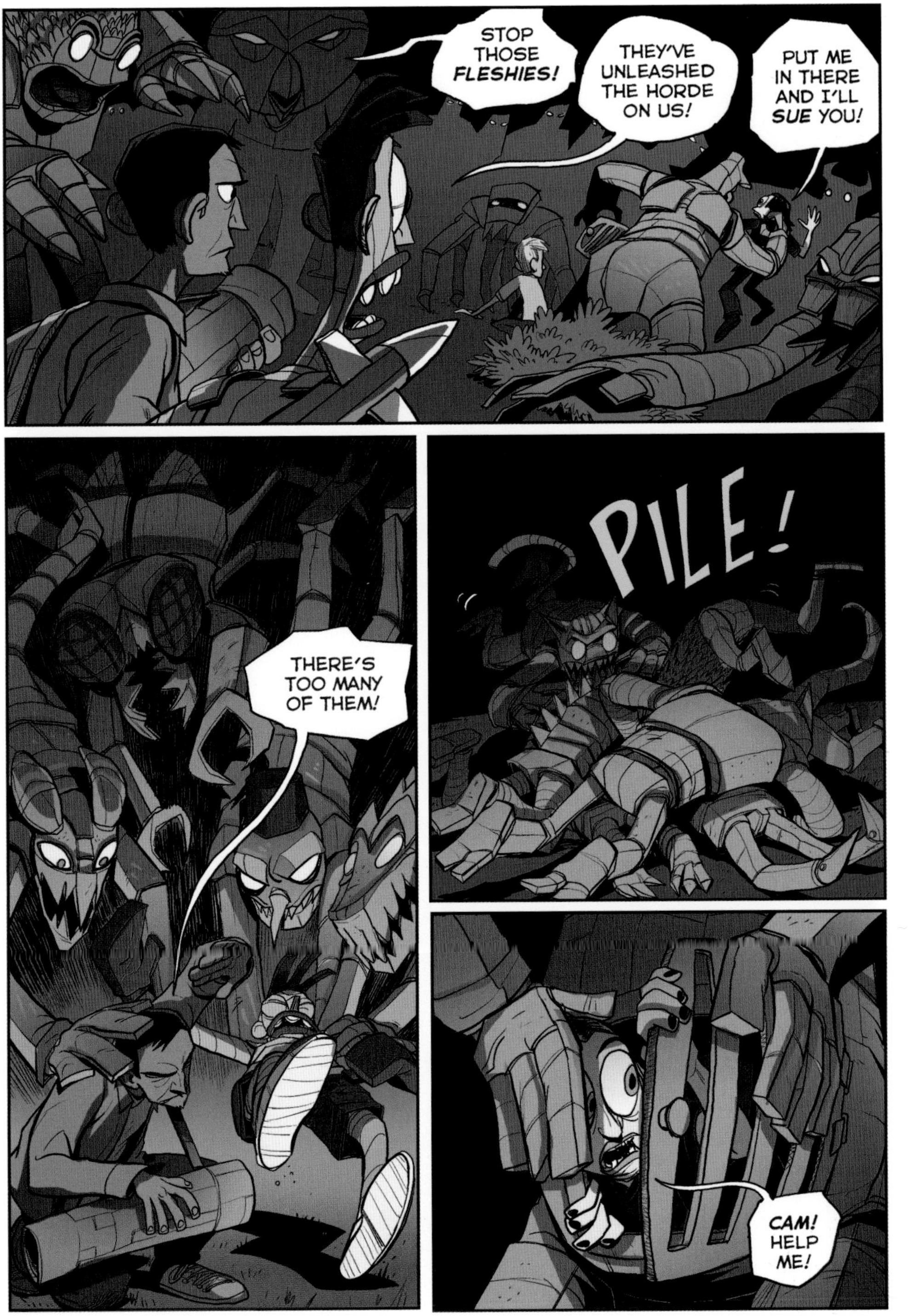
STOP THOSE FLESHIES!
THEY'VE UNLEASHED THE HORDE ON US!
PUT ME IN THERE AND I'LL SUE YOU!
THERE'S TOO MANY OF THEM!
PILE!
CAM! HELP ME!

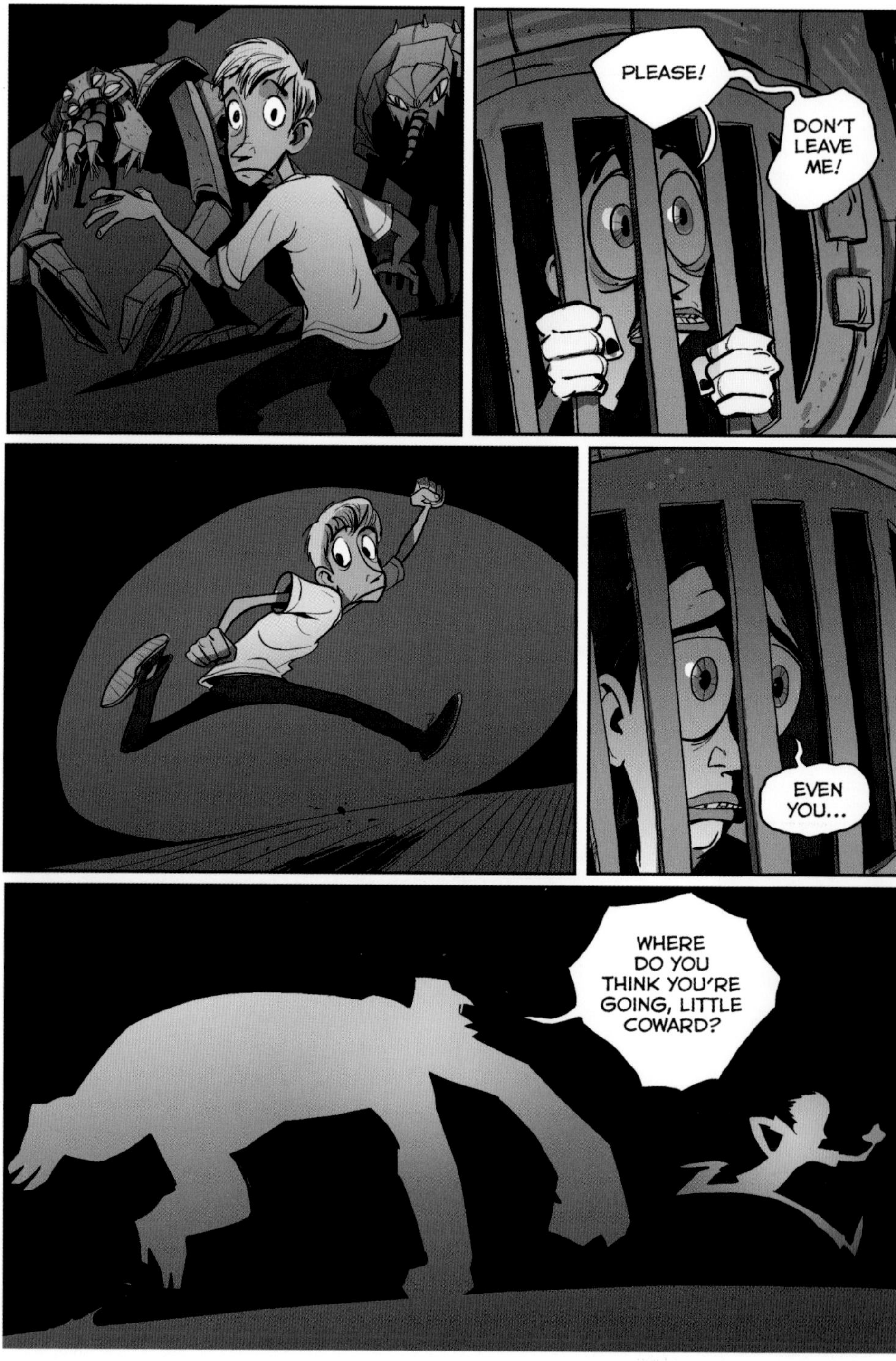
PLEASE!
DON'T LEAVE ME!
EVEN YOU...
WHERE DO YOU THINK YOU'RE GOING, LITTLE COWARD?

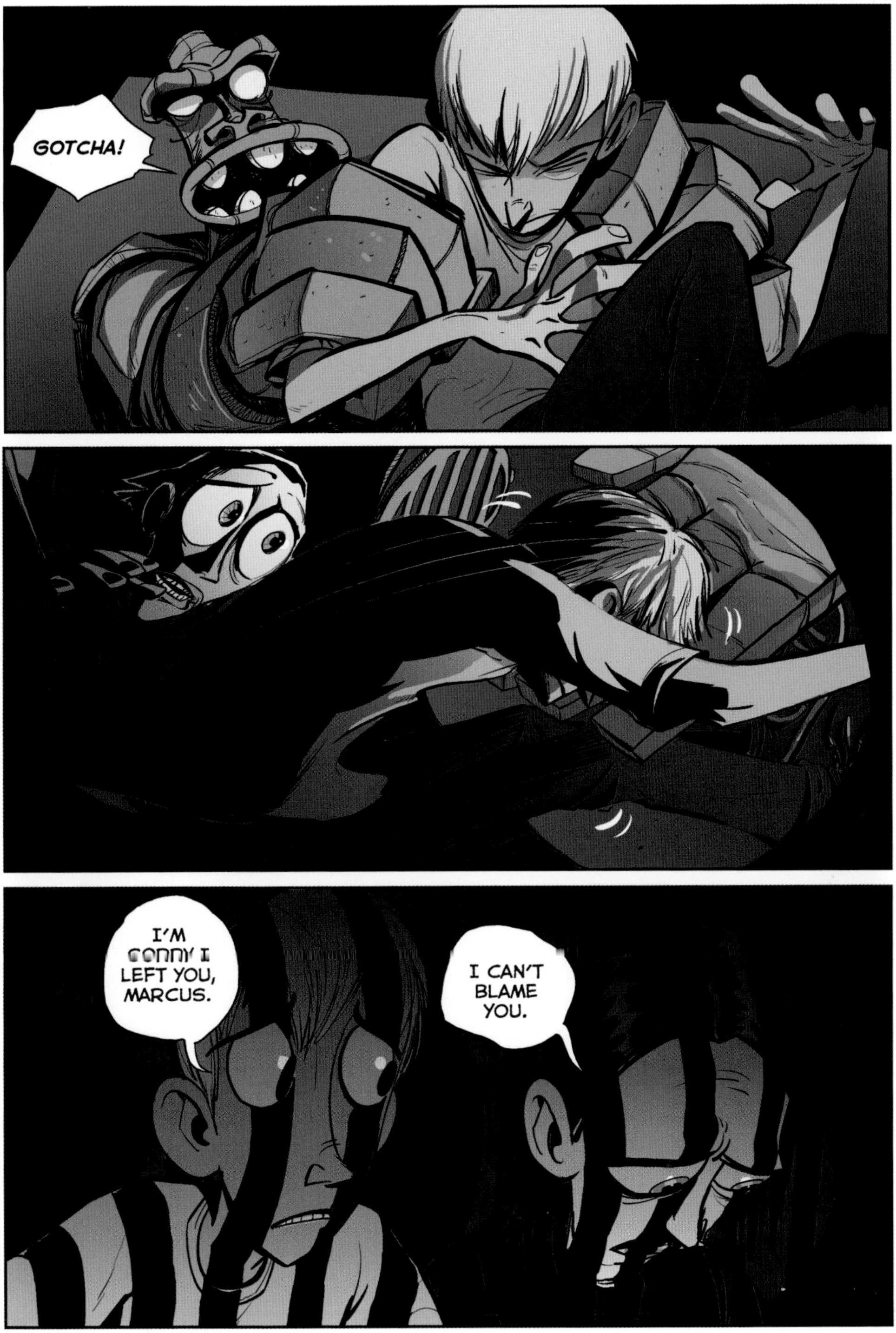
GOTCHA!
I'M SORRY I LEFT YOU, MARCUS.
I CAN'T BLAME YOU.

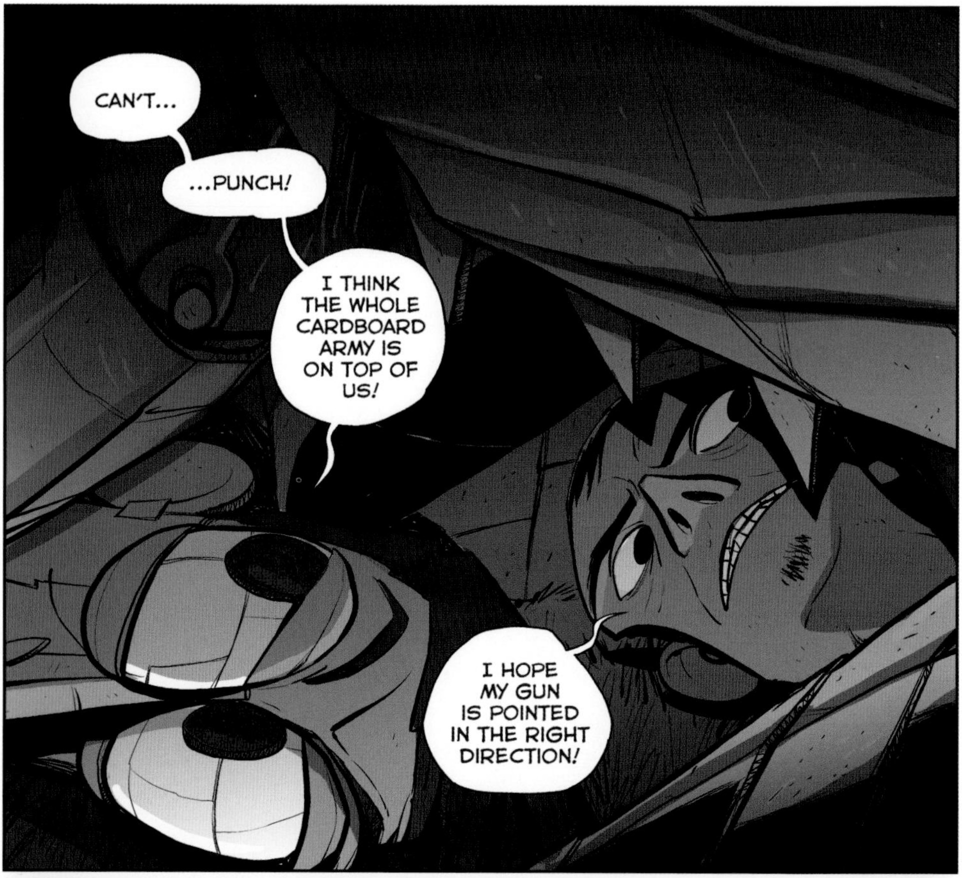
CAN'T...
...PUNCH!
I THINK THE WHOLE CARDBOARD ARMY IS ON TOP OF US!
I HOPE MY GUN IS POINTED IN THE RIGHT DIRECTION!

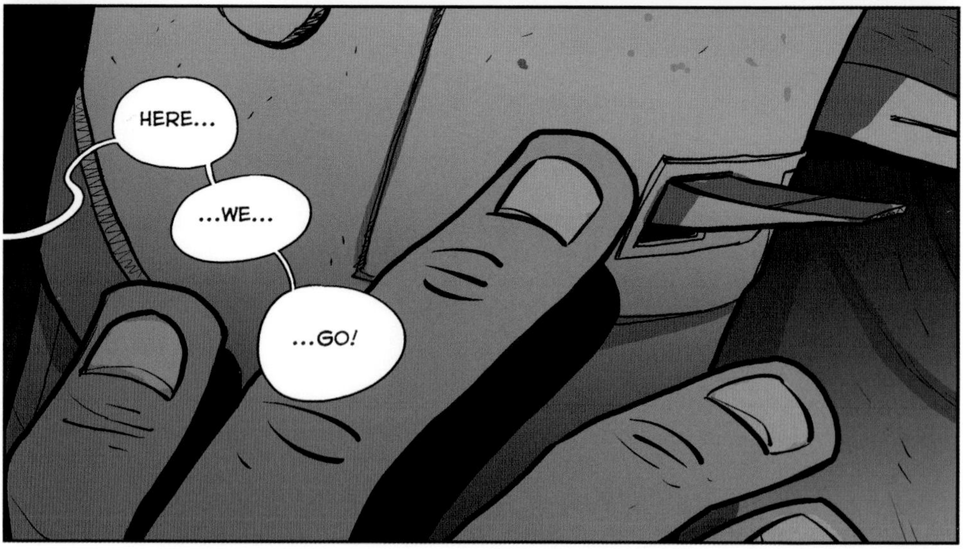
HERE...
...WE...
...GO!

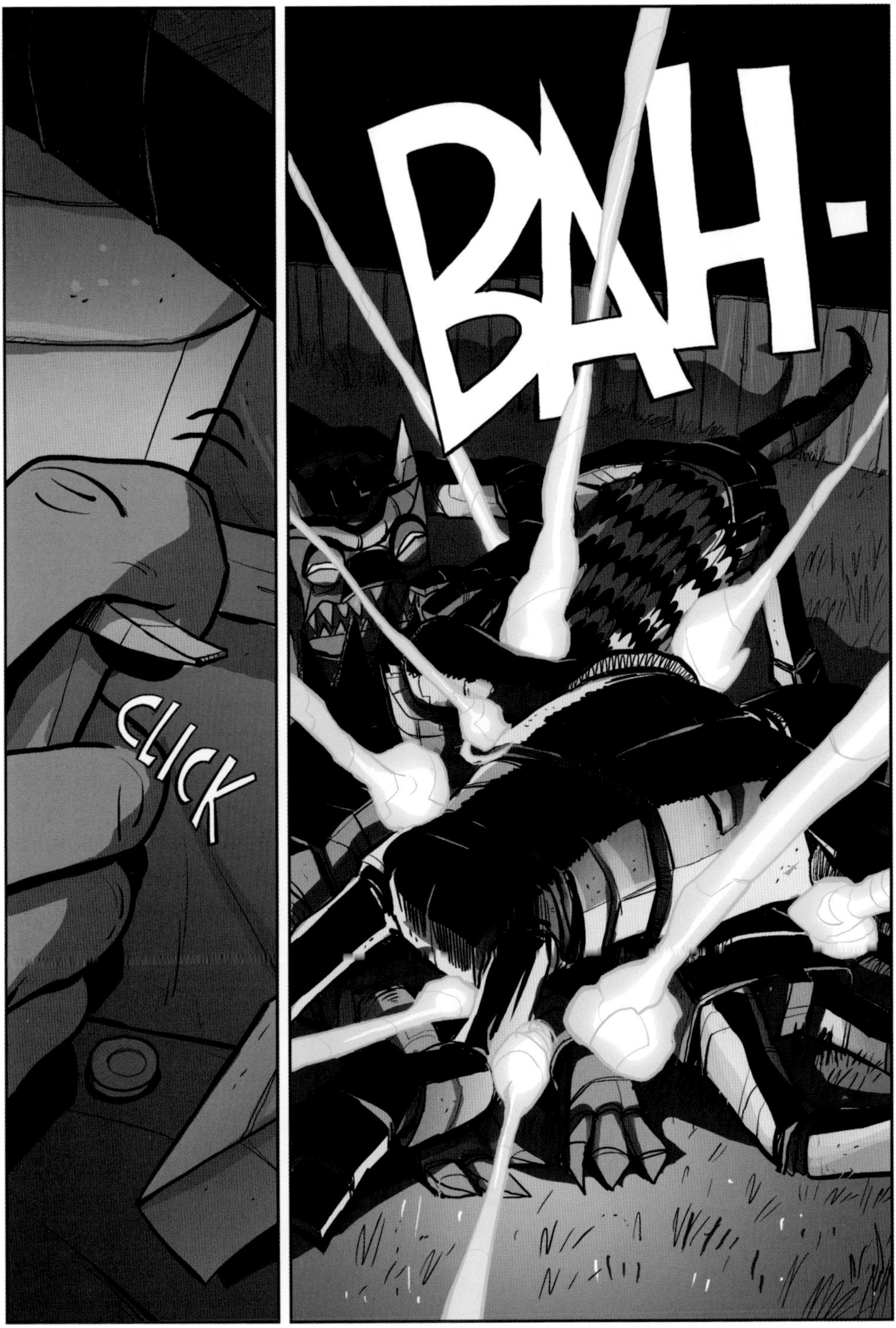
CLICK
BAH-

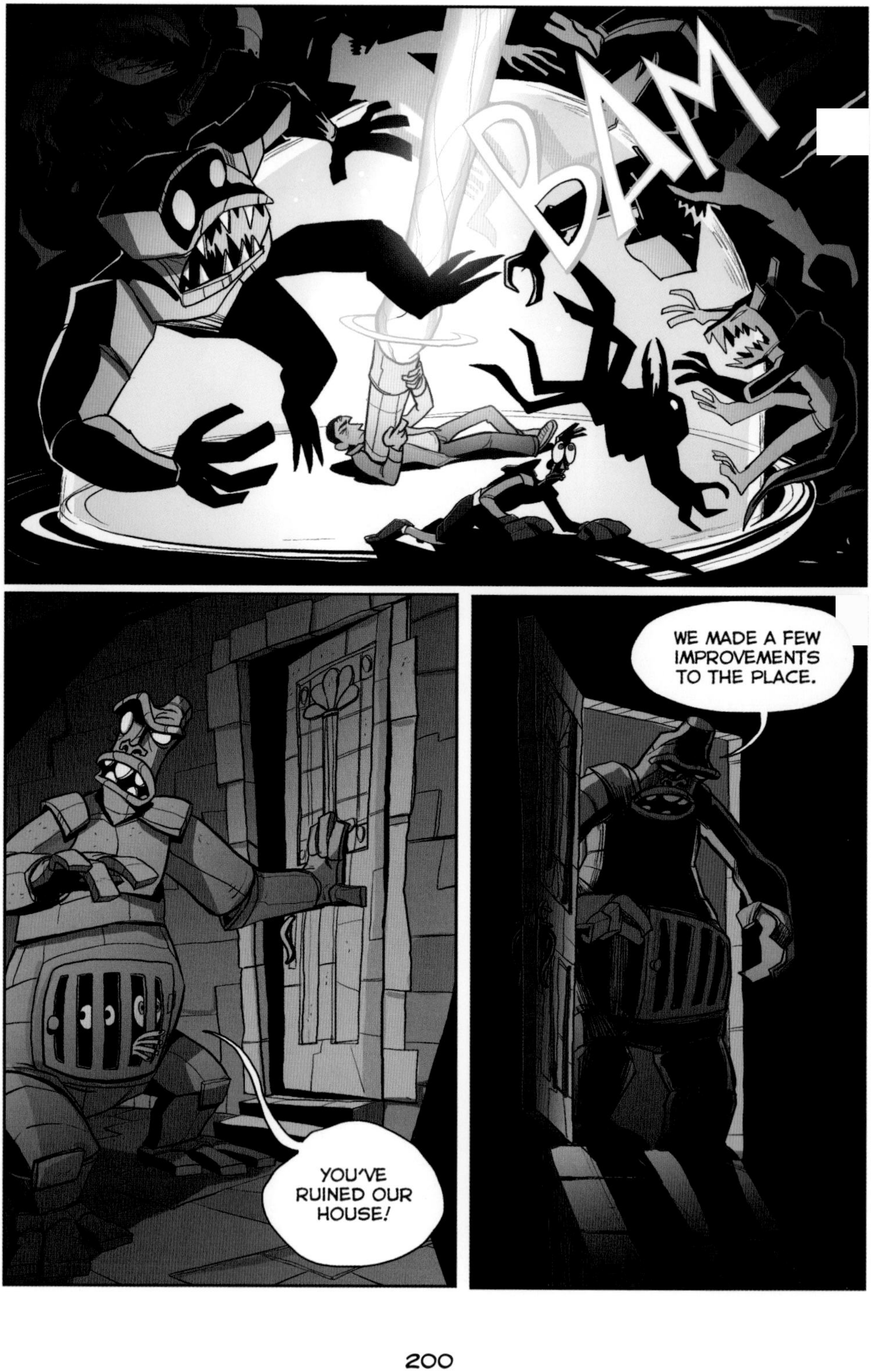
BAM
YOU'VE RUINED OUR HOUSE!
WE MADE A FEW IMPROVEMENTS TO THE PLACE.

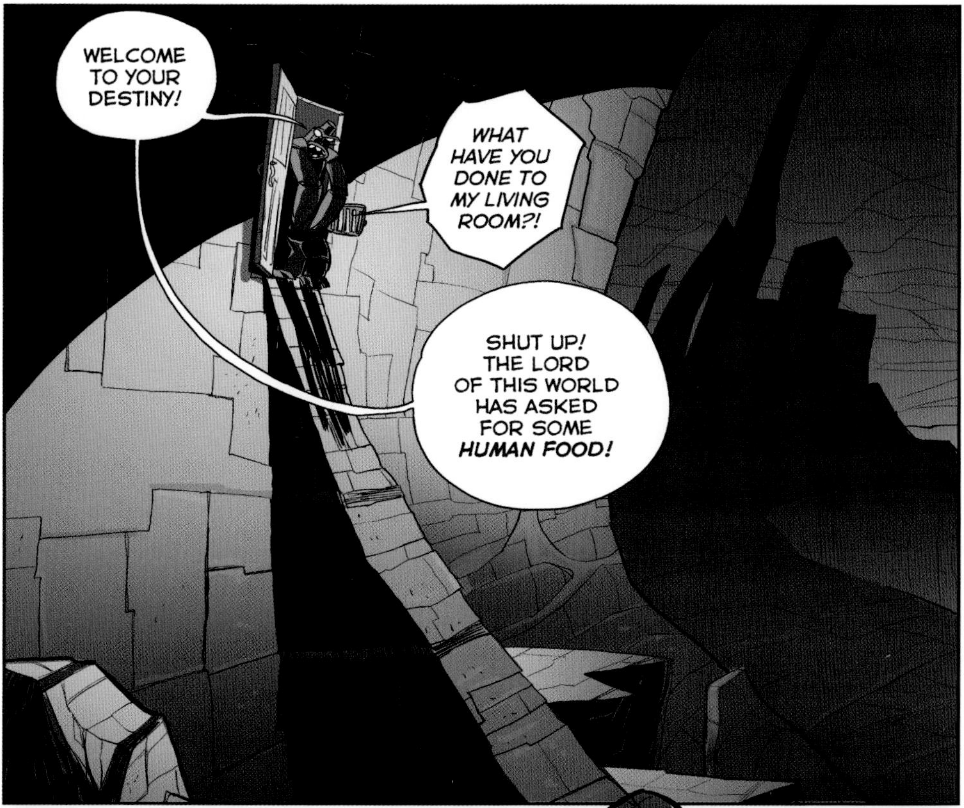
WELCOME TO YOUR DESTINY!
WHAT HAVE YOU DONE TO MY LIVING ROOM?!
SHUT UP! THE LORD OF THIS WORLD HAS ASKED FOR SOME *HUMAN FOOD!*

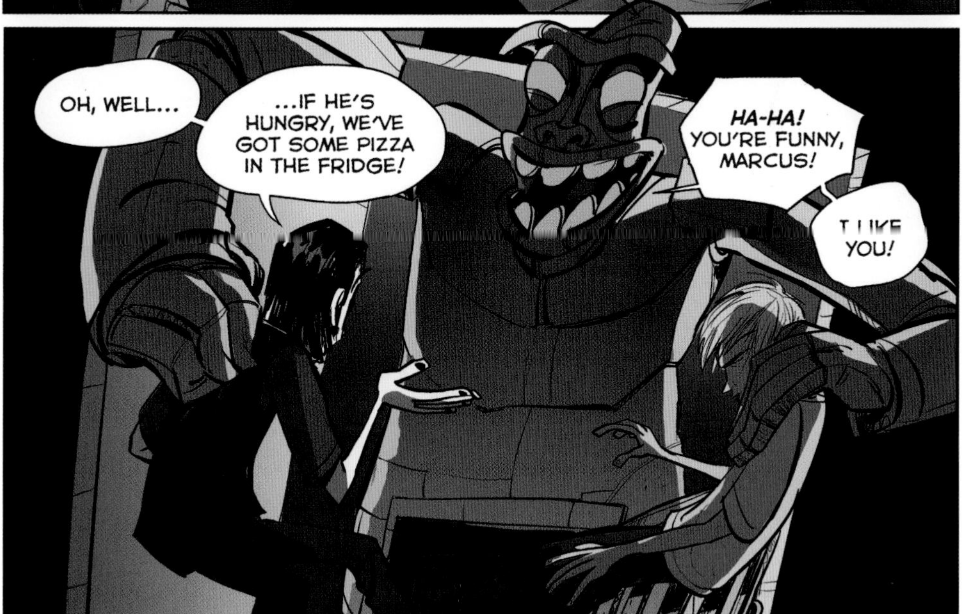
OH, WELL...
...IF HE'S HUNGRY, WE'VE GOT SOME PIZZA IN THE FRIDGE!
HA-HA! YOU'RE FUNNY, MARCUS!
I LIKE YOU!

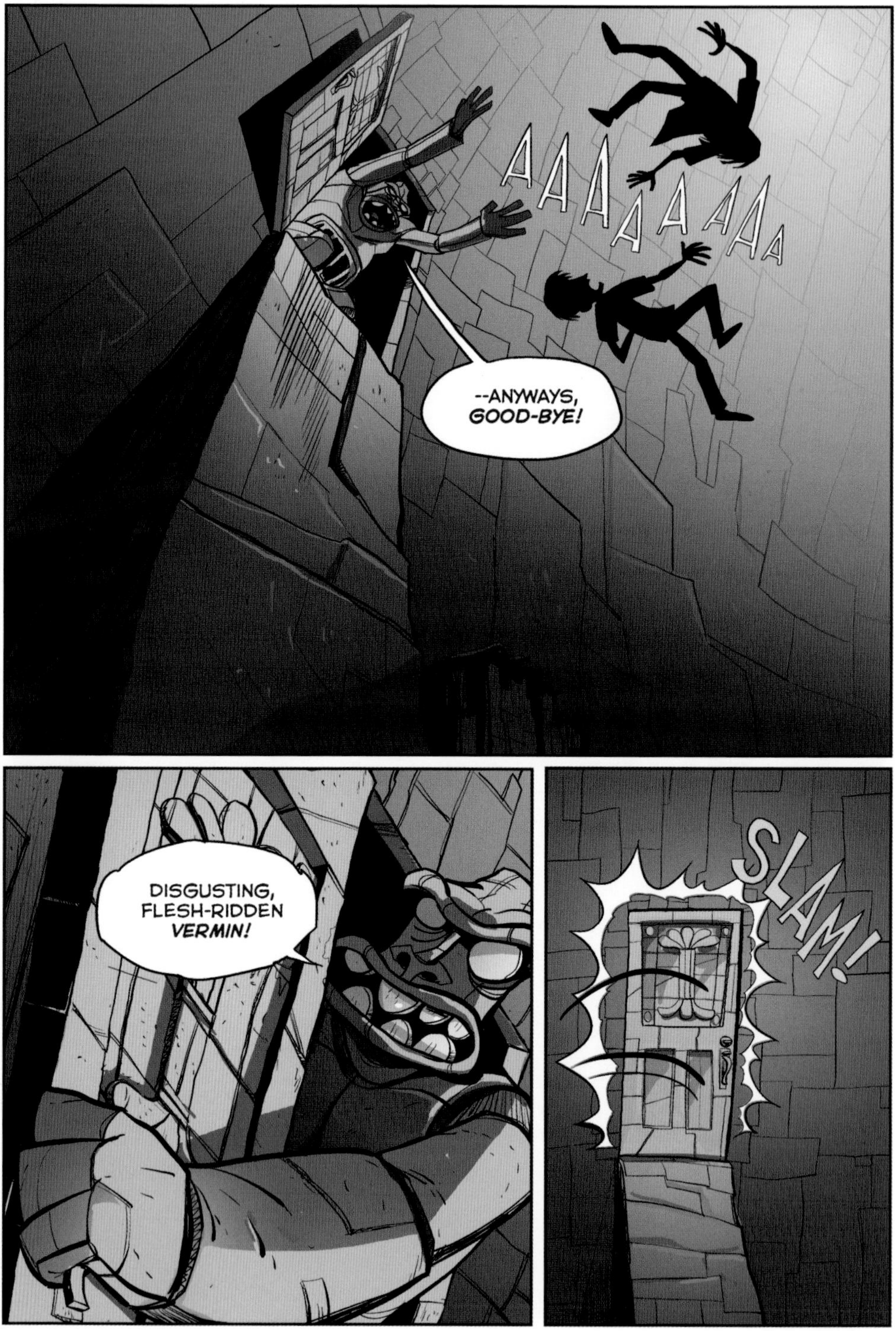
AAAAAAAAAA
--ANYWAYS, GOOD-BYE!
DISGUSTING, FLESH-RIDDEN VERMIN!
SLAM!

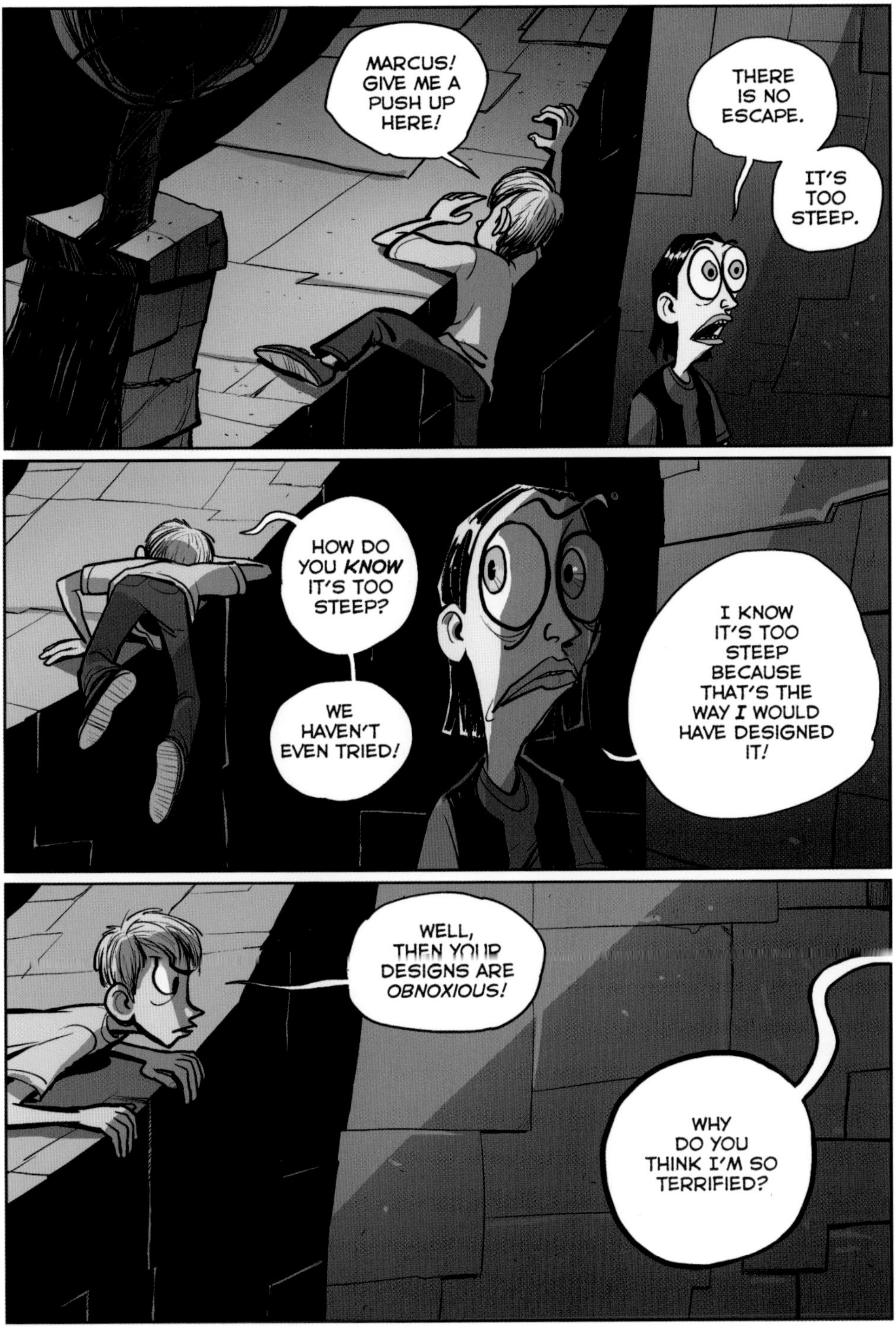
MARCUS! GIVE ME A PUSH UP HERE!
THERE IS NO ESCAPE.
IT'S TOO STEEP.
HOW DO YOU *KNOW* IT'S TOO STEEP?
WE HAVEN'T EVEN TRIED!
I KNOW IT'S TOO STEEP BECAUSE THAT'S THE WAY *I* WOULD HAVE DESIGNED IT!
WELL, THEN YOUR DESIGNS ARE *OBNOXIOUS!*
WHY DO YOU THINK I'M SO TERRIFIED?

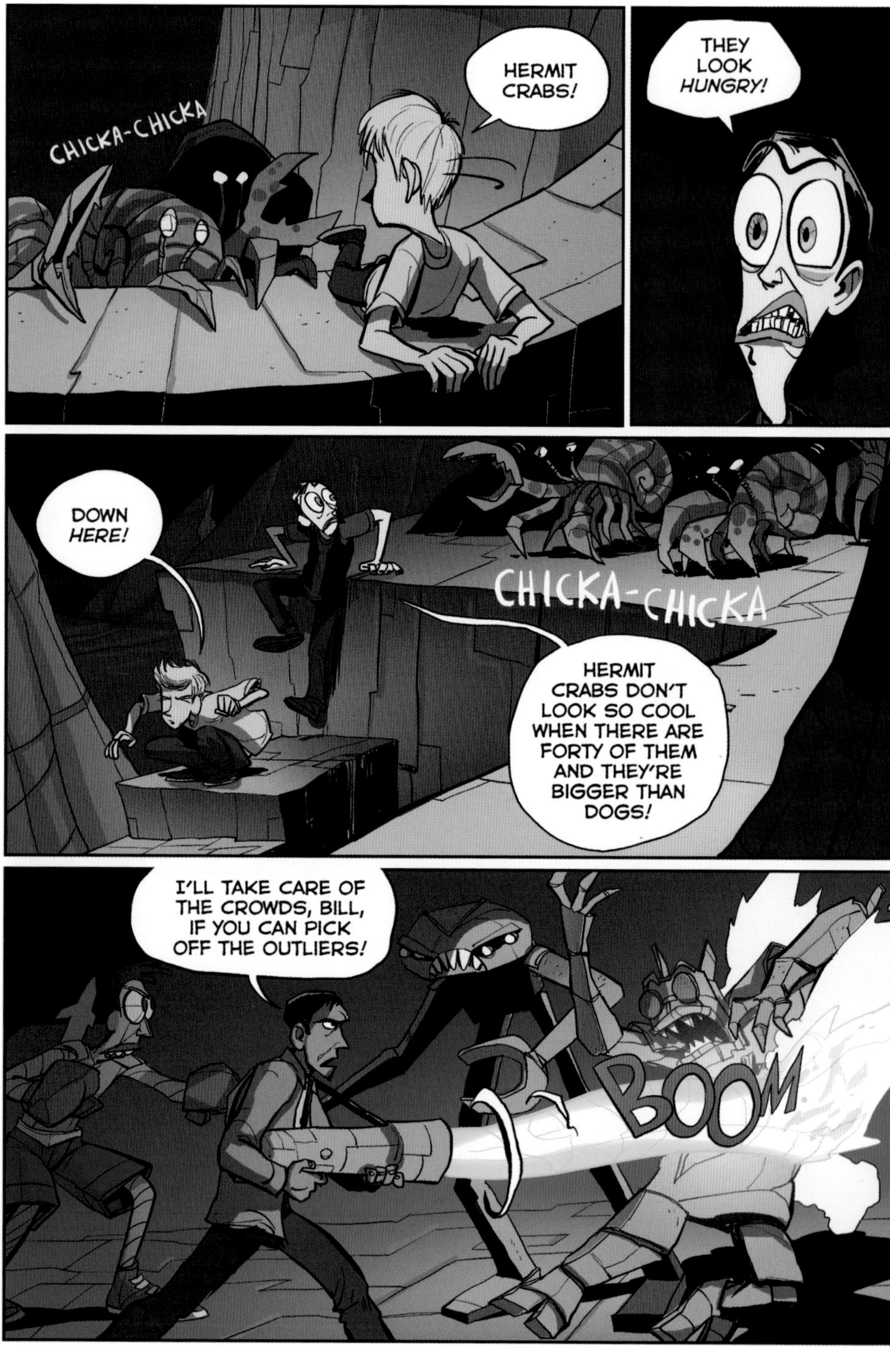
CHICKA-CHICKA
HERMIT CRABS!
THEY LOOK HUNGRY!
DOWN HERE!
CHICKA-CHICKA
HERMIT CRABS DON'T LOOK SO COOL WHEN THERE ARE FORTY OF THEM AND THEY'RE BIGGER THAN DOGS!
I'LL TAKE CARE OF THE CROWDS, BILL, IF YOU CAN PICK OFF THE OUTLIERS!
BOOM

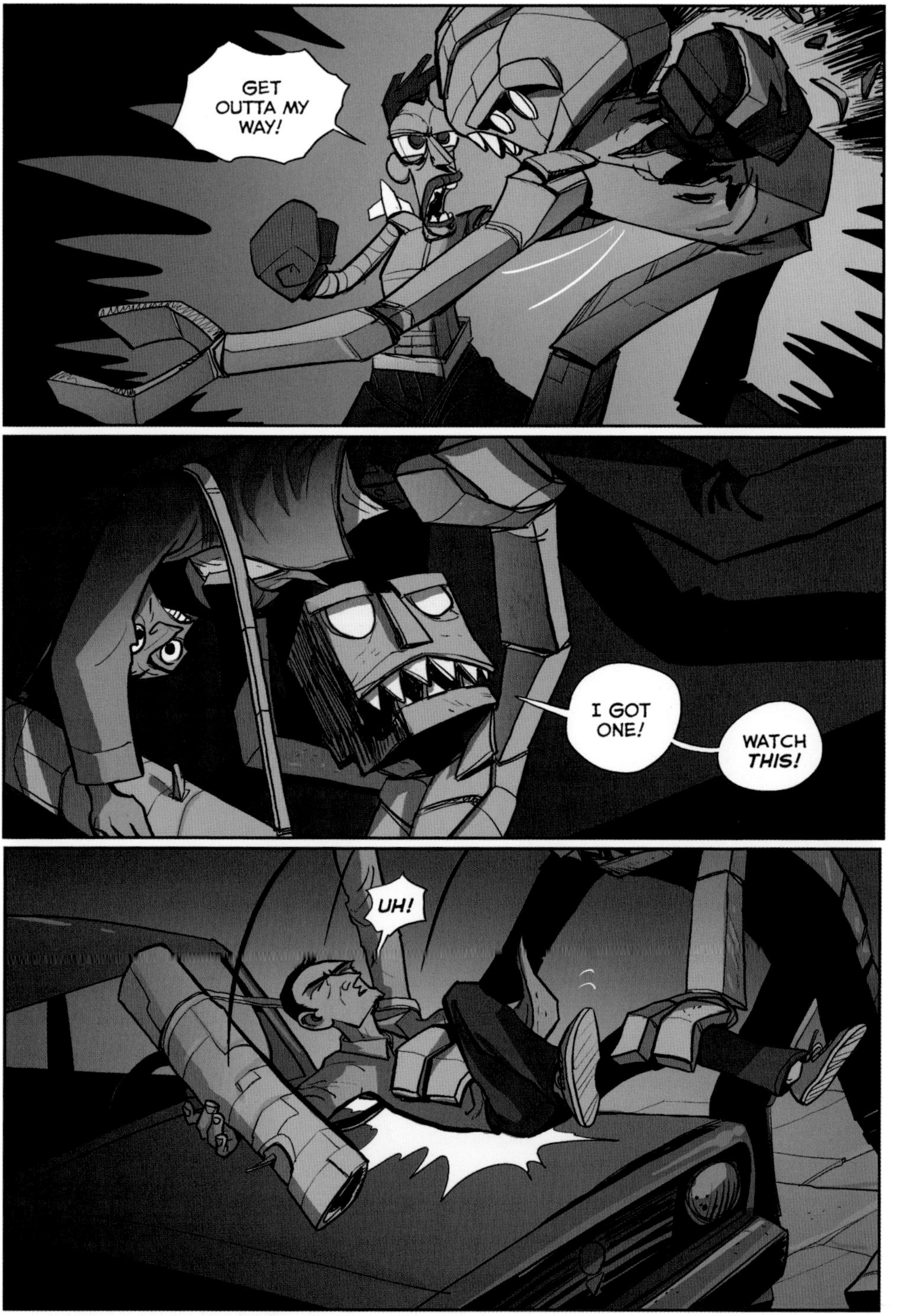
GET OUTTA MY WAY!
I GOT ONE!
WATCH THIS!
UH!

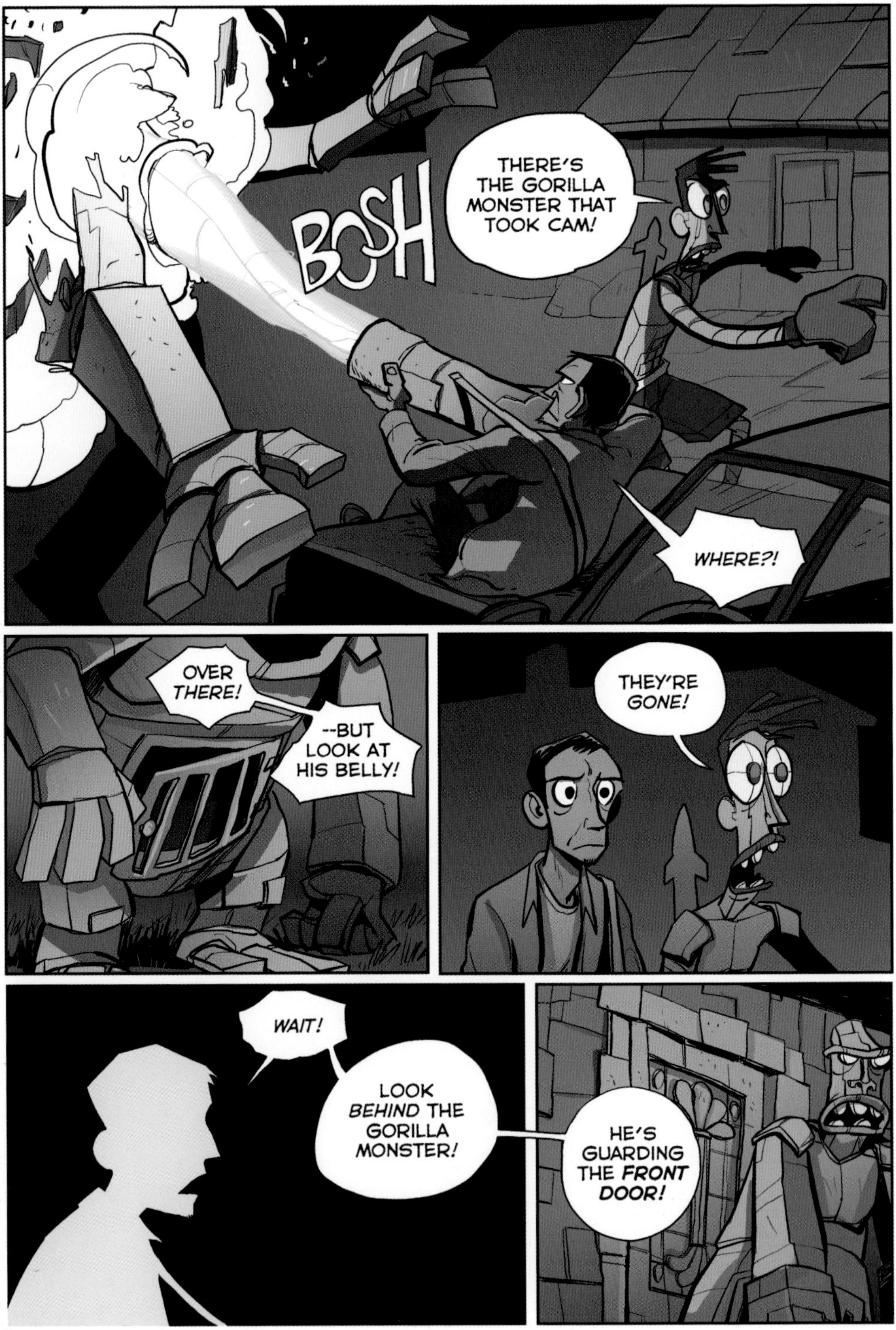
THERE'S THE GORILLA MONSTER THAT TOOK CAM!
BOSH
WHERE?!
OVER THERE!
--BUT LOOK AT HIS BELLY!
THEY'RE GONE!
WAIT!
LOOK BEHIND THE GORILLA MONSTER!
HE'S GUARDING THE FRONT DOOR!

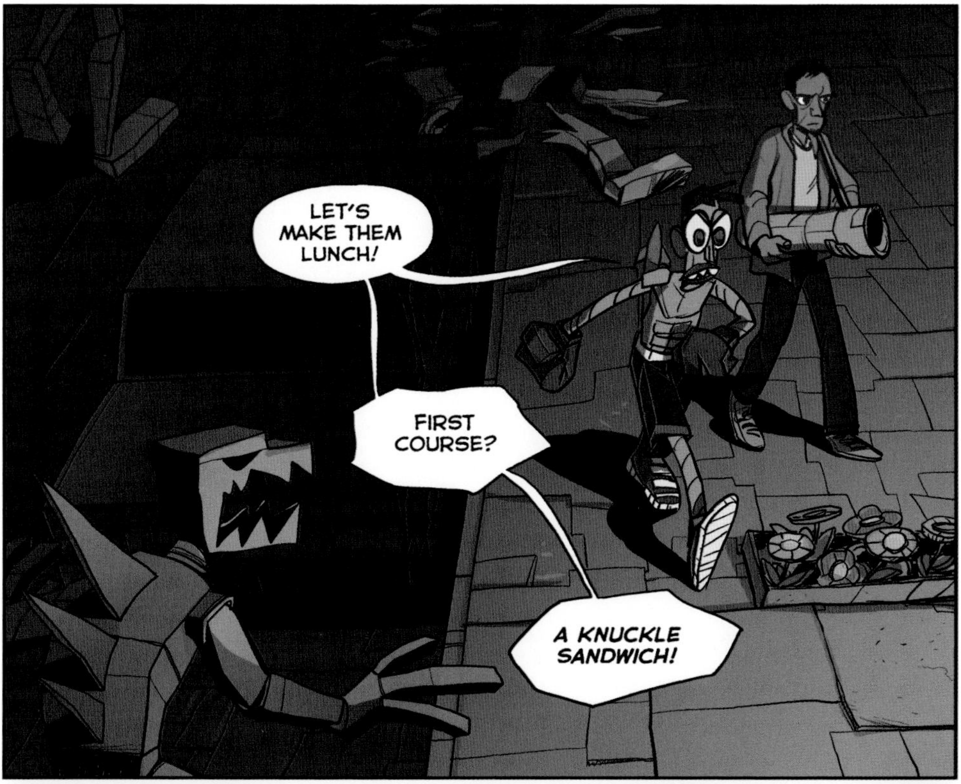
LET'S MAKE THEM LUNCH!
FIRST COURSE?
A KNUCKLE SANDWICH!

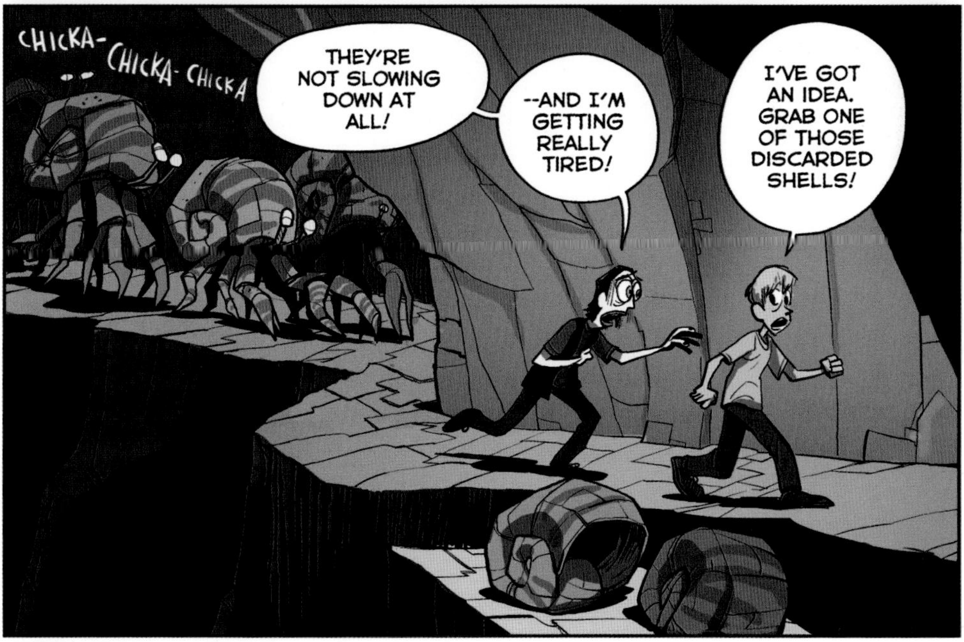
CHICKA-CHICKA-CHICKA
THEY'RE NOT SLOWING DOWN AT ALL!
--AND I'M GETTING REALLY TIRED!
I'VE GOT AN IDEA. GRAB ONE OF THOSE DISCARDED SHELLS!

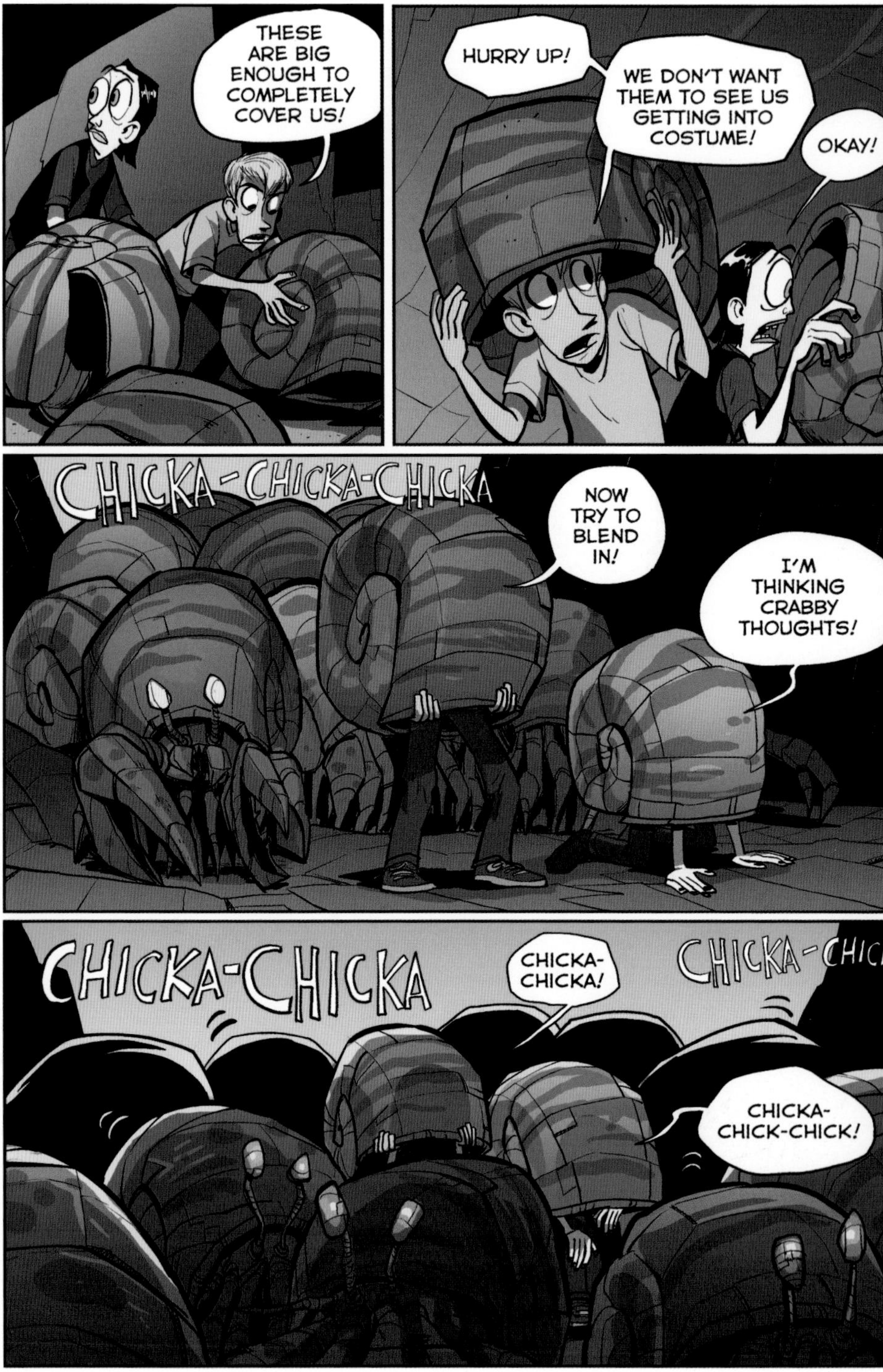
THESE ARE BIG ENOUGH TO COMPLETELY COVER US!
HURRY UP!
WE DON'T WANT THEM TO SEE US GETTING INTO COSTUME!
OKAY!
CHICKA-CHICKA-CHICKA
NOW TRY TO BLEND IN!
I'M THINKING CRABBY THOUGHTS!
CHICKA-CHICKA
CHICKA-CHICKA!
CHICKA-CHICKA
CHICKA-CHICK-CHICK!

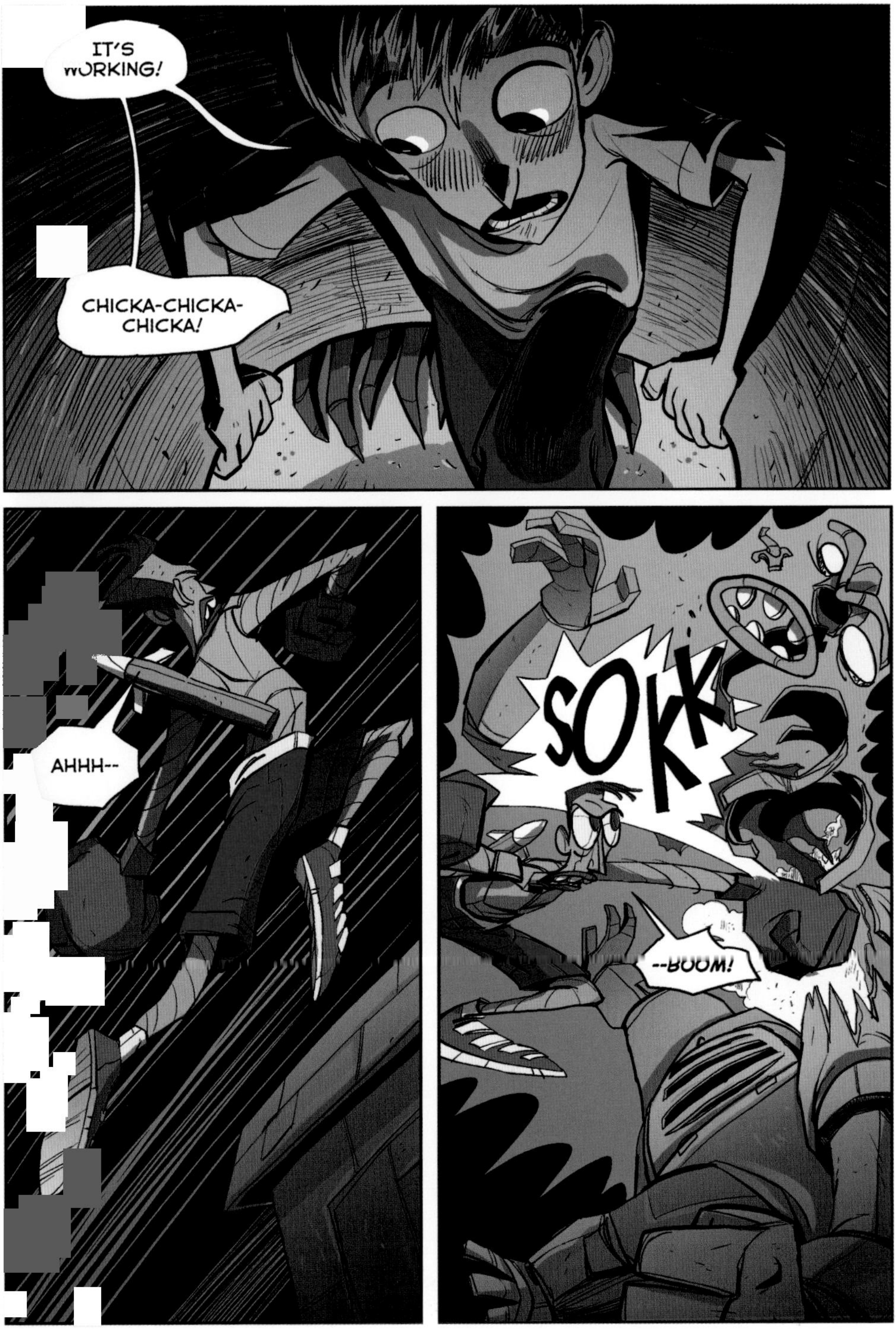
IT'S WORKING!
CHICKA-CHICKA-CHICKA!
AHHH--
SOKK
--BOOM!

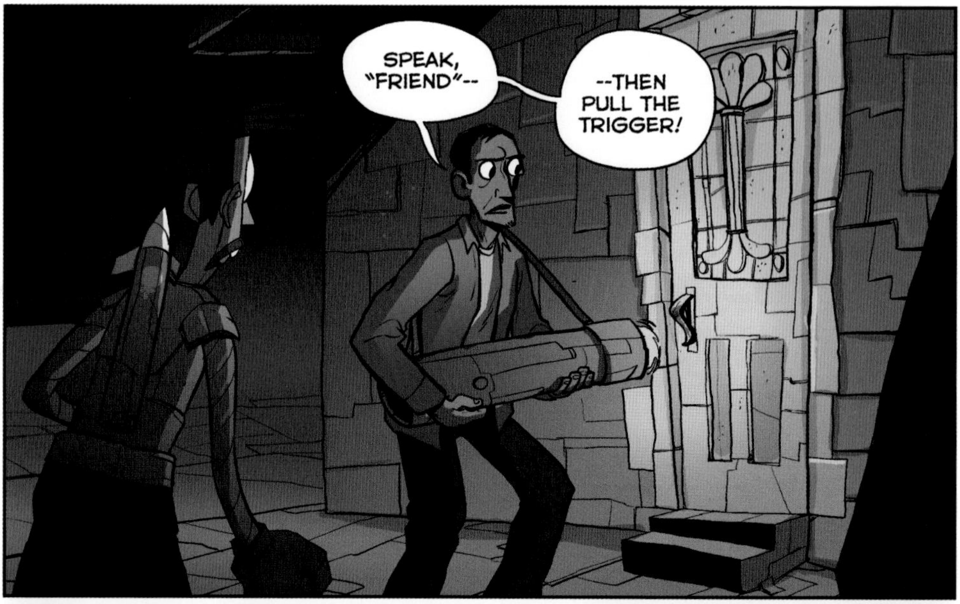
SPEAK, "FRIEND"--
--THEN PULL THE TRIGGER!

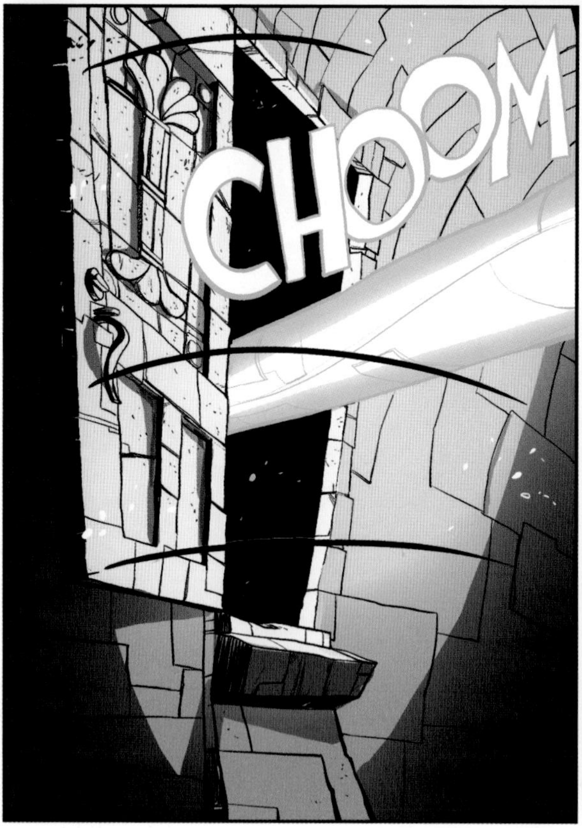
CHOOM

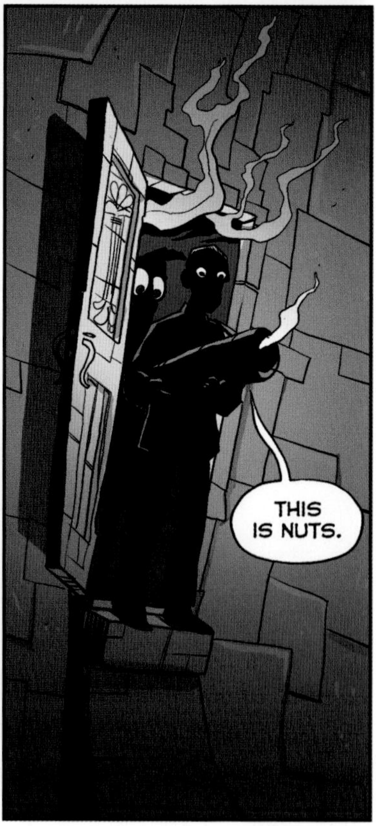
THIS IS NUTS.

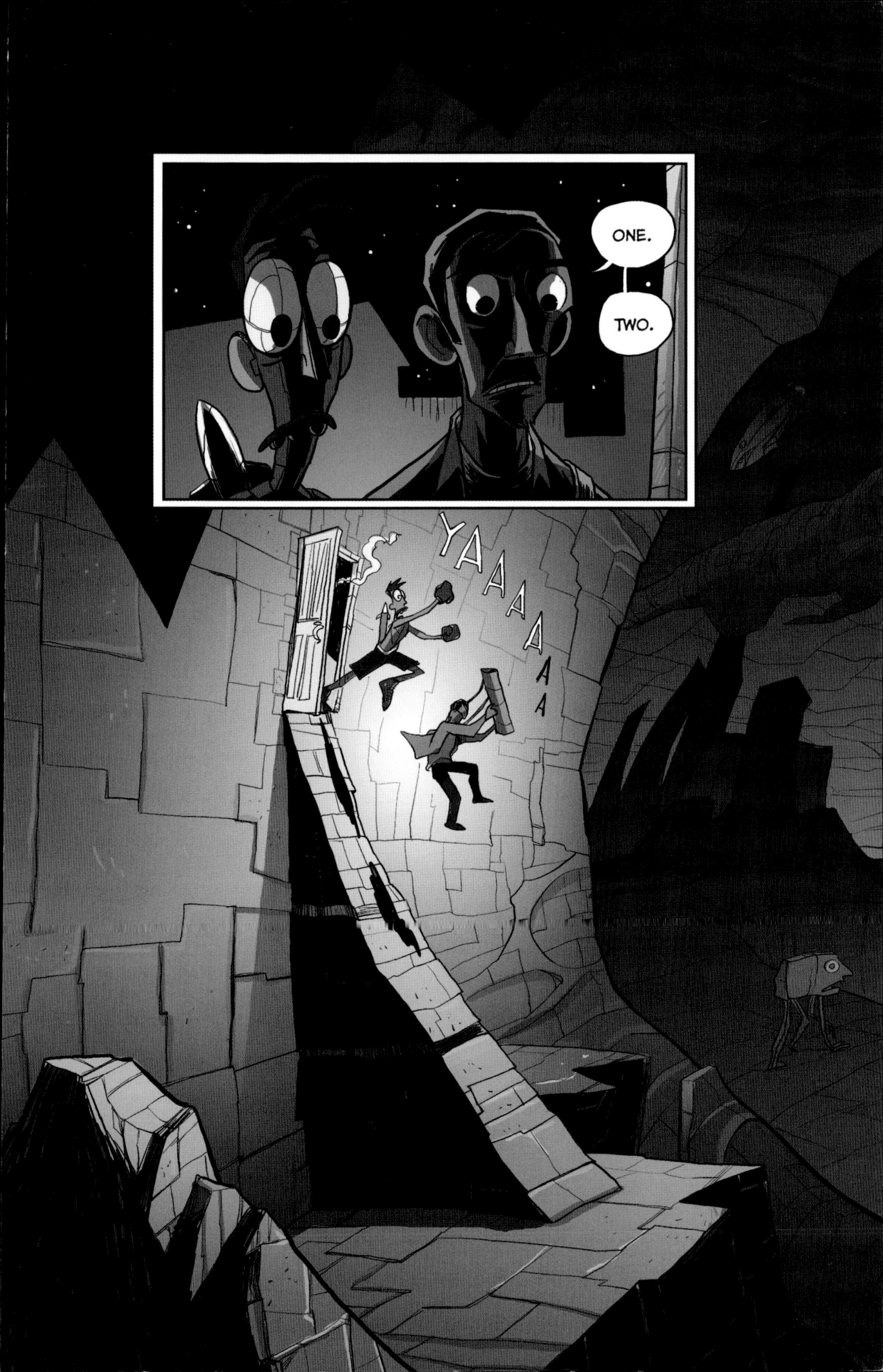
ONE.
TWO.
YAAAAAAAA

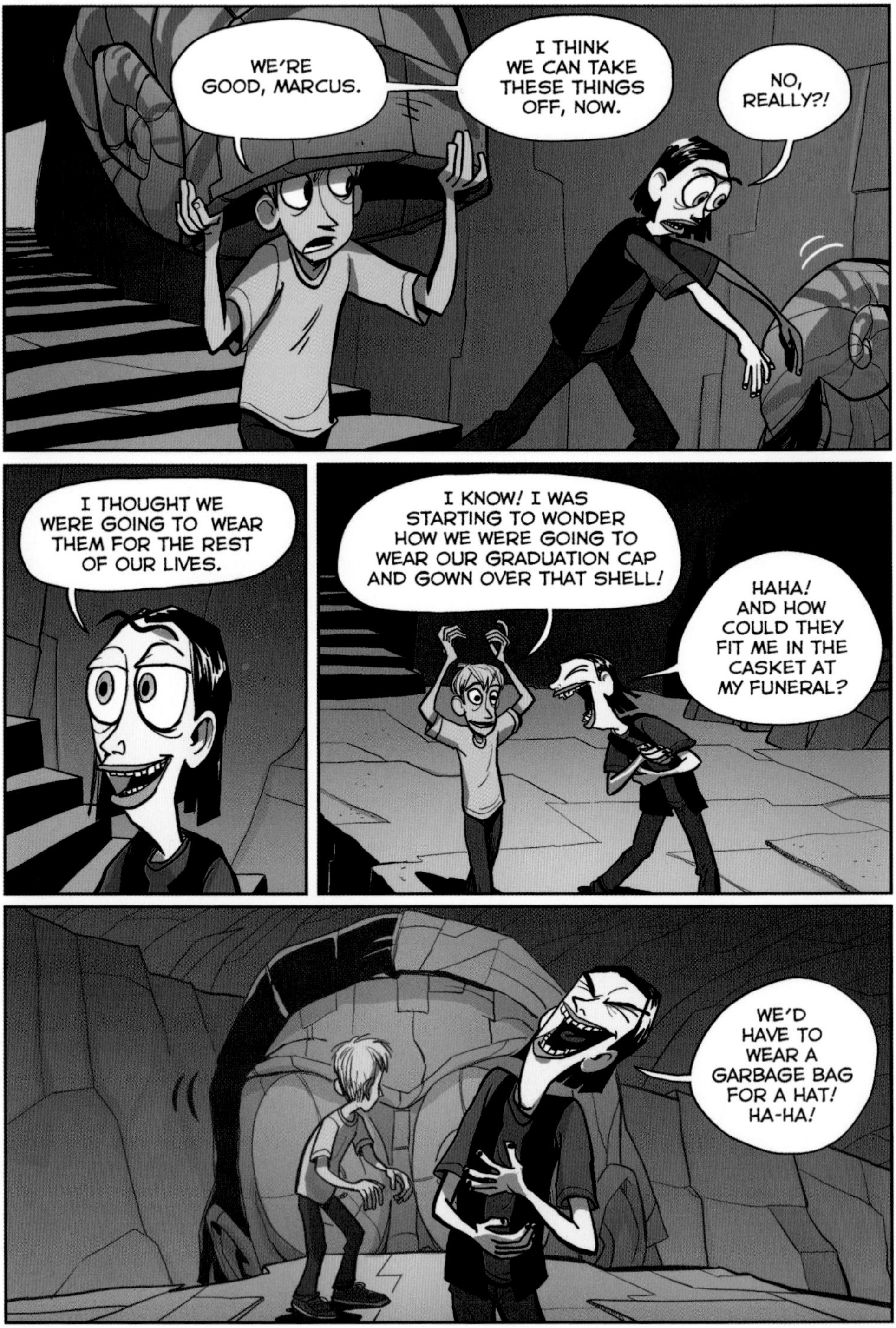
WE'RE GOOD, MARCUS.
I THINK WE CAN TAKE THESE THINGS OFF, NOW.
NO, REALLY?!
I THOUGHT WE WERE GOING TO WEAR THEM FOR THE REST OF OUR LIVES.
I KNOW! I WAS STARTING TO WONDER HOW WE WERE GOING TO WEAR OUR GRADUATION CAP AND GOWN OVER THAT SHELL!
HAHA! AND HOW COULD THEY FIT ME IN THE CASKET AT MY FUNERAL?
WE'D HAVE TO WEAR A GARBAGE BAG FOR A HAT! HA-HA!

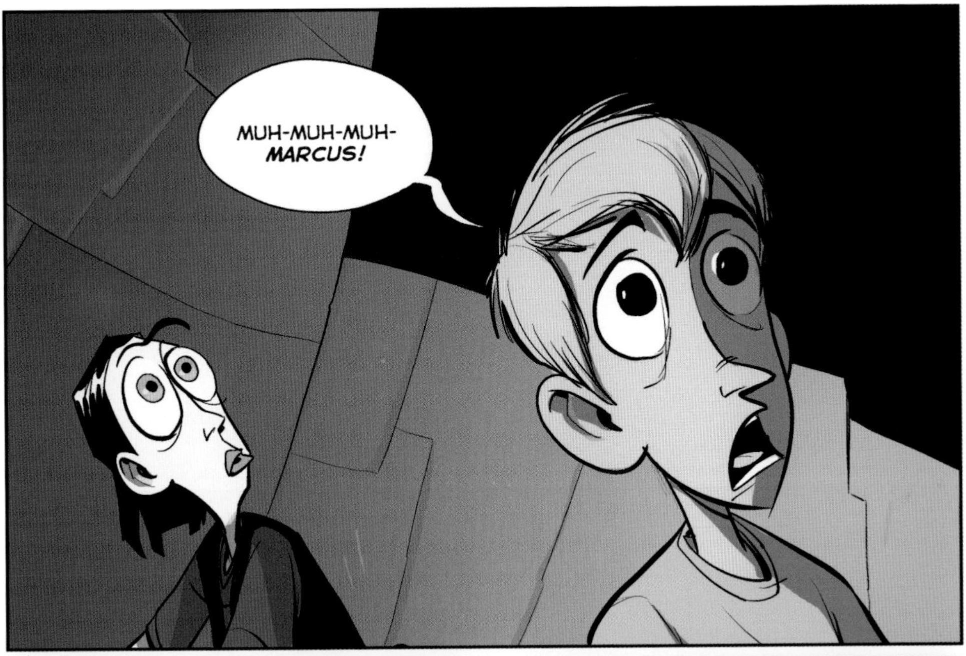
MUH-MUH-MUH-
MARCUS!

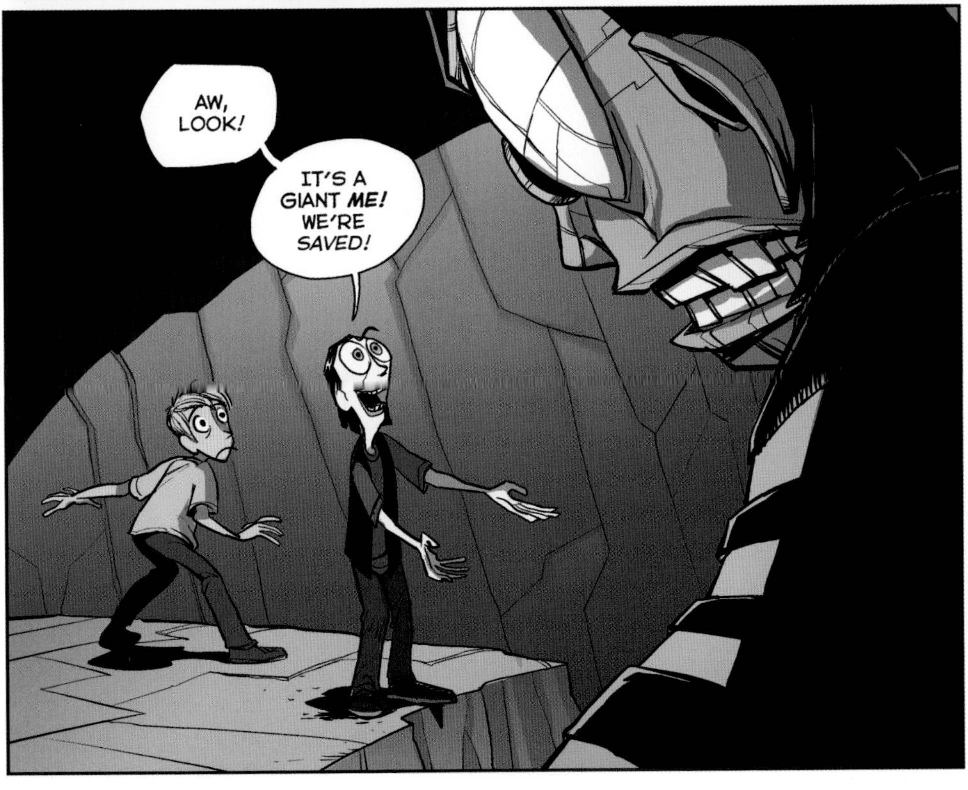
AW, LOOK!
IT'S A GIANT ME! WE'RE SAVED!

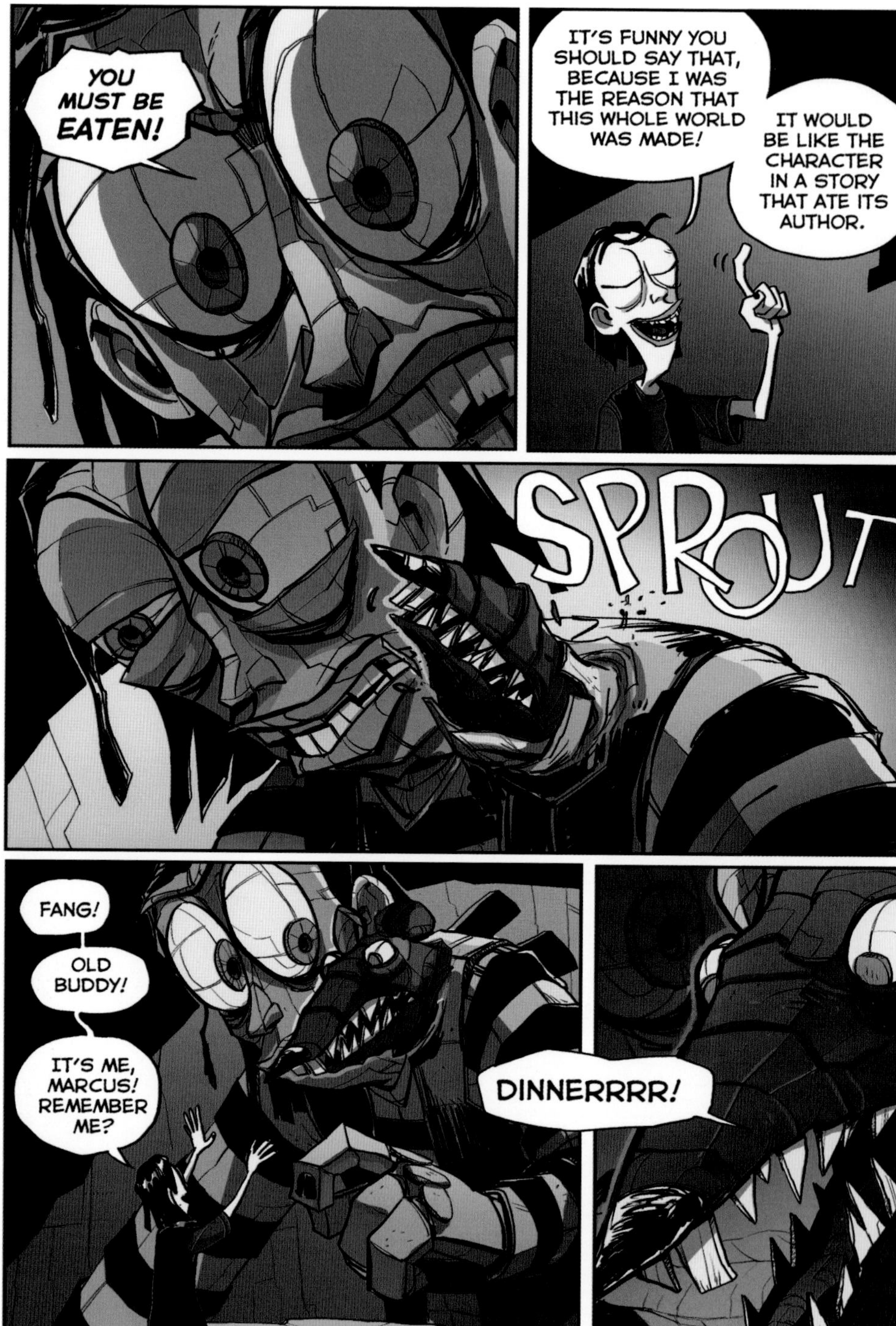
YOU MUST BE EATEN!
IT'S FUNNY YOU SHOULD SAY THAT, BECAUSE I WAS THE REASON THAT THIS WHOLE WORLD WAS MADE!
IT WOULD BE LIKE THE CHARACTER IN A STORY THAT ATE ITS AUTHOR.
SPROUT
FANG!
OLD BUDDY!
IT'S ME, MARCUS! REMEMBER ME?
DINNERRRR!

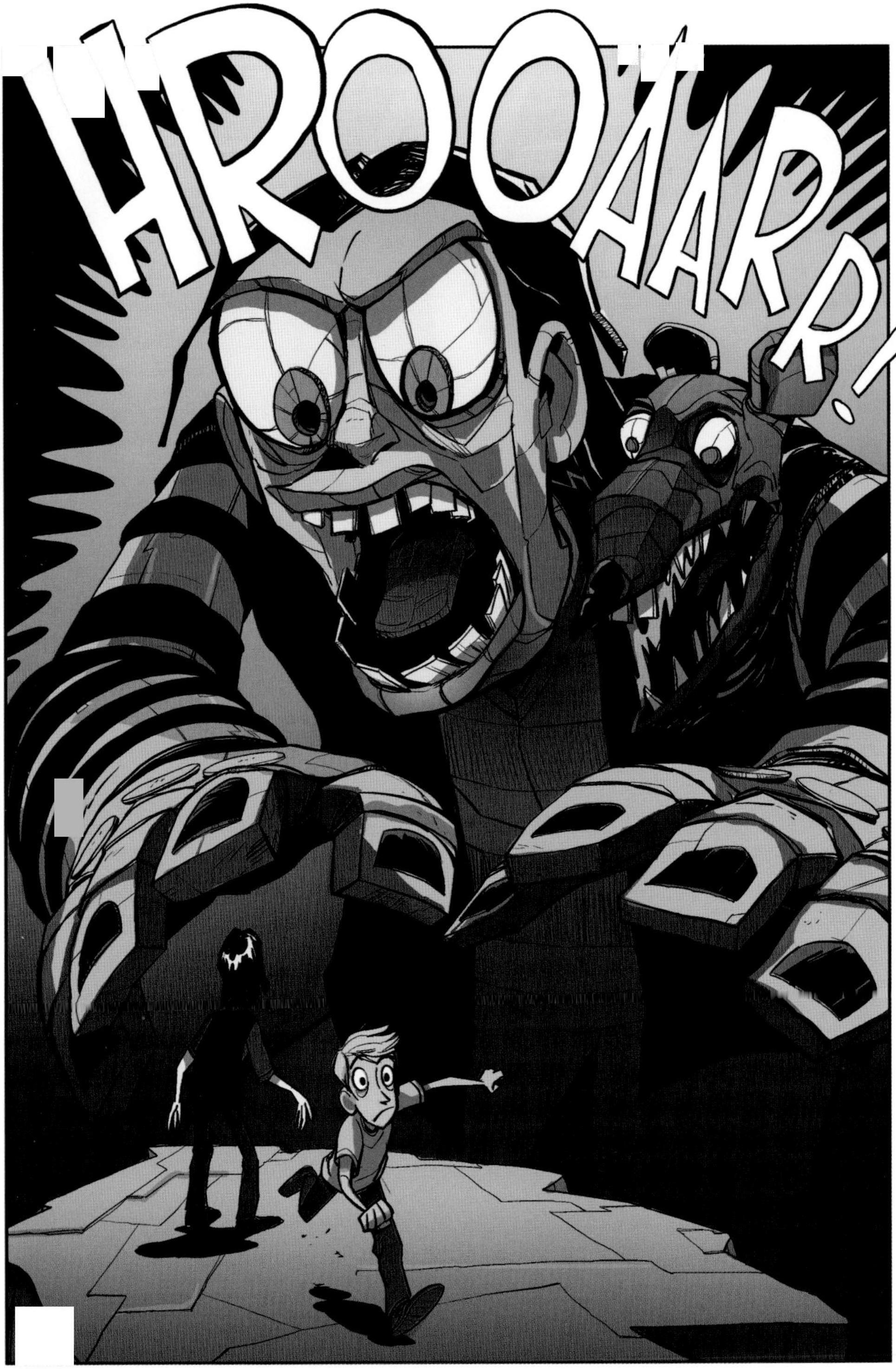
HROOAARR!

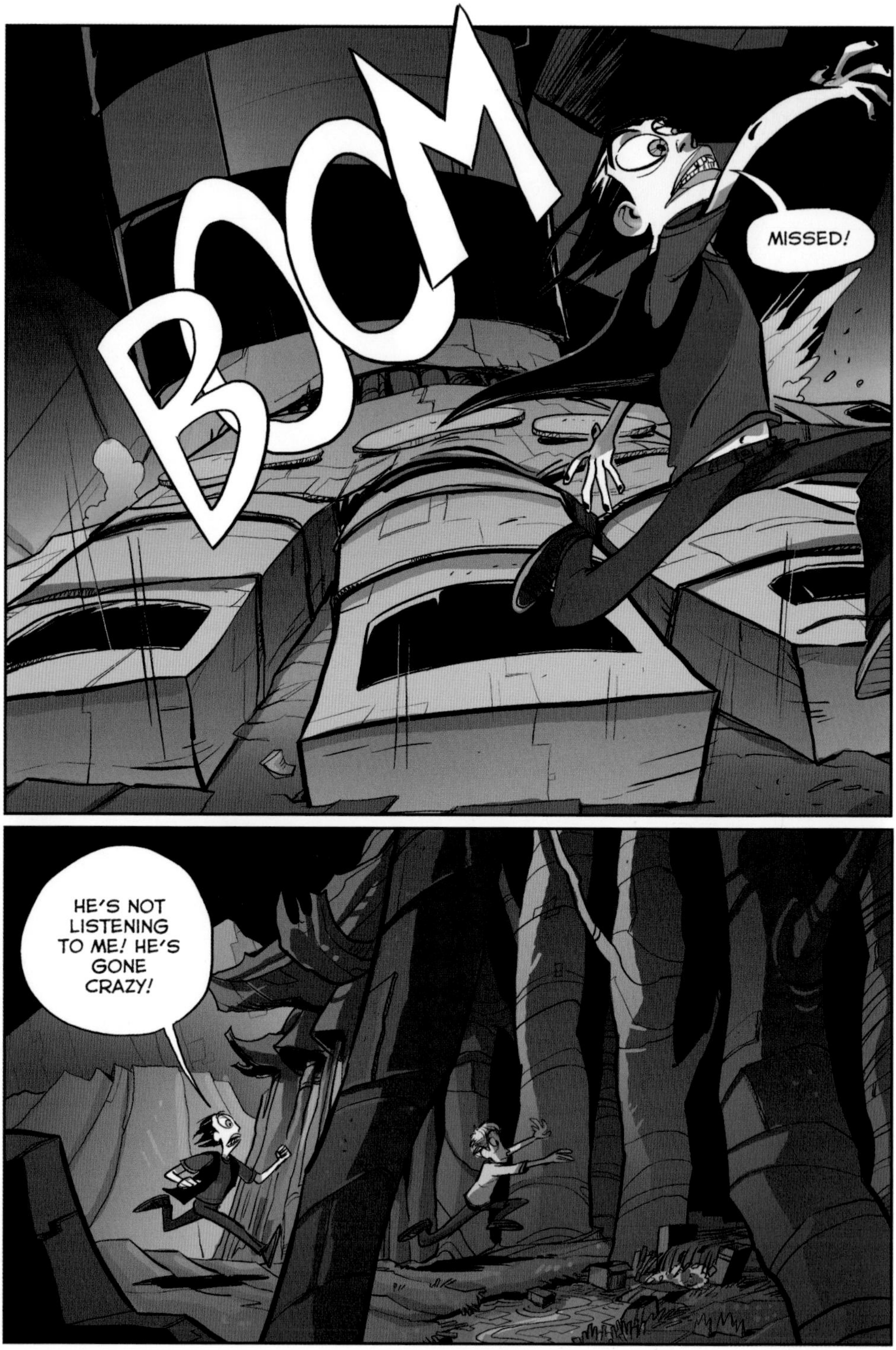
BOOM
MISSED!
HE'S NOT LISTENING TO ME! HE'S GONE CRAZY!

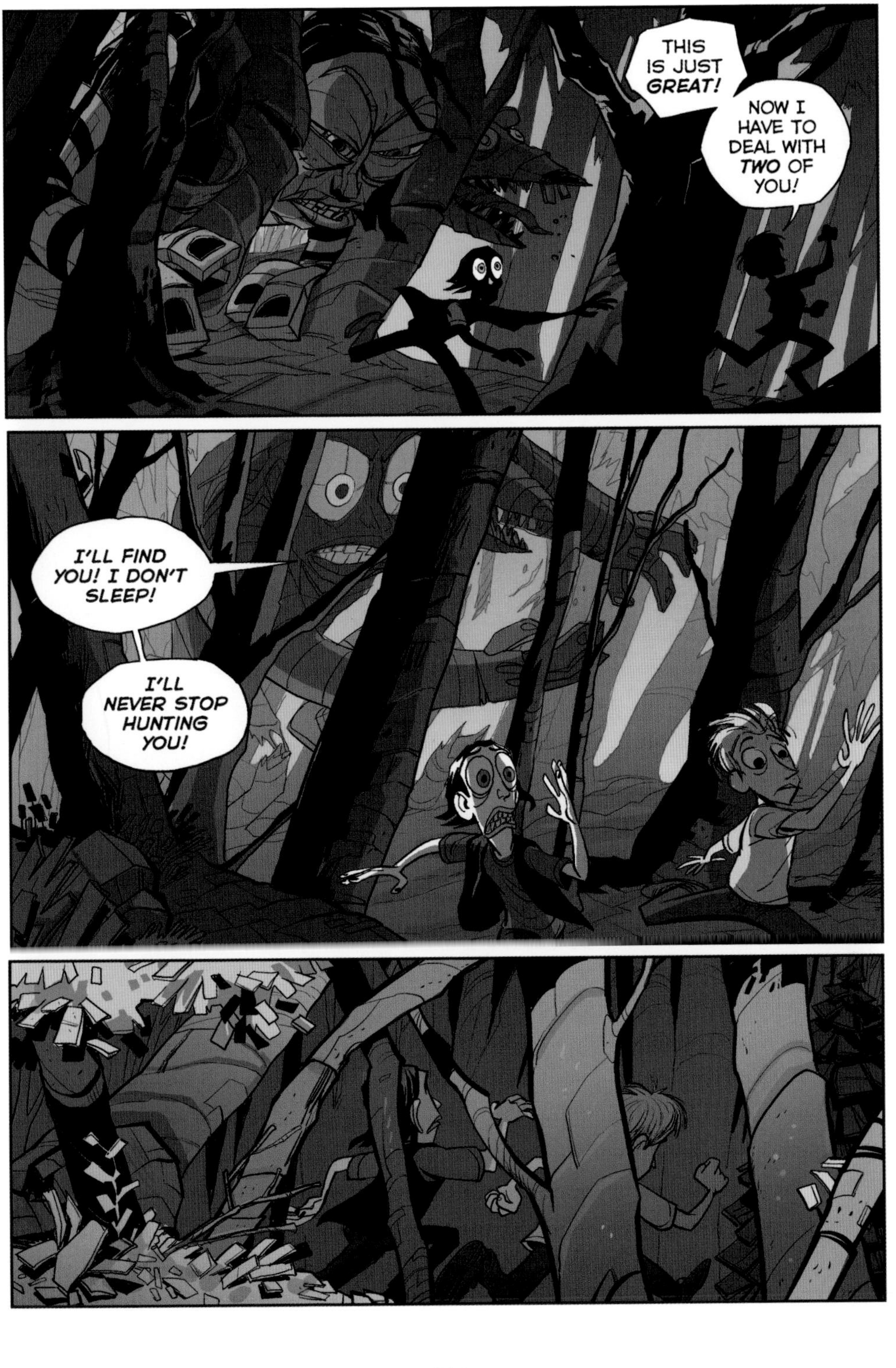
THIS IS JUST GREAT!
NOW I HAVE TO DEAL WITH TWO OF YOU!
I'LL FIND YOU! I DON'T SLEEP!
I'LL NEVER STOP HUNTING YOU!

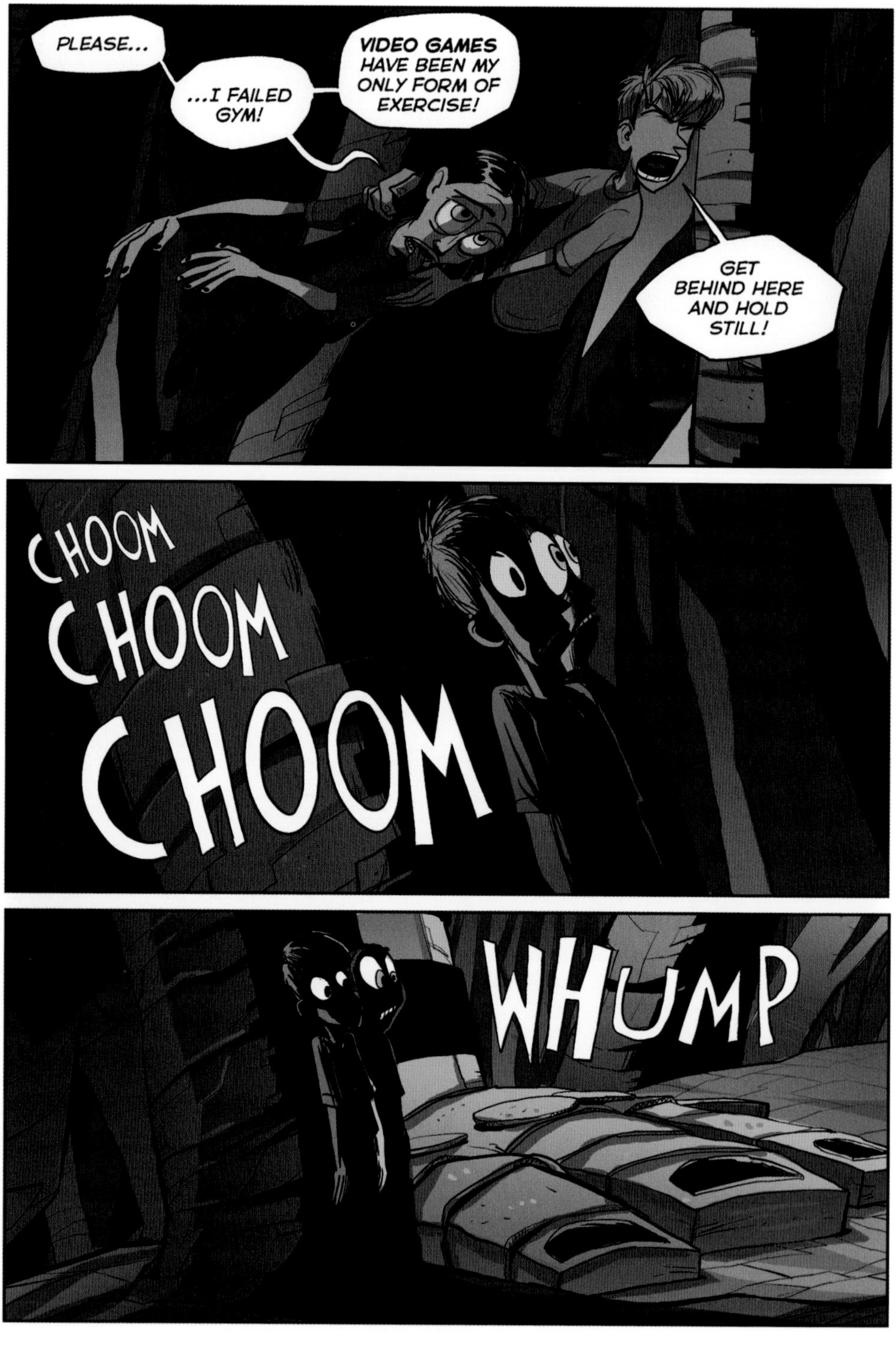
PLEASE...
...I FAILED GYM!
VIDEO GAMES HAVE BEEN MY ONLY FORM OF EXERCISE!
GET BEHIND HERE AND HOLD STILL!
CHOOM
CHOOM
CHOOM
WHUMP

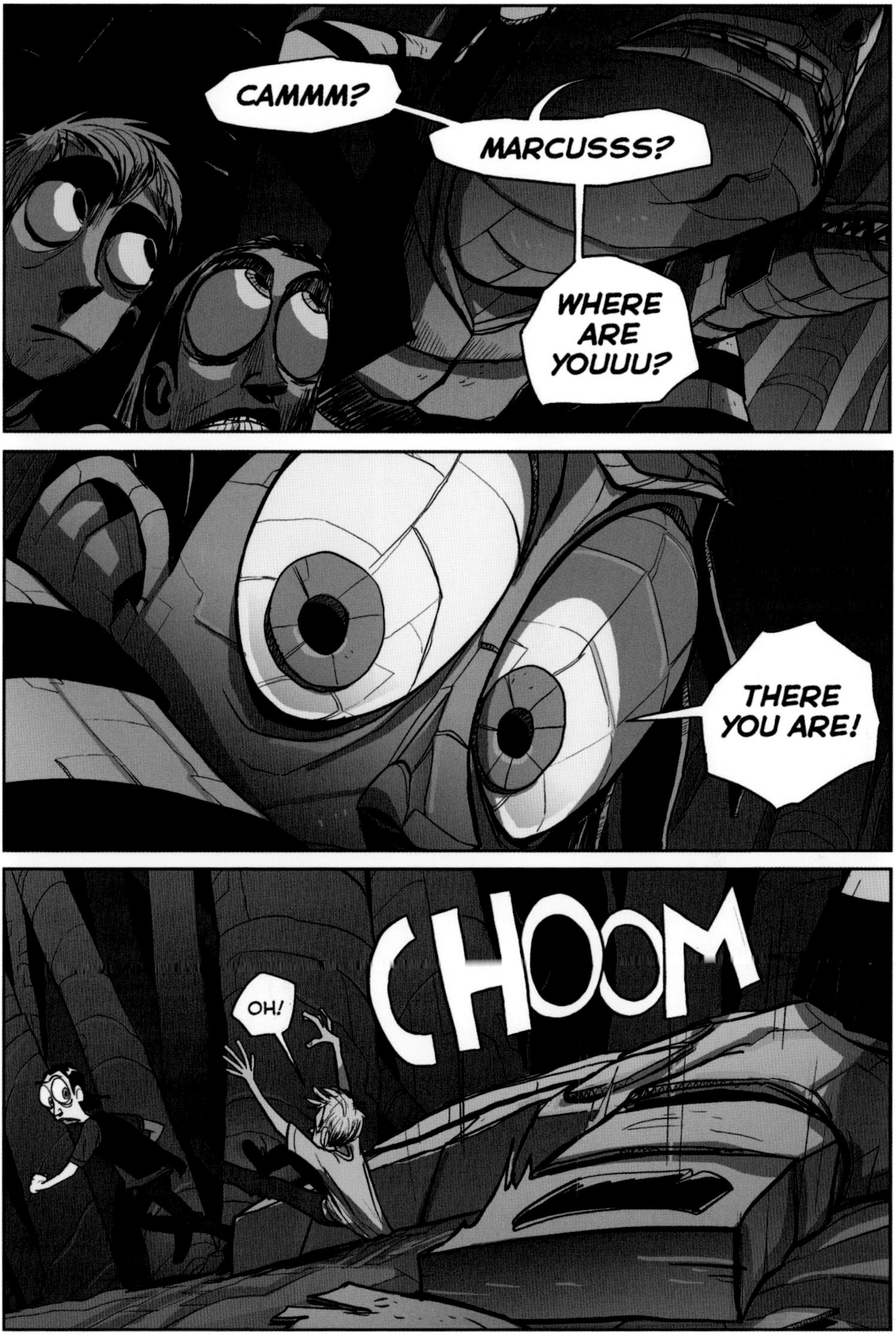
CAMMM?
MARCUSSS?
WHERE ARE YOUUU?
THERE YOU ARE!
CHOOM
OH!

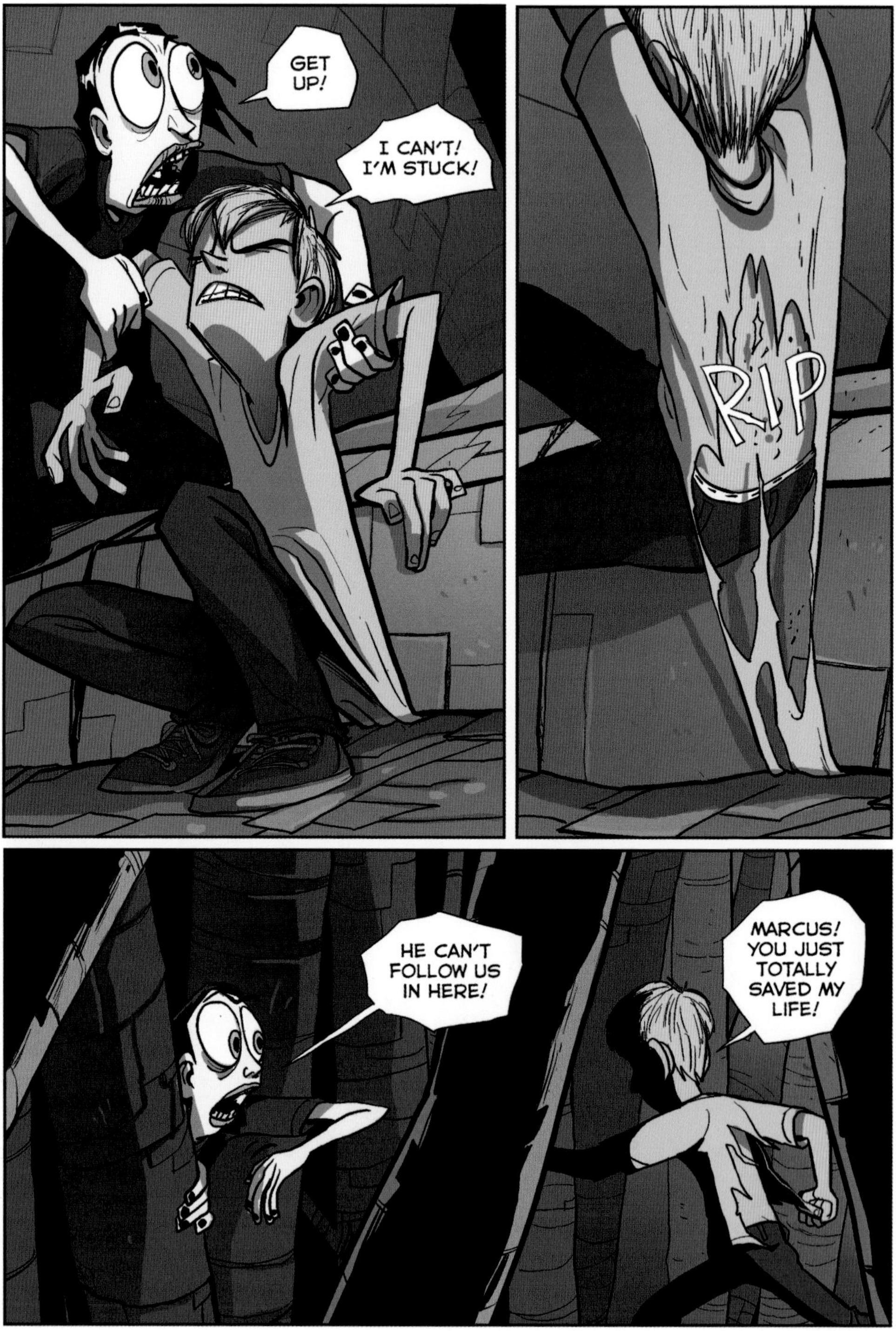
GET UP!
I CAN'T! I'M STUCK!
RIP
HE CAN'T FOLLOW US IN HERE!
MARCUS! YOU JUST TOTALLY SAVED MY LIFE!

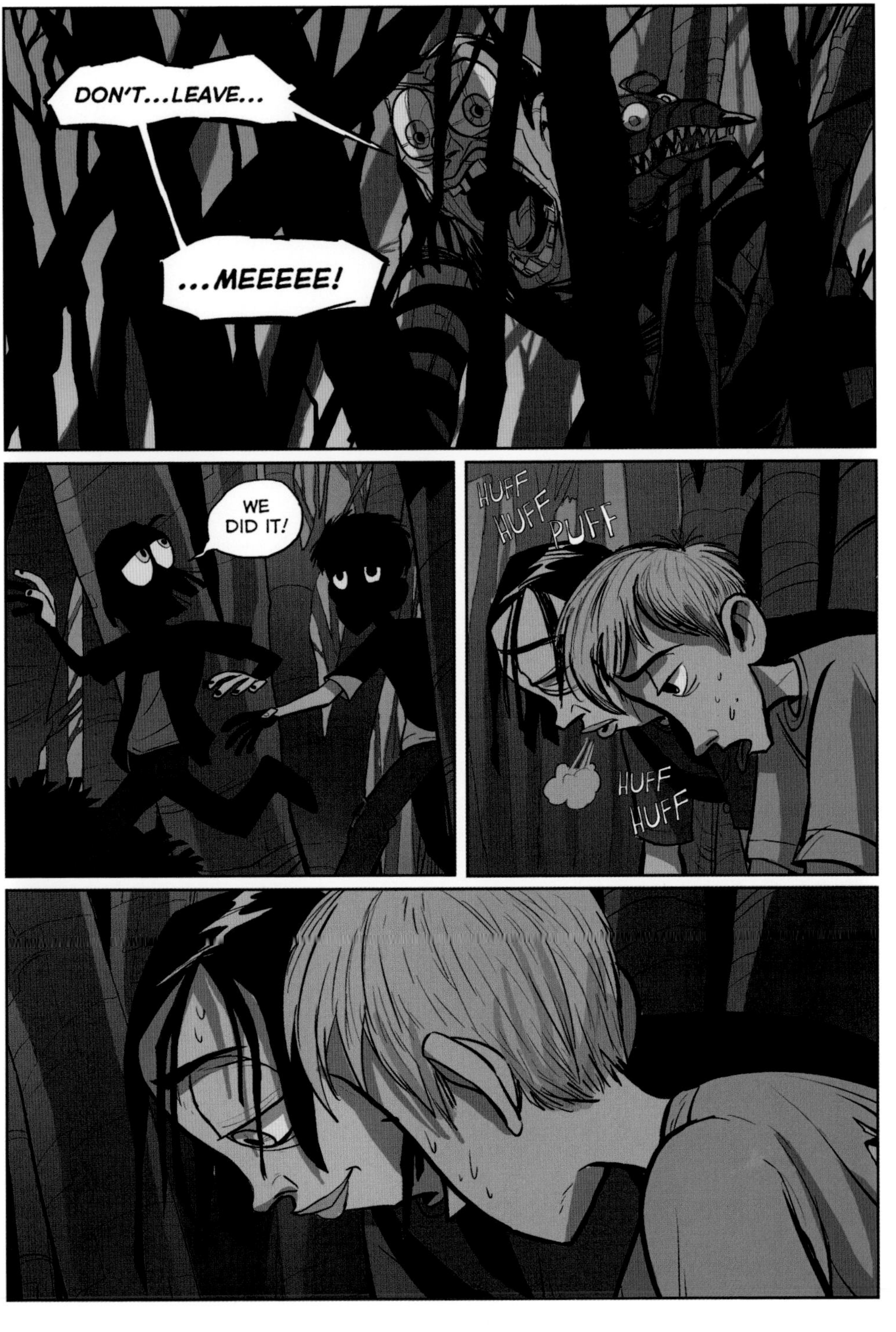
DON'T...LEAVE...
...MEEEEE!
WE DID IT!
HUFF HUFF PUFF
HUFF HUFF

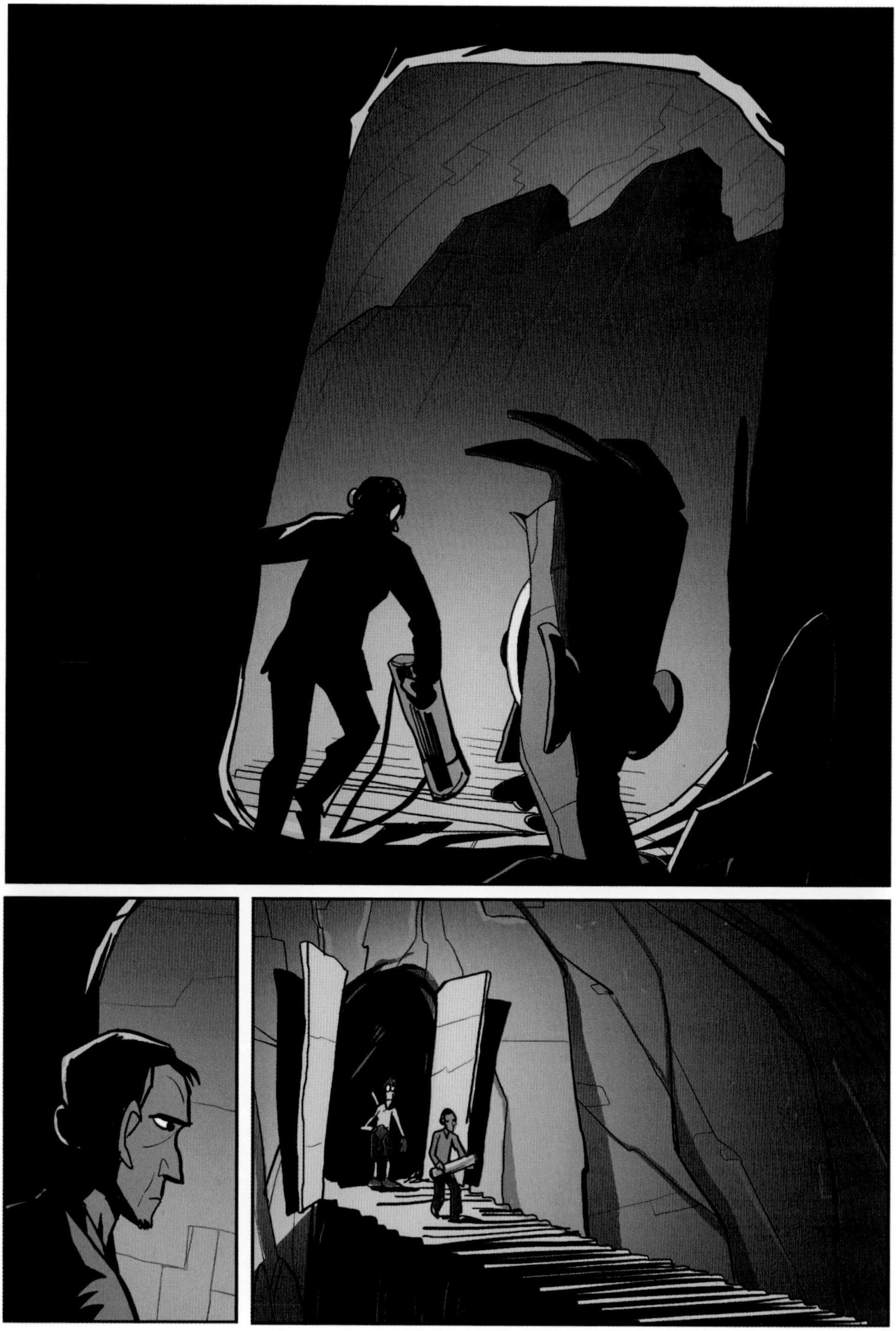

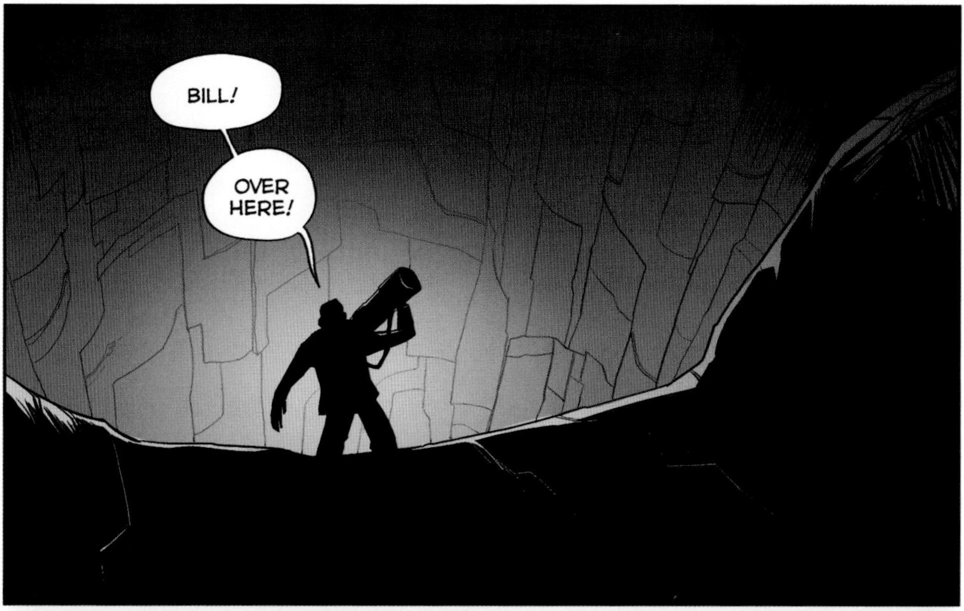
BILL!
OVER HERE!

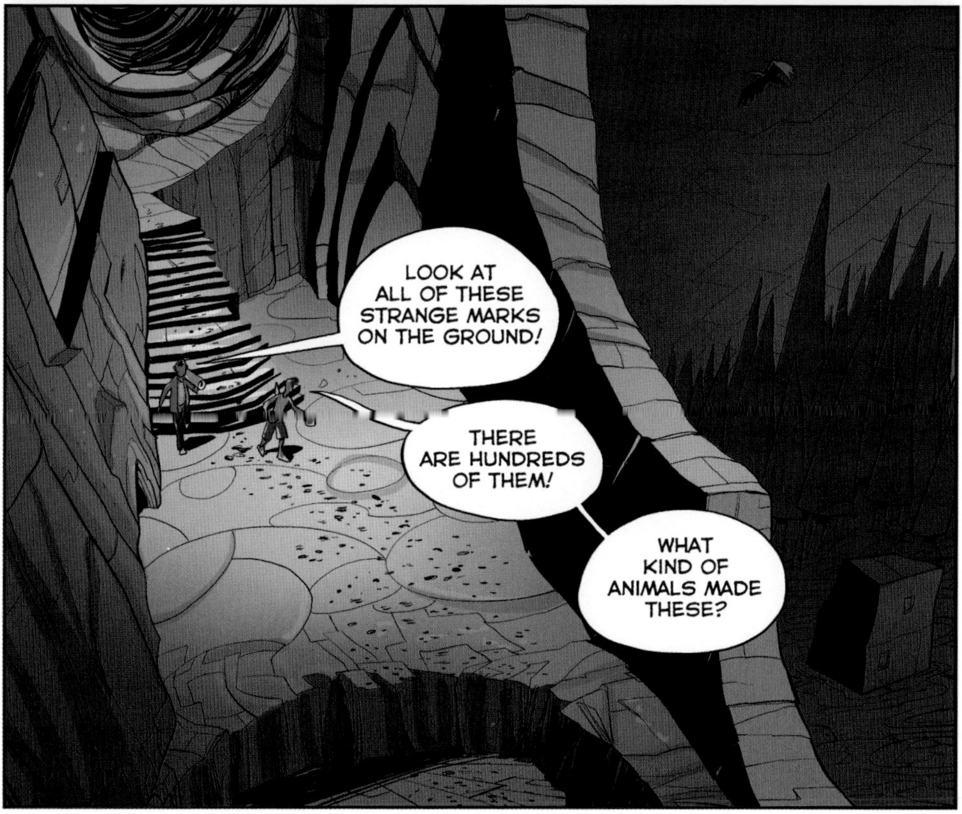
LOOK AT ALL OF THESE STRANGE MARKS ON THE GROUND!
THERE ARE HUNDREDS OF THEM!
WHAT KIND OF ANIMALS MADE THESE?

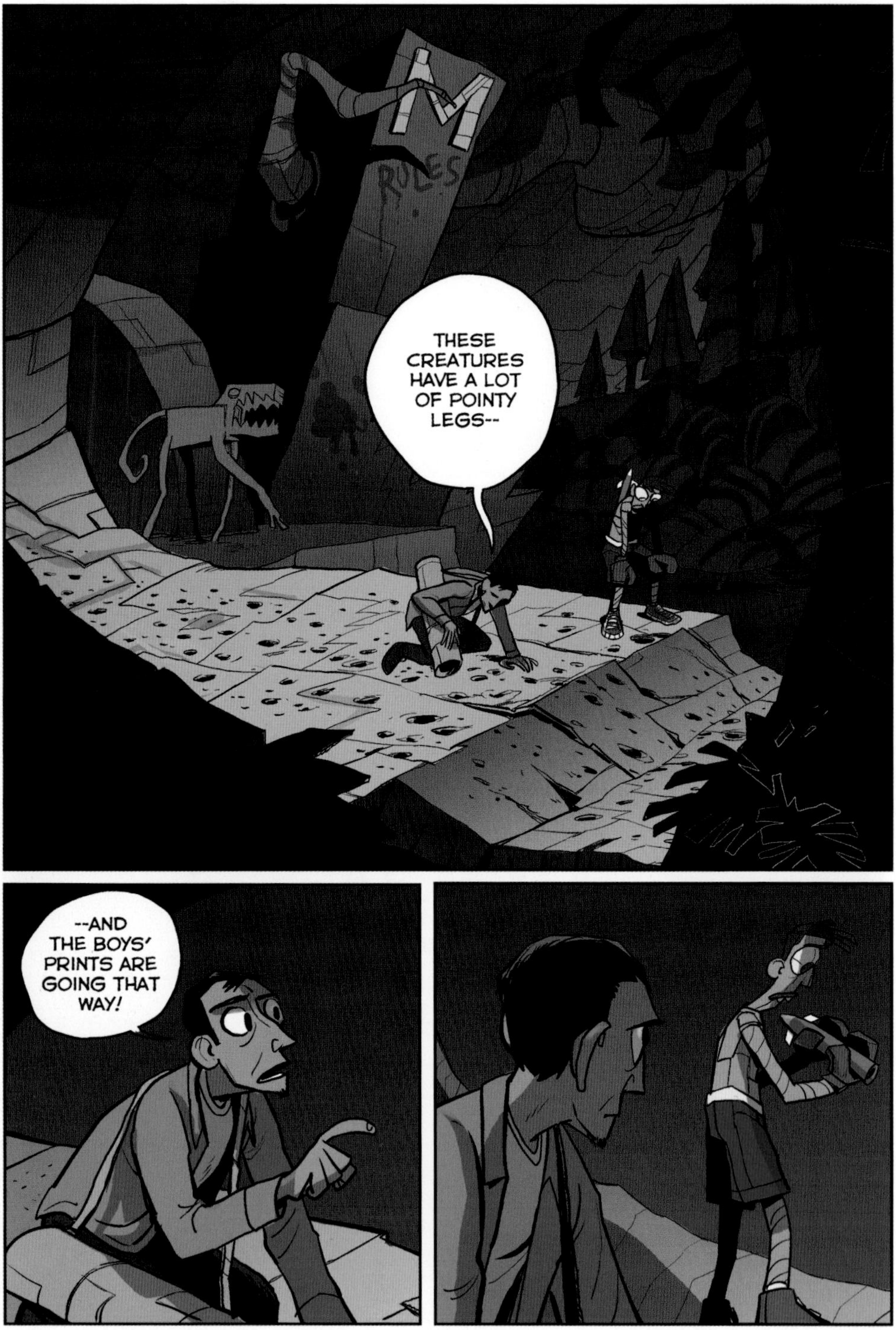
M
RULES
THESE CREATURES HAVE A LOT OF POINTY LEGS--
--AND THE BOYS' PRINTS ARE GOING THAT WAY!

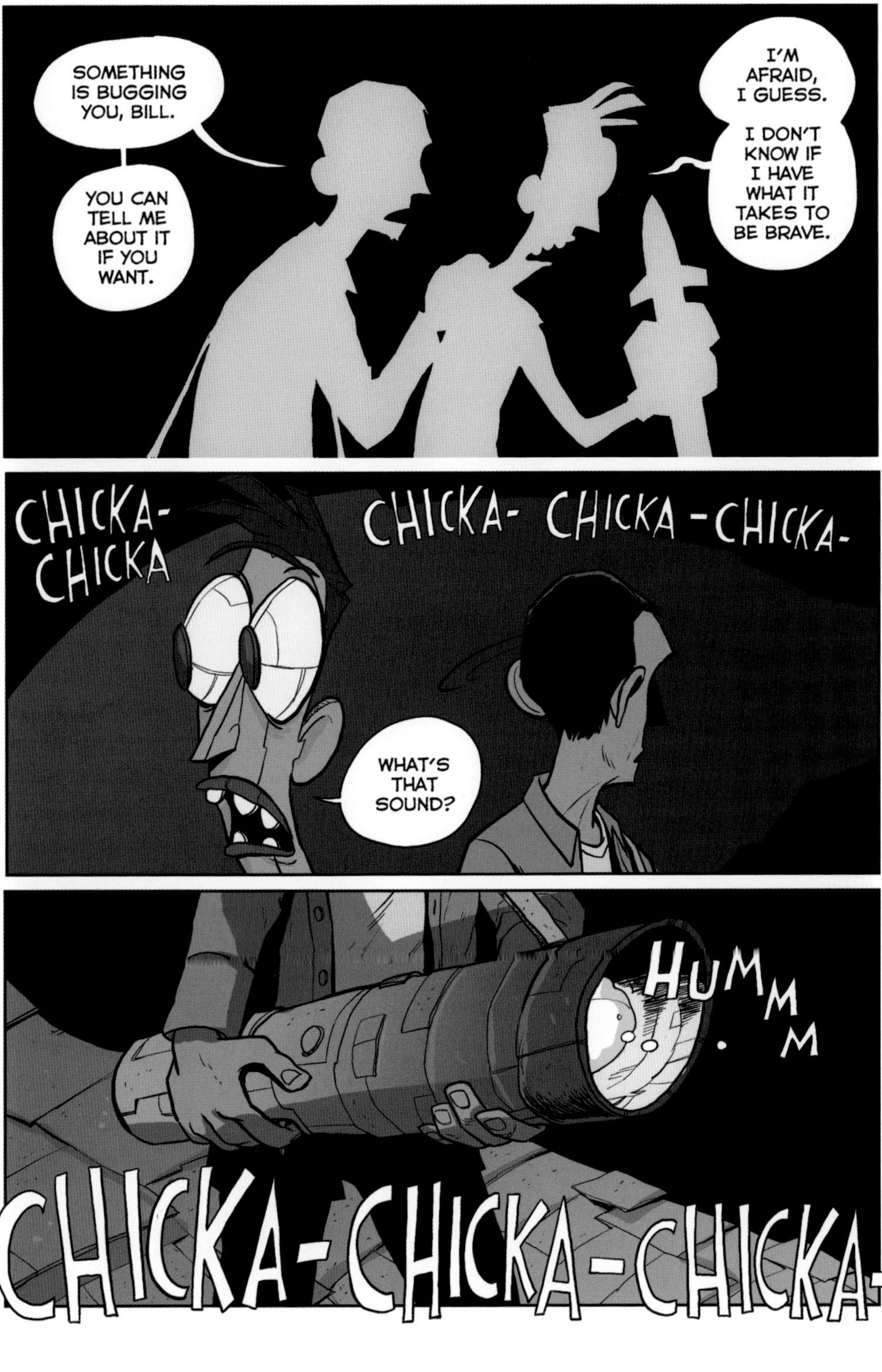
SOMETHING IS BUGGING YOU, BILL.
YOU CAN TELL ME ABOUT IT IF YOU WANT.
I'M AFRAID, I GUESS.
I DON'T KNOW IF I HAVE WHAT IT TAKES TO BE BRAVE.
CHICKA-CHICKA
CHICKA- CHICKA-CHICKA-
WHAT'S THAT SOUND?
HUMMM
CHICKA-CHICKA-CHICKA-

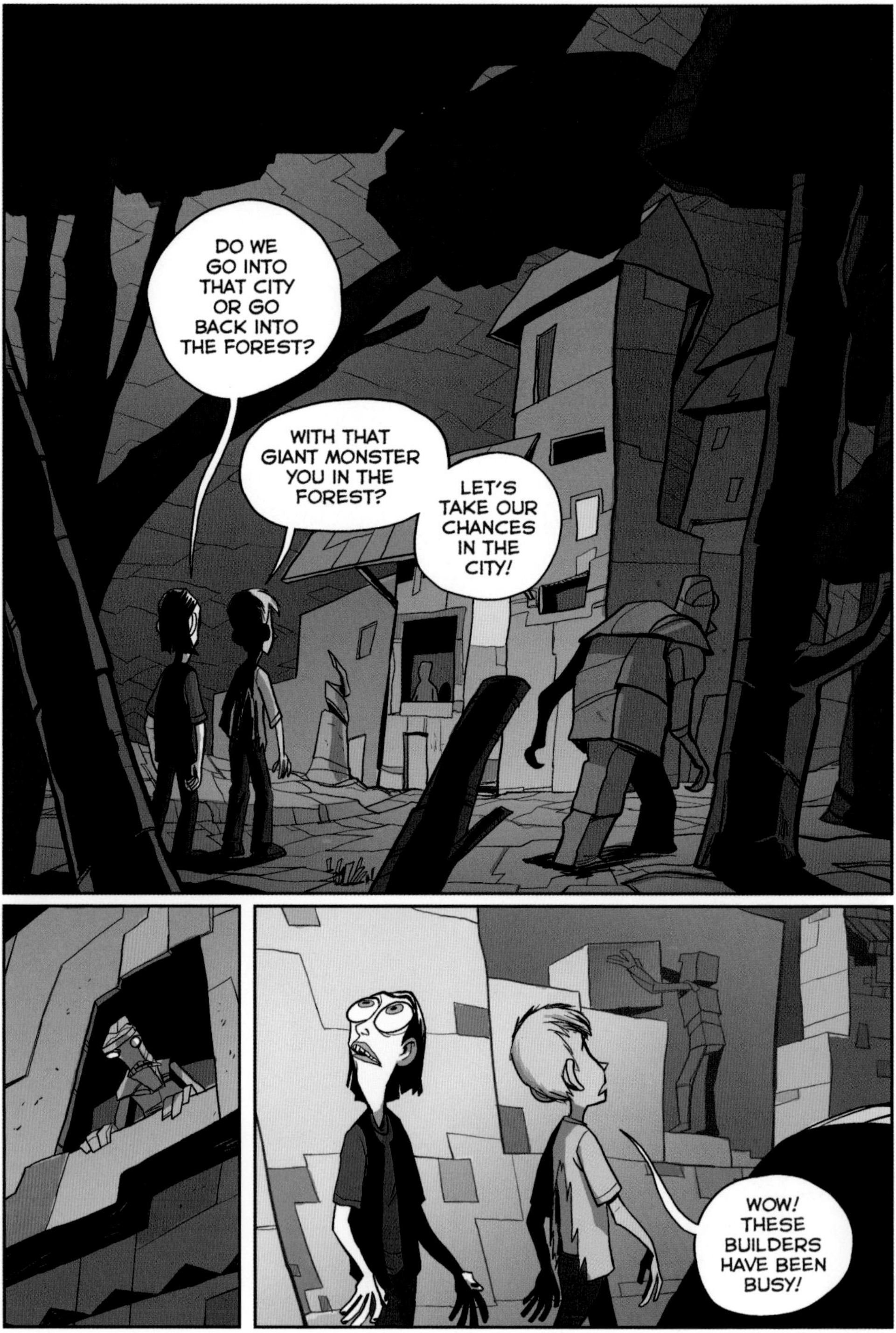
DO WE GO INTO THAT CITY OR GO BACK INTO THE FOREST?
WITH THAT GIANT MONSTER YOU IN THE FOREST?
LET'S TAKE OUR CHANCES IN THE CITY!
WOW! THESE BUILDERS HAVE BEEN BUSY!

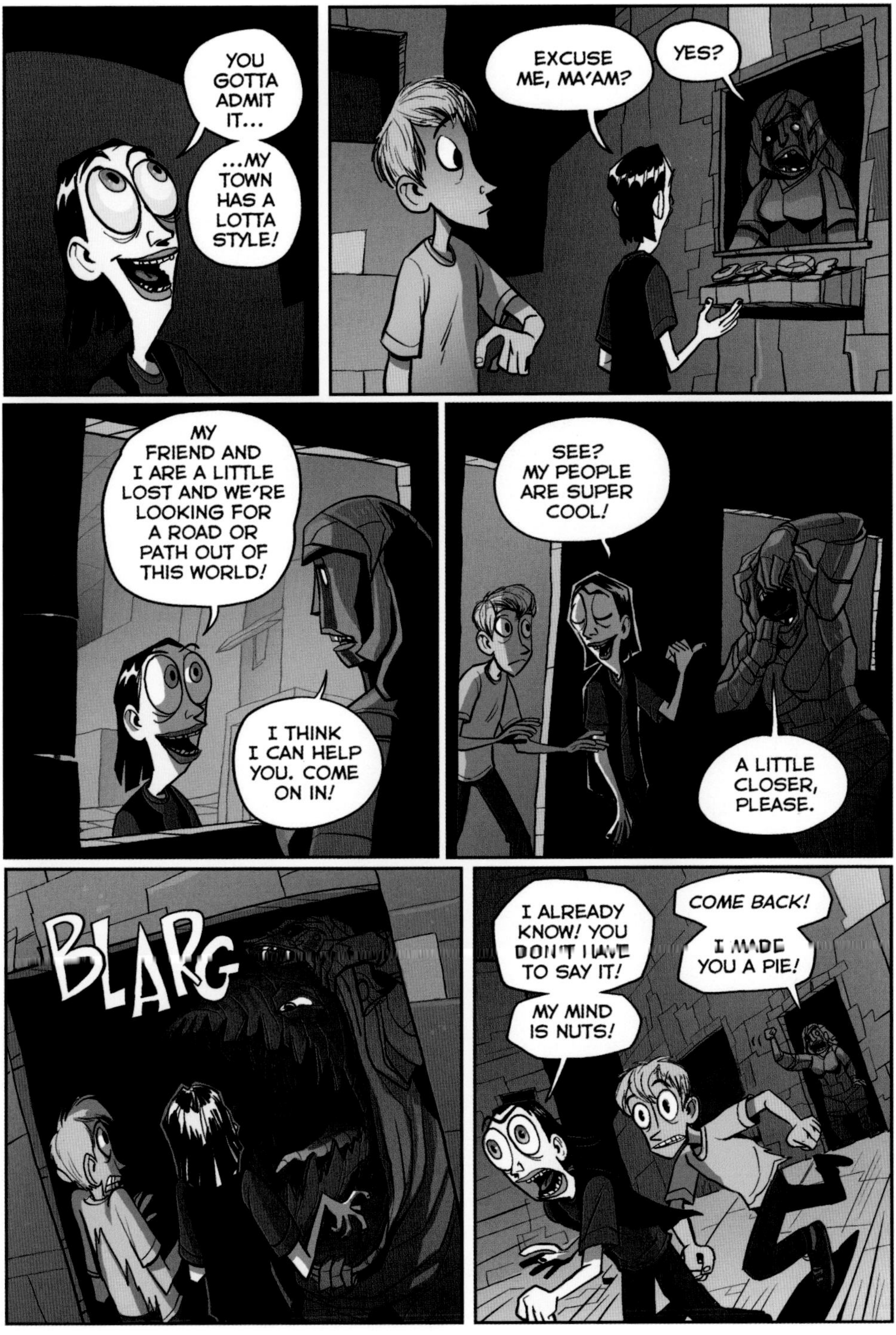
YOU GOTTA ADMIT IT...
...MY TOWN HAS A LOTTA STYLE!
EXCUSE ME, MA'AM?
YES?
MY FRIEND AND I ARE A LITTLE LOST AND WE'RE LOOKING FOR A ROAD OR PATH OUT OF THIS WORLD!
I THINK I CAN HELP YOU. COME ON IN!
SEE? MY PEOPLE ARE SUPER COOL!
A LITTLE CLOSER, PLEASE.
BLARG
I ALREADY KNOW! YOU DON'T HAVE TO SAY IT!
MY MIND IS NUTS!
COME BACK!
I MADE YOU A PIE!

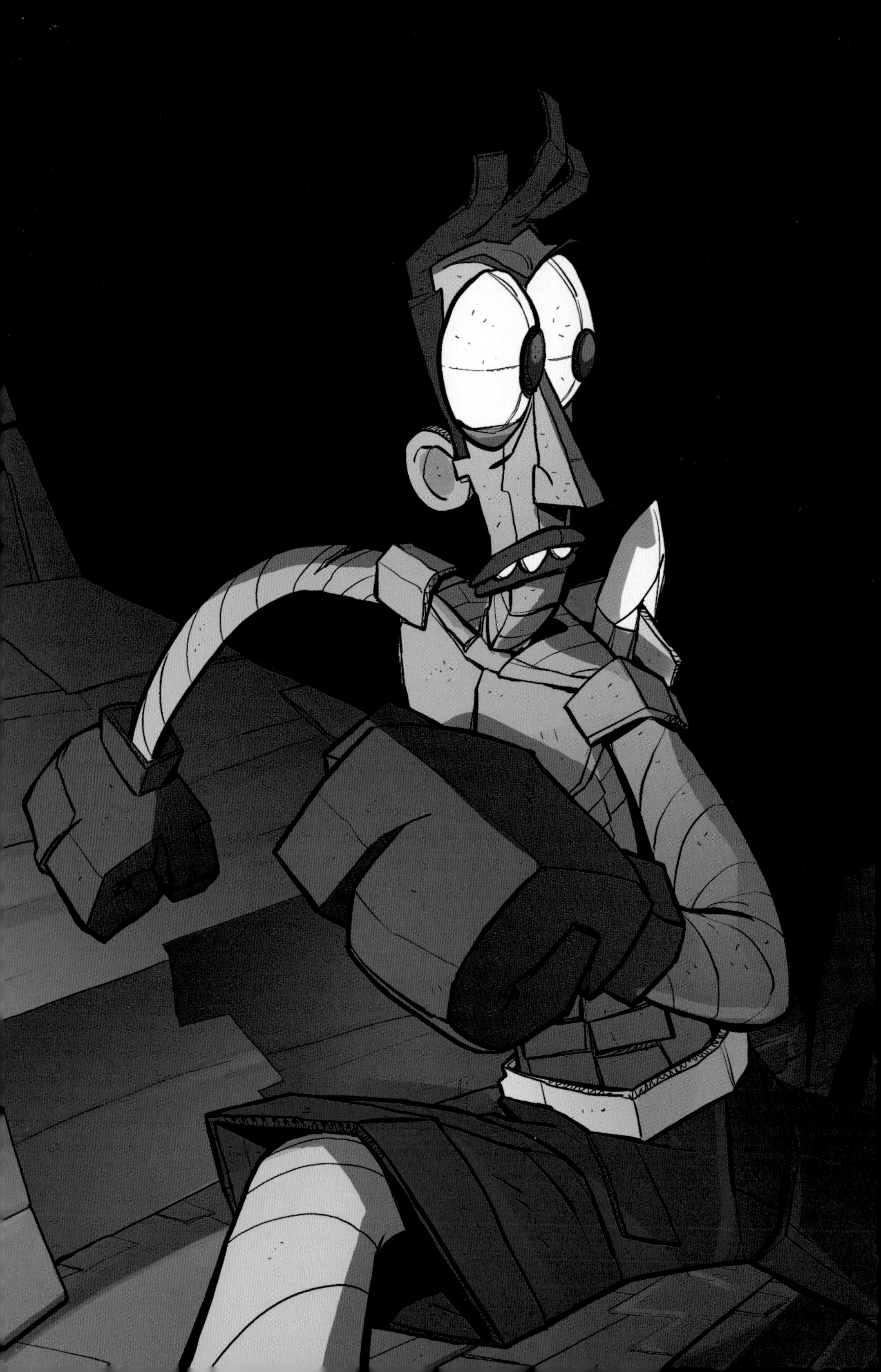

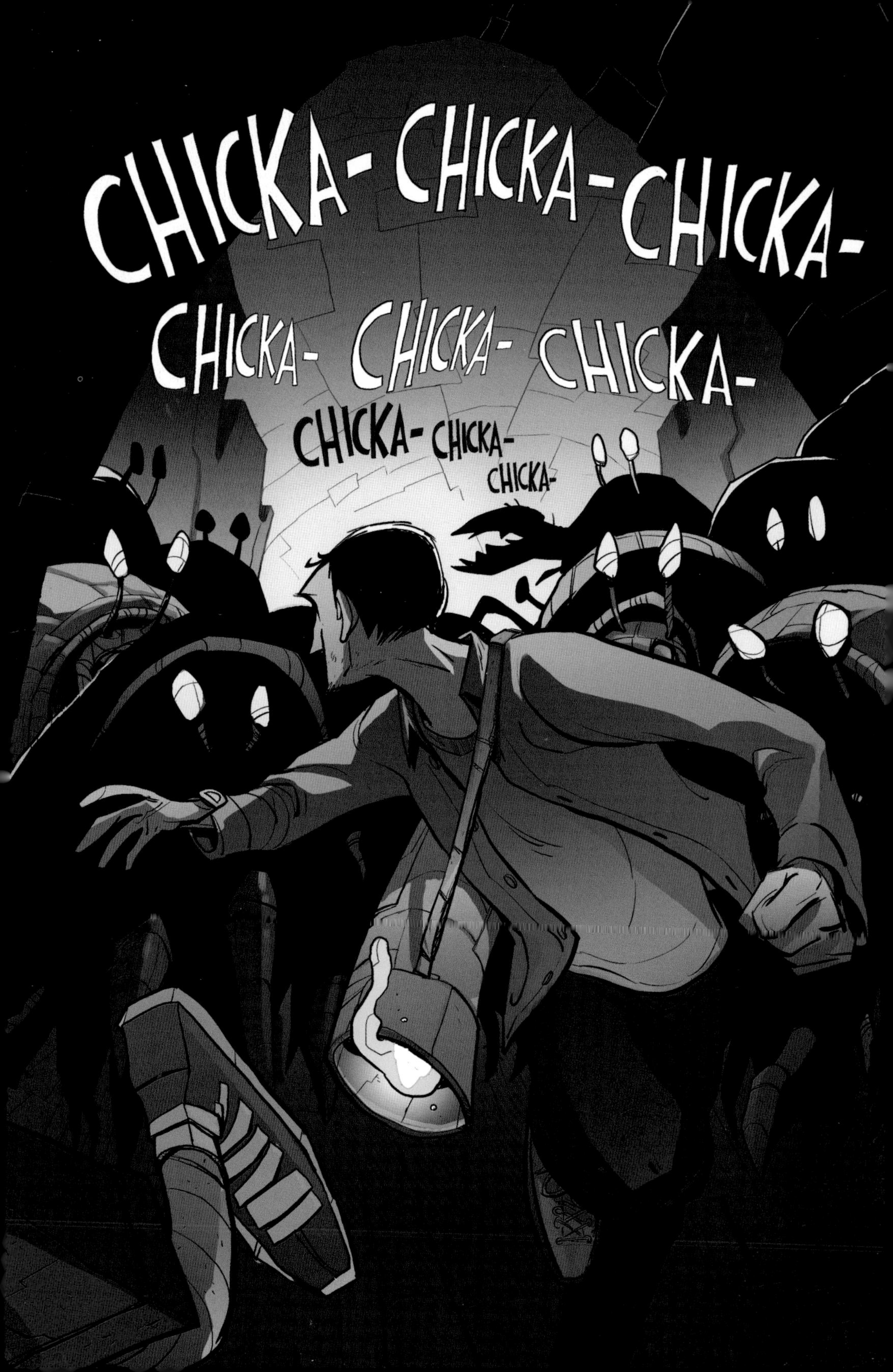
CHICKA- CHICKA- CHICKA-
CHICKA- CHICKA- CHICKA-
CHICKA- CHICKA-
CHICKA-

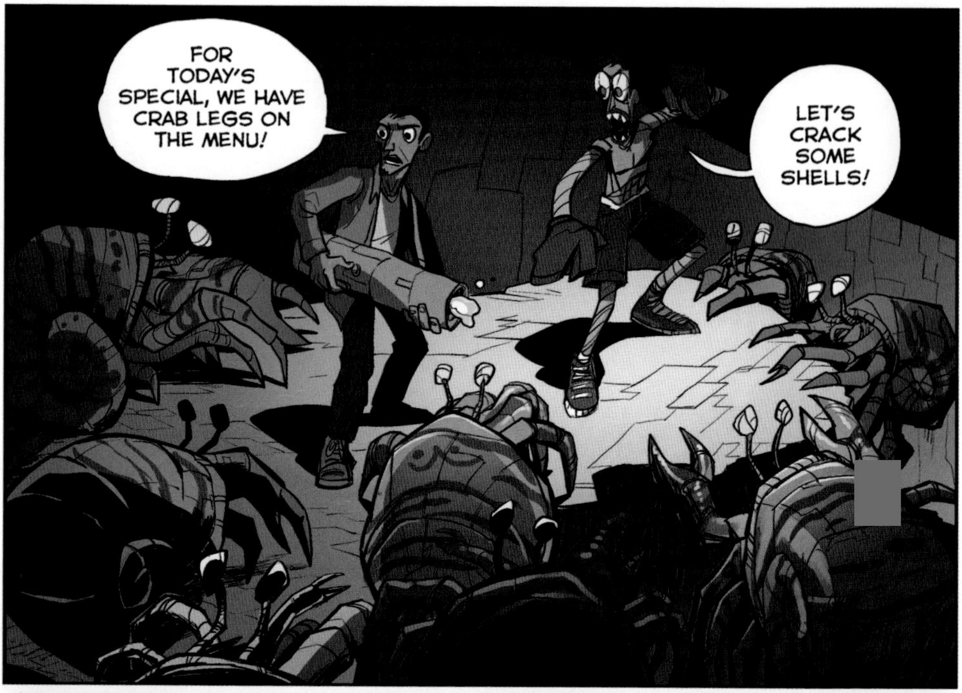
FOR TODAY'S SPECIAL, WE HAVE CRAB LEGS ON THE MENU!
LET'S CRACK SOME SHELLS!
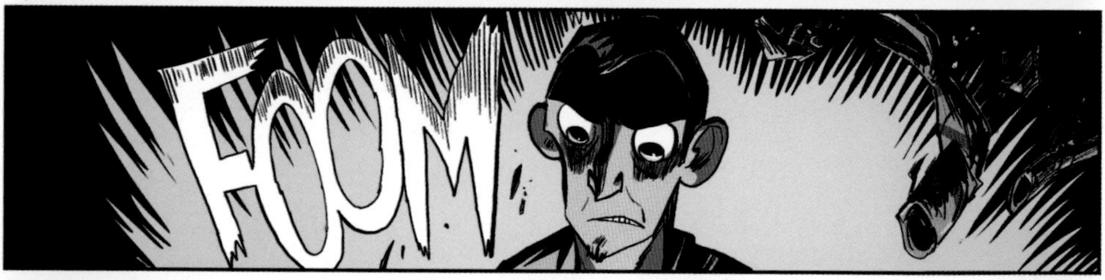
FOOM
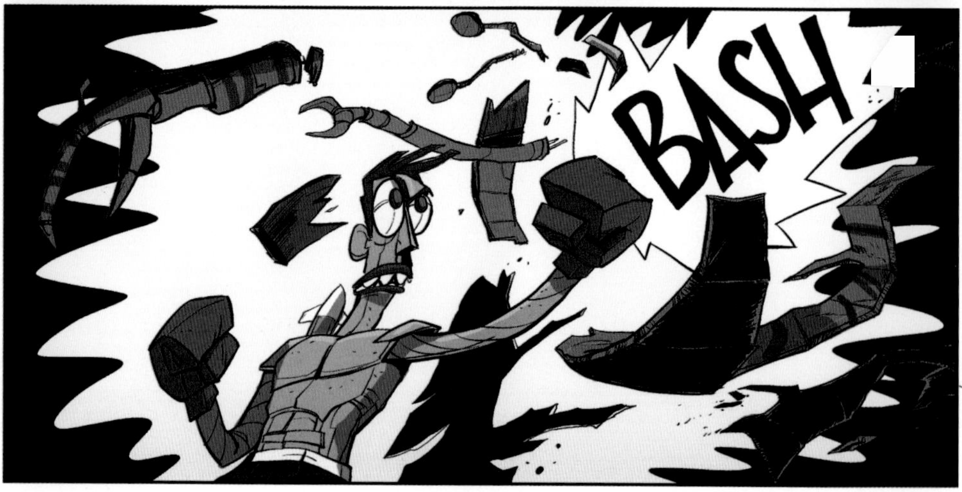
BASH

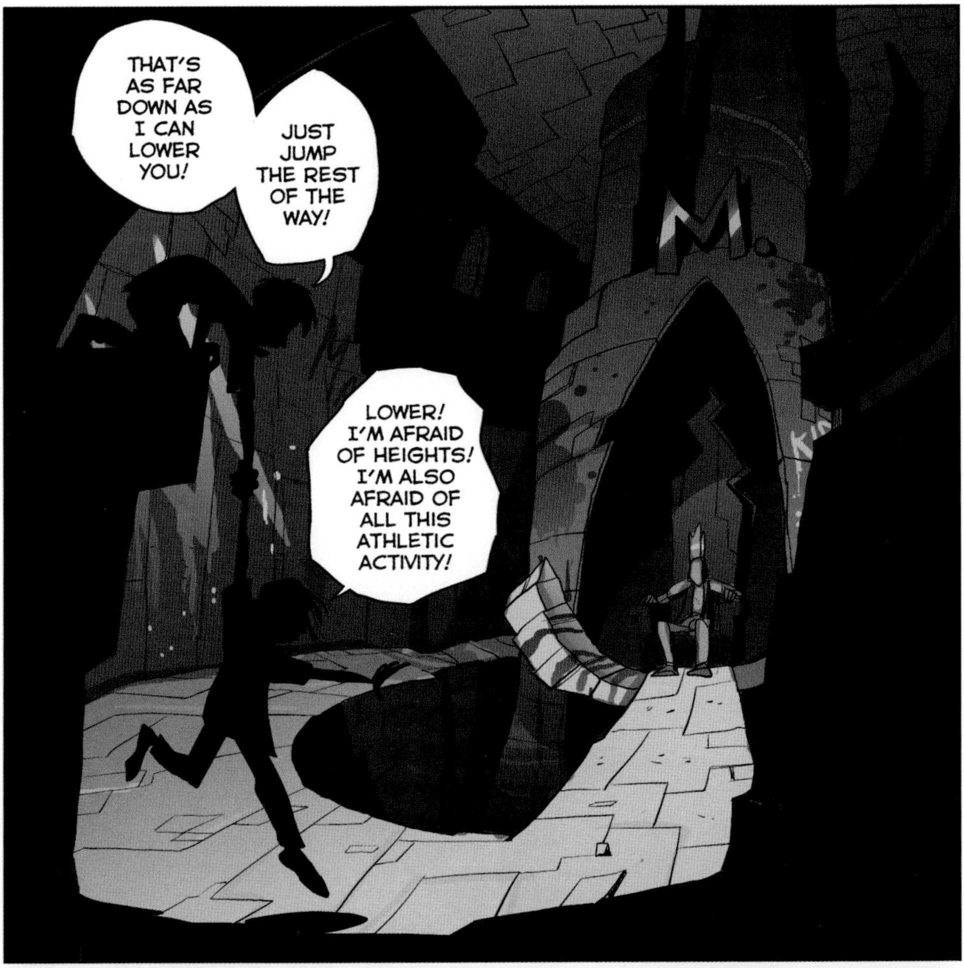
THAT'S AS FAR DOWN AS I CAN LOWER YOU!
JUST JUMP THE REST OF THE WAY!
LOWER! I'M AFRAID OF HEIGHTS! I'M ALSO AFRAID OF ALL THIS ATHLETIC ACTIVITY!

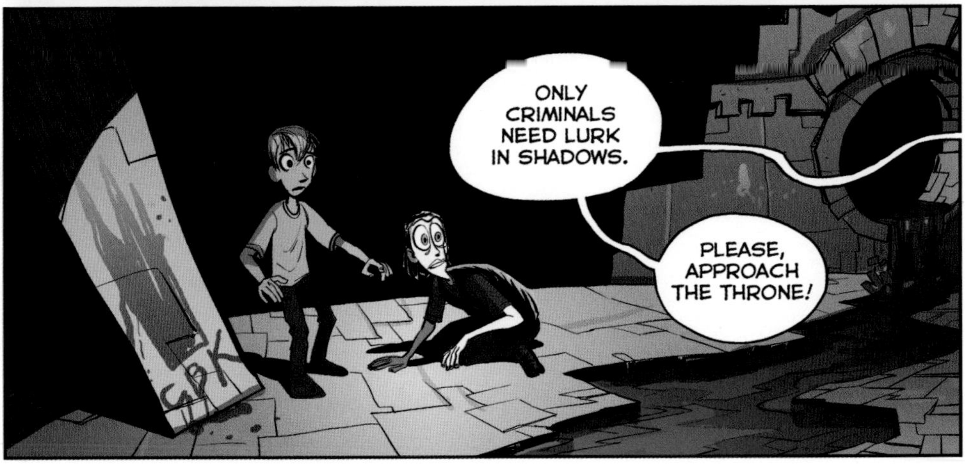
ONLY CRIMINALS NEED LURK IN SHADOWS.
PLEASE, APPROACH THE THRONE!

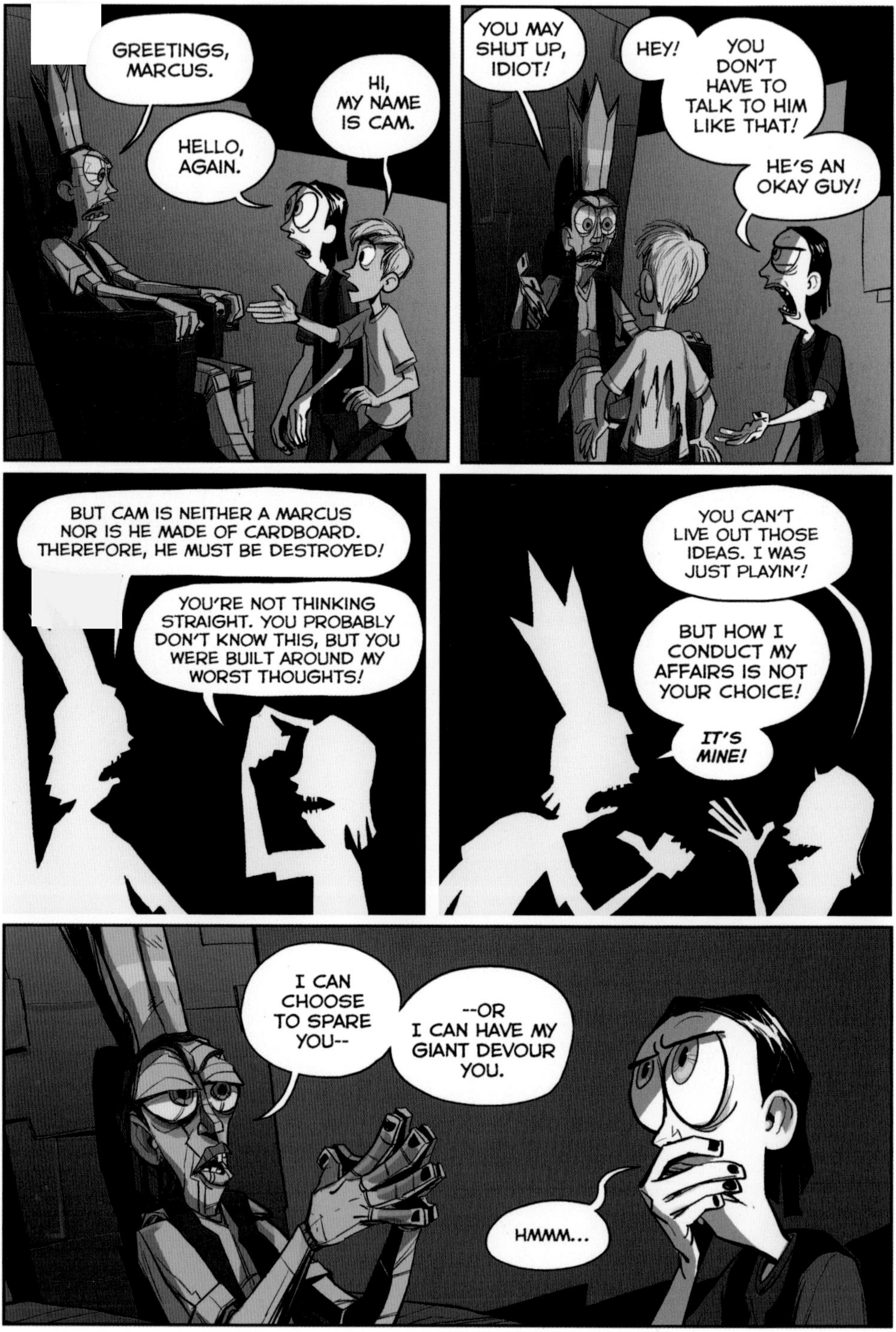
GREETINGS, MARCUS.
HELLO, AGAIN.
HI, MY NAME IS CAM.
YOU MAY SHUT UP, IDIOT!
HEY!
YOU DON'T HAVE TO TALK TO HIM LIKE THAT!
HE'S AN OKAY GUY!
BUT CAM IS NEITHER A MARCUS NOR IS HE MADE OF CARDBOARD. THEREFORE, HE MUST BE DESTROYED!
YOU'RE NOT THINKING STRAIGHT. YOU PROBABLY DON'T KNOW THIS, BUT YOU WERE BUILT AROUND MY WORST THOUGHTS!
YOU CAN'T LIVE OUT THOSE IDEAS. I WAS JUST PLAYIN'!
BUT HOW I CONDUCT MY AFFAIRS IS NOT YOUR CHOICE!
IT'S MINE!
I CAN CHOOSE TO SPARE YOU--
--OR I CAN HAVE MY GIANT DEVOUR YOU.
HMMM...

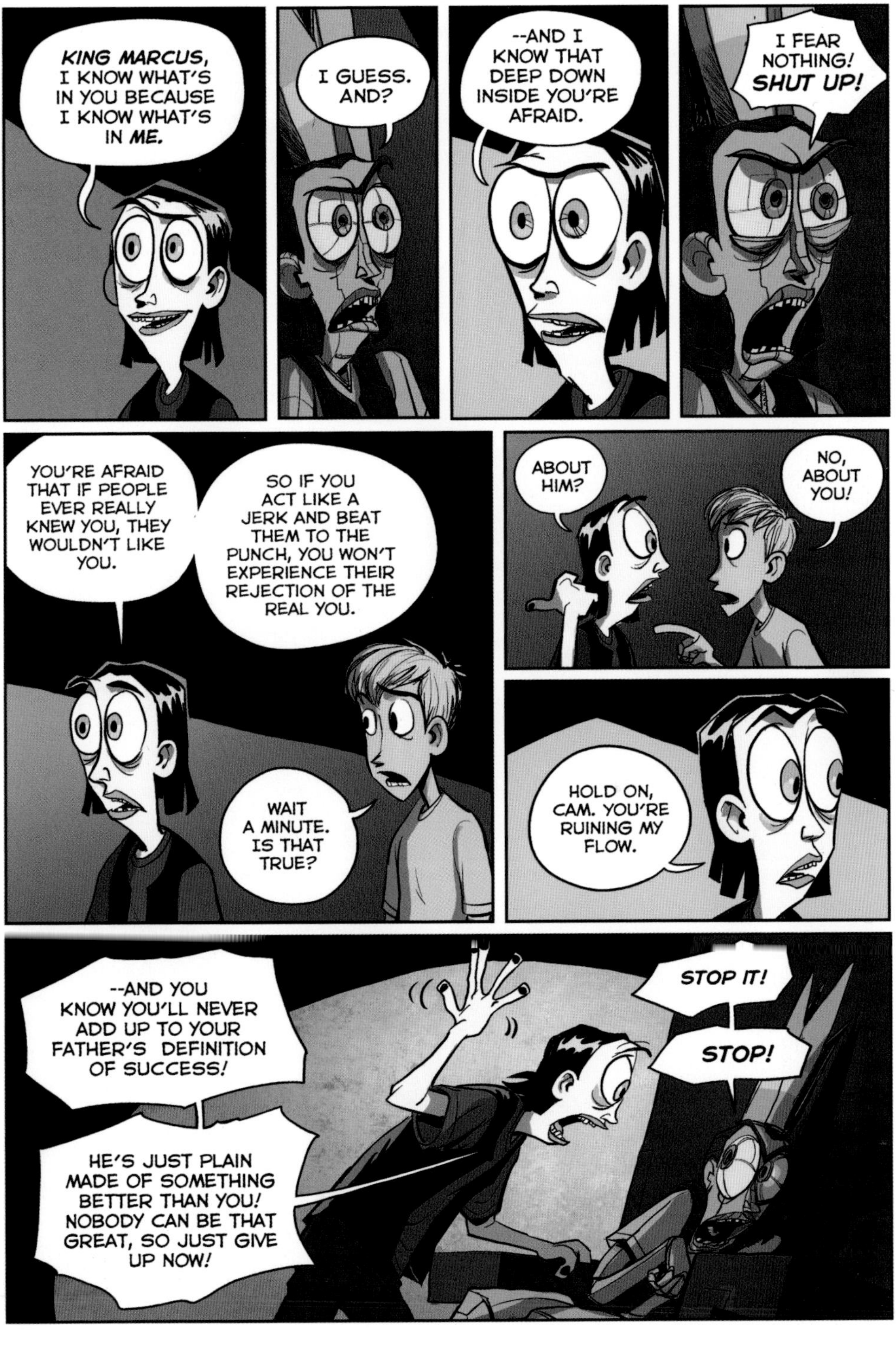

KING MARCUS, I KNOW WHAT'S IN YOU BECAUSE I KNOW WHAT'S IN *ME.*
I GUESS. AND?
--AND I KNOW THAT DEEP DOWN INSIDE YOU'RE AFRAID.
I FEAR NOTHING! *SHUT UP!*
YOU'RE AFRAID THAT IF PEOPLE EVER REALLY KNEW YOU, THEY WOULDN'T LIKE YOU.
SO IF YOU ACT LIKE A JERK AND BEAT THEM TO THE PUNCH, YOU WON'T EXPERIENCE THEIR REJECTION OF THE REAL YOU.
WAIT A MINUTE. IS THAT TRUE?
ABOUT HIM?
NO, ABOUT YOU!
HOLD ON, CAM. YOU'RE RUINING MY FLOW.
--AND YOU KNOW YOU'LL NEVER ADD UP TO YOUR FATHER'S DEFINITION OF SUCCESS!
HE'S JUST PLAIN MADE OF SOMETHING BETTER THAN YOU! NOBODY CAN BE THAT GREAT, SO JUST GIVE UP NOW!
STOP IT!
STOP!

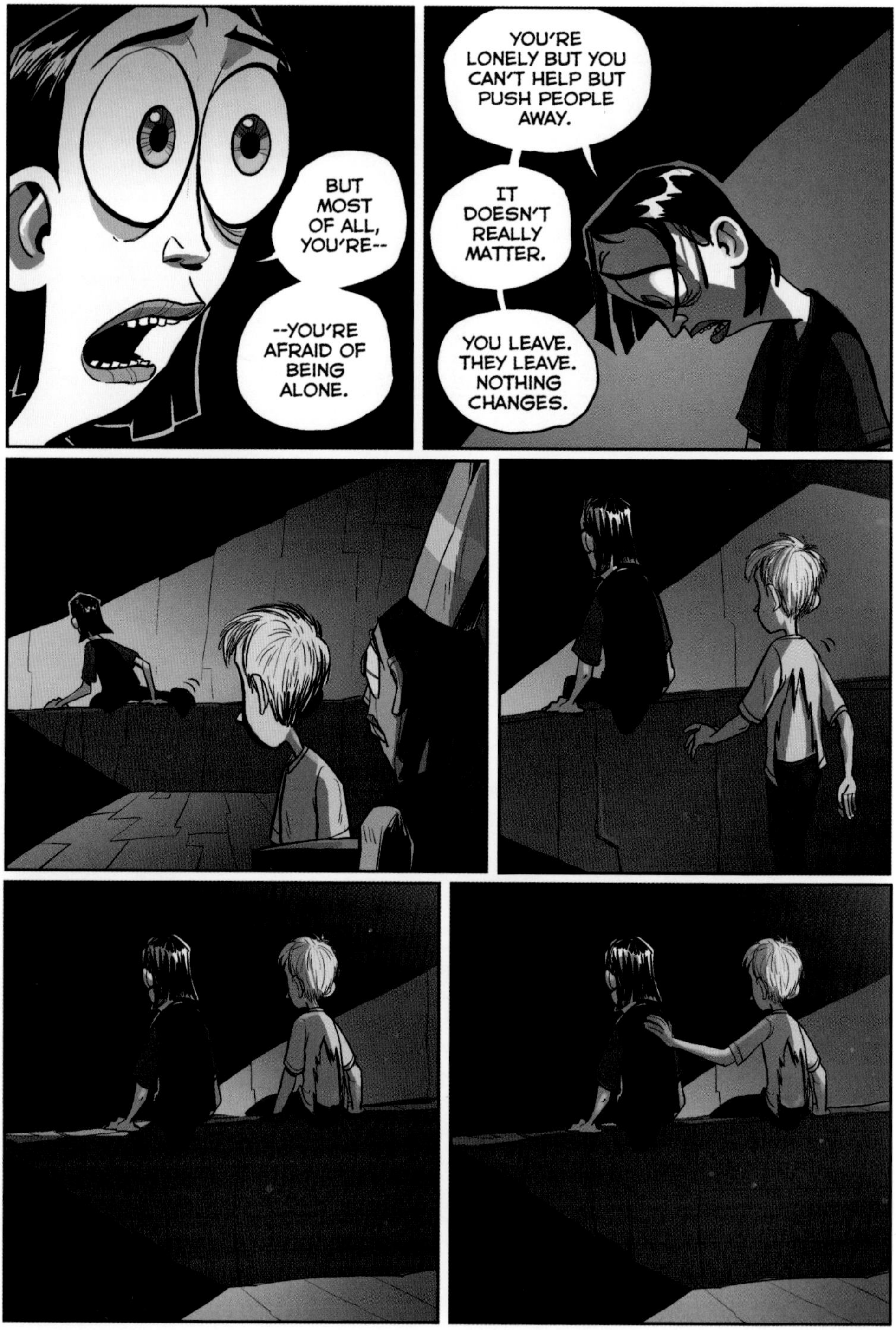
BUT MOST OF ALL, YOU'RE--
--YOU'RE AFRAID OF BEING ALONE.
YOU'RE LONELY BUT YOU CAN'T HELP BUT PUSH PEOPLE AWAY.
IT DOESN'T REALLY MATTER.
YOU LEAVE. THEY LEAVE. NOTHING CHANGES.

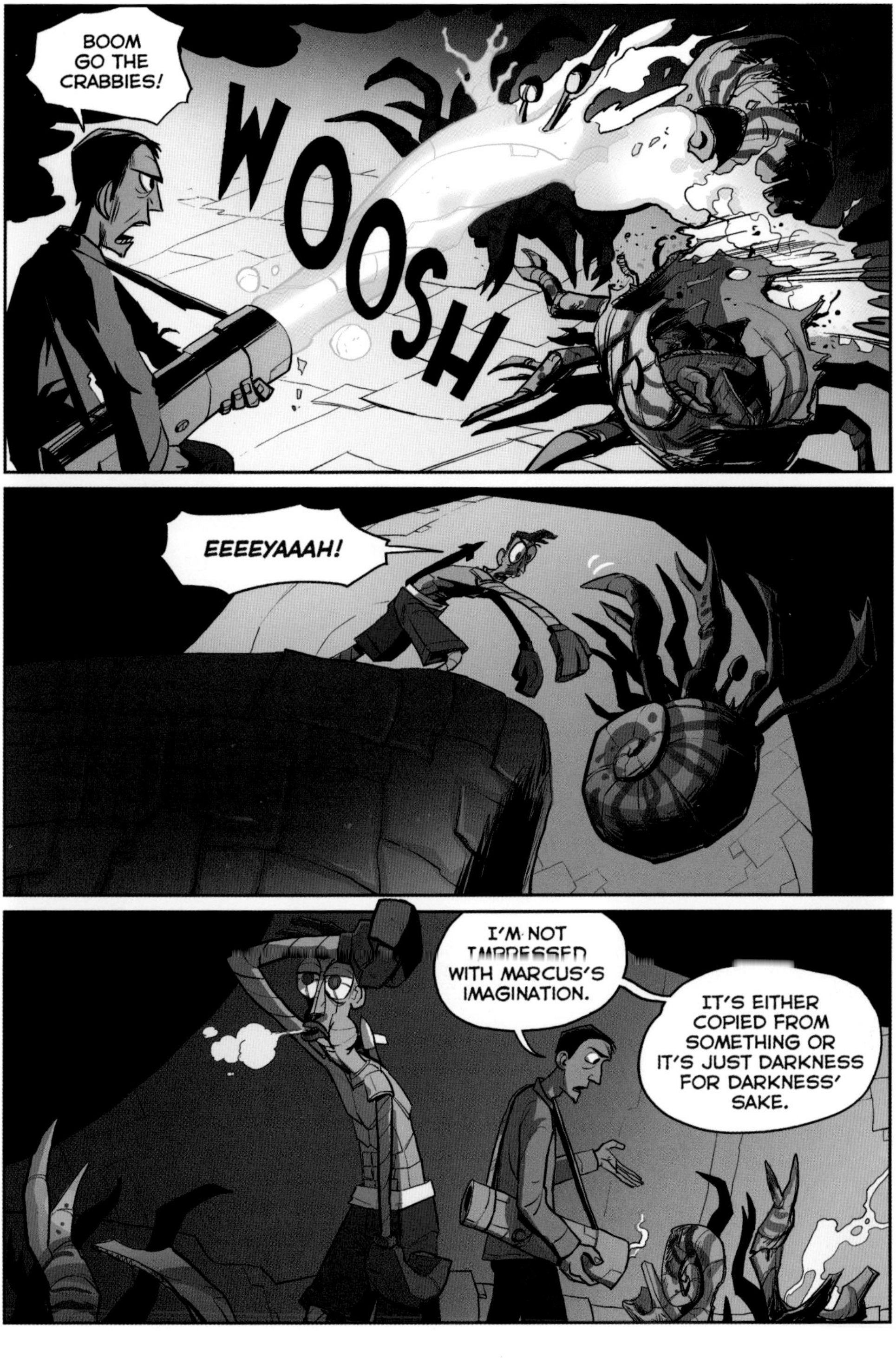
BOOM GO THE CRABBIES!
WOOSH
EEEEYAAAH!
I'M NOT IMPRESSED WITH MARCUS'S IMAGINATION.
IT'S EITHER COPIED FROM SOMETHING OR IT'S JUST DARKNESS FOR DARKNESS' SAKE.

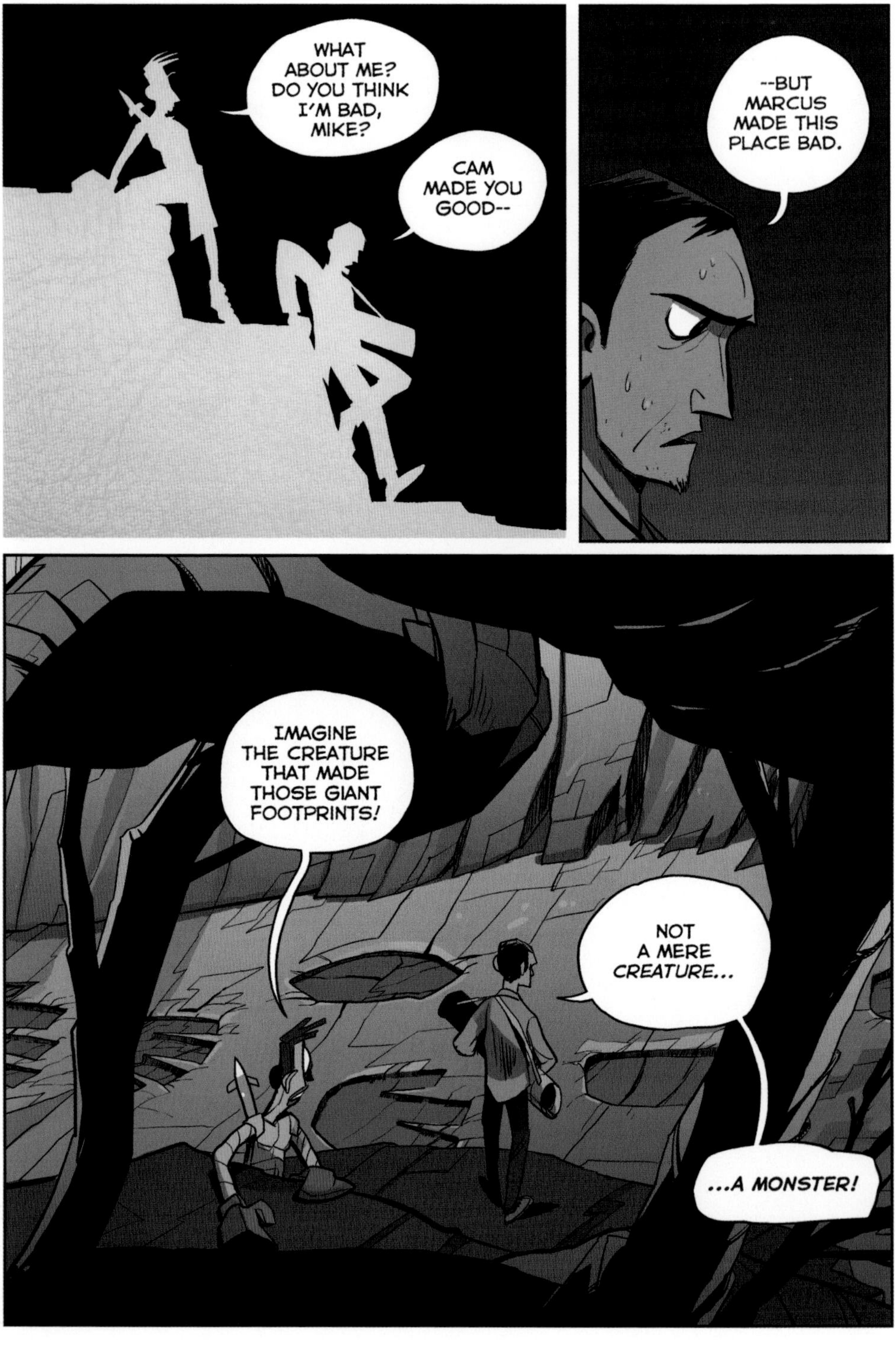
WHAT ABOUT ME? DO YOU THINK I'M BAD, MIKE?
CAM MADE YOU GOOD--
--BUT MARCUS MADE THIS PLACE BAD.
IMAGINE THE CREATURE THAT MADE THOSE GIANT FOOTPRINTS!
NOT A MERE *CREATURE*...
...A MONSTER!

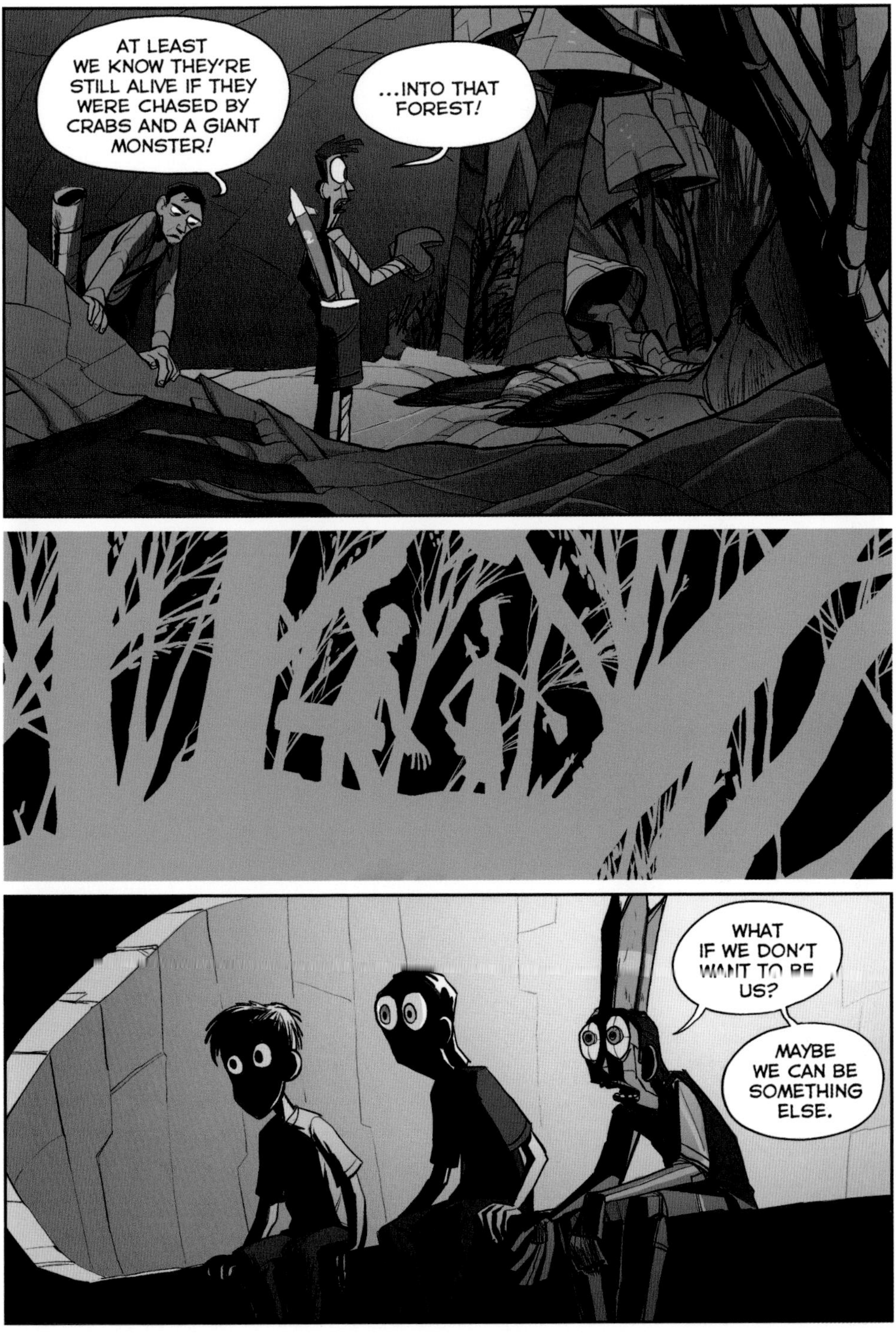
AT LEAST WE KNOW THEY'RE STILL ALIVE IF THEY WERE CHASED BY CRABS AND A GIANT MONSTER!
...INTO THAT FOREST!
WHAT IF WE DON'T WANT TO BE US?
MAYBE WE CAN BE SOMETHING ELSE.

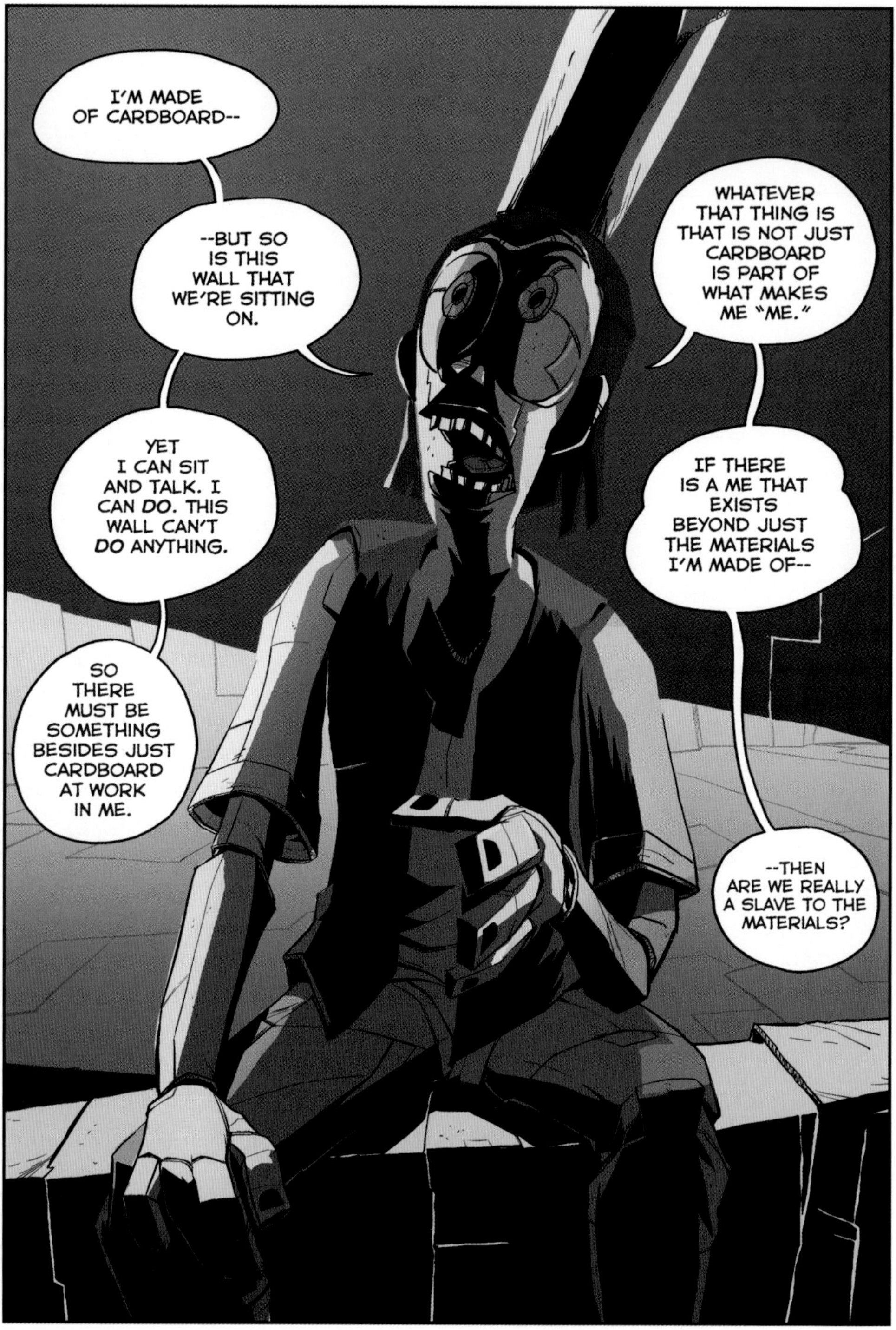
I'M MADE OF CARDBOARD--
--BUT SO IS THIS WALL THAT WE'RE SITTING ON.
YET I CAN SIT AND TALK. I CAN *DO*. THIS WALL CAN'T *DO* ANYTHING.
SO THERE MUST BE SOMETHING BESIDES JUST CARDBOARD AT WORK IN ME.
WHATEVER THAT THING IS THAT IS NOT JUST CARDBOARD IS PART OF WHAT MAKES ME "ME."
IF THERE IS A ME THAT EXISTS BEYOND JUST THE MATERIALS I'M MADE OF--
--THEN ARE WE REALLY A SLAVE TO THE MATERIALS?

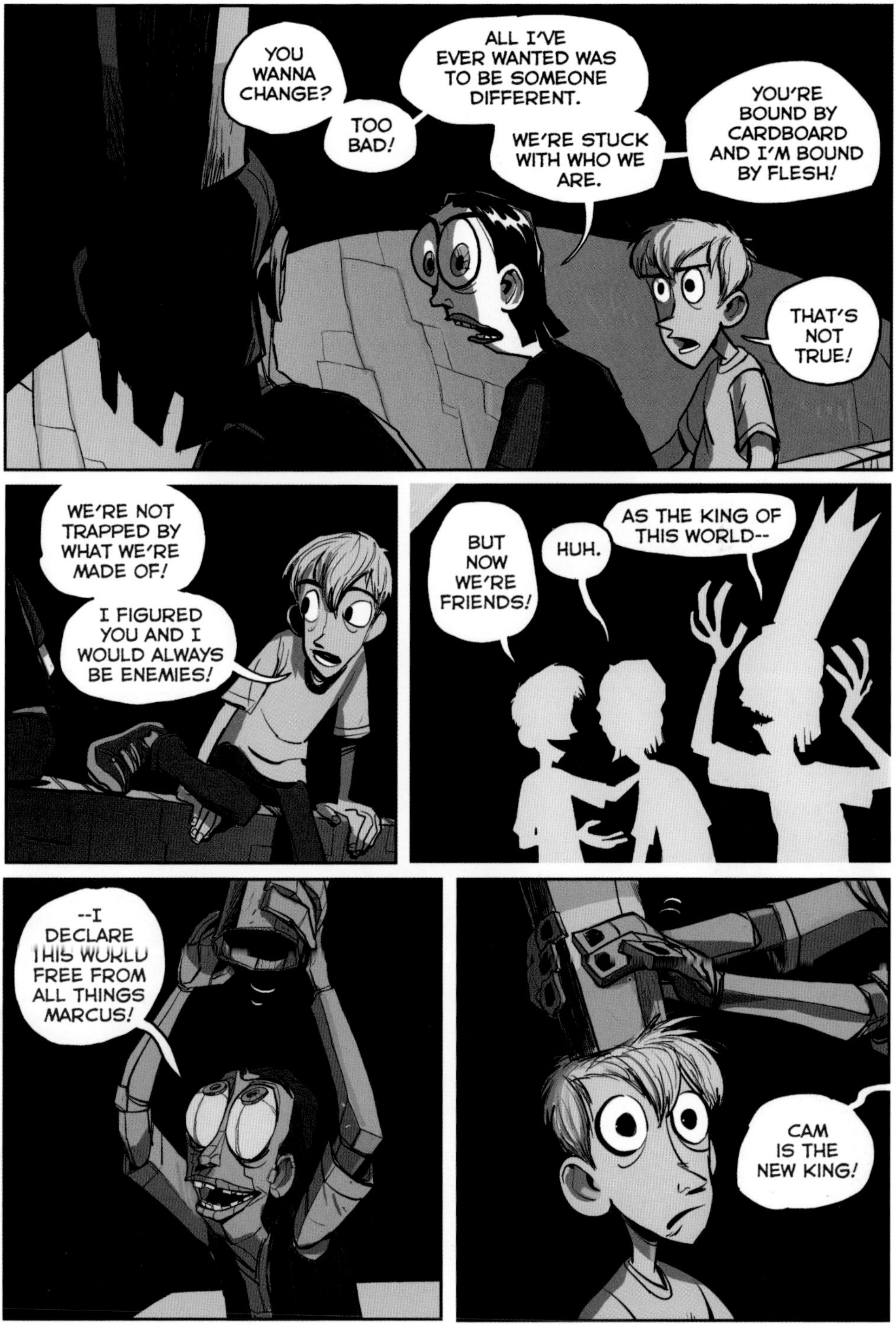
YOU WANNA CHANGE?
TOO BAD!
ALL I'VE EVER WANTED WAS TO BE SOMEONE DIFFERENT.
WE'RE STUCK WITH WHO WE ARE.
YOU'RE BOUND BY CARDBOARD AND I'M BOUND BY FLESH!
THAT'S NOT TRUE!
WE'RE NOT TRAPPED BY WHAT WE'RE MADE OF!
I FIGURED YOU AND I WOULD ALWAYS BE ENEMIES!
BUT NOW WE'RE FRIENDS!
HUH.
AS THE KING OF THIS WORLD--
--I DECLARE THIS WORLD FREE FROM ALL THINGS MARCUS!
CAM IS THE NEW KING!

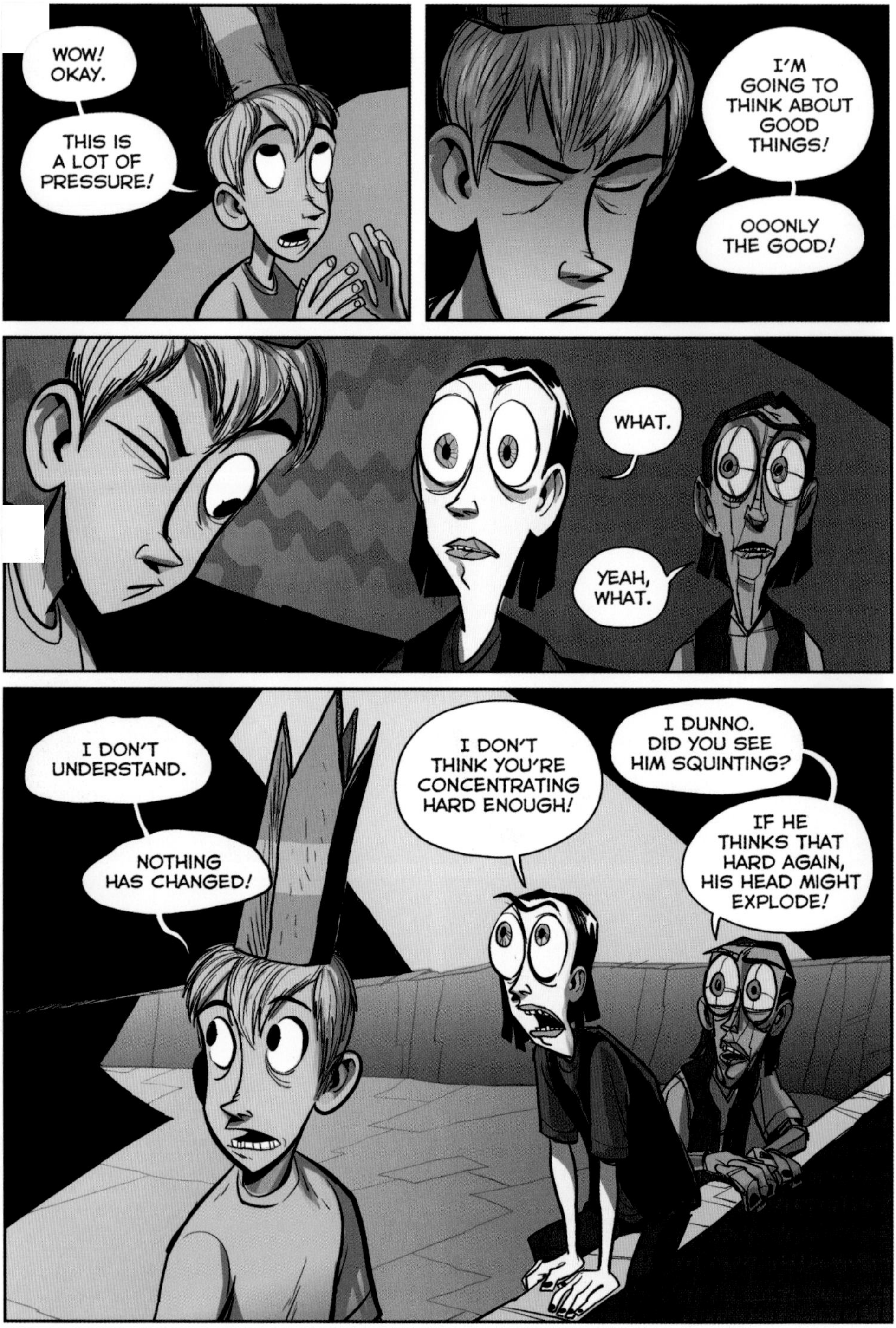
WOW! OKAY.
THIS IS A LOT OF PRESSURE!
I'M GOING TO THINK ABOUT GOOD THINGS!
OOONLY THE GOOD!
WHAT.
YEAH, WHAT.
I DON'T UNDERSTAND.
NOTHING HAS CHANGED!
I DON'T THINK YOU'RE CONCENTRATING HARD ENOUGH!
I DUNNO. DID YOU SEE HIM SQUINTING?
IF HE THINKS THAT HARD AGAIN, HIS HEAD MIGHT EXPLODE!

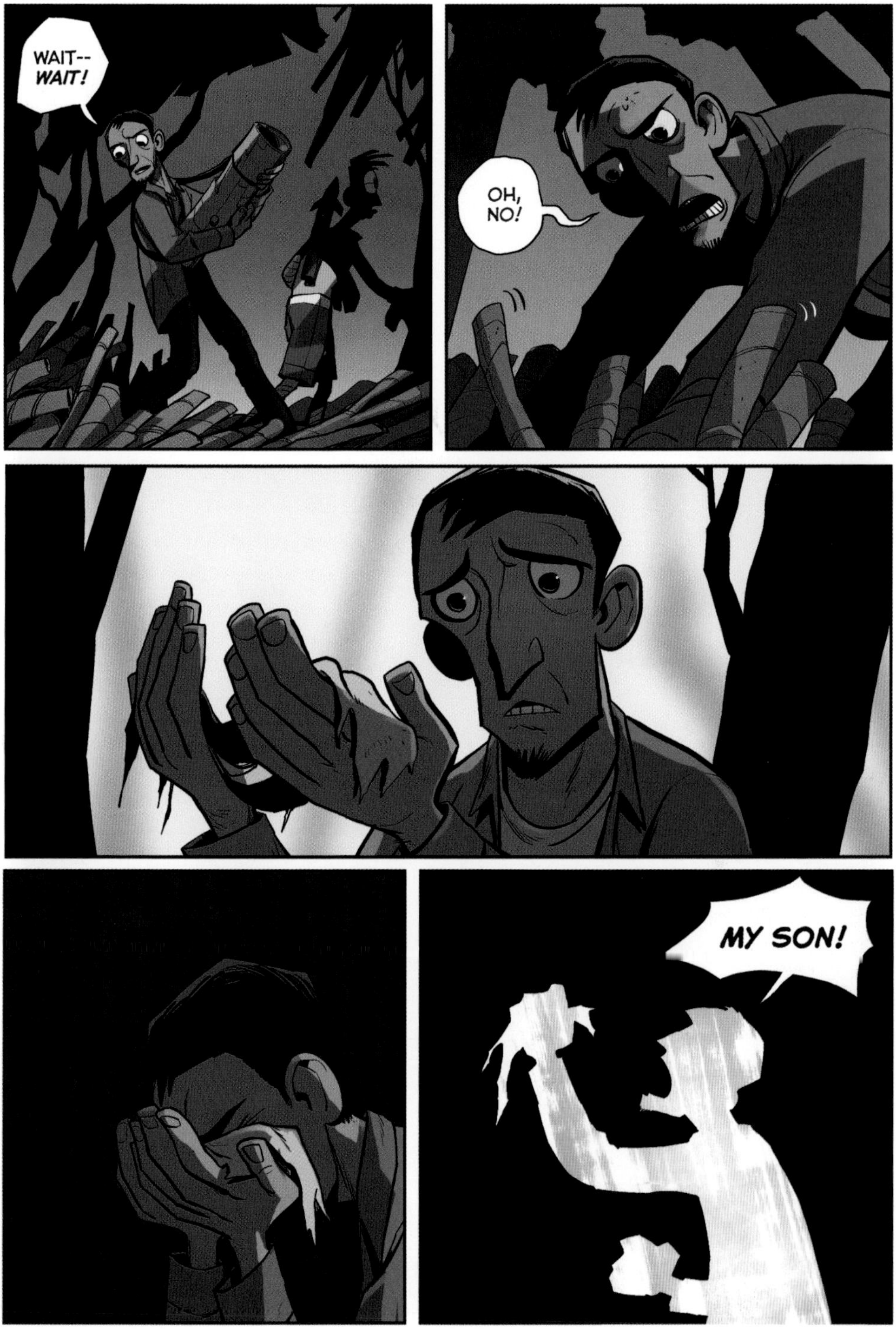
WAIT--
WAIT!
OH,
NO!
MY SON!

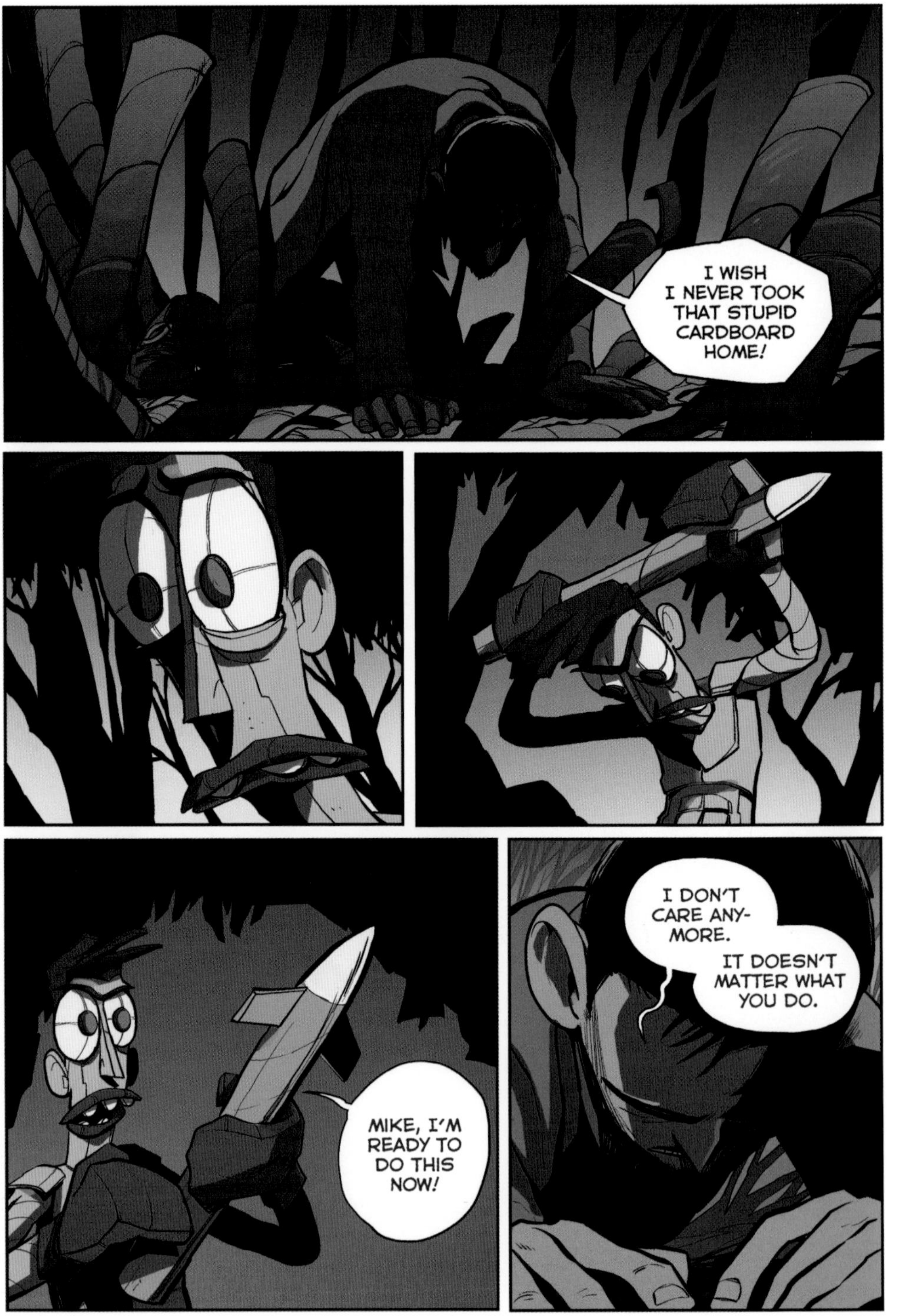
I WISH I NEVER TOOK THAT STUPID CARDBOARD HOME!
MIKE, I'M READY TO DO THIS NOW!
I DON'T CARE ANY-MORE.
IT DOESN'T MATTER WHAT YOU DO.

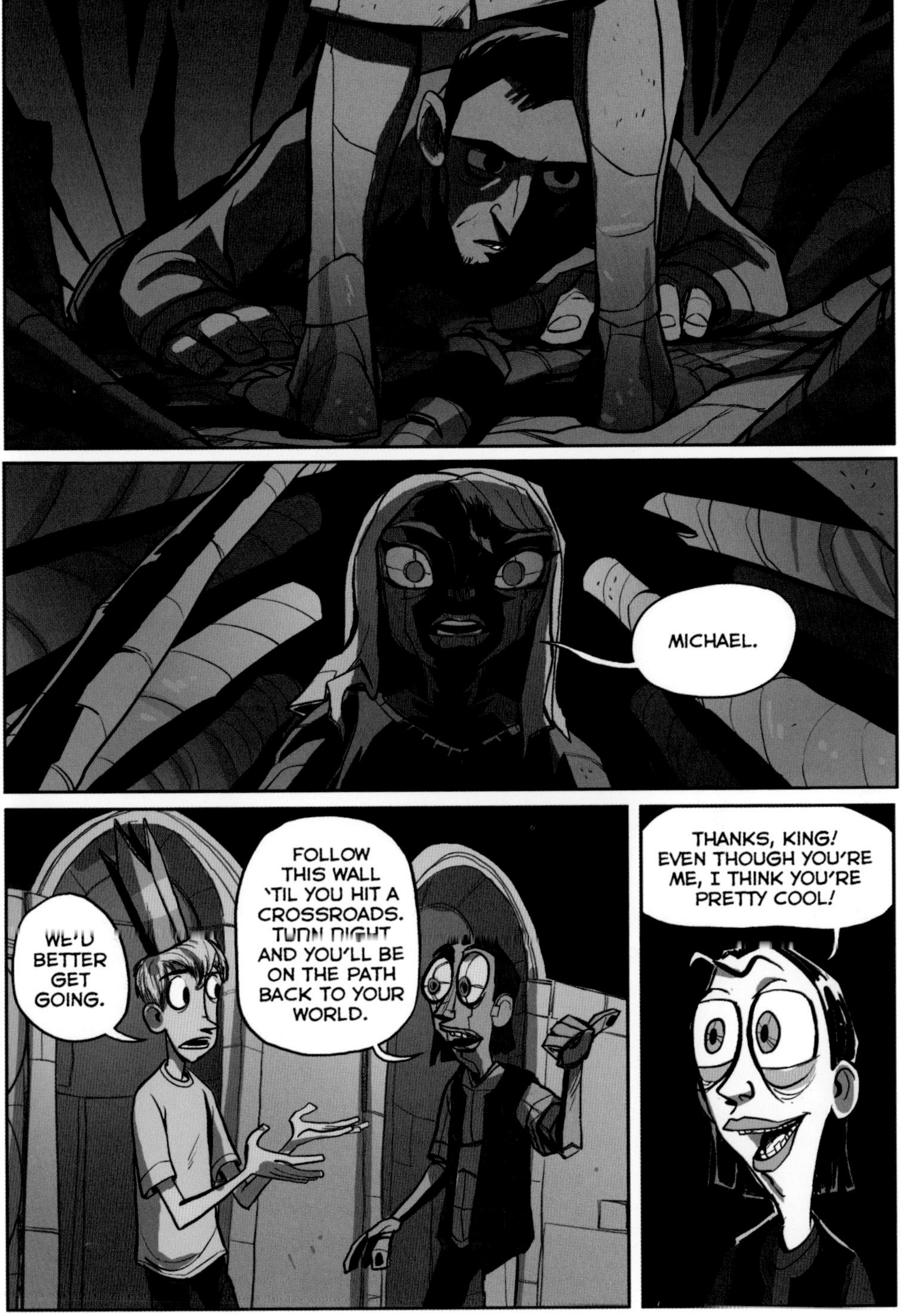
MICHAEL.
WE'D BETTER GET GOING.
FOLLOW THIS WALL 'TIL YOU HIT A CROSSROADS. TURN RIGHT AND YOU'LL BE ON THE PATH BACK TO YOUR WORLD.
THANKS, KING! EVEN THOUGH YOU'RE ME, I THINK YOU'RE PRETTY COOL!

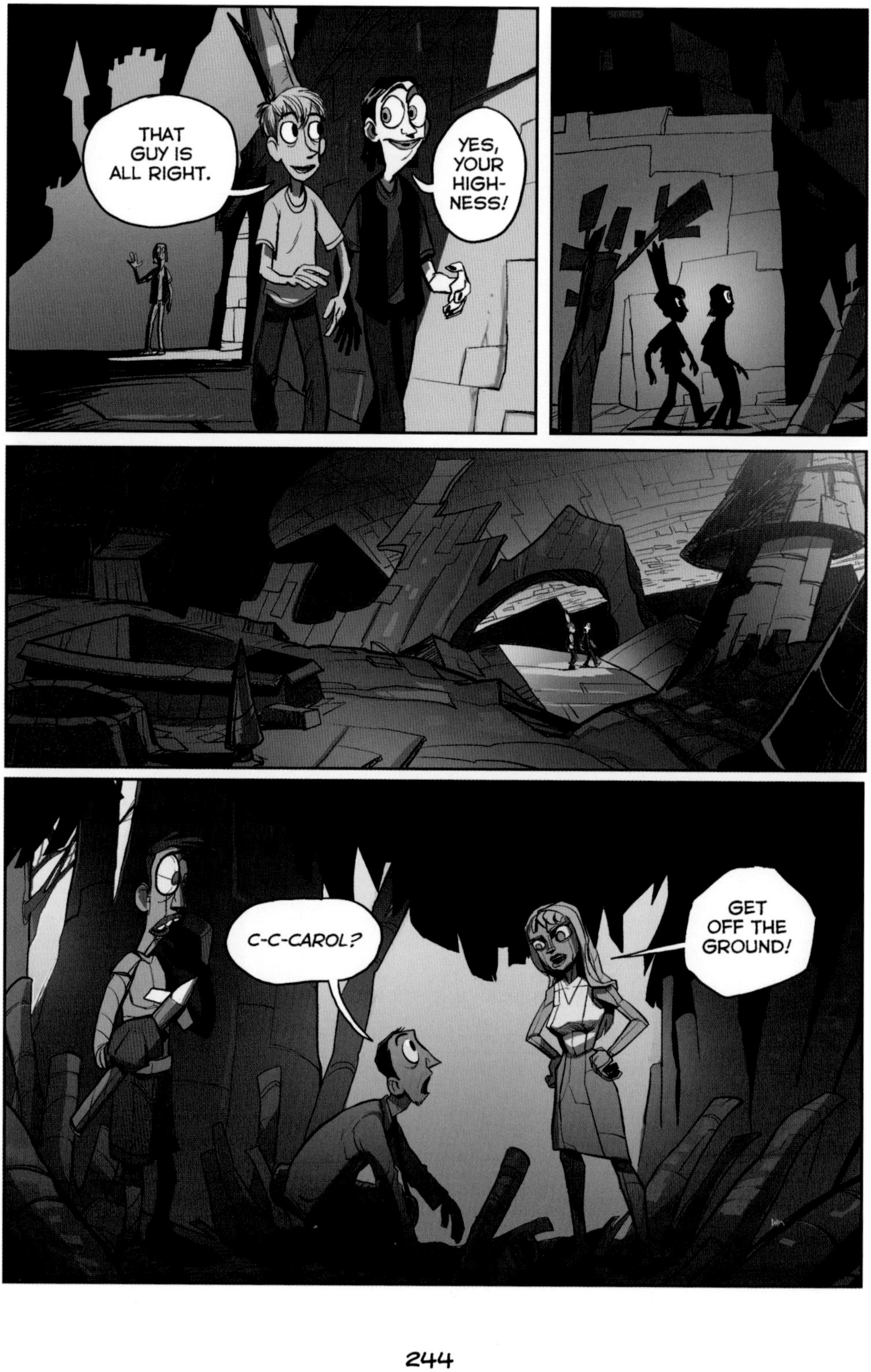
THAT GUY IS ALL RIGHT.
YES, YOUR HIGH-NESS!
C-C-CAROL?
GET OFF THE GROUND!

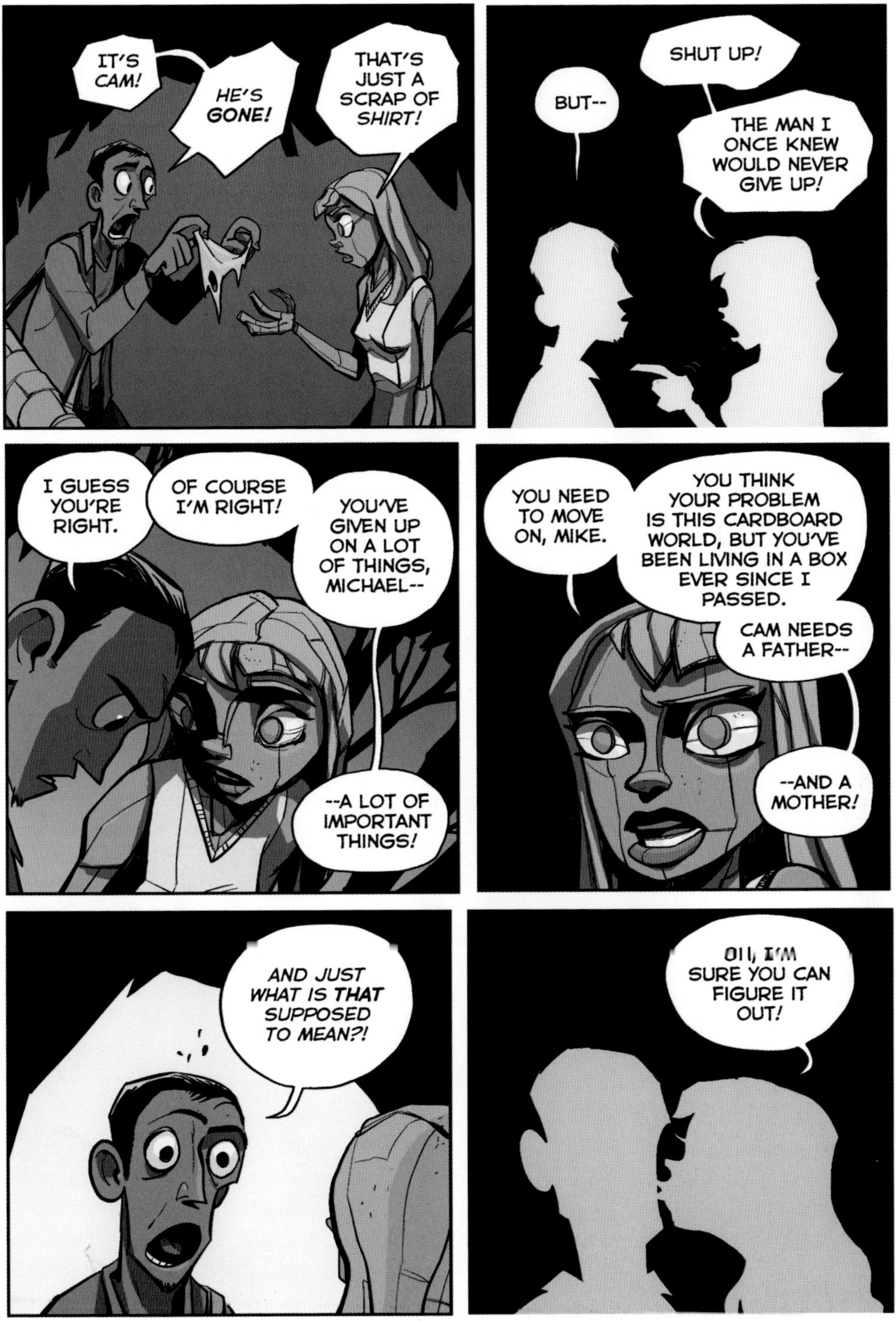
IT'S CAM!
HE'S GONE!
THAT'S JUST A SCRAP OF SHIRT!
BUT--
SHUT UP!
THE MAN I ONCE KNEW WOULD NEVER GIVE UP!
I GUESS YOU'RE RIGHT.
OF COURSE I'M RIGHT!
YOU'VE GIVEN UP ON A LOT OF THINGS, MICHAEL--
--A LOT OF IMPORTANT THINGS!
YOU NEED TO MOVE ON, MIKE.
YOU THINK YOUR PROBLEM IS THIS CARDBOARD WORLD, BUT YOU'VE BEEN LIVING IN A BOX EVER SINCE I PASSED.
CAM NEEDS A FATHER--
--AND A MOTHER!
AND JUST WHAT IS THAT SUPPOSED TO MEAN?!
OH, I'M SURE YOU CAN FIGURE IT OUT!

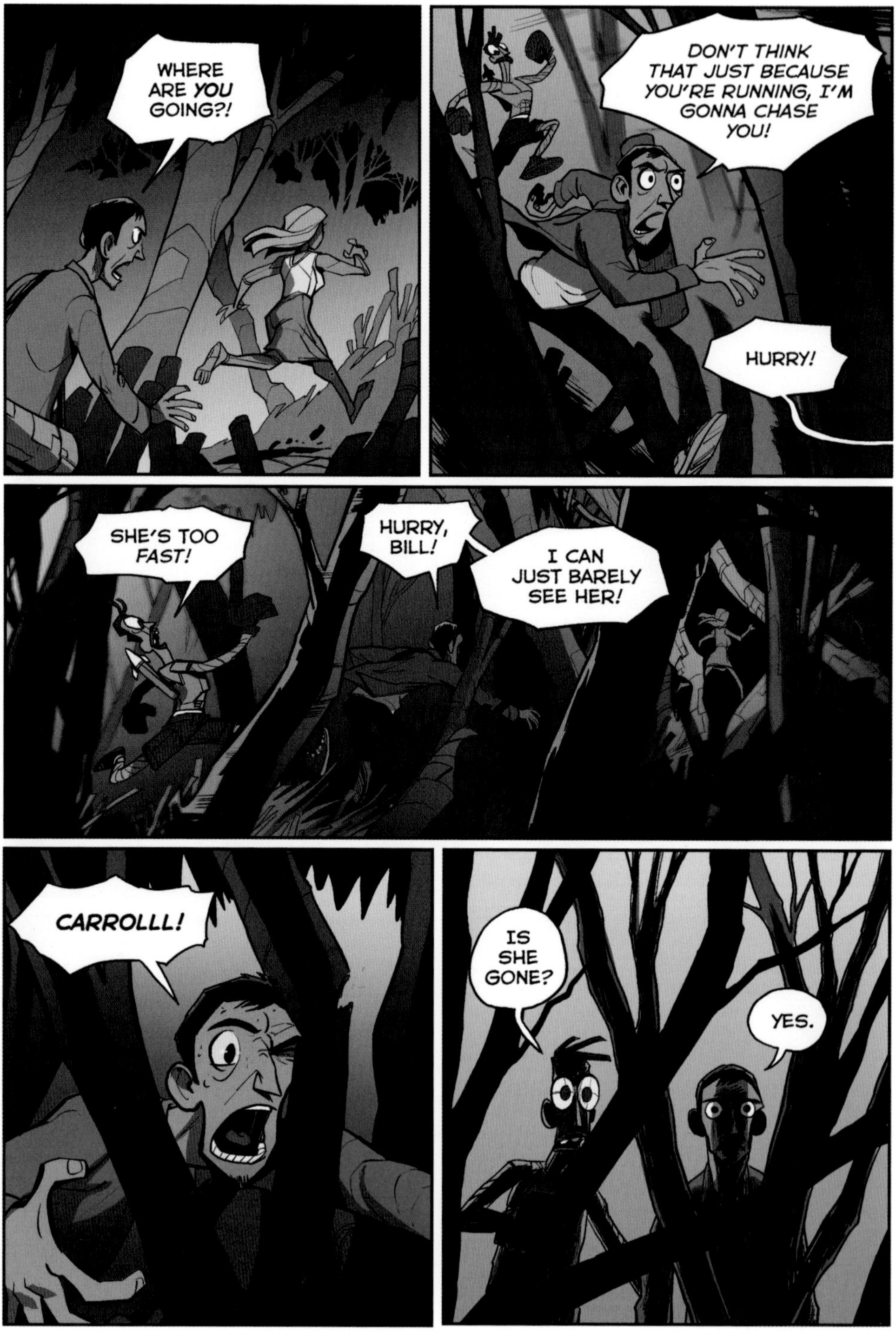
WHERE ARE *YOU* GOING?!
DON'T THINK THAT JUST BECAUSE YOU'RE RUNNING, I'M GONNA CHASE YOU!
HURRY!
SHE'S TOO *FAST!*
HURRY, *BILL!*
I CAN JUST BARELY SEE HER*!*
CARROLLL!
IS SHE GONE?
YES.

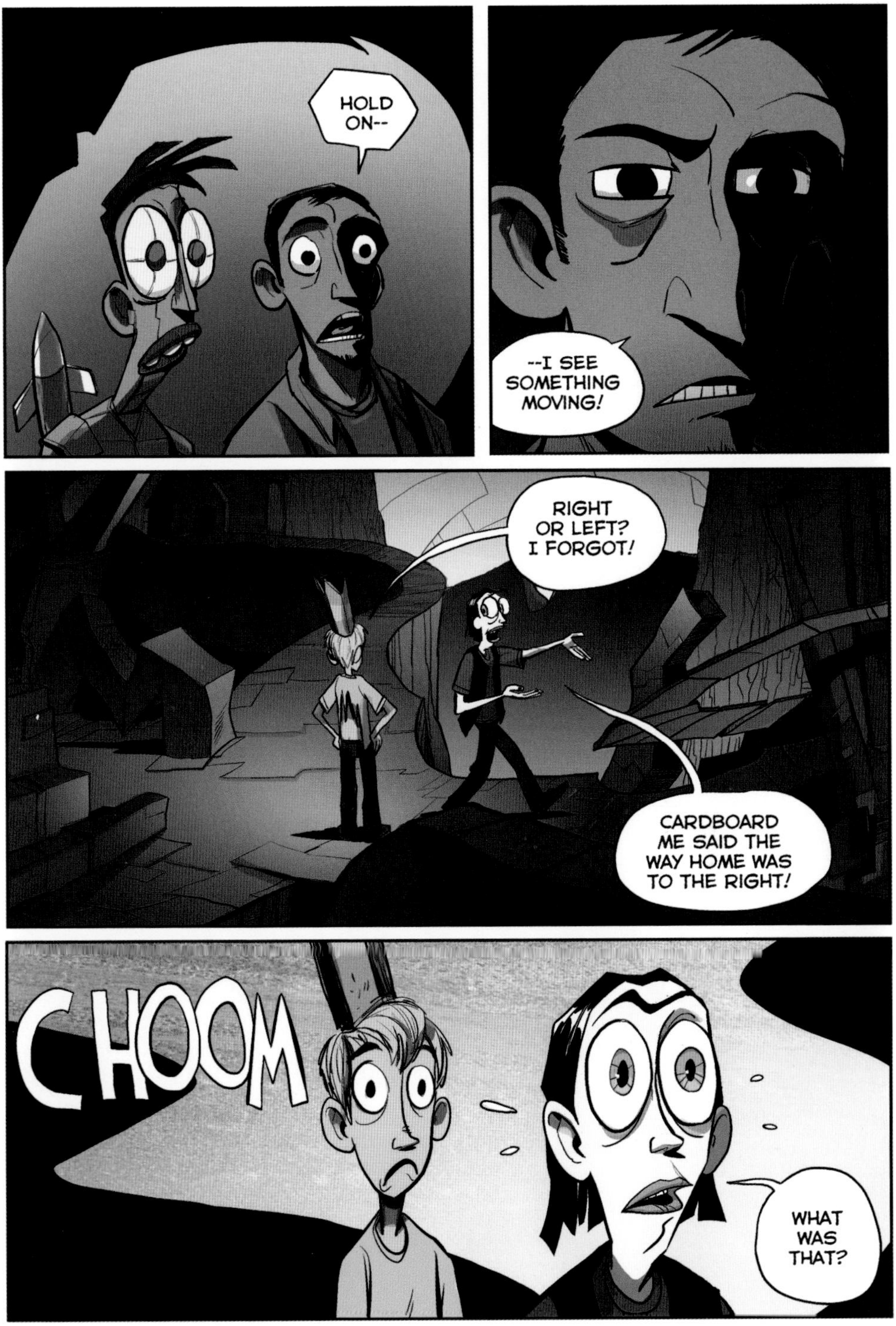
HOLD ON--
--I SEE SOMETHING MOVING!
RIGHT OR LEFT? I FORGOT!
CARDBOARD ME SAID THE WAY HOME WAS TO THE RIGHT!
CHOOM
WHAT WAS THAT?

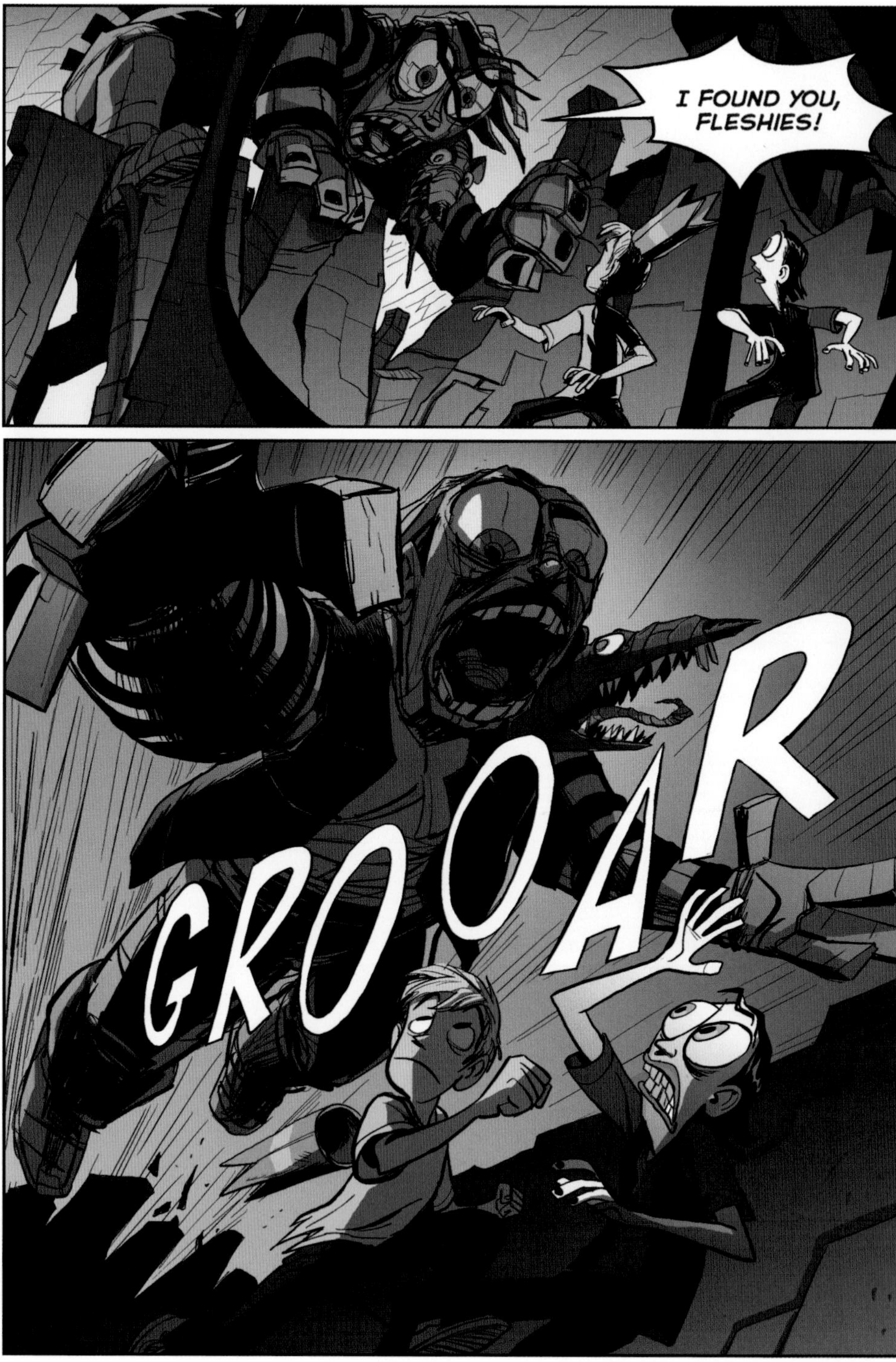
I FOUND YOU, FLESHIES!
GROOAR

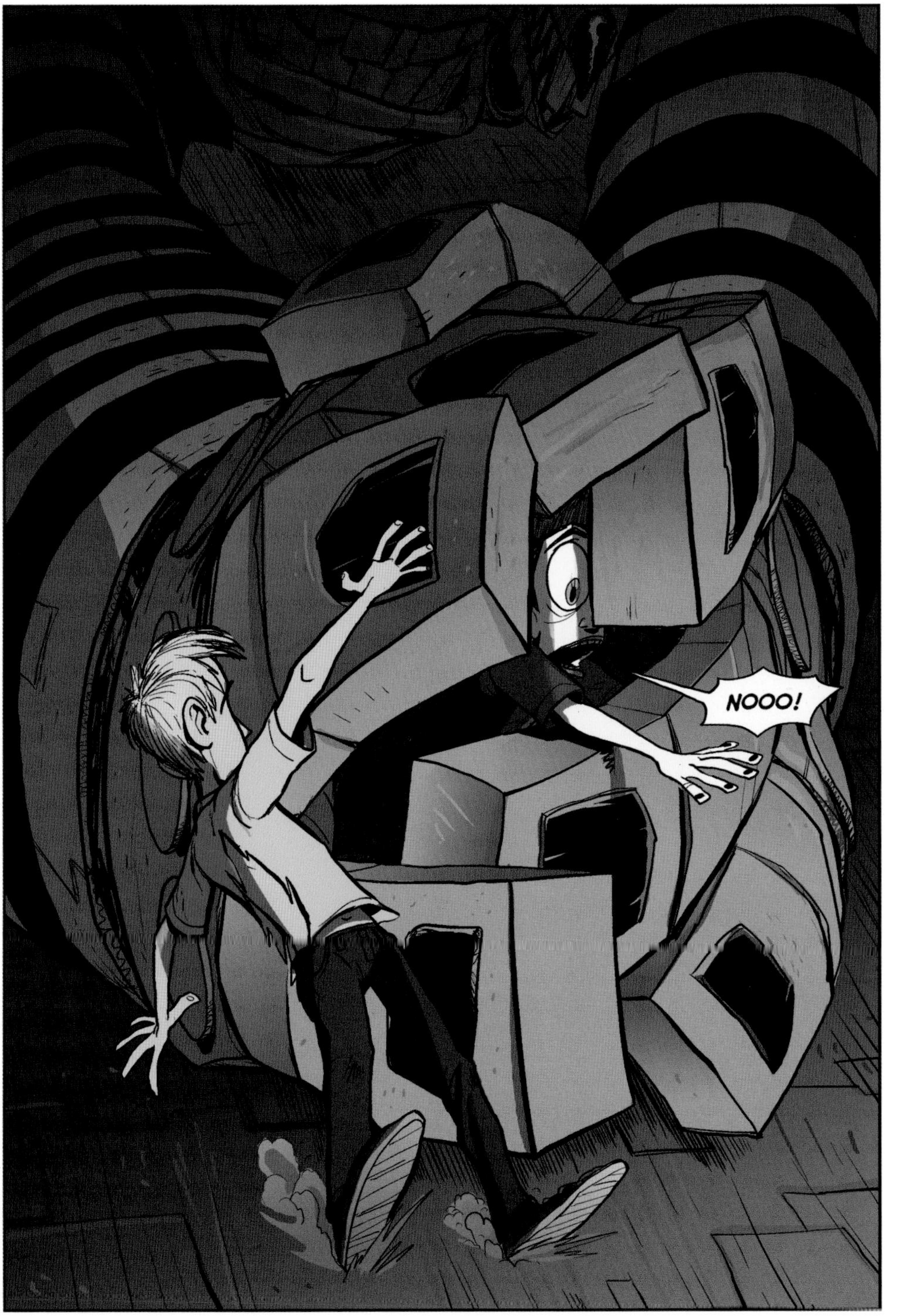
NOOO!

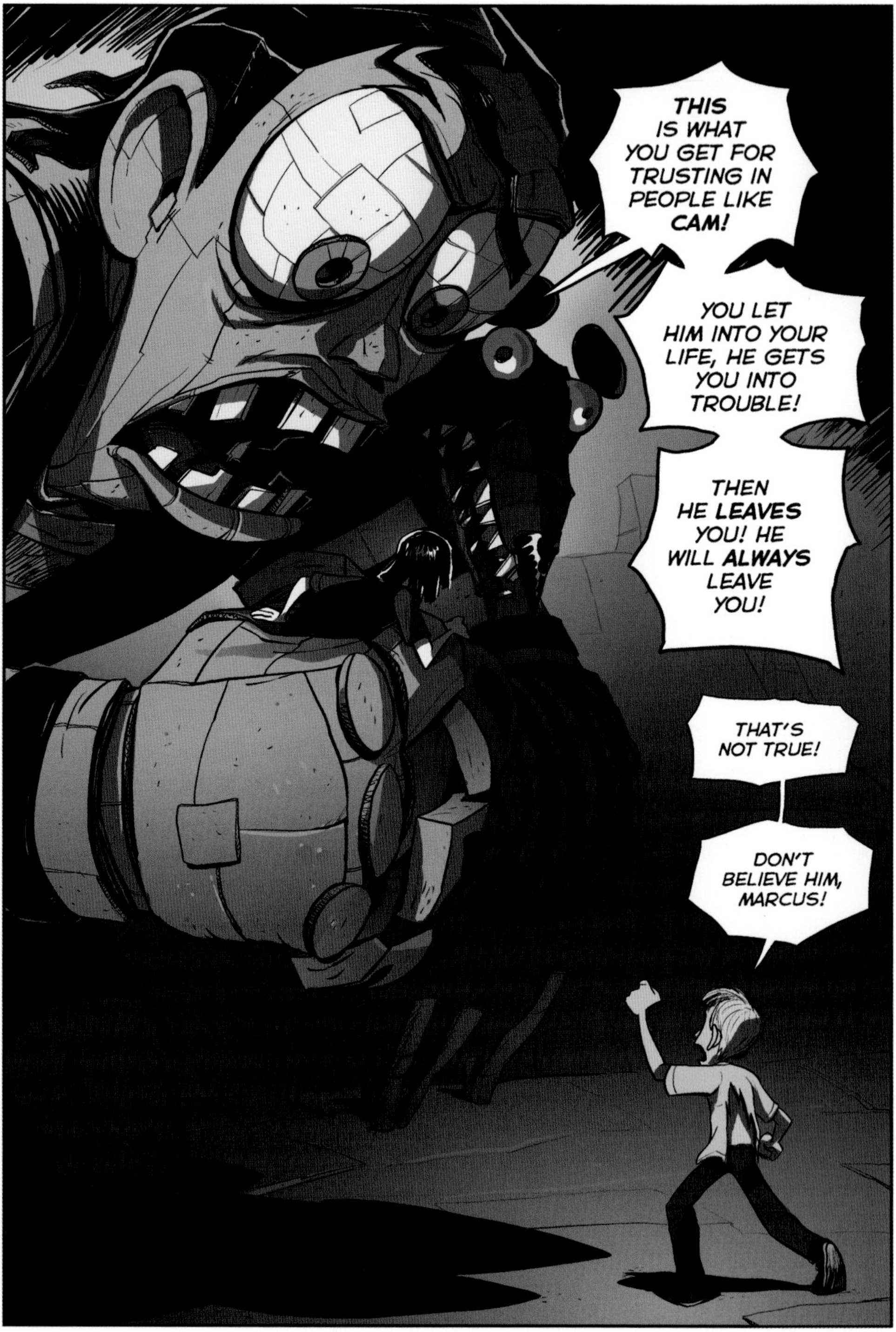
THIS IS WHAT YOU GET FOR TRUSTING IN PEOPLE LIKE CAM!
YOU LET HIM INTO YOUR LIFE, HE GETS YOU INTO TROUBLE!
THEN HE LEAVES YOU! HE WILL ALWAYS LEAVE YOU!
THAT'S NOT TRUE!
DON'T BELIEVE HIM, MARCUS!

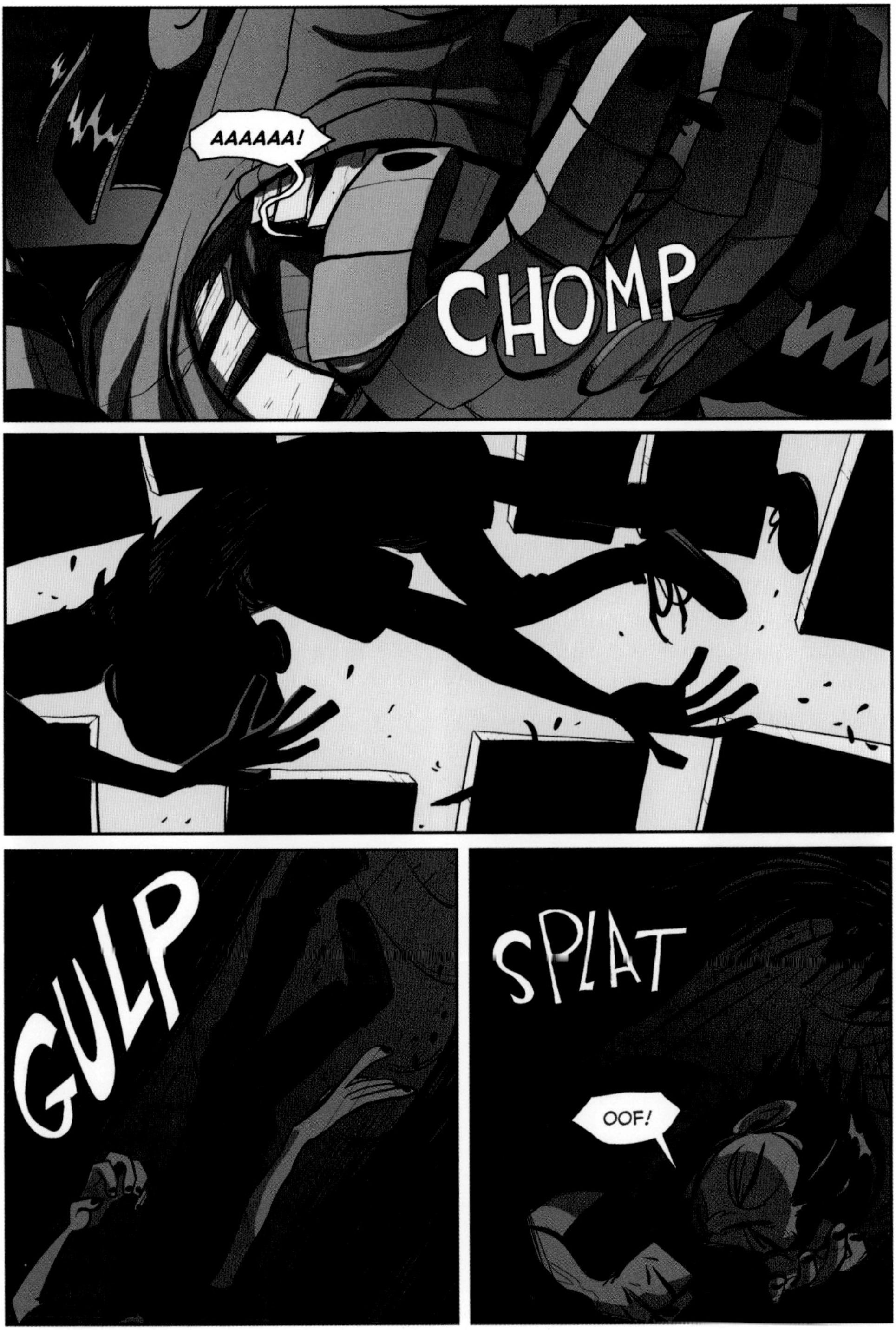
AAAAAA!
CHOMP
GULP
SPLAT
OOF!

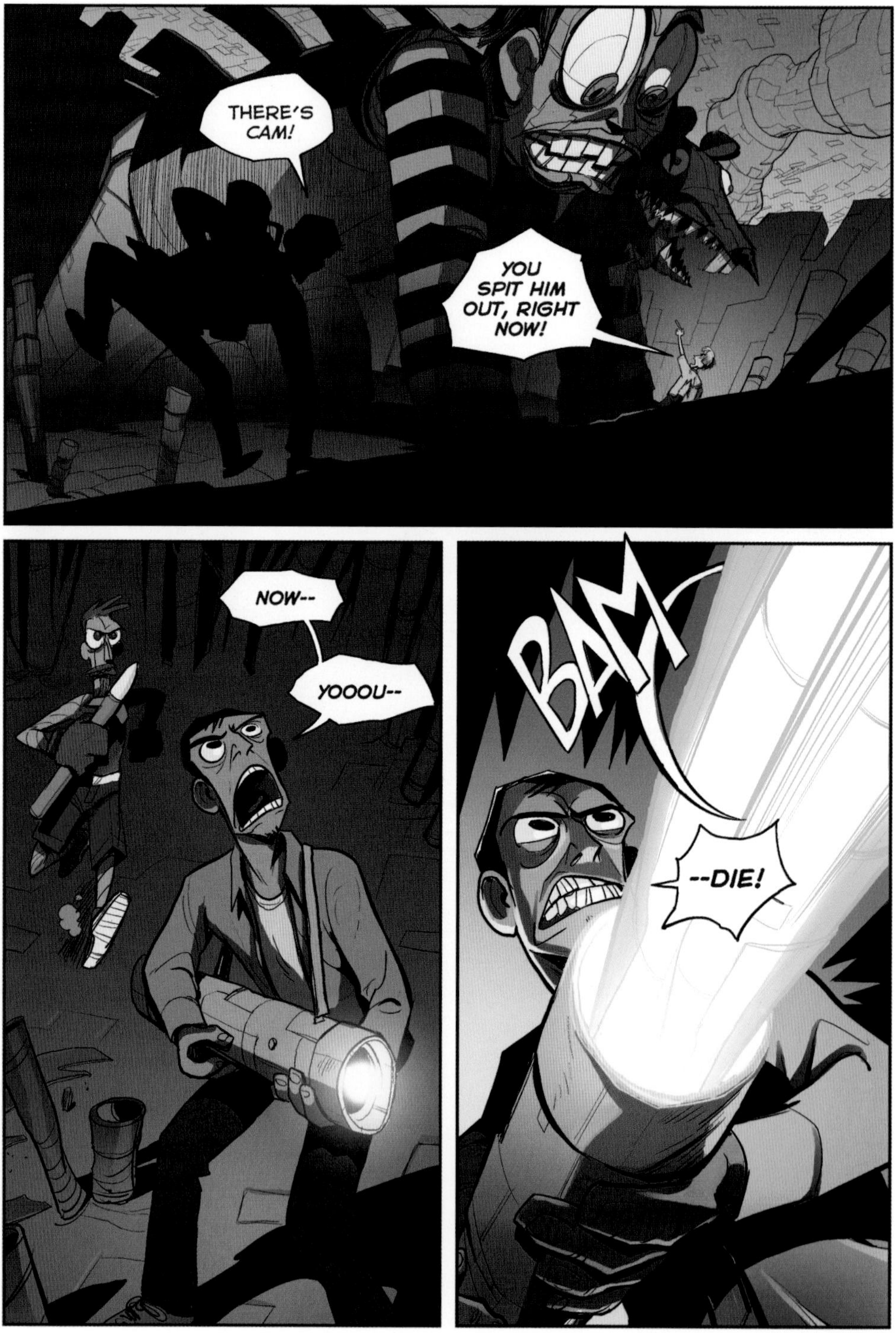
THERE'S CAM!
YOU SPIT HIM OUT, RIGHT NOW!
NOW--
YOOOU--
BAM
--DIE!

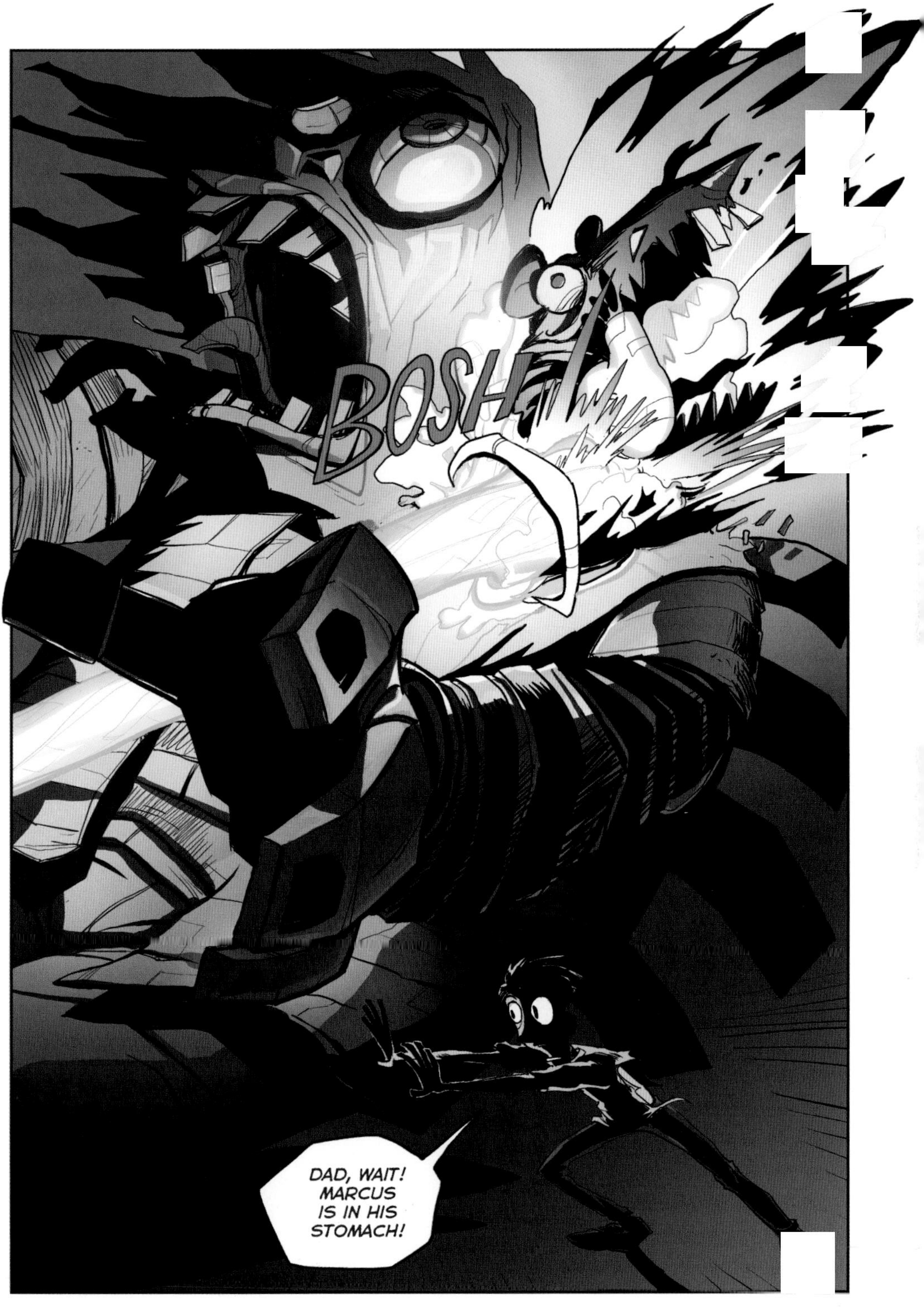
BOSH!
DAD, WAIT! MARCUS IS IN HIS STOMACH!

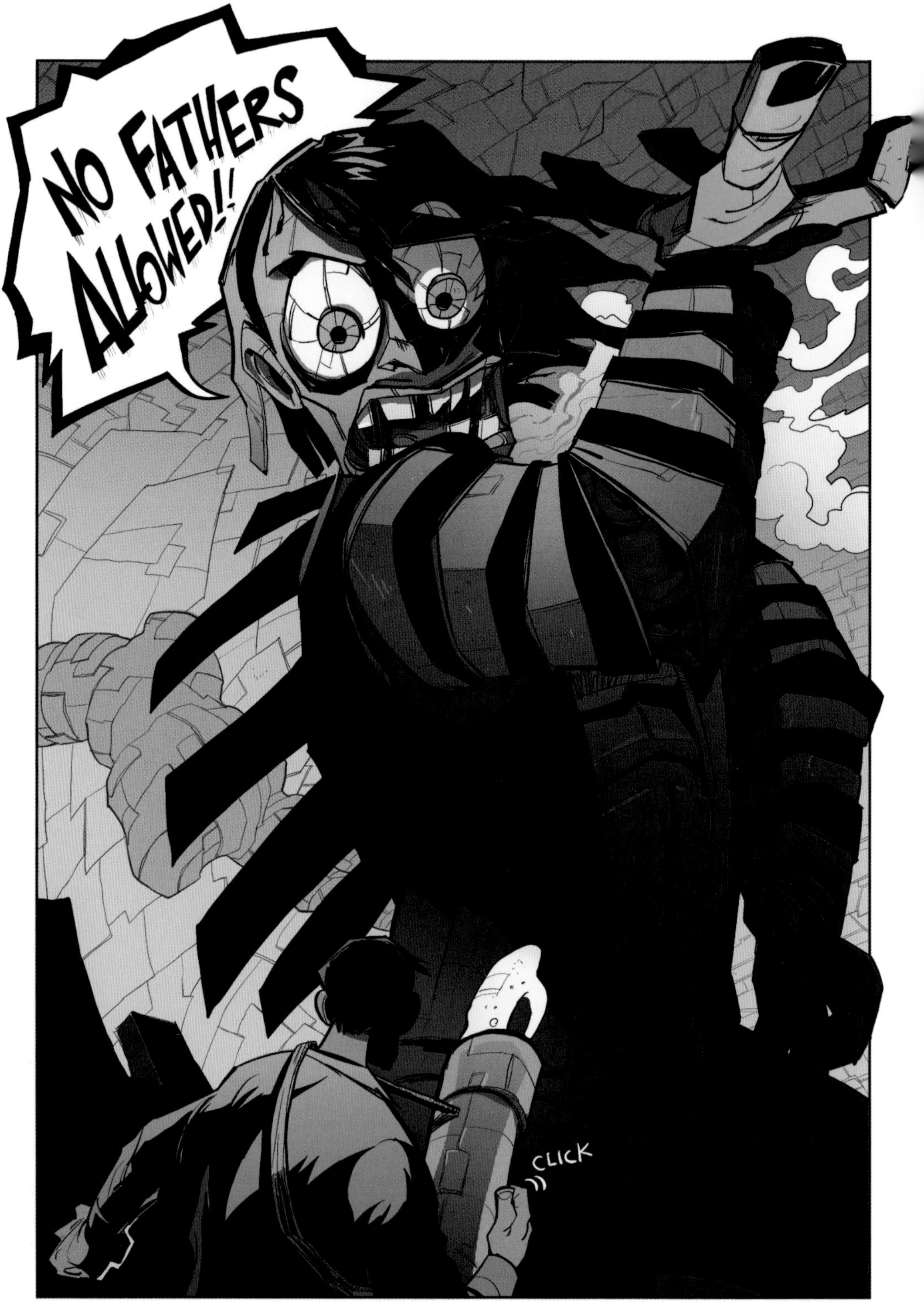
NO FATHERS ALLOWED!!
CLICK

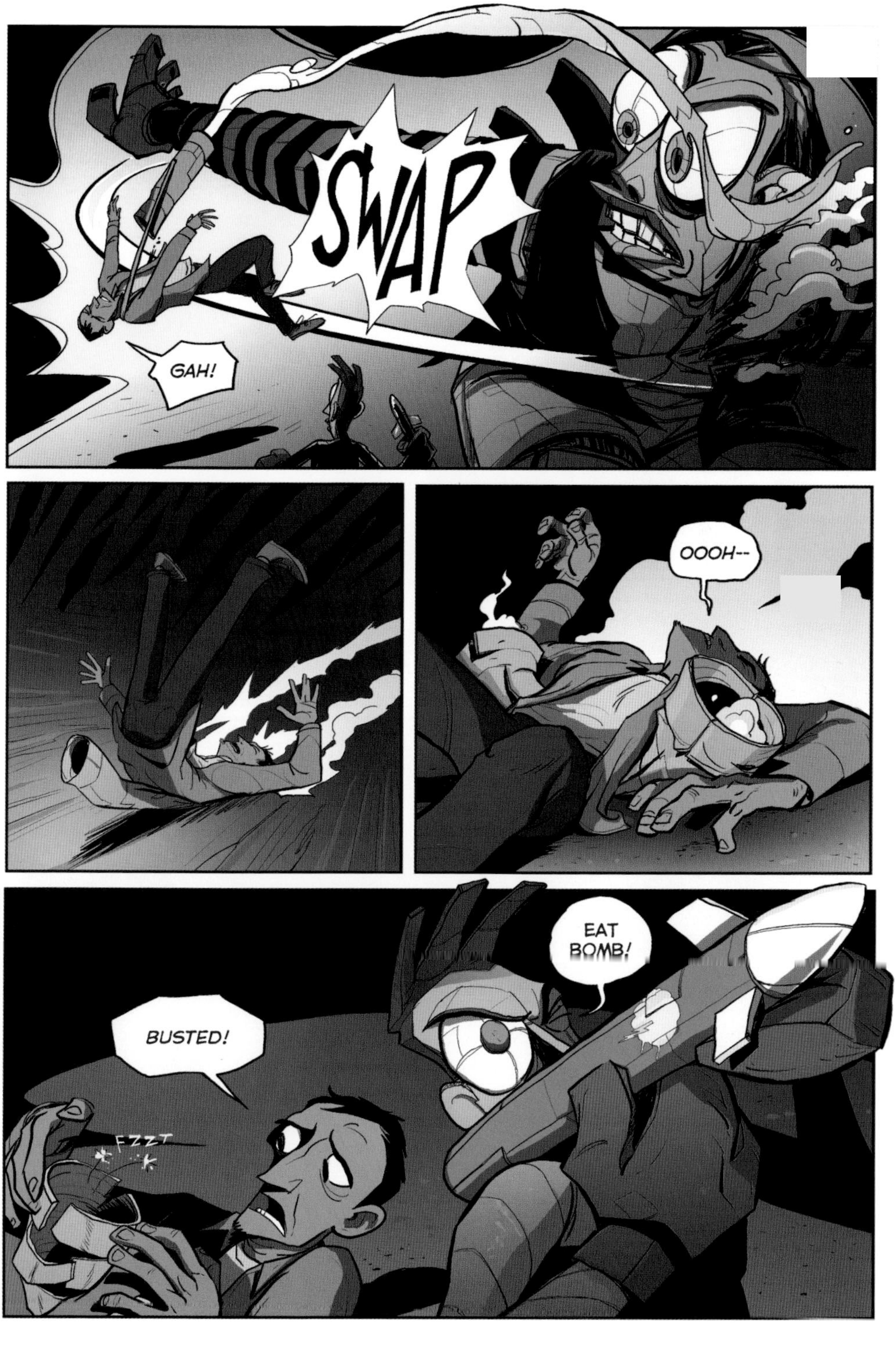
SWAP
GAH!
OOOH--
BUSTED!
EAT BOMB!
FZZT

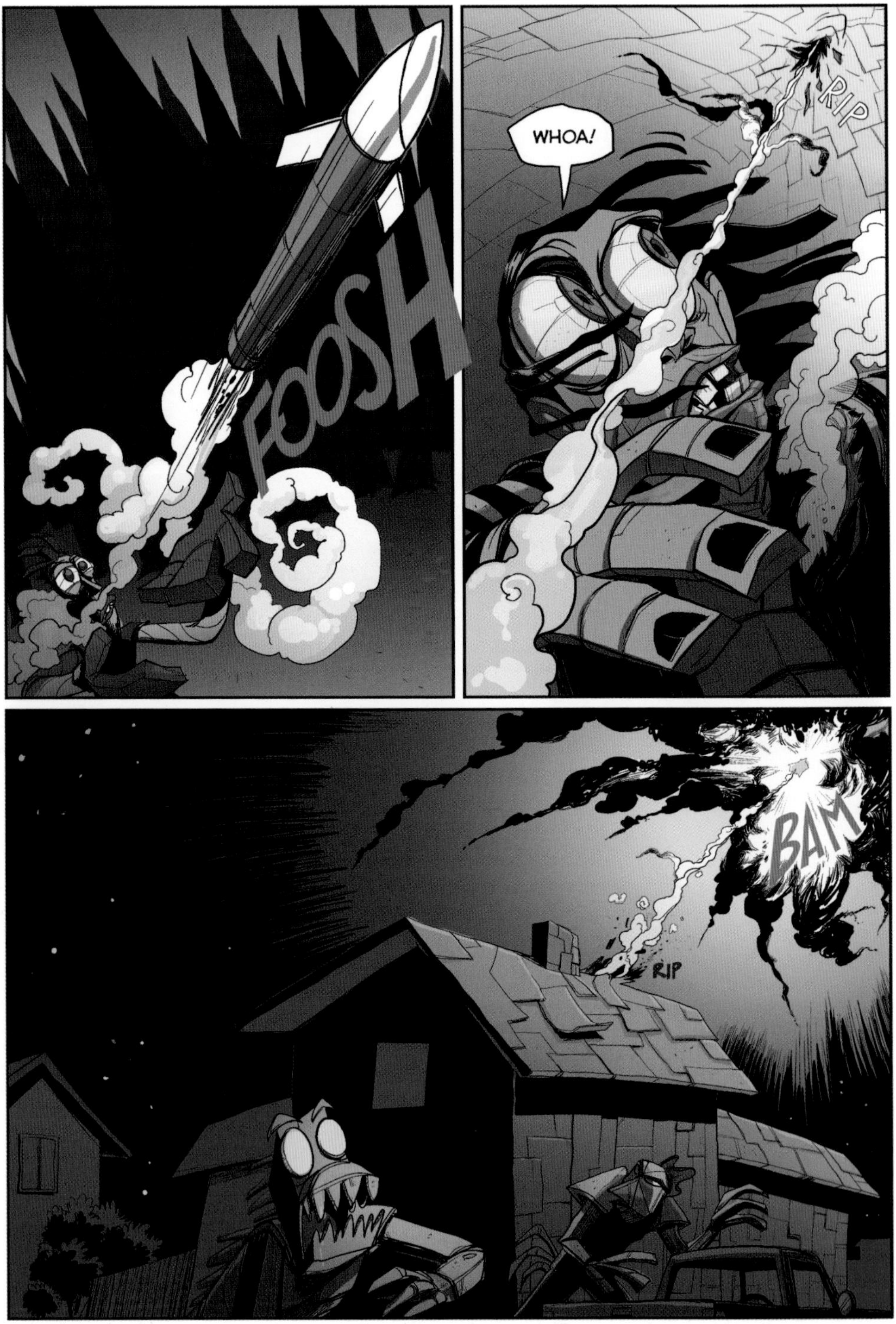
FOOSH
WHOA!
RIP
RIP
BAM

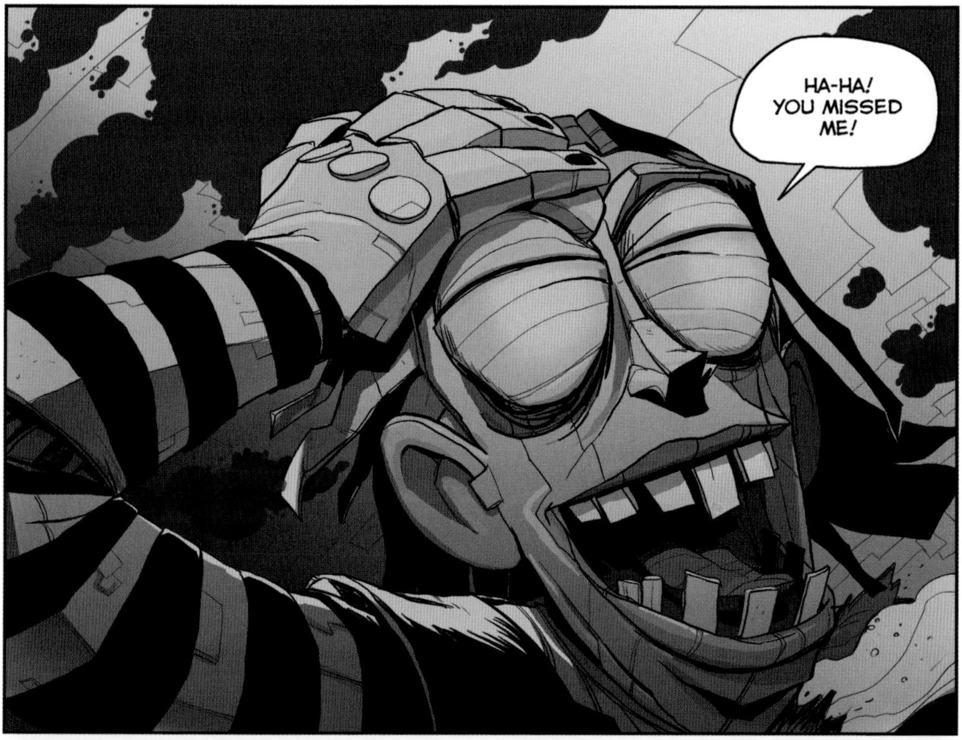
HA-HA! YOU MISSED ME!

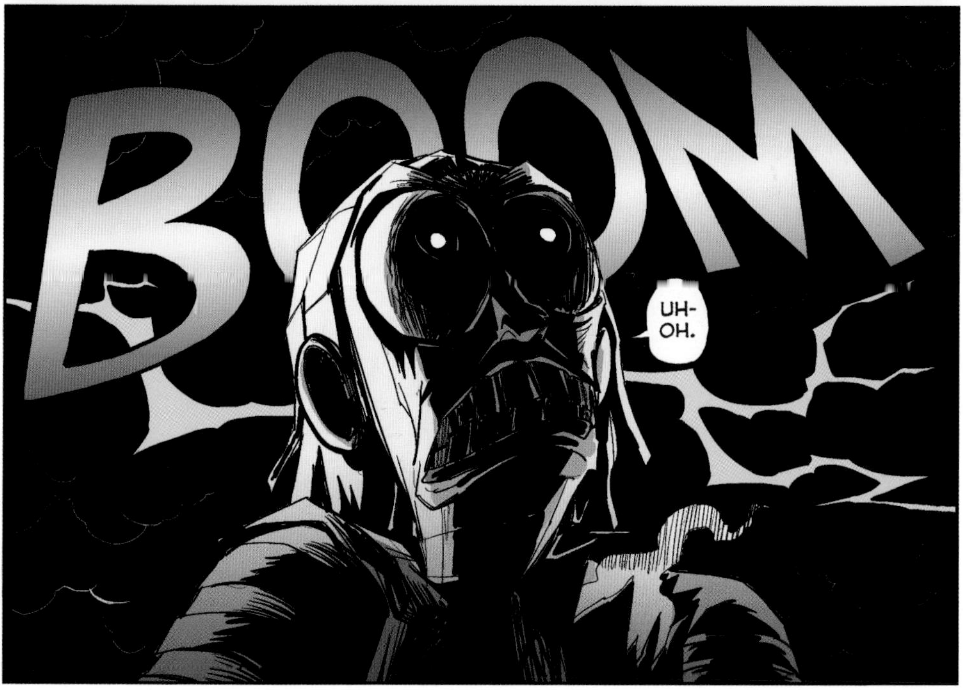
BOOM
UH-OH.

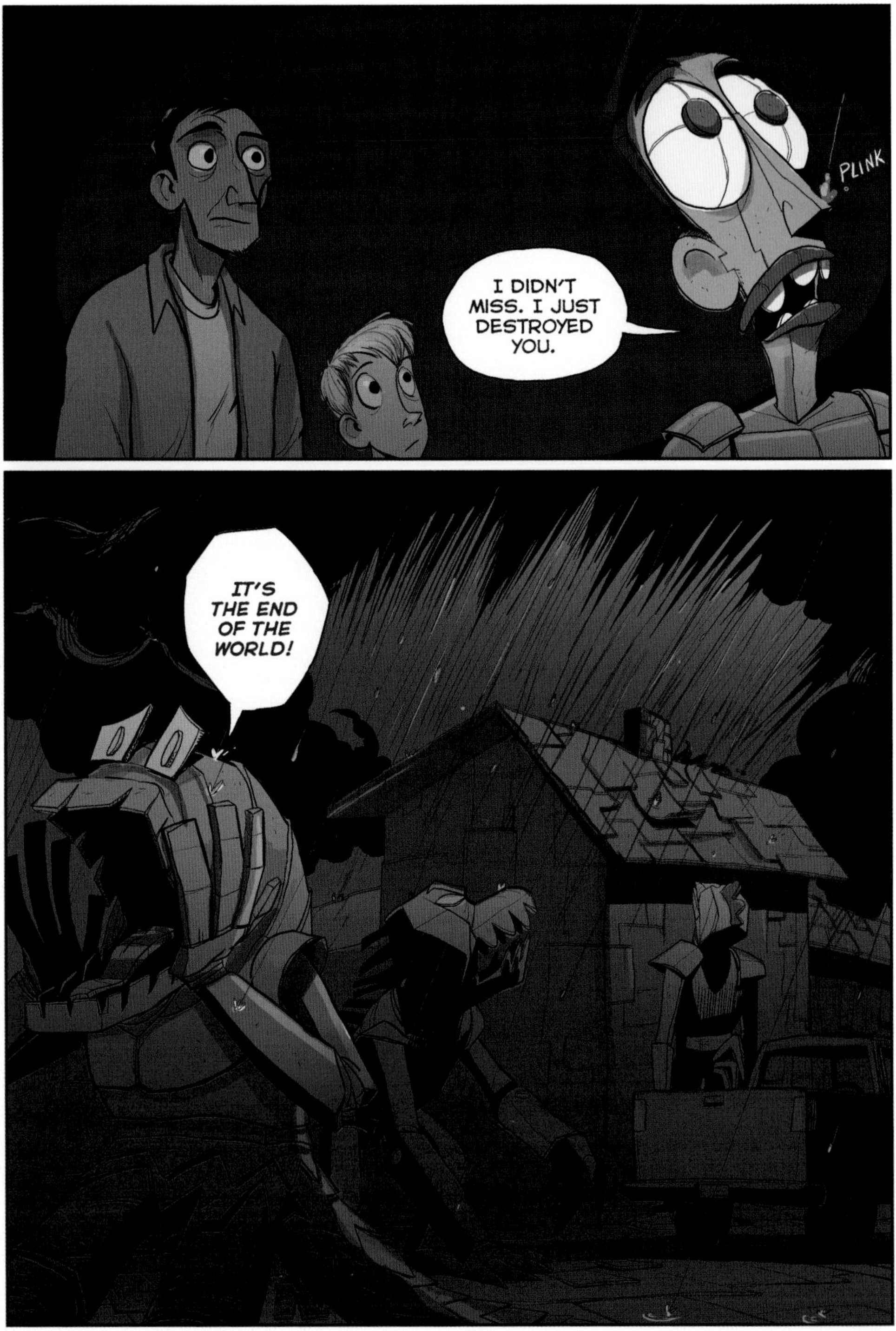
PLINK
I DIDN'T MISS. I JUST DESTROYED YOU.
IT'S THE END OF THE WORLD!

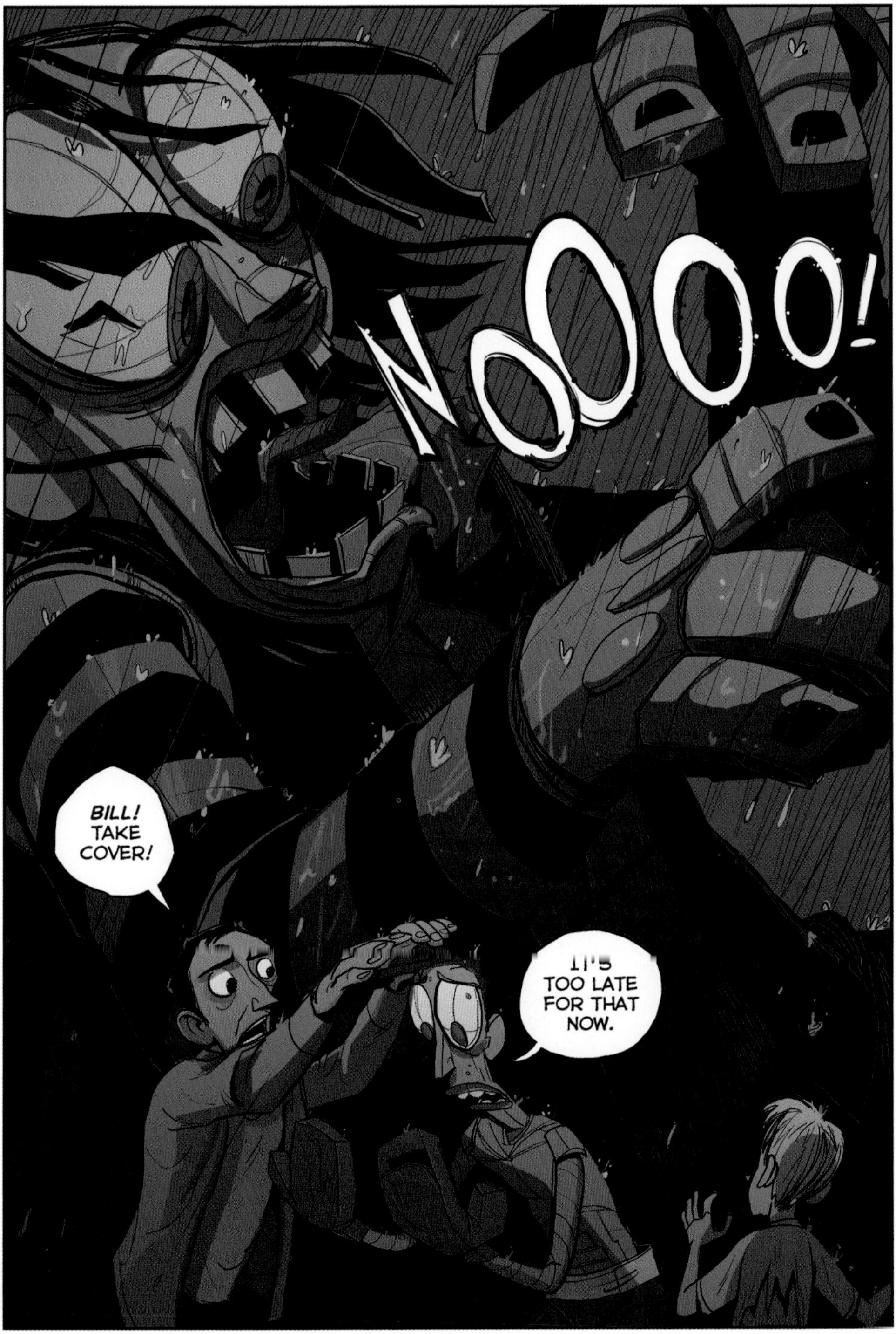
NOOOOO!
BILL! TAKE COVER!
IT'S TOO LATE FOR THAT NOW.

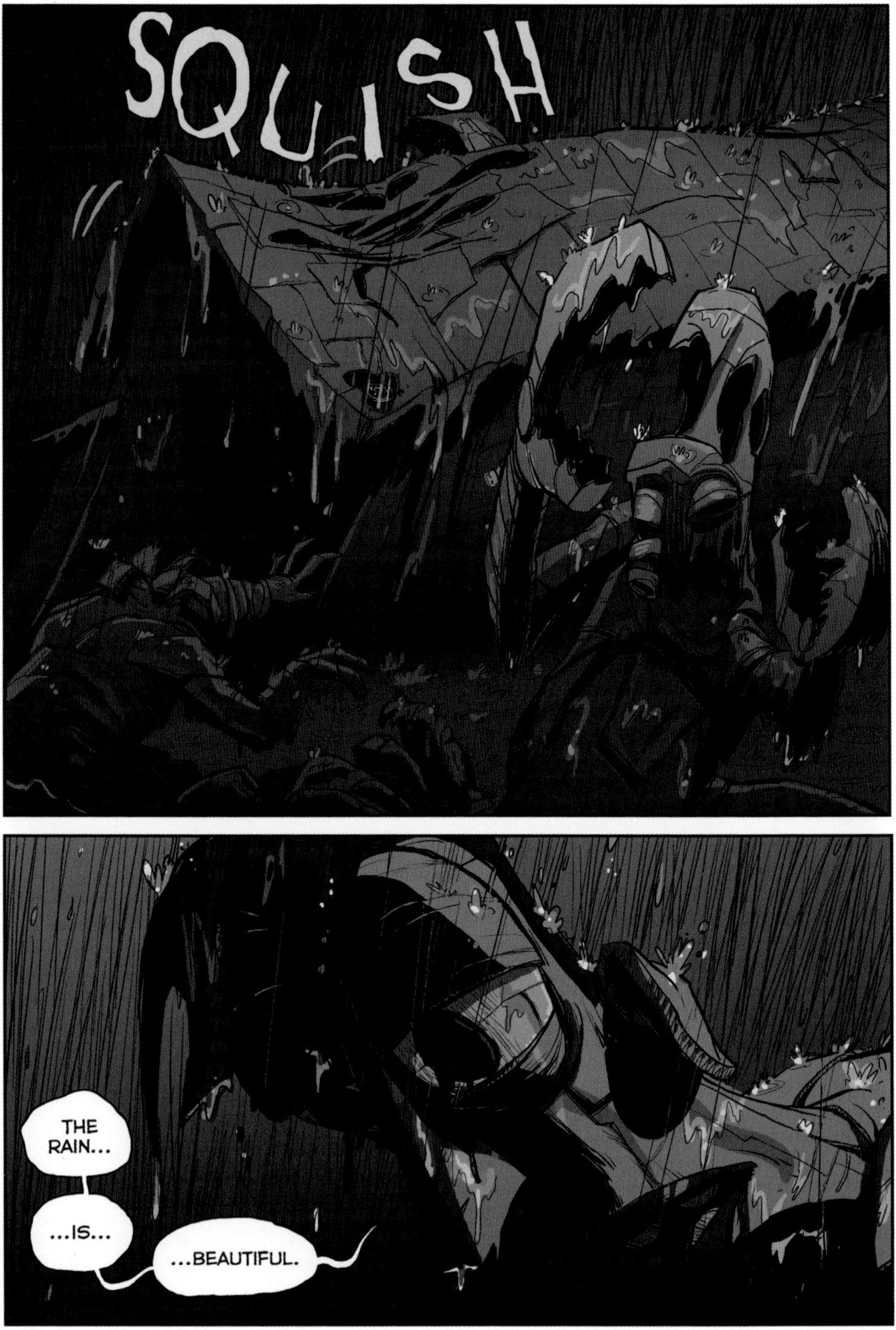
SQUISH
THE RAIN...
...IS...
...BEAUTIFUL.

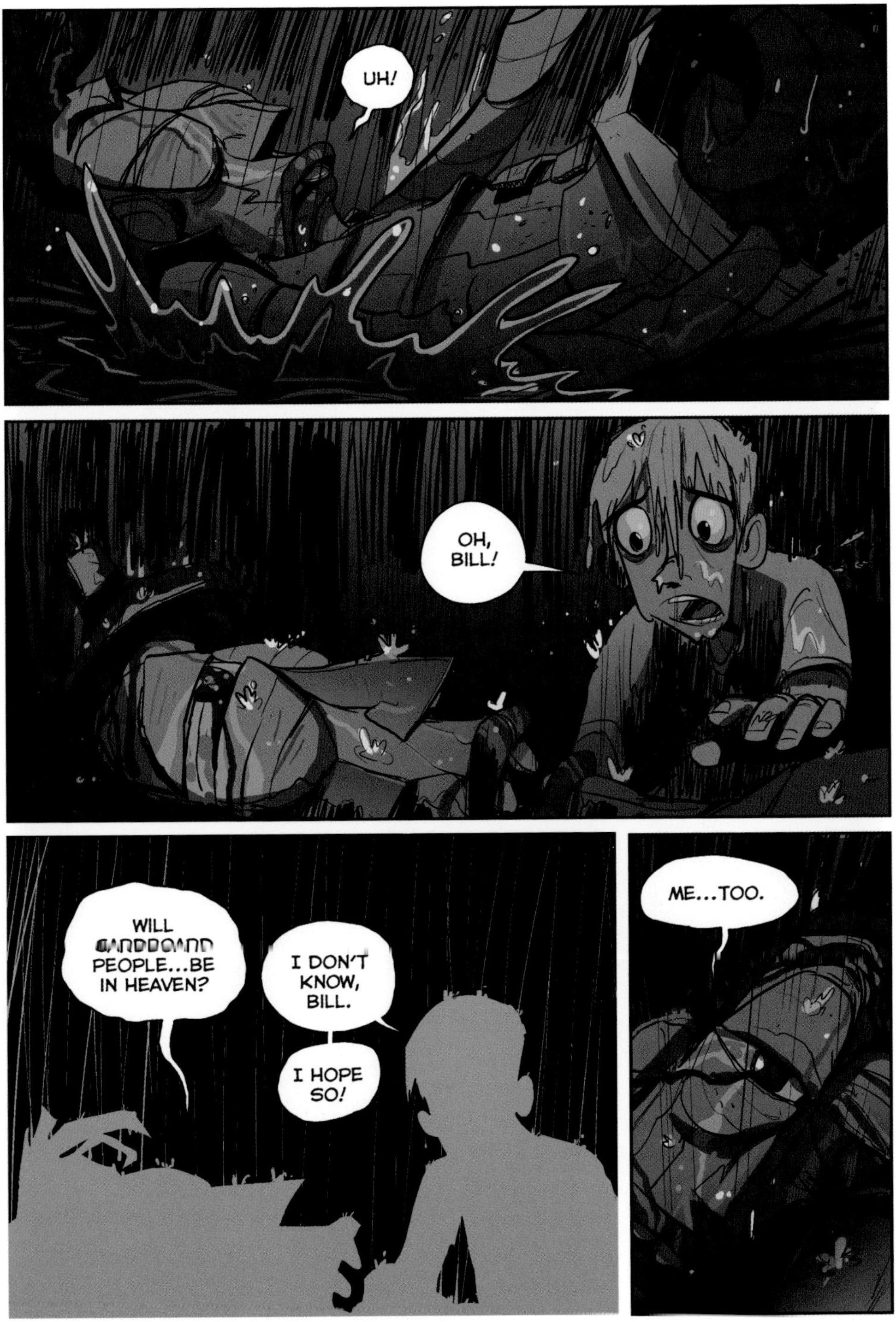
UH!
OH, BILL!
WILL PEOPLE...BE IN HEAVEN?
I DON'T KNOW, BILL.
I HOPE SO!
ME...TOO.

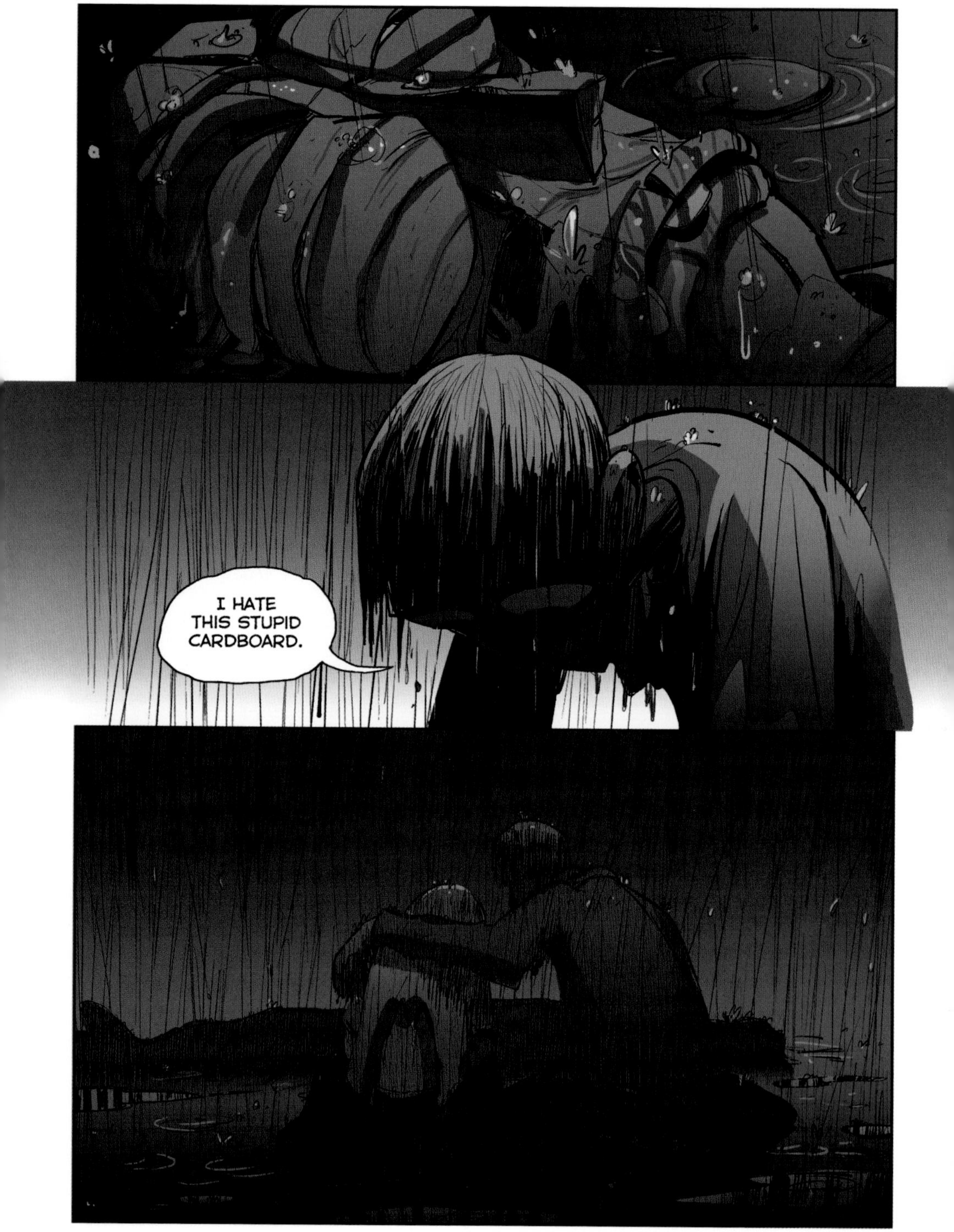
I HATE THIS STUPID CARDBOARD.

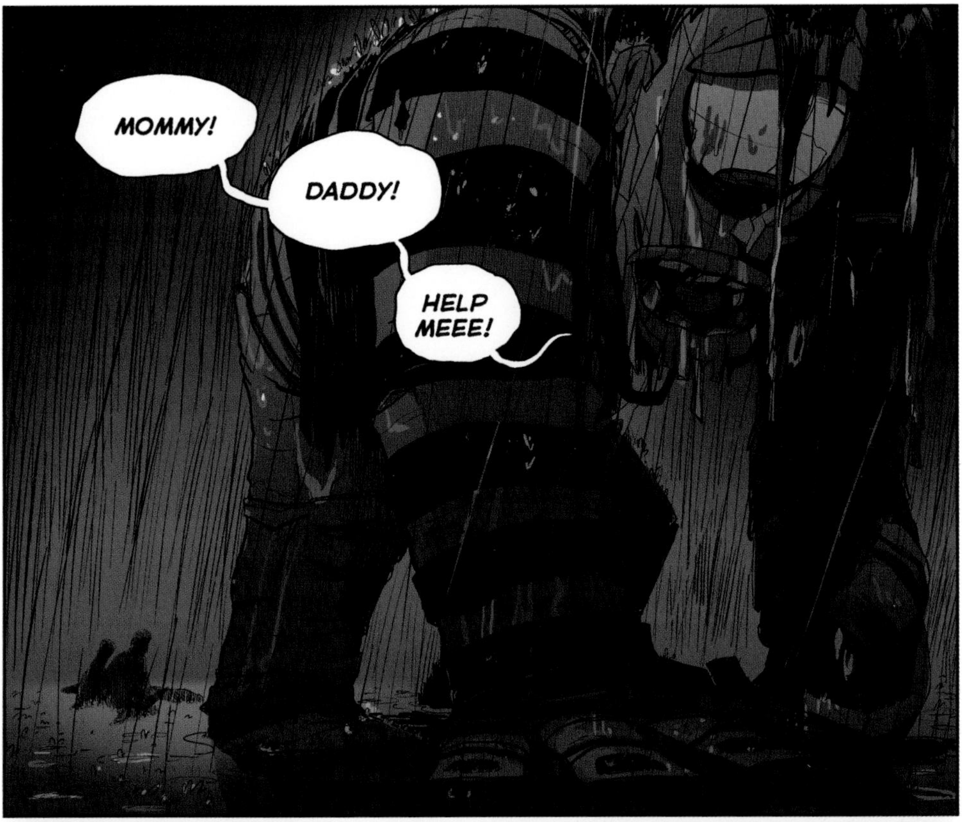
MOMMY!
DADDY!
HELP MEEE!

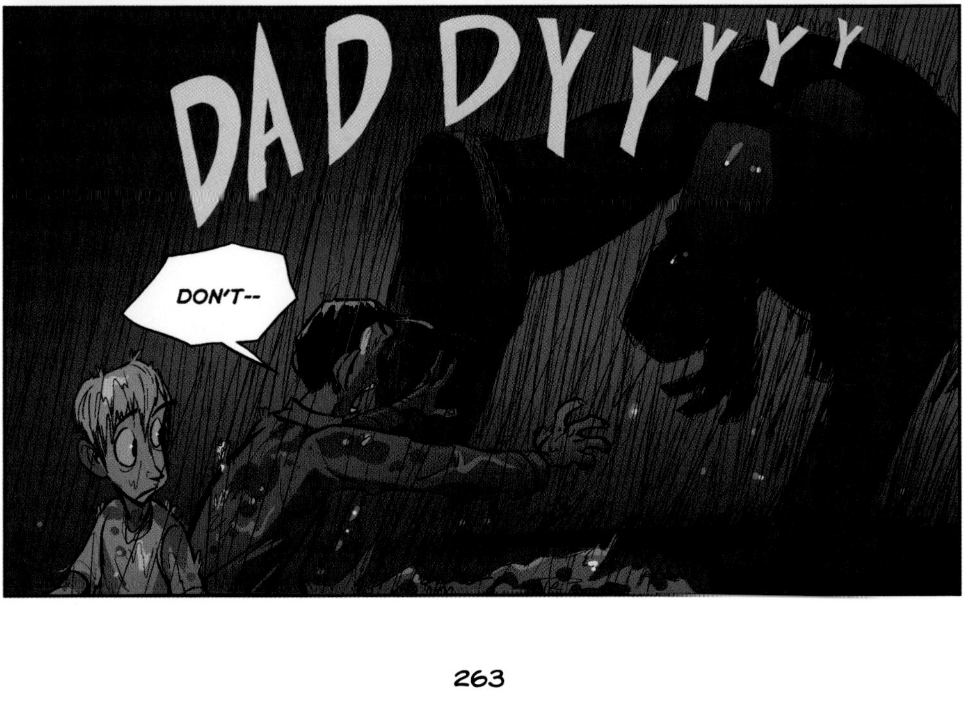
DADDYYYY
DON'T--

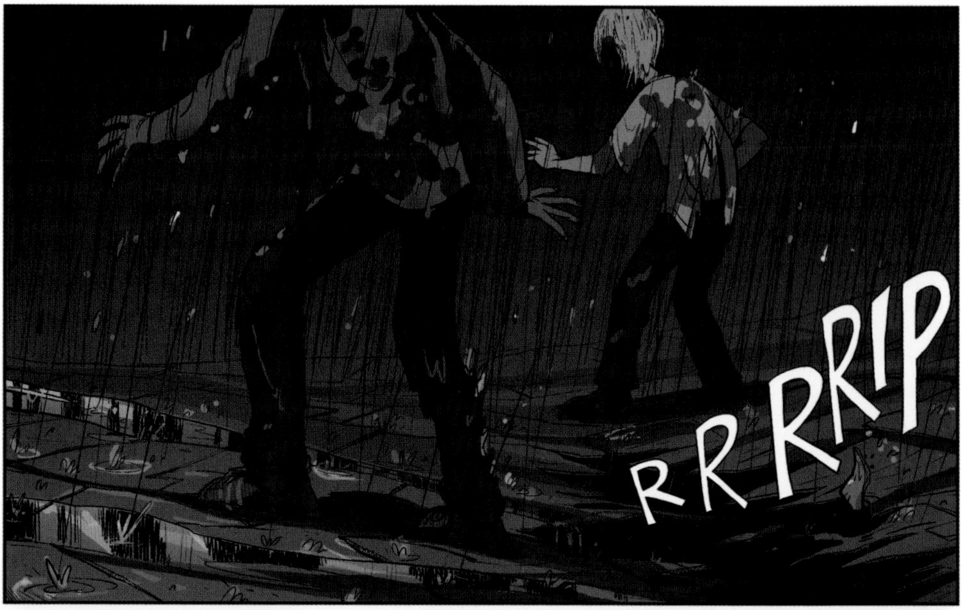
RRRRIP

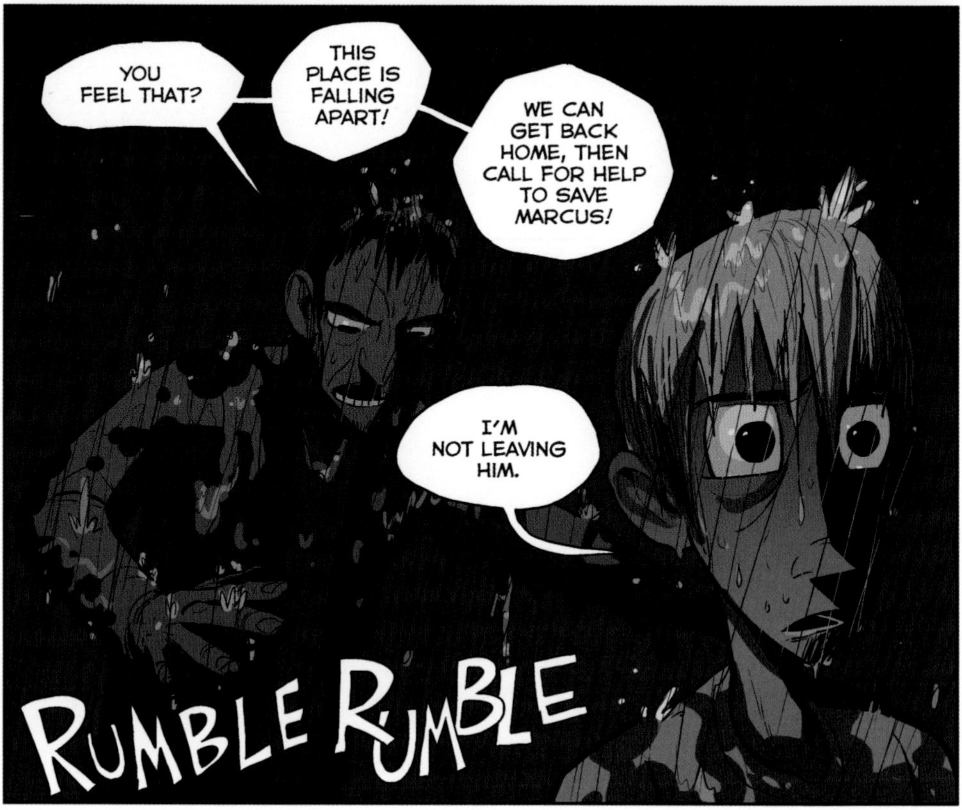
YOU FEEL THAT?
THIS PLACE IS FALLING APART!
WE CAN GET BACK HOME, THEN CALL FOR HELP TO SAVE MARCUS!
I'M NOT LEAVING HIM.
RUMBLE RUMBLE

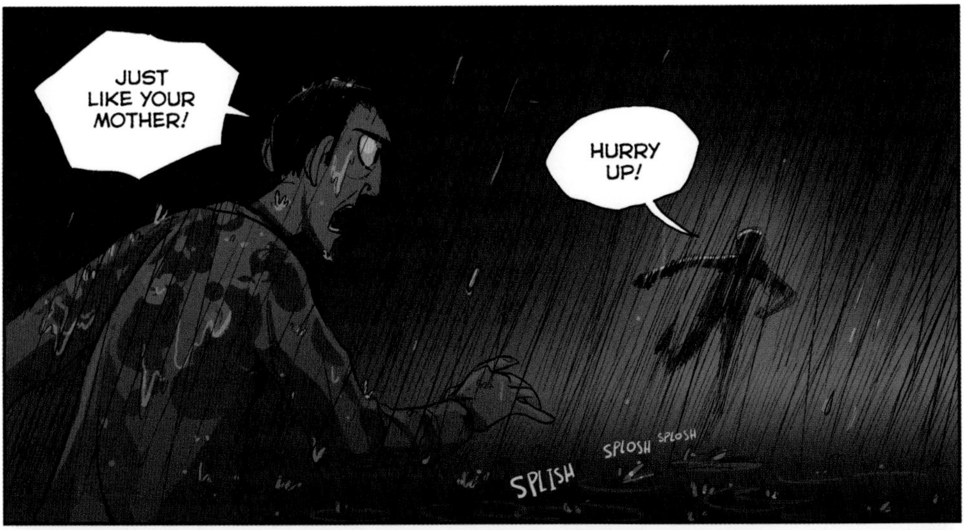
JUST LIKE YOUR MOTHER!
HURRY UP!
SPLOSH SPLOSH
SPLISH

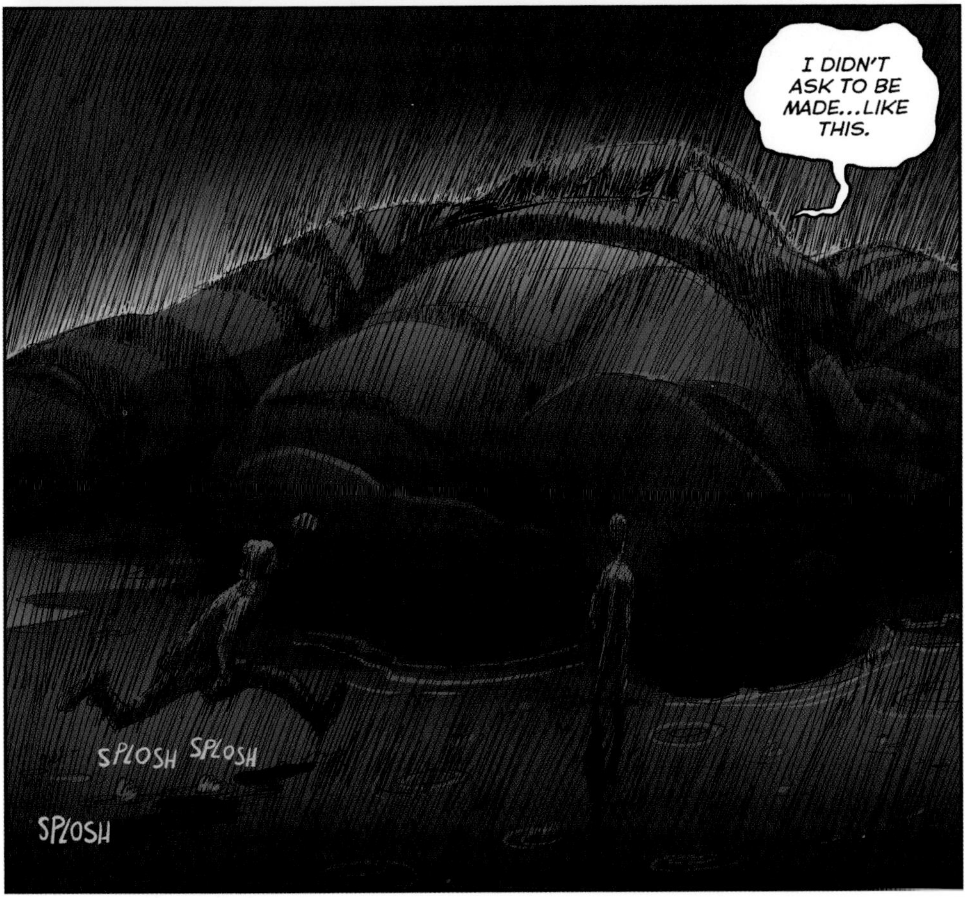
I DIDN'T ASK TO BE MADE...LIKE THIS.
SPLOSH SPLOSH
SPLOSH

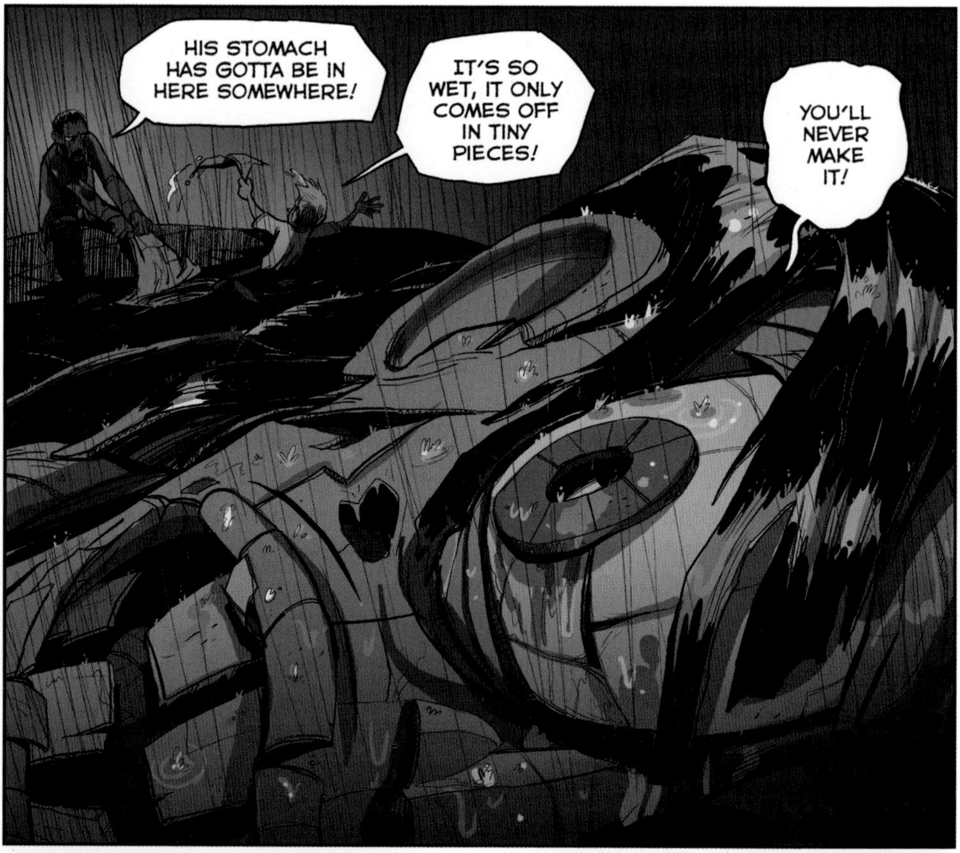
HIS STOMACH HAS GOTTA BE IN HERE SOMEWHERE!
IT'S SO WET, IT ONLY COMES OFF IN TINY PIECES!
YOU'LL NEVER MAKE IT!

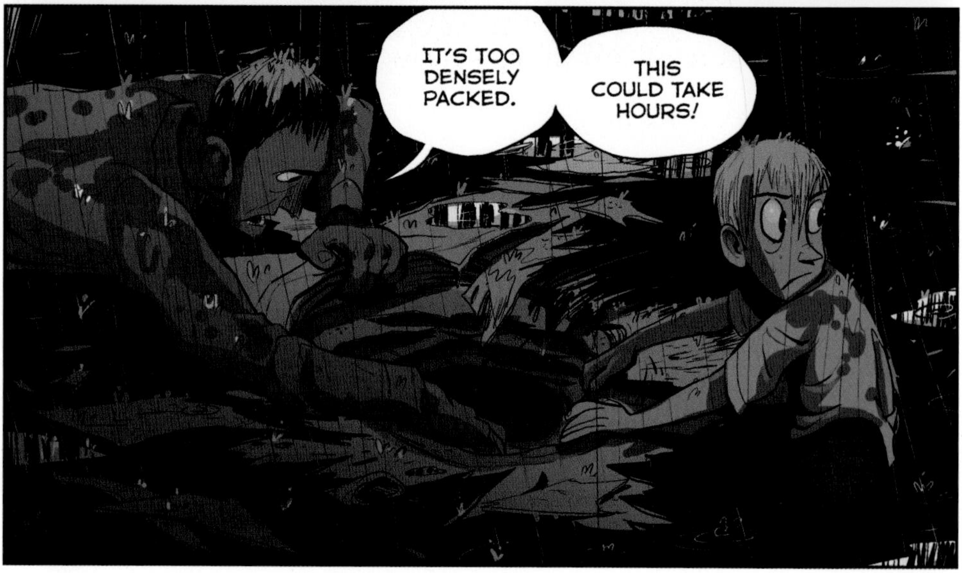
IT'S TOO DENSELY PACKED.
THIS COULD TAKE HOURS!

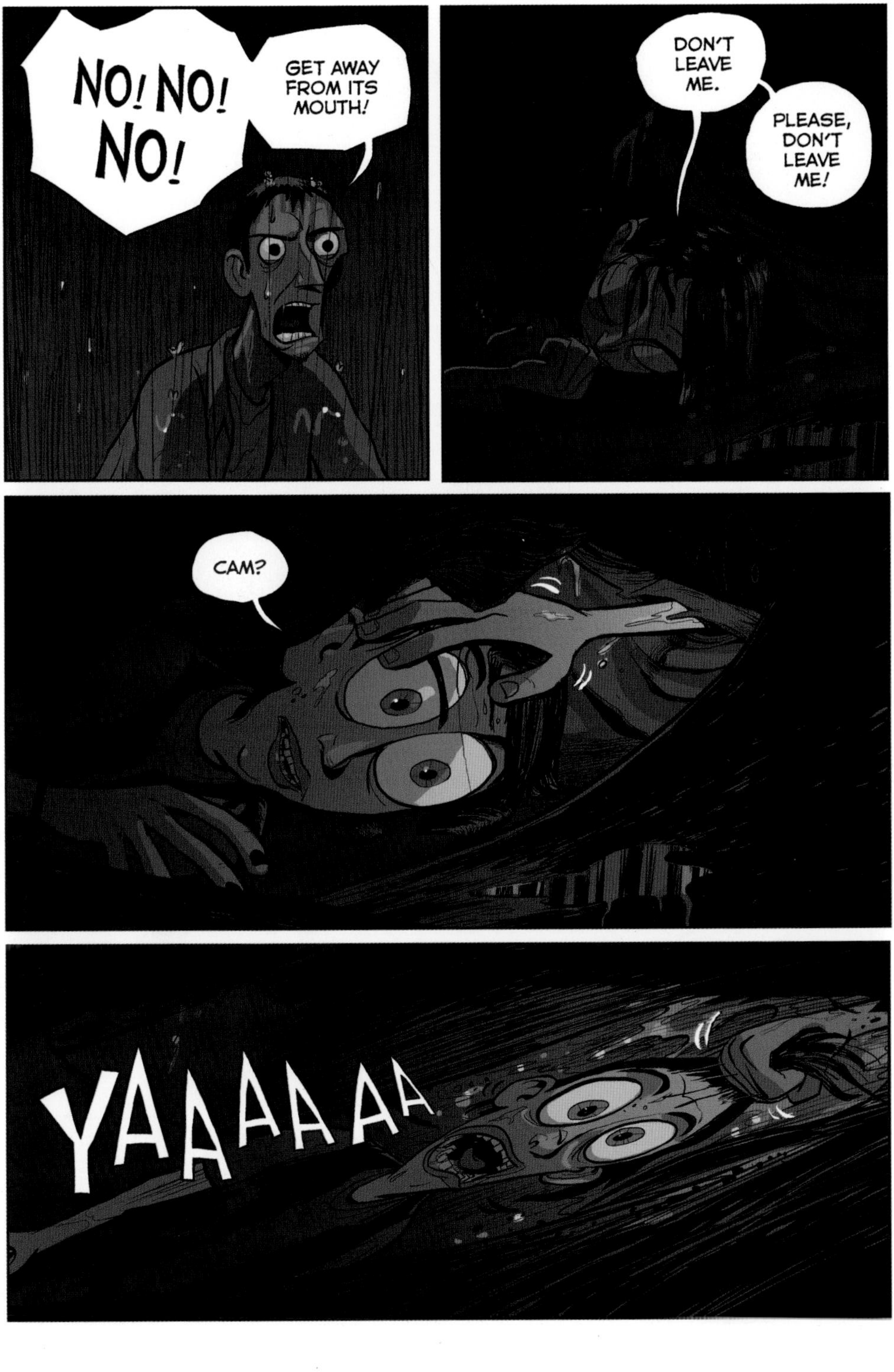
NO! NO! NO!
GET AWAY FROM ITS MOUTH!
DON'T LEAVE ME.
PLEASE, DON'T LEAVE ME!
CAM?
YAAAAAA

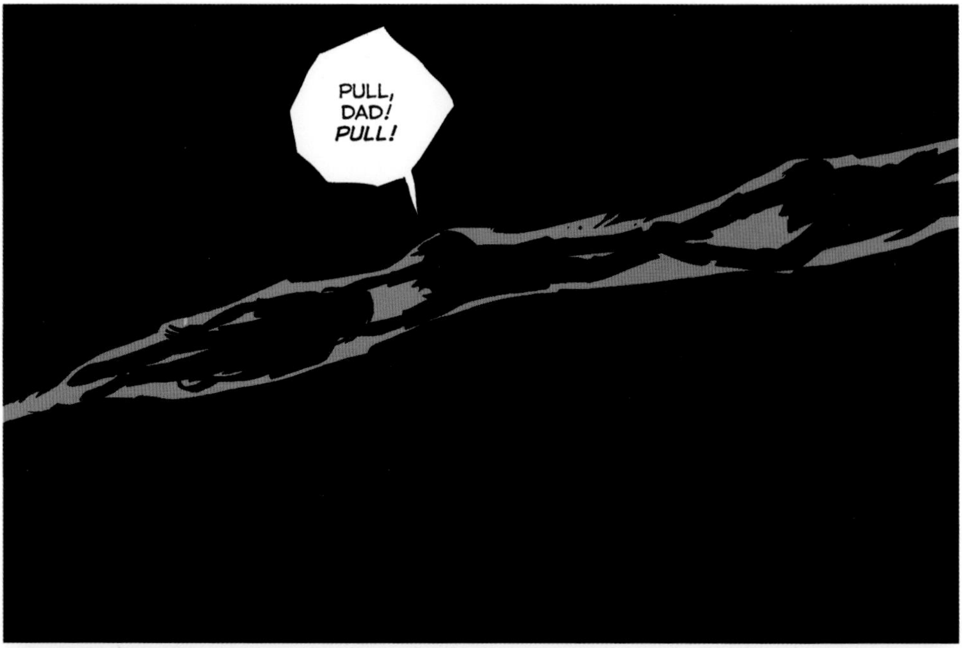
PULL, DAD! *PULL!*

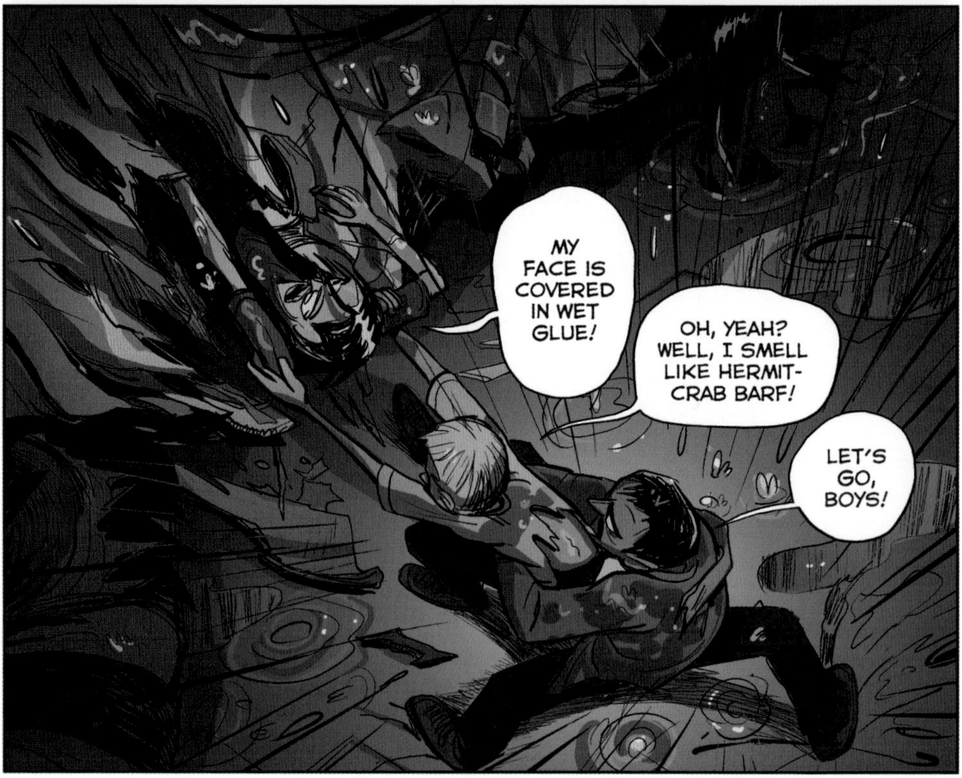
MY FACE IS COVERED IN WET GLUE!
OH, YEAH? WELL, I SMELL LIKE HERMIT-CRAB BARF!
LET'S GO, BOYS!

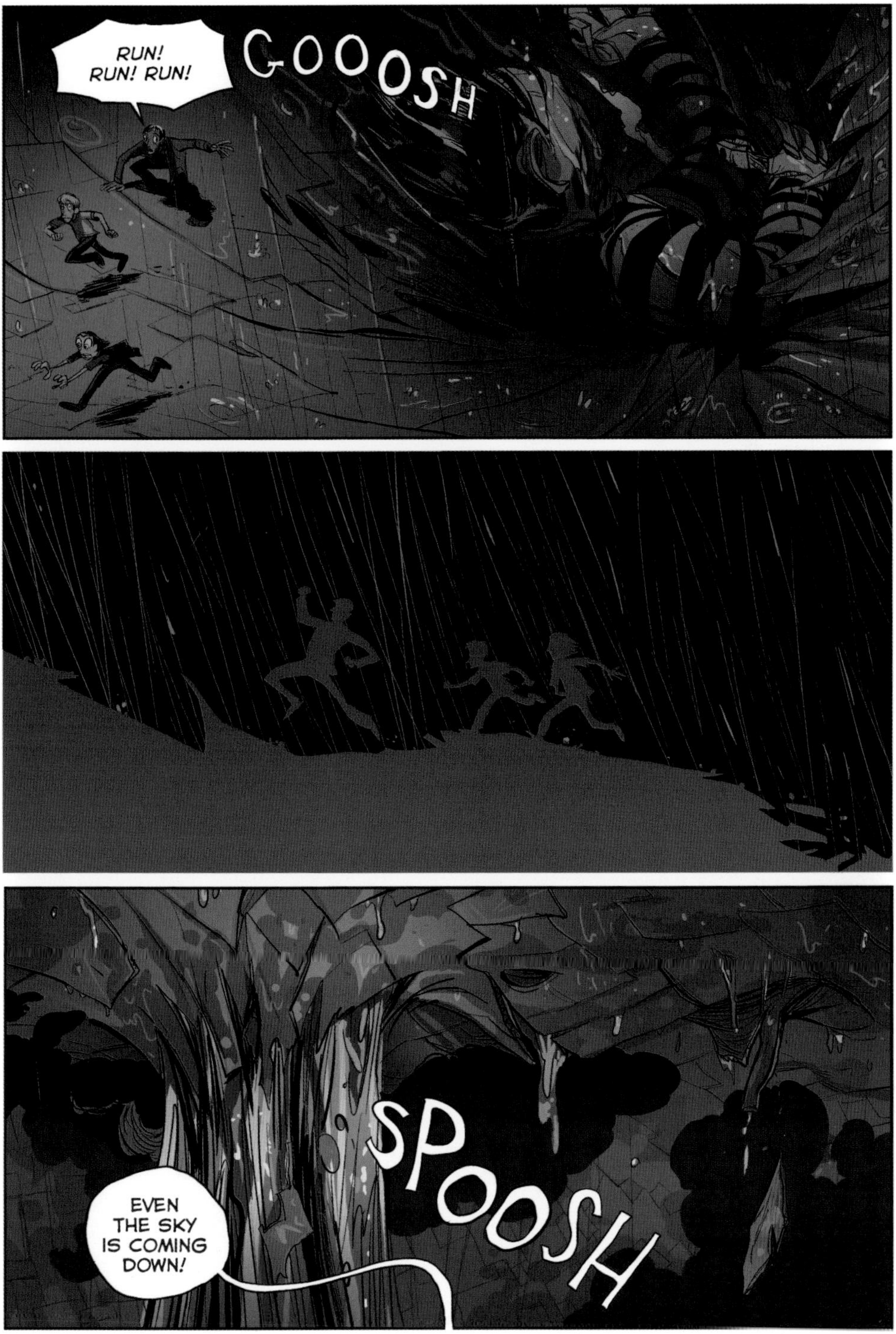
RUN! RUN! RUN!
GOOOOSH
SPOOSH
EVEN THE SKY IS COMING DOWN!

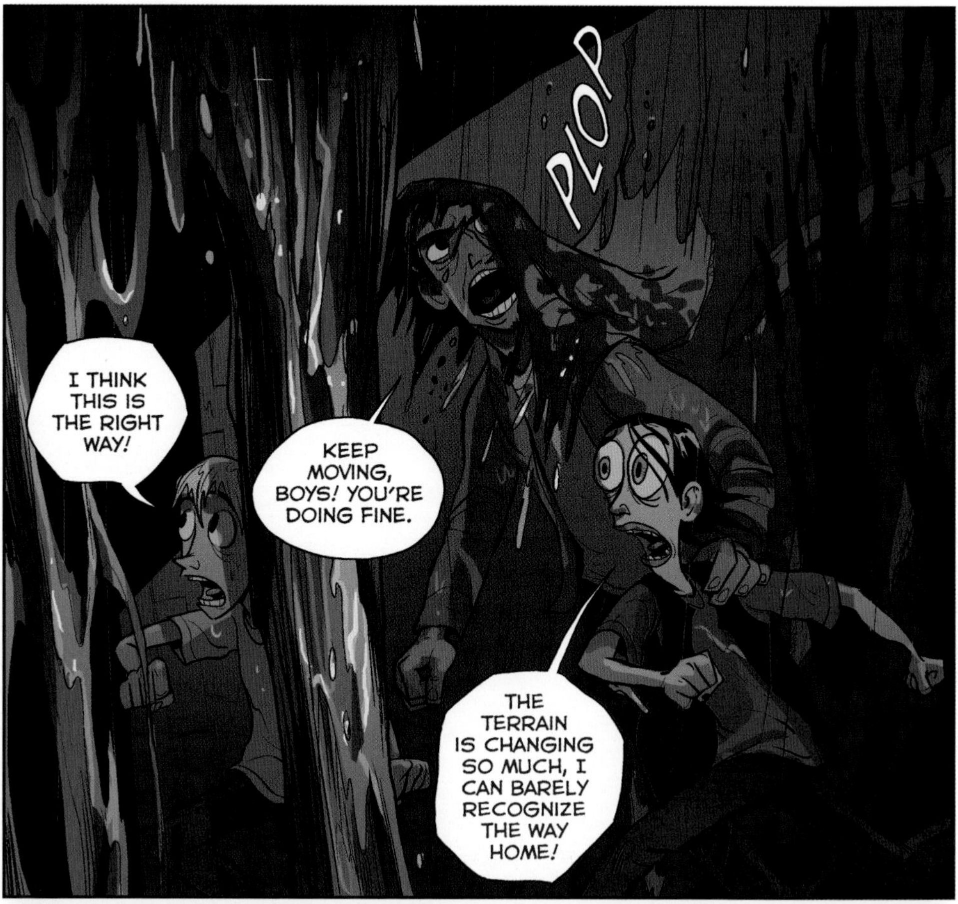
PLOP
I THINK THIS IS THE RIGHT WAY!
KEEP MOVING, BOYS! YOU'RE DOING FINE.
THE TERRAIN IS CHANGING SO MUCH, I CAN BARELY RECOGNIZE THE WAY HOME!

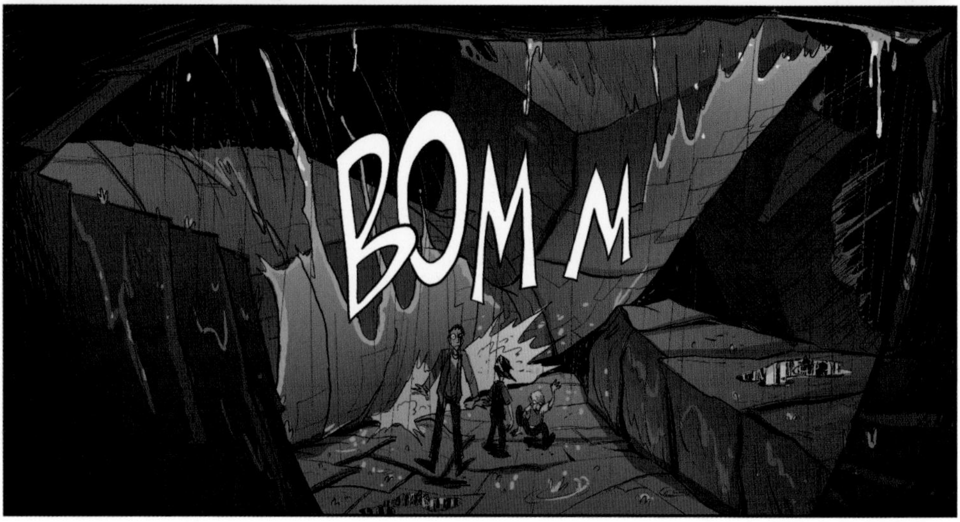
BOMM

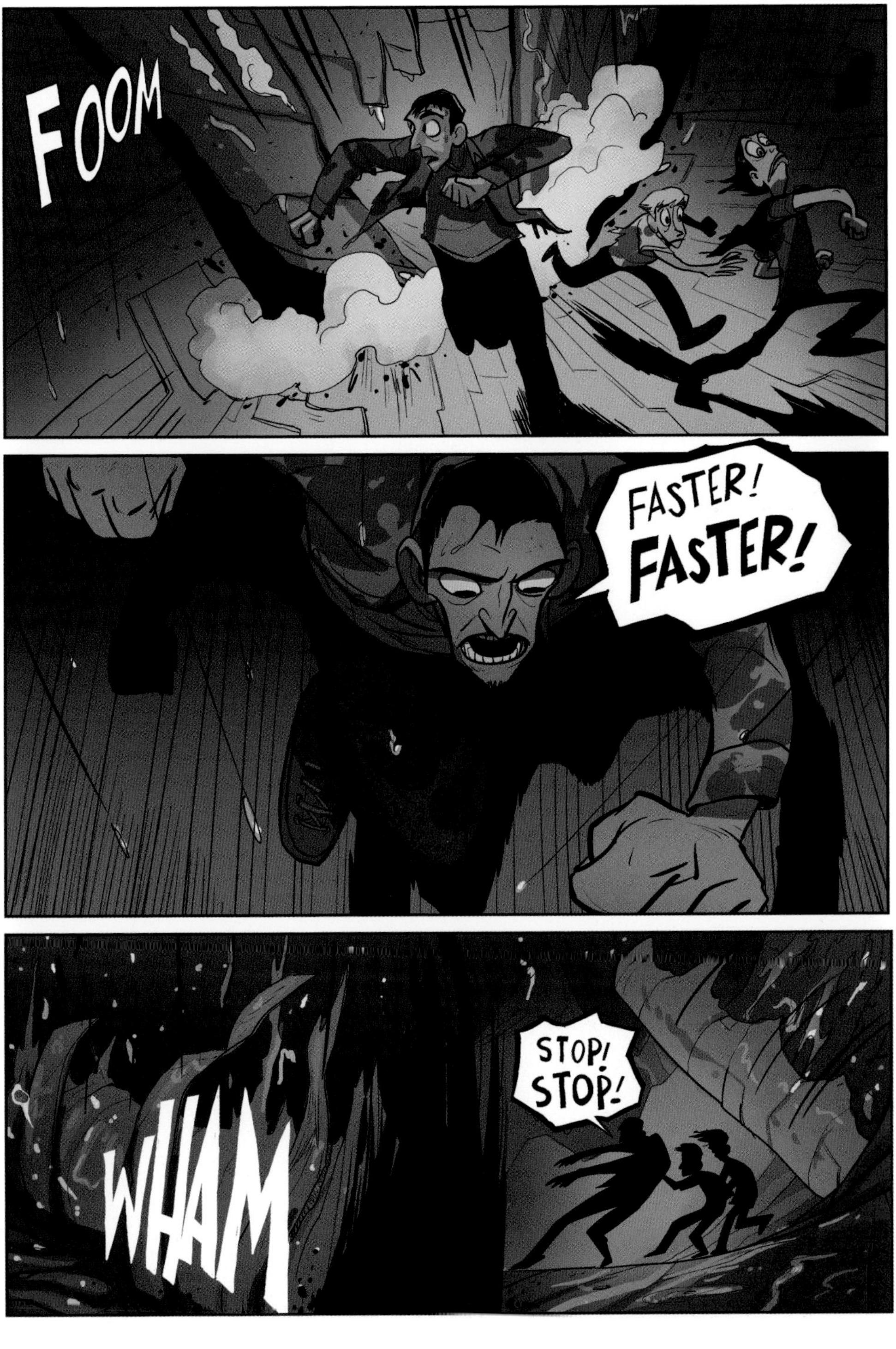
FOOM
FASTER! FASTER!
WHAM
STOP! STOP!

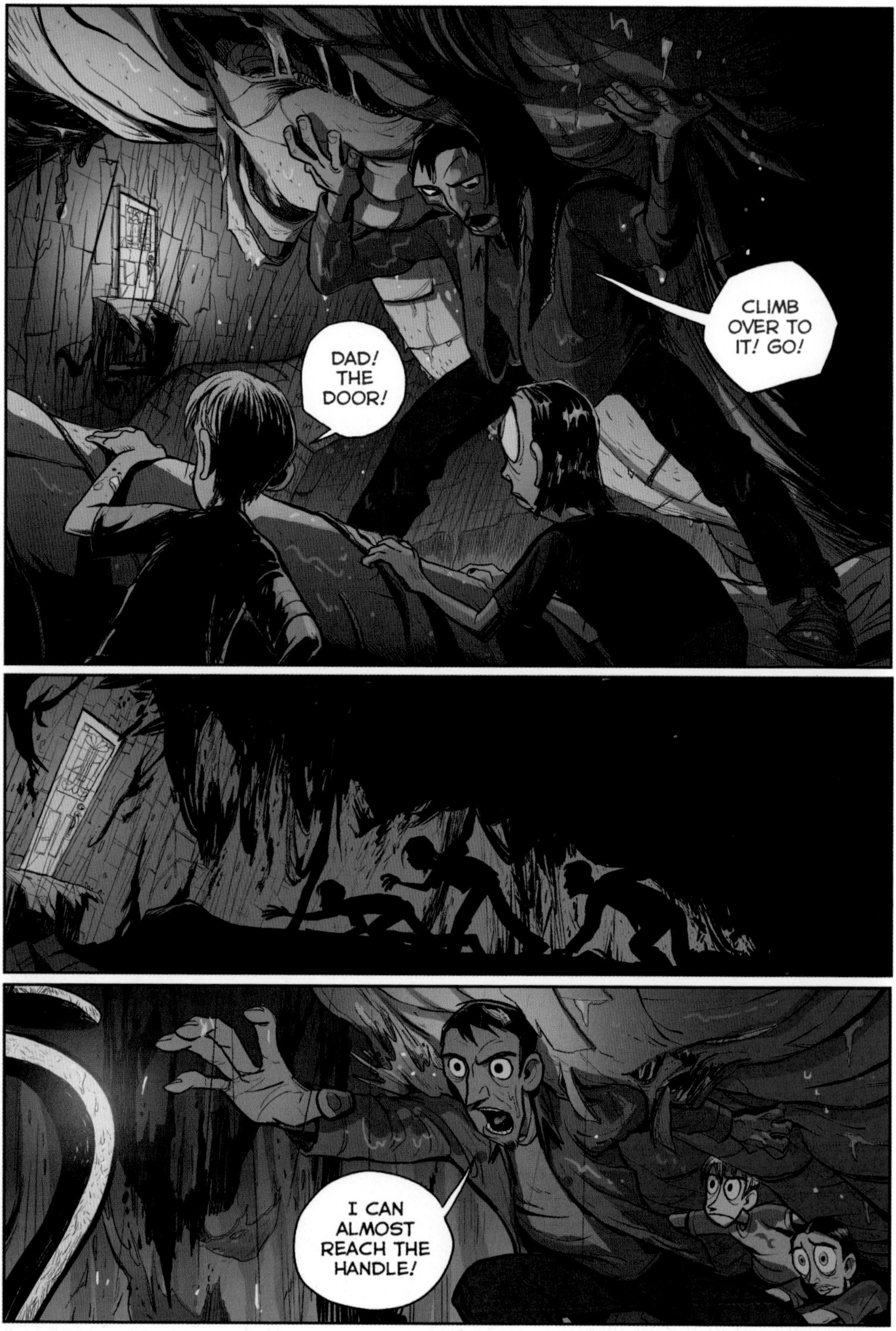
DAD! THE DOOR!
CLIMB OVER TO IT! GO!
I CAN ALMOST REACH THE HANDLE!

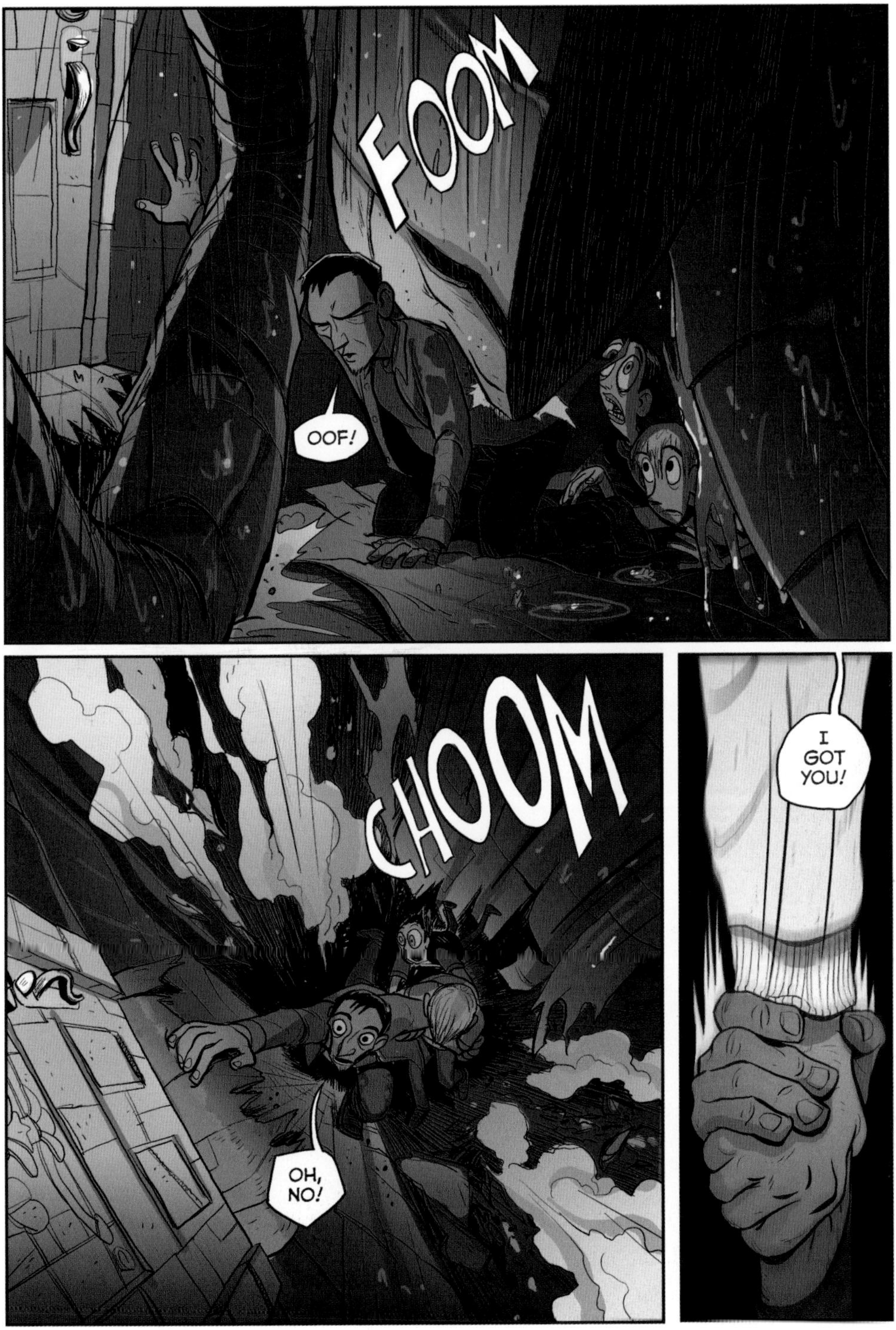
FOOM
OOF!
CHOOM
OH, NO!
I GOT YOU!

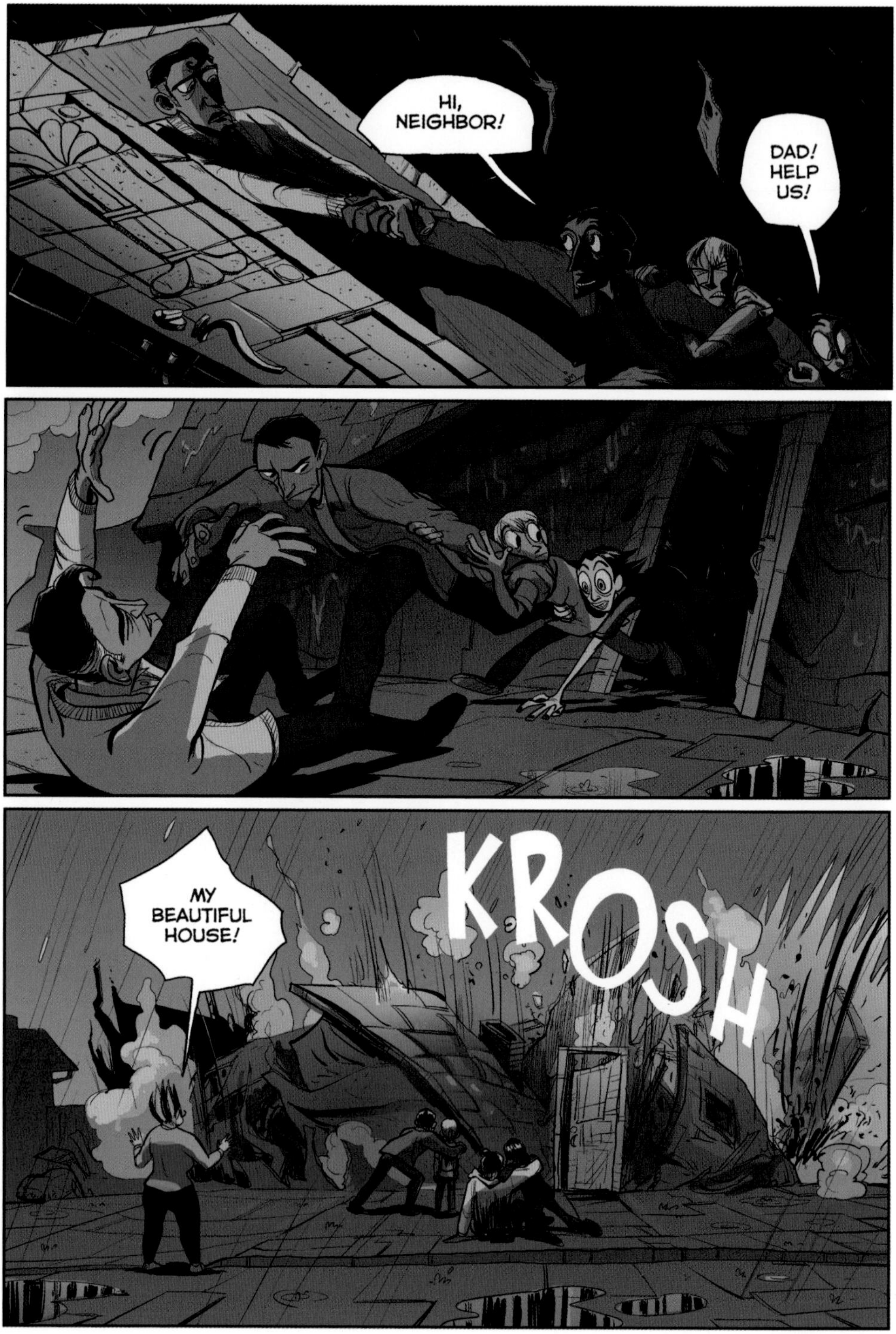
HI, NEIGHBOR!
DAD! HELP US!
MY BEAUTIFUL HOUSE!
KROSH

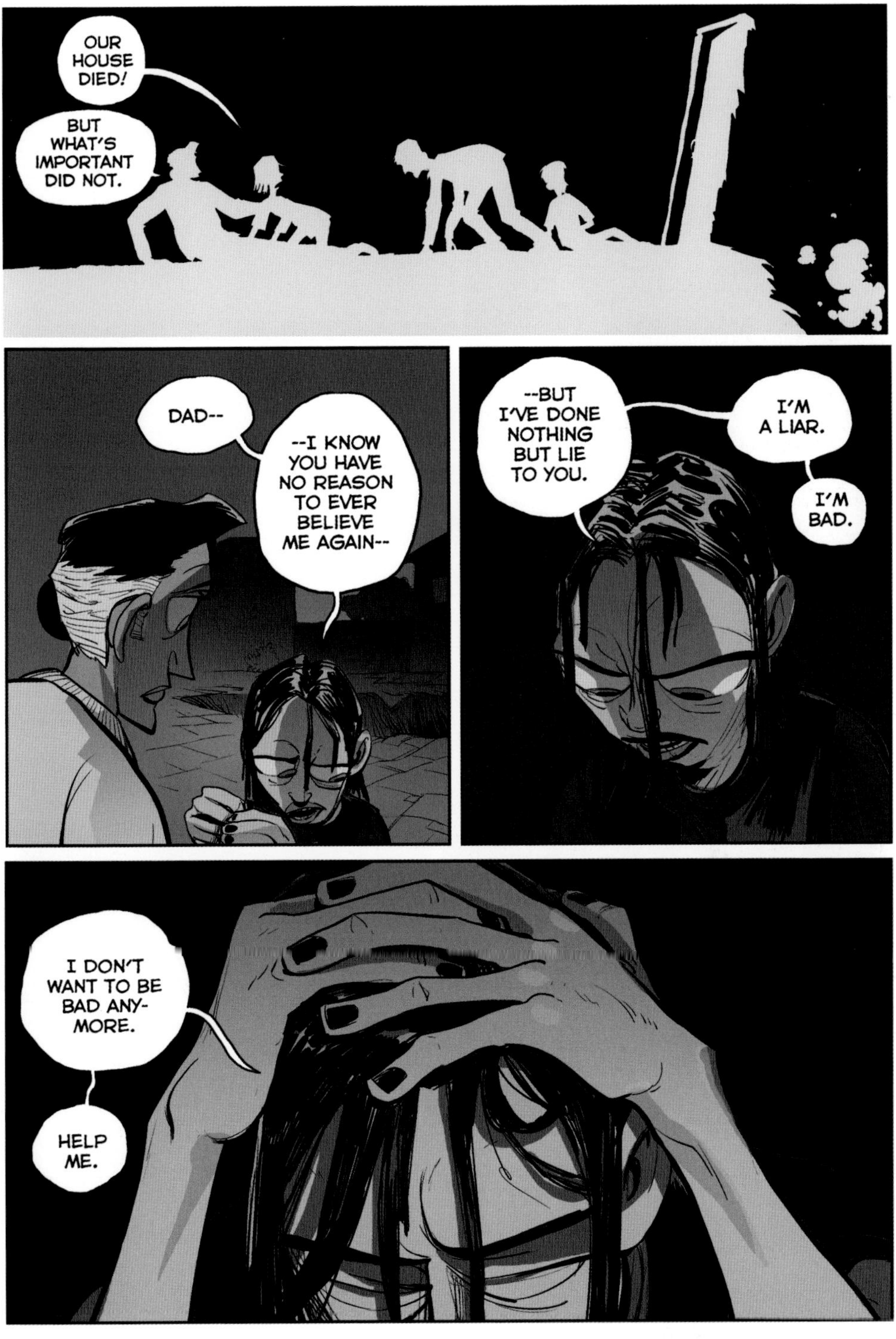
OUR HOUSE DIED!
BUT WHAT'S IMPORTANT DID NOT.
DAD--
--I KNOW YOU HAVE NO REASON TO EVER BELIEVE ME AGAIN--
--BUT I'VE DONE NOTHING BUT LIE TO YOU.
I'M A LIAR.
I'M BAD.
I DON'T WANT TO BE BAD ANY-MORE.
HELP ME.

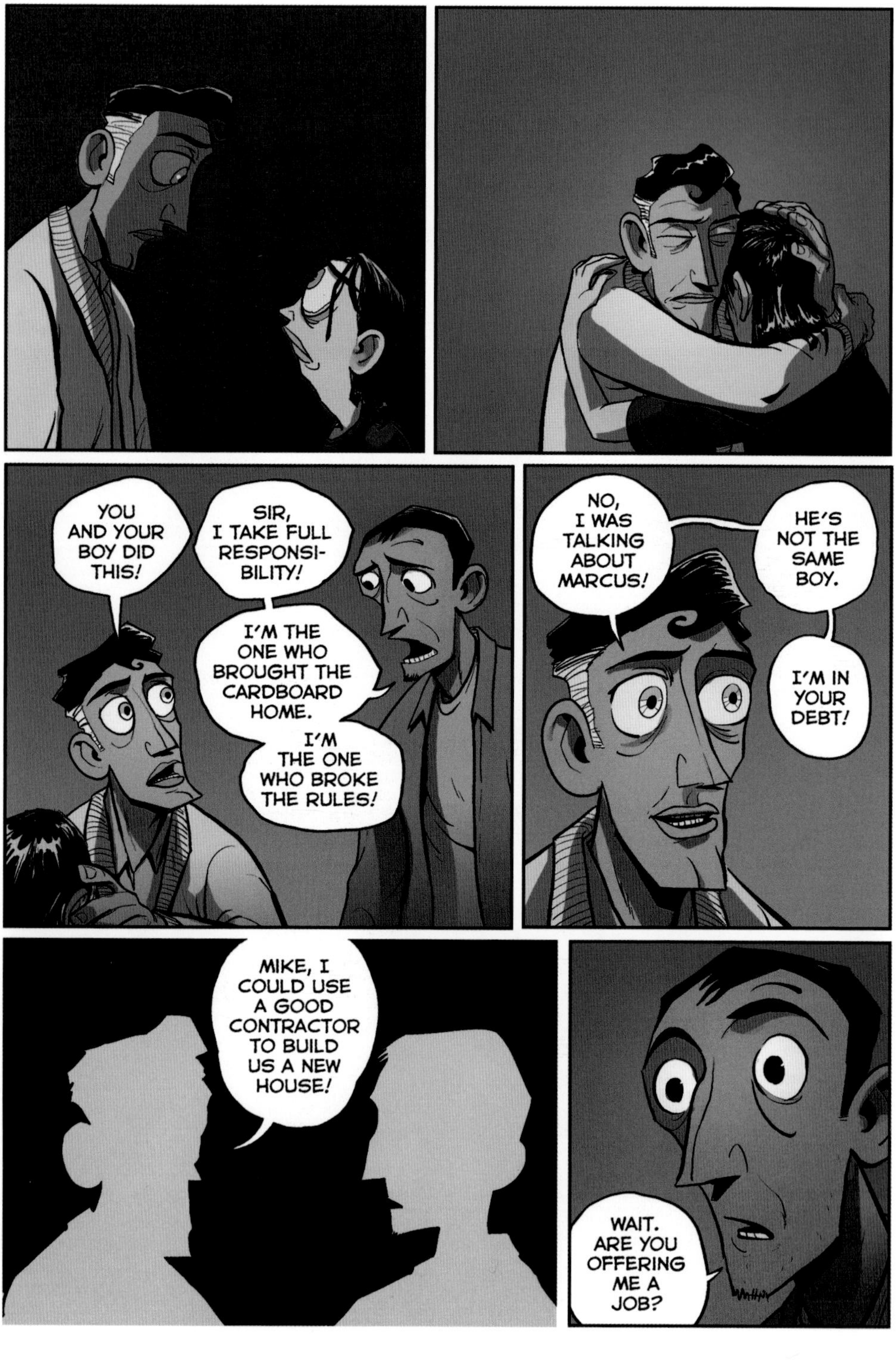
YOU AND YOUR BOY DID THIS!
SIR, I TAKE FULL RESPONSI-BILITY!
I'M THE ONE WHO BROUGHT THE CARDBOARD HOME.
I'M THE ONE WHO BROKE THE RULES!
NO, I WAS TALKING ABOUT MARCUS!
HE'S NOT THE SAME BOY.
I'M IN YOUR DEBT!
MIKE, I COULD USE A GOOD CONTRACTOR TO BUILD US A NEW HOUSE!
WAIT. ARE YOU OFFERING ME A JOB?

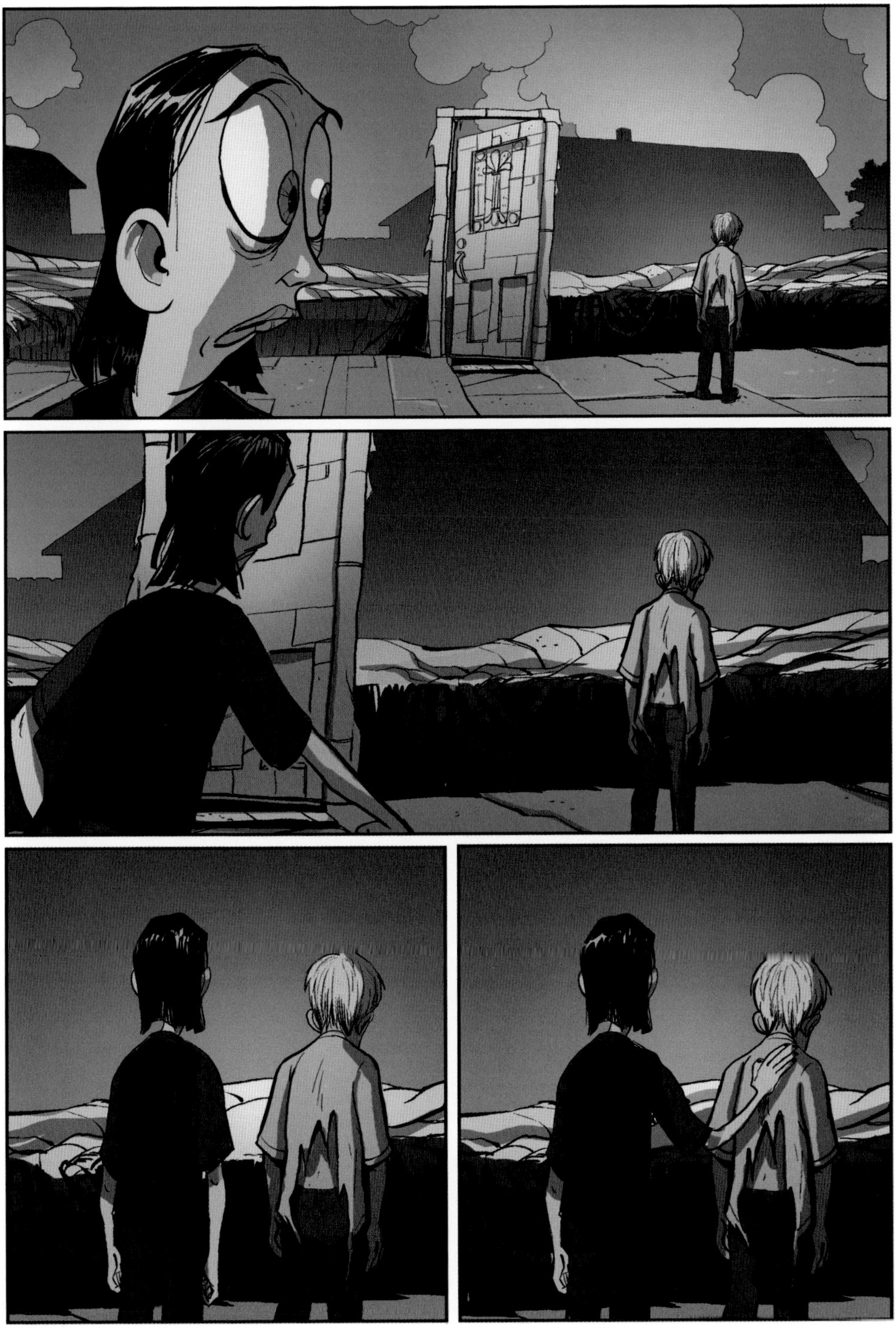

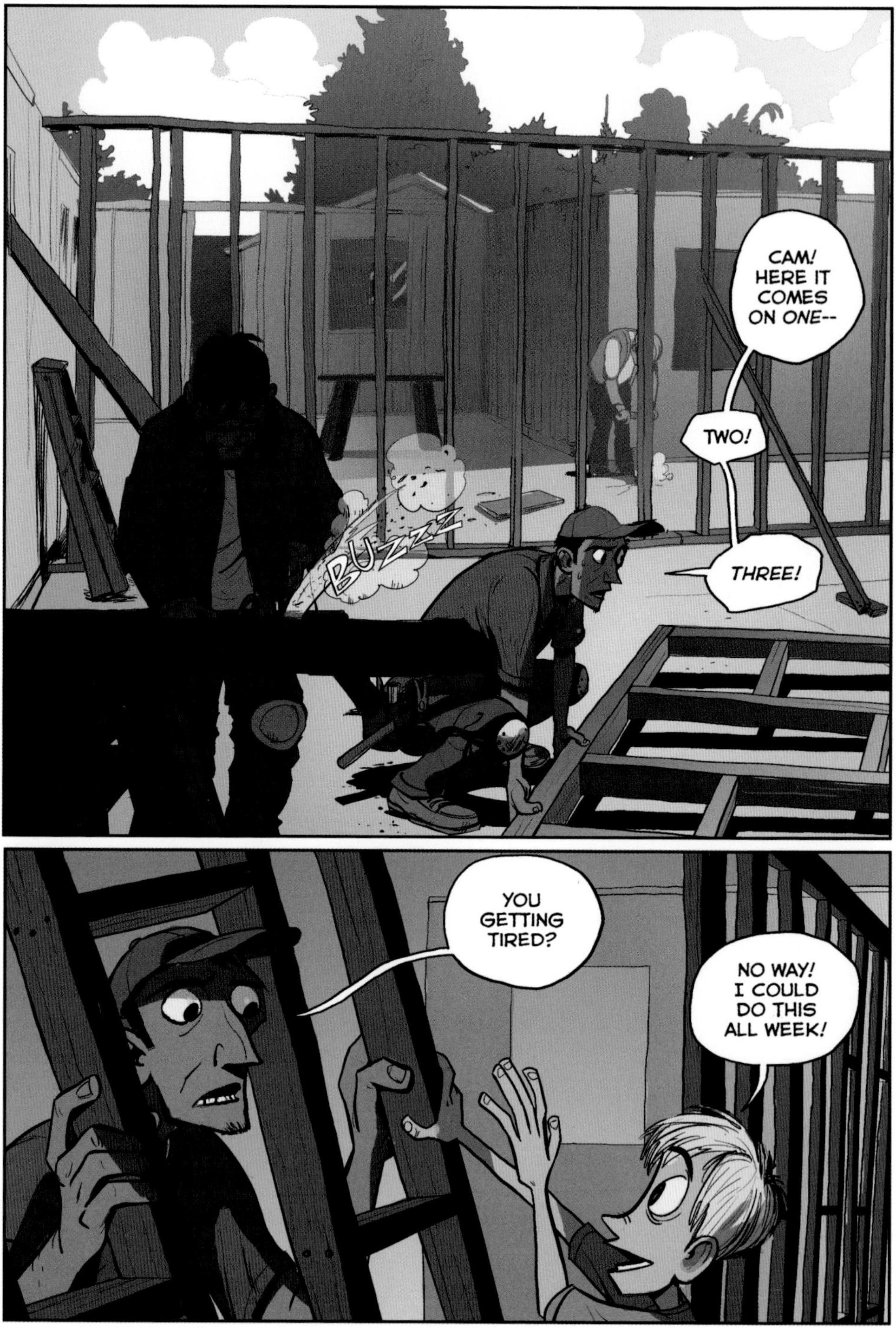
CAM! HERE IT COMES ON ONE--
TWO!
THREE!
BUZZZ
YOU GETTING TIRED?
NO WAY! I COULD DO THIS ALL WEEK!

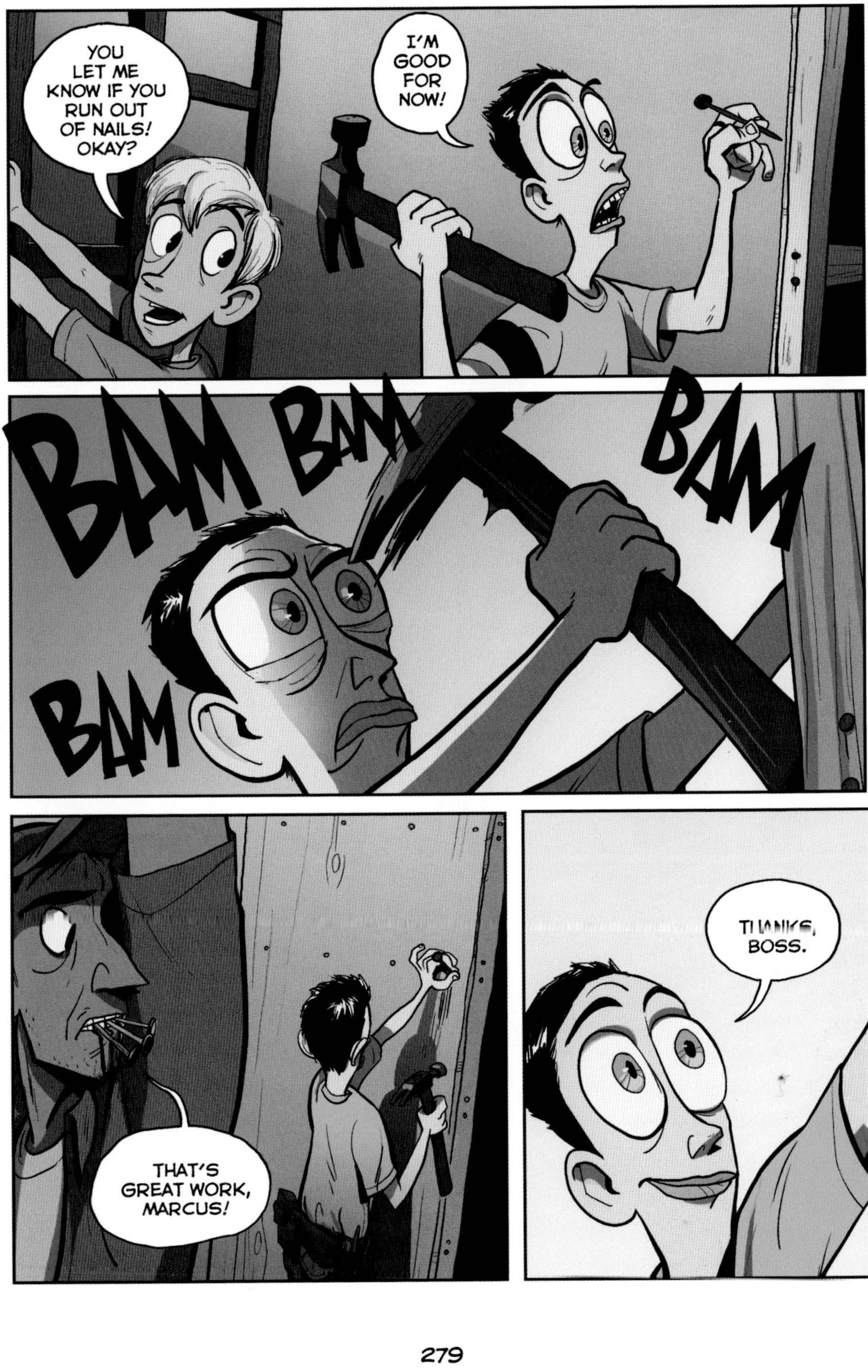
YOU LET ME KNOW IF YOU RUN OUT OF NAILS! OKAY?
I'M GOOD FOR NOW!
BAM
BAM
BAM
BAM
THAT'S GREAT WORK, MARCUS!
THANKS, BOSS.

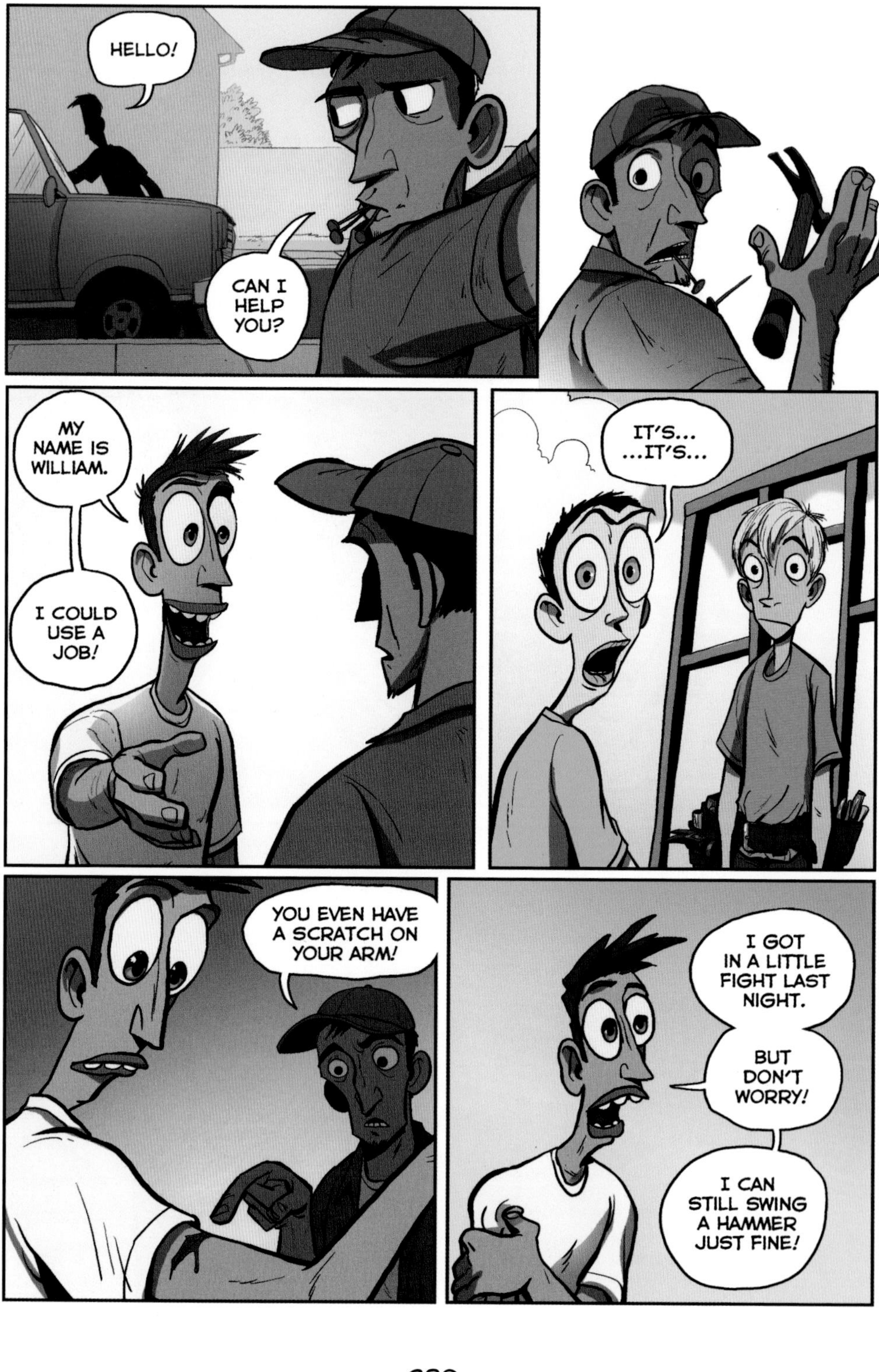
HELLO!
CAN I HELP YOU?
MY NAME IS WILLIAM.
I COULD USE A JOB!
IT'S... ...IT'S...
YOU EVEN HAVE A SCRATCH ON YOUR ARM!
I GOT IN A LITTLE FIGHT LAST NIGHT.
BUT DON'T WORRY!
I CAN STILL SWING A HAMMER JUST FINE!

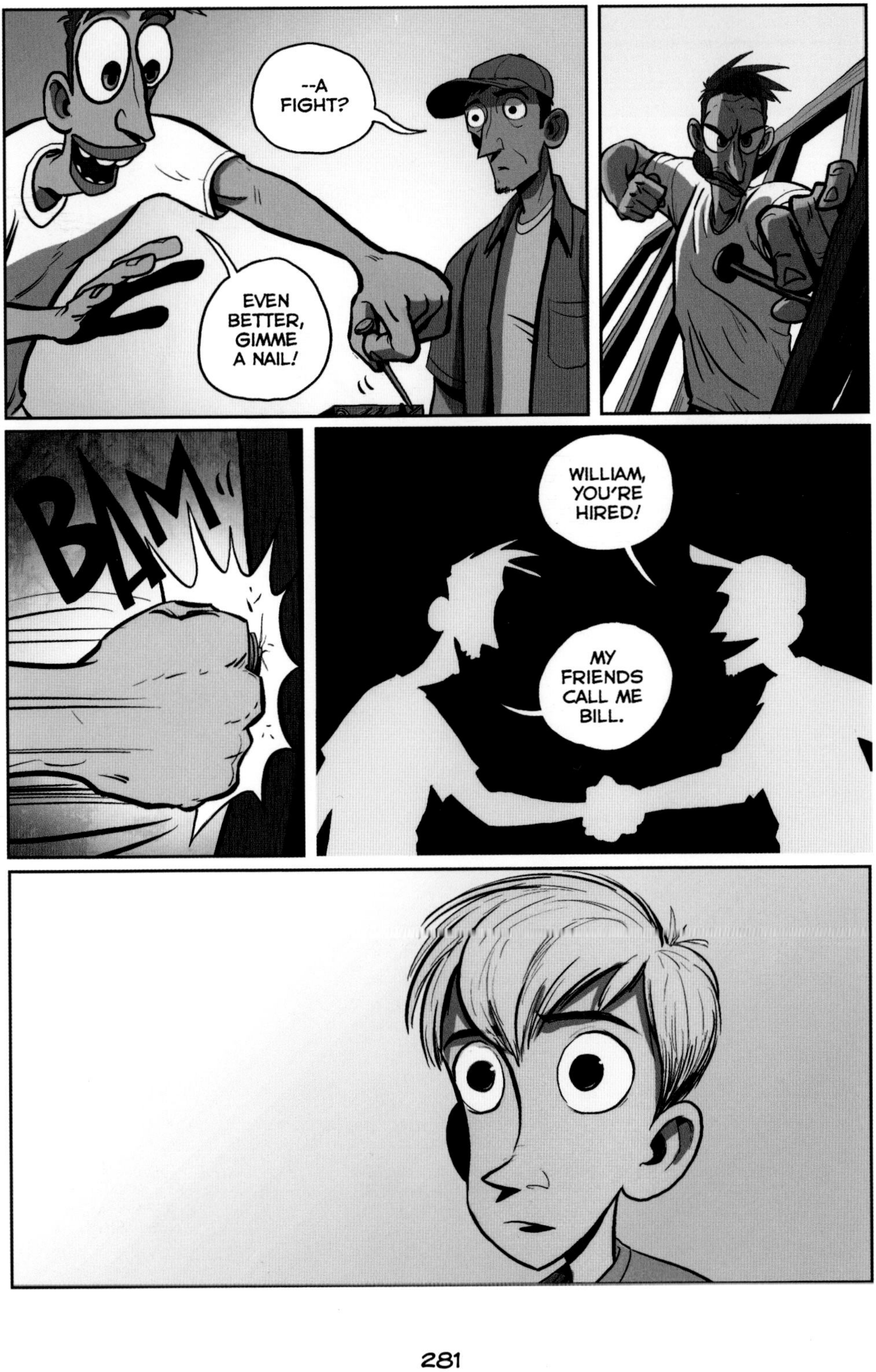
--A FIGHT?
EVEN BETTER, GIMME A NAIL!
BAM
WILLIAM, YOU'RE HIRED!
MY FRIENDS CALL ME BILL.

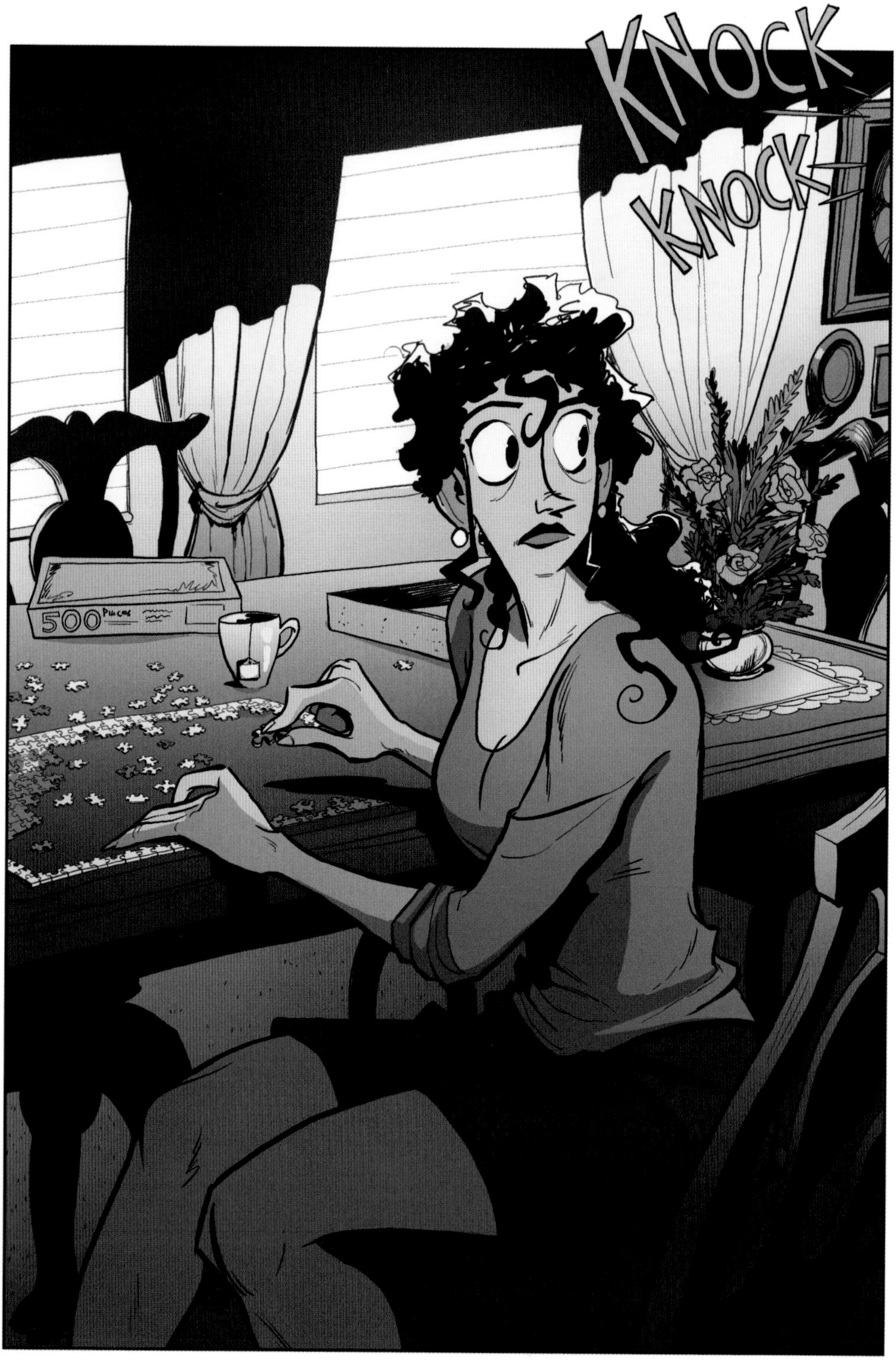
KNOCK
KNOCK
500 Pieces

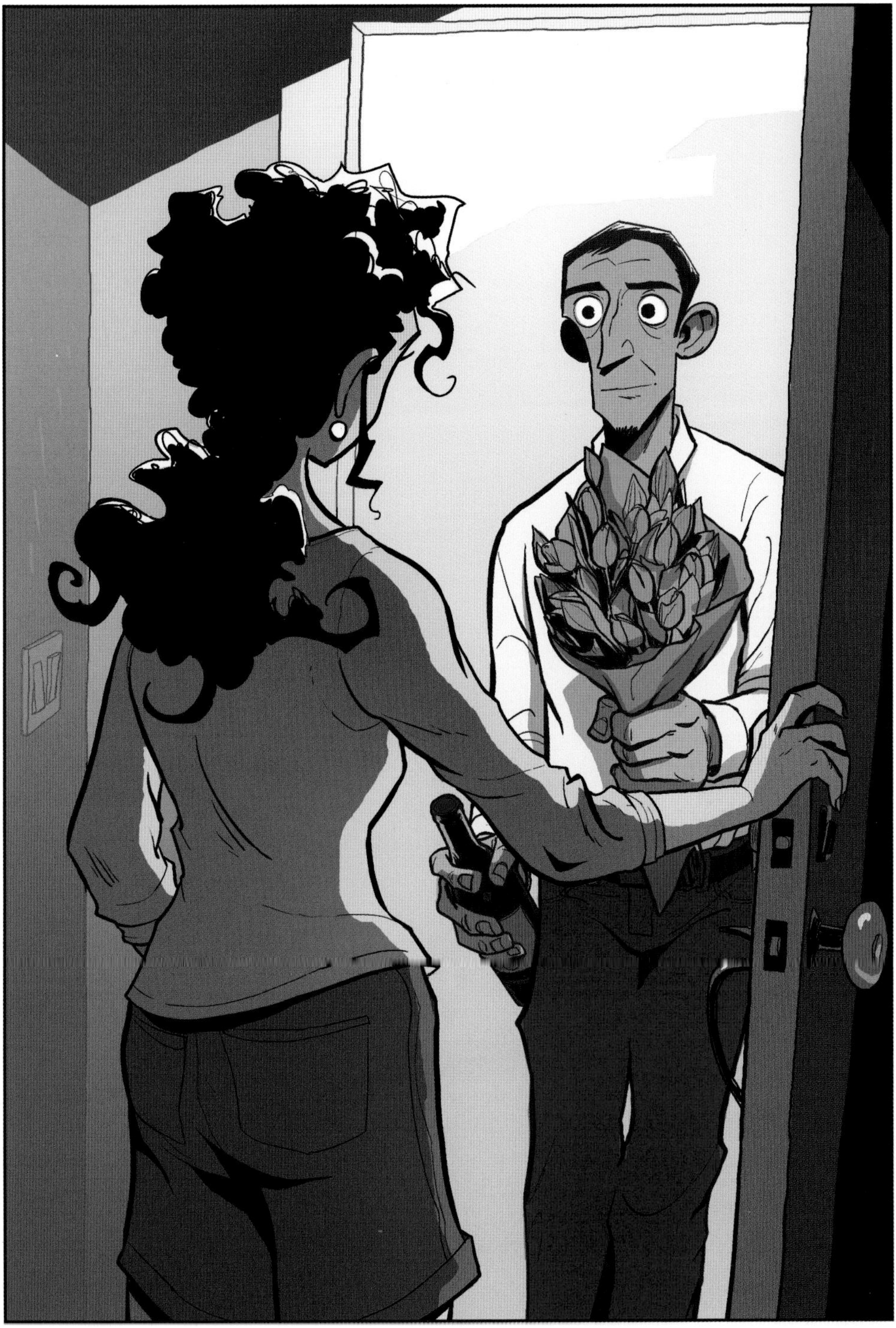